PRAISE FOR *FURYBORN*

"Legrand's epic feminist fantasy is scary, sexy, and intense, set in a world made rich with magic, history, and a gorgeously imagined literary tradition."

  —Melissa Albert, *New York Times* bestselling author of *The Hazel Wood*

"*Furyborn* is an addictive, fascinating fantasy. Truly not to be missed, this story…will have you on the edge of your seat."

                        —Kendare Blake, #1 *New York Times* bestselling
                              author of the Three Dark Crowns series

"A veritable feast of magic: mystical beings, ruthless power struggles, and gorgeously cinematic writing that will sweep you off your feet."

                        —Traci Chee, *New York Times* bestselling author
                              of the Sea of Ink and Gold series

"Immersive and intricate, *Furyborn* is a kick-you-in-the-teeth and grab-you-by-the-heart tale of two queens."

                        —Roshani Chokshi, *New York Times* bestselling author
                              of *The Star-Touched Queen* and *A Crown of Wishes*

"Lush, riveting, and full of intrigue, *Furyborn* is a gripping read that grapples with questions of power, fate, and our abilities to change the world."

  —S. Jae-Jones, *New York Times* bestselling author of *Wintersong*

"Epic in scope, endless in imagination, this book will grab hold of you and refuse to let go."

                        —Amie Kaufman, *New York Times* bestselling author of
                              the Illuminae Files series and the Starbound trilogy

"A captivatingly imaginative world filled with intrigue and deception. *Furyborn* will leave you breathless and aching for more."
—Lisa Maxwell, *New York Times* bestselling author of *The Last Magician*

"Legrand has created magic on every page. Flawed, smart, and fierce heroines kept me dazzled and breathless. Explosive and stunning."
—Mary E. Pearson, *New York Times* bestselling author of The Remnant Chronicles and The Jenna Fox Chronicles

"Captivating and lovely, volatile and deadly. *Furyborn* is a sexy, luscious shiver of a book."
—Sara Raasch, *New York Times* bestselling author of the Snow Like Ashes trilogy

"Two very different and fascinating young women, a delicious villain, nonstop action, and heart-pounding romance. A fantastic read!"
—Morgan Rhodes, *New York Times* bestselling author of the Falling Kingdoms series

"Beautiful, brutal, heart-stopping, and epic, *Furyborn* is a world to lose yourself in—just bring weapons. It's dangerous there."
—Laini Taylor, *New York Times* bestselling author of *Strange the Dreamer* and the Daughter of Smoke and Bone trilogy

"Epic and unforgettable. I was captivated by the story of two powerful young women fighting to survive in this vivid, unique fantasy world. A must-read!"
—Amy Tintera, *New York Times* bestselling author of the Ruined trilogy

Also by Claire Legrand

The Empirium Trilogy
Furyborn
Kingsbane
Lightbringer

LIGHTBRING

LIGHTBRINGER

THE EMPIRIUM TRILOGY · BOOK 3

CLAIRE LEGRAND

sourcebooks
fire

Published by Sourcebooks Fire, an imprint of Sourcebooks
P.O. Box 4410, Naperville, Illinois 60567-4410
(630) 961-3900
sourcebooks.com

Library of Congress Cataloging-in-Publication data is on file with the publisher.

Printed and bound in the United States of America.
LSC 10 9 8 7 6 5 4 3 2 1

For my mom,
who loves me

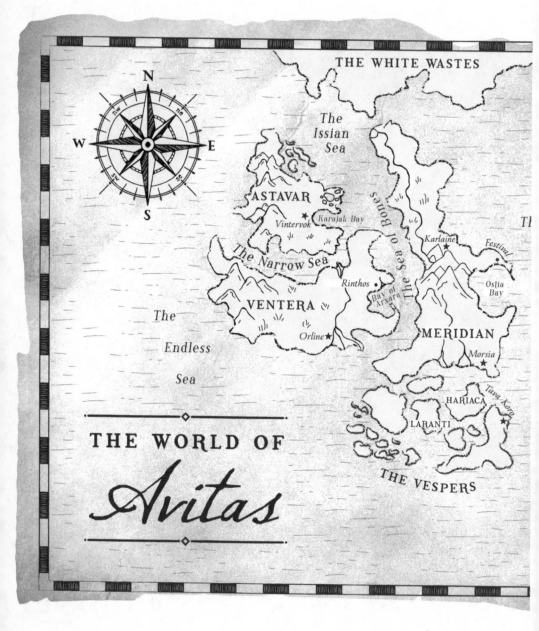

THE WHITE WASTES

The Issian Sea

ASTAVAR

Vintervok   Karajak Bay

The Narrow Sea

VENTERA

Rinthos

Bay of Arxara

Orline

The Sea of Bones

Karlaine

Festival

Ostia Bay

MERIDIAN

Morsia

HARIACA

Tava Kor

LARANTI

THE VESPERS

The Endless Sea

THE WORLD OF
Avitas

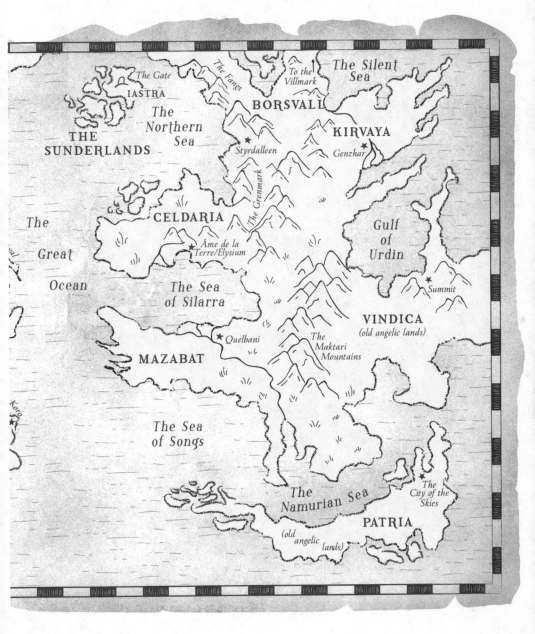

A BEAST
AND A LIAR

"You who fight for your fallen loves, your ravaged coun-
tries, listen closely: There may come a time when the
Emperor appears before you. Perhaps your beauty will
catch his eye, or your talent will do it, or your strength.
He will smile and seduce. He will flatter and promise.
Do not trust him. Fight him until your very last breath.
Fight for those you have lost. Fight for the world that
might have been, and yet still could be."

—*The Word of the Prophet*

Simon crouched near the ice-frosted rock, knife in hand, lips chapped
with cold, feet scabbed and calloused in his worn boots, and watched
with hungry eyes as the hare approached.

It was a gangly white thing, not yet fully grown, and Simon knew that
it would be more fur than decent meat, but he also knew that he was
hungry and would devour anything he could kill.

He knew little else besides that.

The hare paused, close enough that Simon could see its whiskers twitch.
It stared with dumb fear at the world, waiting for death to come. Around
them, the broad brown plateau stretched for cold, solitary miles, glimmering white with morning snow. Flakes drifted silently from a thick gray sky.
Soon, the real snows would come. Simon knew it. The hare knew it.

Only one of them would survive to see it happen.

The hare crept closer. It had caught the scent of a hunter, its pale nose quivering, but could not find him.

Simon had always been good at hiding, and since landing in this awful, unfamiliar wilderness nearly a year ago, he had grown even better at it.

The hare crept closer. Simon could smell its musk, feel the heat of its frightened body. He leapt for it, fell hard upon it, slashed its throat before it could run.

Too hungry to make a fire, he skinned his kill with a few quick strokes of his knife and then tore at the haunches with his teeth. He ate. He did not drop his knife.

He had learned, over the past year, never to drop his knife.

Then, strings of bloody meat hanging from his teeth, the hare half-eaten, Simon heard a sound. He dropped his supper and whirled, ready to either kill or run.

Instead, he stared through the snow.

A figure stood not far away, watching him. Simon squinted. It was a man. He wore a long black coat trimmed with fur. The coat had square shoulders and a high collar and fell to the ground in sweeping folds that matched the jet of his softly curling hair. He cut a beautiful figure there, sharp and clean against the wintry brown vastness of the plains Simon now knew as home.

Behind him, the world hushed. He could no longer hear the distant crack of shifting ice or the harsh mountain wind. He could hear nothing but the wild beat of his own heart and the footsteps of the man coming toward him.

For Simon knew this man. He had once feared him, even hated him. But so much time had passed since those last terrifying moments in Âme de la Terre that even the sight of an enemy was welcome.

The man placed a gloved hand on Simon's bowed head. A soft cry of longing burst from Simon's lips. Groping blindly upward, he found the man's hand and grasped it desperately with one of his own.

"It's you," he whispered. He was no longer alone. An animal ecstasy overcame him. He let out a harsh, croaking laugh.

"It's me," said the angel named Corien. He knelt and looked closely at Simon.

Simon stiffened, his other hand tightening on his knife. Black eyes, lightless and endless. He had never seen such a thing. He bared his teeth, poised on the balls of his feet.

But Corien only smiled. "What is your name?"

Simon's mind was a whirl of confusion. Here was the man who had invaded his home, who had killed hundreds of his neighbors and thousands of Celdarians.

Here was the angel who had slipped inside the mind of his own father and urged him to jump off a tower to his death.

For a wild moment, Simon considered leaping on Corien as he had on the rabbit, opening that smooth white throat the same way. But Simon had seen the swiftness with which angels could attack. Corien would stop him before he could even raise his knife.

He could run, but that was unthinkable. For a year, he had lived alone in the wilderness, his body worn to mere bones and mangled skin. For a year, he had spoken only to himself and to the beasts.

His furious tears spilled over. "You know my name, don't you?" he whispered fiercely. "Can't you see?"

Corien was quiet for such a long time that Simon felt a cold drip of fear down his back and prepared himself to run. Always, he was preparing himself to run.

"I do know you," Corien said softly, but he seemed puzzled. "I know you, and yet I don't."

A swift, seeking presence entered Simon's thoughts, as if sly fingers were pulling aside the folds of his mind to see what lay beneath. He knew what was happening even though he had never felt it before. Dark stories had rippled through Celdaria in the months before and after King Audric's death. Terrible stories about humans driven mad, humans left pale and broken in the ruins of sacked villages.

This was what it was like to be invaded by an angel.

Simon held still, hardly breathing, quaking in the snow, as Corien moved through his mind. A voice slid against Simon's ears, kissed his neck, traced the lines of his scars. The voice hissed words Simon did not understand, and they spiraled louder and faster until his mind was an unbearable din. He felt as if he were being shaken, held above an abyss and flung to and fro as whatever ravenous thing lived in the abyss howled.

Simon cried out and tried to run, but Corien grabbed his arm and his chin and pushed him against the ground with his cold gloved hands. A pressure filled Simon, from his skull to his toes, until he feared his body would burst open. Words rose inside him, pulled by a great force. Soon they would spill out and scatter like insects, hissing *Simon, Simon, Simon,* and they would devour the world.

Then, at last, there was quiet.

Simon gasped in the dirt. Above him, Corien's face was tight and hard with an emotion Simon could not read. It had been so long since he had seen a face.

"I do know you," Corien said quietly. His words fell like rain against metal; Simon felt each one in the back of his teeth. "Somehow, I know you. I see that your name is Simon Randell. You are nine years old. You are a marque. Or, rather, you were a marque, which I knew. This is why I came to you. I sensed an unusual presence in these mountains and followed the long trail of it here to find you. Marques do not exist now. Did you know that, Simon? Very little that is remarkable still lives, except for me."

His black gaze roamed over Simon's body, the thick tapestry of scars on his face and hands. Simon felt his mind shift, accommodating Corien's intrusion. Simon's jaw clenched. He sat stiffly. He would not be afraid. He held his breath.

"I begin to see more," Corien whispered, unblinking. "Your journey forward in time scarred you horribly and almost killed you. You weren't always this ugly." He smiled, and yet the rest of his face, beautiful and pale, did not move. "But you aren't ugly, are you, Simon? Beneath that map of scars, you are quite a fine creature."

Simon struggled to sit up, and when Corien helped him, his gloved hand at Simon's back, Simon flushed. He straightened his posture and lifted his chin, trying to remember how to be a boy. His mind tilted and spun. So, he was far in the future now. He had suspected as much from some terrible instinct gone dormant in his blood. He had whispered it to himself many a night. But now he knew it was true.

Frantic questions crowded him. *When*, exactly, was this future? How much time had passed between then and now? What was this world? Corien's eyes were black, and Simon could not travel, and he wondered: Could these strange things be connected?

What had happened to the empirium?

And why was Corien looking at him so oddly, as if seeing something in Simon's face of which Simon himself was ignorant?

Corien's gaze was cold and impenetrable. "She died beside me. I bled for decades, and even when I was whole again, my mind was not. Is that why, when I look inside you, I can see only elusive shadows and hear little else but your own endless, thudding fear? Is it that my mind has been battered by the years, Simon? Simon Randell. I know your face, but I don't know why. Who are you? Who do you fight for?"

"Fight for?" Simon shook his head. "I fight for no one."

Corien considered him for a moment longer, then said, "Ah, well," and stood, brushing the snow from his coat. "I came here looking for something that could help me. I suppose I have found merely a lost boy."

"Wait!" Simon cried, for Corien had turned to leave, and he simply could not bear being left alone again. He crawled after Corien and grabbed the hem of his coat. He curled up against his boots, miserable as a beaten dog, and there was a small burst of fear in his chest as he considered what he was about to do, but he had long ago stopped feeling shame.

For it was Rielle's death that had ripped him from his home and brought him here. It was her selfishness, her inability to control her power, that had ruined the world and left him abandoned, alone, without his magic.

He pushed past his fear and clutched Corien's arm. He pressed his forehead hard against Corien's sleeve, gathered up his hatred of the dead queen, and sent it hurtling at the angel standing before him so he would see, so he would understand.

"I am from Celdaria," Simon said, trembling. "I have seen the daughter of Rielle. And, my lord, I will fight for you."

He waited. There was silence above him, terrible and heavy. Though Corien was not touching him, Simon felt the weight of a hard hand on his neck.

"I held her on the night she was born," Simon said, the words spilling out fast. "I was the son of Queen Rielle's healer. He hid me from you. And that night, I was frightened. I watched my father jump…" His throat closed. He growled to clear it. He had not cried in months and would not do so now.

"I saw him fall," he said. "And Queen Rielle was dying, and the baby, she was alone. I heard you screaming for the queen, my lord—I saw you beating against her light. And I didn't know what to do, my lord, so I took the baby, and I tried to travel with her somewhere safe. I thought I would take her north, to Borsvall, where King Ilmaire could protect her. I thought that if Queen Rielle died, she would kill me too, and her child."

Simon looked up, shivering. He could not see Corien's face through the blur of tears and snow.

"But something went wrong. Time caught me, my lord, and took me here. I have lived alone for months. I can find no one. I have walked and walked."

He was wailing now, wild and unthinking in his despair. He hated the sound of it, how small it made him seem, but now that he had talked to someone he knew, someone from the Old World that was his home, he knew he could not bear solitude again. If Corien left him, Simon would die. He would throw himself upon the rocks. He would follow the snow-cat trails and let the creatures feed on him.

Corien was very still, then knelt slowly to take Simon's face in his hands. He had removed his gloves. His skin was white and smooth.

"You are in Vindica, little Simon," he said, kindly, "in the wilds of what was once angelic country. You are on the high plains of the Maktari Mountains. Of course you are alone; of course you are cold."

Simon let himself be drawn against Corien's chest and sobbed into his coat. He held himself still and fought hard against the worst of his tears. He could prove that he was indeed a creature worth keeping.

"Don't leave me, please, don't leave me," he whispered. "Take me with you, *please*, my lord."

Corien stroked Simon's long, matted hair. "You loved your father very much. You should hate me for killing him. I did kill him—I see that now too. You should want to kill me for that, but you're so afraid of being alone again that you'll gladly go with me if I tell you to. You'll do whatever I say for the chance to be with someone who knows what you've lost." He laughed, a frayed sound.

"Yes," Simon whispered, shivering in Corien's arms. He felt the angel in his mind, gently probing. "I'll do whatever you say, my lord."

"Such a weak mind, so unguarded and scraped thin," Corien marveled, his fingers soft on Simon's cheeks. "You're remembering things you've tried to forget, and I can see each memory as clearly as if it were my own."

Simon was remembering, yes, in the midst of these tears and this horrible rising fear, this desperation to keep Corien close to him. He could not *stop* remembering.

He remembered Queen Rielle thrusting her infant daughter into his arms on the night of her death. He remembered her shadowed eyes sparking gold, and the sour charge to the air as the room burned bright behind him. He remembered Corien crying out in the queen's rooms, the sound savage with grief. He remembered looking out into the night and summoning the threads that would carry him and the child safely to Borsvall.

And there was his father, gripping his head and stumbling onto the terrace outside the queen's rooms. Toppling over the railing, falling fast to the ground below.

And there were the dark threads of time, gripping Simon, tearing at him. The pain of that, and of how for the first few weeks after arriving here, he had hardly known himself, had been more beast than boy. He had forgotten how to speak. He had run on all fours, bleeding and burned, screaming at nothing.

"And the child?" Corien crooned, caressing him still. "What happened to her?"

"When I awoke here, she was gone." Simon dug in his pocket for the scrap of blanket he carried there. Every time he slept, he buried his face in it. Sometimes he screamed into it. He bit down hard on it and tugged, rocking in the dark.

Corien considered that for a long moment. "She could be here. She could be anywhere. She could be nowhere."

Simon swallowed hard. His heart pounded like hooves against rock. He was a stampede. He held so still that his thin body burned with tension.

"Yes, my lord," he whispered.

"Then a marque will be useful. Even one whose magic is dead and gone."

Then, Corien froze. Simon felt a shift in his mind, and then a sudden, hard stillness, as if something had lodged deep within him and would never move again.

Corien pulled away to stare at him, and the expression he wore now was so different from what had been there before that Simon quailed and tried to move.

But Corien held him fast.

"I see it now, in your face," he whispered. His black gaze raked across Simon's every scar. "You are the man I saw when Rielle's daughter came to her that day, on the mountain…" A single soft laugh. Something cleared in his face, and Simon did not understand what it meant, nor did he comprehend anything Corien was saying.

"You are Simon Randell," said Corien. He touched his temple, his slender fingers trembling. "Of course you are. And now you are here." He kissed Simon's brow, and at the touch of his cold lips, a warmth bloomed in Simon's body, steadying him.

"And now," Corien whispered, "you are mine."

"Perhaps I can reawaken my magic, my lord," Simon blurted eagerly. Something had happened between them, though Simon did not know what. All he knew with certainty was that he would never be alone again. "I've tried, but alone I've failed. Maybe with you…"

He stopped, flushing under Corien's keen black gaze. What did Corien see when he looked at him? For the first time, Simon felt the humiliation of his ruined skin.

But Corien only held out his hand, and with the other, he gently lifted Simon's chin. Simon squirmed in his grip.

"Yes, Simon." Corien smiled. His fingers closed around Simon's own. "Maybe with me."

Then Corien's mind claimed him.

The pain came without warning. Simon was staring up at Corien, and then Simon was screaming, but no sound escaped his lips, for Corien would not permit it to. Something—some awful, insistent presence—was splitting Simon's skull apart, tearing at each thought he had ever known, each memory living inside him. Searching for truth. Hunting for lies. It was unlike anything he had ever felt. Before, Corien had barely swept his mind.

Now, he was unmaking it.

"I am sorry, Simon." Corien smiled down at him, watching him writhe in his arms. "The world is a strange place, and there is no stranger part of it than the twists and turns of time. I must know for certain that you are mine and mine alone. I must know I can trust you."

Then he pressed his cheek to Simon's brow and whispered, "We have much work to do, you and I."

It was the last sound Simon heard before his mind shattered.

— 1 —
RIELLE

"'But how did it happen?' many have asked. 'How was one zealot able to convince all of angelic kind to turn on their human brothers and sisters? We all share the world. Why was he not deemed a lunatic and punished for his bloodlust?' The answer is simple: Kalmaroth was an irresistible force never before seen in our world—and I pray he will never be seen again."

—The writings of Zedna Tanakret,
Grand Magister of the Baths in Morsia,
capital of Meridian, Year 287 of the Second Age

Rielle kept her face hidden in Corien's cloak.

She pressed her nose to the fine dark cloth and inhaled his scent, holding her breath as long as she could. His smell soothed her; she devoured it.

She peered out from under the cloak's hood as Corien killed each person in the merchant's party. It was swift, efficient work, and she watched it through a glaze of calm that, distantly, disturbed her.

But when she thought about that too hard, it hurt her head, so she decided to stop thinking about it and instead watched Corien kill.

There were four men, all of them wearing heavy coats and boots to ward off the November chill, and they never raised a weapon against him. Why would they? He was a vision, approaching them with his wide smile and his cheekbones that seemed cut from pale glass, his black hair clinging to his forehead and his slender white frame shivering in the snow. A piteous figure, and lovely too. It was no wonder that the merchants had drawn their carriage to a halt when they spotted him on the roadside, waving his sputtering squat torch like a beggar. He could have forced them to stop, but he delighted in being able to manipulate them even without using his angelic power.

She waited until all the men were dead, their frames bent in the dirt and their frozen faces contorted with horror, before lowering her hood. One man lay near the carriage, arms outstretched as if he had been trying in his last moments to scramble inside.

Rielle stepped over his wide, staring eyes, gray and glassy, and climbed inside the carriage with a tiny satisfied smile. It felt like an odd sort of smile, affixed to her face rather than summoned by her own will. But it was warm inside the shabby carriage, and she did hate feeling cold.

She pitied the man though. She pitied all of them. At least she thought she did. She couldn't think much about anything without her thoughts veering off into a calm gray sea draped with fog. She didn't understand where the fog had come from, but she liked when it enveloped her. It was warm and still, like an old quilt.

Touching her temple, blinking hard, she recalled, with monumental effort, the pain that had drummed against her skull as Corien and Ludivine warred inside her thoughts these recent weeks. If either of them had turned the full force of their angelic might upon her with an aim to kill her from the inside out, they could have done so easily. The pain of dying in such a way would be extraordinary.

No, Rielle did not envy these men.

But she was safe now, far from Ludivine, and she hadn't heard her loathsome voice in some days now, and of course Corien would never hurt her. Even thinking of him mollified her, like the embrace of sleep after a long day.

Rielle peered out through the frosted window and into the forest, an impenetrable black on a storming, moonless night.

It was foolish to worry that anyone else had seen them. Corien had told her this, and she repeated his words to herself. This stretch of the eastern Celdarian border was remote, he had reminded her, the unkind terrain dense with forests, mountains, and cliffs. Roads were few and ill kept. And the coming storm was rumbling closer, spitting snow and lightning. Any traveler of sound mind would stay home, safe and warm.

And yet, Rielle realized, her thoughts moving sluggishly as she tried to order them, the dead merchants had braved the night, eager for coin. If anyone else came upon them, if they caught a glimpse of her face and knew who she was, they would interfere. They would send word back to the capital. They would try to capture her in hopes of a reward from the crown, and she would have to dispose of them, ruin their trail of whispers and messages, and that could become...untidy.

I would let no one escape us. Corien's thoughts slid inside her mind like the glide of a palm across her skin. *If anyone saw you, I would kill them, or you would, and I would glory in the sight of you.*

She blinked up at him. *Would I?*

You would, and I would kiss you after, he said, and then came the thought of him kissing her brow and her cheeks, and if her heart was still in uproar, she could not feel it and didn't care to.

She was content, wrapped in Corien's cloak. She wished to live forever inside it.

Across from Rielle, the little Kirvayan queen Obritsa climbed into her own seat, her face pinched, strips of her pale-brown skin visible above her ragged collar, under her fall of white hair. Corien insisted upon saving Obritsa's strength for at least another week and traveling by foot instead. The girl was exhausted, having threaded herself, Artem, and Corien across the continent to Celdaria in time for the royal wedding.

A marque, secretly pretending true humanity as part of a revolution brewing in Kirvaya.

Rielle barely noticed the girl. She smiled a little to be polite, which was more than the staring little brat deserved. Then she shifted sleepily within the voluminous folds of Corien's cloak and reached out to him. He was outside the carriage giving orders to Artem, Obritsa's devoted guard, who would drive the restless team of snow-dusted horses onward and east.

Hurry and come back to me, she pleaded. *Please, Corien.*

His voice teased. *So easily can your loneliness best you. Patience, my lovely one.*

And all at once, her calm vanished.

Suddenly, the comforting fog was gone, and Rielle was alone, trapped with her own thoughts somewhere deep in her own dark mind. She tightened her grip on Corien's cloak, panic crawling up her arms. Her body felt swollen and heavy, and she didn't understand why. She stared at Obritsa, who watched her, frowning, and then Rielle looked away and shut her eyes, for she could not quite remember where she was, and this frightened her. She wondered if she was locked away, caged in a high tower, or if she was in a carriage in eastern Celdaria, or perhaps out on a soft gray sea with no one and nothing for thousands of miles.

In this empty space, a sudden roar of memories swelled, and Rielle's eyes filled with tears.

It was not so long ago—only six days past—that she had stood in the gardens behind Baingarde. She remembered this now. She saw it plainly. Amid the mounting haze of this fear she could not explain, figures manifested. Audric. Her king. Her husband, now. Her dearest love. Only six days ago, he had turned away from her, his face twisted with loathing. He had commanded her not to touch him.

You're the monster Aryava foretold, he had said. *A traitor and a liar.*

And what home was there in the world for a traitor? What heart would spare love for a liar?

She touched her temples. Her mind whirled with bewildering images, each fighting to rise faster than the last, and she could not find her breath. *Corien? Where are you?*

Rielle, I'm sorry, I was gone for too long, came his voice, and then he was climbing inside the carriage to greet her.

She reached for him, feeling pathetic and small, and yet she could not stop herself. The memory of Audric's scorn, his disdain and hatred, was too close, too fresh. She had shed her wedding gown some miles back in the woods and now wore an ill-fitting woolen dress Corien had stolen from some farmer's daughter he had found coming home alone from the market. The wool was scratchy and far too hot. She raked her fingers across her skin. She remembered the chaos of the capital as she had fled from it, thousands of people reeling from the revelations in the vision Corien had shown them.

No, not a vision—a truth.

Their new queen had killed the father of Ludivine and Merovec. She had killed her own father, and her mother too. She had killed their late beloved king, Audric's father.

And she had lied about it. She had lied, and had nevertheless been crowned by the Archon's own holy hands.

Rielle shut her eyes, her lips pressed together in a tight line. Perspiration beaded at her hairline. A din of screaming voices circled back to her—those belonging to the people she had sworn to protect, first as Sun Queen and then as the newly crowned queen of Celdaria. She had sworn this, and then she had abandoned her people. Their voices calling out her name were cruel black birds of memory winging in tight spirals on the winds of her mind:

Kingsbane!

Kingsbane!

Kingsbane!

She twisted Corien's cloak hard. She was not ashamed of who she was, of what she was, and yet fear and guilt flooded her like twin rivers set afire, and she did not understand where she was now, or who this girl was who stared so closely at her, or where her own sweet gray fog had gone, so calm and quiet.

"Listen to me." Cool hands cupped her face, and when she opened her eyes, Corien was there, dipping his head to kiss her. He gathered her into his lap and held her close until her trembling ceased.

"I hate them," she whispered against his neck. "And yet I ache to think of leaving them all, of running away in the night like a villain."

Corien's laughter was soft. "You are a villain. At least in their simple eyes, you are. Let them think that. Let them hate you. They are nothing, and you know it."

"Yes, but..."

She stopped before the words could form, but of course Corien had already heard them.

"You miss him?" he asked quietly.

Rielle felt the girl's sharp eyes upon them. Obritsa was her name, she remembered, her mind roaring back to itself with Corien there beside her. Rielle pressed her palms against the solid broad reach of Corien's chest and resisted the urge to fling out her hands, scorch Obritsa's impertinent, keen-eyed face, and teach her a lesson. The thought cheered her; she'd forgotten, in her fear, that she *could* scorch. She could maim and pulverize. She could unmake.

Hush, now. Corien's voice stroked her silent. The hot ripples of anger rising beneath her skin flattened and stilled. *We need her,* he reminded her. *Gentle, Rielle. Do not overtax yourself. Hear me. Hush, my love.*

Rielle's thoughts smoothed out. Contented, heavy-lidded, she heard the distant crash of gray waves and felt faint with relief. Fog crept over her eyes, and she welcomed its softness. It was unnecessary, even silly, to get angry right now and call upon her power, or to be afraid, for of course she would always be safe with Corien. She understood that now. She remembered it.

She mumbled in mind-speak that Obritsa would have to learn not to stare and would also have to learn to transform her constant haughty expression into something less imperious, something more fitting of a servant. The moment they arrived in the north, Rielle would order Obritsa elsewhere, out of her sight, until she was needed again.

Of course, Corien said mildly. *But now is not the time. I asked you a question, my love. Don't you remember?*

Did you? She leaned her heavy head against his shoulder.

Do you miss him? Answer me, he said lightly. *Answer me now.*

Rielle had trouble scraping together her thoughts, but this troubled her only briefly, for the fog was creeping fast through her mind, sweeping away all worries. *I have known him all my life*, she said at last.

And you love him still, and that fire cannot simply be snuffed out overnight. Corien stroked her hair, which fell wild and uncombed down her back. He sighed, sounding tired. *I understand that. But you see now, don't you? You see the truth of him.*

For a long moment, she did not speak. It was so difficult to think.

"He hates me," she whispered at last against the curve of Corien's ear. "He does not understand me."

Corien kissed the bridge of her nose. "He is too small to understand you. All of them are. They see a monster. I see a god in the shape of a girl." His hand slid down her arm to rest on her hip. "They see a beast to be tamed. I see a divine creature aching to be set free."

Rielle's eyes drifted shut as he kissed her brow. Through her mind's fog came images—secret visions of Corien's ardor, and how he longed to demonstrate it, and how passionately he wished they were alone.

But she could not fall with him into the haven of their shared thoughts. Not yet. She had one question, and she fought the fog pulling her under long enough to ask it.

"Tell me this: Is he safe?" Rielle's words tumbled out clumsily. "Is he well?"

A tiny ripple passed from Corien to her, along the sweet cord of their linked minds, as if a small pebble had been thrown into still water.

"He is safe." Corien said nothing else aloud, but Rielle heard him clearly inside her mind.

Someday, he told her, *and soon, I hope you will understand what must be done.*

"I wish I didn't love him," she replied, her voice the thinnest of threads. A strange sleep she did not particularly want was pulling her under. "I wish to worry for him no longer. Someone who hates me as he does deserves no piece of my heart."

I can help you with that. If you'll allow it.

Her exhausted body screamed in protest as she pulled back from Corien to study his face. Her mind was a confusion of hurt and weariness. She burned to no longer be walking or riding in a rattling carriage. A carriage—how strange. Why a carriage? She tried to ask and found she could not speak. She wanted to rest. She wanted to kiss him.

A small cord tugged insistently at her from a distant corner of her mind—the darkest, smallest corner that existed behind a locked door to which she no longer had the key. Which was troubling. Wasn't it? Shouldn't she possess the keys to her own mind?

But when her gaze met Corien's, her discomfiture disappeared, and there was a spray of clean gray sea foam against her face, and the fog of clouds drifting above it kissed her knees, her belly, the back of her neck. Her shoulders slumped. Her frown slipped. The empirium, forever simmering just beneath her skin, lapped steadily at her edges, and the thought occurred to her, in a quiet bloom of happiness, that she never again had to keep that powerful tide from rising. Not here. Not with Corien.

I can help you with that, he had told her. *If you'll allow it.*

He would help her forget her old life. He would help her learn to unlove Audric.

I see a divine creature aching to be set free.

"I'll allow it," she said at last, and then slipped so swiftly into sleep that her last thought before the dimness took her was one of alarm, quickly forgotten.

ELIANA

"Tameryn, Tameryn, Tameryn. I say her name every night before sleep, in hopes that the word, like a prayer, will bring forth some goodness from the empirium, some kind force that will cushion the blow of my endless night-mares. Savrasara, Tameryn, wherever you are. Come back to me. We need you. I need you. You carry my heart, and without you I am lost. What have we done, Tam? My God, what have we done?"

—From the journals of Saint Nerida the Radiant, written during the Angelic Wars, stolen from the First Great Library of Quelbani

Onboard Admiral Ravikant's prized warship, in a small holding cell in the vessel's bowels, Eliana rubbed her wrists raw.

Once—only weeks before—those wrists had worn slender golden chains and flat, round castings she had fashioned herself at the Forge of Vintervok.

Now, they wore chains of a different sort. For the first few days aboard the ship, which she largely spent heaving up her guts onto the wooden floor of her cell, Eliana had ignored the new weight on her arms, the metal links rendering her helpless and inert. She had lain in her own sick, refusing to eat the food the admiral's soldiers brought her, until at last she had been hauled upright and brought to a cargo hold, where they had stood her atop a grate and dumped bucket after bucket of icy-cold seawater over her until she stood clean and shivering, her teeth chattering. They had unbound the chains then—three silent adatrox, as two black-eyed angelic soldiers stood smugly at the door—and they had stripped her of her sodden clothes and dressed her in fresh ones. A large linen shirt, woolen trousers.

Then they refastened her chains, and when they turned her toward the door to escort her back to her cell, Admiral Ravikant stood at the threshold, hands clasped at his waist. An angel in possession of Ioseph Ferracora's body.

Eliana's heart dropped at the sight of her adoptive father's face—the dark hair and sharp chin that were perfect duplicates of Remy's. The short, muscled body she had once thought reassuringly solid and now saw as grotesque, a bullish facade.

The black eyes that held nothing inside them, emptier even than her windowless cell.

Admiral Ravikant watched her in silence, and she could only stare at him, her mouth dry and her heart beating fast.

When he spoke, it was in Ioseph Ferracora's voice, all its warmth gone, and Eliana wanted to be sick once more, though she had no food left in her stomach.

"Dirty yourself like that again," he said, "and I'll come back with your brother and demonstrate how ingenious a dealer of pain I can be. Refuse to eat another meal, and I'll truly grow angry."

He left without another word, and though she hated herself for it, as the adatrox brought her back to her cell, Eliana searched the ship's dim corridors for familiar ash-blond hair, a trim profile, a gleam of ice-blue eyes.

Your eyes are like fire.

She could not stop hearing the sound of her own voice in her memory—nor could she stop feeling the ghost of his hands upon her, the echo of his lips.

But the shadows shivering in the ship's labyrinthine hold were only angels in stolen skins and dead-eyed adatrox marching mindlessly after their masters.

Simon was nowhere to be found.

Eliana twisted her wrists against their bindings, though not to free herself, for she had determined that to be a futile task. Even if she escaped her chains, even if she somehow made it past the guards standing sentry outside her door, what then? What would she do? Dive into the middle of the sea and swim to safety, dragging Remy along behind her through the waves?

Once, not so long ago, she could have concentrated on the twin metal cages of her castings and used their solidity, the smooth anchors of the discs in her palms, to draw fire from the gas lamps lining the hallways and urge them into great bursts, scorching anyone who tried to stand against her.

But now, she could not find even a scrap of will to attempt summoning her power. Without her castings, she was a shell, scraped free of its meat and tossed into the waves. Reaching for the empirium would result only in bitter disappointment. She sensed it as surely as she smelled the tang of her own blood in the air, leaking from the wounds on her wrists.

There was an absence in her now—a great impassable void between the power lying in wait within her and the capacity of her mind to do anything more than stare blankly at the wall as Admiral Ravikant's ship bore her ever onward across the Great Ocean, toward the eastern continent.

Toward Celdaria.

Toward the Emperor.

The chafing of her wrists' tender flesh against the unyielding metal chains provided her with a perverse comfort there in the endless dark. A constant burning pain that reminded her where she was, that she was a prisoner, that her castings had been wrested from her. That one of her fathers was dead, his body long ago turned to ashes by his own lover's will; that her other father was also dead, his corpse overtaken by an angel for ill use.

That one of her mothers was dead, too, by her own hand.

And the other…

The moments when she thought of Rielle were the moments in which Eliana strained against her chains with a fevered sort of hunger.

She could have killed her.

When Simon had sent her back to the Old World, to the foothills of those unfamiliar Celdarian mountains, she had encountered her mother—had locked eyes with Rielle, had breathed the same air—and she had lost focus, allowing fear to overtake her. At that most crucial moment, she had fumbled, missing the opportunity that would have solved everything and prevented all of this—*this*, being a prisoner aboard this immaculate ship, the scent of which sat foul and heavy upon her tongue; *this*, the sound of Remy's horrified despair as he had cried out, weeping, at the sight of Ioseph's altered, black-eyed face.

This—the moment she had turned upon the pier on the shores of Festival and seen with her own eyes the terrible sight of Simon shooting their allies one by one, barking out angelic commands that the imperial soldiers had rushed to obey.

Eliana could have stopped it all from happening. She could have, but instead she had entertained the foolish thought of peace, of conversation and understanding between her and the greatest evil the world had ever known: Rielle Courverie, born Rielle Dardenne. The Blood Queen, the Kingsbane, the Lady of Death.

Eliana could have killed her, but she had tried to talk to her instead. *Talk to her.* As if a creature so vile would ever have the presence of mind or the desire to talk about ending the disastrous war of her own making, still raging a thousand years past her horizon.

And who had engineered that meeting? Who had sat with her and Remy and helped Eliana craft just the right sentences to say in Old Celdarian?

Simon. She forced herself to say his name, first in her mind and then out loud, hoping that soon the sound of it, the rhythm of the syllables, would stoke in her not a hollow, numb despair but rather a rage, cold and clean.

"Simon," she whispered. She stared into the relentless darkness. "Simon. Simon."

She pushed hard against her bindings, rubbing, twisting.

Maybe she would hit bone, if she worked hard enough at it.

Maybe she would bleed herself dry.

—◆—

One of them must have reported to him what she was doing.

Keys jangled in the lock. The door to her cell opened, and clipped bootsteps approached her. She recognized those footfalls. They tore her from a fitful sleep, and she watched in breathless horror as he crouched before her, arms resting lazily on his knees. He was in silhouette, his shape black against the lamplit corridor outside her cell, but she caught the faint gleam of his eyes.

She made herself stare at him, unblinking and unafraid, though that was a lie she was certain he could see through. Her body was weak, malnourished, and the sight of him sparked in her a rage too violent to bear. She quaked at his nearness. Her fingers twitched. She imagined clawing at him.

"Simon," she said, and her voice, at least, emerged steady and flat, as she had intended.

"You're hurting yourself," he observed. "I cannot allow that."

The sound of his voice was both familiar and utterly, horribly foreign. She had never heard it so cold, so devoid of passion, humor, anger. It held only brisk efficiency, his every word clipped and unfeeling.

"I don't care," she replied—a sulky child's response, but she could manage nothing better.

"The Emperor has requested that you arrive unmarred and healthy."

"The Emperor can go fuck himself, and you can join him."

She looked for the man she knew in his shadowed face and saw nothing, not even a ripple of scornful amusement. He rose to his feet and stepped aside as the pair of imperial guards waiting at the door entered in silence.

"Take her to B Deck," he ordered. "The Blue Room."

Then Simon turned on his heel and strode away, his long, lean body moving with the same sinuous grace it always had. His departure made her wild. If she'd had the freedom to do it, if she had been sure it wouldn't result in some awful fate for Remy, she would've launched herself at him, wedged her fingernails into the scarred furrows on his face, torn strips of flesh from his neck, and ripped out his throat.

Leaving her only seconds after showing himself for the first time in days? That she could not abide.

"Don't go," she blurted, desperate. Awful as he was, he was the only thing she knew in this terrible place. She felt that she had begun to lose pieces of herself, huddled in the dark like a kicked animal, but seeing him kneel before her, wishing viciously for his death—and to be its dealer— had awakened her.

He ignored her, striding on.

Frantic, she lunged against the guards' grips on her elbows. "I assume the Emperor has plans for me. Won't those proceed more quickly if I come to him informed of my situation rather than ignorant of it?"

He paused a few paces from the door and glanced back over his shoulder. "The Emperor's plans will proceed quickly, regardless of your ignorance." Then, to the guards, he said, "You have your orders."

He was gone soon after, and as Eliana was escorted out of her cell and through an endless, softly rocking maze of carpeted hallways, she began to doubt that he had ever been there at all.

—◆—

After that, she was never alone.

They brought her to a spacious apartment on one of the upper decks. A plush carpet of midnight blue stretched beneath a pale violet ceiling, the painted wood embellished with depictions of unfamiliar constellations. A chandelier hung from the rafters, links of crystal shivering as the boat rocked and hummed, and the bed was massive, a monstrosity of periwinkle and indigo satin that seemed to leer as a trio of angelic attendants undid Eliana's chains and tugged off her clothes.

Two guards watched the doors, and four more were stationed at the windows, past which stretched a glimmering blackness—the ceaseless waves, a touch of moonlight. The sight of the world beyond the ship shattered something fragile and tender in Eliana's throat, and as the attendants cleaned and bandaged her wrists, she swallowed hard against tears.

In the adjacent bathing room, they scrubbed her from head to toe with steaming water that poured from a gleaming brass faucet. Their movements were brisk but not violent, and Eliana wondered what exactly the Emperor's orders had been. If she did her utmost to goad them into hurting her, would they indulge her?

If she tried to kill herself, put an end to all of this before the Emperor could, would he slip inside her and hold her hostage inside her own mind, preventing her from doing anything except lying on that giant blue bed in silence until the ship made port in Celdaria?

She laughed a little at the image, and once she started, she could not stop. As the attendants worked soap through her shoulder-length cap of curls, hysterical laughter spilled out of her. Eliana watched herself in the mirror as they combed through her dark-brown hair, its waves and loose curls, its knotted snarls. The sight reminded her numbly of Dani Keshavarzian, who had cut her tangle-prone hair to her jawline, back in Willow. Thinking of Dani, of the Admiral's Jubilee, of everyone dead on that beach in Festival, she expected tears, but none came.

The attendants smoothed creams into her skin, its pale-brown color and warm olive tones painted wan and shadowed by the dim candlelight. They softened and plumped her as they might a hunk of meat. Then they dressed her in a shapeless nightgown of violet silk and retreated, leaving her alone with her six guards.

One of them pointed at the bed. "Sleep."

She obeyed, because if she stood for one more moment on her shaking legs, she would collapse, and she could not bear the indignity of angelic soldiers dragging her unconscious to her bed.

She climbed atop it, wobbly as a newborn foal. The perfumed scent of the soaps the attendants had used made her gag. She sank into her pillows, turned away from those twelve staring black eyes, and for the first time since waking aboard the admiral's ship, she wept.

—◆—

For days, she lay in quiet agony among the piles of blue silk that had become her entire world.

And in her dreams, he visited her.

First he was Remy, being dragged away down that endless red corridor of which she'd first dreamed in Astavar. She chased after him, running for miles along the blood-sodden carpet, but whoever or whatever was pulling him was too fast for her, too strong, and the end of the corridor was quickly unraveling, the pieces of it exploding outward like shards of shattered red glass.

Then he was Ioseph, the father who had raised her, lying on a clean white table in a clean white room, being cut open by angels in clean white robes. Each of them wore one of the masks she had seen at the Jubilee in Festival: a metallic black raven, a smiling brass fox, an ivory peacock studded with turquoise jewels. Ioseph screamed as the angels' knives pierced him, and then a funnel of black came spinning down from above, forcing itself into his mouth, his nose, his gaping chest.

Next he was Simon, coming to her in the little room at Willow with the slanted ceiling and the tiny hot stove, the bed tucked into the corner. His muscles trembled as he moved inside her, and his arms around her were warm and strong. They steadied her and they pinned her and they exhilarated her. He placed his palm against her forehead, and the warmth of that gentle touch soothed her. She followed the quiet trail of his touch down, down, down into a hot black tunnel buried deep in her mind. Her own heartbeat drummed faster and faster in her ears, so loud it shook her chest, and suddenly she wanted to leave Simon, she wanted to run from him and never look back. But she couldn't free herself from his arms. She was trapped there in the little bed, in the spiraling tunnel, with the boom of her heartbeat drowning her, choking her, and his mouth was upon her, his fingers pressing between her lips, against the tender curve of her neck, and she craved the pressure of his touch even as she despised it.

"Your eyes," he whispered into her hair, "are like fire."

A terrible scorching heat bloomed inside her. It started in her belly and grew and rose until she was pressing the heels of her palms to her cheeks, burning her fingers on the twin firepits where her eyes used to be, and Simon's laughter was everywhere, a roughshod accompaniment to her racing heart.

Harkan's voice rose through the crackling inferno: *El, if you can do something, do it now!*

She saw herself kneeling in the mud outside the city of Karlaine, pressing her glowing hands into the terrible wound on Remy's stomach—

A sucking swoop of sound, then silence. Darkness.

"Ah." A little sigh. Smooth words stretched around a smile. "There you are."

She turned in her bed at Willow, in that little room with the slanted ceiling, rain tapping its cold fingers against the windows. Sitting in the corner, in a chair draped with Simon's clothes, was a man in black, white fingers steepled at his lips.

His smile widened when her eyes alighted upon him, and the sight of him sitting there, content in his amusement, was such a flawless portrait, so startlingly beautiful, that Eliana found herself weeping anew.

"Welcome home, Your Highness," he said to her, and then rose, the shadows of the room converging on him, shaping the clean black lines of his cloak, his coat, his hair—

—◆—

Eliana awoke as the ship shuddered, then stilled.

The endless rocking was no more, and outside the windows of her blue room there was sunlight, a broad pink sky, a pair of gliding white gulls.

She sat up, her shaking limbs slick with sweat. Bedsheets ruined, eyes burning, cheeks raw and wet.

When the door opened, Admiral Ravikant strode into the room. Eliana's three attendants flanked him, opulent fabrics draped over their arms.

"We're here," she croaked. She had not used her voice in days, perhaps weeks. "Aren't we?"

The admiral's smile was jubilant, the ghost of her father's face alight with an expression of frenzied joy she had never seen him wear.

"Get dressed," he commanded. "He is waiting for you."

→ 3 ←

AUDRIC

"Fear not, Celdaria: The traitor Audric Courverie no longer sits on Katell's sacred throne. The murderous Kingsbane has fled in fear. At last, the mysterious attacks plaguing the eastern borders, leaving our citizens pale and disfigured in their homes, will end. At last, we will find justice for what we have lost. At last, the House of Sauvillier will bring Celdaria's enemies to their knees. Look to the capital and rejoice, for though the crown was weak, it is now strong once more. All hail His Majesty Merovec Sauvillier, the True King of Celdaria!"

—A royal decree issued upon Merovec Sauvillier's assumption of the Celdarian throne, November 8, Year 999 of the Second Age

Audric would have flown for days, if Ludivine had let him.

In the sky, with only the low clouds and Ludivine and Atheria for company, he was almost able to forget everything that had happened. He existed in a soft gray world, even when the sunlight hit him full on, so brilliant and hot that beads of sweat rolled down his brow and back and pasted his clothes to his skin.

His clothes—trousers of the finest wool, boots polished to a faultless shine, a tunic of emerald silk, an embroidered coat of white and gold that hugged his trim torso.

The clothes he had worn to his wedding only days earlier.

"Hush," Ludivine told him the first time memories of that night managed to penetrate the numb fog that had fallen over him. She rode behind him on Atheria, arms wrapped around his waist, cheek pressed against his back. "There's no sense in thinking of that now. Not until we're safe."

Safe. He laughed, but only a little. He hadn't the energy for more than that, and certainly not enough to talk to her, even if he'd wanted to.

And he didn't want to.

He spoke to Ludivine only once, after she convinced him to stop in a small wood near the southern shores of Celdaria. They had to fly carefully, and only at night. Audric had allowed Ludivine to dictate the terms of their travel, too weary and heartsick to protest. It was soothing to be directed and carried. Directed by an angel, carried by a godsbeast.

Again, he laughed. Each time he did, Ludivine's concern butted gently against him like that of a fussing mother. Several times, he considered turning around, shoving her off Atheria, and watching her plunge through the clouds to the ground. The only thing that stopped him was the hope that she might be useful in finding Rielle and convincing her to come home.

A callous, selfish thought, perhaps. He hoped Ludivine could sense it. He hoped it sat as heavily on her heart as his last memories of Rielle sat on his. He hoped it suffocated her.

Atheria alighted soundlessly in a grove of oaks and shook out her wings. Audric felt her great black eyes watching him as he stood between two gnarled trunks and looked north, toward home.

Ludivine touched his arm. "You didn't abandon them."

"I did," he said flatly. "Let's not pretend otherwise."

"If you had stayed, Merovec would have killed you."

His grip on Illumenor's hilt tightened. "I can protect myself."

"Of course, but that is something we could not have risked."

He rounded on her. "Why? Because with me dead, you would have had to work harder to bring Rielle home?"

Ludivine's pale gaze was steady. "It would have broken my heart to lose you."

"That doesn't answer my question."

"It is nevertheless true."

"Surely you don't expect me to believe that anything you say is true."

She watched him quietly for a moment, perhaps hoping that her steady silence would wear him down, that he would apologize for his unkindness, that he would draw her into his arms and kiss her brow as he had always done.

But instead, he watched her with the patience of a mountain until she was the one to look away and sink heavily onto the grass.

"I have made a grave error somewhere," she muttered, "but I cannot see it."

"Your error was in thinking you could control us like pieces in a strategy game," Audric snapped. "You thought you could scheme with Rielle, keep her all to yourself, and still protect her from him somehow. You convinced her to hide the truth from me, and you ushered her through the trials, and you encouraged her to practice the art of resurrection, which is exactly what he wants of her, and you did all of this without consulting anyone."

As he spoke, he grew angrier. His fury did not erupt, but rather overflowed steadily. The world was a whirl of dim light and roaring sound, but he stayed put where he stood and breathed through the heat of his anger.

His fight with Rielle was too fresh for him to make the same mistake twice and push away his strongest ally in the war for Rielle's allegiance.

If it could even still be won.

And the fact that he had to think of such things—Rielle's *allegiance*, as if she owed that to him or anyone—disgusted him so thoroughly that he realized with a swift, quiet turn of understanding that he hated himself utterly.

He stared down at Ludivine, steeling his heart against the sight of her sitting there with slumped shoulders, staring bleakly at nothing, a lock of mussed golden hair come loose from its crown of braids.

"All those months ago, when the Borsvall soldiers ambushed me during the Boon Chase," Audric said, "and Rielle lost control of her power while saving me—you could have stopped her then, isn't that right? You could have entered her mind and subdued her, kept her power secret. She would not have been found out. No trials, no Sun Queen."

"I could not allow you to die," Ludivine said hollowly.

He waited a beat, then crouched before her. "Because you love me?"

"Because Rielle loves you."

The words gutted him. Did she still? He might never know. "Because you wanted her to love me. You wanted us to love one another, and wed, and you wanted us to have children, maybe, for each of these things would have bound her more securely to me, to the crown. To you."

Ludivine flinched. "Because if you had died, it would have broken her heart."

"And in her heartbroken state, she might have done something rash. Fallen into the arms of one ready to soothe her grief. As she has now done, despite all your efforts."

"I didn't—"

"Perhaps you could even have stopped the assassins themselves in their tracks." He realized it for the first time, baffled that it had never occurred to him before. Had she prevented him from deducing the truth? "But you didn't stop them, because you *wanted* Rielle's power to erupt. You wanted her to start exploring it. Why?"

Helplessly, Ludivine opened her mouth and shut it again, her pale, slender hands clenched on her thighs. "It's not as simple as that, Audric—"

"And if you had told me the truth about my father's death," he interrupted, "I could have helped her. I could have helped *you*. We could have been a united front, you and I. All her fears, all the guilt she carried after what happened at the fire trial. Those last minutes with her father. The nightmares that no doubt plagued her—her own, and Corien's too. I could have helped her bear every one of those burdens. But you denied me that choice. And you denied her the comfort I would have given her, the peace I could have helped her find."

Ludivine's eyes shone with tears. "I did what I thought was best."

"You're a fool," he said harshly. "Selfish and prideful. If not for you, she might still be with us."

Atheria knelt at his approach. He mounted her without saying another word and waited for Ludivine to climb up behind him. She settled herself between the godsbeast's massive black-tipped wings and took a shuddering breath.

"I won't apologize," Ludivine whispered once they were in the air. The wind nearly swallowed her words.

"Nor should you ever again try to convince me that you did it all for love," Audric said. "If I hear that once more, I'll be through with you. I'm nearly there already."

Atheria took them swiftly across the sky. Each feathered pulse of her wings was a low, soft drumbeat that shook Audric's chest.

He did not speak to Ludivine again.

—◆—

The coast of Mazabat appeared first as a white sliver on the horizon, an unsteady smile capping the glittering winter sea.

As they approached, Audric saw the grim truth of what Mazabat had endured since Rielle's visit months before: an endless barrage of storms, all of them rippling out from the weakening Gate. Eroded beaches strewn with debris stretched from horizon to horizon. Beyond the coast, miles of forest had been leveled by wind, and the city of Quelbani looked half-made with many of its towers toppled and even the larger temples stripped of their roofs and windows.

Examining the ruined landscape, his heart sinking, Audric didn't notice the people lining the outermost crest of beach until the sky exploded into flame.

Atheria swerved, her wings pounding the air sharply to redirect their course, and let out a fierce scream of anger.

Audric wound his hands into her mane and squinted through the brilliance. A field of fiery starbursts hovered along the shore as far as he could see in either direction. There were so many, and they were so close together, shifting restlessly like trapped fireflies, that they formed a net, effectively blocking Atheria's approach.

Only a single narrow aisle of empty air was left untouched—a corridor guiding them to shore.

"They're controlling our descent," observed Ludivine.

"I don't blame them," he replied, and stroked the arch of Atheria's neck. "Go on."

She snorted, her long ears flattening back against her skull. He could feel her muscles trembling with the effort of hovering there, as if treading water.

Closing his eyes, Audric concentrated on the sunlight caressing his scalp, the back of his neck, his fingers clutching Atheria's mane. He leaned down, pressed his cheek against the chavaile's velvet neck.

"I trust you, Atheria," he told her quietly. He held his palms flat against her coat, imagining that he could send all the channels of power weaving through his body—even those he could not sense—into Atheria's own. He was no angel, nor was he Rielle, who seemed to converse with Atheria as easily as she would with any person.

But then, Atheria was no horse. She was a godsbeast, superior to them all, closer to the empirium than anyone or anything except, perhaps, for Rielle. He hoped she could somehow understand him, feel reassured by his trust in her.

"If danger awaits us on the shore," he continued, "then you may certainly turn away at once and carry us to safety." Feeling foolish, he added, "Do you understand?"

Atheria's ears swiveled, forward and back, as if listening to a world of sound his own ears could not detect, and then, after another moment of hesitation, she plunged down toward the sea, following the path the Mazabatians' fire had made for them.

For the first time since his wedding night, Audric felt something other than despair—a small spark of joy, weak and flickering, quickly snuffed out.

They waited on the beach—an orderly arrangement of royal soldiers some two hundred strong. Fifty were firebrands, their arms trembling with exertion as together they held fast the net of fire stretching along the coastline.

As soon as Atheria's hooves touched the sand, the firebrands lowered their castings and staggered. Some collapsed. Audric was not surprised; such a display of unwavering power was not easily managed even by the most skilled elementals—not anymore, in this quiet age. Healers in white robes rushed forward to tend to the firebrands, and as Audric watched them, he thought of Rielle, of the brilliant web of power she had created to stop the tidal wave from destroying the Borsvallic capital of Styrdalleen.

Hers had been a shield even more massive and dazzling than this display created by fifty firebrands combined—and after, she had not collapsed. She had been tired, yes, but she had stood strong and tall, and her eyes had glittered, and she had moved toward him with a supple, languid grace as the people of Styrdalleen cried out in adulation.

Audric tried to push these thoughts of Rielle aside and failed. She would forever be a refrain cycling under the surface of his every thought, his every word. He could see her so clearly—smell her, feel her—that for a moment he could not move, the colossal weight of his anguish pulling at him like a dark tide.

Atheria shifted, whickering softly.

Audric forced himself to dismount and held up his hands. Hundreds of eyes followed him; raised bows and nocked arrows and brandished castings tracked his every movement. The air shimmered with contained elemental power, as if the beach were a heat mirage.

"Will your firebrands be well?" Audric called out.

A nearby soldier, her lapel decorated with an array of jewel-colored medals, her dark curly hair clipped short and neat, stepped out of the ranks. Audric guessed she was a commander.

"Drop your casting, Lightbringer," she ordered. "And please be reminded that you are vastly outnumbered here and that the rules of extradition do not apply to deposed kings. It is only due to the generosity of Queen Bazati and Queen Fozeyah that you have been allowed entry to our country."

He obeyed, lowering Illumenor to the ground. "I understand. And I must express my deepest sadness about the damage these recent months have brought to your beautiful city."

The commander said nothing. Her proud eyes cut to Ludivine. "Lady Sauvillier. It is your brother who now sits on the Celdarian throne."

"As surely as no elemental power runs in my veins," Ludivine replied, stepping forward with her palms raised, "so does my loyalty lie only with my true king, Audric Courverie."

"That will do," said a deep, rich voice, and then the wall of soldiers parted to reveal a brown-skinned woman in a gown of vivid azure. Her long black hair cascaded down her back in coarse ringlets. Sweeps of amber and cerulean highlighted her grave brown eyes, and around her neck she wore a heavy triangular pendant on a golden chain.

"Queen Bazati." Audric knelt in the sand. "I thank you for allowing Lady Ludivine and myself to land on your shores, and I would like to make a formal request for asylum. Though I know the news from Celdaria is alarming, I hope you will remember the centuries of friendship our two nations have enjoyed—"

"Oh, get up." Queen Bazati of the royal house of Asdalla helped him rise, then drew him into a fierce embrace. "You ate at my family's table when you were hardly higher than my knee. Once, if you'll recall, you threw up on my temple gown right in the middle of prayers after you stole a whole sack of sweets from my kitchen."

He managed a small smile as she pulled away from him. "Then I suppose my request for asylum is granted? I promise not to get sick on any of your gowns."

The queen did not return his smile. Instead, she searched his face for a long moment, then shook her head. "What happened, Audric?"

The compassion in her voice opened a chasm between his ribs, and for the first time since he had awoken alone in the gardens—Rielle gone, and the captain of his guard bearing down on him with disgust and hatred flaring bright in his eyes—Audric felt the hot press of tears.

"I don't know," he answered honestly. "Nothing good, Your Majesty."

She nodded and hooked her arm through his. Her gaze flickered once to Ludivine, and Audric thought he read displeasure in her expression, as if she wished he had arrived in Mazabat alone.

A sentiment to which he could certainly relate.

"I'll have rooms in the royal wing made up for you," she said to him as they walked up the beach toward the shredded tree line and the white stone roads of Quelbani beyond. Citizens sorted through piles of rubble, and crews of builders worked on high scaffolding to repair stripped stone facades, but still the city shone as if no wind could hope to dull its light. As a boy, Audric had relished his family's trips to the Mazabatian capital, for its reputation as a place of scholars, research, and the medicinal arts was unrivaled, its libraries the grandest in the world since the angelic libraries on the southern continent of Patria had been destroyed during the Angelic Wars.

But now, as the sounds of the bustling city met his ears, he found himself wishing, with a longing so simple and keen that it stole his breath, that he could turn around and go home.

Never had he imagined not having a home to return to.

✦◇✦

The apartment the queens had prepared for him was airy and simply but luxuriously appointed—walls of whitewashed stone, trailing ferns of lilac and forest green hanging from the ceiling in brass pots, wind chimes singing merrily from the balconies.

He declined the queens' invitation to supper as politely as possible and was glad when Ludivine retreated without a word to her own chambers down the corridor.

The sun was setting. Beyond his windows, which had been thrown open to admit the cool night air, the sky was dim with tangerine light, its clouds tinted lavender and rose.

He was alone.

He watched the sky for as long as he could remain standing, and then he began to shake from his tense shoulders down to his aching calves. The exhaustion and numbness of those long days traveling aboard Atheria were coming to claim him at last, but the sight of his bed was unbearable. Clean and neat and white, the headboard a masterwork of stained teak carvings and polished blue stone, it was lovely and inviting, but it was not his.

It was a stranger's bed, slept in by countless dignitaries over the years. His own bed was at home, in Baingarde, and had cocooned him as he moved with Rielle in the deep hours of the night, when everything else was still.

Outside, on one of the broad terraces, Atheria touched down with a cheerful little chirp, her mouth full of feathers. She had caught a hawk for supper.

It was the sight of her that undid him.

His grief slammed into him like the tidal wave he had watched Rielle subdue. He couldn't tear the image of her from his mind—a glowing savior, a fire-limned queen riding her immortal steed to save the world.

"Oh, God," he choked out, sinking to his knees, and then all at once, his fury, sorrow, and regret burst up his body, from belly to chest to throat, and he threw his head back and screamed, his arms rigid at his sides.

Quickly, his sobs rose up to claim his voice, and he wept there on the soft white rug, his hands buried in his dark curls. His chest was an agony of pain, as if a blade had cleaved it in two.

He would not have minded if that happened. He could not imagine waking up the next day, and the next, and the next, in this place that was not his home, his throne taken from him and his own, his love, his Rielle gone from him, driven away by his own anger, his stupid, vicious jealousy, his wounded pride.

He did not hear the door open, nor did he hear Ludivine pad barefooted across the floor. He did not realize hours had passed, that the sky was dark, or that he was hungry, shivering on the floor. That he was so tired his bones ached, or that Atheria was pacing in a frenzy of worry on the terrace, chirping like an agitated bird.

But when Ludivine sat beside him and opened her arms, he turned into her, seeking comfort as blindly as a child. She did not send him any reassurances with her mind, and for that he was grateful.

He held on to her, his sobs raw and heaving. He felt Ludivine's lips in his hair.

"I'm so sorry, Audric," she whispered against his temple, her words thick with tears. She stroked his damp curls, said his name again and again.

The sound of her voice reminded him to breathe.

— 4 —

TAL

"My darling Tal. I'll send this to that inn we love, in Beaulaval, in hopes that it will reach you. No word from Audric yet. Things are changing quickly here. Merovec's soldiers stop citizens on the streets. They barge into homes unannounced, patrol neighborhoods constantly. Searching for something, but what? When any of us try to offer counsel, or ask what Merovec is trying to do, we are dismissed. More later, but for now I must tell you that Odo Laroche and I, we've begun what you might call a resistance effort. Those who are loyal to Audric. You'll think it rash, but you aren't seeing what I'm seeing. We've named ourselves Red Crown. Don't laugh. None of this is funny, and we've got to do something. I miss you. Be careful. Trust no one. Bring her home."

—Encoded undelivered letter from Miren Ballastier, Grand Magister of the Forge in Âme de la Terre, capital of Celdaria, to Taliesin Belounnon, Grand Magister of the Pyre, dated November 15, Year 999 of the Second Age

Safely hidden under his heavy woolen cloak, his hood drawn up to shield his sodden blond hair, Taliesin Belounnon, Grand Magister of the Pyre, entered the buzzing tavern hall of the Glittering Mare and headed straight for the goddamned barkeep.

It was a chill night, and the ferocious winter storm that had swept down from the north earlier that day showed no signs of abating. But inside the crowded Glittering Mare, so named for Saint Katell's legendary godsbeast, the air was damp and thick.

The barkeep glanced up as Tal approached. Her mouth thinned, so much like Miren's when she was cross—her red cap of curls was, similarly, eerily reminiscent—that Tal had to avert his eyes.

"If you're going to drip water all over the place," she said, "then it's double the price for everything we've got."

From underneath his hood, Tal met the woman's eyes and gave her a tiny grin, the sort of charming, cockeyed smile he had for the most part put to rest since being ordained Grand Magister.

For the most part.

"Are you certain about that?" he asked. "Happy to wring out my cloak a few times and give the place a good scrub."

The barkeep's frown deepened. "You think a joke and a nice smile's enough to make me change my mind?"

Tal stifled a sigh. He was tired and cold, and his boots and socks were completely soaked, and his shield casting, strapped to his back underneath his cloak, was unfairly heavy, and all he wanted in the world was a drink, all to himself, without anyone bothering him or complaining about the state of his clothes.

As soon as his mind formed the thought, he knew it for a lie.

All he wanted in the world—all he *really* wanted—was to look behind him at the dozens of drinking, gossiping, shouting people jammed into the tavern and see a pale young woman with wild dark hair and bright green eyes. She would be standing there, the crowd swirling obliviously about her, and when her eyes locked with his, her face would crumple with relief, with exhaustion. She would run toward him, arms outstretched, and he would gather her close, smooth down the tangles of her hair, kiss her tearstained cheeks. He would reassure her that she was safe at last, that he would take her swiftly home.

Her name curled on the curve of his tongue. It was a word familiar enough to have a flavor, tart and explosive, as if he'd bitten down on a ripe summer berry. *Rielle.*

He had to look. He could almost *feel* her standing there, frightened and tired, heartsick and homesick.

But when he turned to glance over his shoulder, he saw only the tavern and its customers, only the high-raftered ceiling and the shutters drawn tight against the storm.

He closed his eyes briefly, a sharp pain twisting in his throat. This wasn't the first time he had sworn that she was there—just behind him, just beyond that turn in the road, just beyond that copse of trees. Her echo had accompanied him for days as he searched the Celdarian wilderness, and it was that remnant, that pull, that had him convinced she was always near, that he was getting closer to finding her.

Either that or she was dead, and it was only her memory that haunted him.

But he couldn't imagine that the world would survive her death. And if it could, somehow—if everything could stay as it was even though she no longer breathed the air that kept them all alive—then theirs was a world he no longer wished to inhabit.

He lowered the hood of his cloak, shaking the tangles out of his rain-soaked hair—and shaking loose thoughts of Rielle. Maybe, at least for a few minutes, he could clear his head and find some peace. He glanced up, offering the barkeep a pretty view of his pretty face, as well as a rueful smile that succeeded in making her blush.

"Forgive me," he said, chuckling. "It's been a horrible, long day, I've been traveling for many horrible, long days, and my temper is frayed. Do you have a rag? I'll sop up this mess of mine and leave you be."

"Oh, stop charming me," the barkeep scolded as she moved away, but he'd seen her mouth twitch, and when she returned a few moments later, it was with a steaming mug of cider and two white rags.

"Clean yourself up, and then you can pay for the next one," she said with a wink that reminded him, once again, so utterly of Miren that he lost the capacity to speak.

Instead, he smiled at the woman, found an unoccupied stool, and sat hunched over his drink. Hot and spiced, it loosened some of the knots in his chest, but it did nothing to soothe the headache that had been steadily pounding against his temples since he'd left Âme de la Terre. He had worked diligently over the past several days to keep his thoughts of home fleeting, skimming over them as he might the spines of books he had no interest in reading.

But the cider wasn't excellent only at loosening knots, and soon he was nursing the dregs while thoughts of home whirled and raced through his mind.

It was driving him mad, not knowing what was happening in Âme de la Terre. Word of Audric's ousting and Merovec's assumption of the throne had made its way across the country. Judging by the several hushed conversations taking place around the room and the furtive, curious glances thrown at the door each time it opened, the citizens here in the little village of Tavistère had heard the news too.

Tal gripped his mug and closed his eyes, trying not to think of Miren alone back in the city, dealing with Merovec Sauvillier.

Merovec Sauvillier, king of Celdaria. King Audric, gone into hiding.
Queen Rielle, vanished into the night.

The whispered words floated around the room, and each time they met Tal's ears, the sounds curdled inside him like some horrible blockage he couldn't dislodge. His only consolation was the knowledge that if Audric were found and killed, Merovec would ensure that particular piece of news traveled quickly. Until then, there was some measure of comfort to be found in the confused speculation regarding his whereabouts.

"Here." A fresh mug slid into view. The barkeep was watching him curiously. "You look like you need at least a few more of these."

Tal managed a weak smile. "I'll pay for the third one, then?"

"Keep me engaged in fascinating conversation, and you won't have to pay for any of them. You look like you have some fascinating conversations brewing in that pretty blond head of yours."

"Fascinating," Tal agreed. "Startling. Disturbing."

The barkeep's eyebrows raised. "You know how to intrigue a girl, Wet Cloak."

"Aiden," he lied, with another smile.

"Rosette." She propped her chin in her hands and grinned back at him. "So? A deal's a deal."

And suddenly, Tal wanted nothing more than to confess everything. "I left my home to do something very important," he said instead, his throat constricting. "And I left behind someone I love."

"Why couldn't they come with you?"

Miren's face flashed before him—sharp-chinned and mischievous. A dense field of freckles across pale cheeks. Soft red curls that gleamed like molten copper in the candlelight of their bedroom.

And then, the last night he had seen her, in the gardens behind Baingarde—her face hard and solemn, her eyes bright but full of resolve. She had stayed behind in the capital to be Audric's eyes. A loyal spy for the deposed king.

Be brave, she had whispered against his mouth under the garden pines, and then hurried back to the castle before he could even begin to craft the goodbye she deserved.

"Because," he said at last, rubbing his forehead, "she has an important thing to do as well. Too important to abandon her post, as it were."

"Quite significant people you two must be," Rosette mused, a single finger tapping against her lips. "I don't suppose you'll tell me what these grave tasks are?"

"I'm afraid not."

"You've been sworn to secrecy, have you?"

He placed a hand on his chest and bowed his head. "Sworn to secrecy and bound with gilded chains of honor."

Rosette's smile widened. "I do love when brooding men laden with noble secrets enter my establishment."

Tal's tired mind struggled for a reply. He had drunk too much cider; his thoughts were clouded and sloppy. Miren's face and Rielle's face collided and combined—short red curls and long dark waves. Rielle's echo once again touched his shoulder, sharp and sudden as a gust of wind, and he clenched all his muscles against it.

"I know you're not really there," he muttered, pressing his fingertips hard against his temples.

"Aiden? Are you ill?" Rosette touched his arm. "You've gone so pale. I like you, but you had better not get sick on my counter."

The door to the tavern hall slammed open.

A desperate shout rang out. "The pale mark! They're here! The pale mark! My daughter! Someone, please, they're here! Someone's here!"

Rosette stepped back with a choked cry.

Tal turned, his vision pulsing with the rhythm of his headache, and saw a man standing at the open door, the storm raging at his back. In his arms was the body of a young woman, her limbs rigid, her face twisted into a grotesque, bone-white mask of horror.

Panic snapped through the Glittering Mare like spitting flames. Those nearest the man staggered back as if the girl in his arms carried a foul sickness. Others cried out and hurried for the doors, the windows, the stairs leading up to the boarding rooms.

Tal stood, hot-cold dread flooding down his arms.

He had heard of this "pale mark." King Ilmaire of Borsvall had written to Audric about it, and reports of it from their own soldiers had arrived in the capital week after week in recent months. At the borders of both Celdaria and Borsvall, villages and military outposts alike had been plagued by these unexplained deaths—people killed swiftly in the night. By shadows, was the rumor. There were whispers of beasts, though none of the reports on Tal's desk had managed to describe anything comprehensible.

Some of the dead had been massacred, their bones scattered and their flesh in shreds; others were left lifeless with no wounds on their bodies. The only clue as to what had happened to those mysterious corpses, report after report noted, was their unnaturally pale faces, each and every one of them distorted in horror as if, in their last moments, they had been unmade from the inside out.

A cold hand touched Tal's arm. He turned to see Rosette staring at him, her eyes glazed over with a gray film and a smug smile splitting her face. Tal lost his breath.

She cocked her head sharply to one side. "Too late, Tal."

Her neck snapped with a horrible crack; her eyes cleared. She collapsed, smacking her head against the countertop.

Tal staggered back. Those nearest him screamed and fled. He knew very little about angelic behavior, but Rielle had told him everything that had happened to the late King Hallvard of Borsvall just before he died, and as he stared at Rosette's frozen eyes, her bone-white face twisted in agony, a horrible chill swept across his skin.

Angels.

Corien.

Rielle.

"Too late, Tal!" A new, male voice crowed the words, and by the time Tal found the source, the man—bearded, gray-eyed, smiling madly—was already falling, his neck broken, his face bleached and twisted.

"Too late, Tal!" A serving boy, hardly older than fifteen.

"Too late, Tal!" A woman trying to calm her crying children.

The trail of their broken bodies taunted him, monstrous white faces leading him toward the door. Tal shoved past the panicking crowd and the poor sobbing man falling to his knees at the threshold. His daughter's body tumbled to the floor.

Outside, the storm sucked the air from Tal's throat. Black rain battered him like needles. He unbuckled the straps across his chest and withdrew his shield, then used it to scoop up a broad plate of flame from the oil-soaked torches sputtering at the tavern door. Several people cried out and jumped back, but he ignored them, racing through the crowded, muddy yard. The terrified cries of the horses stabled in the inn's barn pierced the air. Their hooves pounded against their stalls. There was no fire, besides that of his shield; they were afraid of something else.

Only when he reached the trees at the yard's edge did he stop to listen. Not to the cries of those back at the inn. Not to the storm.

Instead, he listened for Rielle.

His body trembling with rage, he closed his eyes, gripped his shield hard, and called upon the empirium with more desperation than he ever had before.

The empirium is in every living thing, and every living thing is of the empirium, he prayed.

Burn steady and burn true. The flames lining his shield grew, snapping and hungry.

Burn clean and burn bright.

Rielle had uttered those same words the day of the fire trial. They had recited them together, again and again, as the burning replica of her parents' house spewed ash and sparks at their feet.

But then...feathers had fallen instead of flames. Brilliant and fire-colored, all of Rielle's making.

Rielle, where are you?

Her echo skipped past him, almost playful. A cold snap across his abdomen.

He ran after it through the dark woods, sodden branches whipping at him, the only light that of his blazing shield, and when he emerged into the clearing where she stood—he knew it, he *knew* she was there even before he saw her, he could feel it, he could feel *her*; he had begged the empirium to find her, and it had, for once, cleanly and completely obeyed him—the pulsing pain in his head exploded.

He crashed to his knees; his shield flew away, the flames extinguished. He fell forward on his hands, and when he looked up, the world tilted, and he saw her for only a moment.

She wore a long, dark cloak so large it swallowed her. Her wet hair clung to her cheeks.

Their eyes locked, and even as his vision darkened, his skull screaming as if it were tearing itself in two, he recognized that look in her eyes. He had taught her for years; he had practically raised her.

She was frightened.

He reached for her, his arm shaking. "Rielle, darling, it's all right, I'm here—"

But then he could no longer hold himself up, and as he watched from the mud, immobile and dazed, a white-haired girl with pale brown skin carved a ring of light from the air at Rielle's feet. He didn't understand what he was seeing. Was the girl a marque?

There was a sweep of darkness, swift movement, a snap in the air. A tall man, the wind whipping his coat.

Then the light was gone. And so was Rielle.

All that remained was a voice that did not belong to her. It was soft and refined and highly amused.

It said, *Too late, Tal.*

And then it kicked him hard into oblivion.

RIELLE

"For millennia, the angels lived only in the skies. After the first angel ascended from the dust of old, the rest of her kind were born—from clouds and comets, from high astral winds. Luminous and ageless, they studied the stars and the empirium beyond. It was not until the angels at last noticed humans living in the world below that they descended, too fascinated to resist what were to them repulsive, remarkable creatures with fleeting lives and enviable powers. To the humans, the Great Descent was a rain of fire upon the world, beyond the work of any elemental. Chaos ruled. Countries were unmade and borders erased. Humans scattered far and wide, leaving the nations we now know as Patria and Vindica free for the angels to claim as their own."

—And Fire Fell From the Skies: The Great Angelic Descent
and How It Changed the World, a collection of scholarly
writings compiled by Lyzet Taval,
of the First Guild of Scholars

Rielle had not yet mastered the art of traveling through Obritsa's threads with any sort of grace.

The third time she stepped through the humming ring of light she had come to despise, she managed to keep her balance for only a moment before her knees buckled.

The ground came at her fast, a flat, hard stretch of red dirt scattered with sharp pebbles that pierced her tender palms.

She looked up, swallowing against the faint urge to be sick that always seemed to accompany traveling by thread, and discovered she was at the bottom of a narrow canyon of towering red stone. There was a roaring river nearby, carving its way through the rock with white foam and a black current. The sky was bright with sunset, casting an eerie crimson light across the flat canyon walls, into which intricate designs had been carved. Rielle picked out familiar shapes: Winged angels soaring through cities crowned with high towers. Great sleek warships pushing toward a distant shore. Stars and moons dotting the canvas of red rock in various configurations, like some sprawling map left behind by a mammoth traveler.

"It's beautiful," she said softly.

"Of course it is. Angels made it." Corien approached her with his left hand outstretched. "This is Samandira, the entrance to Eridel. One of the greatest cities in Vindica, long ago. A place of study and enlightened thinking. Universities where angelic scholars worked to unravel the mysteries of creation. Libraries containing thousands of works examining the nature of the empirium. Before humans destroyed it," he added lightly. "The war did much damage. And then, after our imprisonment, thousands of humans journeyed here to demolish what remained. For years they have done this—undoing everything we accomplished. Pillaging the ruins."

Rielle knew the lightness in his voice was false. After he helped her to her feet, she laced her fingers through his. His black cloak and trousers, once immaculate, had grown filthy from their relentless traveling. Looking up at his face, so fine and smooth in the wash of red light, she felt a surge of fondness—and of pity.

She touched his cheek. Her dirty fingers smudged his pale skin. No words she could say would be of any comfort, and she was still uncertain if comfort was something she wished to give.

But she could not stop herself from touching him.

Her life had become a series of frantic episodes—dashing east, from one city to the next, either on foot or on horseback or in whatever carriage Corien stole from people on the road, none of whom could resist his coaxing voice, his tear-bright pale eyes, his promises of a wild rut in the trees, if only they would grant use of their horse and cart.

He enjoyed toying with them, these hapless humans who were at first content to let him slip inside their minds while gazing upon his exquisite face—until they realized too late what was happening and began to scream in fear.

At first, Rielle had looked away whenever this happened. The sight of them was awful—their faces convulsing and contorting—and then, when they dropped to the ground, the heavy, hard thud. All the color gone from their faces, their expressions those of absolute terror. She knew Corien was capable of violence, but these had seemed such unnecessary, cruel instances of it that she refused to watch.

At first.

Now, she found herself peeking more and more often. It wasn't that she enjoyed their pain, exactly. It was that she enjoyed the display of his power, and he knew she enjoyed it, could feel her tired delight pressing up against his thoughts right before he killed them, and knowing he was delighted brought her some comfort. She was desperate for comfort. Her head would not stop hurting, and she hated her stolen dress.

She hated, too, how strange her body felt some days, how inexplicable sickness came over her without warning until she was forced, mortified, to heave miserably while Corien held back her hair with a tenderness that nearly made up for the indignity of being sick in the dirt.

So, she watched him kill, craving his delight and approval with vaguely troubling desperation. But every time a jolt of alarm rattled her, it disappeared as quickly as it had come.

You're like me, she had told him five days past. He had just stepped away from a gray-haired man, wizened but strong, and let him fall to the ground. The man had been a shepherd, a fact that made Corien laugh for reasons he hid from Rielle when she tried touching his mind.

I've been telling you how alike we are for months, he replied, amused, as he stepped over the corpse to approach her. *Why say this today?*

You don't enjoy hurting them. That's not what makes you do it. Her heart pounded at his nearness. Each hungry pulse buoyed her chest higher and higher until she felt ready to float off the ground. She was so tired—she was always tired in a muddy sort of way, as if she were perpetually slogging through a gummy swamp—and the exhaustion only lifted when he was near.

You enjoy your power, she told him. *You enjoy what you can do, and the feeling of rightness that fills you when you use your mind as it was made to be used.*

Corien considered her for a moment, and then, his breath hot against her mouth, said, *You're only partially correct, my darling. For I do love my power, yes, but in fact I very much do enjoy hurting them. All of them. Every single one.*

Then he had kissed her, long and hard, until her slight sick dismay at his words had vanished, until she had forgotten about the dead man at her feet and all the other bodies they had left in their wake.

She wasn't even entirely sure where they were traveling.

When she had asked Corien, only once, he had answered by sending her his thoughts, but they were so jumbled and confusing that thinking about them hurt her eyes, as if she'd gazed directly at the sun. She was forced to look away from them, and soon she had forgotten all about her questions, only occasionally noticing them there on her mind's horizon before they disappeared once more.

We must continue on, Corien told her. *That's all that matters.*

He was right, of course. They had to keep traveling southeast. There was no need to know more than that.

They rested only when Obritsa needed it, which was far too often for Rielle's liking. Didn't she understand? They had to keep moving. It was important, and Corien didn't care for delays.

But the horrible girl could only carry them a hundred miles at a time before collapsing from exhaustion, which forced them to stop far too often and rest for a night or two in some dreadful filthy inn, or in a shabby cottage after disposing of its occupants, or even out in the open, in the dirt, like beasts.

And in this blur of interminable eastward movement, during which every day brought a new landscape, an unfamiliar dialect or style of clothing, each of which made Rielle feel more unsettled, more alarmingly far away from home, Corien was her only anchor. The only steadfast thing that knew her and loved her.

So, on the dry, flat bank of the canyon river, she touched him. She touched him as often as she could, even when the nausea of traveling through Obritsa's threads left her shaking and damp with sweat.

"Do you want to stay here for a while?" she asked, ignoring Obritsa's muted cries of pain as the girl caught her breath nearby. "We could explore the ruins. Maybe artifacts remain that we can salvage."

Corien's gaze softened, which happened only when he looked upon her face. The relief of this constancy brought tears to Rielle's eyes. He was a bright moon shining down upon the gray, fog-draped sea in which she now lived.

He kissed her brow. "For a night. We'll find an old house, an angelic house, one that used to be as grand and glorious as you, and sleep there until dawn."

Then, without turning, he addressed the girl and her guard.

"Onward, Your Majesty." He loved mocking Obritsa, which tickled Rielle. "You and your noble companion may lead the way."

He pointed down a broad footpath that followed the river, waited for Artem to trudge ahead and Obritsa to limp after him, her small body trembling with exhaustion. Artem loomed over her, tall and sturdy, with light-brown skin and shaggy brown hair, his eyes bleary and troubled. Tied around his torso with six leather straps, resting against his back and shoulders, was an enormous canvas pack. Every time Rielle looked at it, her head spun and her throat tightened until she was forced to look away, then promptly forgot it existed. This happened again now, and when she swayed, Corien's hands at her waist steadied her.

Then he lifted her palm to his mouth and drew her other arm through his. So joined, they walked on.

—◆—

It wasn't until later that night, curled up on a filthy pile of furs and blankets they had found—most likely, Corien had said with contempt, left behind by one of the roving bands of treasure-hunters that roamed Vindica's ruined cities, seeking angelic loot—that Rielle remembered seeing Tal.

The memory returned as she slept, slamming into her with the force of a physical blow. Her eyes snapped open, and she barely managed to stifle a sharp cry.

Several things occurred to her simultaneously:

Corien was sitting a few paces from her, gazing out the open window of the manor house they were occupying for the night. The ceilings were high and the corridors wide, designed to accommodate the flaring wings of angels who stood at least eight feet tall. The proportions made Rielle dizzy. His eyes were open but glazed. When she slept, he often used his mind to "work," he had told her, refusing to offer more information. He was doing that now, his chin propped in his hand as if he were lazily inspecting the horizon for clouds.

So occupied, he hadn't yet realized she was awake—nor that she had remembered the memory he had hidden from her. Tal, lying in the mud, reaching for her, calling for her. *I'm here, Rielle!* And with that single heartbreaking memory came all the others, right on its heels. The fog in which she had lived vanished, and she saw everything clearly at last, as if she had been violently thrust from darkness into stark light.

She had to leave. *Now.*

Rising shakily to her feet, Rielle's eyes flooded with furious tears. She now understood with devastating clarity how she had been living for the past fortnight. It seemed obvious now, and she raged to think of how stupid she must have seemed, how pliable and senseless.

With his power, Corien had muddled her mind, then dragged her across the world through Obritsa's threads. Oblivious, Rielle had let him lead her, and in the moments when her memories had threatened to resurface, her power flaring in protest, he had increased his hold on her and pulled her back into a numb, padded cage. He had coaxed her to sleep and rewarded her with fevered dreams.

Swallowing a sob, trembling with the effort of staying quiet, Rielle silently stood and crept away from him. The stone floor was squalid; her feet carved a ragged path through long centuries of dust and decay.

That he would keep so much from her, that he would deceive her so fully, that she had seen Tal not long ago, that he had been mere yards from her—and yet Corien had prevented them from speaking, had taken the choice from her, had not even allowed her to remember the moment, or *any* moment he did not want her to…

On her feet, she edged backward out of the room, not daring to blink, pushing hard against her fury and disappointment and the grief of her recovered memories until she felt dizzy. She saw it all unfurl unimpeded before her: her wedding, and the vision that revealed she had killed King Bastien; Audric shouting at her in the gardens; fleeing the city; following Corien's voice into the forest outside Âme de la Terre until, at last, she had collapsed into his arms. And then…

And then, nothing. A gray ocean. Occasional flashes of color. A dreamscape of Corien's making. A stolen carriage. Tearing her wedding gown from her body as she wept, then staggering through a black Celdarian wood in her shift and boots until Corien found her, forced her into a gown still warm from its previous wearer, kissed her until her crying ceased and she found herself drifting on a quiet gray sea once more.

And *Tal*—oh, he had called for her. In those trees, on that storming night near a firelit inn, he had fallen to the ground and reached for her. He had been following her, he must have been—searching for her, hoping to bring her home.

Rielle reached the door, her breath tight and thin, her eyes burning as she stared at Corien and willed him to remain still. It was unusual that he would be so distracted by his work that he wouldn't notice her awakening.

But whatever the reason for it, she had to take the chance to run. *I see a divine creature aching to be set free*, he had told her, while tightening the chains that bound her to him.

Freedom. A grand joke. She had been a dog on a leash; she saw that now with a scorching immediacy that felt like she had swallowed lightning.

Her thoughts roaring with panic, she glanced at the unconscious lumps in the far corner of the room that were Artem and Obritsa, kept frozen in a deep sleep crafted, of course, by Corien. He was arranging all of this, and she could trust none of it, and now where was she? Nowhere. Far from home, in a ruined land that had once belonged to angels.

Once Rielle had stepped backward over the threshold and into the vast corridor outside—the ancient, crumbled ceiling open to the house's upper floors and then to the star-salted sky above—she ran.

—◆—

She did not make it far.

She raced through a series of courtyards tucked between the grand, pillared houses in the nearby neighborhood, each abandoned garden overgrown with scrubby trees and twisted dry brambles. Ducking underneath a crumbled stone arch flanked by two figures—one without a head, the other with misshapen lumps on its back that must once have been wings—Rielle looked back over her shoulder.

The moon was half-full, and the air was cold; her breath came in rapid puffs. Black ruins touched with silver loomed over her, scorched with ash that did not fade. Each was marked by a blow of an ancient elemental fist, scars neither time nor weather could scrub away. She could smell the magic even now, centuries later. Smoke on the wind. Mud ripe with rain. The tang of bloodstained metal.

She turned again—and ran straight into Corien.

He grabbed her arms, but before he could speak, before he could wrap her once again in his thoughts and numb her to his liking, she exploded.

Her fury summoned the empirium, and it joyfully obeyed.

Fettered for too long, her power surged up through her body and erupted from her palms. She whipped him with it. He flew across the garden, hit a pillar; his head cracked against the stone. He slid to the ground but wasn't down for long.

Shaking his head, he staggered to his feet.

She flung out her arms at him as if shoving closed a great door. Her power hurled him into the air, pinning him against a shattered lattice of corroded ironwork curving upward from the courtyard walls. Had it once been an aviary? The thought of winged angels keeping birds caged and clipped for their amusement was perverse. Rielle's fury spiked higher.

She shoved her hands into the air. Corien's body jerked against the iron.

"Rielle," he gasped, "please, listen—"

"You should have trapped me again the moment you realized I'd gone," she growled, stalking toward him. "Wrapped me up in that mind of yours that you so love. Kept me dead asleep like Obritsa and Artem. Perhaps you thought you didn't need to. Perhaps you thought I'd see you again and forget to be angry."

"It's happened before," he pointed out, and even dangling from the lattice, he was unsettlingly beautiful, his eyes bright, his petulant mouth practically begging her to kiss it. "You love my companionship. You can't deny it, Rielle."

She couldn't, but his soothing voice was such an obvious attempt to placate her that if she'd had hackles, they would have risen to her ears. "I will deny whatever I wish." She flexed her fingers, twisting cords of the empirium around his body. "I will use my power however I wish."

Corien's pale eyes flashed. She felt his mind reaching for hers and pelted him with a rapid-fire stream of pebbles she summoned from the ground. He howled with pain as they rapped against his face.

"Don't try that again," she commanded. "Don't lie to me again or cloak my thoughts with yours, or I'll kill you. I'll burn you as I did all those months ago, and this time I won't stop. You'll crisp on the ground, and I'll watch your ashes flake away."

"You won't," he gasped, blood now dotting his face. "You love me."

"I wish I didn't," she said bitterly.

"I fascinate you, darling."

"As would your death."

He laughed. How he could laugh while hanging helplessly from the noose of her power charmed her despite her refusal to be charmed.

"You deceived me," she said quietly.

He did not respond for a long moment. "I did," he agreed at last.

She held him in place ruthlessly, her power unyielding. But her chest ached. She despised her hot eyes, her tingling nose, and the fact that he would be able to feel the birth of every tear.

"You didn't need to," she said. "I was there. I was with you. I had come to you. I had…" She hesitated. Everything was too fresh; her recovered memories had scraped her raw. "I had left Audric, left my home, to come to you."

"I know."

"You knew you didn't need to lie to me, and yet you did it anyway."

"I did need to."

Impatience lashed through her body; her power tightened its sizzling grip on him, making him cry out. She saw the slick black gleam of blood on his neck, his hands. If she pressed a bit harder, she would scorch away his skin.

"I don't understand," she told him, her voice choked. "You promised me freedom and have given me the opposite. I came to you because I had no one left. I could trust no one, but I trusted you."

"I know."

"You *knew* me, and you weren't afraid."

"I still do, and I'm still not." His gaze held her gently, and she bristled at the tenderness there, even as she craved it.

"You love me," she declared.

"More than I have ever loved anyone in my long life," he answered at once.

Her heart skipped in its cage. "Then why?"

"Because I know you still love him," he muttered. She watched in fascination as despair swept his face clean of guile. "I know you still love *them*, even as you hate them, and that this is all new for you. You're tired, and yet your blood roars unceasingly with power that makes you tremble with both desire and terror. I know you're afraid to be far from home. I know you miss the familiar. And I did not want that fear to take you from me."

"It would not have been fear that took me from you, if I had decided to leave. It would have been my own self, my own will. And you denied me that choice."

"I could not allow it."

"You could not *allow* it?"

He huffed out an impatient breath. "Rielle, this is a critical time. You've come so far with your abilities, and I'm more proud of you for it than I can express, but now things are changing. It is time to move forward, and I cannot risk losing you."

She scoffed, her vision blurring as tears rose. "You cannot risk losing me, or losing my power?"

"They are one and the same."

"Either you are afraid to lose what my power can do for you, or you're afraid to lose me, Rielle. The woman. Because you love me."

"And can it not be both?" he said with a touch of irritation. "Even your mind allows you to experience many emotions at once. You cannot conceive of how many mine can hold."

With a growl, she flung him hard to the ground. He landed flat on his back and lay there gasping soundlessly.

She crouched beside him, her hands aching with the urge to touch him and soothe the pain of his stolen body before it could restore itself. She knew she could do it; with a mere glancing thought, she slipped into the realm of the empirium and saw the brilliant map of his body laid out before her. She counted the throbbing red-and-black blossoms of light where his body had been battered by her anger—sixteen altogether.

But first he would hear her speak.

"I know what you want from me," she breathed. "You've gently turned me away from it whenever I've had enough wits about me to ask questions. I see that now. And I see clearly what you want. You've teased me with the

idea for months. You want to help me find the remaining four castings."
Now that her memory had cleared, she remembered what was kept in the
massive pack strapped to Artem's back. She understood why looking at it
always made her feel sick, the air drawing tight and hot around her. That
pack held castings. Marzana's shield. Grimvald's hammer. Tokazi's staff.
Corien had stolen them from Âme de la Terre on the night of her wedding,
and their trapped power pulled at her.

"And then," Rielle pressed on, "when we have all seven, you want me to
use them to open the Gate and release your many vengeful kin. You want to
provide me with bodies—millions of human bodies, emptied of their minds,
thanks to you—and you want me to resurrect every invading angel. Give
each of them a corpse, a body they can actually hold on to. A permanent
anchor, since most of them aren't strong enough to hold on to a body for
long. Isn't that right? You want me to bind them to new bodies, fuse them
into being using the empirium, grant them more power than they've ever
had. You want to use me to win this, your second and final war."

She could not bear it any longer; she stroked Corien's bleeding cheek,
and where her fingers grazed his burned skin, it became whole and white
once more. He trembled at her touch, his eyes fluttering with relief. And
desire, even now. Even after she had hurt him, even as he lay bleeding, he
wanted her. The shadows of their shared dark dreams fluttered at the edges
of her mind.

"But what do *I* want?" she whispered. "To repair the Gate and trap the
angels in the Deep for another thousand years? Or do I want to open it, as
you would have me do? Do I want to release the millions of bloodthirsty
souls teeming on the other side?"

"Bloodthirsty." He coughed, still catching his breath. "We are hardly
that. It is justice we seek."

"Of the cruelest sort possible."

"What was done to us was cruel. We will return the gesture in kind."

"And when you lead this army of resurrected angels, where do you see
me? Where do I fit into this grand picture of yours, Kalmaroth?"

He hissed in anger at her use of his angelic name. She smiled a little, enjoying the sting of his wrath. His thoughts betrayed him whenever she uttered the word; he hated that angel, the one who had failed, who had fallen screaming into the Deep.

"You will lead the charge at my side," Corien answered, his voice tight with pain. His fingers touched hers. "You will show the people who would have caged you forever how mistaken they were to think they ever could."

She could hardly breathe. Even holding herself back from him, even with the wall of her unwavering power between them, she felt his heat, his ancient will, as keenly as if they were moving together at last, as they had done in mind but never in flesh.

"And if I chose to help you," she whispered, "what would I become?"

Wincing, he raised himself onto his elbows. "Your truest self. You would rise to greater heights than any being that has ever lived."

There was a fever in his eyes, a relentless white plain of conviction. She would have thought it an absurd thing to say—*greater than any being that has ever lived*—had she not felt that same delicious certainty turning in the back of her mind ever since she was small, even before she was old enough to understand what it meant.

She tried for a scornful smile. "You flatter me."

"You know I don't. Not now. Not with this." He touched her hand. "Rielle, this is what I offer you: If you help me in this war, in this great work I've planned for an endless dark age as my people suffered in the Deep, I will help you achieve everything you have ever ached to know. The ecstasy of joining with the power that made you."

Quite against her will, her blood leapt to life at his words. The world sizzled around her, as if she were a ball of fire flung hard into a frozen sea. She stared at him, seeing the words he did not say, and shuddered down to her bones.

"And would you have me find God for you, Corien? The source of the empirium? Is that what this is? One war is not enough?" Her thumbs toyed with his lips, which opened at once. His teeth scraped her skin. "Would you use me to destroy and supplant the force that made us?"

"No, Rielle. It is *you* who would be God, not me. A kinder, more glorious God than whatever permitted humanity to condemn my kind to eternal suffering. And I would serve you gladly."

For a long moment, neither spoke. Then Rielle looked away, unable to bear the intensity of his gaze, and ran her hands over the slender lines of his body, knitting closed every wound she had dealt him.

"I would have healed in my own time," he pointed out, his voice a trembling thread. Her touch was light; she refused to grant him more pleasure than that.

"I prefer to heal you myself," she said, pretending calm even though she knew he would sense the lie.

When she finished, Corien was himself again, unhurt and unruffled, smiling up at her. She helped him to his feet, her cheeks warming.

"Come, my glorious tormentor." He kissed her hand. "My miraculous queen. Together, we will right the many wrongs that have been done, and then, our war won, we will find the empirium's source at the heart of creation. We'll rend it from the stars and remake its heartless throne into one you deserve."

"You assume I have agreed to help you, or that I ever will," she managed with dignity.

"No, my beauty. It's only that with every breath you draw, I feel how deeply you crave more than this small, pale world will ever be able to give you."

Rielle could say nothing to that. She had thought the same thing herself, and he knew it. Refusing his arm, she returned to lead the way back to the abandoned manor house, feeling cold in the still mountain air and unsettled, her mind heavy and muddy—and then she realized, just after Corien did, what their argument in the ruins had done.

A beat of silence, and then he grabbed an ancient, cracked vase from the floor and flung it against the nearest wall with a roar of fury.

The house was empty. Obritsa and Artem—and the three castings—were gone.

← 6 →

ELIANA

"They say Elysium's towers pierce the clouds, that it's as white as the highest snows. They say it glitters day and night with the stolen jewels of dead cities. They say there are thousands of desperate people on the bridges, scream- ing to be let inside, and more arrive every day. Cowards and traitors, all of them. Pathetic wretches. But if the doors opened up for me, I'd be right there with them. I'd kill my own brother to get inside the Emperor's city, if I had to."

—Collection of stories written by refugees
in occupied Ventera, curated by Hob Cavaserra

The Emperor's city was a gargantuan sprawl of spires and turrets on a high flatland, surrounded by a circular chasm spanned by a dozen slender white bridges.

It glittered like a careless spill of jewels, thousands upon thousands of them, every facet finely crafted, every tower winking in the chill sun- light. The air was thinner than Eliana was accustomed to. Since they'd made port at the coastal city of Luxitaine, their caravan of fine carriages had climbed and climbed until now, in the most mountainous region of Celdaria, they had at last reached Elysium. The mountains ended abruptly, and then there were rocky plains, and then a great chasm ringing the city. It had once been Âme de la Terre, the capital of Celdaria, a city Saint

Katell had crafted after the war. Home of the Lightbringer. Home of the Blood Queen. And Eliana's own home too, she supposed, even now with its altered name and an ancient angel on the throne.

Elysium. Thanks to Remy, Eliana was familiar with the angelic roots of the word. *Paradise. A state of bliss or delight.*

A giggle sprouted in her throat, and she let it rise. There was no point in hiding her growing fear. The Emperor would dismantle any mask she wore.

She sat on the velvet-cushioned bench in the fourth carriage of eight—the fourth and finest—and laughed, ruffling neither the angelic guards sitting on either side of her nor Simon, who sat silently on the bench opposite her. It was the kind of laughter that brought tears along with it. She didn't even bother to wipe her face. She laughed and cried and looked out the window.

Once, she would have inspected the landscape, noted the number of watchtowers along the nearest stretch of the city wall, estimated the wall's height and circumference, made quick, careful note of how many miserable people were clustered on either side of the bridge they were traversing. Hundreds of thousands of people lived in the mountains surrounding Elysium, and thousands more arrived every day, begging for entry and crowding the chasm bridges, eager to supplicate at the feet of angels.

But Eliana didn't think it mattered now, counting the towers and counting the refugees and wondering about the chasm circling the city. What could she do with that information, surrounded by angels who could sense any escape plan the moment it began forming in her mind?

Nothing. She could do nothing with it. She had nothing, and she *was* nothing, and she had no one.

She flexed her naked hands; their bareness repulsed and terrified her. She couldn't sense the empirium; her mind was an endless expanse of choking black wool. Remy sat in another carriage, and she had not been allowed to see him, even after an embarrassing display on the Luxitaine piers that began with begging, progressed to screaming, and ended in exhausted silence.

"Where are you taking me?" she asked. It was a stupid question, given the view out her window, but she could no longer bear the quiet.

Simon's cool gaze flicked up from the thin leather-bound notebook he had been writing in intermittently since they had left Luxitaine three days prior. "Elysium."

She thought she had grown used to the new awful flatness in his eyes. She was wrong. She dug her fingernails into her thigh. "Where in Elysium?"

Simon turned a page and resumed writing. "The Emperor's palace."

"Where in the palace?"

"The receiving hall."

"Which receiving hall? I imagine there must be several, this being a palace."

One of the guards, his broad chest emblazoned with the winged imperial crest, shifted with what Eliana hoped was irritation.

But Simon remained indifferent. The pages of his notebook were lined with meticulous script. "His favorite one."

Eliana tried to sound cheerful, hoping it would unnerve someone other than herself. "And what will we do there?"

The carriage glided to a halt. Simon closed his notebook. He didn't smile, not even cruelly. Eliana wished he would.

"Soon you'll see for yourself," he replied, then exited the carriage with the kind of easy, efficient grace she'd once admired and now despised.

The guards helped her out and into a broad stone yard where everything was white—the cobbled ground, the stone walls, the thin November sky overhead, the lack of sound. Wherever Remy was, they were keeping him out of her sight. At some point during her numbness, they had passed through one of the city gates, and now Eliana could no longer hear the wailing wretches crowding the bridges outside the city. She wondered how many of them had fallen into the chasm, charging desperately after the carriages in hopes of breaching Elysium's walls.

As she thought of the chasm, a memory returned to her.

Remy had read it to her from one of his stolen books back home in

Orline, in a life that seemed distant and absurd to her now: *And on the final night of that old gilded age, the Blood Queen pulled the oceans from their beds, called down the sun's fire, uprooted the mountains, and all that Celdaria once was, all that the world once was, collapsed under the weight of her rage.*

With Remy's dear voice echoing in her mind, Eliana realized that the chasm was where mountains had once stood. Mountains her mother had obliterated on the last night of her life.

Once again, Eliana flexed her bare hands and called for the power she had fought so ferociously to understand.

Nothing answered.

She nearly resumed laughing. Of course nothing answered, for she had become nothing, a wreck of her former self, and it was a relief to know it. A powerless Sun Queen would be of no use to anyone. But if they returned her castings to her, that would be the real danger. Her mother's power in her blood, her castings around her hands once more, and the Emperor's mind directing her exhausted one. His control supplanting hers. His will consuming her own. Encouraging her to try again. *Insisting* she try again, and again, until eventually some exhausted spark of power would alight, and it would all be over. He would have her—a Sun Queen puppet to play with as he liked.

A frightening giddiness overtook her as she imagined the angels clawing at the scraps of her mind, searching for a weapon they would never find.

Fists clenched in her chains, Eliana bit her lip until it bled.

She would take her own life before she allowed her power to rise for the Emperor's use.

They passed through a white archway, then across another stone yard and down a flight of steps into a series of tunnels. They were dark and cold and twisting, clearly designed to confound intruders, and in the close, damp air, Eliana began to feel as queasy as she had when she and Harkan had first boarded the *Streganna*, when the black lily's poison sat thick in her veins.

Thinking of him—his warm, dark eyes, his arms steady around her, how he had accepted her even on her meanest days—Eliana's eyes grew hot. She stumbled; a guard caught her elbow. It was possible, she told herself, that Harkan hadn't died. She hadn't seen him on the beach in Festival. Simon hadn't shot him as he had shot so many others.

It was possible. It was a tiny, timid hope. It turned in her heart like a tender bud working hard to open, and she clutched it with every ounce of tired strength left to her.

The world around her was changing. She noticed it dully, her vision unfocused. A polished marble floor. Ceilings high and dark, glittering with painted stars—silver and gold, violet and crystalline blue. Tall windows of painted glass cast streams of colored light across a tall, narrow room. Amber and rose, turquoise and jade.

Admiral Ravikant led the way, hands clasped behind his back, his gait easy and sickeningly familiar. Her father's steps, slightly altered. Then Simon after him, quiet but clearly comfortable, the tension missing from his shoulders. He had been pretending before, Eliana realized, and now he was not. Now he could relax. Now he was himself.

A wash of human-shaped color to her left, startlingly near, caught her eye.

She faltered, foundering in the grip of her guards.

It was a statue. A woman.

One of many.

"Come, come," said Admiral Ravikant. His voice bounced with glee. "No dawdling."

The guards pushed her onward, and Eliana obeyed—but she hardly noticed any of them.

Instead, she stared at the women.

It was a gallery of women, some carved out of stone, some blown from glass, others assembled from thousands of miniscule colored tiles. Women of golden brass, women fashioned from plates of steel and copper wires, women painted with splashes of color and hung from the walls.

Eliana's skin prickled as they passed between the frozen figures. They seemed too exquisite to be real, even the grotesque ones boasting a strange sort of beauty, and there were too many of them, so many that Eliana felt unbalanced, as if the world had tilted askew. It was an obsessive collection, packing the room from wall to wall with seemingly no logic to their arrangement.

And then, passing one, Eliana stopped, jarred to a halt by a sickening realization.

She stared at the sculpture before her—a woman of glittering black stone, her limbs impossibly delicate, her proportions elongated and alien. She was on her knees, her body arched in obvious agony, her arms and head flung back and left vulnerable to the fury of the skies. Innumerable gilded flames sprang from her arms, her fingers, the ends of her streaming, wild hair. Her gown only half clothed her, its hems and collar shredded. A starburst of gold paint gleamed on her chest. Two more shone in the flat places where her eyes should have been, and two more marked her open, rigid palms.

Eliana tensed. The woman's open mouth was also gold, the deepest visible parts of her throat painted as though bright red fire were crawling up her throat.

She was screaming.

And Eliana recognized her.

Looking around as the guards shoved her on, she recognized all of them. They were all the same woman, over and over, her features sometimes exaggerated or caricatured, but always recognizable, always familiar. Eliana had seen them herself, weeks ago, centuries ago, back in Celdaria, in those woods where Rielle had tried to kill her. In those woods where Corien had slipped inside her mind and said, *What a life you have led. What interesting company you keep.*

They were all Rielle. Every one of them was Rielle.

Rielle, painted in angry thick strokes of oil paint, standing alone on the edge of a cliff overlooking a red sea, the sky afire with countless stars. Rielle, a mere girl, abstract and cheerful, formed out of tangled wires splashed with garish colors, one arm reaching for a feather that hung suspended in the air.

"Impressive, isn't it?" Admiral Ravikant asked with a knowing smile. They had come to the gallery's far side, where narrow twin doors stood locked, their bronze handles cast to resemble wings. "His Excellency is a skilled artist."

What interesting company you keep. Corien's words were beginning to roar, cycling through Eliana's head in a vicious loop. *What a life you have led.*

Her gaze flew to Simon, her skin icing over with understanding. Had he always planned to betray her? Or was it their ill-fated, ill-planned journey to the past that had changed him? Had Corien seen Simon in her mind on that awful day—his allegiance to the Prophet, his devotion to Eliana, his fervent belief in her ability to save them all—and had that somehow changed everything? Was Simon altered when they arrived back at Willow, infected, his loyalties belonging to the Empire?

Simon had said he would not be affected by their travels through time, that as the weaver of the threads, he would be immune to any changes to the future world, as would she. But perhaps he hadn't really known, or he'd been lying even then, eager to please her, eager to complete his mission and alter the past to save the future, hoping to somehow, miraculously, avoid the worst. Or hoping that the worst would find him.

And where was the Prophet in this new, altered future? Whoever they were, how had they let this happen?

Did the Prophet even exist?

Admiral Ravikant pushed open the doors. "And now, sadly, I must leave you. Orders are orders." The admiral lifted Eliana's bound hands to his lips. "We will meet again soon, Lady Eliana." He glanced at Simon. "Commander."

Simon inclined his head and said nothing.

Then he was gone, the angel in her father's skin, gliding back through the gallery with the guards at his heels, and Simon was pulling the doors closed, and it was only the two of them in an enormous shadowed room— gleaming parquet floors, massive framed paintings of angels in flight, gigantic windows with the drapes pulled nearly to, allowing in only thin streams of light that cut the floor into eighths. The ceiling was high. Three levels of curtained mezzanines bordered the room on three sides. It was a room meant for dancing, for elaborate ceremonies.

And at the far end, a grand staircase coiled down from the third floor like a fat polished serpent. Eliana could not feel a breeze; the air was still. But something was moving in the shadows on the staircase—a gathering, a pull and push of darkness that shifted and curled, coalescing.

Simon led her forward, his hand hard around her upper arm. It was only then that she realized she had been standing frozen at the closed doors. The shivering shadows on the staircase entranced her, so she did not fight Simon's grip, but when they stopped ten paces from the foot of the stairs, sweat beaded on her forehead, and her palms turned clammy. She wanted to run and hide from whatever was coming down the stairs; she wanted to stay and look it in the eye.

A faint sensation of intrusion toyed with the edges of her mind. Invisible coy fingers, plucking and stirring. She shook her head as if to shake off drowsiness, and her vision shifted violently, a discordant sound scraping against her skull. Flashes of images appeared with each blink: a man in black sitting on a throne. A woman standing in a field of fire.

Eliana herself, ankle-deep in a shallow pool of black water, reaching for the star-dusted sky.

She touched one of the stars, and it burned her fingers. She tried to yank away her hand, but the star had fused with her skin and was bleeding down her arm, flooding her veins, bubbling up her throat to disintegrate her tongue.

The images abruptly disappeared, leaving her unbalanced. She watched the shadows gather as they floated down the stairs, joining to become a teeming black heart, and wondered wildly if a beast was coming for her, some feral, starved creature set loose from the city's dungeons.

She shook herself, blinking hard. She could not trust her mind. Of course she couldn't.

What nonsense, came a voice she recognized, sliding happily into her mind like a wriggling cat. *Your mind is the only thing you can trust. It will show you what you must do to survive.*

She looked up, eyes burning, and watched shapes emerge from the shadows, until at last there were boots and trousers, a fine white linen shirt, a long black coat, unbuttoned, knee length. A smiling face, pale and elegant. Eyes black and liquid. Soft dark hair curling against cheeks and nape.

The Emperor. *Corien.*

"And here you are at last," he said. "The daughter of my great love. Time tried to separate us, Eliana, but we managed to find each other eventually, didn't we?"

His voice was smooth and clear, so inarguably lovely that it sickened her. She could barely speak, her throat closing with fear. "Where is my brother?"

"I'll tell you if you help me. I'll bring him right here, and you'll never be parted from him again."

Stricken, she stared at him. "If I help you."

He laughed softly. "I can't tell you how delighted I am to finally have the opportunity to learn everything about you." He paused, his smile widening. "Well, I *could* tell you, in fact. I could make you feel my delight as keenly as I do. I can make you feel whatever I want you to feel. I could make you want to kiss me. I could make you rub yourself against me like a groveling dog."

Circling her, he fell silent, and when Simon stepped away, Eliana felt the absurd, mortifying urge to reach for him and keep him close, despite everything.

"Awful, isn't it? To love someone so very deeply? To love them enough that you would lose yourself to them, lose everything to them, if it meant they might stay beside you a little while longer?" There was mockery in Corien's voice, with sympathy close behind. "I loved like that once, as you know. I loved many times before that, but never again since. It's lonely to be loveless for a thousand years. Lonelier still to build an empire from the ashes of a world destroyed by your own mistakes, and to do that not once but twice."

Corien stopped before her, close now. He considered her face, and she fought desperately not to blanch under that terrible unblinking scrutiny.

"Tell me where Remy is," she said, her jaw clenched tight.

"I won't make such mistakes a third time," he said, as if she hadn't spoken. "I'm sure you've guessed that. I've had centuries to plan for this moment. My hatred has grown for centuries. My hate for you, Eliana, and for all of your kind. My hate for the deceitful woman I loved. My hate for a God that would condemn me to this endless fate of war and grief and torment."

Corien's gaze was thoughtful, his voice calm. "Can you comprehend how deeply I hate you? I'll allow you to attempt imagining it for a time, until I decide to share the feelings with you directly. I hate you, and yet I love you, in a strange way. It's an unsettling dichotomy I long to tear from my mind, but I can't—it's lodged there, it's part of me. I love you because you are hers. I loathe you because you are his."

With no warning, he seized her chin, turned her face left, then right, inspecting her, and she was too terrified, too baffled, to react.

A small smile curved his lips. "I see her there." He waved with his free hand, his voice lilting. "I see you, Rielle!" Then he released her, wistful. "You have her sharp jaw, her cheekbones. But you're lithe where she was soft, and darker than she was. And you've his mouth, his nose. His great brown cow eyes."

It was the mention of Audric that jarred her, awakening within her a surprising spark of defiance. Of the Lightbringer she knew only the old songs, Remy's beloved tales. The dilapidated statue near the river in Orline—King Audric, proud and sad, mounted on the chavaile that had once been loyal to the Blood Queen, both of them looking toward the rising sun.

Eliana bristled at the derision in Corien's voice. *Cow eyes.* As if the Lightbringer had been a mere pitiful beast.

"Considering all your mighty power," she said, forcing the words through her teeth, "I'm surprised it took you so long to find me. I arrived in this time eighteen years ago. Surely your angelic mind should have found me much sooner than this. And yet you needed a crude human tool to scour the world and do your work for you."

She refused to look at Simon.

But Corien only spread his arms, palms up. "You're right, of course. If our world was as it should be, if my beloved hadn't permanently damaged the empirium when she died"—he gestured to his ink-black eyes—"I would have found you within hours. My former glorious mind would have found you at once, right where you lay in Rozen Ferracora's arms, and would have held both of you immobile until my soldiers came to fetch you. And then they would have slit Rozen's throat, and Ioseph's too, which would have been a shame, because out of all the bodies Ravikant has possessed, Ioseph's is his favorite. But perhaps that's only because he was so eager to see the look on your face when you realized what your adoptive father's body was being used for."

He clasped his hands, gazing at her with an admiration that reeked of mockery. "I saw it, you know. I saw everything that happened that day. My soldiers are my eyes and ears, and I saw you on that beach, your hands blazing as you ran toward the water. Oh, dearest Eliana, you were so full of hope. It was really quite charming. I saw your face when you realized Ravikant lives in Ioseph's body. And then, when Simon shut you into your cell? Splendid. A magnificent portrait of disbelief and devastation. It was almost like I could see your heart breaking. Which has always struck me as an odd expression. A heart can't *break*, can it? It can burst, it can be torn to shreds, it can be stomped upon and smeared across the ground, but it can't break in the way a bone does."

He spoke too quickly, his black eyes bottomless and glittering. He seemed elated to be looking at her, like a delighted child reunited with his best friend. Eliana's stomach turned. She couldn't contain a small, panicked sob.

"Please," she said, focusing on the one thing she could think of clearly, "let me see my brother."

He ignored her, smoothing back a lock of hair that clung to her damp cheek. "Can you imagine if you were mine instead of his? Your mother's beauty added to my own? My angelic beauty, of course. How I looked before the Deep took me. My God. You would be a vision. And!" He clapped his hands. "You would have wings on your back, just like Simon once did! The sign of a marque. Isn't that right, Simon?"

"Yes, Your Excellency," said Simon from somewhere behind her.

"Do what you're going to do and be done with it," Eliana spat, tears hot in her eyes. "You're going to hurt me. So hurt me."

Corien's smile faded. "How disappointing. You seem to have inherited your father's lack of humor."

"I also inherited his lack of tolerance for evil despots." She felt dizzy with fear but forced herself to look straight at him. "I know what you want. You want to use me as a weapon, to finally eradicate humanity, as you failed to do with my mother. I won't help you. You'll have to kill me." She grasped wildly for ammunition. "You can't force me to do what you want—not on that scale, and not with the power I possess. If you could do that, you would have done it with Rielle."

A flicker of anger passed over Corien's face. She latched on to it, startled. "Ah, see? There's something about the power she had, that I have. Something surpassing yours, something you can't touch."

"So it would seem," said Corien evenly.

"You had to persuade her to join your cause before she would do what you wanted," Eliana continued, emboldened by the mutinous look on his face. "And now you'll have to persuade me, only you'll fail. I'll never do what she did. I'll never help you kill my own people."

"Oh, my sweet, stupid child." Corien smoothed his thumbs across the slick arches of her brows. "You think I want to use you to eradicate humanity? I've nearly done that on my own. It's only a matter of time until the rest of you are gone. No, what you will do is sit there and watch, mute and bound, while Simon uses the power you have so helpfully resurrected to send me back to find your mother."

Eliana stared as Simon approached, the strength she had summoned vanishing in an instant. Of course. It was not about her power, not anymore.

It was about his.

And she was the one who had reawakened it.

Desperate, she tried to stand, to run at him, but she remained helpless and frozen to the floor. She struggled, straining against bonds she could not see. Pain exploded at her temples.

Corien clucked his tongue. "Spare yourself, Eliana. Angelic chains are unbreakable."

She tried to scream; he stifled her voice. In horrified silence, she watched as Simon, not three steps from her, raised his arms and began to pull thin, pale strands of light from the air. His brow furrowed only slightly, his posture impeccable.

Eliana blazed with anger as she watched him work. Once, she had thought his magic beautiful. The memory of his face, softened with wonder at his own power, scorched a furious path inside her, and for a single crystalline moment, she was wiped clean of all terror and knew nothing but the solid, sharp blade of her anger.

Once, she had sat beside him in the gardens of Willow and mended a scar on his chest. They had held each other, whispering of old wounds and what had been done to them. They were more than their wounds; they were more than their anger.

Once, she had awakened in him a power, and he had used it to send her to a time centuries past.

But this time was different.

The glowing threads Simon pulled from the air snapped at every tug. He struggled to fashion their floating scraps into a ring, but the faster he reached for them, the more quickly they dissolved, and soon they were gone entirely.

Sweat beaded on Simon's brow. His blue eyes fixed on some distant point in the dim receiving hall, he reached for more light, but nothing came to him. The room was quiet. He was a man alone, arms trembling in empty air.

Simon let his hands fall. His shoulders were high and square. He did not look at Corien.

But Corien was looking at him, all amusement gone from his face. "Why have you stopped?"

"I cannot do it," Simon replied tightly.

"Of course you can. You did it before. That's why you're here now, with me. You sent her back in time, and now you're mine." Something sharp flickered in Corien's eyes. His cheekbones were white knives in the shadows. "Do it, Simon."

Simon hesitated, then raised his arms once more, but after a long moment of strained silence, he cried out and fell to the floor, shuddering and pale. The air remained dark. Threadless.

Eliana's head buzzed with terror. She tried to move away from him, but Corien's mind held her fast.

"Again," Corien said coolly.

Simon obeyed. The dark room ached with tense silence. Then, at last, he dropped to his hands and knees, heaving.

"Again."

Kneeling, Simon raised his arms, every muscle straining as if in his hands he held a mountain.

Corien stood over him, watching without expression, and when Simon pushed himself to his feet at last and stalked a few paces away, breathing hard, still Corien watched him and said nothing.

Then his quiet black gaze fell on Eliana.

She tried to look away, but he did not allow her even a blink. Her eyes burned, and her lungs ached. She longed to gulp for air but could only suck in thin scraps of it. She tried to scream, and Corien's will swallowed her voice.

"I see," he muttered at last. He looked from her to Simon, then to her again. "I see."

Simon turned, his eyes watery and red, his skin sallow. "Your Excellency, I apologize, I don't know what's happened—"

"I do." Corien came to Eliana and stroked her cheek. "I think you're nothing without her, Simon. And I think you've made her angry."

Eliana stared back at him, triumph blooming like fire in her heart. But before she could try to speak, she fell abruptly into a thick fog.

Corien was everywhere and nowhere. She heard him whisper but could not see his face. She was being moved about like a doll, her legs carrying her against her will. She felt rough hands on her neck and arm, guiding her. She caught a glimpse of sunlight, a chamber of gold, a rustle of black fabric. Simon's silhouette. Shadowed figures moving swiftly. The echo of Corien's laughter. A clipped order: *Make sure she eats. Make sure she sleeps.*

A vision took her: herself sleeping comfortably in a white nightgown, on a white bed, in a white tower, with a white shore far below. She knew it was a lie and tried to resist it, tried to punch her way to freedom, but the vision was too powerful, and it claimed her.

She was the Eliana sleeping in a strange white bed, and as she dreamed, she smiled, and knew nothing of grief, and was content.

A cool hand stroked her back. *Sleep, Eliana. There is much work to do, I see. More than I had imagined. Sleep. Dream.*

She obeyed.

AUDRIC

"Merovec has begun calling elementals before him in the Hall of the Saints for questioning. From among our citizens and from his own ranks. We've heard he asks them if they know where Rielle has gone. If they speak to angels. If they are loyal to him, or to you. He does not allow the magisters to witness these proceedings—only the Archon, and only because he stopped using his magic upon his election, decades ago. What the Archon sees during these long hours, we do not know. Odo and I are doing what we can to comfort families and quietly grow our efforts with Red Crown, but the air is rank with confusion and fear, and we must move slowly."

—Encoded letter from Miren Ballastier
to the exiled king Audric Courverie,
dated November 19, Year 999 of the Second Age

At home, when Audric had been unable to sleep, he had never minded.

He had his books for solace, the royal archives to disappear into, the gardens and catacombs to wander. As a child, he'd had his cousin Ludivine and his best friend, Rielle, who had never minded being woken up for a nighttime expedition down to the kitchens for sweets or joining him in exploring an unfamiliar wing of the castle. Baingarde was massive, an ancient and rambling construction, the secrets of which Audric had spent his entire life unraveling—just in time, he reflected wryly, to be driven away from it.

And then, of course, in recent months, sometimes he had been unable to sleep simply due to the sheer joy of knowing Rielle was there beside him in his bed. He would close his eyes and imagine their lives together, a golden future stretching on for decades.

At night, with Rielle beside him, he found it easier to ignore the dangerous reality of their changing world.

But here in Quelbani, in the queens' palace, there was no solace to be found, and Rielle was so far away that the distance between them felt incomprehensible.

He tried reaching for her. Once, on that awful day when the fanatical members of the House of the Second Sun had taken their own lives on Baingarde's steps, Ludivine had connected the thoughts of all three of them at once. At the time, Audric had thought it a careless mistake made by Ludivine in a moment of panic and horror.

Now, he could be sure of nothing.

But perhaps something of that three-person mental link remained. Some ragged, hair-thin thread he could access if he was lucky.

As if he had ever been lucky.

Another wave of weariness swept through him. He stopped restlessly pacing through his rooms to stand at one of the windows. Closing his eyes, he thought of Celdaria: the twelve snowcapped mountains encircling Âme de la Terre; the verdant farmlands in central Celdaria; the glittering canal cities hemming the southern coast.

Rielle? He felt tentative, embarrassed, as he reached out into the breezy Mazabatian night with his thoughts. *Are you there?*

He waited tensely for several minutes. He sent pleas out into the night, apologies, declarations of love.

Where are you?

Are you safe?

Rielle, I'm so sorry.

I love you, my darling, and I always will.

My light and my life, please come back to me.

But no answer came, and he gave up at once with a frantic sort of desperation, his mind a storm of barely suppressed screams.

He turned away from the window, dragging his hand through his curls, and then, the futility of his attempt slamming into him with dizzying force, he burst out onto the terrace, frantic for fresh air.

Some fifteen feet away, Atheria lay in her bed. Audric had asked his Mazabatian attendants to bring her cushions, as Rielle had done at home. It was a ridiculous sight—the massive, muscled godsbeast sitting primly on her pile of tasseled velvet, her enormous wings folded around her body like a feathered shell—and made him feel so homesick for his bedroom, and Rielle in it, and Atheria just outside, and his people sleeping in their beds in the city below, that his tired eyes filled with tears. He stood beside Atheria and leaned heavily on the stone railing.

"She may not even be in Celdaria by now," he said, gesturing vaguely toward the north. "She could be anywhere. I might have been sending my thoughts to the wrong place. I *can't* send my thoughts, not like she can—not like *they* can—and I'm stupid for trying."

Atheria pressed her nose against his hip, her nostrils flaring.

"I should ask Lu to help me, but I don't want to ask her for anything."

With a soft, curious trill, Atheria rested her muzzle on the railing beside his elbow, as if sensing she should comfort him but not particularly wanting to leave her pillows.

"But," Audric continued with a weary sigh, "that feels like a sort of stubbornness I should work through and not allow to control me." He glanced at Atheria. "Isn't that right?"

The chavaile, momentarily distracted, snorted at a white moth that had alighted on her leg.

"Right. Thank you. An excellent talk."

Irritable, and irritated with himself for feeling irritable, he resumed pacing, this time on the terrace. His exhaustion was so complete that he felt not quite intact within his own body, dizzy and parched. He hadn't truly slept since arriving in Quelbani four days ago, and he had hardly eaten. His dreams were shapeless and menacing, and every time he woke, it was with Rielle's name on his lips.

A horn announced the arrival of a boat in the nearby harbor. He squinted, following the line of the lantern-lit shore, and at last saw a ship out on the dark water—squat and plain, lit by the rising dawn. There was activity on the beach. Rushing figures, casted lanterns sputtering to life.

A joyful thought came from Ludivine: *It's Sloane, and Evyline, and the Sun Guard. They're all alive and safe.*

Audric stood motionless at the railing, watching the ship bearing his fellow Celdarian exiles glide toward the shore. Exiles loyal to him, who had risked their lives and abandoned their country to help him. He knew what they would want—to help him take back his throne, to help him find Rielle.

Audric could not imagine those things ever happening. His mind felt clumsy with despair; he couldn't clear his thoughts and didn't want to try. He was convinced the fuzzy, twisting grip of grief would never release him and had come to feel glad for it, for if the grief left him, he feared some sort of anchor would be dislodged. He would dissolve without it, simply float away and no longer exist—which wasn't the most terrible thing he could imagine.

The most terrible thing had already happened.

He walked calmly to the doors of his apartment and ensured that they were locked.

Please make sure they are well fed, he said, not directing the thoughts toward Ludivine but knowing she could hear them nevertheless, his cunning, beloved little liar. *And that they are given comfortable places to sleep and tended to by healers, if required.*

What's happened? She was alarmed by something in his voice.

I've lost the woman I love and the home I love, he thought, *and I fear that before this is all over, I will have to choose between them.*

Ludivine was silent for a long time. *Are you going to hurt yourself?*

He laughed aloud, bitterly. *Wouldn't you be the first to know?*

The truth was, he thought he might hurt himself eventually, but at the moment, even thinking about doing so required more effort than he could muster. He made his way to the bed, stripped off his tunic, his trousers. He stood staring at the tall, claw-footed mirror until he could no longer stand the sight of himself—his lean brown limbs and mussed dark curls, the shadows under his eyes, his chapped lips. He saw himself as Corien must see him, as Merovec and the Mazabatian queens must see him—ineffectual. Small. Craven. Dim and shabby beside his matchless Rielle. A mere human, soft and gullible. Someone had taken his throne, and he had run away and let him have it.

The Lightbringer, they called him. But in his tear-bright eyes, he saw nothing of light, nothing of the king he had once dreamed of becoming. He thought of Illumenor lying dark and quiet beside his bed and considered tossing it into the sea. His vision a glittering sheen, his throat a hot column of tears, he climbed into bed and closed his eyes. He didn't think he would be able to sleep, but the stillness, at least, was peaceful. His limbs felt heavy with it.

If he could stay like that forever, he decided, even if it meant never leaving this bed, never seeing Rielle again, never setting foot on Celdarian soil again, he would be glad, for it would probably save everyone a great deal of trouble in the end.

Why fight any of this? He sent the thought to Ludivine, neither expecting nor wanting an answer, and let his sorrow come for him like rising black water.

◆

Audric awoke only two short hours later when a wave of ice-cold water came splashing down onto his face.

Lurching upright with a gasp, he blinked awake and tried to make sense of what was happening. He had barely wiped his eyes when it happened again—a cold pane of water crashing down upon him.

Drenched, he tried to scramble out of bed, fumbling for Illumenor. But the linens were soaked and tangled about his legs, and he flailed as he stumbled to his feet, catching himself against the bedpost with a hissed curse.

He whirled, abruptly furious. It was full morning; sunlight was streaming through the windows, and his body sparked with it. Anger drew heat and light to his palms, which itched to hold his sword.

"Cover yourself," snapped a familiar voice. "The princess is here, and she's getting an eyeful."

Audric wiped the wet hair out of his face, blinked, and saw two people standing a few paces away. One was Sloane Belounnon, Grand Magister of the House of Night—Tal's sister, a prodigiously talented shadowcaster, and obviously annoyed. She still wore the fine black-and-blue suit she had worn to the wedding many days ago, though the fabric was now smudged with travel grime, as was her pale face. Her sleek, shoulder-length black hair was bundled messily at her nape.

Beside her, grinning, the castings around her wrists buzzing with recent use, was Princess Kamayin Asdalla—her skin a rich, deep brown, her hair kept short in tight, black curls. Underneath her crisp white jacket, a delicate golden chain cinched her iridescent gown at the waist.

She waved cheekily at him. "Good morning."

Audric clutched the sodden linens to his hips. He only briefly thought about trying for some kind of dignified greeting. "What was that for?"

"Because you knew we had arrived and yet didn't come down to greet us," Sloane said briskly. "The entire Sun Guard has been out of their minds for the entire journey, wanting us to go faster, because in the absence of the Sun Queen, they want to protect you, the Lightbringer. And if you could have seen the look on Evyline's face when she was informed that no, King Audric would not be coming down to greet her because he was still in bed and did not want to be disturbed...I could slap you. That woman has come to love you and Rielle so deeply, it's as if you're her own children, and she has left her family and her friends and her life behind in

Âme de la Terre to come help you—they all have—and this is how you thank them for their sacrifice?"

For a moment, Audric couldn't speak. She was right, of course, and it shamed him so completely that he shrank into himself. His numbness resettled around him after being temporarily shaken by the rude awakening, and he found that he didn't care if Princess Kamayin saw him naked. He dropped the linens and retrieved his trousers, his rumpled tunic.

"Well?" Sloane's voice bristled with impatience. She had always been the sharper one, and Tal the softer. "What do you have to say for yourself?"

He shrugged, weary but resolved. "I can't see them."

"You can't see them," she repeated flatly. "And what is that supposed to mean? How dare you spew that shit at me."

Kamayin's eyebrows shot up. "If anyone talked like that to my mothers, they'd spend the rest of their life in a dungeon."

"Sloane's known me since I was born," Audric mumbled, tugging on his tunic. "She talks to me like that all the time."

"Only when you deserve it." Sloane folded her arms over her chest. "What do you mean, you can't see them?"

"I mean…" He trailed off. How could he possibly explain that if he saw Evyline, and Fara, Ivaine, Maylis—Rielle's devoted guards—it would be like losing her all over again? How could he describe the dark tide rising higher and higher inside him, blacking out all thought and feeling, leaving him numb, erased, irrelevant? Or his anger at Ludivine for her manipulations, his anger at Rielle for leaving him, his anger at himself for pushing her away?

And more than anything, his anger at Corien, which remained a distant thing, so titanic and boiling that his mind couldn't fully grasp it and instead focused on the more immediate things, the smaller furies, the paler fears.

He looked at Sloane, helpless. "I can't see them," he said again in a whisper, and something changed on Sloane's face. A softening. Slight, but real.

She nodded slowly, gave him a tight smile. "You should go back to sleep." She came to him, straightened the collar of his tunic, glanced up at his dripping hair, and declared, with a kinder smile, "And you look terrible, it must be said. I'll come again this afternoon to help you prepare for tomorrow."

"Tomorrow?"

"We're meeting with the queens—you, me, Ludivine, the Sun Guard, the royal advisers, and the Mazabatian high magisters. A war council."

"And me," said Kamayin, turning her wrists as her castings hummed. The spilled water evaporated; soon the bed was dry. "I'll be there too."

"I'm not meeting with anyone," Audric said automatically. The very idea of facing all those watching eyes made him want to sleep forever.

"Fine, then. I suppose Merovec will remain on your throne, Corien will destroy us all, and meanwhile, you'll be here, hiding in your bed, letting Miren's reports go unread while she and everyone else at home live every day in confusion and fear."

With that, Sloane marched out of the room, and when Kamayin quietly followed suit, a strange urge to be near another person flared inside Audric's chest. He thought of calling for Ludivine and immediately decided against it.

"Wait, please," he said.

Kamayin turned, watching him curiously.

"I am…" He paused, struggling to speak. He couldn't bear to stand any longer and so sat on the rug, leaning back against the bed. "Could you sit with me for a while? If you have duties that need attending, I understand."

"I'm a princess," she said, not unkindly, "not a physician or one of your servants. Besides, we hardly know each other."

"I know."

"Wouldn't you rather Lady Ludivine sat with you?"

He couldn't keep the darkness from his voice. "No. I don't want to see her just now."

Kamayin nodded. "I always worry she's poking around in my head."

"A reasonable fear."

"But you still love her."

"Of course."

Kamayin blew out a breath. Then she sat down next to him and hugged her knees to her chest. "It's really terrible, what's happening. What may happen. To all of us, I mean."

Audric leaned his head back against the bedpost. "Yes."

"I've been reading all about the Angelic Wars with my friend, Zuka. To prepare, you know. I don't skip past the grisly bits. I read everything. I'm a bit obsessive about it. I've never seen a war."

"I'm sorry that you may have to."

Kamayin was quiet for a moment. Then, more softly, she said, "It's also terrible, what's happened to you. If I were you, my love gone and my home taken from me, I'd not get out of bed for an entire year. At the very least. My mothers' advisers would have to drag me out, kicking and screaming."

"And if they casted water at you while you slept?"

"They wouldn't dare," she said matter-of-factly. "They would be too afraid to throw anything at me, and rightly so."

Audric smiled a little and said nothing. He didn't feel words were required of him. It was a relief, sitting quietly beside someone who seemed content to do all the talking. Someone who understood the reason for his grief but did not feel it herself, or ask him to explain it.

He slept, and when he awoke, stiff on the floor, it was dark, and Kamayin was gone, but she had left him a neat stack of books on the bedside table, and a note: *From my own personal library. Novels with happy endings. If you bend or tear even a single page, we shall no longer be friends.*

He retrieved the topmost book—*The Hawk and the Dove*. Then he crawled into bed and held the book to his chest for a long time, breathing in the scent of paper and ink, and thought of home.

◆

He did not go to the meeting the next morning, despite Sloane's threats.

Her justified fury made him all the more disgusted with himself. The angrier he became at his own inability to face what must come next, the further he sank into a toxic whirl of despair. He recognized his self-pity and still could not extricate himself from it. He knew a walk in the fresh air would benefit him but refused to leave the unwashed cocoon of his blankets. He began to wonder if someday Sloane might actually drag him from the bed kicking and screaming, but he imagined he had a while before she attempted that.

It was much easier to turn away from the look of disappointment on her face and pretend she wasn't there, so that was exactly what he did.

⟶◆⟵

Four nights after Sloane and the Sun Guard's arrival, Audric awoke from a gluey, uncomfortable sleep to a strange series of shuffling sounds.

He blinked the sleep from his eyes and saw Atheria's head resting on the mattress near his outstretched arm. She had settled herself on the floor by his bed and was staring at him with her enormous dark eyes.

"Sleeping in here with me now, are you?" he asked quietly.

She blew a hot breath on his fingers. He loved her snorts, her chirps in the morning as she watched the sky and imitated birdcalls. He knew she could bite clean through his arm if she wanted to with those sharp predator's teeth, but in the quiet darkness, she was gentle beside him, a warm, familiar weight.

That night, he dreamed of riding Atheria. They flew east, toward the sunrise; he was tired and heartsick, but his sword arm was strong.

⟶◆⟵

Audric did not attend the war council's second meeting either. He knew when it was happening; Sloane visited every day to remind him of the date. She admonished and wheedled him by turns. Only once did she resort to begging.

"Merovec won't know what to do when he comes for them," she said quietly, and they both knew who *he* was. "Merovec thinks he can vanquish angels, but he doesn't know them like you do. He's hard, intransigent. And he doesn't know Rielle." She crouched beside him, her eyes bright with tears. "Audric. The day may come when she turns on Celdaria. You know this. And you know *her*. When that day comes, you may be the only one who can stop her."

"I won't hurt her," he said, his voice so raw and vicious that it startled him as much as it quite obviously startled her. "Don't ask me to do that. Ask me anything but that. Say it again, and I'll never forgive you. And damn you anyway, Sloane, for being so persistently heartless."

She stared at him for a moment, and then something in her deflated, as if she were seeing him clearly for the first time and finally realizing the depth of her disappointment. His shame was blistering; he revolted himself.

Sloane did not visit him after that, not for days, and then something happened without explanation one morning when Audric woke from a few hours of restless sleep. It had been eighteen days since the Celdarian entourage's arrival. Nearly one month since he had last seen Rielle.

He rose from his bed with a sense of tranquility that disturbed him, like a sea ominously still before a gale. He stood silently in the center of his bedroom, barefoot and bare-chested, and recognized that he existed on a knife's edge. On one side was the third war council meeting, which would begin downstairs in an hour. He could dress and wash himself, trim the beard that had grown a bit wild. He could attend the meeting and by doing so face the impossible, inevitable heartbreak on the horizon.

On the other side was an ending. He could take his own life and let the rest of them sort everything out on their own.

He considered the idea, examining it as a healer might inspect a wound that needed stitching. For several long minutes, he wavered. Atheria watched him keenly from the terrace, mid-breakfast, her kill maimed at her feet.

Then, Audric took a long, slow breath and walked to the bathing room. He splashed water on his face and inspected his hair, rubbed his bristly cheeks.

I love how easily you can grow a beard, Rielle had told him on many occasions, gazing dreamily up at him. She loved to nuzzle her smooth cheek against his rough one. *My brilliant, beautiful, noble, scruffy bear-king*, she had said on one particular occasion, drunk on wine and on him, and he had burst out laughing and then kissed her until they were both trembling and ready.

In the mirror, his reflection smiled faintly.

Forty-five minutes later, dressed in borrowed clothes that were looser on his frame than they had been a month ago, feeling like a fawn on new legs, Audric opened the door to Queen Bazati's council chambers, found Evyline—square-jawed, gray-haired, her face open with sudden hope— and nodded at her. His grief and sorrow still lived inside him and always would, and he imagined there would yet be days when getting out of bed was an indescribable torment.

But today, he was standing.

"I'm sorry," he said to Evyline and to all of them, staunchly ignoring Ludivine's pale profile to his left. "I needed time. I'm ready now."

⟶ 8 ⟵

ELIANA

*"As an elemental, you must learn a certain control that
other humans, who cannot touch the empirium, will never
know. Your body—every muscle, every thought, every feeling—is inexorably connected to the deepest fabric of the
world. Unchecked, your anger could lash out and shatter
a window, send a kitchen blade flying. Your despair could
crack the earth beneath your mother's feet."*

—The Path to the Empirium: A Meditation
on Elemental Practice by Velia Arrosara,
Grand Magister of the Firmament in Orline,
capital of Ventera, Years 313–331 of the Second Age

When Eliana awoke, she was in the white room from her dreams.
Rafters of ivory and pearl gathered at nine points across the
ceiling like clusters of bleached stems. The bed was enormous, draped in
white. Pale gauzy curtains hung from each post. The floor was smooth
white stone. Thick white rugs surrounded the bed and abutted the empty
hearth. Beside the nearby window, two delicate armchairs faced each
other, awaiting conversation.

Bouquets of crimson flowers sat in vases at her bedside, near the windows, on the tiny dining table, their curling red petals providing the
room's only color.

As she inspected it all, Eliana smiled. What a lovely room the Emperor had given her. How thoughtfully decorated it was, and how thoughtful to have left her so many attendants, should she require help with something.

There were ten, all women, silent and glassy-eyed as they stood against the pale walls. Their hair was cropped short and white robes covered them from neck to toes.

"Good morning," Eliana called out cheerfully. She stretched and yawned, then swung her legs out of bed and into the cool air. Someone had bathed her, dressed her in a thin white nightgown. Such a generous host, the Emperor. She wondered distractedly if all angels were so kind.

She discovered that beyond the bedroom, there was a sitting room, a receiving room, a bathing room, and a dressing room, all in shades of white—cream and eggshell and vanilla, cloud and snow and sand. The drapes had all been pulled wide open; sunlight drenched the rooms. The red flowers emitted a sharp, sweet perfume so powerful it made her tongue tingle.

She buried her face in their petals and breathed deep.

Then she went to the bathing room to look for a mirror. If she were to see Corien today, she ought to make herself presentable. But she could not find a mirror, or a comb, or jewelry, or pins for her hair.

"Strange," she said aloud, then shrugged and forgot she had ever thought such a thing.

Double doors marked the exit to her rooms—two huge pieces of white stone engraved with perfectly symmetrical diamond patterns.

She tried the doors, and they opened without a sound.

The corridor outside was broad and pale. Windows lined each side, their lace curtains fluttering in the breeze. Beyond the windows bloomed a profusion of flowers and greenery. Birdsong trilled from a cloudless blue sky.

Merrily, she continued on her way, wandering down empty white corridors. The sun was warm on her bare toes. She caught glimmering dust motes with her fingers.

At last, she came to a single door standing ajar in a wall of gleaming pale wood.

Her heart lifted at the sight, though she could not have said why, and when she pushed open the door, she let out a cry, for there was Simon, sitting at a desk with his feet up on a windowsill. He turned to her and smiled broadly. He stood and came toward her with three long strides, and she met him in a pool of sunlight at the room's heart. When she threw her arms around his neck, he lifted her off her feet and buried his face in her hair.

"There you are," he said, and she squirmed happily in his arms, pulled back to gaze upon his face.

And froze.

It was wrong. It was all wrong.

That face, so smooth and smiling, was not Simon's. She remembered now—there ought to have been scars. He was scarred all over; he had been burned and cut. But this man holding her was healed and happy. No shadows turned in the bright blue of his eyes. His smile was open and easy.

"No," she whispered, and pushed back from him.

He released her, brow furrowed. "What is it, love?"

She whirled around to face the door and screamed, "No!"

She woke in her white room, drenched in sweat. The sunlight was gone. It was the deep of night.

Across the room, sitting in a chair by the window, was Corien, washed silver with moonlight.

"That wasn't real," she said, staring at him, her heart racing high in her throat. Even now that she understood her dream had been a lie of his creation, she wished she had never woken from it, and she hated herself for that.

She could still feel Simon's arms around her, and the feeling of lightness in her heart as she had wandered those halls bright with sunshine.

Tears came to her eyes. Her chest ached with longing. The pinch of hunger returned to her stomach; she had not eaten since she had first woken in this room, since she had beaten her fists raw on the locked doors.

"That wasn't real," she whispered again.

Corien shrugged eloquently and rose to his feet. "It could be," he said, and left her alone with her staring guards.

When Eliana awoke, she was standing on a white shore.

Gentle, warm waves lapped at her feet. The sand was soft, and behind her, on the dunes, clusters of thin pale grass rustled quietly in the wind. She tasted salt on her lips. The air was clear and light. She put her arms out to feel it and rose up onto her toes. Maybe she would fly. She was happy enough for it.

"El!"

She turned and smiled.

Remy was coming up a trail through the dunes, his arm linked with that of a kind-eyed boy with light brown skin and dark hair he kept long and knotted at his nape. Remy kissed his cheek, then ran to Eliana with a basket in his hands. She watched him fondly. At seventeen, he was the gangliest boy she had ever seen, and taller than she remembered. Had he grown even since leaving for the market that morning? The sea wind ruffled his dark hair. His eyes were bluer than the sky.

He grinned down at her and held out his basket. "I remembered."

She pulled back the basket's covering and saw a bushel of strawberries, each bright and red as blood. When she bit into the first one, the taste burst open in her mouth.

She sighed, closing her eyes. "I could die from happiness."

Warm hands slid around her waist, gently pulling her back against a broad chest.

"Please don't," Simon murmured. "Stay with me."

She turned to him with a smile.

"They're perfect," she said, and when he bit into the fruit she held up for him, his teeth grazed her fingers, and she shivered with delight, but then she caught a strange scent on the air. A sharp sweetness that did not belong.

"What is that?" she asked, before recognizing it—a floral perfume, cloying and familiar.

She cried out, bolted from Simon's arms, ignored Remy calling her name, and ran.

She awoke not in bed but on Corien's arm. They were walking together along a breezeway of his palace, overlooking the city of Elysium. White spires pierced the sky. A gown of black velvet cinched with a gold sash kissed her legs with every step.

She thought of the sea, the soft shore, Remy's bright smile.

Corien pointed with his walking stick at a nearby tower capped with bronze tiles and winged figures carved from white stone. The polished scarlet jewel at the top of his cane glinted like an evil eye.

"That is the Tower of the Singing Skies," he said lightly. "In Patria, in the City of the Skies, when an angel died, the temple choirs took to the air and sang laments for three days without ceasing. If only you could have heard it, Eliana. If only you could have seen us at the height of our glory."

He wanted her to weep, to wail and beg, but Eliana refused, even once she had returned to her room. She wasn't truly alone there, after all.

She would never be alone again.

—◆—

When Eliana awoke, she was in a house that resembled her home in Orline.

A tall, narrow house, all its windows thrown open to the morning. Polished tile floors, thick rugs in the sitting room, the bedrooms, her father's study.

She found Ioseph Ferracora in the kitchen, chopping vegetables, humming a tune. Eliana grinned as she watched him. It had been so long since she had seen him like this, relaxed and cooking breakfast. For years, he had been at war, but now he was *home*, and she couldn't stop looking at him. He was fair-skinned with ruddy cheeks, shaggy dark hair like Remy's, and he had a stubborn square jaw and square shoulders. A stranger wouldn't expect him to possess any sort of grace or gentleness. But Eliana knew better.

He could whittle the finest little figurines—woodland creatures with legs thin as twigs, robed saints crowned with stars. When she woke from nightmares of the war that had nearly claimed him, he held her as tenderly as if she were a newborn.

Ioseph set down his knife, and Eliana came up behind him and hugged him, wrapped her arms around his big barrel chest and pressed her face to his back. When he laughed, she felt it in her ribs.

"What's that for?" he asked, pulling her around to face him.

She gazed upon his rugged features, his beard-roughened cheeks. Her own felt likely to split open from her smile.

"It's for nothing," she answered. "It's for everything. I've missed you, Papa."

"I know, my sweet girl," he told her, and kissed her cheek. "But that's all past now. We're together. We're a family, and we're safe."

A merry shriek flew at them from the next room, which sent her father's mouth quirking. He retrieved his knife and gestured with it toward the door.

"You'd best get a handle on that man of yours," Ioseph warned, laughter in his voice. "He and Remy will wake the neighbors."

Eliana turned to see Remy race into the kitchen and Simon tumble in just after him. Simon caught him, scooped him up into his arms, and Remy howled with laughter, pounded his fists against Simon's shoulders.

"He cheated, El!" Remy shouted. "He cheated at king's cards, and I called him on it!"

"Ah, but I would never lie to you," Simon proclaimed solemnly, and then, over Remy's head, he gave Eliana a sly wink that left her wobbly at her father's side.

But something was wrong, she thought, watching them tease and laugh. Ioseph approached them with mock sternness, hands on his hips, and proclaimed something Eliana could not understand, for she was suddenly distracted. She stared at the back of her father's head, watched Simon set Remy on his feet and ruffle his hair, and that was it, she realized—*that* was the wrongness of it.

Remy was too small. He was a tiny child again, not the gangly boy she knew. And Simon's face was smooth and full of light, the shadows gone from under his eyes, and Ioseph...

"Father?" she asked quietly.

He didn't respond, his back to her, but something was wrong, or at least she thought it was, and she needed to look at Ioseph Ferracora straight on. She needed to see her father's warm, dark gaze, the amiable lines around his eyes, and feel reassured that this strangeness turning inside her was simply a fancy, the echo of a dream.

She touched his shoulder, but before he could turn, she saw his reflection in the mirror hanging across the room.

Mouth frozen in a smile, eyes black as twin hollows.

"You should have let yourself dream," said Ioseph, but the voice was not his, and came from over her shoulder.

She whirled, but when she opened her eyes, it was to find herself twisted on the floor of her room. Her nightgown clung to her, soaked through with sweat.

Corien stood above her, clearly amused.

"You insist upon turning every sweet thing I give you into a horror," he told her, and then pulled her to her feet and held her as she wept. She curled her fingers into his black coat, wishing she had the strength to claw at him. But the dream he had sent her had left her trembling. Her arms were liquid, useless.

"It could be like that," Corien whispered against her damp hair. He rocked with her as if soon they would dance. "Life could be happy again, Eliana, if you let me make it so for you."

She knew he was right, and she shut her eyes with an ache in her chest, remembering the warmth of her father's smile. Her quiet home in Orline. Rozen Ferracora's garden, the kitchen table strewn with Rozen's tinkerings. Remy safe in his bed, reading aloud from one of his books, and Harkan asleep just across the way.

◆

When Eliana awoke, Simon was standing over her, an urgent light in his eyes. A sword glinted at his hip; strapped to his chest were two revolvers.

"We don't have much time," he said, helping her sit. "Listen carefully, for any moment he will discover I'm gone, and all will be ruined."

She stared at him. "What are you talking about?"

"It's a ruse, Eliana. It's all been a lie." He found her hands and kissed them. "I'm sorry for it, but it was the only way to protect you. I could not risk your life." His voice broke as he spoke against her fingers. "It's been torment to deceive you. Every moment I see you suffer is agony."

Relief flooded her body, her skin tingling. She felt light-headed, weightless.

"I don't understand," she said, but left her bed to follow him. He had gathered supplies. He was holding out a cloak to her. At the door, Remy kept watch. His hair was shaggy, unkempt, and fell to his shoulders. Bruises marred his skin as if he had borne the fall of a hundred fists, but his eyes gleamed triumphant in the moonlight.

"We have one chance to escape, and it's tonight," Simon said, ushering her toward the door. "Follow me."

But she refused, planting her feet at the threshold. Something was wrong. There was a sharp metallic patter in her mind, and she could not dislodge its rhythm. It was familiar. She had heard it before.

"El, we have to leave!" Remy whispered from the door.

"Gunshots." She looked at Simon, the memory rising fast. "You shot them all in Festival. You gave orders to the angels."

He hissed out an impatient breath. "It was all a lie, Eliana. Aren't you listening?" He grabbed her wrist. His grip was awful, merciless. "Walk. Now."

But she knew the truth: She could trust nothing she saw. Her entire world had become lies of Corien's making.

She awoke quietly in the dim light of her room, her face wet with tears, and found Corien sitting on the edge of her bed.

"I've hoped for that," she said, her voice cracking with exhaustion. None of her sleep felt true anymore. "That there was a reason for it all besides deceit."

"I know," said Corien, his voice a croon of sympathy. He touched her cheek, rearranged her mussed hair.

Fresh tears turned her white room shapeless and bright. "What a fool I am," she whispered. "What I fool I have always been."

"I can make this stop," came his tender voice, wheedling and kind. "You know I can. All I ask for in exchange is—"

"I'll die before I help you." She glared at him through her tears, trembling with a sudden spike of rage. "You can send me a thousand sweet lies, a thousand nights of promises, a thousand dreams of everything I wish for and everyone I have ever loved, and my answer will be the same."

His silence then was utter, terrifying in its stillness.

She waited, tense, trying to decipher the black expanse of his gaze, and when the burning of her eyes became unbearable and she blinked at last, he was gone.

◆

When Eliana awoke, she was in the white room from her dreams.

"Good morning," she called out cheerfully to her attendants. She stretched and yawned, then swung her legs out of bed and into the cool air. In her nightgown, she wandered the broad sunlit hallways of her home and wondered, as she always did, at her own wild fortune. She heard birdsong and hummed along. She plucked a red flower from a vase and inhaled its sweet perfume.

At last, she came to twin narrow doors of dark polished wood, their bronze handles fashioned into flaring wings.

Corien stood at the threshold, wearing a brocade coat of ebony and midnight blue. The embroidered pattern glinted iridescent, like a blackbird's feathers.

Eliana's joy died. A lie. It was a lie. This was not her home. It was Corien's.

"No," she said, and stepped back from him. Soon she would awaken. She knew the pattern by now. She would come to in her room and see him watching her, listen to him comfort and coax her.

Guards arrived at her elbows, forcing her forward into the shadowed receiving hall where they had first met.

"Another dream?" She laughed, grasping wildly for bravado. "I didn't realize you would be so tiresome."

Corien said nothing, gliding past her.

"I have a gift for you, Eliana," he said smoothly, and as Eliana followed him, stumbling between her relentless angelic guards, two figures in the shadows came into view.

Simon, his eyes flat and cold, his body all tidy sharp lines in the black imperial uniform. Square shoulders, gold buttons, red sash.

And Remy, standing beside him, thin and pale and dressed in a plain tunic and trousers, the fabric torn and stained. Eyes wide, hands in chains, lip bloodied.

Eliana's stomach lurched, but she stayed where she was. She clenched her fists and kept her voice calm. "I've seen this before. I've seen a hundred Remys, and some of them looked just like this."

"Remy Ferracora," said Corien, circling the room. "A famed storyteller, I've heard."

"El?" Remy's voice was hoarse. His eyes darted wildly from Eliana to Corien to the doors. "What's happening? Where have they been keeping you?"

Eliana did not reply. She would not participate in this. Not again. Not ever. For too many nights, she had believed what she saw. She had attempted escape. She had been home in Orline with her father, with Harkan. She had been on a white shore with Simon, in a gray cottage that was all their own.

Never again. She swallowed hard. She said nothing.

Remy glanced fearfully at Corien. "Can I go to her?"

"Of course." Corien gestured magnanimously. "Cherish this."

Remy flew into her arms, but Eliana's dreams had felt real before. She looked away, doing nothing, saying nothing. Corien was watching as he circled them, hands behind his back. There was a slight smile on his lips.

She would give him nothing.

"Where have you been?" Remy pressed his face against her arm. His thin body trembled. "I called for you, and you never came."

"I'm sorry," she replied distantly. "I've been busy."

Remy pulled back to frown at her. "What's wrong with you? Don't you care where I've been?"

Eliana refused to look at him. If she looked into the eyes of one more creation of Corien's mind, he would win.

"Tell me," she said, indifferent.

Remy paused, uncertain, and then said quickly, "It's a place of many rooms. I don't know how many. I can't count them. It's underground, dark and cold. I hear them all around me. Thousands of voices, screaming and crying and laughing." He hesitated, glanced at Simon. "*He* brought me there, the first day he arrived. He put me in my room."

Ah, and now Corien would bring Simon into the lie, try to draw her in that way. "I see. What room?"

"The place where I'm kept." Remy stepped back from her, and now his voice turned fearful. "Why aren't you looking at me?"

"Sad, isn't it?" Corien approached, his face alight with glee. "To see her so changed? I suppose she doesn't care about you anymore."

Remy moved away from them both. "What have you done to her?"

"The question you should be asking," said Corien, "is what will I do to you?"

Suddenly, Remy's body seized where he stood. He jerked left, then right with choked cries, then fell, his jaw smacking hard against the floor, and began to scream.

For a moment, Eliana stared at him, frozen with horror as his screams tore at her and her blood roared.

Then she turned her back on him, looking instead at the closed doors.

"I won't be your plaything anymore," she said tightly.

Corien came around to stare at her, his expression one of mocking surprise. "And instead you will allow your own brother to be? I thought I knew you well."

She stepped away from him. Behind her, Remy's screams rent the air asunder. Her arms erupted in chills. She made for the doors. Any moment now, she would awaken in her bed, rested and triumphant, and Corien would be the fool, not her.

"The daughter of the noble Lightbringer," he mused, keeping pace at her side. "Who would have thought you could be so cold?"

She reached the doors. When she spoke, her voice shook with anger. "End this. Wake me."

Corien leaned against the wall beside the doors. "Oh, Eliana. You don't understand. Here, I'll help you just a little. Every passing minute I remain in your brother's mind is a year gone from his life. Maybe more. Every mind is different." He shrugged. "Leave, if you wish."

Eliana stared at the door, at her hand upon the bronze wing, and a slow, sinking dread came over her. A high whine sounded in her ears; she heard the sound of Remy's skull hitting the floor. He was convulsing.

Corien's face was full of pity she could not trust. He removed piles of gold from his pockets. "Here," he said gently, and began to fasten the familiar thin chains around her wrists. The twin discs of her castings settled in her palms, smooth and cold.

Corien smiled. "There, you see? When the mood strikes, I can be most generous."

She stared at him in horror, knowing this was just what he wanted, then turned back to Remy. Her castings were unblinking cold eyes against her sweating hands.

She crashed to her knees at Remy's side, fumbled to lift him, held his head in her lap. His eyes were glazed; spit foamed at his lips. She held on to him, desperate to soothe his shaking, but he did not see her. He stared at the ceiling, clawing the air, and then he began clawing at himself, his fingernails tearing at his arms, his cheeks.

Eliana caught his arms, held him tight against her body.

"Release him," she cried. "What are you doing to him?"

"I'm forcing him to relive the moment my body was torn from me," Corien said calmly. He was close now, watching them from above. "When I was driven into the Deep by your ancestors and stripped of all physicality. My skin flayed, my bones crushed, my veins sucked dry by the universe itself. The empirium dismantling me in an abyss where nothing is allowed to exist save for its own raw power." He drew in a slow breath, exhaled. "As you might guess, it was an agony I cannot possibly describe. No one who hasn't felt it can know."

He crouched for a better look, his black gaze fixed on Remy's thrashing body. Eliana sensed a great focus within him, a terrible concentration that connected everything he was to everything Remy was, small and helpless in her arms.

A faint smile played over Corien's face. "After this, perhaps Remy can help me describe it to you. Our little wordsmith."

Sitting on the ground with Remy dying in her arms, she realized with a sick jolt of fear that this was a horrible parallel to that moment in Karlaine: Remy's abdomen torn and bloody, her own vision a field of empirium gold, her hands submerged in his wound, knitting him whole once more.

And Simon behind her, holding on to her, an anchor in that savage moment of awakening. Against her cheek, he had whispered, *I'm not letting go.*

"You know how to end this, Eliana," Corien said quietly. "You know what you must do."

She sucked in harsh breaths, fighting with all her might to still Remy's body, but it was impossible. She could not fight Corien alone, not without using her power, and if she managed to summon it, Simon might manage to summon his.

"I will die before I help you," she said through her tears.

Abruptly, Remy's thrashing subsided.

He was limp in her arms, drenched with sweat. Trembling, he stared at the ceiling, his lips moving soundlessly.

"Remy, can you hear me?" She held his cheeks, pressed her forehead to his. Against the cold chains of her castings, his skin was blazing hot.

"Talk to me. Please, say something."

He did, in a whisper so faint she had to ask him to repeat it. "Kill me."

Eliana's blood froze. "What did you say?"

His bleary gaze locked with hers. "Kill me, El. Then he can't use me against you like this."

From the shadows, Corien stretched, his joints popping. "God, it really can be hard work to dig and dig like this, to implant. To focus so singularly on one mind while also controlling thousands of others. Quite painful, really, if that's a consolation of any kind?"

"He's done nothing to you." Eliana swiped at her eyes with shaking hands. "He's an innocent."

"So were many angelic children who suffered the same fate Remy just lived through," Corien returned calmly. "And they didn't wake up in their own bodies afterward, alive and whole. Isn't he lucky?"

Then Simon spoke. "If you care about him, you'll do as you're commanded and spare him the pain." The quiet whip of his voice shocked Eliana, jolting her. How could she ever have thought him warm, passionate, selfless? His mouth quirked cruelly, as if he knew her thoughts. "Or perhaps you don't care about him," he added. "Maybe you're as good a liar as I am."

"Why is he here?" she asked Corien, choking on her own voice. "I won't beg him for help. I won't beg either of you."

Remy's hand tightened around hers. A small smile touched his mouth.

Corien glanced Simon's way. "I have to make sure he's still mine, don't I? I can understand how the two of you—his pretty little charge and her sweet pup of a brother—might melt the very coldest of hearts. So I'd like him to see every moment of this. I'd like to test him. He likes it when I test him."

A private smile passed between the two of them. Eliana searched for the telltale adatrox gray in Simon's eyes but saw only the familiar bright blue.

He was not under Corien's control. He was, at last, utterly himself, and as Eliana sat with Remy limp in her arms, the truth of how alone she was in this place, how she had only herself to turn to for strength, settled against her tired bones like silt in dark water.

She turned to face Corien, a desperate plea on her lips.

He was there at once, kneeling at her side. "You can have everything I've shown you. Every happiness, every peace. I'll end this, Eliana—this life of yours, all its violence, all its sacrifice. Your brother will be safe. He'll be so happy, and so will you. Alive, healthy. Safe. *Safe*, can you imagine? For once in your life."

He stroked her cheek with the backs of his fingers. "I can end your fight, if you only do this final thing for me. Let your power rise, as it once did. Share it with Simon, as you once did."

Even with Simon watching from the shadows, compliance hovered on Eliana's lips. She could taste the words. *Yes*, she longed to say. *You've won. Both of you have won.*

But something stopped her, some last shred of defiance, and with a sharp sound of frustration, Corien gripped her head and shook her.

"I must go back to her, Eliana," he whispered, tears in his eyes. "I must find her. Open up. Give us your power. *Send me back.*"

◆

When Eliana awoke, she was in the white room from her dreams.

Corien sat beside her on the bed, and Simon stood behind him, waiting, and her dull-eyed adatrox guards surrounded the room, white-robed and silent.

Her castings, intact around her hands, were warming.

And Remy…Remy was nowhere. Remy was gone. What had he said? *It's a place of many rooms. It's underground, dark and cold.*

Imagining Remy trapped in such a place, years and years of his life torn from him, Eliana's grief and anger became physical, an exhausted explosion of heat that swept through her body. She could not stop it from coming, nor did she want to. She wanted it to rise and consume her, the rooms in which she now lived, the palace that had become her entire world, and spit out the ashes like poison.

She pushed away from Corien, stumbled out of her bed, and fell hard to the floor. Her hands slammed against the white stone, and at the impact her castings bloomed with light. They were twin nets of fire around her hands, and she could sense, in that moment of white-hot clarity, countless cords of energy bursting furiously to life at her desperate, unknowing command.

The world shuddered—an earthquake, an explosion. The windows of her bedroom shook in their frames. Her guards stumbled.

In the silence that followed, Eliana huddled on the ground, her vision sparking with light, her fingers splayed across the stone floor. She panted, dizzy and heaving, every muscle trembling.

And in her palms, her castings buzzed—alive, now, and waiting.

At the sight of them, horror punched her in the gut, and her vision cleared as terrible understanding set in.

She immediately grasped for control. Anger coursed through her still, and a terrible sadness clutched painfully at her throat, but she could not allow that to beat her. Corien could weave a thousand beautiful lies for her every day for the rest of her life. It would not matter. She could not allow this to happen, not ever again. She imagined shoving against her castings, turning them cold and dark once more. She imagined her power returning to the deepest corners of herself, hidden and untouchable, like shadows retreating fast at midday.

But it was too late.

Beside a humming, pale ring of light, Simon stood with raised arms, both of them shaking with obvious effort. But when he stepped through the light and disappeared, he emerged the next moment at the far side of the room. He took a single staggering step before falling to his knees, gasping for breath, and when he looked up at Corien, it was with a tired triumph.

Such a little thing, a mere skip across a single room, and he had not touched the threads of time.

But the threads of space he had found were brighter than those he had summoned upon her arrival in Elysium. Stronger, more reliable. It was a start, and Eliana had allowed it to happen. She had *made* it happen. She had lost her grip on her power, let it rise as she had when Remy lay bleeding in her arms, and again on the beach in Festival, and again—awfully, guttingly—in the gardens of Willow with Simon's heart beating under her hands. That one small moment had been enough.

Her stomach plunged fast, a swift fall of ice.

Corien smiled, wide and slow.

"Excellent," he said quietly. "Now we can begin."

‑ 9 ‑
NAVI

"The last queen of the Vespers? Oh, we all loved her. Her consort died at sea many years ago, left her a young widow, but she kept building her ships, and she raised seven children to be the sweetest little crownlings you could ever hope to meet. Then the Empire came to the capital, killed her and six of her babies on the steps of the Ivory Palace. But her seventh child, little Brizeya, was never found. Some think she was swept out to sea, where the waves laid her to rest beside her father. Others think she still lives, planning her revenge. I think of that poor child every night. If she does still live, I hope she never learns her true name. There's nothing left for her here. There's nothing left for any of us."

—Collection of stories written by citizens
of the occupied Vespers, curated by Hob Cavaserra

They had been traveling through the Kavalian Bog for six days and two hours, and Navi was convinced they would never find their way out.

Glaring ahead through the strange yellow-tinged fog that choked the air, Navi gripped her oar hard and rowed.

Ruusa, the head of her personal guard, did not like that Navi was rowing. She was one of only four of Navi's personal guard who had managed to escape the Empire's invasion of Astavar and flee to safety with Navi, her brother Malik, and their friend Hob.

It had been weeks since they had left Astavar, weeks since Navi's healers had administered the crawler antidote Eliana and Harkan had stolen from Annerkilak. Ruusa, however, was still not used to the idea of Navi being well. She scolded Navi for working so hard at the oars. Navi would wear herself out. Navi must guard against exhaustion in case some dormant scrap of crawler serum remained in her blood.

But rowing was the only thing keeping Navi sane. Rowing and recreating in her memory a map of the Vespers.

They were on one of the Vespers' northernmost islands, Hariaca. Once they crossed this awful, endless swamp, they would follow the Hezta River to the island's southern coast. From there they would traverse the Amatis Shallows on foot to the island of Laranti.

And there, at last, Navi would meet with the leader of Red Crown in the Vespers. A woman, Hob said, named Ysabet. She would be able to help Navi mobilize the Red Crown soldiers scattered throughout the Vespers—a massive nation comprising thousands of islands ranging in size from the enormous and city-choked to the minute and remote—and prepare them to travel across the Great Ocean to the Emperor's city, Elysium. They would gather an army of rebels and strays, then sail to Eliana's aid, ready to help her destroy the heart of the Empire.

If, that is, Eliana was still alive by then. If she hadn't already been tortured into madness or coerced into allying with the Emperor.

Or, God forbid, willingly *agreed* to ally with the Emperor.

It was at a small Red Crown safe house in Meridian that they had learned the devastating truth: the brutal onslaught of imperial forces at the city of Festival and the capture of Eliana by Admiral Ravikant, who commanded the Emperor's navy.

Navi closed her eyes. She had not yet managed to think of Eliana without tears rising.

"Eliana will not help him," Navi muttered in Astavari. "She is too strong for him. She will not break."

It was a familiar refrain, something she voiced aloud whenever she needed reassurance.

"Of course, my lady," answered Ruusa blandly, also in their native tongue.

"Her mother may have joined the angels, but Eliana is not her mother."

"That is true, my lady."

"She is stronger than Queen Rielle."

At that, Ruusa blew out an impatient breath. "My lady, you did not know Queen Rielle, so you cannot know that Eliana is stronger than her!"

Navi smiled wryly. "For days you've been listening to me recite my little prayers. I was wondering when you would stop saying, 'Yes, my lady,' and 'Of course, you're right, my lady,' and yell at me instead."

Ruusa's mouth was a thin line. She glared at the trees they glided between, each slick with slime and draped with thick vines. The four boats carrying the other members of their party were nearby, their pale lanterns shining faintly in the gloom. A warm, overripe stink rose from the stagnant water like that of flowers gone brown in their vase.

"I did not yell, my lady," Ruusa muttered. "I was very careful not to yell."

"That depends on one's definition of yelling, I suppose."

Ruusa was quiet for a moment. "I am sorry, my lady. Please forgive me."

"There is nothing to forgive. I encourage impertinence in my guards, Ruusa. You know this."

"Of course, my lady." Ruusa paused. "It's only that I don't want you to be disappointed."

"Disappointed by what?" Navi asked, already knowing the answer. Fear curdled in her heart. She refused to acknowledge it.

"By *whom*."

"Ah."

"Lady Eliana has brought you nothing but trouble since you left Orline. Were it not for Lady Eliana, you would not have been captured by Fidelia in Sanctuary. You would not have had to endure torture, nor would you have been experimented upon and administered the crawler serum."

"Now, you can't know that," Navi said lightly. "I might have been captured anywhere by Fidelia. And if I had been without Eliana there to save me, I would be a crawler by now."

"And then," Ruusa went on, unimpressed, "it was the Empire's desire to find Lady Eliana that brought them to Vintervok. It was *her* they wanted. *She* is why they stormed our city, my lady, our *home*. I know I was not born in Astavar, but it had become my country, just as it has always been yours, my lady, and when it bleeds, so do I."

The pain in Ruusa's voice was too raw for Navi to ignore. She caught the eye of the sandy-haired, sunburned boy sitting across from her, who was listening intently but pretending not to. He was one of their strays, fifteen years old, his family murdered during an Empire raid. He'd attacked their camp one night somewhere in the southern dust-woods of Meridian. Ruusa had wanted to kill him for it, but Navi had not allowed it, and now he was loyal to her, ready to fight the Empire. His name was Miro. Since Navi had saved his life that night in the dust-woods, he had never looked at her with anything but fervent reverence.

Of course, he knew nothing of her true identity. None of her strays did. They knew her only as Jatana, just as they knew Malik only as Rovan.

That they were the last survivors of the Astavari royal family would remain a secret. She and her brother were Red Crown; they hated the Empire. That was all Miro and the others needed to know.

Navi smiled at the boy. "Miro, would you mind rowing for a while?" she asked in the common tongue.

He quickly took her place, and once Navi had settled across from Ruusa, she resumed speaking in Astavari. "My darling Ruusa, please know that I hear you. I know you have left your home, a place that had become a haven to you, and that everyone you love was there."

"Everyone I love but you," Ruusa corrected promptly.

With those words, Navi felt something within her give way, and her eyes stung with tears. As she pushed her people south, she had refused to think much on what they had left behind. But oh, how she wished she could crawl into Ruusa's lap, as she had many times during her childhood, and ignore every impossible thing that lay ahead.

Ruusa gave Navi a keen look. She knew Navi's expressions well, particularly the one that preceded impetuous embraces. "Not now, Your Highness. Not in front of everyone."

Navi smiled and blinked her eyes dry. "Very well. Somehow I will restrain myself."

"Excellent, my lady."

"But I will tell you this: I know you grieve what you have lost. I grieve as well. I think we will grieve for the rest of our lives. With every step we take away from our home, grief braids itself more tightly into the fabric of our deepest selves. And just as I cannot pry my grief from me, discard it, and move on without it, I also cannot let go of my hope."

Navi placed her hands on Ruusa's. The two other rowers in their boat slowed their oars to listen. One was Taya, one of Navi's guards, and the other was Edran, another stray that had joined their humble ranks on the coast of the Narrow Sea. Like their other new recruits, he couldn't understand Astavari, but he watched Navi with wide, adoring eyes.

"I must believe that Eliana is the Sun Queen for whom we have prayed all our lives," Navi said, willing Ruusa to see in her eyes only her conviction and none of her fear. "I must believe she has the strength to withstand every bit of cunning and cruelty the Emperor will use against her. Please understand that when I speak of her in this way, it is not to dismiss your anger or your sorrow, but rather to express my belief—for myself, and for everyone trusting us with their lives. My belief is my hope, and hope is the light that shines even on the darkest night."

Ruusa was silent, her gaze steely. Miro watched their exchange with breathless attention, his oar forgotten.

At last, Ruusa's expression softened so subtly that Navi knew the others would not notice.

"I understand, my lady," said Ruusa, "and I forgive you."

Navi squeezed her hands in thanks.

Then, as she reached for Miro and his oar, the swamp shuddered.

It was more than a simple tremor, which could have been explained away in this volatile part of the world. It rumbled on, unending, and when Navi tried to call out, she found that something had stolen her voice.

She gripped the sides of the boat, struggling to breathe, her mind racing.

Volcanoes and quakes were ordinary occurrences. New islands formed, and old islands split into pieces. The Vesperian people—thousands of sprawling families, hundreds of cultures, united by the love of their late queen, who had been murdered during the Empire's invasion—depended on reports from the Saterketa, scholars who specialized in reading and predicting changes in the earth.

Their guide, Bazko, had told them this on their first day in the bog, when spirits had still been high and Bazko himself had been bursting with conversation. He was loyal to Red Crown and would help them safely navigate the Kavalian Bog, famous for the sheer number of travelers who had met gruesome ends in its waters.

Over the past six days, Navi—eager to trust, desperate for help—had nevertheless grown skeptical. The first time Bazko had told them that they would soon be leaving the bog for cleaner waters had been two days ago.

And now the swamp was quaking, no end to it in sight, and there was a high-pitched whine ringing in Navi's ears that she couldn't shake. Higher and higher it climbed. One glance at Ruusa told her she wasn't the only one to hear it.

Bazko sat dumbfounded in the prow of their lead boat, clutching his seat and looking about wildly. He pressed his left ear to his left shoulder and raised his right fist in the air: a command to stop.

The rowers of the other four boats in their party pulled up their oars. Navi searched through the yellow-gray shadows for Malik, her brother, who sat tensely in the boat to her left. The eerie swamp light painted his golden-brown skin with shadows. Then she looked to the right; in that boat sat Hob, broad-shouldered, his skin a dark, rich brown. Navi often turned to these men for comfort. One she had loved all her life; the other she had come to love over the past few months.

But now, they looked as frightened as she did, and a cold terror gripped her heart as she wondered if they would die here, if the swamp would open up and swallow them.

The shudder continued, and Navi counted through it. The putrid water rippled, rocking their boats. Insects and snakes dropped from their branches into the water. Long-legged birds flew off in droves.

Then, silence. Absolute and sudden. Navi's ears rang, but the awful whining noise was gone.

"What was that?" Miro whispered after a moment. He started to stand, clutching his oar like a weapon. "What's happening?"

Ruusa pulled him back into his seat. "Hush, boy."

Navi waited for their guide to call out a signal, some sign that he knew what that quake had been, but Bazko said nothing. He slowly lowered his fist, looking around at the others like a child desperate for guidance, and it occurred to Navi how small they were, how insignificant in the grand, unknowable scheme of the world.

How many strays had they recruited? Wiping away the sweat dripping down her brow, she counted quickly to make sure they were all still safely in their boats. Thirty-one. She, Malik, Hob, Ruusa, her three other living guards, and thirty-one people who were either so desperate to escape their loneliness or so obsessively hungry for revenge against the Empire that they had agreed to brave the Vesperian wilderness with a young woman who spoke of legends as if they were real, who could promise nothing except the hope of a distant fight. A journey to the Emperor's city. An assault on the place he called home.

The rescue of a princess who would save them all, if only they could reach her in time.

Navi swallowed against the sour taste in her mouth. What was she thinking? How could she and this tiny army she had made possibly mount any sort of offensive against inexhaustible imperial troops?

She was wrong to hope, foolish to even try. Her home was lost. Her *world* was lost. And scrabbling for survival like this, clinging to wild imaginings of victory, was not only an undignified way to pass what would doubtless be her final days but also a great unkindness to those who followed her. These rootless people, so desperate for even the smallest glimmer of salvation.

She closed her eyes, her palms clammy with dread. What had she done? Where was she leading them, and what lies had she tricked herself into believing?

"All is well," Bazko called out. His laughter was unconvincing. "Quite the quake, wasn't it? Not to worry. They don't call the Vespers the Ever-Shifting Lands for nothing."

Ruusa touched Navi's elbow. "Jatana, here, drink some water. Hold on to me."

But when Navi opened her eyes to accept Ruusa's canteen, something distracted her—a strange, jagged, flickering darkness, as if a seam had been ripped open in the air. No, not flickering. *Shifting.* Like a light seen through calm waters, only it was hovering *atop* the water perhaps forty yards away. Threaded with shades of gold, violet, and the plum-blue of a bruise, it hovered, waiting.

And something about it—the faint sheen of gold, the particular quality of its rippling movement, its very existence, like something from an Old World tale—reminded Navi, for reasons she could not articulate, of her lost friend.

Eliana.

A chill kissed her neck. She stood slowly, ignoring Ruusa. Splinters of darkness branched off the shape in the air like cracks in glass. She watched them grow, holding her breath, listening to the others cry out in wonder.

Then, the splinters stopped. A hundred spider legs of darkness hung suspended in the air and grew no more.

A feeling tugged at Navi's breastbone, urging her toward something, or perhaps away. She did not understand what it meant, but the longer she stared at this hovering shape, the sicker she felt.

But she had to look at it. She had to move closer. Something had happened, something to do with the empirium, and this was proof of it. The quake, and now this. Navi had to know what it was. Was Eliana hurt? Had she been killed, and now the world was breaking?

"There." She pointed. "Do you see that?"

"I see it!" Miro scrambled to crouch beside her, rocking the boat and making Ruusa curse. "Is it a fire?"

Navi retrieved Miro's oar. "We must go to it, quickly."

Ruusa did not move. "Whatever that is, we should stay far away from it."

Navi's patience had vanished, replaced by a frantic need to see this thing, to touch it. A wild thought came to her that Eliana could be on the other side of it.

"You will pick up your oar," she said to Ruusa, her voice calm but sharp-edged, "and help me get to that thing before it disappears, or you will condemn yourself to being forever a disappointment in my eyes."

It was a harsh thing to say, and Navi hated saying it, but soon they were moving, Ruusa rowing in abashed silence. Malik called after her, and Hob too, and Navi heard their splashing oars, but she did not look back at them, because as Ruusa and Taya and Edran and Miro brought her closer to this floating splintered eye, something changed.

Inside the eye, in the midst of those swirling dark colors, shapes grew, like dropped ink spreading in water.

Navi couldn't look away. This impossible thing had fastened hooks to her heart. If she tried to break away, her chest would open like a crack in the earth. What *was* it?

"You're not going fast enough," she muttered, and then, seeing that the water had grown shallow, she leapt over the side of the boat and plunged into the swamp.

Soon after, Ruusa's oar hit the ground. Navi heard the bottom of their boat wedge into the mud, heard Miro exclaim in fear, but she could not stop moving forward.

"Navi!" came Hob's voice. "Stop!"

"Something's inside it!" she called back to him.

A creature in the water brushed past her leg. She hardly noticed it, climbed up a slight rise in the sucking mud. Past the bruise's smudged rim spun slow shapes, like whorls of smoke.

Navi yanked her foot free of the muck, found solid ground. From the side, the bruise was hair thin, nearly disappearing as she gazed at it.

But moving around it, she saw that, from a different angle, it was wider, like a suspended dark mirror. Thin, bright-blue sparks crackled around its edges, like small fingers of lightning. If she could only touch this strange blemish in the air, push aside some of its tangled shadows, she would be able to see what lay inside it. She would be able to *understand*.

Her feet were moving too fast. She tried to slow down, move away, but the very air was tugging her forward. She stumbled over her own feet, reached out to brace herself, but she did not fall. Her arms went rigid, fingers pulled toward the dark unblinking eye. In a flash of terror, she understood that this thing, whatever it was, had a will.

It *wanted* her to come close.

It wanted her to touch it.

Her fingers brushed the air around it, and a horrible pressure bore down on them, then on her hand and wrist, her arm, her elbow.

She glanced down in horror, a scream lodged in her throat, and then, the darkness mere inches from her face, a crack like lightning flashed before her eyes.

A thousand images became clear to her in that single shocking instant, as if countless lifetimes had been forced into her mind all at once. Strips of skin unfurling from bone like long black tongues. Hands reaching for help that would not come. A million howling voices, a cacophony of fury.

A glittering city that had no end. Beasts with wings like scythes.

A maw immense enough to swallow the world, black and fathomless.

Navi flew back, stumbling. Something had broken her gaze. Hands seized her arms and legs, tugged her back into the swamp. She fell, inhaled murky water, came bursting back up with a gasp.

She hit something solid, and there was Malik, knee-deep in the muck, Hob and Ruusa just behind him. They helped her climb back into the boat and then shoved it away hard, away from the rise of land and the black seam crowning the air above it.

She hit something solid, and there was Malik, knee-deep in the muck, Hob and Ruusa just behind him. The men helped her and Ruusa climb into their boat and then shoved it away hard, away from the rise of land and the black seam crowning the air above it.

Then Malik and Hob scrambled back into their own boat, which had pulled up just beside hers, both of them dripping and breathing hard. Miro took off his shabby coat and draped it tenderly around Navi's shoulders.

She clutched it closed at her throat, and only then did she realize that her fingertips were coated with a thin sheen of blood.

Watching the darkness glide away from them as her friends rowed hard in the opposite direction, Navi began to weep.

Malik watched her gravely from his boat. "What was it? What did you see?"

Navi could not begin to describe it. Her head ached as the images buried themselves in her mind. She felt them crowding the walls of her skull, too big for her, too ageless.

A fleeting thought came to her: If this was even a pale echo of what Eliana felt, living with such power, then it was astonishing she had not yet shattered.

"It was the Deep," Navi whispered. "I know it was, though I cannot explain how. The things I saw, how they pulled at me..." She shook her head. "That shape, that *thing*, it is a tear between here and there. Something has opened, and I don't know why, but beyond it, past that seam, is everything we have ever feared."

Ruusa stared, her freckled face gone horribly pale. As he rowed, Hob's mouth was set in a grim line.

"Eliana often spoke to me of the Gate," Navi continued, locking eyes with Malik. "You know of it too. Father and Papa—they told you, just as they told me. Most people in our world think it only a rumor. They look at their black-eyed attackers and convince themselves there are no angels still living. But we know better."

Malik looked grim. "And you think that…that *thing* is another Gate?"

"I think it could be someday. I think the quake we felt was something much bigger than simply a shift in the earth. I think it was a shift in the empirium, that Eliana is still alive and fighting." Navi stared at the distant black eye, hovering half-hidden in the trees. Fear tickled her throat.

"And I think," she said quietly, "that if we mean to help her before it's too late, we must hurry."

✦ 10 ✦

RIELLE

"Dearest sister, you may have heard that I am dead, and while it's true that Merovec Sauvillier nearly beat the life out of me, he didn't finish the job, though I wish he had. Two friends rescued me. No, I can't tell you their names, though you would like them both. I'm no longer Merovec's prisoner. I wanted to tell you that, at least. But I cannot come home. I've heard what happened in Âme de la Terre. I know Audric and Rielle are gone. I could not warn them in time. I failed them, just as I failed to save Father. I never wanted his crown. That was always your secret wish. You'll be better for our people than I could ever hope to be. Find Audric. Help him as you can. They will call me the Craven King, for abandoning you. They'll call me the Abdicator. Well, let them. Lying near death, I realized home had never felt like home to me. Now I choose to live, and find a place where I actually fit, for however long we've all got left in this darkening world. I'll miss you, but I'm not sorry to be gone."

—Encoded letter from King Ilmaire Lysleva to his sister, Ingrid, dated November, Year 999 of the Second Age

Corien found Obritsa almost at once, pinning her and her guard in place with his mind. But in the brief moments after her escape, she had traveled more than a hundred miles.

They would have to retrieve her on foot.

For three days, Corien raged in silence as they traveled the scrubby, mountainous landscape of Vindica, its cliffs and canyons, its plains cut by thin rivers. His pace was ruthless. He hardly spoke to Rielle; when he did, it was in clipped commands.

Come here.

Walk faster.

Kiss me.

He kept his promise; he no longer cloaked her thoughts. When he pulled her against his body in the dark, Rielle grabbed his collar and met his mouth with hers.

When she obeyed him, it was because she wanted to obey.

Then, on the fourth day, they found Obritsa.

Rielle knew it as soon as she opened her eyes from a restless two-hour sleep. They had stopped racing through the night only when Rielle, exhausted, had stumbled over a crack in the ground and nearly tumbled off a cliff-side path. Now, curled up on the floor of a shallow mountain cave, she opened her eyes just as Corien stopped pacing.

"Get up." He was wild, his hair hanging in greasy strands. He yanked Rielle to her feet. "They're close."

"Unhand me." She ripped her arm from his grip. "I can walk on my own."

"Then keep up. And watch where you step." His pale eyes glittered in the moonlight, and he wore a hard smile. "I have her. She can't move. I have both of them."

Rielle struggled to match his stride, her side cramping. He was hiding his intentions from her, and the expression on his face alarmed her.

They found Artem first in a cluster of wind-twisted trees. On his stomach, limbs askew. Alive, Rielle assumed, but certainly not moving. The pack holding the castings had fallen and split. Marzana's shield glinted silver; Grimvald's hammer hummed quietly in the dirt.

Past him was Obritsa. Corien had hold of her with his mind, and yet she was still crawling away slowly, as if moving through tar. Tears streamed down her face from the effort. Her face was gaunt, her lips cracked. Rielle realized, startled, that the girl must have been trapped in this clearing for days, crawling and desperate, trying to escape Corien's hold.

He stalked toward Obritsa, grabbed her tangled white hair, yanked her to her feet. She did not cry out. Instead, she kneed him in the groin, twisted out of his grip. That startled him; Rielle could feel his surprise. She watched in astonishment as the girl whipped a crude knife out of her boot—a jagged piece of stone sharpened into a blade. Obritsa swiped at Corien as he lunged. Her knife sliced across his chest. He roared in fury, backhanded her. She crashed to the ground. Her knife flew into the trees, and she scrambled for it.

Corien found her first.

She collapsed with a scream. Her small body twisted in the dirt like a beached fish.

"You thought you could run from me," Corien said, crouching over her. "You thought you could beat me."

"I did," Obritsa gasped out. "For three days I beat you."

Corien's face twisted with fury. "I don't need to touch you to hurt you, but it does intensify the feeling." He lowered his hand to her face, pressing her cheek into the dirt. "Don't you agree?"

Obritsa's shrieks were animal, unintelligible. A low moan sounded from Rielle's left—Artem, still immobile on the ground, a soft groan of distress the only thing he could manage as Obritsa writhed.

The sound was so pathetic that it embarrassed Rielle. And if Corien kept going, he would kill the girl. They would be stranded here—wherever *here* was—and would have to covertly secure transportation through coercion, manipulation, and murder. Doable, but messy.

Rielle was too tired for messy, and the sight of Obritsa's legs kicking, her fingernails scraping the ground as she tried to push away from Corien, turned Rielle's stomach. A desperate feeling touched her—a sense of being pinned down, of being caged—and she realized Obritsa's fear was spilling out of Corien's thoughts and into her own.

The Kirvayan queen was a tiresome brat, but this was not the way to punish her.

Rielle stepped forward. "Release her."

"Oh, but she ran away," Corien said sweetly. "She must be punished."

"You'll punish the life out of her, and then we won't have a marque to help us. Release her, now."

"Like a naughty dog, she ran off and made us chase after her." Corien clucked his tongue. Obritsa's back arched, her scream cracking with sobs.

"And it's your fault she was able to run away," Rielle pointed out.

Obritsa's screams subsided to awful choked whimpers.

"Release her," Rielle commanded.

Corien growled an angelic curse but did not relent.

"Fine," she said sharply. "You idiot."

A flick of her wrist, and Corien flew back through the trees. He hit one spine-first, then dropped into a bed of tangled undergrowth.

Lightheaded, Rielle stood over Obritsa as the girl was sick in the dirt. Artem, his breathing labored, pushed himself onto his hands and knees.

"Korozhka," he wheezed, then spoke to the girl in Kirvayan as he crawled toward her. Rielle knew enough of the language to translate: *My queen, my dearest heart, I'm here. If you live, then I live. If you die, then I am no longer.*

At the naked tenderness in his voice, an unwelcome pang shook Rielle. A door inside her unlocked and gave way, and a flood of images claimed her vision.

She saw herself in Baingarde, sleeping peacefully in her bed with Audric on her left and Ludivine on her right. Limbs sprawled across pillows. Audric snoring. Ludivine's eyelids restless with dreams. They were young. It was a thing they often did in childhood—sneaking into each other's rooms, reading books and playing games, eating cakes stolen from the kitchens until they fell asleep in a pile like a pack of tired puppies. It was before Ludivine died, before an angel took her place. Before the trials. Before Corien.

Rielle froze, seeing but not seeing Artem and Obritsa's embrace—Artem smoothing Obritsa's dirt-streaked hair, Obritsa whispering fiercely, tearfully, against his collar.

Rielle's body was there in the wilds of Vindica, but suddenly her mind was at home in Celdaria.

Another vision came. She was playing a game of snaps at a sticky table in Odo's tavern. There was Audric, losing cheerfully, his curls damp from the heat and his smile broad. And there was Ludivine—an angel now, though they didn't know it—leaning in close, pressing a kiss to Rielle's cheek.

Rielle shook herself, stepping away from Obritsa and Artem.

Ludivine had found her at last.

"Go away," Rielle whispered. "I don't want you here."

In answer, another image appeared: herself in Garver Randell's shop, listening patiently as the boy Simon taught her the names of the bottled tonics arranged on his father's shelves.

And another: herself, barefoot, lounging on her terrace, nestled against Atheria's belly with a book in hand.

And another: herself in Audric's bed. Bedsheets tangled around her legs, her skin flushed pink with Audric's kisses, her fingers buried in his curls.

"Stop!" Rielle spun around and searched the trees. "Get away from me! I don't want you here! I left you!"

Come home, came Ludivine's voice, distant and distorted. Rielle could feel the miles between them, how difficult it was for Ludivine to form words. *Please, Rielle. Come home to us. Come home to me.*

"Never," Rielle said, the word a choked sob. She staggered away from the Ludivine who wasn't there. She put up her hands to fend off the image of herself smiling dreamily up at Audric. Touching his face. Bringing him down for a kiss.

"I'm never coming back," Rielle whispered. She leaned hard against a tree, glaring into the darkness of this land she did not know.

You ache for home.

"I have no home," Rielle snapped. "I am a monster. Don't you remember? 'You're the monster Aryava foretold. A traitor and a liar.'"

Audric was angry and afraid. He regrets saying those things. He doesn't believe them. Ludivine's thoughts were growing stronger, more frantic. *Rielle, he loves you still. He wants to help you.*

Rielle's tears spilled over. Her fingers dug into the tree's rough bark. "I need no help. I've made my choice. Respect that and leave me."

A pause. *I haven't yet told him about the baby,* Ludivine said quietly. *It isn't my place. I told you I wouldn't, and I haven't.*

The baby.

A wave of shock swept over Rielle. The last of the memories Corien had hidden from her was suddenly washed clean, sparkling like a diamond in her mind.

Unbidden, her left hand went to her belly. She had always had a bit of plumpness there, but now it was more pronounced. With sickening clarity she understood the sickness that had plagued her, the uncomfortable swollen feeling of her body.

Oh, Rielle. Ludivine's voice was gentle. *Had you forgotten?*

A memory came to Rielle of the girl on the mountain, months ago—the young woman who claimed to be her daughter. They had fought. She had said her name was Eliana.

Rielle turned away from the memory, shook her head to clear it. A lie, she reminded herself. Some trick of Corien's. It meant nothing.

Then, a crack in the brush. Shuffling movements.

Rielle whirled around and whipped her arm through the air, knocking Artem and Obritsa flat. They lay stunned in the trees a dozen yards away. A short-lived attempt at escape.

I've forgotten nothing, Rielle snapped. She no longer had the voice to speak aloud. *I remember every lie you've ever told me, Lu, every lie you convinced me to tell. You didn't tell us you were an angel until it aligned with the picture you wanted to paint for the Celdarian people—a picture of me as a savior and a resurrectionist. You didn't tell me the truth about how the saints tricked the angels into the Deep because you didn't want me to mistrust you or to fear that you were manipulating me into aiding some kind of vengeful scheme on behalf of your people.*

Rielle was dizzy with anger. She shoved every scrap of it toward the presence of Ludivine, which made her head throb, for she was assaulting her own mind. *You told me to lie to Audric, and I did, and I hate you for it almost as much as I hate myself. You're a snake and a coward. I hate you.*

A beat of silence. Then Ludivine spoke. *You're lying, darling.*

Rielle stormed through the trees and found Corien immobile and gasping where she had thrown him. Impatient, she swept her hand up his body. He barked out a curse as his spine snapped violently back into place.

"Stop her, please," Rielle choked out, kneeling beside him. "She's in my head. I don't want her there."

Rielle, no, wait—

But then Ludivine was gone. In her place was a welcome warm cleanliness. A locked door. A mind swept clean.

Rielle sank into Corien's arms and fumed, shivering, letting him stroke her hair and croon angelic endearments to her. *Ishkana,* my beloved. *Daeleya-lira,* my heart, you are safe.

Even as he soothed her, the grief sat hard in her throat, as if someone had screwed it into place. Yet she was giddy with relief and a vicious gladness.

"I'm never going back," she whispered. "I have no home."

"Your home is here, with me," Corien said, his mouth against her hair. "Your home is wherever we are."

But there was an emptiness in her, one that Corien hadn't yet been able to fill. With Ludivine's echo fresh in her mind, memories of home clung fast—Audric's warm laughter, Ludivine's softness, the scents of cinnamon in the kitchen and mountain snow on Atheria's wings. Ale and fried potatoes in Odo's tavern. The sweet floral perfume of the whistblooms surrounding the Holdfast. Candle smoke and prayer incense, rich and heady, in Tal's office.

"The two of us together," Corien insisted. "*Together*, Rielle. That's all that matters."

But Rielle knew—and so did he, she could sense it—that as much as they both wanted that to be enough, it wasn't.

Not yet.

First, she would have to let this strange new life, the loneliness of it, the sorrow still aching inside her, finish breaking her heart.

And then she would have to rebuild it.

—◆—

Five days later, they were on a stolen supply ship, sailing southeast across the Namurian Sea.

Corien had convinced its crew to massacre each other, sparing only enough of them to dispose of the others' bodies and keep the ship afloat afterward. They drifted through their duties with gray, unseeing eyes—tending the sails, manning the rudder, swabbing the decks clean of their shipmates' blood.

Rielle huddled in the captain's quarters, a scratchy wool blanket wrapped tightly around her. They were in pursuit of the nearest casting— the arrow of Saint Ghovan. For months, Corien had been tracking the Venteran Obex, the ancient guardians sworn to protect the casting. They had abandoned their customary post and were instead now traveling at an obscene pace across the world, never stopping for long, using marques to jump from place to place.

Weeks earlier, their trail had ended abruptly on the southern continent of Patria, which had centuries before been the heart of the angelic empire. For weeks, the Obex had stayed in one place. Hiding. Waiting.

Had the Obex exhausted their power and energy? Were they stranded, their employed marques depleted, and ready to make a desperate final stand in the ruins of Patria?

"Or is it a trap of some kind?" Corien had mused two days earlier as he lay in the late captain's bed with Rielle curled at his side. "Do they know I'm tracking them? Are they planning an ambush?"

He had laughed at the idea, and Rielle, weary, seasick, had smiled weakly against his sleeve. The smooth sound of his laughter was a gorgeous rarity. She clung to it.

"I do hope they'll try an ambush," he'd said, lazily stroking the curve of her back. "Wouldn't that be amusing, my love?"

In his voice, she had heard what he expected of her: If the Obex were indeed lying in wait, planning an ambush, he wanted Rielle to kill them before they had the chance to attack. Dissolve them. Scorch them.

He wanted her to unmake them.

And I will watch you, Corien had whispered in her mind. *My glorious queen, burning our enemies where they stand. Taking what is ours. Beginning our great conquest.*

Now, on the floor, Rielle wrapped her long hair into a knot at the base of her neck and held it in her fist. She was too tired to think about unmaking anyone at the moment. Her pregnancy was a sickness; her joints ached, and her stomach churned.

And her mind would not quiet. Even through the door Corien had pulled shut and locked twice now, Ludivine persisted. She whispered and wheedled. She sent endearments and thin threads of memory.

Rielle ground the heels of her palms against her temples in tight circles. "Lu, go *away*."

"If you want to see her," said a small voice from across the room, "I can send you to her. Not all the way there in one go, of course, but eventually. It would be a start. Maybe he wouldn't attack me, if you were with me."

Rielle lifted her head, staring blearily.

Bound in the opposite corner, the girl-queen Obritsa met Rielle's gaze. It was the first time she had spoken since Corien had taken Artem belowdecks just after they'd claimed the ship as their own. Where the Kirvayan guard was kept and what games Corien was playing with his mind, Rielle did not know.

"Isn't that what you want?" Obritsa continued. "To see Lady Ludivine? To see them both? You didn't have time to say a proper goodbye, after all."

Rielle closed her eyes. "I didn't want to say goodbye."

"I saw you on the night of your wedding. You were devastated. There was agony on your face. You didn't want to leave them, and yet you did. You felt you had no choice."

"I was glad to leave them," Rielle snapped, pressing her fingers against her forehead. Miniature storms of power crackled between her knuckles. "I should have done it sooner."

"You forget that you visited my palace, Lady Rielle," said Obritsa. "I saw all of you together. I saw you with Prince Audric. *King* Audric, now. The love between you was not a lie."

Rielle's heart pounded in her ears. "Our love was not a lie then," she said stiffly. "Now, it would be."

"If you say it, I suppose it's true."

"I could disintegrate you with a snap of my fingers, and you know it. Considering that, it seems odd that you would insist on provoking me."

If Obritsa felt fear, Rielle could not see it. The shadows under Obritsa's tired eyes made her face look sunken, yet her poise was impeccable. She was a spy, Rielle knew—a weapon planted on the Kirvayan throne by revolutionaries determined to overthrow the elemental ruling class. And now she was the prisoner of an angel.

Rielle looked away. The girl was an asset, nothing more. She deserved neither admiration nor pity.

"He's busy, maybe even distracted, but he won't be for long," Obritsa said quietly. "If you want to see Ludivine and Audric again, you should act quickly, and you know it."

Rielle rose unsteadily, hating the new plumpness of her body. Thoughts of the child growing inside her crested bitterly, but she fought against them. She couldn't think about the life inside her just yet, nor the danger it might pose. She couldn't think about how furious she was with Corien for keeping the truth of her child from her, even after he had promised her no more lies. He had apologized; she had accepted. That should have been enough.

Rielle paced. Corien was up on the deck, overseeing his new, gray-eyed crew. She knew that even as he worked his mind would be elsewhere, in a thousand different places across the world and in the Deep. It was possible that, right now, in this moment and perhaps for a few more, he would be distracted and not looking at the captain's quarters, where Obritsa's words lingered in Rielle's ears, and a seed of doubt had begun sprouting slowly in her heart.

But the girl was right; at any moment, he would return to them. In an instant, he could reach for her, and hear everything they said.

"It's taken us weeks to travel this far," Rielle said quietly. "I wouldn't be able to get to Celdaria and back before he realized we were gone."

"No, you wouldn't," Obritsa agreed.

"He'd find us before we could get very far."

"Most likely."

"And punish us. You most of all." She blew out a sharp breath. "What a stupid idea. You're stupid for suggesting it."

"Undoubtedly." A beat of silence. "But wouldn't it be worth it to try?"

Rielle breathed slowly through her nose, fighting for calm as nerves bubbled hot in her chest, rising higher and higher. *Was* it worth it to attempt leaving? She imagined being back in Celdaria, in the familiar halls of Baingarde. She could confront Audric, know for certain that he was alive and well. Demand an apology for what he'd said to her on their wedding night.

Punish him, if she decided to. Reject him forever.

She could plant her feet on Celdarian soil once more, ride Atheria up to Mount Cibelline's highest slopes and gulp down the crisp mountain air until her lungs burned.

But what would she find beyond that? What life could she find there after everything that had happened?

She turned to the nearby wall, pressing her palms against it, her head pounding in time with the rocking of the ship. "I cannot."

Obritsa's voice tightened with impatience. "You claim to want freedom, and yet you allow him his chains." Then, in an urgent whisper: "Lady

Rielle, if you'd seen what I've seen at his base in the north, the things he does in the mountain beneath his fortress—"

Then, abruptly, Obritsa stopped speaking.

Rielle whirled just in time to see the girl stiffen. Her eyes glazed over, and she slumped back against the wall.

The door flew open, and Rielle hurried toward it, met Corien at the threshold with a kiss.

"I want to get rid of them," she said breathlessly, her mouth against his, "as soon as we have the casting and take it to...what do you call it? Your base?"

"The Northern Reach," he said, voice flat, not responding to her touch.

"Yes. As soon as we get there, get *home*, can we rid ourselves of her?" She gestured at Obritsa. "We can find another marque. I don't like this one. The sight of her repulses me. Such a scrawny little thing."

It was a pitiful lie. Obritsa was quite obviously beautiful, and Corien knew Rielle thought so.

His fingers curled at her waist. His lips hovered over hers. "Your dress is getting tighter. We'll have to find you a new one."

"Several new ones, please? Lacy ones, and velvet. Gowns that feel nice against my skin." Rielle ran her hands down his torso, paused at his belt, then moved lower. He drew in a sharp breath. This was new, a place she had touched in the dreamscape of their minds but never in reality. Her body fluttering with nerves, she leaned closer and whispered against the skin above his collar, "Things that feel nice as you take them off of me."

He caught her wrist, kissed her racing pulse.

"Stay at my side, Rielle," he said, "and you'll get everything you want."

A thrill of fear touched her skin. He knew she had been speaking to Obritsa; she had sensed that the moment he entered the room.

She grinned up at him, pretending they didn't both know she had been offered the chance to escape him and had come close to taking it.

Pretending that she knew exactly what she wanted and that it was as simple as the kiss with which she now claimed him.

After a week on the sea, they reached the enormous island of Patria, a country of lush rain forests, high plains, and towering volcanic mountains.

Once, it had teemed with angels.

Now, it was a land beautiful in its desolation, echoes of luxury dusting every abandoned street. Broad plazas of cracked marble, spiraling towers capped with copper gone green and black, neighborhoods of slate-roofed manor houses and crumbled apartment buildings bordered with stately columned terraces, all laid out in impeccably designed grids. Wings of bronze and ivory capped peaked roofs, street markers, overgrown gardens.

But in the centuries since the angels' defeat, the land had devoured every construction. Bright green vines with ravenous-looking white flowers spilled out of courtyards. Twisting black trees climbed through shattered glass ceilings. In the heart of a sunlit neighborhood stood a cavernous library, its shelves bare and its floor strewn with rotting books.

"The City of the Skies," Corien announced as they stepped across the library's threshold. Overhead, the ceiling was a broken tapestry of colored glass. "The heart of the angelic empire. This is where the empirium raised the first angel from the dust and breathed the gift of long life into her lungs before sending her to live among the clouds."

Rielle turned away from him, her gorge rising. She knew that story quite well. Many times, Audric had read it to her from his favorite collection of angelic lore. Even now, she could hear his warm, rich voice shape the words, imbuing it with the rhythm of song.

Corien turned sharply to glare at her.

Their eyes met, a hundred warring words on her tongue.

Then the Obex found them.

It was an ambush indeed, just as Corien had hoped for, and a pathetic one. As soon as the first arrow flew—whizzing down from behind the spiked parapet of a crumbling watchtower adjacent to the library—Rielle's exhaustion faded, and her instinct erupted.

Afterward, she didn't recall slaughtering them. Their faces, how they had staged their attack, where they hid, what they wore, how many there were, how many of them were humans and how many were marques employed by the Obex—Rielle knew none of this and didn't care to know.

She knew only that there were weapons flying at them and that it was time to kill.

It was over in moments.

Glorious, fire-hot moments during which she could feel neither the edges of her own body nor the earth under her feet. Her power had been waiting for this moment, brewing under her skin as she slept and fretted; as she huddled, miserable and sick, on the stolen ship; as she hid from the tenacious scraps of Ludivine's voice in fevered dreams of Corien's making.

It had been waiting for weeks, an animal pacing in its cage, and when it broke free of her, the explosion of power knocked Obritsa and Artem to the ground. Rielle remembered blackness rising up and taking her, replacing her eyes and lungs with gold.

Later, she came to slowly. On her hands and knees, on a shattered marble floor, she panted. A red sun of blood circled her, its rays wet and shining. There were no bodies; flakes of bone drifted slowly through the air like snow. A hum filled Rielle's ears, and she couldn't determine if it came from somewhere far away or from deep inside her ribs.

She fumbled through shards of shattered marble, clods of fresh earth. Her hand landed on a long, heavy piece of metal, and when she lifted Ghovan's arrow free of the rubble, her vision cleared.

She sat in a tableau of utter destruction.

The library was gone, its ruins demolished. Piles of dust and stone were scattered across the uprooted foundations like snowdrifts. Curls of black smoke crowned each of Rielle's fingers. She cradled the arrow in her arms and smiled, her skin buzzing. She felt the cords of Saint Ghovan's arrow snap into place as it connected to Saint Marzana's shield, Saint Grimvald's hammer, Saint Tokazi's staff. A web of power that fed her own and painted her skin in veins of bright color.

She heard something heavy being dragged and looked up to see Corien kneeling a few paces in front of her. He'd found a body, still intact—one of the Obex, she assumed. She'd missed one.

Corien caught her wrists before she could destroy it.

"Wait," he said, his voice coming through a churning sea of color. She blinked, and blinked again. Perhaps her vision wasn't so clear after all. She could see the black and white of Corien's familiar form, the faint sheen of red coating the ground, but beyond that, all was gold—gold behind her eyes, gold beneath her fingernails, gold at the corners of Corien's mouth.

She lunged forward and kissed him, greedy and full of fire. She bit his lips, climbed into his lap. She was ravenous. In her right hand, she clutched Saint Ghovan's arrow.

"Rielle, wait, listen to me." Corien's voice floated down from the clouds. Gently, he detached himself from her. "I need you to try something for me. Now, while you're still hot and humming. My beautiful girl." He pressed a kiss to her brow. His voice was urgent, thrumming with excitement. Or was she herself thrumming? The whole *world* was thrumming, and she had made it so.

Smiling, she touched his face. She'd been drunk before on wine and ale, but that was nothing compared to being drunk on the ecstasy of her own power. She sensed, distantly, that it had never been this good before, never this eager or quick—and never this disorienting. How suddenly it had erupted; how violently it had come over her.

She braced her palms against the ground. "What is it you want?" She laughed at the absurd shape of her hands in the dirt. "Anything. I can do anything."

"I know you can." Corien pushed the Obex's body closer to her. "I have friends here. Many of them. Can you see them?"

He sent her a thought, and she sensed how tentative it was, how careful. He was being *careful* with her in a way he'd never been before.

He was afraid.

She would ask him about that later, but at the moment she was fascinated by the thoughts he was sending her. She became aware of a new presence—a dozen of them, *dozens* of them, all drifting nearby. Consciousnesses. Mighty ones.

"Angels," she breathed, looking around in wonder. "There are angels here."

The empirium granted her vision that her eyes would never possess. Faint shapes drifted through the air, dim and pale, shapeless and anguished. Their voices teemed, whispering. They did not have hands or arms, and yet she felt them reaching for her, imploring. They lacked cohesion. The empirium gold glinting inside them was pale, worn out.

"Those who have escaped the Deep," Corien was saying quietly, "but who are not strong enough to be soldiers, I have sent here, to the City of the Skies, to hide and to wait. For you, my vicious marvel." He paused, a tense, expectant beat. "Will you try? Now, for me? Your power is so vital right now, I can barely…Rielle, I can hardly look at you. You're brilliant. You're *shining.*"

"I am the Unmaker," she said simply, kindly. An explanation. "And I am the Kingsbane. But you shouldn't be afraid of me." This she announced to the air. She felt settled in her own skin, blissfully calm. "Who among you is bold enough to be the first angel reborn? Come forward. Come to me."

A mind approached her, curious and afraid, trying to mask its fear. A child, Rielle thought. A boy. A vision of truth came to her: As an angel, during the First Age, this child had been a creature of alabaster skin, hair that fell in auburn waves past his shoulders, amber eyes flecked with bright green. When the Deep took him, rent his body from him, he had been mere decades old, quite young for an angel.

"Malikel," Rielle whispered. "Don't be afraid. Be reborn."

Her empirium-bright vision took her under. It showed her that the boy, Malikel, was at his core nothing more than stardust. Millions of spinning orbs, each more brilliant than the sun, each connected to all the others—and to the ground Rielle knelt upon, and to the darkening shape of the corpse at her feet. It was an abomination, that corpse. She hated the sight of it. Why would it lie gaping before her like this, so dead and dim, so lifeless, when it could easily be made whole again?

She worked quickly. Her power was endless, brewing like a storm. She followed its reach up to Malikel, tugged on the threads of his mind. Some nearby threads, slippery and elusive, she could not touch, not yet—the threads connecting this place to that place, the threads connecting the moments ahead of her to the moments behind.

Darkly, she thought of Obritsa. It wasn't fair that the girl should enjoy privileges Rielle could not.

"Someday I will travel anywhere and everywhere," she murmured as she knit together the threads she could touch—the physicality of the corpse, the eagerness of Malikel's mind—and dreamt of the threads she couldn't. "Someday, I will travel to the ends of everything and then back to the beginnings. Someday, marques will fall to their knees in envy of me, for I will surpass them."

"Concentrate, Rielle," Corien said urgently, his voice near and far at once. "You're dimming fast."

And he was right. Something was changing so rapidly that it made her falter. Malikel's mind, all his ancient thoughts, were half knitted to this corpse, this body with its brightening light. A braided path brought them slowly together, a connection of the empirium itself—angel to corpse, vibrant mind to dead flesh. The beginning of a new life, crafted by her own will.

But then Rielle's fingers caught on an empirial knot—a snag in the fabric of energy she had woven—and she stumbled in her work. The energy that had come over her as she killed the Venteran Obex bled swiftly from her. It was as if she'd been holding up a palace with her own two hands, lifting it high in the air, and then her muscles gave out without warning and the entire structure came tumbling down. The knots unraveled; the threads of mind-to-flesh and flesh-to-mind slipped from her grip.

She didn't hear Malikel's scream, for he had no mouth, no voice, but she felt his panic, his terror and pain. It wasn't just that the stitches she had created were unraveling.

Malikel *himself* was unraveling.

She felt the essence of his mind unspool. Something at the core of his consciousness was rent open and flew apart, a detonation. The pieces of him went flying, his thoughts reduced to sheer terror, and then he was gone.

Rielle sat back hard on her heels.

The corpse steamed at her feet, now a puddle of blood, bone, and punctured organs. A constellation of sizzling gashes dotted what had once been its torso, and through the gashes blazed a golden light, rapidly fading.

Rielle looked up at Corien through a veil of weariness, and as her exhaustion returned, she began to understand what had happened. The thoughts of the other angels brushed up against her, all of them terrified, all of them astonished and cowed.

"I'm not ready yet," Rielle said at last. "I thought I could do it; I *felt* how close I was. I've *been* close." She cried tears she did not ask for, registered a sadness that felt too far from her to touch. Her mind was wrapped in sheets of thick cotton. She wanted to lie down in the dirt and sleep for months. Her nose and mouth filled with the scent and taste of blood. Her thoughts crested and dove, darting from desire to desire, and she didn't know how to quiet them.

Corien said nothing. He lifted her into his arms, held her close against his chest.

"You need rest," he said quietly. "True rest. We have four castings now. There is time before we need to find the others." He brushed a kiss across her cheek, then whispered, "I'll show you my home. A place of industry and monstrous beauty. The water is black and cold, the snow endless and clean."

Rielle hardly heard him. Her vision tilted, and she tipped into a rocking sea of half consciousness. Following her was Corien's voice, and chasing that, a vision: herself robed in red, haloed with light. Stars and moons rained upon her open palms, waterfalls made from the night sky. At her feet knelt Corien, legions of angels behind him—all winged, all armored.

You will open the Gate, he told her, *and you will remake the world.*

But Rielle heard the doubt in his voice, the fear and worry.

As she spiraled into blackness, another voice came to her from the distant ocean of her power. A voice that rumbled and quaked. A voice of many, and of one. She recognized it at once. It was the endless ancient black of Atheria's eyes. It was the roar of her own blood as she watched her shadow-dragon lick the Archon's cheek, ready to devour him. It was the humming snap of power in her veins when she turned fire into feathers, when she tamed oceans, when she killed, and killed, and killed again.

It was the voice of the empirium, and it burned its cold, pitiless words into her mind like a brand she could not evade:

this power is yours
you are mine
mine is yours
take it
take me
I take you
I rise
I rise
I RISE

→ 11 ←

SIMON

"Do you think I want to write this decree? Do you think I yearn for more death? No, my friend. But do you hear what they call us? Saint Katell the Magnificent. Saint Grimvald the Mighty. And yet we are holding together what remains of this world with only our own tired hands. I don't know if the Gate will stand. But I know what I saw, and I know the true danger of marques just as well as you do. We cannot allow this all to happen again. The world will not survive it."

—Undated encoded letter from Saint Katell
the Magnificent to Saint Grimvald the Mighty, stolen
from the archives of the First Great Library of Quelbani

Simon sat in a chair just outside the Emperor's private study, pretending to read the book in his hands.

But what truly interested him was the young woman sitting nervously across from him.

Her name was Jessamyn, and she was a student of Invictus—the Emperor's private regiment of human assassins, all of them ruthless, all of them devoted to the angelic cause. She had lightly freckled brown skin and a neat braid dyed bright red, which would no doubt change soon. The Lyceum, which housed the Invictus barracks and training yards, was as full of hair dyes, masks, and costumes as a playhouse.

Simon studied her. She was picking her nails, as if sitting in the receiving room outside the Emperor's study was a terrible bore. But Simon knew better. All Invictus operatives were the same. He saw the sheen of sweat at her hairline. He saw her nervous gaze flit to the study's closed door, to the Emperor's secretary at his desk, to the attendants flanking the outer doors, then back to her nails.

She was terrified.

As she should be.

He smiled to himself. Corien would enjoy watching her squirm.

"You're the Invictus trainee, aren't you?" Simon said. "Jessamyn, yes?"

The girl's expression soured, but then quickly calmed.

Simon expected as much. Her teacher had been Varos, an assassin Corien had been fond of, who had recently been killed during the attack on Festival. By *Harkan*, of all people. It was a shame to lose a good assassin, but it was a comfort to know that before Varos died, he had managed to dispose of that Venteran fool.

All of this had been in Jessamyn's report. And in Varos's journal, which Simon had confiscated on the Emperor's behalf, there were many notes about Jessamyn herself—that she was desperate to prove herself to the Emperor. That she learned quickly and struck fast, and that she despised her human name.

What Varos hadn't known, and what Jessamyn herself still did not, was that Eliana had known her, had fought with her—or at least she had known a Jessamyn who had existed but did no longer.

Thanks to him.

"Yes, Jessamyn," she said tightly. "That's correct."

Simon inspected her, head to toe. "Interesting that he would want to speak with a person of so little consequence."

To her credit, Jessamyn only inclined her head—though Simon saw a muscle in her jaw twitch.

"Nevertheless, I hope I can be of service to him," she replied. "Do you know why he wants to see me?"

"The Emperor has heard much about you and is curious. He likes to know which students the Lyceum particularly prizes. He would like to see you for himself and express his sympathy for your teacher's death. Also, a word of advice: You shouldn't ask questions like that." Simon closed his book and fixed her with a cold stare. "It makes you sound like a child, not a killer."

From inside Corien's study came the explosive sound of shattering glass. Jessamyn flew to her feet, reaching for the dagger at her hip.

The Emperor's black-eyed secretary jumped in his chair, and even Simon, who was used to such things, had to blink to adjust his vision, for the secretary's body shifted and blurred, a dark aura forming about his skin.

He bolted out of his chair. He clutched his neck, his chest and arms, and let out a strangled cry before staggering out of the receiving room and into the corridor. Slightly disgusted, Simon watched him go. It wasn't the first time a small disruption had shaken this particular secretary. He was a strong enough angel to hold on to a human body for a time, but not strong enough to keep that hold if something distracted him. His grasp of the empirium was tenuous.

As it was for all but the strongest angels, since the Fall of the Blood Queen.

"Follow him," Simon ordered the waiting attendants. "He's losing cohesion."

They obeyed at once. He and Jessamyn were alone.

"A severance?" she said quietly after a moment. "Just from being startled?"

Simon briskly rearranged the secretary's abandoned papers. "He's young. I've seen worse."

"It isn't fair." Jessamyn faced Simon, her jaw square and her eyes bright. "They should not have to live like this, scrabbling from body to body. They are God's chosen. They deserve better—"

The study doors swung open.

The Emperor stood there, leaning hard against the door. His white shirt—sleeves rolled up to his elbows, hem untucked—was soaked with blood.

He fixed his eyes on Simon. They glittered as if cut from black glass.

As ever, when Corien's eyes fell upon him, Simon felt a sharp chill. It was the delight that came from being sought out again and again as the Emperor's most trusted, his most beloved.

It was the creeping terror that Simon would, after everything they had worked for, continue to fail him.

"They wouldn't shut their fucking mouths about the cruciata," Corien spat. "I've kept them at bay for decades now, for *centuries*, and I'll keep them at bay for decades more if I have to. But I won't have to."

Simon peered past Corien into the study and caught a glimpse of the carnage. Streaks of blood painted the walls and rugs. Maimed bodies in torn black uniforms scattered the floor like debris. Simon recognized the bodies as those belonging to three angelic generals. Only yesterday, the generals had been charged with relieving others currently stationed at the northern front, the Empire's first line of defense against anything that came through the Gate.

Now, the generals' bodies lay ruined on the floor.

And judging by the look on Corien's face, the angels themselves had not survived the meeting either.

Simon chose his next words carefully. Not even he was immune to the Emperor's wrath in moments such as this.

"Your Excellency," he said, "this is the Invictus trainee, Jessamyn, who was at the battle in Festival—"

Don't tell me things I already know, said Corien with such furious force that pain shot through Simon's skull like a knife. It required all his strength to remain standing and to resist apologizing. Few things infuriated Corien more than apologies.

Instead, Simon bore the agony and watched Corien's gaze shift to Jessamyn.

"Three of my generals have been insisting that our defenses against the cruciata are insufficient and that soon we will be overrun," Corien began, his voice now eerily calm. "I got inside their craven minds and killed them, and then I hacked their chosen bodies to pieces." He gestured grandly at himself. "Hence the mess. Tell me, Jessamyn, what do you think about this?"

For a moment, Jessamyn could only stare. Then she sank to her knees and bowed her head. Her hands trembled against the floor.

"Your Excellency, your generals were foolish to doubt you," she said.

"But they're not entirely wrong, are they?" Corien knelt before her. "Look up. I want to see you. That's better. They're not entirely wrong, my generals. More and more cruciata have been worming their way through the Gate. We manage to kill some. Others get away."

"Yes, Your Excellency," Jessamyn managed. "That's true."

Simon stepped forward. Where Corien was taking this conversation, he did not know, but he saw tiny flickers of movement on his pale face, like shadows of things that weren't there, and the sight made him uneasy. At any moment now, the secretary could return, and the attendants. The servants could arrive with the supper meant for Corien's private meal with Admiral Ravikant—or, worse, the admiral himself could arrive early.

They could not see Corien like this, covered in the blood of his own soldiers, madness turning like stars in his eyes. The health of the Empire depended on their ignorance.

Simon stepped forward, knowing with absolute certainty what would come next.

"Your Excellency," he began, "perhaps before supper, we should sort out your study—"

His skull split open, admitting tongues of black fire that plunged down his throat and pulled his spine through his ribs.

The vision was extraordinary, so detailed and violent that for a moment Simon lost himself and swayed. He groped for something with which to brace himself and found the study door.

Seventeen years of living in this palace, and his master's punishments could still surprise him.

You know better, came Corien's voice, regretful and pitying in that way Simon had learned not to trust.

"Don't interrupt me, Simon," Corien said aloud. "I don't like being interrupted."

Simon breathed quietly through his nose, refusing to gulp down air in front of their guest. Let her think it was a mere twinge of pain he had felt.

He watched Corien take Jessamyn's chin in his hand. "Tell me what you know of the cruciata," he said.

"They are beasts from the Deep," she replied, her expression fierce with determination. "They were made aware of us when the angels broke free of their prison."

"When Rielle opened the Gate," Corien corrected her.

Jessamyn flushed. "Yes, Your Excellency."

"And who keeps the beasts from overrunning our world?"

"You do, your Excellency," she whispered. "Your mind engineered the machines that shoot them down as they enter our world."

"The vaecordia. The guns of God's chosen."

"Yes, Your Excellency."

"Yes, and my mind controls those machines," Corien said, "and my mind controls the guards in this palace, and speaks to my generals in Astavar, and speaks to my commanders on the Namurian Sea, and to the adatrox patrolling the streets of Orline. My mind scours the world for the Prophet." He smiled. "My mind is infinite. I am beyond the understanding of anyone who still lives."

Jessamyn's eyes were bright with awe. "Yes, Your Excellency."

The pain had receded enough for Simon to sense that something was wrong. He was seldom alone in his mind. Only when Corien was immersed in his deepest work, or captivated by drink or music, or shut up in his rooms, brooding on memories, did Simon feel that ancient angelic mind relax its hold on him.

But it was happening now, as Corien knelt on the floor before this wide-eyed girl. His mind seethed against Simon's own and then vanished, as if some shining blade had cut him free. Simon saw Corien's shoulders sag and his smile waver, and he had a sudden vision of Corien lunging forward to rip off Jessamyn's face with his teeth.

"You look different, Jessamyn," Corien murmured, leaning close to her. "You look different from what she remembered. I'd like to keep you close. I think it will hurt her to see you. And I would like to keep hurting her, until she can't bear it." He laughed quietly, touching Jessamyn's face and then his. "Until I can't bear it."

Then he considered her for a moment longer, his laughter quieting. "Actually, I've an idea. A grand idea. You see, there's the boy. Remy."

Jessamyn frowned. She cut a swift glance toward Simon, then looked back to Corien. "The brother of Eliana Ferracora?"

"Indeed. He rots in a solitary cell in the heart of Vaera Bashta. You will bring him to the Lyceum and teach him as Varos taught you." He smiled, his gaze distant. "You will turn him cold and heartless. A killer, nothing more than a blade. And he will serve in her queensguard, and every day she resists me will be another day of looking into the eyes of the brother she has helped make into a monster."

Corien gripped Jessamyn's shoulders and bowed his head, his shoulders shaking with silent laughter. "Yes. *Yes.* And there will be no relief from this guilt. Already, she despairs at what has happened to Remy due to her actions. Soon, when she realizes what you've done to her brother, that torment will grow and bloom until she cracks all the way open and I can scoop out all her damnable insides."

He raised his gaze once more to Jessamyn. "I *will* break her. I *will* see my love again, and then all will be as it should."

Jessamyn's expression was hard and eager. "Of course, your Excellency. I will do as you command."

Then Corien rose, swaying, his brow knotted with pain. He turned as if to return to his study, then fell hard against Simon's chest.

Simon caught him, helped him stand. He was muttering two words in Lissar over and over against Simon's jacket:

Burn them.

Simon found Jessamyn staring from her spot on the floor. "Get out of here. If you tell anyone what you've seen, I'll cut out your eyes and feed them to you."

Jessamyn fled at once, and after she had gone, Simon helped Corien into his study and kicked the door shut behind them. The bare floor was slick with blood, the rugs bloated with it. He avoided the body that had once belonged to General Bartamos and settled Corien in the chair nearest the quiet hearth.

For a moment, Simon stood over him, watching him breathe. Corien gingerly touched his own temples, as if they would rupture under the weight of his hands. It was not the first time this had happened, nor would it be the last.

And Simon knew of only one way to steady him when his mind was like this—split by rage and exhaustion, poisoned by centuries of grief. Every day, more cruciata escaped the Gate's pull. Every day brought the world of the Deep closer to their own.

The Empire needed a commander, not a madman.

Simon waited until he had steadied his breathing, until he had arranged his thoughts and felt prepared for what would come next. He was a slate, smooth and clean. He was a hollow vessel, ready to receive what it must.

"You are pushing yourself too hard," Simon said at last, keeping his voice steady. "Even you, mighty as you are, are not indestructible. Not after a thousand years of rebirth and conquest."

Corien laughed softly. "I told her that once. I told her that not even she was invulnerable to death. I told her so many things."

Simon glanced at the windows, each glowing with the yellow light of early evening. Admiral Ravikant would arrive at nightfall. The rugs needed to be removed, the furniture switched out, the floor scrubbed.

He knelt before Corien and kissed his red knuckles, as he had done in rooms even darker and bloodier than this one.

"And, my lord," he said softly, "I must point out that you will have difficulty keeping your Empire loyal to you if you kill any general who comes to your office with a valid concern."

With those words, the air in the room changed. Simon felt Corien lift his head to stare at him, but he kept his own bowed. A thrill of fear pricked his calm. Fleetingly, he thought of that frozen Vindican plateau where Corien had first tortured his mind. He remembered waking days later in fits of agony, feeling as though his mind had been flayed and restitched a thousand times over.

He remembered how calm Corien had been afterward, how kind—tender, even.

"What are you saying, Simon?" Corien asked quietly. "That I am no longer fit to rule? That I should take care to temper my rightful anger, or else those I command, who would still be rotting in the Deep were it not for me, will rise up against me and somehow succeed?"

Simon shook his head. "No, my lord. I only meant that I worry."

"Odd that you should say so," Corien mused, "for *I* worry for *you*. Weeks have passed since Eliana's arrival, and still we remain here. Your power seems reluctant." Cool fingers, sticky and rank, cupped Simon's cheeks. "I think it needs a little encouragement."

And then Simon could say nothing else, for in the grip of those bloodstained white hands, he was no longer Simon. He was a mind in agony. He was a body inert on the floor.

He was a weapon, dismantled by the hands of its master.

— 12 —

AUDRIC

"I write this so that, if I die, and someone comes upon my body, they'll know where I have been and what I have seen. I have wandered north from the place that was once my home and never my home, and have now entered the northern mountain range called the Villmark. I've always wanted to explore these peaks in search of ice dragons, the ancient godsbeasts that Saint Grimvald rode into battle against the angels, but princes and kings are not allowed to wander off into the wild looking for beasts no one has seen in an age. Fortunately, I am no longer a prince or a king, or anything but a man alone."

—Journal of Ilmaire Lysleva, dated
December, Year 999 of the Second Age

Audric dodged Evyline's sword. Then he spun and parried, sending Illumenor's blade slamming into hers.

Evyline had recommended they fight with wooden training swords, but both Sloane and Audric had disagreed. If Audric was going to impress the Mazabatian troops and perhaps persuade some of them to meet with their senators before tomorrow's vote, he needed to show off properly.

He also needed the Mazabatian Senate to vote yes on his petition for military aid. And if Sloane thought a public fight in the barracks courtyard would help achieve this, Audric would do it.

He just wished Illumenor wasn't so damned *heavy*.

Another swing, another parry. He and Evyline danced around each other, their crashing blades glinting in the morning sunlight. For all her bulk, Evyline was fast, her footwork impressive. She thrust her sword; Audric deflected, but it was inelegant. She bore down on him, using the weight of her sword to press him toward the ground. He pushed against her and scrambled away. His boots kicked up dust as he spun around and desperately swung his sword to block hers.

He was beginning to regret declining her offer to use the training swords. Fighting hadn't always been this difficult.

But after eight weeks of grieving, Audric felt thin and fragile, his muscles weak, his stamina eradicated. When he had pointed this out to Sloane, she had dismissed his worries.

"You're the Lightbringer," she had said with a small smile, trying to cheer him. "A few weeks in bed hasn't ruined you."

She was right; he wasn't ruined.

He was, however, exhausted.

And Evyline was tireless. She flung her sword around as though it weighed nothing, dealing one ferocious overhead strike after another. Audric blocked all of them, but only just, and then he turned oddly, and his knees wobbled, making him stumble. He felt the fight's tide turn and saw in Evyline's pale brown eyes that she felt it too. Another shift of her weight, one more blow of her sword, and she would beat him.

Audric glanced over Evyline's shoulder, meeting Sloane's gaze. She stood against a pillar, her arms crossed. He knew very well the worried scowl she wore.

Then Evyline relented, dealing a clumsy, ineffectual blow Audric easily deflected, allowing him to regain some ground. She was letting him win, but he was too tired to care.

She dodged him, but not quickly enough. He spun and caught her blade with his own, pressed his weight down against her. Their audience would think he had trapped her under the pressure of his sword, but it was a lie. This needed to end.

"Do you yield?" he called out.

"I yield," Evyline replied, and they stepped apart, breathing hard. Evyline sheathed her sword and bowed.

"Well fought, Your Majesty," she announced for all to hear.

But no applause followed her declaration, and when Audric dared to look at the soldiers scattered around the yard watching the fight, his stomach sank.

Dozens had gathered—at the barracks windows, in the breezeways at the courtyard's perimeter—and none of them were smiling.

Don't worry, came Ludivine's reassurance, *there will be other opportunities to impress them.*

He resisted the urge to swat her away like a fly. *I asked you not to talk to me like this. This is my mind, and not yours to enter as you please.*

Without another word, she was gone, and the little twinge of pain in his heart infuriated him. Every time she spoke to him, every time he dismissed her, it was like being presented with the full breadth of her lies all over again: Rielle had killed his father, killed Ludivine's father, killed her *own* father—and both Rielle and Ludivine had kept these secrets from him. They had promised him only truth and then continued to deceive him.

Princess Kamayin kept trying to convince him to forgive Ludivine. They would need her as an ally in the war to come, she pointed out.

Audric didn't disagree. He would accept her help when the time came.

But he didn't have to forgive her.

A voice from the gathered soldiers sharply cried out one word in Mazabatian: "Traitor!"

A shocked silence. The word rang in Audric's ears like a struck bell.

Evyline withdrew her sword and took two furious steps forward, making the soldiers nearest her stagger back.

"You are addressing the king of Celdaria," she barked, "and you will demonstrate the proper respect or face the consequences."

"It's all right, Evyline," Audric said, joining her at the crowd's edge.

She reluctantly lowered her sword and stepped back to flank him. "If someone wishes to speak to me, you may come forward and do so. In fact, I welcome it."

A moment passed in which everyone gathered seemed to be holding their breath. Then, to Audric's right, a young soldier, copper-skinned with shining black hair pulled into a tight braid, pushed her way forward, her eyes bright and ferocious. One of her fellow soldiers grabbed her arm, trying to pull her back; she yanked herself free.

"My name is Sanya," she announced, "and I would like to speak."

Audric nodded at her. "Please do so."

"Eight weeks have passed since you arrived," she began. "You sleep in our queens' palace. You eat at their table. You sit in council meetings for hours, but when we ask our commanders for information about what was discussed, they deflect our questions and won't meet our eyes. How are we to know you aren't stalling until your queen can arrive and kill us all? How are we to trust a king whose queen deceived him so completely?"

Low rumbles of agreement swept through the crowd. Soldiers shifted their weight, glanced at each other uneasily. Others watched Audric in silence.

Something inside him quietly crumbled. He had never imagined he would be looked upon with such suspicion, such hostile distrust.

But this was now his world. This was what had come of the choices he had made, and the choices of others that he could not control. He would answer this woman with the truth.

"You can't know for certain that you can trust me," he said calmly. "I understand your frustration and your fear, and I'm sorry."

Another soldier stepped forward—pale and glowering, Sanya's companion who had tried to stop her. "We have heard that your friend, the lady Ludivine, is no human, but an angel."

"That's true."

The crowd rumbled with anger. More voices cried out from behind him, from above: "Traitor! Liar!"

Evyline leaned close. "My lord, we must leave."

"Their anger is valid," he said, stepping away from her.

"Will you send us to die for you?" Sanya called out, her eyes fixed upon him like arrows on their target. "Since your queen showed her face here in the capital, we have faced storms, quakes, and floods that have left much of our country in ruins. And now we will be forced to leave and fight for your throne instead of protecting our home?"

"This is about more than my throne," Audric replied. He knew he should say something better than that, that he should speak eloquently about the importance of all nations coming together as one to fend off the encroaching enemy.

But he was tired, and the escalating force of the soldiers' collective anger felt like stones piling on his chest.

"Many possibilities are being carefully, thoroughly explored and discussed," was all he could manage. "All I can tell you right now is that your queens trust me."

Sanya scoffed, her eyes flashing. "So did your people. And now we hear they're being turned out of their own homes and imprisoned for using magic, even if all they can do is light a single candle. Is that what will happen to us too? Will we all be sitting with our magic beaten out of us when the angels come at last?"

The crowd fell silent once more.

Audric stared at Sanya, unable to speak.

Because she was right: His people had trusted him to protect them, and he had failed them. He had abandoned them to fend for themselves in the chaos of a country on the brink of a war it could not win.

Suddenly, a swirling cloud of shadows descended upon them, encircling both him and Evyline. The shadows held wolves with snapping teeth and leopards with shifting black coats.

Veiled by their darkness, Audric hurried toward the nearest door leading back into the barracks, Evyline behind him. The rest of the Sun Guard waited inside, eyeing the shadows with awe and terror. One of their number, Maylis, muttered a prayer and touched her nape, honoring the House of Night.

The barracks door slammed shut. Sloane strode out of the shadows, which dissolved at her touch. The glass orb at the top of her casting, an ebony scepter, glowed as bright as a flame's blue heart.

"That was my fault," she muttered as they hurried through the barracks, back toward the palace. "We should never have gone out there. You aren't ready for it."

Trying to shake off the memory of Sanya's furious voice, Audric protested. "My sword work is rusty, I'll grant you that, but—"

"I'm not talking about your sword work," she snapped. "I'm talking about your ability to face what's to come and inspire the people whose help you'll need to survive it."

To Audric's left, Evyline grumbled a warning. Sloane sighed and stopped at a turn in the hallway, rubbing her face.

"Don't apologize," Audric said numbly. He couldn't look at Sloane. He wanted to return to his rooms; he wanted so badly to sleep. Maybe it would erase this day from his memory. "You're right, of course."

"Listen to me, love." Sloane gently touched Audric's cheek so he would face her. "I know you grieve. I know your mind has turned against you, and I understand why. But many of us are grieving, and there's more sorrow on the horizon, so I need you—*we* need you—to pick up the pieces of yourself and fight." She smiled sadly. "You are the Lightbringer, and our world is growing dark."

He stared at her through a bright film of tears. Though he towered over her, he felt diminished beside her. A boy being examined by a beloved aunt, only to be found lacking.

"When the moment comes, if it comes," he said thickly, "what if I cannot do what needs to be done?"

Sloane lowered her arm, her gaze solemn. "Then we will all die, Audric. All of us."

A royal page, pink-cheeked and tow-headed, breathing hard, appeared at the hallway's far end and hurried toward them.

"A message for you, Your Majesty," he said with a little bow, and left as quickly as he'd come.

Audric read the letter with dread rising fast in his heart. The message was curt, the letters hastily scrawled.

"The queens are requesting a meeting first thing in the morning," he announced, crumpling the paper in his fist. Tomorrow, the Mazabatian Senate would vote to approve or deny his request for military aid. "There is news from the north."

And whatever it was, he could not imagine it was good.

—◆—

The next morning at nine o'clock, the war council met in the queens' atrium, a circular room capped with a glass ceiling through which sunlight streamed, tinged green from the trees swaying overhead. The walls were a rich terra cotta, the floor tiled in pearl and cobalt.

A massive round table carved from rich red oak sat at the room's heart, around which the war council was seated—Audric, Queen Bazati and Queen Fozeyah, Princess Kamayin. General Rakallo, chief commander of the royal armies. The seven high magisters. Ludivine. Sloane. Evyline, who refused to leave Audric's side.

And this morning, an additional skinny, pale man Audric guessed to be ten years older than himself. He stared at the table, white-knuckled hands gripping its edge.

All Audric knew about him was that his name was Jazan, and that he was a spy. Months ago, rumors of missing children in Kirvaya had piqued Princess Kamayin's curiosity. When she had sent four of her personal spies to investigate, only one—Jazan—had returned.

The room hardly breathed as he spoke.

"He keeps them in little rooms," Jazan whispered, his voice shaking. "Rooms with low ceilings, too small to stand in. When he sends for them, they're taken down beneath the mountains. To his laboratories."

Jazan glanced up at Kamayin. "It's like a whole city, my lady. A city carved out of the ice and black mountains."

Queen Bazati sat rigid in her chair, her dark eyes blazing.

"What does he want with children?" asked Sloane, her face drawn tight with fear. "Why children?"

"*Elemental* children," Jazan corrected. "My lady. Pardon me. They're all elementals. Most of them haven't even come into their magic yet, and I think that's what he likes about them. The things he does to them— with the help of his healers and his soldiers—force the children's magic to awaken earlier than it would naturally, and when this happens, he can control it utterly. He can mold it. Mold *them*." Jazan's voice cracked. "I also think he takes them because it frightens people when children disappear."

Jazan dragged a shaking hand across his face. "Oh, God, he hates us. He'll kill us all. Every single one of us. He'll do it in the worst way possible. We'll die burning. We'll die screaming."

Audric leaned forward. "Jazan. What does he do with them? Experiments, you said?"

"There are monsters in the Deep," Jazan whispered through his fingers. "I heard his healers speak of them. But they're not healers like the ones we know. They're cutters. They're angels in human skins, though not all of them are strong enough to stay anchored to their bodies. Some are, and they stay in the same skins for weeks. There were a few I never saw change. But some of them go through bodies like a soldier goes through gloves."

"You said they spoke of monsters," Audric redirected him gently. "What kinds of monsters?"

"I don't know. They called them by a strange word: cruciata. As far as I can tell, they live in the Deep. And now he's trying to recreate them, or something like them. He and his healers, they make serums, these vile elixirs. They smell like poison, and all the tunnels and caves underneath the mountains reek of it. And then they..."

Jazan looked up at Audric, silently imploring. "There are dragons too. *Dragons*." He laughed a little. "I didn't believe my own eyes at first, but it's true: There are still dragons in the world. Ice dragons from Borsvall. Furred collars and everything, just like in all the paintings. And he's..." Jazan spread out his hands, palms facing up. He looked around the table helplessly, as if desperate for someone to tell him it was all a dream. "He's making *monsters* out of them. He cuts them open and stitches them back together. And there are other beasts, too, that his healers play with and sew together with the dragons, or…God help me, I don't know how they do it. But these beasts, they are abominations.

"And the children… He forces them to forge castings, and he controls their minds while they do it. It's perverse. It isn't right. And the castings the children make—some are for themselves, and some are designed to fit the beasts, like a set of armor shared between child and monster, and… Your Majesties, I think he means to make an army of them. Elemental children with their minds under his control, them and their beasts armored in bound castings. I don't understand how, but… These beasts, they can fling fire just as the children that ride them do. The children shake the earth and bend swords, and so do their beasts, same as any elemental. As if child and beast were one creature, split into two bodies."

"This is impossible," muttered the Grand Magister of the Baths, wringing her freckled hands. "You saw wrong."

"I don't see wrong." Jazan wiped his eyes with bandaged fingers. The wounds he had sustained were minimal.

And this disturbed Audric most of all.

"Why did he let you live?" Audric asked.

"He wasn't even there. Not really. Not in body." Jazan thumped his chest hard. "Not like this. He was off somewhere else in the world, and his generals were running things in his absence. But I heard him." Jazan nodded, laughing a little. His tears spilled over. "I heard him. I'm his messenger. He wants you to know what is coming for you."

"What did he say?" Audric leaned forward. "Do you know where he is?"

"He's in Patria," said Ludivine.

Everyone turned to face her. She sat pale and still, her hands clasped on the table. She met Audric's gaze and held it. "He brought Rielle to Patria. They're after the saints' castings. When they left Celdaria, they had three of them. Now, they have four."

Audric briefly closed his eyes. Of course Rielle would still be searching for the castings—now, perhaps, to open the Gate instead of repair it.

Several people around the table drew in sharp breaths.

"She has Saint Marzana's shield," Audric said quietly, remembering. "Saint Grimvald's hammer."

"Saint Tokazi's staff," Kamayin added. She did not speak of the Obex Rielle had slaughtered to obtain the staff, but Audric saw the memory on her grim face.

"And now, Saint Ghovan's arrow," Ludivine concluded, her expression grave.

"And once she has found all seven," he added, every word heavy on his tongue, "their power may be enough for her to do with the Gate as she pleases."

A hush fell over the room.

Queen Fozeyah glared at Ludivine. "How do you know they are in Patria?"

She hesitated. "I tried to speak to Rielle. I reached out to her. I...I saw her."

Shock jolted Audric. "Is she hurt? Is she well?"

"She's not hurt," Ludivine said slowly. "Not in the way you're thinking."

"Stop speaking in riddles and tell us the truth," he snapped.

Ludivine's calm was maddening. "Her connection to the empirium is much stronger now than it was weeks ago. I was stunned to sense the change in her. It was as though I'd been thrust into some raging golden fire."

Then, a pause. A tiny flinch that Audric was viciously glad to see. He hoped it meant she was hurting in some way that would never heal, just as he was.

"Her power is rising fast," Ludivine finished, "and I don't know how much longer she will be able to control it."

The silence was terrible. Audric leaned heavily against the table, ran his hands through his hair.

For the first time in weeks, he reached out to Ludivine's mind, clumsy and desperate. *Is she afraid?*

Yes. Ludivine's voice was a mere whisper of thought. *And she aches for home.*

Audric pushed back from the table and went to the nearest window. He shut his eyes against the cheerful morning, the lush palace grounds, and tried not to imagine Rielle alone in an unfamiliar country, Corien whispering promises in her ear and the empirium burning her alive from the inside out.

Unfortunately, his imagination had always been spectacular.

"Besides the dragons and the children and whatever unholy beasts they've made," said Sloane, her voice brimming with anger, "how many troops does he have at his disposal?"

"By my last count, five hundred angelic soldiers," Jazan replied, his voice hollow.

"More will come," said Ludivine quietly. "When Rielle opens the Gate, there will be millions."

"*If* she opens the Gate," the Grand Magister of the Pyre pointed out.

"But there are others," Jazan continued. He pulled restlessly at the hems of his sleeves. "Thousands of humans. The angels control them."

Audric turned back to the table, his heart sinking as he began to understand. "He did that to the Sauvillier soldiers the day of the fire trial. He controlled them, turned them against their own people."

"Their eyes were gray," Sloane breathed, her gaze distant. She was remembering, just as Audric was. "Gray and empty, like a fog had fallen inside them."

"The angels call them adatrox," Jazan said. "His generals travel the world collecting them. Thousands of them. They slip inside their minds and remake them as they see fit. They tell them what to do, and the adatrox must do it. I don't think they even know what they're doing. I hope they don't know." Jazan's face fell, lined with shadows. "The things the angels made them do to each other…the things the angels made them do to us…"

He collapsed into sobs, and after Kamayin called for her handmaidens to escort him to the palace's hospital wing, Queen Bazati turned to her and spoke for the first time since the meeting began.

"I have many questions for you, my daughter," she said, her voice low.

"Three years ago, I recruited two dozen spies," Kamayin said, facing her mothers with a defiant gleam in her eyes. "The Starlings. They're very good. Better than your spies, Mama. Don't worry. I fund them myself."

Queen Fozeyah's mouth twitched, but the smile did not meet her eyes. "How enterprising of you."

"Every princess deserves her own private order of spies," Kamayin said, bristling. "When I heard of the missing children in Kirvaya, I had to send out my birds. And it's a good thing I did. Now we know what we're facing."

General Rakallo, the decorated commander who had greeted Audric on the beach, scowled in her chair. "Yes, now we know, and now everything is changed."

"It changes nothing," said Sloane, a bite to her voice. "We suspected Corien would be amassing armies to rise up against us."

The Grand Magister of the Holdfast, his ruddy face pocked with scars, spoke in hushed tones. "But we did not know just how large his forces would be, and we knew nothing about these monsters he is creating."

"I don't even understand how such a thing is possible," Queen Bazati muttered, her hands in fists.

"The common angelic mind, Your Majesty, is extraordinary," said Ludivine. "Corien's mind is far from common. Before the Wars, he was strong. Now, after centuries spent in the Deep, planning his revenge, he is beyond any of us. Even me."

"Except for Rielle," Audric said at once, and as soon as the words left his lips, tears sprang to his eyes. It was the first time he'd said her name aloud in weeks, and the cherished word snatched away his breath.

General Rakallo sighed sharply. "Yes, the only being more powerful than the angel bent on destroying us is the woman who left her home and loved ones to join him. Forgive me, Your Majesty, if I do not find this particularly comforting."

Kamayin abruptly stood, hands flat on the table. "That kind of talk is neither necessary nor productive, General Rakallo."

The Grand Magister of the Holdfast shook his head. "I disagree, Your Highness. We cannot consider Rielle an ally or an asset. She is a weapon, and right now she is in Corien's arsenal."

Queen Fozeyah sat with her fingers steepled at her lips. "Can she be killed?"

Now Evyline was the one surging to her feet, her eyes bright with indignation.

Audric reached for her. "Evyline, please sit down."

Queen Fozeyah held up her hands, the shining dark coils of her hair falling back over her tawny brown shoulders, left bare by the wide neck of her gown. "Queen Rielle is loved by many in this room. But we must ask ourselves these questions and be prepared for any eventuality if we want to survive this."

"Anything can be killed," came Ludivine's haunted voice. "But could we get close enough to do it?" Her desolate gaze moved to Audric. "That I do not know."

"Killing her may not be necessary," Audric said quietly, and he hated how glad he was to see Ludivine's small, approving smile in response.

General Rakallo's mouth was thin with exasperation. "Your Majesties, can we truly trust this man to be part of our strategizing? He is blinded by love. He has been deceived by Queen Rielle before, and he can be deceived again."

"Yes, I love her," Audric said, and he had never meant the words so passionately. As if it were a crime to love her, this fearsome, inexplicable woman with her temper and her bravery and her surprising, glittering mind.

"And yes," he went on, "she deceived me, and when I discovered the depth of her lies, I let my anger and fear overcome me. I told her she was the thing she had feared becoming—a monster. I rejected her humanity; I dismissed everything that is good in her." His voice broke. "And there is so much good in her. Courage and resilience, and such a capacity for love that anyone lucky enough to earn her trust could live off the power of her adoration alone." He looked around at the gathered council, silently pleading with each of them to understand. "I pushed her away. And now she is with our greatest enemy. Were it not for my error in judgment, my weakness, she might still be with us."

He took a slow breath, fighting for calm. "She has been burdened from birth with a great and terrible power. For months she has been judged, tortured, worshipped, and reviled. And despite all of that, she stayed with us—until I made the mistake of condemning her. We cannot win her back without love. And without her, we cannot win."

The room was silent as the council members watched him with varying degrees of pity, embarrassment, sadness. Anger.

"Queen Bazati," he said, his voice steady but his stomach in knots, "Queen Fozeyah, you cannot allow this news from the north to affect today's vote. I beseech you, speak with the assembly before the vote is called. Let *me* speak to them. Celdaria will be the first front of this war— that I can promise you. Corien will want the poetry of beginning his conquest at the seat of my power, and with Merovec on the throne, the city will fall swiftly. He is utterly unprepared to face such an army. He is paranoid and fearful, as the letters from Red Crown attest. I've shown them to you. You've *read* them and have heard reports through your own underground. He does not understand angels. I do. He does not know Rielle." He smiled softly, his heart in tatters. "I do. And if we want her to come back to us, she must have a home to return to."

Then he looked around at all of them, willing them to understand. "To prepare for the true war ahead of us, we must amass as strong a force as possible in the place where Corien no doubt intends to strike first: Âme de la Terre. And before we can do that, I must reclaim my throne. I can do neither of these things without your army. Together, we can be our world's first line of defense against Corien when he comes. Unless you would prefer that he face whatever ragged army Merovec patches together."

Queen Bazati's expression was implacable. "I understand your argument, Audric. I supported your petition to the Senate, as did my wife."

She sighed, staring at the table, and then straightened to address the entire council. "But I cannot speak to the Senate before the vote. Because they have already voted."

Shock rippled through the room.

Kamayin gaped at her mothers, shaking her head slowly.

"What?" Audric whispered. He felt numb with horror. "When? And why?"

"Late last night, we spoke to Jazan with the speakers of all ten Senate chambers," explained Queen Fozeyah. "We wanted the chance to hear his report before you did and assess the situation privately."

"You made that man relive what happened to him twice in the span of twelve hours?" Audric said angrily. "I hadn't thought either of you that cruel."

"It isn't cruelty, Audric." Queen Bazati's gaze was full of pity. "It is survival."

Into the tense silence came a sharp rap at the door. Queen Fozeyah rose and opened it, admitting the high speaker of the Mazabatian Senate—a plump, stern-faced woman with rich brown skin and a cap of tight gray curls. She surveyed the room, her sharp gaze lingering on Audric.

"You have news for us," said Queen Bazati quietly.

The high speaker nodded, then opened a leather packet and began to read.

"On the matter of the petition of King Audric Courverie of the nation of Celdaria," said the high speaker, her voice sharp and clear, "who has requested military aid to invade that country's capital and oust the usurper, Merovec Sauvillier, with the far-reaching objective of establishing a base of defense against potential angelic invaders, the Senate has deliberated and voted. We have taken into consideration the counsel of our queens, the holy magisters, and the Mazabatian people, whose voices have bestowed upon us our power. Our nation has been battered by unprecedented disasters in recent months, and we simply do not have the resources or the bodies to send abroad while we are struggling to clear our beaches, rebuild our farmlands, and gather our dead."

The high speaker paused. "With a final count of one hundred and ninety-two to eight, we hereby move that the Celdarian petition be rejected and that the crown deny their request for military aid."

Audric sat heavily in his chair, watching numbly as the high speaker presented her packet to the queens.

"If you concur with this motion for denial, Your Majesties," the woman continued, "your signatures will confirm the vote. If not, you may appeal the vote in a special session."

Audric held his breath, not daring to speak, and then watched as if through the slow mire of a dream while the queens signed the document that doomed his country and would soon doom them all. He only vaguely noticed the others' reactions: Kamayin rushing at her mothers, passionately protesting; the Grand Magister of the Baths touching her throat in solemn prayer.

Queen Bazati was watching him, her expression compassionate but resolute. Queen Fozeyah led a shouting Kamayin into one of the private studies circling the room.

And the worst thing, the most horrible thing, was that Audric understood their decision.

Why *should* they trust him? Why *should* they send thousands of their troops to fight a futile war that had begun centuries before any of them were born?

If he was going to take back his country and rally the people of Avitas to fight for their Sun Queen and their future, he would have to do it alone.

⟶ 13 ⟵

RIELLE

"From our observations in the Deep, we have divided the cruciata into five distinct groupings based on their closest similarity to creatures known in Avitas: vipers (reptilian), raptors (avian), catamounts (feline), bulls (a strange combination of bovine and ursine characteristics), and nibblers (insectivorous and arachnid, though far larger than is typical in Avitas). Notably, while the nibblers are smaller than the others—and their grouping the least populous, perhaps indicating a lack of strength that makes it difficult for them to navigate the Deep—they are also by far the most ravenous."

—A report written by the angel Kasdeia, surgeon of the Northern Reach, dated August 17, Year 994 of the Second Age

For days, Rielle existed in a black-gold ocean. There, in the most exquisite and fathomless depths of her body, the empirium roared and roiled.

Fleeting moments of awareness illuminated the truth: They were traveling north. She and Corien. The girl, Obritsa; her guard, Artem. They were traveling quickly. Rings of light flashed open, then closed, a faint scent of smoke with each illumination.

The castings Artem carried, now four in number, emitted a new, stronger power that hummed against Rielle's skin like the air before a storm, ready to snap open.

And Corien was close. Rielle felt his mouth against her cheek, the nest of his arms around her. Sometimes she recognized his nearness and met his lips with her own. Sometimes she was lost at sea and cried out for him, but even he could not find her there in the dark shimmering depths.

There, she was utterly alone with the empirium. Its tireless voice was an unending chorus of words too strange and terrible for her to decipher, and she could not plug her ears, nor did she want to. Wrapped up in its waves, she floated and dove and sank and drowned, and she welcomed each lung-crushing moment of pain. She opened her mouth and swallowed black water. She opened her eyes and saw skies scattered with gold stars. She reached out, fingers grasping, and was pulled down into darkness, and she welcomed the fall, because somewhere in the darkness was the answer.

Somewhere in this endless world of the empirium was *more*—more power, more understanding.

Why have you chosen me? She asked this many times. *What do you want with me?*

The empirium answered in incomprehensible words that rattled her bones and cracked her spine, but where she should have felt pain, she felt only warm waves of pleasure. She turned into the tide, let it sweep her down through ecstatic black water. It broke around her, a cold curtain of needles.

you are, rumbled a voice that was not singular but rather all voices, an eternal chorus.

Yes? She held her breath, listening.

Nothing answered her but the constant beat of her heart, the churning pulse of black waves.

Then the empirium spoke again—a boom of noiseless noise that exploded between Rielle's ears:

I will wake

Her eyes snapped open.

She was surrounded by white, and she was in Corien's arms. He held her against his chest, his black hair peppered with snow.

"There you are," he whispered, relief plain on his face. "You've come back to me."

Air burst into her lungs. She coughed, expelling water that wasn't there, and pushed against Corien's chest. "Put me down!"

He obeyed, looking flummoxed, and then Rielle was on the ground near a sweeping flight of black steps. The air repulsed her, as did the rock stretching for miles beneath her and the countless infinitesimal grains of moisture she could sense floating around her. She turned inward, away from the elements that called to her, away from the empirium that lived inside them all. In her head, she heard the crash of black waves, and when she fought them, they thundered ever louder.

"I am just a girl," she whispered, praying it. A lie, and yet it comforted her.

Once she had remembered how to breathe, she looked around and saw that she huddled between two massive doors, each flung open wide. To her left, a sprawling landscape of mountains and ice. To her right, a dark entrance hall lit by torches in iron brackets.

She pressed her forehead to the cool floor—polished tiles of black marble veined with white. She pounded her fists against it once.

Corien knelt silently beside her. "What is it? What happened?"

"I was almost there," she said, hardly able to speak. "I almost understood. I could see it. I could *feel* it. I was swimming toward it, and then suddenly I was here, with you." She glared at him through her tears. "Did you wake me?"

"No," Corien said calmly. "You woke on your own. I was worried..." He hesitated, his jaw working. "I was worried you might never wake again."

Rielle closed her eyes, pressed her brow hard against the tile. It was cold as ice and settled her frenzied mind. "There was an ocean. A great black ocean lit up with gold. I was inside it. It was taking me..."

"Where was it taking you?"

"No, you don't understand. It was *taking* me. It wanted to breathe. It wanted to walk, to see through my eyes." She struggled to sit up, glad he did not try to help. She felt clumsy after days of inactivity, her body strange and heavy. Distracted, she placed a hand on her stomach. The girl on the mountain flitted through her mind, a memory she refused to follow.

"The empirium was claiming me for its own," Rielle murmured, "and I wanted it to have me."

Corien watched her curiously. "If the empirium had taken you, what would have become of you?"

"I don't know. It would have killed me. It would have made me better, or stronger. Or maybe it would have not liked my taste and spat me out. But I would have known, at least, even if it had killed me. I would have understood."

"Understood what?"

Impatience lashed through her. "*This.* All of this." She gestured at herself. "Why I'm like this. Why I *am*. Can't you sense what I mean?"

But when she reached for Corien's thoughts, she felt the startling truth: Only the barest hint of him remained inside her. The rest of his presence was gone, some distance away in the landscape of her mind. Genteel, it seemed, even chaste. Careful. Discreet.

She stared at him, caught between gratitude and offense. "Were you afraid? Is that why you've stayed out of my thoughts?" She lifted her chin. "You thought the empirium might work through me to hurt you. You were disgusted by me."

"Never. I thought…" He paused, at a rare loss for words. "I thought you might want privacy. You were so hot in my arms that it frightened me. I thought me being there, wherever you had gone, would only interfere with whatever was happening. I wanted…" He spread his hands, laughing a little. "Rielle, you are beyond me. I hope someday you can take me with you to that place, and we can learn all the answers we seek together."

He looked at the floor, his brow furrowed. His lashes were thick and dark; Rielle felt a sudden craving to kiss them. She sent him the thought, and his heated gaze snapped up to meet hers.

"I won't pretend to understand all that's happening to you," he whispered. "But I will do everything I can to make myself worthy of you."

For a long time, Rielle could not speak. Instead, she rose unsteadily to her feet and turned away from him, looking out over the world.

She stood at the top of a huge flight of stone stairs, past which sprawled a vast network of ice, rock, fire, and equipment. Soldiers ran drills. Other workers hauled crates and turned the spokes of gigantic metal wheels to open great doors set in the earth. They wore nondescript clothing and obeyed soldiers barking orders in what Rielle thought must be an angelic language. Behind her was a massive fortress of black stone. Inside its entrance hall, silent, masked guards stood at winding staircases.

"The Northern Reach," Rielle whispered. Her breath became clouds.

Corien came to stand beside her. "Home."

She looked up at him—his travel-worn collar, his stiff jaw, the proud gleam in his pale eyes as he surveyed this kingdom of ice he had built out of nothing.

A tenderness overcame her. She turned his chin, brought his lips down to hers. Unbidden, a memory of Audric flashed across her vision; she felt Corien flinch but did not apologize.

"I still love him," she reminded him, thinking of her lingering grief so Corien would easily see it in her mind. "But I'm here with you. He's afraid of me. You aren't. He turned me away. You didn't. That will have to be enough for now."

Corien's expression hardened. "You are a creature of maddening contradictions," he muttered, raking a hand through his hair.

"And you love me for it," she replied. A distant crash of dark waves echoed through her skull. She felt the cold lap of infinite gold against her toes. She touched her head, searching for cracks.

"I've had a suite of rooms made up for you," he said tightly, stepping away from her. "I imagine you'll want to rest."

"No." Audric remained in her mind, his memory warm and steady, even as the rest of her teemed. If she looked at it too closely, pain pricked her chest and eyes like thorns.

But Audric was far away; Audric thought her a monster.

Her mind shivered, exhausted by its own hesitations. She longed desperately for oblivion. She caught Corien's hand, sending him a thought clear and hard as a diamond: *Rest is not what I want.*

The force of her suggestion surprised him; she felt his delight unfurl, softening all his frustrations.

Then Corien pressed his fingers into her palm, called for guards to shut the doors against the cold, and guided her upstairs.

—◆—

Corien was making monsters.

One hung from the ceiling—though this was not one he had made. Rather, it was his model. His inspiration.

"We named them the cruciata," he explained, guiding Rielle through a large room he had called a laboratory. Suspended from the stone ceiling by a series of fine copper wires and steel plates hung a preserved bestial corpse. The beast had six splayed legs, a hide of crimson scales, a long, reptilian snout. Empty eye sockets, long hooked tail, a spine ridged with tiny serrated spikes. Its jaws had been pried open, revealing several rows of teeth.

Corien pointed at the frozen slender legs. "Some can fly. Others lumber. This one is a viper. Its greatest weapon is speed. They propel themselves rapidly across the ground, as lizards do, and can move in near silence."

As he spoke, Corien walked slowly through the room, long black coat trailing after him. He had bathed after their night together, and the dark waves of his hair gleamed in the laboratory's torchlight.

And Rielle listened as he spoke. She really, truly did.

But she also found those ebony locks of his difficult to look away from—mostly because she remembered how silken they had felt against her thighs the night before.

"When your saints created the Gate," Corien was saying, "the act of tearing open the fabric of the Deep sent ripples of chaos through the entire realm. An immeasurable vastness forever altered by the crime of our imprisonment." His voice darkened. "The making of the Gate rent apart countless seams, most too insignificant to consider. One of them, however, opened into the world from which these creatures originate. The crack is small, but it exists, and it is ever-widening. The cruciata are cunning, and the strongest of them, the luckiest, are finding ways to escape their own world and enter the Deep. It has taken them centuries. Even fewer of them have managed to pass through the Deep, ram their way through the Gate, and come here. But more will come. It is only a matter of time."

Rielle's mind struggled to accept the idea that there were other worlds beyond their own, beyond even the Deep. Countless others, Corien surmised, all connected by the immensity of the empirium.

Other worlds. Yet another piece of information Ludivine had neglected to share with her.

Ludivine. *Ludivine.* The more often she said the name to herself, the less it hurt to remember it. Someday, she would imagine Ludivine's face and feel nothing at all.

Someday. But not yet.

"But the Deep stripped your bodies from you," Rielle pointed out, trying to focus. "When the cruciata enter the Deep, does the same not happen to them?"

Corien's expression was grim. "No. They seem to be immune to such indignities."

"Perhaps the empirium saw fit to punish the angels for beginning the war against humans," Rielle offered blithely. Antagonizing him cleared her mind. She could not resist it. "Perhaps the cruciata have committed no such offense."

Corien shot her a dangerous look. "Perhaps."

"I was told about these cruciata before," she said, moving past him. "I heard they originated from the Deep itself."

"Who told you this?"

"Jodoc Indarien. Speaker of the Obex in the Sunderlands. He shot Ludivine with an arrow constructed of a strange metal. He called it a *blightblade*."

Corien stiffened, reading her memory. "He told you only what he knew, which was incomplete."

"Jodoc also said that a cruciata's blood is deadly to angels. Is this accurate?"

"Frustratingly, yes." Corien glanced up at the suspended beast. A line of neat black stitches bisected its belly. "This viper crawled through the Gate some years ago and—clever thing—snuck aboard a trade vessel that had come to the Sunderlands with supplies for the Obex. I don't think the Obex even knew it had broken through. Many angels died during its capture and during the journey here. It's something about the blood. We had to bleed it dry before it was safe to dissect. Even the fumes can be toxic."

"To you," said Rielle. "Not to humans." She blinked guilelessly at him. "So Jodoc said."

Corien's mouth thinned. "On that point, he was correct. My hunters, once exposed to the beast's blood, were pushed from the human bodies they inhabited and completely lost cohesion. Thankfully, others took their places, and I'm confident we'll eventually engineer ways to protect ourselves from their toxins, should we encounter more cruciata in the future."

The suggestion in his voice killed her amusement. She looked straight at him. "You mean if I open the Gate."

He gave her a tight smile. Her use of the word *if* had not escaped him. "I do."

She shivered at the thought. The empirium rippled through her, a dark tremor. Was it afraid or eager? She searched her own heart for the answer but found none.

"I have many loyal to me in the Deep," Corien went on. "Thanks to you, my dear, and your failed efforts to repair the Gate, I can now communicate with them. They tell me the vast majority of cruciata remain in their own world, which we have named Hosterah. If you open the Gate, the risk of a cruciata invasion is slim. If you'd like, you can reseal the damn thing once my people are free. And if any cruciata do come for us before you manage that, you will destroy them."

Rielle sensed a memory. It floated to the surface of his mind and drifted toward hers. It was herself, months ago in the Sunderlands, attempting to repair the Gate and instead cracking it further.

"Is that why you urged me toward it?" She watched Corien closely. "You wanted me to touch it. You wanted to see if I was powerful enough yet to open it."

"In part," he admitted smoothly.

"But you suspected I wasn't ready and that it would hurt me."

"I *guessed* it would hurt you and knew that your failure would help me—and thereby help *you*."

She stepped back from him, reaching for his mind and finding, to her horror, that he spoke the truth. "You astonish me."

"And you yourself wanted to attempt a repair." Corien approached her slowly. "Even if I hadn't encouraged it, you would have done exactly the same. Why shouldn't I have taken advantage of a situation that was already in motion?" He was near her now, his eyes alight with passion. "I have my people to think about, Rielle. Millions of angels, imprisoned and waiting for me to free them. Remember that."

At his words, a bitter thought occurred to Rielle—that Audric, even to help his people, even if everyone expected it of him, would never urge her toward a thing he knew would hurt her.

She shoved the thought at Corien and watched the anger settle over him like a net of flitting shadows.

Satisfied, she lifted her chin and stared him down. "Can you control the cruciata as you can control humans?"

His furious gaze moved across her face, as if searching for a chink in her armor. "No. Their minds are too alien."

"So you are creating your own." Rielle stretched onto her toes to touch the cruciata's stiff tail. "Beasts with blood that won't harm you. Beasts with minds you can influence."

Corien's eyes followed her every movement. "Precisely. Though complete control of their minds remains elusive, we have devised...other methods to manipulate them."

For a moment, Rielle gazed up at the viper, imagining it alive and vicious—twenty feet of muscle and scaly hide, racing across the ground with claws as long as her forearm.

"If I open the Gate," she said slowly, "I could exacerbate the damage done by the saints."

"Yes," Corien agreed.

"Without meaning to, I could widen those cracks in the Deep and bring the cruciata *here*."

"And then you will destroy them, as I've said. You'll blink them to ashes." Irritation colored his voice. "You worry for the people of this world. You worry for those who would not worry for you. Why?"

Because life is precious.

Because it's the right thing to do.

Because I am the Sun Queen. I protect, and I defend.

None of the answers she mulled over rang true. Early in the trials, she had believed such things, had even proclaimed them for all to hear. But maybe she had been lying to herself even then.

Corien was watching her intently. "They don't deserve your pity or your protection. You're more like us then you are like them. You belong with us." A pause. "You belong with me, not with him."

Rielle tried to hold this declaration in her mind but could not find a steady grip on it.

She turned away from Corien to stare at the beast, with which she felt a sudden sick kinship. "I belong nowhere," she whispered.

It was the truest thing she had said in some time.

Corien's fingers brushed the small of her back. "I know you must come to this truth on your own, and I will wait for you to find it, but I urge you to see it *now*: where you belong is at my side."

When she did not reply, he found her hand, pressed his thumb into her palm. "I have been engineering this war for centuries. And at the end of it, you and I will reign over a glorious new world in which the only beasts are our own and will obey our every command."

She drew in a breath and turned to face him. "Show me."

—◆—

He had carved out an entire city beneath the mountains. More immaculate laboratories, staffed by white-robed angelic scholars and lined with metal tables, racks of wicked-looking tools, rows of stoppered vials. Mines and forges that burned day and night. Barracks for legions of mute, gray-eyed soldiers that Corien called adatrox.

"They're human," Rielle said quietly as Corien escorted her through a massive stone hall. On either side, lines of adatrox ran the room's length. They were dark and pale, fat and thin. Borsvallic men, Kirvayan women. Mazabatians. Celdarians. They stood like dolls arranged by a child—rigid, slightly awkward, slightly askew.

As Rielle passed, their clouded eyes did not follow her.

"They will be our first wave of terror," Corien said. "Stupid brutes. Not very creative, but certainly effective."

"How many are there?"

"Seven thousand. In two months' time, I will have ten."

A shiver of fear ran through Rielle as she began to comprehend the scope of his work. She remembered the Sauvillier soldiers at the fire trial—their gray eyes, their muteness, how they had turned on their own neighbors without warning.

Then, there had been dozens of soldiers. Here, there were thousands. Thousands of people ripped from their homes, possessed by angels.

"And you inhabit all of their minds?" Rielle whispered.

"Most. Each of my commanders controls a few squadrons." He glanced her way. Amusement lit up his thoughts. "This frightens you."

"It impresses me. And yes, it frightens me."

He lifted her hand to his lips. "I like impressing you. And I confess, I also like frightening you. It pleases me to imagine you shaking in awe of me, as I have so often done in awe of you. Ah. Here."

He did not give her a chance to respond. She sensed him registering her discomfort, how utterly he had unnerved her, and yet he pushed on gleefully. It was a game between them, a push and tug. She had bested him in the laboratory, and now he was gaining ground.

A game in which the objective is not to win, he thought to her, *but to emerge as equal victors.*

Rielle kept her gaze trained on the path before them. *And if I decide I no longer wish to play?*

Corien did not answer, instead leading her down a series of dimly lit corridors. The air grew hotter and fouler as they walked, and when they emerged into a cavernous room lit from above by an iron gridwork of torches, the stench nearly knocked Rielle off her feet—but she was glad for it. The distraction was welcome, evaporating the tension between them.

"Look," Corien whispered, gesturing grandly. "Little works of art, are they not? The dragons have been particularly helpful to us. Their genetics are robust and versatile."

Rielle didn't know what he meant by that, but she nevertheless approached the edge of a pit carved out of the ground, hot ropes of fear tightening her throat. The pit itself was massive, perhaps three hundred yards square, with a thick iron grating bolted across the top. Around the edge were children, and none of them could have been older than ten. They too had veiled gray eyes, but there was a power to them, as there had not been with the adatrox. Some stood, some crouched. All of them stared down into the pit.

And all of them wore castings.

They were all identical—twin gold bands around the wrists and a gold collar about the neck. Floating through the air, piercing the stink, were familiar scents. Damp earth. Sun-baked stone. Rainwater, smoke, alpine wind. The acrid bite of shadows and the bitter tang of metal.

Rielle stared, her revulsion a swift cascade.

These children were elementals, far too young to be using castings. Her own experience with magic, and Audric's too, had been exceptional; ordinarily, a child might start studying elemental power when they were quite young, but would not forge their casting until at least early adolescence.

"Did they forge their castings here?" Rielle asked faintly.

"They did." Corien's quiet delight kissed her thoughts. "Some took to it better than others."

"And if they refused?"

"I convinced them."

Robbed of speech, Rielle chose to approach the pit and knelt to peer inside.

Beneath the grating, snapping and pawing at one another, were creatures—reminiscent of the cruciata corpse, but ghastlier. Rielle gazed breathlessly upon their beastliness: hulking shoulders, ropy with muscle; stubby wings of flesh and feathers; shaggy dark pelts and scaled hides; beaks and claws. Heads as blunt and huge as anvils. Horns that clacked against the grating and sparked like flint. They gnashed their teeth and swung their heads, moaning as if in furious agony.

And though they were malformed and distorted, each a patchwork of horrors, they all shared certain distinctive features. The tails, for one, and the wings, and the rough, furred hides.

"They're dragons," she whispered. "You've changed them."

"Improvement by way of the grotesque." Kneeling beside her, Corien looked thoughtfully at his creations. "One of my generals started calling them crawlers, as you can't really say that they're dragons anymore, can you? The name has rather caught on. Though so far I've found it impossible to completely control the mind of a godsbeast, our treatments keep them docile, and beyond that, the children's castings bind them like a harness does a horse. And of course, I control the children. Watch this."

He snapped his fingers—for the show of it, Rielle knew. His abilities needed no outward trigger.

Surrounding the pit, the elemental children snapped to attention. Echoes of their hoarse cries rang in the silence. Corien reached for a mechanism attached to the grating, pressed a catch. A door in the grating flew open.

"Show her," Corien commanded, his voice brimming with excitement. As soon as the word left his mouth, one of the children—a young boy, fair of skin and hair, gray-eyed and round-cheeked—raised his banded wrists.

A crawler leapt up from the pit to latch on with cracked claws. Hanging there, it opened its wide mouth and howled.

Every torch suspended from the grid overhead exploded to life. Roaring pendants of flame spewed from their brackets, filling the cavern with blazing light and heat. Metal plates molded around the beast's chest, belly, and shoulders shone liquid with fire, matching the brilliance of the boy's castings.

Rielle stepped back from the inferno, her heart pounding as the truth became clear to her.

The crawler's armor was part of the child's casting, binding them together. A pair of killers, pliable and pitiless. And whatever power lived in a godsbeast was no doubt enhancing the elemental magic the child already possessed.

And Corien...

Corien could control them—the children, and their beasts.

He could control all of them.

✦ 14 ✦

JESSAMYN

"Translated from the formal Qaharis, 'Vaera Bashta' means 'den of sorrows.' This massive, cavernous facility, spanning two square miles beneath the city of Elysium, houses prisoners from every country in Avitas, and was designed by the Emperor, in His infinite wisdom, to torment its human inhabitants beyond repair."

—The Glory of Elysium: An Introduction to the Emperor's City, compiled by the Invictus Council of Five for students of the Lyceum

It happened twice a month, announced by five sharp blasts of the huge brass prison horns—some kept underground, others bolted to nearby rooftops in the city above.

Jessamyn crouched on her perch in the prison of Vaera Bashta and watched the chaos unfold. In the common tongue, it was called the culling. In Lissar, it was *cinvayat*, and in Qaharis, it was *praeori kyta*. A time when all the locks in the prison's fifteen wards were undone, all the doors thrown open.

For three hours, thousands of prisoners were free to do as they pleased, to kill who they wished, to cower in the shadows and hope no one found them—until the angelic wardens forced them back into their cells.

Jessamyn waited until the horn blasts had faded, then jumped silently down from the stone ledge overlooking section E3. The grated walkway below was empty, untouched by the chaos of the culling. It led to the solitaries, and the prisoners kept there were not allowed the same fun as the others. The solitaries were special. Many had personally affronted the Emperor. Conspirators. Dissidents.

Brothers of stubborn princesses who refused to use their power as they ought to.

The wardens had retreated to their offices, food and drink in hand— none of which would quench their thirst or satisfy their hunger, but the act of consuming it, Varos had long ago explained to Jessamyn, was satisfaction enough. At least for a time. At least until it wasn't.

As Jessamyn stalked down the empty walkway, the sounds of violence rang in her ears. Savage shouts as hunters pounced on their prey. Choked, wet cries as death claimed the weak. She caught only glimpses of the prisoners swarming through the dimly lit caverns below. A skinny boy, his shoulder blades protruding from his bare back like a pair of submerged knives, crawled through the shadows and whispered frantic prayers that no one would find him. Someone did; Jessamyn heard his stifled cry, the sound of bone smacking stone. To her right, marching toward the lower wards, a gang of men chanted in Borsvallic, brandishing torches they'd wrenched from the walls. To her left, a gang of half-naked children in filthy rags pounced upon an old man and dragged him to the ground.

They were hungry. For some, this was a time to kill not for pleasure, but simply for a full belly.

When Jessamyn at last reached the solitaries, the culling had faded to an echo. The corridor was carved from black stone, immaculate and silent. Two adatrox guards flanked door 14. Jessamyn prepared to order them aside, but they opened the door and stepped away before she could.

She set her jaw as she breezed past them. She hoped that when the Empire had been elevated to its proper former glory, the use of adatrox soldiers would no longer be necessary. They could be useful tools, she supposed, but she hated their sightless gray eyes, the stupid, jerking way they moved. Controlled by angels, their own human minds flattened and ravaged—the adatrox reminded her of her own humanity, and how weak it was. How easily she could be invaded and manipulated, reduced to some puppet creature, if she failed to prove her worth to the Emperor.

Someday, when she had earned her angelic name, and with it a place as an adviser to the Emperor, she would tell him this. And he would listen.

A tiny chill of pleasure skipped down her arms as she imagined it. Since her appointment with the Emperor the day before, she had not been able to stop thinking of him. Blood-splattered, wild-eyed, and beautiful, whispering to her of the plan they would carry out *together*. Turn the boy Remy into a weapon. Use him to wear down the last of Eliana's will.

Show the little shit of a princess that the one person left to her in the world had become an eager pet of the enemy—all thanks to Jessamyn.

Pride warmed her chest. If only Varos could have seen this day. He would never have doubted her again.

Jessamyn stood tall in the door of Remy's cell. He huddled in the corner. The air was foul and cold.

"Wake up," she commanded.

A moment passed. Remy did not move.

She stormed toward him, grabbed the collar of his prison tunic, and wrenched him to his feet.

"Wake up," she repeated, shoving him away with a snarl.

He stumbled, wide-eyed, and managed to right himself. His bare feet slapped into a shallow dark puddle near the drain in the center of the floor.

In silence, Jessamyn assessed him. He was a skinny bird of a boy. His head barely reached her shoulder. His matted hair had grown wild; his bottom lip was swollen and bloodied. Scratches marred his arms and feet. He stood with his shoulders hunched, his body curled forward as if to protect his middle.

Jessamyn suppressed a swell of irritation. Presenting a mangy, half-dead child to the Council of Five as her new student would make her a laughingstock, no matter the Emperor's orders.

She would need time alone with Remy before anyone at the Lyceum got a good look at him. It was not only her reputation at stake but Varos's as well.

"My name is Jessamyn," she told him. "You will come with me."

She turned and made for the door, but he did not follow. At the threshold, she glared over her shoulder.

"Or would you prefer to stay here?" she asked calmly. "Alone and festering in the dark? Rotten scraps to eat and guards coming every morning to beat you?"

At last, he spoke. "Is where you're taking me worse?"

That surprised her. Such a miserable-looking creature; he didn't look as though he had any wits left about him.

"Better in some ways, worse in others," she answered, for there was no point in lying. She forced herself to gentle her voice. Let him think she could be a friend. "But you will see your sister. In fact, if you do as I tell you, there will soon come a time when you'll be able to see her every day."

His face brightened. In his eyes shone a small light of hope.

Jessamyn frowned as he limped to follow her. So there was softness in him yet.

There would not be for long.

——◇——

That night, Remy sat on a stool in Jessamyn's room at the Lyceum, watching her closely in the mirror.

"Your face is your biggest failing," Jessamyn told him. A silver snip of her scissors. He had bathed, and now she was trimming his hair to a respectable length. "I can see every question you wish to ask, every emotion you feel."

She watched him attempt to school his features into a cold mask. It might have been humorous, had the Emperor's words not still been whispering in her thoughts.

Maybe he was watching them even now.

Jessamyn glared at her muddled reflection in the scissors' blades.

"I understand," Remy told her, his voice carefully even.

"You understand nothing." Jessamyn stepped back to check her work. "And if you want to survive, you will do everything I tell you. You will study, you will practice, you will train. You will eat what I eat. You will sleep when I sleep."

Remy fell silent, watching her as she tidied the room and swept the hair from the floor.

"Why are you doing this?" he asked quietly.

Jessamyn did not look at him. When she had first been assigned to Varos, she had been a mere child. She had slept on a hard pallet on the floor of his bedroom. Many a night, she had lain awake, listening to him breathe and fighting sleep, for she knew she would wake with Varos's hands around her throat and would have to fight him or fail yet another lesson. At first, she had been afraid of such tests.

Later, she had come to crave them.

Remy would be the same. And someday, Eliana Ferracora would see that light in his eyes and know all was lost. There was no reason to fight. There was only the Empire, and the glorious purpose of serving His Majesty the Emperor of the Undying.

Jessamyn found her old pallet under the bed and threw it to the floor. It was brown with dust; the edges were frayed and patched.

Then she turned and found Remy standing very near her, a placid expression on his face.

One glance at the mirror showed her the scissors clutched behind his back. Fool boy.

And she was even more the fool for letting memories distract her.

With a snarl, Jessamyn snapped her hand to Remy's throat, jabbing him in his windpipe. He dropped the scissors and staggered back, gasping for air.

She followed him, smacked her palm hard against his ear, punched him just below his chest. He cried out with pain, fell to his knees. She had seen him favor his left side; he had a bruised rib, she suspected.

In an instant, she had wrenched back his head, one hand in his hair. The other held one of the knives from her belt. She pressed the blade to his throat and leaned so close that her lips brushed his cheek.

"Why am I doing this?" she asked, repeating his question. "Because He has chosen me to guard His works."

She yanked him to his feet, kicked his thigh. He fell once more, onto the pallet she had laid out for him.

Jessamyn followed him. "He has chosen me to receive His glory," she continued. It was the induction oath of Invictus, one she should have uttered before the Five with Varos standing proudly behind her.

Remy scrambled up at her approach, tried to run. She grabbed the stool and threw it past him at the door. It smashed against the wall and splintered; Remy ducked to avoid the flying wood.

"I am the blade that cuts at night," Jessamyn said, following him. "I am the guardian of His story."

She grabbed Remy by his shoulders, forced him back toward the mirror. Standing behind him, her hands hard on his arms, she made him stare at his wide-eyed, tear-streaked reflection. Across his throat, a thin line of blood.

"Someday, you will be too," she said to him. "So the Emperor commands. It's been done, Remy. The order has been given."

Then Jessamyn turned him around, caught him by his chin so their gazes locked. His mouth trembled; his eyes glistened with tears.

"I will help you survive it," she told him, and at least this much was true. "But try to hurt me again, and I'll make you wish you were back in that cell, rotting away in the dark. Do you understand?"

After a moment, Remy nodded. Tears spilled down his cheeks, and Jessamyn fought the urge to scold him for it. This was no ordinary student. She would have to tread carefully.

"Good," she said instead, and nodded toward the washbasin. "That was our first lesson. Now clean yourself up."

⟶ 15 ⟵

ELIANA

"Bring me two hundred musicians. The ones we just disposed of were entirely inadequate, and you knew that when you presented them to me. Bring me composers who write their helpless mortality into every melody, singers with storms of grief in their lungs. Bring me people who wish they could stop listening to the music boiling in their blood but cannot, so they tear it from their bodies the only way they know how—through air and strings and drums and pen."

—Letter from His Holy Majesty, the Emperor
of the Undying, to Admiral Ravikant,
dated May 11, Year 1018 of the Third Age

The words drifted through Eliana's mind on a faint breeze: *Will you hurt me to get her back?*

She stirred from a deep sleep and opened her eyes to a thick white fog. Her tongue was dry and fat, her limbs heavy. She wanted to walk, but she could not stand.

So she crawled.

⟶◇⟵

She reached a courtyard, then a clean hallway padded with a thick blue carpet. Sunlight streamed through arched windows bordered with colored glass, and Eliana found the strength to rise. At the end of the hallway stood a door, and through it, Simon's office.

Her palms tingled at the sight of it.

Inside, she found him beside the open windows, dozing on a chaise with an open book on his chest. A breeze ruffled the pages.

Eliana moved the book aside with a grin, climbed atop him, reached for his face—and then went very still, her hands hovering over his skin.

He had opened his eyes and now gazed up at her with a sleepy smile. "What a sight to awaken to," he said softly.

She scrambled away and fled the room, her heart pounding. She clenched her hands into fists, ordered her buzzing palms to quiet. Around her hands, the chains of her castings shivered and sparked.

Not here. She formed the thought and pushed it down her arms. *Not ever again.*

—◆—

Eliana opened her eyes.

Will you hurt me to get her back?

"I don't know who you are!" she cried. "Who are you?"

No one answered.

She stood at the edge of a strange leafless forest. She did not like the look of it, but there was no choice but to enter.

Moving through the trees, she realized too late that they weren't trees at all. They were bodies in all colors and sizes, naked and staring. Their eyes were black and lidless.

Angels, waiting for her to save them.

The empirium had punished them, had stripped magic from the world.

"Only you can bring it back," one of the bodies whispered, and though it did not move, Eliana felt its fingers clutch at her skirts. "Only you can bring her back."

"Save us," another wailed. "Help us see."

"We are ravenous."

"We are thirsty."

One shivered as she passed. "Touch me. Make me feel again."

"*Find her.*"

Eliana clapped her hands over her ears and ran, the angels' cries chasing after her. Heat from her palms scorched her skin, and her lips were wet with blood, but she kept her hands pressed tight against her skull.

If she was going to burn, she would do it alone.

—◆—

Eliana opened her eyes.

Will you hurt me to get her back?

She stared in horror at the man huddled on the ground at her feet. He had been pummeled; black bruises drew continents across his sallow skin. He clutched his stomach with one hand and reached for Eliana with the other. Between the fingers pressed to his abdomen, the end of his life bubbled crimson.

"It was a ruse, Eliana," Simon said, his voice ragged. "Please, help me. I did it all for you."

Eliana stepped back from him, her eyes burning as hot as her hands. "I can't. I won't." She glanced at the sky. They were on a cliff, overlooking a range of bald mountains. The sky was red with sunset. Rings of blood marked her palms, rimming her castings. They were hot; they were ready.

She denied them. *Not here.* She imagined plunging her hands into an icy pool, how her castings would steam and shrivel.

"Do you hear me?" She raised her voice. The air was strange, thick and close, and it swallowed her words as soon as she shouted them. "I won't help you. I'll die before I help you. I can do this forever."

Simon crawled toward her. "Will you help me? Like you did for Remy. Remember?" And then Simon let out a sharp groan of pain, a tight sob. He blinked hard, shook his head. "Hurry, Eliana. I want to explain. I want to tell you everything. Please, help me."

Eliana turned her back on him and walked away. She heard him cry out, begging for her to come back. Something was attacking him; she heard a chittering sound, like a swarm of bugs, and then the pounding of feet and fists against flesh. A bone snapped, and Simon's scream was hoarse with pain.

"Eliana, *please!*"

She closed her eyes and walked until she had worn holes in her boots and the soles of her feet trailed red prints. It wasn't real. She knew that. None of this was real.

And yet Simon's cry of anguish followed her to the edge of the world.

—◆—

Will you hurt me to get her back?

Eliana opened her eyes to see a young woman glaring down at her.

Clad in the square-shouldered black uniform worn by palace guards, the woman's skin was a honeyed brown, her cheeks sprayed with freckles. Her long braid was a rich, bright scarlet.

Jessamyn.

The memory came quickly: the smooth warmth of Jessamyn's skin as they kissed in that shed outside the city of Karlaine. The relief of her touch, and the peace that came after—until the attack, not an hour later, that had nearly claimed Remy's life.

Eliana recovered quickly. "The last time I saw you," she said, sitting up, "you were punching me. We were on the pier in Festival."

"I remember," said Jessamyn, every word clipped. "Get up."

"Why are you here?"

"The Emperor has assigned me to your escort," came the flat reply. Jessamyn gripped Eliana's wrist, yanked her hard toward the edge of the bed. "He has commanded your attendance at tonight's concert."

So, this Jessamyn was just as relentless as the one Eliana had known.

Two of her adatrox attendants led her into the bathing room. They were exquisitely lovely women, both of them gray-eyed and mute, one with smooth brown skin, the other eerily pale. Their white robes fluttered at their ankles, and around their necks gleamed gilded collars.

As they combed and styled the loose curls that now fell to her shoulders, Eliana watched Jessamyn closely. Though she stood at the door to the bathing room, stationed as any guard would be, Jessamyn seemed restless, unsettled. One finger tapped against her thigh. She held her jaw tightly.

A thought came to Eliana's tired mind. She knew little of the mechanics of time, but still she wondered: Was it possible for anything of her Jessamyn to exist inside this one? Some commonality she could find and use, if she only knew where to look?

Eliana needed to keep her talking. She glanced at the gown waiting on its hook. "So, another concert tonight, then. Orchestra? Choir? A soloist, perhaps?"

"I am not privy to the Emperor's plans," said Jessamyn, "and if I were, I would not share them with you."

"Why did he assign you to my guard?"

"I do not ask the Emperor to explain his orders. I merely follow them."

Eliana's attendants helped her rise, then dried her with soft white towels and began strapping her into an elaborate undergarment that cinched her waist.

"Aren't you curious?" Eliana insisted.

Jessamyn glanced at her, impassive. "No."

Her attendants wrapped her in a plunging red velvet gown. Diamonds spangled its sheer sleeves, and its skirt sparkled with an overlay of gold organza.

"I would be, if I were you," Eliana said. "You're an Invictus trainee, aren't you? You should be out in the world somewhere, carrying out missions. Tending my clothes, escorting me to concerts—you don't find that a little insulting?"

Jessamyn shot her a thin look. "'He has chosen me to guard His works. He has chosen me to receive His glory. I am the blade that cuts at night. I am the guardian of His story.'"

A chill seized Eliana at the reverence in Jessamyn's voice. She cloaked it with a shrug. "If you say so."

There was jewelry to match the gown—two heavy gold rings crowned with flat bouquets of stars. The attendants bent to slide them on and then flinched away from her hands, where the gold chains of her castings glinted. Their smooth brows furrowed slightly. One opened her mouth and let out a muted cry of fear.

"Let me," came Jessamyn's brusque command. She dismissed the attendants and put the rings on Eliana's fingers herself.

"I knew you once," Eliana said, watching Jessamyn's face for any sign of the woman she had known. "You were kind to me then. You kiss as well as you fight."

Jessamyn stepped back to inspect her, frowning. "They forgot your earrings."

Eliana swallowed against a pang of disappointment and lowered her gaze to the floor. If Jessamyn felt any curiosity about such strange remarks, she betrayed none of it, her stony face hardly more familiar than a stranger's, and only at that moment, with a swift ache of despair, did Eliana realize what she had been hoping.

That if the Jessamyn she had known could be reached, then maybe Simon could be too.

"Tell me," she whispered, her voice thick. "How long have I been here?"

Jessamyn retrieved glittering earrings from a cushion on the floor. "Two months."

A moment passed before Eliana could speak again. Two months was longer than she had guessed. Eight weeks she had spent in nightmares of Corien's design, and still she could not be sure if what she had seen of Remy—his thrashing body, his horrible screams—had been the truth or a lie.

Her eyes filled with tears; quickly, she blinked them away. She had not used her castings since that day in her bedroom, when Simon had traveled from one side of it to the other. That was a triumph. That was worth any sacrifice.

But how tired she was of sacrifice.

I'll end this, Eliana. Corien's whispered memory came sweetly, reminding her. *This life of yours, all its violence, all its sacrifice. Your brother will be safe. He'll be so happy, and so will you. Alive, healthy, safe. Safe, can you imagine? For once in your life.*

Eliana blew out a soft, shuddering breath. She pressed her palms hard against her legs.

"Will you hurt me to get her back?" she whispered.

Jessamyn, fastening Eliana's earrings into place, did not respond.

"I keep hearing those words," Eliana said. She wiped her cheeks, careless of the rouge. "I don't know why I'm hearing them. I think someone's trying to tell me something, but I don't know who they are or what they mean to say. *Will you hurt me to get her back?* What does that mean? Is it a warning? A message?"

For a moment, their gazes locked, and Eliana searched Jessamyn's face with a desperation that felt half a breath from madness.

A flicker of feeling crossed Jessamyn's face and was quickly gone. Her mouth was a straight line of annoyance.

"Perhaps a memory," she offered. "With so many angels about, there are often strays." She raised an indifferent eyebrow. "I would suggest you not dwell on it. The Emperor will not appreciate your distraction."

Then she glanced past Eliana, dropped smoothly to one knee, and bowed her head.

Eliana turned to see Corien standing at the threshold, watching them in amusement. He wore a high-collared vest of black brocade, a black velvet coat, a bloodred waistcoat.

"What a vision you are," he mumbled. "If I squint and enjoy a few more drinks, I think I can almost pretend you're her."

He held out his arm, but Eliana refused it. Eyes burning with exhaustion, she nevertheless felt warmed by a sudden calm.

Will you hurt me to get her back?

At last, she knew that voice.

"I need to see Simon," she declared. She flexed her fingers; her castings were cold and dark.

Corien's smile stretched wide. "As my queen demands."

Simon awaited them in a sitting room in the palace's north wing. He wore a dark dress uniform, the knee-length coat buttoned high at his neck and snugly hugging his trim torso. He stood at the window, looking out into the night, and at their entrance, he turned and inclined his head.

"Your Excellency," he said smoothly, his gaze on the Emperor. He avoided looking at Eliana entirely.

But from the moment she entered the room, Eliana did not take her eyes off of him.

"Apologies for delaying the concert, Simon," said Corien, brimming with a quiet, gleeful energy. "I know how fond you are of this composer. But our queen demanded to see you, and it sounded quite serious. I could not deny her."

Then Corien found a decanter on a serving table, poured himself a glass of red wine, raised his drink to them, and settled comfortably on a chaise in the corner. A servant had lit a small fire; the room's bronze light shifted with shadows.

Eliana stood in silence for a moment, tense with uncertainty. Perhaps it was a mistake to be here. She could not allow herself to release even a scrap of anger.

But there was something she had to know.

"I am myself," she muttered, fists clenching and unclenching at her sides. *Not here*, she commanded her castings. *Not ever again.*

Simon watched in silence. On his chaise, Corien smiled over the rim of his glass.

"I was indeed looking forward to this concert," Simon said at last, his voice edged with impatience. "So if you don't intend to speak after all—"

"I will speak," Eliana said quietly, her arms rigid. "That night in Karlaine. We were attacked. There were adatrox. Crawlers. Cruciata."

"Yes."

"You and Remy had been following me, I suppose, since Harkan…" Harkan's name caught in the back of her throat. "Since Harkan drugged me and took me from Dyrefal. The day the Empire invaded Astavar."

"Yes."

That hollow voice, lifeless and cold. Eliana's fingernails bit her palms. Simon wasn't stupid. He must have known what she was about to say, and it infuriated her that he could remain so calm, and it infuriated her even more that she could not allow herself to be furious.

She made her voice steady. "Remy was shot that day. Shot in the gut. He died, and I healed him."

"Yes."

"'Save him, or watch him die.' That's what you said to me." Eliana's mouth soured at the memory. It was mortifying to think of her old, foolish self. "You held me. You told me you weren't letting go of me."

Silence. Not even a shift of weight. He was a lifeless painting, watching her unravel.

Eliana forced the words out. "I let you fuck me."

A tiny smirk played at the corner of Simon's mouth. "And I thank you for that. I needed it."

His words punched her, and her stomach lurched to hear them, but she remained standing. Heat flared in her palms; she hardly noticed it.

"I keep hearing something in my head," she said through her teeth. "At first, I didn't recognize the voice. It was distorted, distant, and my mind's been run ragged. But now I know it belongs to Remy. I've been hearing it for…" She hesitated. In her mind, days became weeks became hours. She didn't *know* how long she had been hearing it.

"I don't know why it's happening," she said at last, "but I've heard Remy say the same phrase dozens of times now. 'Will you hurt me to get her back?'"

She searched every scar on Simon's face, the curve of his bottom lip, the sharp line of his jaw. A bead of sweat rolled down her neck. She imagined striking him with fists of fire, what his face would betray as he burned.

"'Get her back'," she whispered. "Get *me* back. Because Harkan had taken me. It made sense to me that you brought Remy with you when you came after me. You loved me, I thought. You wanted me to be with my brother because it would make me happy."

Eliana approached him slowly. Her gown's heavy train trailed across the floor. "But now I understand. Now I see that you never loved me. Every time you touched me was a lie. So why, then, would you drag along my little brother when you could have moved more quickly without him?"

Simon watched her approach, his expression still as an etching.

"Because you were desperate for my power to surface," Eliana answered. "You wanted to see more than patchy summoned fires and ships sunk by storms. You wanted to see my *real* power so it would awaken yours, and you knew the best way to scare it out of me."

Three steps from him, Eliana stopped. A distant roar of anger churned in her ears. Her body ached with tension. "You shot him."

Simon's smirk returned. His eyes glinted, lupine. "I did. I shot him right in the gut."

With a terrible sharp cry, Eliana lunged at him, her fist raised to strike. He shot forward to meet her, blocked her punch with his own. His fist caught her on the arm, and then the other dealt a hard blow to her stomach. Once, she would have recovered quickly from that, but weeks at sea followed by weeks in the prison of Corien's mind had left her thin and soft.

She staggered from the blow, gulping for air, but the white-hot blades of fury blazing up her spine would not let her rest. She flew at Simon, advancing on him with wild kicks and punches, her throat raw from her screams. He trapped her in his arms; she jabbed him in the ribs with her elbow, then turned and clipped his jaw with a ferocious punch. He faltered; she kneed him in the groin.

As he stumbled, she whirled around, grabbed a vase from a table, and brought it crashing down on his head. He staggered, and when she kicked him, he flew clear across the room and collided with the far wall. Several framed paintings crashed to the floor; he slumped beside them, his face streaked with blood. On his left, the hearth simmered.

Eliana sank fast to the rug. Rage held her shaking in its grasp, turned her vision red and black. The windows cracked in their panes. On the mantle, candles became blazing spears of flame. Beyond the terrace, out in the city, a slender white tower swayed and collapsed. Distant cries of alarm floated up through the palace.

Not here. Eliana huddled in a tight ball on the floor, her clasped hands hidden against her chest.

Not here, not here. She was herself. She was a girl, a child, an infant.

Not here, not ever again. She was clean and swaddled in white. Soft and cocooned, her power a mere whisper. She was not angry. She was not afraid. She would not despair.

As she listened to the palace quake, hot tears of shame rolled down her cheeks. For so long, she had resisted the urge to give Corien any part of herself, had kept her power closed off and quiet—until tonight. Had it been Corien who had planted Remy's voice in her mind, hoping it would provoke her? Or had the memory come from someone else?

She glanced up, saw Simon push himself to his feet and raise his arms, reaching for threads. Faint lights sparked at his fingertips for only an instant before the room went dark once more.

Eliana's eyes fluttered closed, her castings dark inside her fists. When she smiled, she tasted salt.

Then a familiar roar of rage pierced the air, followed by the crash of glass. Someone grabbed her by the hair and yanked her to her feet. Remy's face bloomed in her mind, gaunt and bloody. One eye blue, the other reddened from a cruel punch and ringed with bruises. She wanted to reach for him but would not. She shut her eyes, fought against the pull of his dear voice whispering her name.

It wasn't real. She lived inside a nightmare, that was all.

"I will hurt him again," Corien hissed against her ear, his breath sour with wine. "And again, and again. I show you beauty, I promise you peace at last for *weeks*, and this is what I get in return? You goddamned idiot girl. You're fighting a war you cannot win, and you know it. I will hurt him right in front of you, just like I did before. Yes, that was real, and it will be so again. I will rain agony upon him until you break. Is that what you want?"

He was dragging her across the room, his arm wedged under hers. She struggled against him, but his mind held her fast, forcing her to walk. She felt sick with fear as her legs moved against her will.

"I want to see the concert," she gasped out.

"Oh, no, my pretty one," said Corien, laughing. "It's too late for niceties. Consider the peaceful life I have given you forfeit."

Their progress through the palace was a blur of motion and color, her feet clumsy under Corien's direction. When she came to herself again, blinking rapidly, she stood on a terrace blazing with torchlight. The wind howled, and a quick glance around showed her that they stood on one of the topmost levels of the palace, the space lit by a dozen torches. Two white watchtowers flanked the terrace, and Eliana went cold with horror as she saw Remy dangling from one of them. An angelic guard held him by the collar. His face, bloodied and hollow-cheeked, was framed by neatly trimmed dark hair.

And from the other tower…

Eliana stared at the man hanging in the air, held suspended just as Remy was. She knew the face, but her mind refused to accept what it might mean.

"Father?" she whispered. Her arms were ice.

Ioseph Ferracora stared down at her, his face wet with tears and his eyes no longer black. They were blue, like Remy's. His square chin jutted stubbornly, like Remy's.

"Oh, yes, I've been meaning to tell you this," Corien said cheerfully. "Your father—I'm sorry, the man who raised you; we know who your real father is, don't we?—he didn't die in the Battle of Arxara Bay, as you may have been led to believe. He was alive when Admiral Ravikant found him. And since Ravikant is one of our most talented, one of our strongest, he was able to inhabit your father's body while still preserving his human life, keeping his mind intact and healthy. The admiral, of course, has graciously absented himself for the purposes of our little reunion tonight." Corien gently touched Eliana's cheek. "Isn't this happy news? Ioseph Ferracora still lives after all!"

Eliana could not find her voice. Her eyes locked on to her father's face and wouldn't let go. She could not stop thinking of the vision Corien had sent her—Remy, Simon, Ioseph, and herself, happy and laughing in a sunlit house. And there was every memory from her childhood: Ioseph going off to war; dancing with Rozen in their kitchen; holding little Eliana in his lap after the annual Sun Queen pageant, both of them glittering with gold powder, watching the sun rise while the statue of the Lightbringer towered above them.

The world spun slowly; something terrible was about to happen, and Eliana was helpless to stop it. She made her hands into fists. If her castings awakened again, she was not certain she would be able to dam the flood of her power this time.

Ioseph shook his head. "Don't listen to him, sweet girl. It's all right." His voice shook. Tears rolled down his cheeks and into the beard Admiral Ravikant had kept so neatly trimmed. "It's all right."

"Isn't it happy news?" Corien roared. He shook Eliana hard. "Tell me!"

A sob burst out of her. "Yes. Yes!"

"I'm tired of waiting for you to come to your senses, Eliana," he said hotly against her cheek, "of offering you pleasures, promising you peace. No longer. If I cannot persuade you to reason, I will be forced to break you."

Corien jerked his head at Ioseph's tower. "Save the man who found you in the streets and fed and protected you until he left home to fight a war I started, only to have his body stolen and used like a puppet."

He turned her roughly, made her stare at Remy's tower next. "Or save your innocent little brother, who even now doesn't blame you for all the misery he's endured on your behalf. Try to save them both, and I'll tear their skulls to pieces from the inside out before they even hit the ground."

Then, before Eliana could even draw breath to beg, the guards holding Ioseph and Remy let them go, and their bodies plunged into the night.

TAL

"*Merovec found the Archon's corpse at the doors of the House of Light. He claims the Archon took his own life, but he won't allow us to examine the body. In recent days, the Archon had been pleading with Merovec to end the interrogation of elementals. He was the only one of the Magisterial Council Merovec would allow inside Baingarde; now we are without an ally in the castle. The city is in an uproar. Those loyal to Merovec are looting temples, dismantling them piece by piece. The faithful are desperate, with nowhere to go. Merovec has heard rumors of Red Crown and is personally entering homes unannounced with squadrons of soldiers to search basements and question families. It's as if he thinks we're hiding Rielle in someone's attic. We in Red Crown say this to each other when we need courage: For crown and country, we protect the true light.*"

—Encoded letter from Miren Ballastier, Grand Magister of the Forge, to the exiled king Audric Courverie, dated December 3, Year 999 of the Second Age

Tal reached a bend in the mountain path and stopped to catch his breath.

Below him stretched a sea of red rock—the canyons and mountains of southeastern Vindica. It was a country that had once belonged to angels and now could boast only a hollow, stark sort of beauty, as if the empirium itself had forsaken it. Crumbling cities had been abandoned to the appetite of time, hosting only a population of scavengers, wanderers, and the occasional ambitious acolyte on a solitary pilgrimage.

From his spot on the path, Tal surveyed the horizon, the mountains around him, the darkening periwinkle sky. Even though he wore a long, thick scarf tied around his head and neck, his lips stung, and his throat was parched. The brutal mountain winds, choked with grit, were ceaseless.

Then Ludivine's panicked voice burst into his mind—a sensation with which Tal remained utterly uncomfortable and only allowed because he had long ago realized he could not find Rielle on his own. He wasn't powerful enough. His mind was dull, unimaginative. It always had been. Only a decent elemental talent and a ruthless dedication to studying had secured him his position as Grand Magister.

This truth had always eaten at him. Now that he had been isolated for weeks, its appetite had become monstrous, leaving Tal's mood black and fragile.

I cannot see her. Ludivine's thoughts clawed at him like the frantic grip of someone drowning. *Something's happened. I cannot see her any longer.*

Tal hated mind-speak. *Hated* it. The act felt unholy, made him want to bathe in scalding water.

Is she hurt? He stood rigidly in a patch of scrubby grass, staring at the southern horizon, where a thin black line marked the Namurian Sea, and Patria beyond. *Is she dead?*

He heard Ludivine's exhausted laughter. *Do you think Rielle could die and the world would somehow go on undisturbed?*

Then where is she?

I don't know. I don't know! She's so far from me. So far, and so frightened, Tal. A sob floated to him through whatever perverse connection Ludivine had forged with his mind. *He is keeping her hidden from me. You must find her.*

Tal let out a single bitter laugh. Desperation had kept him moving for weeks; he had hardly stopped to rest, pushing through storms of both snow and dust. He had followed a patchy trail cobbled together from Ludivine's frantic whispers and whatever information he could gather when he dared to stop at inns, travelers' hostels, encampments of nomadic tribes and roving treasure-seekers.

For weeks, he had hardly slept, both his dreams and his waking thoughts full of Rielle. The image of her from that horrible night outside the village of Tavistère tormented him. They had locked eyes; Corien had taunted him. *Too late, Tal.*

That desperation, the memory of her frightened face in the rain, had kept him pushing onward for long weeks, heedless of his aching muscles, the blisters in his boots, the hungry pinch of his stomach.

But now that strength left him all at once, like the bones had been sucked out of him. He sank to the ground and sat unmoving as the wind spat its relentless red sand.

Too late, Tal. Tal laughed, reached up under his head scarf, and scrubbed his filthy hands over his face. *That's what he said to me that night. I suppose he was right.*

Ludivine's voice was grave. In his mind's eye, Tal could see her sitting in a chair surrounded by greenery, her shoulders tense and her hands clasped tightly in her lap.

Tal, you must find her, she thought to him. *If I cannot see her, then you'll have to do it alone.*

"What do you think I've been trying to do?" he spat. He refused to mind-speak any longer.

I cannot leave Audric. He needs me to help him, and the world needs him on his throne.

"I didn't ask you to leave Audric." Tal pushed himself to his feet. That simple act was exhausting enough to make him want to lie back down in the sand and let it bury him. But he had seen a cave a mile or so down the mountain, and he could sleep there for the night.

"I'll search the entire world for her," he mumbled. "I, a single, simple firebrand, will track the most powerful pair of creatures who have ever lived. An angel and a queen of God. And when I find them, she'll surely listen to me. Don't you think? She always has. Not once has she ever defied me."

After a moment, Ludivine spoke quietly. *You sound slightly hysterical, Tal. You should rest.*

If only she were actually there beside him so he could slap her. "I should rest? Do you know, I had not once thought of that. Thank you."

You're no good to her exhausted.

He threw the entire vicious force of his frustration into his thoughts. *And you were no good to her even at your best.*

She recoiled, and Tal had walked half a mile more before she spoke again.

You're right. Her voice came faintly. *I have failed her utterly. I have failed all of you.*

Her despair was honest. Even the distant echoes of it rippling through Tal's mind made his eyes burn. He briefly considered sending her a thought of comfort, though she did not deserve it.

But something distracted him—a flash of light a few hundred yards down the mountain. It shone for two seconds, flickered, brightened, and then vanished.

Tal froze, chills blanketing his overheated skin. The sunlight had dimmed, and the rocks around him had taken on an eerie crimson glow. He was suddenly very aware of how alone he was, and how vulnerable.

He slipped his hand into the pocket of his coat, the stiff fabric caked with sand. Wrapped his fingers around his dagger. Reached for the shield on his back, felt his power pull tight between his body and his casting.

What is it? Ludivine asked.

Nothing good, I'm sure, Tal replied. *Leave me. You'll distract me, and you're too far away to help.*

He felt her hesitation.

Tell me what you find, she said at last.

And if what I find is my death?

Her voice was heavy with regret. *I am sorry, Tal.*

Then, with a subtle shift of sensation in his mind, she was gone.

Flattening himself against the rock, Tal edged his way down the mountain path, which narrowed into a tight chasm between two tall cliffs.

At the chasm's mouth, he waited, breathless, for beyond the cliffs, where the path widened once more, there was a dramatic decline, and then a small clearing of flat stone buffeted by a cluster of boulders.

And in this clearing, a ring of light appeared—small and dim at first, and then it quickly grew and brightened, a shifting darkness at its center. The first light had flickered; this one was steady.

A figure stepped through the ring, followed by a second. An instant later, the light vanished, thrusting the mountain back into darkness. Night was coming; only a faint red glow of sunset remained.

Tal's heartbeat boomed in his ears.

Who these people were, he did not know. But at least one of them was a marque—and Rielle had been traveling with a marque.

He searched the darkness. If she was there, he would have to act quickly. If she wasn't there, he didn't think he could bear it.

"That took far too long," said one of the people below, their voice male and gruff and vaguely familiar. "The earthquake—"

"Tried to kill me and failed," spat the second of the pair. A woman, Tal thought. She pushed back the hood of her cloak and ran her hands through a long fall of wild pale hair. "The whole world's gone mad, Garver. The world itself and the people in it."

Tal's knees shook with relief even as fresh despair tore at him. Neither of these people was Rielle's marque. He pressed his forehead against the wall of stone beside him, still warm from the sun. Palms flat against the rock, he began to pray.

Fleet-seeming fire, blaze not with fury or abandon.

Burn steady and burn true, burn clean and burn bright.

As his mind cleared, Tal realized he knew the name Garver, if it was indeed the same man. Garver Randell was a healer and apothecary whom both Audric and Rielle preferred to any of the royal healers at the palace, much to the healers' dismay. Garver had a son, Rielle had told him. An eight-year-old boy named Simon.

"Avura?" he heard Garver ask below.

"Gone," his companion answered. "Those quakes brought everything crashing down, even the goddamned mountains."

Tal listened, stunned. Avura was one of the larger settlements in the western foothills of the Maktari Mountains, which stretched north to south along the entire length of western Vindica.

Tal had been there only four days ago, following the erratic path of Rielle's trail. The city's population numbered in the hundreds of thousands, and never in recorded history had an earthquake occurred in that region. Certainly not one large enough to destroy so large a city.

The Gate will fall. It was happening just as Aryava had foretold.

Two Queens will rise. One of blood, and one of light.

For years, he had prayed that Rielle was the Sun Queen. He had prayed it so fiercely and so often that he had come to believe it wholeheartedly— that she was good, that she could be neither broken nor corrupted. That if he taught her conscientiously, if he prayed for her with enough conviction, he could ensure she would become the person who would save them.

But none of it had been enough. He had failed her. He had failed everyone. He was no better than Ludivine, incapable of protecting what was most important, and now Rielle was lost. The queen of blood after all, it seemed. The Kingsbane, many called her.

Only Tal couldn't make himself believe that, even after everything that had happened. Not Rielle. He had taught her for years, watched her courage bloom. She was powerful, yes, but she was *good*. She knew what was right and had always strove to do it. He tried to envision her as a bloodthirsty queen on the arm of an angel and refused to believe it, even as his mind easily supplied the images.

"Fleet-seeming fire," he whispered, his hands trembling against the sun-warmed stone, "blaze not with fury or abandon. Burn steady and burn true. Burn clean and burn bright."

Then, light bloomed through his eyelids. The air near him shifted.

Tal whirled and snapped open his eyes just as the light disappeared. Two strong hands grabbed hold of his arms; a cold blade poked at his throat.

"He has a casting," said the person holding his arms. It was the woman he had seen, her voice sharp. "A shield strapped to his back. Call upon your power, elemental," she said quietly, "and I'll plunge this dagger into your throat."

"There is no fire in these rocks," he replied wearily. "You're safe from me, marque."

A faint flush of sun remained at the western horizon, allowing Tal enough light to see the man who held the knife to his throat. He had graying brown hair and ruddy skin, a slight beard, and piercing blue eyes.

The man narrowed his gaze, then used his free hand to rip the scarf from Tal's head.

"I know you," he said, inspecting Tal's face. "Taliesin Belounnon. Grand Magister of the capital's Pyre."

"And you are Garver Randell," Tal guessed. "Healer to the true king of Celdaria."

A pause, and then Garver smiled grimly. "The true king," he agreed, and lowered his knife.

The woman released Tal and stepped around to glare at him. Her skin was pale, as was her hair. Her eyes were even more piercing than Garver's, and her frame was bony and sharp.

"What in God's name are you doing all the way out here?" she asked.

"Praying," he said flatly.

"Yes, and we heard you all the way down the slope. You should watch that in the future. What if I were someone who wanted to kill you?"

"Annick," warned Garver.

"Do you want to kill me?" Tal asked.

"Not at the moment," Annick replied. "But that could easily change. Tell me this, my lord." Her lip curled at the words. He didn't blame her; during the Angelic Wars, when fear of marques had reached feverish heights, the Church had been instrumental in eradicating them. Any survivors of the slaughter had gone deep into hiding.

"We've been tracking a marque for some weeks," Annick continued, "hoping to find an ally in these dark, uncertain times. Whoever they are, they're fast and strong, and it's been difficult to match their pace. Now we've lost the trail—the very same night we find you, a Grand Magister of the Celdarian church, out in the angelic wilds. Do you have an explanation for this remarkable coincidence?"

Tal looked hard at Annick's face, which was too carefully expressionless too trust. Then he glanced at Garver.

"I've also been tracking a marque," Tal said. "I've been following them since Tavistère. Then Terenash, then the Gormar Highlands and Zhirat. I was in Avura only four days ago. Is this also the path you've taken?"

Annick fell into stony silence. Garver frowned, considering him.

Urgently, Tal pressed on. "If there's a way I can help you rediscover their trail, please tell me. I must find them."

"Why would we help you find a marque?" Annick asked, crossing her arms over her chest. "You're of the Church. Out here, you *are* the Church."

"I wasn't even alive during the Scourge! Your quarrel lies with my ancestors."

"And you've done much in your life to make up for their crimes, have you?" Annick said, her eyes glittering. "You've petitioned your magister friends to rewrite the laws to allow me to show the wings on my back and live freely in the world, rather than hide in a cave in the middle of nowhere?"

Garver pinched the bridge of his nose. "Annick..."

"No, I haven't," Tal admitted.

"Then don't pretend innocence," Annick snapped. "Your very blood is tainted with mine."

"Yes, all right, of course you're right," Tal said quickly, "and if I survive the impending doom of the world, I swear to you I will assemble the Magisterial Council and demand that they revisit the Authority doctrines and the registry. But first we have to survive. I must find the marque you've been searching for, and you'll be able to help me track them much more effectively than I could on my own."

He hesitated, then decided what he wanted to say was worth the risk. "I think you're tracking them for the same reason I am. Not to find allies, but to find Rielle."

The quiet that fell over them vibrated with tension. Annick's face was unreadable.

But Garver relented. "The night of the royal wedding, I sensed a marque near the city. A shocking thing, for I knew only two marques existed in the capital, myself being one of them. This one was new and incredibly powerful, much more so than I am. Then Queen Rielle disappeared, and the marque with her."

"And you've been tracking them ever since?" Tal asked.

"With help, and much more slowly than I would like." He glanced at Annick. "Not many marques these days can travel such distances alone. Whoever is with the queen is someone of exceptional power."

"And when you find this marque and Queen Rielle," Tal said, "what do you plan to do, exactly?"

Before Garver could answer, Annick laughed.

"He hasn't gotten that far yet," she replied. "I enumerated for him all the reasons why he shouldn't do this foolhardy thing, and that topped the list. *Not having a plan.*"

Garver bristled. "I couldn't stand by and do nothing."

"No, so you decided to travel right into my bedroom with no warning, toss our son at me with no regard for my poor, shocked wife, and then go traipsing about the world after an angel with no plan other than dragging me along with you."

"*I* can help you," Tal said urgently. "If we can find your marque, we can find Rielle. And if I can find Rielle..." A lump formed in his throat, breaking his voice. "If I can find her, I can free her from him. I can bring her home to Celdaria, where she belongs. Only then will we be safe. If we cannot do this, I fear she'll be forever lost, and the world will fall, just as Aryava proclaimed."

"And what if Queen Rielle does not wish to be free of him?" Garver asked quietly. "What if she went willingly? What is it about you that will convince her to leave him?"

"I love her." The choked words burst out of Tal. "I love her, and she loves me. I have taught her everything she knows. I have protected her all her life."

"And done a piss-poor job of it," Annick muttered.

"Annick!" scolded Garver.

"I know her. I *know* her." Tal looked to each of them, praying they would believe him. "I can reach her. I know I can. I simply have to talk to her. If she hears me, she'll see reason. If I can touch her, hold her, she'll remember home. She'll fight her way free of him if she has to."

After a long moment, Garver glanced at Annick. She said nothing, her expression grave, and nodded once.

"Very well, my lord," Garver said. "We will travel together. We'll rest until dawn, then begin at first light."

Tal's exhausted relief was too immense for words. He directed them to the cave he had found, then settled on the hard ground outside it, under a wide black mouth full of stars. He hooked his arm securely through the strap of his shield, which covered his torso like a burnished shell.

Just inside the cave, Garver sat down heavily and put his head in his hands. Annick settled beside him, looking out into the night.

"I hate being so far away from Simon," Garver said gruffly, after a long moment. "He's a tender-hearted boy, though he tries not to be. He'll worry."

"Quinlan is looking after him," Annick replied. "She has powerful friends. They'll be safe."

"Your wife is entirely too good for you."

"Too true," Annick said, and then added, a grin in her voice, "Do you know, at times like this, I almost find myself wishing you and I hadn't ever stopped loving each other."

"At times like this, I find myself wishing I had no power at all, so I could send your sorry ass to save the world and stay at home with my son."

"*Our* son, you wretch," Annick said fondly, and kissed Garver's nose.

Tal listened to their quiet conversation until his eyes began to drift shut, and for the first time since leaving Celdaria, he fell asleep with a flare of hope burning clean and bright in his heart.

⇥ 17 ⇤

ELIANA

"There are days when I too lose my courage. I hear the screams of the dying, and I think all is lost. But if you learn one thing from my writings, I hope it is this: Whatever pain you have been dealt, the Sun Queen, when she comes, will bear far more. And she will know all the while that, if she surrenders, she will do so at the cost of everything that lives."

—*The Word of the Prophet*

I t was over far too quickly.

Eliana lurched across the terrace, clumsy with terror, and crashed to her knees against the low stone parapet. Ioseph and Remy fell fast toward the ground, their bodies blurred shapes in the darkness.

From the moment Eliana grasped Corien's intent, she knew what her choice would be, and therefore did not hesitate. She could sense the truth in his words: If she tried to save them both, he would kill them, and she would be left with nothing.

But he had known that and had correctly guessed how she would respond to that threat, that she would have no choice but to do what she was doing now—reaching out for Remy's body as it spun and plummeted, desperation making her castings flare to life.

The empirium shifted at her command, the air around Remy weaving itself into a brilliant cushioned net. Eyes glazed, her vision gone golden and supple, Eliana could see the change in the air like the press of a thumb against skin, making the world's flesh stretch and pucker.

Silent tears rolled down her cheeks as she lowered Remy gently to the courtyard below, the clean white stone now marred by something Eliana could not bring herself to look at. Instead, she watched a pair of guards lift Remy to his feet and escort him away until he was lost in the shadows.

She huddled on the terrace, shivering against the parapet. She laid her cheek on the rough cool stone, and as she listened to the sounds of soldiers carrying away Ioseph's body, something broke within her. Not a snap, but a gentle giving way, as if a tree gone soft and half-rotted had been standing too tall in harsh winds and could no longer bear its own weight. An exhaustion unlike any she had felt before fell over her, drawing a thick blanket of numbness over her thoughts.

She barely noticed Corien helping her rise. He smoothed her hair back from her face, wiped away her tears.

"What a waste to make you endure this," he said. "We would make a happy family, if you allowed it. You, me, Remy. Your mother too, once I've found her. I'll let you flay Simon down to his bones if you wish and keep him alive for every second of agony."

Corien's thumb caressed her jaw. He watched her with eyes blacker than the sky above them. "Send me back, Eliana, and you'll never have to feel like this again."

Then he turned and was gone, and Eliana slipped into a quiet dark tunnel devoid of life. When she found light once more, she was on her clean white bed in her clean white rooms, every surface awash in soft moonlight. She curled atop the blankets, shivering.

A crackling sound spit through the room, a warped buzz that reminded her of the sour hiss of galvanized lighting. From a brass funnel affixed to the wall, high in a corner of the room above a bundle of thick wires, came the soaring melody of the orchestra playing in the theater downstairs. The brass device distorted the sound, making it seem as though the orchestra were making music on a distant high mountain.

Eliana did not know how Corien had achieved this, nor did she care. The music struck her ears like the blunt heels of vicious hands, and she let them pummel her to sleep.

◆◇◆

Eliana awoke to the nauseating smell of breakfast arriving.

She watched dully as her white-robed attendants carried dishes to the small white dining table by the south-facing windows—a plate, a bowl, a pitcher, a goblet. The scent of food sat in her nose and mouth like a sour film. Eliana turned away from the neatly set table. If she looked at it for another second, she would be sick.

There was a moment of silence, and then from the doorway came a sharp huff of impatience. Jessamyn appeared, marching over to Eliana's bed in her trim black uniform. A small collection of sheathed knives hung from her belt.

"You will eat every bite," she commanded, yanking Eliana upright. "His Excellency commands it."

Eliana did not resist. Once on her feet, she followed Jessamyn to the table. Her mind felt muddled; to move her legs, to think her thoughts, was to slog through a swamp. She felt as though she had been pulled through a tight chasm into a state that was neither awake nor asleep.

And yet her gaze flitted to Jessamyn's daggers. How easily her thoughts tipped to Arabeth and Nox and Whistler, her own beloved, long-gone knives. Slowly, an idea began to form.

Eliana sat before her breakfast and measured her breathing, allowed her idea to grow. If she moved too quickly, she would disrupt the fog that kept her mind torpid, and Corien would sense what she intended and stop her.

"Eat," Jessamyn snapped, standing tall beside the table.

Eliana lifted a spoonful of mash to her lips. Morning light filtered through the windows; the glass was spotless, and beyond it, a dove perched on the gutter preened its feathers.

Eliana's idea turned and sharpened, steadily taking shape. She could not—*would* not—help Corien. And yet she could not endure more of this. The endless nightly torment, Remy brought before her and abused, the inability to trust her own mind.

This was the answer. She had to end his game before he could win, and this was the only way to do it.

She ate under Jessamyn's watchful gaze. Spoon from bowl to lips until the dish was clean, and then she started on her fruit. A berry popped open between her teeth.

"Where is Remy being held?" she asked. If she was going to abandon him to this place, she needed to hear the truth of his fate. "Is he hurt? Is he being fed?"

"Fed, yes," Jessamyn said after a slight pause. "Hurt, yes, but nothing egregious. The Emperor will make certain he is safe as long as he is useful."

As long as he is useful. Eliana smiled with faint relief. Once she was gone, they would kill him. He would want it that way. He would want her to do this. Two lives in exchange for countless others? A simple equation. If Remy knew, as she did, that it was the only way to win, he would hold the blade himself.

"I had thought of that," she whispered, finishing her fruit. "That he would be kept alive as long as I am."

She reached for a slice of buttered bread. She envisioned the three daggers strapped to Jessamyn's belt but did not dare look at them. A strange peace came over her. She would have to be quick. One last kill for the Dread of Orline.

Remy, forgive me, she prayed.

Then she rose swiftly from her chair and struck Jessamyn hard in the throat.

Jessamyn staggered back and gasped soundlessly, clutching her neck. She hadn't been expecting it. Eliana was weak. She'd gone soft; she hadn't held a dagger in weeks. She hardly looked like a person anymore, let alone a killer.

But desperation gave her new strength. She found the shortest dagger on Jessamyn's belt and wrenched it free of its sheath. Her mind a frenzy of white light and crackling noise, her blood afire with triumph, she thrust the blade toward her own stomach.

Before blade could meet flesh, something seized her—a firm but gentle presence in her mind like a hand around her wrist, pulling her back from the brink.

No, little one. Not yet. We have things left to do, you and I.

Whoever this person was, sending mind-speak into her thoughts as angels did, it was not Corien.

Eliana dropped the knife.

The adatrox stationed around the room remained silent and still. Jessamyn leaned against the dining table with one hand, her other hand at her collar. She did not lunge at Eliana to counterattack. None of the adatrox hurried forward to apprehend her.

Eliana stood slowly, staring. Jessamyn gasped for air. The dove at the window flew away with a soft trill.

We have a moment to speak uninterrupted, the voice told Eliana. *I am deceiving the eyes of your guards, but I cannot shield us for long.*

Who are you? Eliana stepped back from Jessamyn, her heart pounding in her ears. *You're an angel.*

I am a friend.

Eliana spun around, searching for something to attack, but the room remained still and quiet. The only sound was Jessamyn's ragged breathing. *That does not answer my question.*

Not all angels are alike, and not all worship at the Emperor's feet. After a pause, the voice said, gentler now, *Haven't you such a friend? Your Zahra, whom you love?*

Eliana sensed a kindness in this voice, and a great sadness. Her eyes filled with furious tears. *Don't you want me to stop him? This is the only way.*

No. There is another. I don't have much time before he realizes I'm here, and he can't know I'm still alive, which is why I haven't shown myself to you before now. Despite its sadness, the voice held an iron resolve that frightened Eliana, even kind as it was—for in this, at least, the voice matched Corien's own. An indomitable will. Centuries of purpose.

I would have liked more time before coming to you, for your own sake, the voice continued. *These months have been steadily wearing at you. You have suffered great losses, and you have so diligently worked against your power to protect us all that now you can find it only in moments of great duress, pain, or fear. That is why he hurts you so. That is why he promises happiness, only to tear it from your grasp.* A pause. Then, an immense fondness. *What you have endured is unforgivable. I wish I could tell you there isn't more to come.*

Eliana was mystified. Standing in a pool of still sunlight, her unseeing guards staring blankly like statues, she asked again, this time aloud, "Who are you?"

I have many names, the voice replied. *But you know me as the Prophet.*

ᐨ 18 ᐨ

RIELLE

"There is only one known scholarly depiction of Saint Tameryn without her dagger in hand—the frontispiece of a meticulously curated collection of obscure Astavari children's tales. In the illustration, visible only when illuminated by direct sunlight, Tameryn is a child, and though ordinarily her likeness is of grave expression, in this instance she is beatific. In repose among a meadow's flowers, she holds to her breast a white kitten in one hand and a beam of light in the other. No black leopard godsbeast to guard her. No dagger with which to fell her enemies. Not a single shadow in sight."

—A footnote in *The Book of the Saints*

Rielle waited with mounting impatience for the tailor to finish adjusting the fabric of her new gown.

But she could not allow herself to be impatient. She needed to keep her mind as schooled as her face—mostly blank, a touch of imperiousness. The tailor moved quickly around her, pinning fabric, taking measurements. Corien had insisted she have a spectacular wardrobe, and the tailor he had conscripted for the job hailed from Kirvaya. Brilliantly talented, Corien had assured her, and indeed the man had created something exquisite—a high-collared black gown with structured shoulders and long snug sleeves that glittered with artful swirls of tiny gold jewels, a high waist, and a sweeping, dramatic skirt that allowed room for her growing belly.

Exquisite, and yet Rielle could not look directly at it. The black expanse of it, the glittering gold froth at the hem, reminded her of the endless sea of the empirium and how she had nearly drowned in it.

How she had *wanted* to drown in it.

The tailor fussed with a wrap of dark gray fur, draping it across her shoulders.

Rielle locked eyes with her reflection. The same green she had always seen in mirrors now flared with thick bands of swirling gold. The change had been happening slowly over the past few months, and she had ignored it, but could do so no longer. The gold would soon eclipse the green.

Suddenly, she could not bear to stand there any longer. Her stomach was unsettled; she couldn't eat anything anymore without feeling sick. And she was surrounded by horrors. Monsters crafted from dragons and children forced into their magic. Monsters battering at the Gate. A monster who kissed her one moment and crafted abominations the next.

And she herself, the most monstrous of them all.

"We will finish this later," Rielle announced, placing a hand on her belly. "I feel ill and need to rest."

Half a lie, and one that almost made her laugh. She would never be allowed to rest.

As her handmaidens helped her undress, slip into a sleeping shift, and find her furred slippers, Rielle imagined clamping her thoughts between the jaws of a vise, afraid to breathe too loudly. Corien was working somewhere deep in the bowels of the Northern Reach to which he had not yet introduced her. With his mind occupied—directing the movements of angels around the world, communicating with those still in the Deep, working with his physicians to cut and maim—Rielle's own mind was as clear as it would ever be.

But she had to move fast.

As soon as she was alone, she gathered every piece of warm clothing she could find. Her sturdy fur-lined boots, which she had worn earlier that week when Corien gave her a tour of the reeking dragon pens. Thick tights, thick wool stockings, tunic, and trousers, and a long fur coat that fell past her knees. A scarf to wrap around her head and neck and a fur hat to tie down over that.

She fashioned a sack from one of the bedsheets, trying to put out of her mind the recent memory of being tangled in it, Corien's mouth hot on her skin. Her hands shook as she stuffed her makeshift bag full of clothing. Then she grabbed a blank page from the notebook on Corien's desk and a pen and stuffed them into her bodice.

She flew down the hidden staircase that began behind the mirror in the bathing room—a secret passage through which Corien could enter and exit his rooms privately. It was mid-afternoon—the laboratories and barracks, the mines and forges, would be bustling with activity, but the fortress itself was quiet. Rielle hurried to one of the supply storerooms near the kitchens, grabbed potatoes and hard rolls, a few strips of cured elk meat. She couldn't guess what food they would be able to find or where their journey would take them.

She reached out with her mind, wondering if she would feel Corien watching her.

Silence. He was there, but distant, a faint shadow in her mind. He was still working. There was still time.

Inside an empty office that belonged to one of Corien's scout commanders, Anadirah, Rielle found a small leather rucksack with a strap meant to fasten around the torso. She transferred the food into it, leaving the clothes ready and waiting on the floor. Then, with a pounding heart and a face cool as ice, she strode through the fortress to the little room in the east wing where Obritsa lived.

"I will see the marque," Rielle announced to the two adatrox guarding the door. "At once."

They blinked in confusion, their eyes gray and fuzzy, but she stood firm, staring them down, and soon they unlocked the door and stepped aside.

Blood thundering in her skull, Rielle entered the room and shut the door behind her. Whatever angels had been assigned to control those particular adatrox would soon let Corien know what had happened. It was an odd enough thing to risk disturbing him.

Near the blazing hearth, Obritsa sat in a chair, tightly bound by long coils of thick chains. The girl was obviously uncomfortably warm, her pale-brown skin slick with sweat, her gaze bleary. So bound, she would not be able to thread. The art required use of one's hands.

Obritsa looked up at Rielle's entrance, her eyes puffy from crying but her face hard with hatred. "Have you come to kill me at last? Or have you simply come to tell me that my Artem is dead?"

Rielle ignored her, and with a quick lash of power, she dissolved the chains in an instant, leaving Obritsa abruptly free and sitting in a cloud of iridescent ashes.

"We don't have much time," Rielle said, withdrawing the paper and pen from her bodice and beginning to sketch a map of the fortress. "He'll come for us soon. I need you to take me away from here, as far away as you can manage. Bear in mind that we have a long way to go, and I'll need you to keep your strength. I've gathered supplies and clothes and hidden them in a closet down the corridor. We'll retrieve them before we leave. Dress quickly. I think the best route for us to take is due north, through the White Wastes. We'll cross the ice fields and the pole, then enter Astavar from the north."

"Your sudden change of heart is surprising." Obritsa's eyes glinted with a new sharp light. "He showed you, didn't he? You saw what he's been making. The elemental children he stole from my country. He keeps them in cages. In his laboratories, he perverts their magic and turns tortured godsbeasts into monsters. You saw it all."

Rielle paused in her work. Memories of the last few days lingered in her mind like scraps of nightmares. She longed to chase after them, examine what Corien had done and marvel at the inventiveness of it.

She longed to condemn him for it and personally see to it that he was punished.

The contradictions of her own heart made her want to scream.

"The Gate must not be opened," she said, refusing to look at Obritsa. If she glimpsed a single smug smile, she would burn it off the girl's face. "These abominations he has made are crimes against the empirium."

Then she braced herself, holding still and silent, as if uttering the words would bring him crashing through the door.

But the only sound in the room was the crackling fire. She released a shuddering breath.

"We'll destroy the castings we already have. I know where they're kept." She pointed at her scribbled maps. "You will take me there first, and then to the castings. That will create a distraction, perhaps slow him down. We'll go to Astavar next, find Tameryn's dagger."

"Are you capable of destroying them?" Obritsa asked, watching her closely. "They were forged by the saints."

Rielle laughed a little, distractedly scratching at her temple. "I'm capable of anything. Now, quickly, while I am still myself. Before anyone gets to me."

She closed her eyes, pushing against the distant rumble of the empirium, the nibbling of its black-gold waves. Her scratching fingers drew blood.

"You can't touch me," she whispered. "You can't have me, not yet."

Obritsa sounded slightly alarmed. "Who are you talking to?"

Rielle ignored her. "If you want to stop him, you'll do as I command. *Now*."

The girl rose from her chair, then hesitated.

"Artem is too heavily guarded," Rielle said at once, "and we've lost enough time as it is. We'll have to leave him behind." She thrust the map at Obritsa. She could feel the edges of her control fraying, her thoughts spilling out. "Hurry, damn you! He'll come for me at any moment!"

Her mouth in a thin line, her eyes hard and glittering, Obritsa worked quickly, her deft fingers summoning bright threads from the air and crafting them into a humming ring of light. She glanced at Rielle.

Rielle stepped through the light, and Obritsa followed shortly after.

The threads unraveled with a simmering hiss, and the ring collapsed, snapping shut.

They dressed hurriedly in Anadirah's office, Obritsa dwarfed by the too-large furs. A gentle pressure was building in Rielle's mind, her thoughts shifting into a familiar configuration.

"Hurry," she whispered, her fingers shaking as she tied her scarf and hat into place. "He's coming."

Obritsa, eyes wide, summoned more threads. They stepped through the ring and into a small unadorned room of stone in one of the fortress's towers, just as Rielle had instructed—but horror overcame her as she realized the truth.

The room held only one casting: Saint Marzana's shield, sitting alone in the center of the floor. Pale shafts of wintry light from four different windows intersected on the shield's battered face.

Obritsa closed her threads and turned. "Where are the others?"

Rielle stared at the shield, a hot white rage rising within her.

Corien had separated the castings, hidden them individually throughout the fortress, and he hadn't told her.

The last tattered cords of her control snapped.

She screamed in fury and flung her hands at the shield, calling the empirium to her in an incandescent wave of power. The room exploded into gold, every fleck of dust, every trace of air and moisture illuminated with brilliant light.

Obritsa threw up her arms to shield her eyes.

A high, discordant hum pierced the air—the shield vibrating on the floor. Then, with a loud crack, it shot toward the ceiling, shattered into dust, and was gone. All that remained was a charred spot on the floor and a spiderweb of cracks that spanned from wall to wall. The room quaked violently, the ceiling swaying overhead.

Rielle sagged to the floor, her mind bursting with stars. Her bones and muscles ached, her teeth and the space behind her eyes pulsed with pain— but beneath it was a depraved, wriggling pleasure. There was a delicate tingling in her fingers and toes, a supple energy playing at the ends of her hair and crackling along the soft lines of her skin.

She sensed a light nearby, turned slowly toward it as if moving through water.

"Go, Rielle," said Obritsa, her voice tight with fear. "Hurry. The tower is falling."

A loud snap split the air, and the floor gave way beneath Rielle's feet as she stepped through the ring of light hovering in the air to her left. She felt Obritsa right on her heels and heard the threads snap closed behind them as they fell together into a white world of snow.

The air was so cold it immediately stole Rielle's breath. She pushed to her feet, gasping, and fumbled to put on her gloves. Beside her, Obritsa adjusted the rucksack on her shoulders.

They stood on a glacier, a low range of gray-and-white mountains behind them. A few hundred yards ahead of them gleamed a black grin of water shot through with icebergs. And in the distance, dark mountains that pierced the clouds.

Rielle's heart pounded as she watched them. Those mountains marked the Northern Reach, and she had escaped from it. From *him*.

And as soon as the thought formed, he found her.

Rielle, what have you done? He groped for her, his fingers brushing against her wrist, his voice caressing her neck. His anger tugged at her chest; she was supper, caught in a snare. *The shield, Rielle! How could you do this to me? To us?*

Rielle cried out, "Again, Obritsa! North!"

The girl obeyed, her wide frightened eyes the only things visible behind her layers of furs.

Rielle went first, Obritsa close on her heels, and as Rielle passed through the ring of light, Corien's roar of fury struck the back of her neck like a whip.

◆

They landed in a deep drift of snow.

Rielle choked on it, the fresh white powder up to her chin, and pawed around for Obritsa. She found the girl's gloved hand, held tight to it, then sent out a burst of power that melted every flake within ten feet of where they stood. Water gushed to the bare black ground in a brief cold torrent.

Gasping and coughing for air, her furs drenched, Obritsa nevertheless did not hesitate. She summoned more threads, each drifting in a cloud of steam as the snow once again closed in fast around them.

A vision settled before Rielle's eyes: the black fortress at the Northern Reach, a gaping hole at the corner where the tower she had collapsed had once stood.

She blinked, and then Corien was beside her, cloaked in black and gray furs. He had left his face bare, and in the relentless snow, his pale-eyed beauty was even more startling.

"What is the point of this, Rielle?" he asked her. "What are you hoping to achieve?"

Though he was not truly there, he was real enough in her mind, and Rielle swayed toward the promise of warmth in his arms.

But then she turned away from him, remembering the cruciata corpse hanging from the ceiling, the stolen Kirvayan children crammed into cages, the crawlers howling in their pit.

"You lied to me," she told him. "You never told me what you had been doing, what atrocities you have made real. I may be a monster, but I am not so monstrous that I can permit the abuse of children and godsbeasts."

Corien laughed gently. "You're confused, darling. You're tired. I understand. Come home to me. Come home and rest." His voice slipped down the curve of her back. "Remember how good I made you feel, how you came apart again and again under my hands? Remember the power of that, the *rightness* of it? You belong here. You belong in my arms, Rielle."

Teeth chattering in the cold, Rielle shouted at Obritsa, "Faster, please!"

"Our throne awaits us," Corien said urgently. "If monstrous acts are required to achieve that, then so be it. It was a monstrous act that was done to me and my people. All great work must start somewhere, and what our future holds will be glorious enough to burn away any memory of the grotesque and cruel. You want this more than anything. I can feel it. I *know* you, Rielle."

Obritsa looked back over her shoulder. "It's ready!"

Rielle hurried toward the ring of light shining above the snow.

"You're lying to yourself!" Corien roared. "Without me, what will be left of you? You'll be alone! You'll never find—"

Rielle stepped through the threads, and his voice disappeared.

—◆—

They landed on a steep icy slope. Rielle immediately skidded, then caught herself on a nearby rock.

But Obritsa could not find her footing and slid past Rielle with a sharp cry of fear.

Rielle reached out and stopped her, freezing Obritsa in a net of power that held her sprawled motionless in the snow.

As Rielle felt herself begin to slip, her grip on the rock failing, inspiration bloomed. She touched the empirium and sent a gentle wave of power rushing out over their little stretch of mountain. Snow and ice became mounds of downy grass dotted with wildflowers, and the air turned balmy and sweet.

She collapsed into a cool patch of clover, breathing in the smell of green.

Corien's voice came quietly. *I'm ashamed of how I spoke to you. I was afraid when I realized you'd left me. I'm sorry. I was cruel, and I lied to you. Rielle, you'll never be alone.* His voice held stifled tears. *And I'll never stop loving you. I'll never abandon you or flee from you or flinch away in fear. Queen of my heart, I was made for this. I was brought into this world to love you.*

Obritsa crawled through the grass to Rielle's side, helped her sit up. She had summoned more threads, a ring of them humming cheerfully at Rielle's toes.

"It's time," said Obritsa, panting. "Come. It's fading fast."

The girl was right. Rielle looked blearily around to see her meadow's grass withering, the blooms turning black. Her focus was too scattered, her fear and anger running rampant.

She pushed herself to her feet, turned away from Corien's soft pleas, and passed through Obritsa's threads to whatever lay beyond.

—◇—

On a clear night in the White Wastes, Rielle and Obritsa sat with their backs against a squat low cliff, looking out over a magnificent vista of snowy fields. The world was white and flat as far as Rielle could see. Above them, a sky of stars and twisting lights—green and violet, turquoise and amber. The legendary Astavari sky.

Obritsa—exhausted, her power depleted—rested her head against Rielle's shoulder. Rielle stroked the girl's arm through her furs.

Corien was quiet, only the barest shade of color on her mind's horizon. Rielle knew she should be worried about what that could mean, but she was too tired for worry. They had been pushing themselves ruthlessly across the White Wastes for days, and this was the first time they had seen the stars.

"We're almost there," she murmured to Obritsa, who was growing heavy with sleep.

A thin vein of power tickled the edges of Rielle's awareness. The crooks of her arms tingled; she rubbed her boots together, restless. The casting was close, and it was calling to her. In her mind's eye, she saw Saint Tameryn in battle, riding her black leopard and flanked by a pack of shadow-wolves she had summoned with her casting—an elegant dagger with an ebony hilt.

Rielle closed her eyes. "We're so close," she whispered. "I can feel it."

—◇—

When Rielle stepped through the final ring of light that would bring her to Saint Tameryn's casting, she was tense and ready, her power humming eagerly at her fingertips.

She stood in an immense cavern at the edge of a vast, clear lake. Bounteous greenery covered the cavern walls—tangles of creeping vines trimmed with glossy jade leaves, clusters of tiny white flowers that hung like clouds. The lake's shore was a broad expanse of black stone glinting with flecks of amethyst. A gentle breeze ruffled the water, and though there was no window to the outside world, sunlight gently suffused everything Rielle could see.

Obritsa came up quietly beside her, lowering her furred hood. Chunks of snow fell to the ground. "Saint Tameryn's cavern," she whispered.

Rielle closed her eyes, breathing in the gentle air. Here, the casting's call was insistent and clear. Its power showed her a vision: Saint Tameryn in a sleepy-eyed embrace with Saint Nerida. One with golden-brown skin and a head of glossy dark waves, the other ebony-haired with pale skin kissed golden by the sun. Entwined in a white bed beneath a canopy of leaves, they glowed with happiness.

An echo of their love bloomed in Rielle's heart, the memory carried on the current of the casting's power, and it was so overwhelming, so vivid in its purity, that Rielle felt choked by it. Dashing the tears from her eyes, she resolved to leave this place the first moment she could, for it brought memories of Audric too close.

She swept her gaze across the cavern and found a circular belvedere made of stone, sitting on a plinth out on the water. A low wall connected it to the shore.

Standing amid the belvedere's columns were three men in gray robes, each with a familiar sigil embroidered on his chest—a high, square tower, and above it an eye. One of the men was already frantically pulling threads from the air, which made Obritsa draw in a sharp breath.

The Astavari Obex, and one of the marques who served them.

Rielle stormed toward them at once, Obritsa hurrying behind.

"Relinquish it," Rielle called out, "or I will destroy you."

One of the Obex clutched Tameryn's dagger behind his back. "Lady Rielle, please, you must listen to reason—"

"I warned you," Rielle said. There was no time to argue with them, nor to spare them. Still some fifty yards from them, she sent fists of power flying, grasped their hearts in her blazing hand, and stopped them, as she had done to her father, to King Bastien, to Lord Dervin. But she was better at it now—swifter, more efficient. Their deaths were painless; she made sure of it. Tameryn's dagger clattered to the ground. The marque's threads unraveled and disappeared.

Rielle crossed the wall to retrieve the dagger, then rejoined Obritsa on the shore. The girl looked utterly unsurprised by what Rielle had done. Instead, a faint smile brightened her tired face.

"We did it," Obritsa said breathlessly. "I did it."

"You did well," Rielle agreed, and then held up the dagger, tilting its blade to catch the light. She tried not to think about how elated Audric would be to stand in Saint Tameryn's beloved retreat, but her mind was a vicious traitor.

"Take us to the surface," Rielle instructed. "Somewhere remote. That waterfall we passed in the mountains. Take us there."

Obritsa frowned. "You won't destroy it here?"

Rielle tightened her grip on the dagger. She waited until her eyes were dry and her mind free of the imagined Audric, standing awestruck on the shore.

Then she said quietly, "No. Not here."

—◆—

They rested under a cluster of pines in the mountains some distance north of Astavar's capital, Vintervok. Not far from them, a slender waterfall tumbled down a black rise of stone. A thin mist pervaded the air, softening every leaf and limb.

Obritsa slept soundly on the bed of her furs, snug between Rielle and a boulder velvet with moss. Shadows stretched deep and dark beneath Obritsa's eyes, and her cheeks were hollower now than they had been in the Northern Reach. But then, so were Rielle's. She had seen her reflection in the nearby river and had hardly recognized the person staring back at her.

She left Obritsa sleeping and wandered through the trees until she found a tiny clearing encircled by pines. There, she stripped down to her tights and thin tunic. Alone, free of the thick layers of clothing and with no companions but the trees, she felt less brittle and found it easier to breathe. She sat on a soft bed of moss, leaned her head back against the trunk of a pine, and gazed at the sea of needles swaying above them. Her palms still tingled from destroying the dagger, and she had a passionate desire to sleep for a solid month. But they could not rest for long. The prolonged quiet meant Corien was planning something—or that he knew something she did not.

Rielle rested one of her hands on her belly. Sometimes the new shape of it revolted her, and she would come close to summoning her power and ridding herself of the creature inside her once and for all. She had neither the time nor the energy for the changes it had wrought upon her body, the new exhaustion of moving herself through the world. And it belonged not only to her but to Audric, and with that particular chain around her, she could never truly be free of him.

Other times, she felt such a tenderness for the child she carried that it left her faint. Absently, she traced her fingers across her skin, wondering how it was faring after such wild days of travel. She wondered too if she should see a healer—and that made her think of Garver Randell, his little shop that smelled of herbs and resin, and Simon, looking up at his Sun Queen with shining eyes.

What they must think of her, sitting at their dinner table back in Âme de la Terre, wondering how they had been so thoroughly deceived.

How they must have come to despise her.

Head in her hands, Rielle blinked to clear her burning eyes, and suddenly, though she had not commanded it to, her vision flickered, and when it settled, the forest around her had been redrawn in shades of shifting gold.

An exhausted sort of dread washed over her body, even as her mind came alive with desire.

this power is yours

"No," she moaned, covering her ears. "Not now."

I wake

The empirium's presence was cold and infinite, its whisper ageless, its might unthinkable. It rose to her surface like a behemoth of the sea coming up for air. Rielle shut her eyes against it, willing her vision to be small and pale once more.

this power is yours

take it

take me

I RISE

"I can't," Rielle whispered, tears rimming her lashes. "It's too much."

Her hands crackled with heat, and she flattened them against the dirt, hoping the press of the earth would satisfy their hunger.

Then there was a shift in the air, a thickening of the world's quiet that muffled all other sounds. The rush of the waterfall softened to a dull rumble; the wood's chatter hushed.

Rielle looked up and saw a faint vision: an airy room lined with fluttering curtains. Windows framing a white city. A terrace piled high with flowers.

And standing before her was Ludivine, faint but smiling. Golden-haired and pale in a gown of soft rose. Beside her stood a man in a green tunic, his dark curls mussed, his brown skin warm with sunlight.

Rielle's breath caught. "Audric?"

19

NAVI

"May your ship sail true
and your fires burn bright.
May your heart think of me
while the stars shine their light."

—Traditional Vesperian traveler's prayer

M alik had been gone for five days, two more than it should have taken him to travel to the island of Laranti and return with Ysabet, the Red Crown leader Hob had arranged for them to meet. A woman, Hob's contacts in the underground had said, whose influence in the Vespers was unmatched.

But Malik had not yet returned. Navi couldn't sleep for worrying about him.

Instead, she sat up late in her shabby canvas tent, staring at the damp, curling sheets of paper on the table she and Hob had fashioned out of an old tree stump. Beyond the tent flap, clouds of angry flies swarmed, kept at bay by the foul-smelling oil their guide, Bazko, had sold to them for what Navi suspected was an exorbitant price. But she had gladly spent it, even though the coin they'd managed to smuggle out of Astavar—and exchange for Vesperian currency before word of the invasion spread— was disappearing fast. The bog's flies were ravenous, each the size of a thumbprint.

"Forty-seven," Navi breathed, looking over the encoded list of names before her—the latest count of everyone they had recruited to their little army of strays. Red Crown loyalists, refugees, orphans. "It isn't enough."

"No," Hob said simply. "It is not."

"We have to move faster, somehow. I hate being stuck in this awful place."

"It was the right decision, to stay and keep watch over the fissure."

Navi drew in a long, slow breath, hoping it would bring her some semblance of calm.

It did not.

The tent's canvas and some hundred yards of swamp stood between her and the fissure to the Deep, but Navi could still feel it pulling at her. The shape of its dark, jagged eye had stamped itself on her vision, as if she had stared too long at a bright light. Nothing had emerged from the fissure, and the tear had not grown larger.

But the swamp had grown eerily quiet since the fissure's appearance. Navi had the sense that she wasn't alone in holding her breath, waiting for the next quake and what it might bring.

The tent flap opened, and Miro ducked inside, looking miserable. He dragged his sleeve across his grimy face. "My lady, may I sleep in here until my next watch? The flies are eating me alive."

"Yes, of course." Navi gestured to a battered leather tarp that served as a bed for anyone who needed it, and once the boy's breathing had evened out, she returned to Hob, wiped her brow with a rag from her pocket, and then hid her face against the damp cloth.

The only sounds were Miro's light snores, the buzzing flies, soft shuffling and clanking noises as others moved around the camp, everyone's voices hushed as if afraid to disturb the swamp's unnatural silence. Somewhere nearby, those on watch were slowly patrolling the water.

"What was I thinking, Hob?" Navi whispered. "This is madness."

"I think I would call it rash courage, perhaps," Hob said evenly, "but not madness."

She looked up at him, exhaustion making her eyes sting with tears. "An army to crush the Empire. That's what I said I would build. That's what I told Malik as we fled Astavar. And now I have forty-seven people in a bug-infested swamp, waiting for me to do something extraordinary while a door to the Deep stares at us day and night, and Malik, who has gone to meet our supposed ally, has been gone for far too long. Have I sent him to his death as well?"

"There is no supposing. Ysabet will help us."

Navi let out a tired laugh and rubbed her eyes, willing her tears to dry.

"You trust me, don't you?" Hob said gently.

"That you have told me what you think is true? Yes, I trust that. But a woman I've never met?" Navi stared bleakly at her list of names. "I have failed Eliana."

"We've done nothing yet. You have not had the opportunity to fail her."

Navi made a soft, frustrated sound. "And that inaction could be the thing that kills her, the thing that kills us all. Or maybe..." She sighed, wiped her face once more. She had never sweated so much in her life. "Maybe it's arrogant, even idiotic, to think that whatever I could do would be of any help to her."

"You'll drive yourself mad thinking *coulds* and *maybes*."

Navi knew he was right. And yet, the world shrank around her even as it expanded. She felt the truth of her own smallness, the enormity of the world, how much pain and sorrow it contained.

She rose, rolling her shoulders. A walk might clear her mind, even if it meant facing the flies.

Then the lamps outside the tent, dotting the camp like dim fireflies, went out one by one. Muted, startled cries arose from the night.

Hob stood swiftly, blew out their own lamp, drew his sword, and roused Miro. Navi bent to retrieve her revolver, a crude thing they'd bought in Morsia's underground market. She was grateful to Hob for dousing their light; already, her eyes had begun to adjust.

A voice called out from the center of camp. "You who claim this camp.

You who calls herself Jatana. If you want the man Rovan to live, you will empty your hands of whatever weapons you carry and come forward at once."

Navi stood at the tent flap, her heart pounding. Jatana and Rovan: her false name and Malik's.

Whoever these people were, they had her brother.

Navi dropped her revolver into the mud, ignored Hob's whispered warning, and stepped outside.

Immediately, someone grabbed her and roughly shoved a sack over her head. She kicked out and hit a shin, shoved her elbow into something fleshy, but then hands seized her arms, and Navi could no longer stand. The sack, she realized, swaying, had been soaked with a sharp, foul-smelling substance meant to knock her out.

She growled in frustration, heard Hob bolt out after her. Through the sack's woven fabric, she saw a distant pinprick of bruised blue light—the fissure's eye, lidless and staring, watching her struggle without remorse.

Then she saw no more.

—◇—

Navi awoke to a fresh breeze. Sunlight kissed her arms and neck.

She no longer wore a sack over her head. Instead, a rag had been tied tightly around her eyes, leaving her nose and mouth free to breathe the salty air. She shifted on her hard seat; her hands were bound with cloth. It occurred to her that the world was rocking.

A gruff voice sounded overhead. "She's awake."

Another voice, sharp and authoritative, said, "Let me see her."

The blindfold removed, Navi squinted in the bright light, and after a moment, she saw that she was sitting in a small, narrow boat. Across from her on a low bench sat someone wrapped in earth-colored shawls—some with beaded fringe, others hemmed in pink silk, all of which obscured the person's true shape and size. A dark scarf covered their head, hiding scalp and hair, and over their face they wore an oval mask fashioned of small metal plates bound together by links of chain. Slits marked the nose and mouth.

Quick glances left and right showed Navi that other boats floated nearby, three figures in each. One person sat to work the oars. The two others stood, spears in hand, all of them trained on Navi.

The masked person spoke in a low, rich voice. "You are Jatana of Meridian."

Navi stared evenly at the mask. "I am."

"Why are you here?"

"You took me from my camp and brought me here."

The mask was silent for a long moment. "You come to the Vespers in hopes of meeting Ysabet of Red Crown. You want soldiers. You want weapons. You want to hurt the Empire."

Navi said nothing.

"Fourteen years ago, the Empire claimed the Vespers in the name of His Holy Majesty the Emperor of the Undying," the mask continued. "Those who would work against him are considered traitors to the Empire. We, his humble servants, are tasked with bringing traitors to the capital for judgment. But we are perfectly capable of performing executions ourselves."

Sweat rolled down Navi's back. The breeze did little to temper the scorching sun. She realized she hadn't seen Malik in either of the other boats, nor the two people who'd gone with him to meet with Ysabet. She wondered if they were now dead at the bottom of the sea and if she would soon join them. She held her tongue, resisting the urge to lean over the side of the boat and search the water for her brother.

"What would you say," the mask continued, "if I asked you to declare your loyalty to the Empire or else lose your life at the hands of my guards?"

The soldiers raised their spears, their bodies tensing as if ready to throw.

As the boat bobbed with the waves, Navi imagined the cool, blue world of the ocean floor. It would not be such a terrible place to rest.

And if she was going to die, she would do so with love for Eliana on her lips.

"I would say that the Queen's light guides me," she replied, looking steadily at the mask's unreadable plated face, "and that her fire will burn the Empire to the ground."

And then, remarkably, the masked person said, "Excellent."

They whipped out a dagger from under their clothes and leapt at Navi. Pounced on her, pinned her to her seat, and held the dagger's blade hard against her throat.

Navi froze, fighting the urge to struggle. Through the gaps in the plated mask, brown eyes met hers.

For a long moment, that bright gaze searched her face. Then the masked person relaxed, stood, returned their dagger to its sheath. Navi caught a glimpse of the iridescent copper blade—the same metal as that of the box inside which Zahra had been trapped.

Navi felt a bitter pang of longing. What she wouldn't have given to hear the wraith's voice suddenly drift down from the sky.

The masked person called out a command in a Vesperian dialect Navi did not know. The soldiers in the nearby boats relaxed, lowering their spears. The rowers resumed their work, pushing the boats toward a small black island on the horizon.

Navi's attacker untied their mask and unwrapped the scarf from their head, revealing a slim, ruddy-faced young woman, her skin marked with freckles and one rather large white scar. She shook out her shaggy, chin-length hair, bleached white from the sun, and shrugged off her layers of shawls. Beneath it she wore snug brown trousers over slim shapely legs and battered knee-high boots. The collar of her white tunic gaped open to reveal two knotted cords of leather tied around her neck.

"Apologies for the dramatics," she said, gesturing noncommittally with a lazy flick of her hand. "And for the knife. But I don't trust anyone until I've looked them in the eye and held a blightblade to their throat. You understand."

Navi, shocked into speech, said, "I do, actually." Then she paused, wondering. This was a much younger woman than she had been expecting, perhaps only a year or two older than Navi herself. "You are Ysabet?"

Ysabet raised an eyebrow. "And you are Navana, princess of Astavar."

"My name is Jatana." Navi wrinkled her brow, feigning confusion, but her heart lurched with sudden fear. "You know this."

"What I know," said Ysabet, looking out to sea as the island grew larger and nearer, "are the stories I've heard from the north. A princess working in Lord Arkelion's maidensfold as a spy for Red Crown. A death-defying escape. An alliance with the notorious Wolf. Rumors too of a girl with miraculous powers. Some say she is the Sun Queen. A fleet of imperial warships sunk by a freak storm in Karajak Bay. An army of monsters. Astavar invaded at last and fallen. The kings dead, but no royal children found. And now, a girl named Jatana and her brother arrive on my islands, wanting to meet me. Wanting to build an army."

Ysabet paused, then turned to look back over her shoulder.

Navi's chest ached with fresh sorrow, but she held Ysabet's curious gaze and did not flinch.

"We may be scattered, here in the Vespers," Ysabet continued, "and our number much smaller than I would like. Red Crown is weak in these islands, but it still lives, and my crows fly far." Ysabet hesitated. Her voice was hard, but there was something soft to the bow of her mouth. "I know what it is to lose your family, Navana. The unfairness of it. The agony of grief. This is why I fight. You are among friends here. I simply had to see you for myself before I could be sure."

"And my brother?" Navi asked, raising her chin. She would hide her astonishment and her heartbreak. This Red Crown queen would not rattle her. "His companions?"

"*They* are probably resting, like the reasonable people they are. *He* is no doubt pacing lines into my floor as he awaits your arrival. Not sure we'll ever be true friends, he and I. Don't think he'll want to forgive me for frightening you as I've done. Ah, well." She flashed a little grin at Navi. "You and I can be friends instead."

Navi was not sure how to respond, so she chose not to. They sat in silence as their small fleet of boats approached the island that was no longer so distant. As the waves brought them closer, she noticed how comfortably Ysabet sat in the prow, patiently watching the island near.

Then there was a rumble deep in the water. Even the air seemed to tremble. Navi noticed one of the island's black peaks spewing steam.

Ysabet caught her staring. Her lips quirked. "Not to worry, princess. Raratari is not set to erupt for another three months. I have two Saterketa scholars in my employ, and they have never been wrong in their readings of the earth."

"Hopefully this will not be their first mistake," Navi said, irritated that her alarm was so obvious.

Ysabet laughed, then stood in the prow and called out commands to the other boats. They passed through a wide mouth of rock and into a black cove, and Navi's jaw dropped, for the cliffs ahead of them began to open—two massive doors tugged apart by some hidden mechanism Navi's mind burned to inspect. The doors moved slowly but quietly for their size. Ingeniously crafted to resemble rock, disguised by grime and vegetation, they opened to reveal an inner hidden cove. And in the water sat an enormous dark ship, half-built. Cannons glinted on its lower decks.

Navi joined Ysabet at the prow, gazing in wonder as they glided past. It was gigantic, easily matching the size of an imperial warship.

"It's beautiful," she whispered.

Ysabet glanced over. "My mother designed it. The last plans she drew before her death, and one of her only possessions my uncle managed to save. I've enhanced her ideas myself. Uncle says I've the same gifts my mother had. An eye for design. A mind for building."

That stirred something in Navi's mind, some distant memory that nagged at her to look closer. She had long ago heard of someone in the Vespers, some figure renowned for shipbuilding. But she dismissed the thought, not allowing herself the distraction. Though she knew very little about sea craft, she appreciated the ship's bold, sleek lines. It radiated efficiency and confidence, and even as it sat there, docked, it seemed to hum with an eagerness to *move*.

"She looks fast," Navi observed.

Ysabet crooked a quizzical smile at her. "You know ships, do you?"

Navi swallowed her slight twinge of embarrassment. Maybe Ysabet's amusement was a good thing. "No," she admitted, "but I like the look of her."

That made Ysabet beam. "Such a short time we've known each other, and already you know just how to make me preen."

Utterly disarmed by the sight of Ysabet's broad grin, Navi fumbled for a witty response—and then heard a shout.

She looked up and cried out in relief, for Malik stood on one of the rope bridges strung along the cove walls. She waved back to him, then clasped her hands at her chest and whispered a soft prayer.

Ysabet watched her carefully. She sat and crossed her arms, leaning back against the prow. "I started building her not knowing what to do with her," she said quietly. "For years I'd been fighting little battles, flitting from island to island and stabbing the Empire here and there like a mosquito. Stealing weapons, raiding their warehouses. Hating myself for not being able to do more. Hating the people of the Vespers for not fighting harder, which was unfair of me, but there it is.

"And then," Ysabet said, leaning forward, elbows on her knees, "I heard of this astonishing girl. The Sun Queen, say those who still pray to the empirium, hoping it will come back. And then I heard of Astavar falling, and I realized we're approaching something. A precipice, maybe. And I could either sit and wait for the world to fall out from under me, or I could do something, even if it was stupid and wild. So I took out my mother's plans after years of keeping them locked away, and I started to build. For what purpose, I did not know. But if I was ever in need of a ship, I would have one. Then I heard about you, and for the first time in ages, I felt something I liked. I felt hopeful again."

Ysabet's brown eyes held a fervent light. "What do you want, princess?" she said quietly. "Why do you fight? If you had an army, what would you do with it?"

They had reached a small pier. The two soldiers in their boat jumped out and tied it off with thick knotted ropes. Navi remained inside, staring at Ysabet with her heart in her throat. Not for weeks had she felt this surge of energy, this willingness to hope. She hardly dared trust it.

"The Sun Queen lives," Navi answered quietly. "She is dear to me, a friend I love with my whole heart. And she needs my help. Had I an army, I would sail to Elysium and fight for her. I would show her she is not alone."

"And would you die for this friend?"

"For her," Navi said, "and for everyone."

One of Ysabet's soldiers reached down to help her up onto the pier. She waved him off, her gaze fixed on Navi.

"This ship, once she's built," she said, "will be able to make the ocean crossing in three weeks. She's got guns, and she's got weapons stores that would make an imperial general salivate."

Navi laughed softly in astonishment. "Three weeks? That's as fast as an imperial warship."

Ysabet grinned. "My mother was good at what she did. I'm even better. But a fast ship is nothing without a mission to guide it."

Navi glanced back at the cannons standing proudly in their docks. She recognized the design. "Those are imperial cannons."

"I like to keep my people busy."

Navi heard the little dip of darkness in her voice, the glint of an inner shield. She held Ysabet's gaze and placed a gentle hand on her arm.

"I have also lost many," she said quietly. "I know what it feels like to know you live because others have died, how the grief sits in you like a stone you cannot dislodge. I have to believe that if they could see us now, they would be proud of our fight and would not regret their part in it."

Eyes bright with tears, Ysabet gave her a wry smile. "A princess, indeed. You have a way with words, Your Highness."

"And you have a ship, while I have a mission."

"And you have an army."

"A small one."

"As is mine." Ysabet clasped Navi's hands and squeezed. "But together, our troops are not as few. Together, they are stronger."

Navi grinned, breathless with rising joy. What a relief, to no longer be so alone. "You'll help us, then?"

"Yes, princess. We'll help each other. I'll push my people until they wish they loved me less so they could allow themselves to hate me. A month, I think, is all we'll need."

Ysabet bent to brush her lips across Navi's knuckles. Then she jumped out of the boat and onto the pier, shouting commands at the soldiers who waited nearby.

And Navi sat for a moment, catching her breath. The warmth of Ysabet's lips lingered on her skin. She folded her hands against her chest and held them there until her thoughts steadied. Malik was coming fast down the pier, his smile bright and broad. Her brother, still alive, and so was she.

Eliana, she prayed, *hold fast to your iron heart. Stay strong. We are coming.*

20

AUDRIC

"*The most remarkable thing has happened. I've met an ice dragon. A godsbeast, a creature of lore made flesh. Her name is Valdís, and she travels with one of the Kammerat, the legendary dragon-speakers—a man named Leevi. He looks to be Audric's age, perhaps a year or two younger than I, and has told me an astonishing story. Leevi and Valdís have escaped a place called the Northern Reach. For long weeks they've been traveling to the High Villmark, where other Kammerat live in secret, guarding their dragon companions. Valdís has been ill, poisoned by angels, and I think Leevi might have killed me when I stumbled upon them, were it not for Valdís, who sensed in me the blood of Grimvald and found strength Leevi says she hasn't shown in months. Tomorrow, we will ride together to the Kammerat. Leevi wants them to help free the others imprisoned in this angelic fortress. He says I, as Borsvall's king, can help convince them. But how can we hope to win a war against beings so cruel and ingenious? I don't know the answer, but I do know this: Tomorrow, sweet saints, I will ride a dragon.*"

—Journal of Ilmaire Lysleva,
dated January, Year 1000 of the Second Age

There she was—Rielle, in some distant Astavari forest, surrounded by ferns and brambles. Damp curls of hair clung to her cheeks and neck, and she sat in a bed of moss, wearing only dark tights and a thin white tunic, her hands and clothes stained with mud.

Audric nearly fell to his knees at the sight, fighting every instinct he possessed not to rush toward her at once. He tried to say her name, but it came out a whisper.

"Audric?" Rielle stared up at him, her cheeks wet with tears, her eyes shadowed and sleepless.

"Yes, I'm here. But not for long." He took a halting step forward. He remembered Ludivine's warning: pushing the boundaries of the mental connection she had reawakened between the three of them, forcing the vision beyond its limits, could cause it to lose its cohesion immediately—or worse, draw Corien's attention.

"He'll find me soon," Ludivine said, behind him and to his left. Through the link of their minds, Audric could feel her trembling with exertion. Waves of longing butted gently against him, and he found it comforting to know that Ludivine was also in agony—to see Rielle, and yet not be able to touch her. A torment that stole away his breath.

"I've been practicing, Rielle," Ludivine said, "growing stronger, working to extend the reach and stealth of my mind, but it still requires…" She paused, and Audric felt the breath of her exhaustion pass through him. "It requires enormous effort, and I have much still to learn."

Rielle watched them in silence. Wherever she was, the light shifted, drawing out a strange gleam in her eyes.

"Darling, are you hurt?" Audric asked, struggling to keep his voice calm. "How are you feeling?" He searched her body for signs of injury and drank in all the things he had missed—the wild dark fall of her hair, the turn of her jaw, the space she occupied in the world. He imagined her warmth, the sweet weight of her body beside him, her head tucked under his. She seemed softer, somehow, even though her shadowed face was worryingly gaunt. Clearly, she was neither sleeping nor eating well.

Suddenly, he could no longer stand there and pretend to be strong. If he didn't touch her—even only this pale, half-real brushing of his mind against hers, buoyed on the river of Ludivine's power—if he did not reach out to her, cup her face in his hands, rest his brow against hers and feel her breathe with him, the ache in his chest would consume him. If he could not protect her, could not help her, he could at least try to reach for her.

He hurried forward, choked out her name, ignoring Ludivine's backward tug of alarm—but Rielle scrambled away from him. As if he would hurt her, as if he had cornered her.

Immediately, Audric stepped back, his stomach pitching with shame.

"I'm sorry," he whispered. He held up his hands. Tears built behind his eyes, but he refused them. "There is no excuse for the things I said to you that night. I understand why you left. Rielle…" But the memory of their wedding night, the bitter echo of what it could have been, was too terrible, too heavy, and it cracked his voice in two. "I am so sorry, my love."

Rielle watched him in silence, her gaze bright and hard. It flickered to Ludivine, then back to him, and then, saying nothing, she rose to her feet and smoothed her hands down the front of her tunic, flattening it against her torso.

Audric nearly laughed with relief to see her standing there, her shoulders square and tense. Because there she was—his beloved, his Rielle—and there were her arms, there was the dip of her throat, the folds of tunic and trousers around her every curve.

He saw the change at once, and at the sight of her rounded stomach, her swollen breasts, he let out a small, strange sound that was neither laugh nor sob.

A smile flickered across Rielle's face. There was a soft light in her eyes, and he rejoiced to see it.

But he could not quite dislodge the sudden fear that jumped into his mind. It was a horrible thing to wonder, a jealousy that deserved no place in this moment.

Was the child his? Or was it Corien's?

He dismissed the thought as soon as it formed. The child was Rielle's, and he would love it with all his heart.

"Oh, Rielle," he breathed, smiling, and his desperate longing to hold her in his arms was a spear through his chest. "How are you feeling? Are you seeing a healer? I know you must be frightened and worried. The prophecy—"

"I saw that," she said, her distant voice thistle-sharp. "I saw your face." She let her arms fall, her hands in fists and her eyes snapping with fury. "*That's* the first thing you think after all this time apart? Whether or not the child is yours."

Audric's heart sank. "No, Rielle, that doesn't matter to me. The first thing I thought was how relieved I am to see you unhurt."

"Liar," she said coldly. Her gaze sparked an angry gold. "Rest assured, Audric—*you* were the one who did this to me. All of this."

A violent force sliced the moment in two, falling between them like the drop of an ax.

Audric staggered back and collapsed, his head and shoulders forced to the floor, and by the time he was able to move again, the wood had disappeared, and so had Rielle.

He was in his apartment in the palace of Queen Bazati and Queen Fozeyah, and apart from Ludivine, he was alone.

His vision spinning, despair sewing his throat shut, Audric pressed his brow and fists into the soft rug. Vaguely, he heard Ludivine moving, and he looked up as she settled beside him, her face sweating and pale. Beyond her, the open windows framed a calm sea, the sun cheerfully lighting the water, the city, the ravaged beach. Darkness brewed at the horizon kissing the open sea, painting the sky a buttery slate blue.

"He found her," Ludivine said, gently touching his knee. "I'm sorry. There was nothing I could do." She drew in a shaky breath. "He is stronger than he has ever been."

Audric said nothing. He found the edge of the rug, where Rielle's image had been moments before. He pressed his palms against it, hopelessly seeking the warm echo of her body.

After a long moment, Ludivine said softly, "The child *is* yours, Audric."

"I wasn't lying when I said it doesn't matter to me." The words were ash in his mouth and came too late. "She'll be terrified regardless, and she'll hate it and love it too, and that I can't help her through this is a great unkindness dealt to us both. One I deserve but she does not."

"I should tell you that Rielle knew before your wedding, as did I."

Audric laughed bitterly. It was agony to imagine a world in which he and Rielle would be able to celebrate and worry together. He would dote on her, provide her with anything she desired. She would have everyone in Âme de la Terre fussing over her—or no one, if she preferred it.

"You knew a piece of information that was important for me to know," he said, "and yet you kept it from me? Astonishing. Unprecedented."

Ludivine was quiet. "She told me not to tell you. I could not ignore that."

"If I'd known..."

He stopped himself, looked away.

"If you'd known," Ludivine said, "you would have treated her more kindly in the gardens? You would have stopped to think? You would have shown your child mercy and understanding that you did not grant your wife?"

Audric stared at the floor until he recovered his voice, then glared at Ludivine. His blood was a quiet drum of anger.

"If I'd known," Audric said tightly, "we would have had this joyful thing between us, a light to illuminate the darkness of that day. An anchor to help us weather its storms. You're not wrong to accuse me of rashness, of foolishness, even of unkindness. But I am not alone in my mistakes. And none of that absolves you."

Ludivine met his eyes for a long moment. The feeling of her own shame rose to meet his.

"Absolution," she said at last, "is something I neither seek nor deserve."

"On that, we can agree," he said, which was perhaps unfair, but he could feel himself slipping back into the quiet black depths that had ruled his life for those first long weeks in Mazabat, and the hopelessness of that feeling, the inevitable weight of it, acted upon him like a drug, plying his tongue.

He rose, gathering the shreds of his voice, and sent her a silent dismissal.

"Thank you for your help," he said aloud. "It was a gift to see her face again."

Ludivine hesitated, then gently opened up all her love to him before leaving him to his solitude and the escape of sleep.

◆◇◆

Not two hours later, Audric awoke to the feeling of rain on his face.

Audric, hurry, came Ludivine's urgent voice. *They need you.*

The doors to his apartment burst open. Evyline rushed in with the rest of the Sun Guard.

"My king, we must move quickly," Evyline said, her gaze darting to the windows.

Audric sat up and wiped his face. Atheria stood near the bed, shaking out her wings and mane. She pawed the rug, nostrils flaring.

Audric, glancing past her, immediately saw why.

He hurried to the windows, beyond which the world was dark, the tide high and furious. Huge churning waves spilled across the shore. Trees shook at a slant in the roaring wind. Even the castle seemed to sway. The sky swirled black with clouds, illuminated by jagged fans of lightning. Bells from the city's seven temples chimed, faint through the howling storm.

Quickly, he found his clothes, threw on his jacket, pulled on his boots.

"Are they evacuating the city?" he asked.

"Yes, my king," Evyline replied. "But there is much confusion, and many of the roadways are already flooded. They have seen hurricanes before, my king, especially in recent months, but have always had adequate time to prepare."

Audric found Illumenor beside his bed. When his hand closed around the hilt, the familiar tremor of power flew from palm to shoulder. "Why did no one wake me sooner?"

"It came upon us in minutes, my king. Ten minutes ago, it was a clear day, the clouds distant."

An ill feeling brewed in Audric's chest. This was the Gate's doing. "It is no ordinary storm, then."

"I had wondered, my king," said Evyline gravely.

A wave of screams from outside drew them out onto the terrace, where sheets of rain rippled like black veils. Atheria used her wings to shield them from the worst of it.

Audric squinted through the storm. What had once remained of the damaged beach had disappeared beneath climbing waves that must have surpassed one hundred feet, more whitecap than water. He watched in horror as great piles of wreckage swept out with the tide—bungalows and piers, the lookout towers that dotted the coastline, the market district, an entire neighborhood of apartments. With each wave, another piece of the city fell into the sea.

Ludivine appeared at his side, her expression solemn.

"How many people have died?" Audric asked her.

"Five hundred and two," she said quietly.

"Where is Kamayin? The queens?"

"Organizing their elementals near the water, trying to fend off the worst of it."

Audric turned at once and climbed onto Atheria's back. He reached down to Ludivine, helped her settle behind him.

Evyline lurched forward. "My king, no!"

But Atheria had already pushed off into the wild air, and soon the terrace was far behind them. The chavaile dove through the rain and wind, dodging chunks of debris—uprooted trees, shattered wooden shutters, shards of roof tiles, black sprays of dirt and rock. As they flew, Audric surveyed the devastation below. Churning water surged through the flooded streets, carrying wreckage and drowned animals. The citizens of Quelbani climbed frantically for higher ground.

Atheria brought them to a broad stretch of road that had become the new shoreline, littered with seaweed, shells, and beached fish. Queen Bazati and Queen Fozeyah directed squadrons of elementals. Earthshakers struggled to stabilize the sodden ground. Windsingers, arms in the air, wrangled what wind they could.

And Princess Kamayin, her gown plastered to her body, the castings around her wrists flashing like trapped stars, shouted orders to a band of waterworkers gathered in a triangle. Their efforts subdued a crashing wave, shoving it back toward the sea—but more waves were just behind it, relentless and raging, and though Kamayin's elementals fought valiantly, a helpless panic was writ plain on their faces.

They knew this was not a storm of the natural world.

They knew they might not survive it.

Audric guided Atheria down to land beside the queens, then leapt to the ground and drew Illumenor. The sun was distant, diminished by the storm and the late hour, but Audric nevertheless felt light everywhere around him. The infinite, familiar warmth of it, forever bright beyond the clouds, tugged at his heart like the rhythm of a long-beloved song.

As he focused on the connection between him and the light, on the power speeding faster and faster through his body, Illumenor began to glow. And when it had reached a brilliant shine, Audric released the tension in his body, directed his power outward, and cast broad rays of sunlight in a circle, himself the blazing heart.

He held the light in place, his mind gripping the vibrating reins of his power. The heat turned the rain to steam before it could hit the ground, and while standing within the bounds of Audric's light, the elementals nearest him could wipe their faces and catch their breaths.

As he held his power steady, Audric glanced to his left and noticed Sanya, the soldier who had confronted him in the training yard. She was not, it seemed, an elemental. Instead, she was working with other soldiers to build high piles of debris and canvas bags filled with sand.

"Sanya!" he called out. "Bring me chains, rope—anything that can hold against the wind. The strongest things you can find!"

Sanya, her face screwed up against the lashing rain, leapt to obey, calling others to help her.

Kamayin rushed over, the castings around her wrists still faintly aglow, her soaked brown skin gleaming in Audric's casted light. Beyond her, the queens continued shouting commands.

"What are you planning?" Kamayin cried.

Audric yelled to be heard. "I think I can break apart the storm."

Kamayin's gaze flitted over his sword, his arms. "You're strong enough for that?"

An image flashed into his mind—Rielle riding Atheria out to meet the tidal wave that threatened Borsvall's shores. How brilliantly she had burned against that dark wall of water, a beacon of hope for everyone who saw her.

He held the image close, aching with love. "I can do it. Lu, help them as you can. Focus their minds, boost their confidence."

He expected her to protest, but she simply nodded, her pale eyes grave, locks of gold hair gone dark against her cheeks.

A burst of screams made Kamayin turn and cry out in despair.

Audric glanced back in time to see a massive wave bearing down on a section of beach some thousand yards away. The wave crested with a roar and then crashed down hard, flattening everything in its path.

"Here!" Sanya rushed over along with another soldier. Between them, they carried a length of huge, sand-crusted chain and a coil of sodden rope.

Audric called out to everyone gathered, "I'm going to release the light! Prepare yourselves!"

Elementals and soldiers alike turned back toward the storm, their expressions resolute. The windsingers raised their arms, and Audric felt the air tighten as they focused their power.

Then he released his hold on his own. Illumenor darkened, as did the beach. The rain crashed back down, and the soldiers resumed constructing their wall.

Audric climbed onto Atheria, shouting over the rain and wind, "The chain! Tie it around us! Tight, but not enough to hurt her!"

Sanya and the other soldier, Kamayin, and Ludivine all hurried forward, helping Audric wrap the lengths of chain around his legs and waist and around Atheria's stomach until he was anchored snugly in place between her trembling wings.

Then, reading his intentions, Atheria knelt, looked over at Sanya, and snorted.

Sanya hesitated, clutching the coil of rope in her hands. "My lord...the storm will blow your godsbeast from the sky."

Audric raised his hands, Illumenor gripped between them. "As tight as you can, Sanya. Tighter than you think you should."

Sanya shot him a single worried look, then hurried to obey, wrapping the rope several times around his hands and Illumenor's hilt, so tightly his hands bloomed with pain.

More screams rose from behind him, at the city's edge, but he did not turn back to look.

Ludivine sent him a sharp hot wave of encouragement. *Go, my darling.*

Audric closed his eyes, sending Atheria a silent apology.

"With the dawn I rise," he prayed. "With the day I blaze."

Then he roared, "Fly!" and Atheria pushed hard off the sand and into the air—where the wind immediately knocked them violently to the side. Atheria recovered fast, her wings beating furiously.

The storm was immeasurable, colossal. Wind howled and wailed, pounding against them as the waves below battered the shore. Atheria fought hard to stay aloft, bowing her head against the wind. Feathers were ripped from her wings and went spinning off into the clouds. Her body quaked beneath him, and he knew a lesser creature would already have been decimated.

Ahead of them towered a black wall of clouds, lit with lightning.

Past that, said Ludivine in his mind, *lies the eye of the storm. It is calmer than the rest.*

Audric closed his eyes, forcing past the fear racking his body to focus his thoughts and envision the task ahead. It was a wild theory, one that was very possibly wrong: that a burst of raw power, if it was strong enough, if it struck true, could shift the empirium itself and break apart the storm at its foundations.

Such an act could also kill him. If he threw every scrap of his power at the storm, what would be left of him without it?

But he could not dwell on thoughts of death. Instead, Audric imagined himself and Atheria flying through that thick wall of clouds, then bursting into light and safety on the other side.

And the vision of Rielle stayed with him like a swell of warmth in his heart—she and Atheria, a small starburst of light fighting that raging wall of water in the Northern Sea.

Audric forced open his eyes and saw nothing but furious black clouds. A blast of wind slammed into Atheria, knocking their course askew and sending Audric's stomach down to his toes. But then Atheria pushed herself back up, battling the wind's relentless fists.

A bolt of lightning erupted so close that Audric's head rang with the crackling heat of it. His teeth ached, and his mouth and nose filled with a sour, hot smell that reminded him of the acrid stench that had scorched the air when Rielle had tried and failed to mend the Gate.

His body buzzed with energy that was not his own. It came from the storm, this Gate-made hurricane. It raged against his skin, it burned his lungs, and he began to fear that he had made a terrible mistake, that whatever he could do would not possibly be enough in the face of such godly power. The Gate was made in a time of bloodshed and desperation. This storm's very nature, its lineage, was that of fury.

Shakily, he reached out with his mind. *Lu?*

I'm here, came her steady voice. *And so are you, Lightbringer. Show yourself.*

Audric closed his eyes once more, sucked in a breath, and thrust his hands into the air, Illumenor clutched tightly between them.

Immediately, the wind caught the broad blade and sent them spinning until Atheria righted them and pushed forward with a piercing cry.

Audric, his head reeling as if he had been struck, faced the spitting clouds and began to pray. *With the dawn I rise.*

Memories flooded him: himself as a child, training in the royal gardens with Magister Guillory, every fern and pine of that shadowed green world ornamented with sunbursts he had pulled down from the sky.

With the day I blaze.

His eight-year-old hands, pudgy and sweaty but nevertheless steady in the air, keeping those countless lights suspended and slowly turning. Nearby, watching proudly, his mother and father, arm in arm.

And now, even caught in the thrashing storm, Audric felt the sunlight rising around him, responding to the call of his power. Illumenor blazed in his hands, so bright he could no longer see past it. Its brilliance was his entire world, and it burned its shape into his eyes.

Then a concentrated gust of wind burst to life behind them, pushing them forward into the black wall of clouds.

With the dawn I rise.

He realized, as the Sun Rite raced through his thoughts, that the push of wind had been too precise, too focused, to be natural. And the feeling of it—teeming with hope and gratitude, vibrating with power—confirmed his guess.

The windsingers down below had sent this wind to him. Together, they had mustered up enough power to help him and Atheria make this last desperate push.

With the day I blaze, Audric thought, his hands tingling with power, and when he and Atheria burst through the wall of clouds and into the storm's eye, his relief was so immense that he cried out, and his power erupted with joy. Energy coursed through him, so violent and vivid that he felt certain it would tear him in two. He imagined the full breadth of the storm, sprawling black and angry over the sea, and the infinite layers of the empirium that wove through it like panes of golden glass. They touched the clouds and the lightning, the blade in his hands, the power in his veins. Broad spears of light exploded from Illumenor, and the world blazed white and hot.

In the ringing silence that followed, his vision slowly returned to him, though his head pounded with pain that blacked out half the world. Dimly, he realized that Atheria was flying desperately back to shore. He looked around, blinking darkness from his eyes. The storm had lost cohesion, its clouds scattered and quickly disintegrating. Calm winds rushed past him, cooling his scorched cheeks as Atheria bolted over the water.

He felt a dull ache pounding up his arms and looked down at his hands.

Illumenor's hilt glistened with blood. His palms screamed with a blistering agony so ferocious it stabbed his teeth.

Ludivine reached for him, the gentle wash of her tenderness muting all sensation. Soon, he could feel no pain.

You can let go, Audric, she told him. *They're safe.*

He did, letting his arms drop. Swaying on Atheria's back, woozy, he watched firewheels of color spin before his eyes. He wondered if he was dying, if he would ever see Rielle again, and what she would think when she learned what he had done. Then he collapsed against Atheria's neck.

◆◇◆

Gently, at the sound of a familiar voice calling his name, Audric began to stir, and he only let himself rise to wakefulness because the voice was Rielle's.

He followed it skyward, pushing through the painful weight that pressed against him, this pressure that wanted to bury him. An immensity of exhaustion.

Then he saw her—his love, his Rielle, dressed in white, her hair loose and her face shining with love. She reached for him; she bid him climb.

But when Audric opened his eyes, her name on his lips, the vision vanished. It was only Ludivine looking down at him. She sat beside him on the bed, her eyes shining with tears.

"I'm sorry," she whispered. "I had to wake you. I couldn't wait any longer to see your eyes again."

Audric turned away from her. Tears rolled down his cheeks.

Ludivine came around the bed to sit beside him. Gently cradling one of his bandaged hands, she raised his wrist to her lips and kissed it.

"You did it," she whispered. "The storm broke. Your power shattered it. You *unmade* it, Lightbringer. The sea is calm. You saved the city."

Audric breathed until his grief loosened its black hold. A question came to him, even as his heart still ached.

Ludivine smiled softly, reading his question. "Yes. *Yes*, Audric. They all saw you do it. They watched Atheria fly. It was like nothing they had ever seen. They stood on the beach, and the elementals felt it the moment your power erupted. The shock of it sang through their bodies and sent their own power blazing. They told the soldiers, and the soldiers told the people, and now the city speaks of you and the saints in the same breath." She touched his face, and he was so tired that he forgot to be angry with her and pressed his cheek into her palm.

Ludivine trembled as she kissed his brow. "Now, come. They're waiting for you."

"Who?"

"*Everyone*."

A small hope sparked inside him, drawing him to his feet. He allowed Ludivine to help him dress. All the while, he gazed at his hands, then sent her a silent inquiry.

"They will heal," she replied gently. "The queen's personal physicians treated you. They are enormously skilled, and say the empirium seems to be aiding their own treatment. They say that within a week you will be able to take off the bandages. Within two, you will hold Illumenor once more."

He nodded, wobbly and cotton-mouthed. He leaned hard against Ludivine as they proceeded downstairs, Evyline and the Sun Guard just behind them. When they reached the Senate hall, Audric pulled gently away from Ludivine, ready to walk on his own.

But then the doors opened, and Audric stared, his pulse rising fast, for not only had the entire Senate gathered—all two hundred members, robed in the colors of their districts—but so had their aides, their advisers, the Magisterial Council. Hundreds of soldiers and civilians. As he passed General Rakallo, she placed her hand on her chest and bowed low. They were *all* bowing. They sank to their knees, touched their lips, chests, and foreheads in prayer.

On the room's central dais, the queens rose from their seats. Princess Kamayin, beaming, came forward and pinned to Audric's lapel a blue iris—one of the most prized flowers in Mazabat and the symbol of the crown.

The high speaker of the Senate stepped forward with a scroll in her hands, and Audric listened in weary shock as her voice rang through the hall.

"On the matter of the petition of King Audric Courverie of the nation of Celdaria," said the speaker, "who has requested military aid to invade that country's capital and oust the usurper, Merovec Sauvillier, with the far-reaching objective of establishing a base of defense against potential angelic invaders, the Senate has decided to reconsider our previous decision. We have taken into consideration the counsel of our queens, the holy magisters, and the Mazabatian people, whose voices have bestowed upon us our seats of power."

The high speaker glanced up at Audric, her face unreadable. "We have also considered recent events, including the hurricane that nearly destroyed our capital and the actions of the Celdarian king in that moment of crisis—actions that could have cost him his life."

She paused. "Our final vote is unanimous. We hereby move that the Celdarian petition be revisited and accepted and that the crown approve the king's request for military aid—first for the purpose of reclaiming the Celdarian throne, but more importantly, to provide assistance in the war against the angel Corien and any conflicts that may follow thereafter."

Then the high speaker presented her scroll to the queens, rolling it out flat on a stand of polished wood, and at last gave Audric a small smile.

"If you concur with this motion to approve the Celdarian petition, my queens," said the speaker, "your signatures will confirm our vote."

Queen Bazati stepped forward, her head held high, and signed the paper with a flourish. Then Queen Fozeyah added her own name with a broad smile.

Kamayin rushed to Audric and threw her arms around him, and he watched over her shoulder, his head roaring with disbelief, as everyone in the hall rose to their feet and erupted into thunderous applause.

⭢ 21 ⭠

JESSAMYN

"To the white towers of Elysium—to these I pledge my every bone. To the glory that once was and the glory that will be—to this I offer my every sinew. To Him, the Light Undying, I devote every inch of my flesh."

—From the initiation rites of novitiates
to the order of Invictus

Jessamyn ducked Nevia's fighting staff as it cut through the air, then shot back up and met the staff with her own.

Fighting was good. Fighting helped her forget the horrible thing she had done.

For nearly an hour straight, she had been fighting with Nevia in one of the Lyceum's sparring yards. She refused to stop, not even to wipe her face, which was lucky, because Nevia had a reputation for ruthlessness and would not have agreed to rest.

That ruthlessness was why Jessamyn had left Remy in her room in the middle of his lesson, marched into the barracks, and tossed a staff to Nevia, which had made the older woman grin in her wolfish way.

Now they fought, the yard's doors and windows lined with onlookers. Recruits with their own staffs at the ready, eager to jump in should Jessamyn relent. But Jessamyn could not possibly relent.

With each strike, with each blow she delivered and received, she felt some of the wild fear within her diminish, though her mind still spun with the memory of what had happened in Eliana's rooms the day before.

How was it possible that this gaunt, mute, joke of a girl—who had once been a formidable assassin, supposedly, though Jessamyn couldn't imagine that—could have bested her? Jessamyn, student of one of the greatest assassins Invictus had ever employed? Jessamyn, virashta of Varos? She had told herself it was lingering grief over his death that had distracted her. But this was no comfort, for it indicated a softness to which she had long thought herself impervious. A human softness Varos had tried to beat out of her.

Nevia's staff grazed her arm, making Jessamyn grunt and stumble. She regrouped, spun on the thin, flexible sole of her sandal, and smacked Nevia hard on the shoulder, then again on the hip.

And still she could not stop thinking about what would have happened if Eliana had succeeded in killing herself, what the Emperor's punishment would have been.

What his punishment might yet be.

Thinking about it made her sloppy. Nevia spun fast, whacked Jessamyn on the head with her staff, then used it to strike Jessamyn's feet out from under her. She fell hard, knocking her chin against the ground. Stars burst across her vision, and she tasted blood, but the shame was far worse.

Nevia circled her. "I never did understand what Varos saw in you," she said. There was no malice in her voice, simply a bewildered curiosity.

Then a set of doors to Jessamyn's right flew open, and everyone but her—Nevia, the watching trainees—fell simultaneously to the ground.

The Emperor stormed into the yard, a fur-trimmed cloak thrown about his shoulders, and as soon as Jessamyn locked eyes with him, her body stiffened, her bones snapped rigid. She blinked, and the world shifted.

She was alone in the yard. The sky was gray, the buildings of the Lyceum black and windowless. The world vibrated—the air, the Lyceum, the stone underfoot. A child's sketch given furious life.

In this strange, shaded world, the Emperor was glorious—eight feet tall, slender and long-limbed, his face an exquisite configuration of sharp cheekbones and bright, pale eyes, his hair a shifting black cloud. His clothes floated about him in dark whorls. From his back fanned a set of enormous wings—bright where they burst from his shoulders, tipped in shadow.

Jessamyn cried out, her knees buckling. She wanted desperately to look away. He was too beautiful, too brilliant. She should not be looking at him. Her human eyes were too small for it.

But the Emperor held her in place with his mind, forcing her to stare. She felt him slipping into her thoughts like a snake through a crack in stone. Soon she would shatter, the taste of his fury on her lips as metallic and sour as blood.

"You brought knives into her room," he said, his voice jagged and booming.

He was too immense for her. His mind in hers made her head ache and her eyes burn with a searing heat. His fingers were deep in the folds of her thoughts, digging, twisting.

The world flickered, then changed.

Jessamyn watched in horror as Nevia and the others reappeared—though now they were emaciated, wild-eyed. They bashed their heads against the walls until their faces were soaked in blood. They leapt on each other and tore with their teeth, feasting.

Jessamyn choked out, "My lord, please—"

"You have been trained by my finest fighters," the Emperor said, "and yet you were stupid enough to present Eliana with weapons. Your idiocy astounds me."

A crow swooped down from the sky and pounced upon a small song-bird. Jessamyn watched the crow stab the bird's chest, rip at its throat, and shake it. With its great black beak, it tore away chunks of flesh and tufts of feathers.

Jessamyn's heart pounded faster and harder. She was frantic to cover her ears, but she could not move her arms, because she no longer had any. Instead, her wings flapped and fluttered. She was the songbird in the dirt, and the crow pecked at her, broke her ribs, peeled off strips of her flesh. The crow's eyes flashed a brilliant white, as blazing as the Emperor's angelic eyes had once been, and she knew that this darkness, this huge, roaring weight bearing down upon her, clawing at her, was the crow, yes, but also the Emperor, forcing open her mind.

"Forgive me, Your Excellency," Jessamyn managed, her throat in shreds. "I grieve for Varos—"

"Your grief is laughable beside my own," the Emperor replied. He was a shifting column of darkness, hovering over her face as if considering a kiss. She saw his white eyes, wanted to close her own against them, but she had no eyelids. She wanted to scream, but she could not open her lips. When she touched her face, she found that her mouth had disappeared, in its place a flat plane of flesh.

"Tell me," murmured the Emperor, "why did she stop? What did you see?"

Jessamyn stood whole beside her own body. She watched her other self, mouthless and lidless, twitching in the Emperor's grasp.

"She jabbed me in the throat," Jessamyn said, watching calmly. "She pulled a dagger from my belt. She thrust the knife at her stomach, then stopped before the blade could touch her."

"What did she look like in that moment?"

"Her eyes grew hazy." It was fascinating to Jessamyn to see what her body looked like when it was in agony. How her muscles distended, how copiously she wept. "She dropped the knife." Jessamyn paused, remembering. The memory was distorted, as if she were watching it through a veil. "She asked a question. 'Who are you?'"

The world exploded into brilliant white light, the air shrieking at Jessamyn's ears.

At last, blackness.

She opened her eyes, gasping, and stared up at the midday sky. The Emperor was gone. She thought she heard the sound of his boots clipping stone. Nevia and the others roused themselves from the stupor the Emperor had held them in, each of them blinking and disoriented.

And only then did Jessamyn realize how strange it was that the Emperor had asked her what had happened in Eliana's rooms. He seldom left the girl's thoughts, after all. His mind should have shown him the answer.

Which meant that—even though Jessamyn had never imagined it possible for anyone to match the Emperor's strength—something, someone, somehow, was shielding the truth from him.

—◆—

The following evening, Jessamyn strode through the Lyceum toward the library. She felt sharp around the edges, her skin ill-fitting. She had spent the entire day stationed outside Eliana's rooms while the Emperor worked.

It rankled her that listening to the girl's screams could affect her so. She was Invictus, the student of Varos. She had heard worse. She had *done* worse.

And yet, she could not put from her mind what the Emperor had done to her in the fighting yard the day before. It was as if Jessamyn had died on the ground beneath the Emperor's hands and had been reborn a shaky, jumpy version of herself.

A hard knot of fury rose in Jessamyn's throat as she stormed through the Lyceum's shadows. All of this was Eliana's fault. She refused to capitulate, and so the Emperor's temper unraveled.

Jessamyn had heard the whispers at the Lyceum over the past few weeks, fearful and furious: More cruciata were pouring through the Gate every day. The Sunderlands were lost, the Northern Sea choked with beasts. Thousands of angels patrolled the Celdarian and Borsvallic coasts, standing between Elysium and an invasion of monsters, and they used the Emperor's vaecordia to cut down beast after beast from the sky. None had yet made it past the front line to the mainland, angels were losing their stolen human vessels by the dozens, the toxic blood of the cruciata forcing them to abandon their bodies, and the Empire was struggling to supply them with fresh ones quickly enough. Some angels had even themselves succumbed to the beasts' poisonous blood, their intangible, bodiless minds splintered beyond repair.

The front would not hold forever.

Jessamyn scanned the library for Remy, her heart pulsing with an unfamiliar, angry fear she couldn't seem to shake. Her mind felt hot and choked from it. Eliana had the power to seal the Gate and rid the Empire of this problem forever, but she refused to use it. If the Emperor could not break her in time, her inaction would doom them all.

And, Jessamyn thought, it was possible that the Emperor was no longer strong enough or sound enough of mind to crack Eliana's defenses. It had been months since her arrival, and still the little lost princess had not been beaten.

Jessamyn held her breath, waiting for punishment to descend from the skies. Some angel would hear her treasonous thoughts and come for her, drag her to the palace, and let Admiral Ravikant carve her to pieces.

But the library remained dark and quiet. At the far end, a small lamp glowed. A dark-haired figure bent over a book. Remy, studying at his favorite table. Jessamyn blew out a slow breath.

When Varos had been alive, her loyalty had been absolute, her obeisance fervent and unthinking. But now Varos was dead. Jessamyn had witnessed firsthand the Emperor's erratic state of mind. The Lyceum was full of whispers, and monsters were flooding the world.

For the first time, Jessamyn was feeling the slow turnings of doubt. And she hated it. Doubt was weakness; doubt was betrayal.

There was only one thing to do. She needed to push Remy even harder through his training. Present him to the Five and to the Emperor, and then to Eliana. Jessamyn imagined watching the girl's face fall as she realized what had been done to her brother—and with it, her will to fight.

Reassured, Jessamyn shook out her arms as if to shake off dust, then darted into the long dark rows of bookshelves and moved swiftly toward where Remy sat, intending to catch him unawares.

But by the time she arrived at his table, he was gone. The book was still open, the lamp glowing softly.

Jessamyn let out a low curse, grabbed a dagger from her boot, and whirled around, but Remy was not distracted by seditious thoughts and moved faster.

He darted out of the shadows and seized her. Blade against her throat, a sharp jab to her solar plexus. He twisted her arm, nearly succeeded in disarming her.

Nearly.

She recovered quickly, cut him quick and sharp on his bicep.

"You walk too loudly, kaeshana," Remy said. He released her, the edge in his voice glinting silver. "You crashed through the library doors like an animal. Did you think I wouldn't hear?" It was the first time he had spoken since whatever it was the Emperor had done to him two days ago, whatever had made Eliana want to take her own life.

"I felt generous," Jessamyn said. "Thought I'd give you a fighting chance."

Collecting her scattered thoughts, fighting a swell of irritation that he had managed to catch her so completely off guard, she moved around the table to look at him.

In the months since Remy had come to Elysium, he had grown taller. Nearly two inches, she guessed. And now that he had lived in the Lyceum for weeks, he stood straight rather than hunched like a prisoner. The light in his eyes was sharp, focused. He clasped his hands behind his back, waiting for her orders. The deferent student, with his neatly combed dark hair and his long tunic's tidy collar. On his cheek was a fading cut from their sparring session the previous week.

Jessamyn glanced at the book he had been reading, a brown-papered text written in scripted Old Celdarian. It was part of every Invictus trainee's schooling—gaining fluency in the languages of the Old World, the angelic languages, and every modern tongue.

"Are you finished translating?" she asked.

"Nearly," Remy replied.

"Nearly isn't good enough. You should have completed the entire volume by now." Jessamyn slammed the book closed and kicked over his chair. The crash was thunder in the quiet, cavernous room. "We'll go to the training yards. We'll fight until dawn, and then you'll sit here and finish, and you won't eat until you do."

Remy flinched but kept his eyes straight ahead.

"That would be a mistake," he said evenly. Only the barest tremor in his voice betrayed his nerves.

Despite herself, Jessamyn was impressed by his defiance. "Oh?" She came around to look at him, peering close. "Have you gone mad, little virashta? Have my fists beaten your brains out of you at last?"

Remy was quiet for a moment, then dared to look at her. His face was hard, but there was a pity in his eyes that unnerved her.

"Fighting with me until dawn would be a mistake," he told her. His voice cracked, neither boy nor man. "You need rest, and if you go back to the palace without sleep, you may make another mistake and displease the Emperor."

Jessamyn stared at him, speechless.

"I saw what happened in the yard yesterday," Remy said, looking away. "I snuck into one of the attics and watched you fight Nevia. I saw it when he came for you. He was too distracted to realize I was there, I think. I saw the others fall. I saw him attack you."

Remy's mouth twisted; he was biting the inside of his lip, a nervous habit Jessamyn had broken him of their first week together. She should have struck him for it, but she was too shocked to move.

"And I heard what happened to Eliana," he added, his eyes bright. "I heard it was your knife she almost used. Everyone's talking about it."

"Everyone," Jessamyn said, quietly reeling.

"Here at the Lyceum. I notice things, when you're not here. I sneak around and spy, as you've taught me." Then he looked at her again with a ferocity that startled her. "I don't think you should fight me tonight. I think you should rest. I think you'll need to stay sharp."

Jessamyn finally managed a soft laugh. "Such a devoted student you are. I'm touched by your concern. You, who hate me and would probably love to see me executed or exiled by the Council of Five. Thrown out into the tent cities for the refugees to devour."

"It doesn't matter whether I hate you," Remy replied. "You need to stay alive and in the Emperor's favor. And you being alive is good for me."

The library's shadows suddenly felt oppressive, as if they held the weight of many staring eyes. So he had overheard whispers. Her fellow trainees, no doubt, gossiping about her rumored failure. Jessamyn laughed, circling Remy so he would not see her face and how he had shaken her.

Then she whirled around and kicked him in the small of his back, sending him flying forward into the table.

"I need to stay sharp?" she snapped, swallowing the revolting fear curling at the back of her throat. "So do you, little virashta. And if you think you can weasel out of a fight tonight, you are gravely mistaken."

Remy glared at her over his shoulder, wiped the blood from his lip.

Then he launched himself at her, and Jessamyn felt herself relax with her first savage blow to his head. They would fight until *she* decided it was time to rest.

They would fight until Remy remembered his place—and until she remembered hers.

RIELLE

"There are scholars who believe the empirium to be a conscious force, kind and merciful, a gift from a benevolent God. Others believe it to be inherently indifferent to the life it has made. I posit that the empirium and God as some have conceived it are one and the same. It is neither unkind nor particularly benevolent. It simply is—an incomprehensible essence that I, for one, am glad I cannot knowingly touch."

—The Unknowable Essence: An Examination
of the Empirium by Humans Without Elemental Magic,
a collection of essays compiled by Celdarian librarian
Vaillana Morel for the First Guild of Scholars

Raindrops landed on Rielle's cheeks, and she turned up her face to welcome them.

She spread her arms wide, because a terrible heat surrounded her, and in her blood raged an inferno. She was desperate for the cool splash of rain.

But the rain was hot, and when it hit her lips, there was a pungent thickness to it, a red tang. Something coiled tight in her chest, and when she opened her eyes, she saw that the drops wetting her face were not water but blood.

She was standing in a shallow pool of it on a cliff-side overlooking a rocky line of coves. Her memory slowly returning, she recalled that Obritsa had taken her to Meridian's eastern shore in pursuit of the Meridian Obex and Saint Nerida's trident. The wind from the ocean below gusted up into her blood-matted hair. Waves crashed and roared like beasts battling for meat, and the horizon flashed with lightning.

Many storms, Rielle learned, casting her power out across the flat plane of water and reading the words the empirium had etched upon it. A thousand storms rippled out from the Gate and carpeted skies across the world.

Rielle laughed, licking her lips, and braced her palms against the slick ground. The earth rippled at her touch, for her hands were still blazing hot. The humming echo of Saint Nerida's destroyed trident lingered against her skin. A shattered arrow lay at her feet. The Obex had actually tried to shoot her, as if she were some ordinary attacker. How they had screamed just before she unmade them.

Rielle looked over her shoulder and locked eyes with Obritsa. The little traveler, the Kirvayan queen, with her tangled white hair and her light-brown skin gone sallow with the storm. The girl glimmered, gold painting her hands where the empirium lay waiting for her to thread. Gold painting her mind, with all its meticulous control and focus. There was gold in the ocean, and gold in the sky, and a pulsing gold underneath the black rocks and the restless ocean, rising, rising.

"Well?" Rielle rasped, mocking. "Have you anything to say?"

Obritsa's furs were also streaked with blood. Flakes of charred flesh lingered in the air, but she did not flinch away from them.

Instead, she held Rielle's gaze and said, "Have you ever considered killing him?"

Rielle laughed. The hairs stood up on the back of her neck. "Kill him?"

"You could, I think." A flake of ash stuck to Obritsa's eyelashes. She paid it no mind, her face blank as washed stone. "Obviously you can destroy bodies. I think you could destroy him too, if you wanted. Unmake his truest self from the inside out. A mind, a body—they're the same, aren't they? At their deepest level, they are of the empirium, just as everything is."

"Could I kill him?" Rielle tried out the words, but the thought slipped through her mind like a sharp-toothed eel, vicious and elusive. It wriggled its coils inside her, and its eyes were as pale as Corien's in his moonlit bedroom, its plump flesh the sleek obsidian of his hair. She had destroyed that angel Malikel in Patria, though it had been clumsy, unintentional. Could she do the same to Corien, who was so much stronger? Would he even allow her the chance?

Rage flared swiftly inside her. She stalked toward Obritsa and knocked her flat. The girl's head hit a soft spot amidst the rocks, a flat patch of black mud. Rielle saw the angry red-black flare of the pain in her skull and the stars blinking fast across her eyes.

"You will not speak of that, or of him, ever again," Rielle hissed. Only a short hour ago, she had been tired down to her bones. Now, blood all around and her veins sizzling with the violence of destruction, she was reborn.

Obritsa stared up at her, breathless. "I should have stopped you from killing the Obex. You are not yourself. Your eyes are changing so quickly. Gold devouring green."

"Stop me?" Rielle smiled wide. "You could never."

And then she felt a change in the air, this air that obeyed her and was in her and of her, this air that would gather into a bludgeon and crush Obritsa into the earth if Rielle so desired. It shifted and folded, allowing room for three more bodies on this black cliff thrusting out into the sea, and when Rielle looked up, she saw two rings of light snapping closed. Her nostrils stung with the familiar smoky scent of threads, but these did not belong to Obritsa.

They belonged to two marques—a man Rielle knew, and a woman she didn't. The man was tall and blue-eyed, scruffy of face and hair. The woman was tall and lean and pale. The man lowered his glowing hands, his body stiff with tension—and his face, Rielle thought, softening with pity, even as he was so obviously afraid.

"Garver?" Rielle whispered. The sight of him was incongruous and deeply unsettling. She imagined ridding the world of him with one swipe of her arm through the air. She did not want to think of home, of Audric with that jealous question twisting his face, and yet there was Garver, reminding her of it all simply by existing.

Another man stepped past Garver, and this was worse, this was a blow that left Rielle unsteady on her feet and shaking with anger that he would have come after her, that he could have found her here. He was shaggier than he had ever been, and thinner, his tangled blond hair gathered in a messy knot.

Tal. Her heart constricted around the word.

He was hurrying toward her, his face alight with joyous relief, and all at once, Rielle realized what he would see—her, spattered with blood, her hands pinning Obritsa to the dirt. A ruin of ash and death encircling them.

The last time he had seen her had been on her wedding night. She had been a gilded creature, trussed up in lace and velvet, stupid and happy, and she had still been slender then, her belly and face not so plump as they were now.

"Rielle! Oh, sweet saints, thank God you're all right," he said, the words bursting from him. When he reached for her, a bolt of terror cracked through her like lightning.

"Get away from me," she snarled, not releasing her hold on Obritsa. The girl would run; the strange little alliance between them had doubtless been shattered the moment Rielle attacked her. Without her, if Rielle couldn't snatch Garver or his friend before they threaded themselves to safety, she would be stranded here on this awful, storm-bitten coast, and it would take Corien months to retrieve her.

Tal startled to a stop, the joy falling from his face. His gaze flitted across the cliff-side, the blood-sprayed rocks.

Their eyes met. "Rielle, it's all right," he said, as if placating a child. "I understand what happened here."

She laughed. As if, with his simple mind and unexceptional talents, he could understand anything of what she felt or what she was.

He approached her, hands raised. "You don't have to be ashamed. You're destroying the saints' castings, aren't you? You've chosen not to open the Gate." There was a small smile on his lips. "I knew you wouldn't help him. I knew you would come to your senses. You were angry and afraid. I understand that."

"Come to my senses?" She glared up at him through her lashes. The world pulsed in shades of amber and bronze. "You know nothing of my mind, and you never could."

"But I want to, Rielle." He slowly knelt, so their eyes were level. "I want to know what you see. I want to understand everything that hurts you."

Between them, Obritsa struggled in Rielle's grip, her breathing fast and thin.

"You can't." A great frustration reared up in Rielle. Tal's ignorance disgusted her. "My might is beyond the reach of any man who lives."

"Maybe, if you come home with me—"

"Home?" A tiny laugh escaped her. She drew in a shuddering breath, which pulled tears from her eyes. Her voice was a mere quaver. "I have no home."

"Yes, you do." Tal's voice held an immense gentleness, and she couldn't bear it, that he would dare to be gentle when she felt so brittle, so sticky with blood.

"Get away from me, Tal. You've said you love me. Show me that, and obey my wishes."

"Your home is in Âme de la Terre," he said, undeterred, "with me, and Audric, and Ludivine. Queen Genoveve, Sloane, Miren." Tal glanced over his shoulder, where Garver stood grimly. "Your friend Garver Randell and his little boy."

Rielle felt the moment Corien took hold of Obritsa's mind. The girl's body slackened under her hands, and with relief Rielle scrambled away from her, left her sprawled. Garver started toward Obritsa immediately, but Rielle flung out her arm and shoved him back into the tangled brush, far from the cliff's edge. The pale woman, his companion, ran after him with a sharp cry.

Tal tensed. "Rielle, please. Come home with me. You don't have to run anymore."

"And what shall I do, when I go home with you?" She crouched in the dirt, her smile turning vicious. "Shall I parade through the streets, greeting my many admirers? Shall I compose a song to accompany the curses they will throw at me? Tell me, Tal, what rhymes with Kingsbane?"

"Rielle. It won't be like that."

"You're lying to me." She shook her head, harsh laughter rising, and touched her aching temple. "Everyone's always *lying* to me. Audric said he didn't care, that it didn't matter, but it does. He can't hide that from me."

"If you come home, if you tell everyone what happened, they'll understand. They will accept you."

"They hate me," she whispered, "and they always will, and you know it."

Tal opened his arms to her, and his face was so soft, so open with love, that Rielle, tired as she was, her head pulsing with pain and her mouth sour with death, let him come. He held her against his chest, his hand gingerly cupping her head. He pressed his mouth against her hair, heedless of the blood.

And for a moment, Rielle closed her eyes and allowed it.

But then Tal began to speak.

"You were confused," he said softly. "He slipped into your head and tricked you. I understand."

Rielle pushed him away and scrambled to her feet. Her eyes blurred with tears, and she hated that he would see them and think her in need of comfort. She pulled the tears into her palms, turned them to fire, and threw them to the ground, where they stuck and grew.

Tal watched the flames in wonder. The shield strapped to his back seemed pathetic beside them, a toy fit for a child.

"I was not tricked," Rielle spat, clear-eyed. "I wanted to leave. I wanted him. He isn't afraid of me. He adores what I can do, and he wants me to do more."

He stared up at her from the rocks, stricken. "Of course he does! He wants to use you!"

"He wants us to work together, as one."

"And what lies at the end of that work? Everything you love will be destroyed. Everything you know, gone."

"If I decide to spare anyone, he will allow it."

"Listen to yourself!"

"He loves me, Tal."

"So do we." He stood, his shield sparking as his anger rose. "We love you, Rielle, and will not ask of you any bloodshed."

"What if I want bloodshed? Will you still love me then?"

He hesitated, and that was enough.

Rielle stepped back from him. "I see it on your face. What I am terrifies you. It revolts you."

"No, love—"

"A shadowed life, hiding away in soft rooms, praying for calm, appearing only to water dying crops or cool a hot summer wind, is not a life I want. I would die in that life, no matter how much love you claim would surround me."

There was something happening to Tal's face, a shrinking. His muscles drew tight and thin, and his eyes shone with sadness.

"Rielle, that's not what your life would be," he said. "You would live under everyone's protection. We would slowly reintroduce you to the people, bring petitioners to court to ask questions, voice their concerns."

"And until it was safe for me to walk freely again, would I sit docile by Audric's side, our child in my arms? A devoted wife and queen, silent with shame? Begging for pardon? Trying to persuade everyone who looked at me with disgust that it wasn't an angel's child in my arms? Would I have to present her to the magisters every month to prove no marks of black wings had formed on her back?"

"No—my God, no, that's not what would happen. I swear to you, Rielle. It would take time, but—"

"Stop *lying* to me!"

Tal's knees buckled. Rielle watched him fall, her body drawn tight with anger. She saw the places where he hurt—his skull, his chest, his stomach. Dark wounds from the grip of her power. His light was so pale, so ordinary. The empirium within him was a mere pallid sheen. She marveled that she had never noticed it before.

"You know there is nothing left for me there," she whispered. "Perhaps there never was."

"Your family is there," Tal gasped, reaching for her. "Your friends, your teachers. Whatever Corien has made you believe, you are not a monster whose only power is destruction. You are *loved*, Rielle."

"You lie!" She flung her arms at him, her palms rigid with anger. He tried to stand, and she shoved him back down. He pushed uselessly at the air and clawed at his throat. His eyes were bulging; his veins stood out like cracks.

"I would have died for you," he gasped, twitching on the ground. A terrible black sound spilled from him, raw in its grief, and Rielle saw the flash of power in his eyes just before he let out a strained roar. He wrenched his arm behind him, fighting her grip so hard that he snapped bone, and then, his face white with pain, he seized his shield.

It blossomed, a wreath of flame. Rielle saw Garver huddling in the brush some yards away, the pale woman helping him sit. A small flame flickered in Garver's hands—a crudely constructed torch. At his feet was a tattered bag of supplies.

Rielle faced the fire Tal threw at her, and for a single crystalline moment, her eyes were infinite and pitiless. Thousands of tiny bindings shivered before her, millions of spinning empirium stars, all waiting for her command. Inside her, a hundred doors swung open on their hinges.

It was easy to turn the fire back toward its shield. Tal let out a choked cry, swiftly silenced.

She ensured it was a fast burn.

Even monsters were not always without mercy.

◆

Hours later, a whisper lifted Rielle to her feet.

She licked her lips and tasted ashes, then saw Corien standing on the cliff's edge. She felt him sifting carefully through her mind. A stag edging into a meadow after a storm. He was afraid she would run again.

She laughed, a faint burst of air. "I have nowhere to run to now," she whispered. She touched her wet cloak, and her fingers came away black with ruin.

And you don't have to, Corien said, the vision of himself offering an embrace. She pressed her cheek against his chest, seeking the idea of warmth he sent gently through her mind, but even that brought her little comfort. She was numb to it. Her fingers tingled with fire. She stared blankly at the fading gold spot on the ground where Tal had once been.

Such a lonesome feeling it was, to understand the full truth of her own grotesque impossibility—and a perverse relief to understand, at last, with Tal's ashes striping her furs, that she could never go home.

Corien held her, murmuring things she did not hear, but then another voice spoke to her, a cold clarion call, and she turned her face to the northeast, listening.

Corien's vision-self watched uncertainly as she pushed past him to the cliff's very edge. *What do you hear?*

She thought of how to explain it to him—how the voice belonged to the boundless thing stirring inside her, and how much more clearly she could understand it now that her eyes had been opened by the burn of Tal's fire. For years, this thing inside her had been awakening, and now, at last, it stretched its limbs, opened its wide, dark mouth.

She remembered the black-gold sea that had taken her after she killed the Obex in Patria. And now it returned, lapping against her, and she was not afraid of it. It lived in her veins, and she welcomed its endless will. How it pulled at her, nibbled at her. Both feeding her and hungering for her.

Turning, she faced Corien. At his feet was Obritsa, lying flat and still. The brush beyond her was empty. Garver and his companion had fled, Rielle supposed, or perhaps she had killed them too. Imagining it, she felt nothing.

Rielle, tell me what you're thinking, Corien insisted, worry coloring his voice.

"I must go to the Gate." Her mouth moved, and she was there inside her own body, and she was everywhere, spilling across the world on the backs of storms. She was herself, and she was the hungry black sea inside her, and she was the ocean bashing against the rocks below. She laughed. The

Gate. Of course. "It is the only thing left to me," she whispered. "I have made my choice. Now there is only this. Me, and my power, and the things I command it to do."

And me, Corien added quietly.

Rielle ignored him. She looked out over the waves and saw nothing but infinite layers of gold. A sea of stars, shaping the world. They blinded her, but she could not tear away her gaze.

"It calls me," she said, "and I must answer."

Corien nodded and disappeared. The next instant, Obritsa sat up, her eyes glazed, Rielle's fingerprints stamping her throat. Though Rielle could see the girl struggling to resist Corien's commands, she nevertheless raised her hands, summoned threads, wove them into a circle. Rielle walked through them to a wet black island in the middle of the ocean. The wind knocked her to her knees.

Don't be afraid, Corien said, his voice a rope of love, guiding her. She clung to it. *I'm here with you. I've been coming for you for weeks now. I'll meet you there, my beauty.*

Rielle hardly heard him. Obritsa followed her through the threads to the black island and then began again. Her haggard face was frozen in concentration, her eyes Corien-fuzzed.

Another ring of light. Rielle passed through it, and then Corien sent a map of the Great Ocean into her mind, a long chain of meticulously drawn islands that took a scattershot path across the waves.

I don't need that, she told him, for her own map was more accurate. As they traveled, the empirium rippled black-gold against her ribs, and she laughed, and she wept with fear and longing, for she had never felt it so pronounced, so eager. Not even when her shadow-dragon had licked the Archon's face. Not even hours before, when she had killed the Obex in Meridian. Tal's face appeared in her mind, anguished and full of love, but the empirium rose up and swallowed it.

Another island in the Northern Sea. At her right, Celdaria's coast stretched like a distant dark ribbon. Seeing it, she felt nothing.

The next ring of light brought her to Iastra, the largest island of the Sunderlands, and the huge square plinth of stone upon which stood the Gate.

Obritsa fell to her knees, her face pinched with pain. Corien had released her. She huddled on the ground and heaved.

Rielle stepped over her and walked unhurriedly to the Gate. Arrows flew at her; shouts rose up from the perimeter. The Obex, standing guard, had suspected she was coming. There was the call of a horn and running footsteps across stone.

She raised her arm, silencing them all. It did not amuse her that they would try to stop her. It was simply pitiful. Their bodies dropped behind her, all forty at once.

The Gate towered, a monument of shifting light bordered by stone. Rielle floated toward it, her feet barely touching the ground. The empirium pushed her on, and her own glittering muscles carried her, and it astonished her that months ago she had stood in this very spot. She had looked up at the Gate, the dozens of cracks floating across the surface of its strange light, black and violet and white-blue like flames. That girl had thought herself strong enough to mend this thing the saints had made.

What a fool she had been in so many ways. Thinking of it, Rielle blazed with an anger cold and pure as starfire.

The empirium filled her ears, roaring for her.

I am yours

That she had thought she needed a few humans' flimsy castings—or anything but her bare hands—to make or unmake what she desired seemed ludicrous now. She laughed, giddy with astonishment.

you are mine

Rielle stepped onto the ancient dais and plunged her hands into the Gate.

Power coursed through her, an ageless current that turned her blood blazing hot and shook her bones. She gripped the fabric of the empirium, marveling at how thick it was here at the Gate, how tightly bound, how desperate for release. It rippled like the flank of some great beast. She pushed away from her body, and with each gained inch, lightning burst from the Gate, striking her again and again—her brow, her chest, her hips. Her belly, where her child grew.

Unexpected, the desperate fear that lashed her heart.

Do not let her die, she told the empirium as the Gate burned her, and she thought she felt within its thunderous hunger a reassurance, sent from nowhere and everywhere:

she will rise

A girl, then, as she had guessed. Rielle smiled as she opened the Gate wide, rending asunder all that the saints had spilled so much blood to achieve. She pushed and tore until she stood in the Gate's mouth, her rigid arms outstretched and her head flung back to the skies. Furious tides of power ripped through her every seam and remade them with stitches of gold.

A howl rose above her, as if all the winds had gathered in celebration.

Rielle barely managed to open her eyes, tears streaming down her cheeks. But even blurred, the escaping angels were glorious—a swift cascade of shadow, the echoes of jointed black wings.

They poured from the Gate's light, a river unleashed. Some touched her as they flew, with their minds and their supple cool nothingness. A barrage of frenzied gratitude, of triumphant rage, and Rielle shook as they coursed past her. Images pelted her: The flutter of glossy wings, flares of light joining them to bodies sleek and gleaming as seals. Hair that flowed like silver streams. Towering cities capped with spiraling turrets.

How long she stood there, Rielle could not measure. When at last she fell to her hands and knees, she lay weeping, smiling through her tears. Her body vibrated with a thousand bruises; her skin hissed with fire. And yet she was alive, and her hands were bare, and there was the proof of what she was: to do this monstrous thing, she had needed only her own self.

Corien was frantic when he came for her. Though she felt his pride in her, his dazzling joy at the sight of his freed people, she heard that little hitch in his heart, the fear that betrayed him.

My love, my beauty, he crooned, sending comfort to her. His thoughts cooled her, a false poultice for her burns. He sent her an image: his flesh-and-blood self, his beautiful stolen body, blazing toward her across the Northern Sea on a black ship. He was coming to bring her home.

You did too much, he told her. *Look at you, my glorious one. I'm almost there.*

I am more even than this, she replied, surprised by how her thoughts had deepened and coarsened, accommodating a different voice. She felt Corien startle and wondered through her euphoric haze of pain if on some future day, she would stop speaking altogether. If someday when she opened her mouth, the empirium alone would speak, her own voice consumed and silenced.

✦ 23 ✦

ELIANA

"Saint Ghovan the Fearless forged his casting on the high cliffs of western Ventera during a furious storm. The ocean was a far, wild thing, endless and terrible, and the forging fires were so great they burned his hands, but he held onto the pain, for it reminded him of the thing he was beginning to understand he must do. He had seen the darkness in his father's eyes, the secrets in his father's palace, and so he began to craft secrets of his own."

—*The Book of the Saints*

Eliana dropped to the floor, drenched in sweat.

She lay flat on the carpet and gulped down ragged breaths. Her head pounded along the searing paths where Corien had just been, a swift, booming drum of pain.

He crouched beside her and smoothed the wet hair back from her face.

"Let's try again," he told her kindly. "You were going to kill yourself. Then you stopped. Why?"

It was difficult to find her voice. "I couldn't leave Remy. He wouldn't understand."

"Liar. He would have. He's not so changed that he no longer understands sacrifice for the greater good." Corien's voice twisted with mockery. "Tell me the truth."

Eliana closed her eyes. Her body shook, seized by feverish chills. "I can't," she whispered, which was the truth. Whenever she tried to think about what had happened, a confusion of shadows blocked her way. She reached for her thoughts, ready to arrange them so Corien could see, for if she had to face another day of this—his mind raging through hers, his black gaze relentless as she thrashed in pain on the floor—she would die.

If only he would let her.

But as always, the memories slipped from her grasp.

"I can't tell you," she said again, and forced open her eyes to glare at him. A spark of defiance snapped inside her. She pressed her cold castings against the floor and relished the bite of their chains. "And even if I could, I wouldn't. You can tear at me all you want. You'll never find what you seek, and you'll never see my mother again. She's dead. I'm all you've got now, and I'll fight you until one day you lose your temper and kill me. Then you'll be alone forever."

She smiled, exhausted laughter bubbling in her throat. "An eternity trapped behind black eyes in a gray world full of broken magic you can't touch, eating food you can't taste and drinking wine that turns to ash on your tongue. Wondering every morning if this will be the day that finally tears you out of the body you stole and leaves you stranded, unable to take another. I don't envy you. Poor thing."

Corien watched her for a long moment. The silence filled Eliana with a slowly climbing dread.

"Please don't," she whispered, full of regret. "I didn't mean it."

"You did, you awful bitch," Corien said. "I hope it was satisfying."

Then he came for her again, his will hard and cold as a knife kept sharp for the hunt. It sliced through her skull and everything that lived there. It peeled her back, layer by layer, until she forgot her determination to fight and went rigid with animal screams.

◆

At night, Eliana wept or lay in knots of pain. She sometimes slept, but sleep often brought visions from Corien, indescribable nightmares that left her convinced she had died, that the agony of her mind had at last killed her. Then she would realize she was still alive and feel frantic with despair.

But her guard watched her closely, and Jessamyn—red-eyed, her skin strangely wan, as if she too were finding sleep elusive—no longer carried her knives. They were all careful to present her with nothing she could make into a weapon. She ate every meal with her hands.

Occasionally, a faint whisper of thought brushed against her, and she remembered that a voice had spoken to her kindly, that a gentle mind had stayed her hand that day.

She dismissed it as delusion.

There was nothing kind or gentle left in her world.

—◇—

Awaken, said the voice in Eliana's dreams, *but slowly*.

She walked along a flat gray beach, scattering sheets of sea foam. Carefully she edged into the water until it closed over her head.

Her eyes opened.

She was in her rooms in Corien's palace, but there was a new stillness to them, a thick hush, and with it came a single tentative memory.

Afraid to even think the word in case he should hear, she sent out the question nevertheless: *Prophet?*

I am here, answered the voice, the very same one as before. *We must move quietly, Eliana. I cannot be with you for long. Not yet.*

Eliana lay like a stone in her bed; the damp sheets clung to her. The morning sun drenched the room, suffusing it with heat, but if she moved, he would find her.

Where have you been? Living in Corien's palace, his presence never far from her and her days filled with the tireless wrath of his mind, she now understood well the focus required for mind-speak. *You stopped me from killing myself. You said we had things to do. Then you left me.*

I know. The Prophet's voice was neither masculine nor feminine. Soft but steady, it came to Eliana through layers of heavy silt. She sensed the Prophet was trying to hide. *I am sorry for that. I had to stay away until his anger faded. I knew he would be looking for me after what happened that day.*

Corien's name rose to the top of Eliana's thoughts on a dull wave of fear.

Careful, the Prophet cautioned. *Do not think too closely of him when we speak. You may alert him to my presence if you do. If you must think of him at all, allow your thoughts to slide over the idea of him like water over rocks.*

But it was too late for sliding water. A drum of panic beat against Eliana's ears, and all she could think of was his name. *Corien.* His thoughts squeezing like hard fingers inside her skull. *Corien.* His presence invading her dreams with flashing teeth and hands slick as snakes. *Corien.*

He's coming. The Prophet's voice was already fading. *I'm sorry. I will return, little one.*

Eliana felt the Prophet leave like a needle sliding free of its cushion. When Corien came, it wasn't to hurt her. Silently, he crawled into her bed, wrapped her in his arms as a lover might, curled his body around hers.

He held her for hours, crooning angelic lullabies against her neck. She resisted the urge to break away from him and fought the pull of sleep, thinking instead of a soft-water river flowing quietly across a bed of smooth gray stones. Soon, fuzzy and limp, she hardly noticed the black eyes burrowing into her skull from behind, like nesting beetles plump with eggs.

Awaken, but slowly.

Eliana opened her eyes to see her rooms washed silver with moonlight.

Will you show me your face, angel? It had been twelve days since she had last heard from the Prophet. She had made sure to keep count, a thing she had long ago given up, for each day had seemed an impossible burden.

Now, each moment buzzed with anticipation as she waited for the Prophet to return, and the endless days felt lighter.

Not yet, said the Prophet, voice full of regret. *Let's have a conversation, you and I. How long can we talk before he stirs, I wonder?*

What would you like to talk about? Eliana glanced at the adatrox flanking her door. Jessamyn was not there, but she would come in the morning. *How each day I live on is a torment? How worn thin I have become in body and mind? How far my power feels from me now?*

I already know all of these things, said the Prophet gently. *But if it would help you to tell me, please do.*

Eliana breathed in silence for several minutes. She imagined her little river running soft across its stones.

Every day I imagine ending my life. She let the thought flow along the river's calm current. *You should have let me. You claim to be a friend of humans, but in fact you've doomed us all.*

It feels cruel to beg your patience, but I beg it nevertheless. The Prophet sent a feeling upstream, where it lapped against Eliana's toes. It was too subtle to read clearly, but it warmed Eliana, and she imagined hiding forever inside it.

What am I waiting for? What will we do?

Unfortunately, we must move slowly. We must glide through the water between us and guard against any ripples that might wake the beast lying in the depths. Do you understand?

Eliana settled carefully against her pillows, pretending sleep. *And then? We move slowly, you said. Toward what?*

A beat of silence, and then the Prophet's thoughts darted swift as silver minnows into the cracks of Eliana's mind.

A second chance.

A shiver slipped down Eliana's body. *I don't know what you mean.*

Tell me about home, the Prophet suggested. *About Orline.*

I cannot. It hurts me. Too much death, too much sadness.

But what about the good things? Tell me about Remy. About Harkan. Past the grief, there is light still, even if only in memory. Tell me about that light.

Eliana waited several minutes before she could form a steady thought.

When Remy was very small, she began, *he was terrified of storms. I would wake to find him shivering beside me in my bed. Sometimes not even stories were enough, not even songs. One night we made a tent out of my quilt, strung it across a corner of the room with lengths of twine. Inside it, we piled blankets and pillows, his books, the shells Harkan had gathered for me when his father took him to the sea. It was a fortress, and inside it, no storm could touch us.*

As Eliana spoke, she settled into the embrace of the Prophet's presence. So unlike Corien's—firm, but never invasive. A froth brewing gently at the edges of her mind.

Very good, said the Prophet, once Eliana fell into silence. *Fifteen minutes. He is coming, but this was an excellent beginning. I will return, Eliana, when it's safe. Trust me.*

How can I? Eliana whispered.

But the Prophet had already gone.

—◇—

The days between the Prophet's visits stretched on like dark roads with no end. For weeks, they met in secret, and the carefully hidden memories of their conversations gave Eliana something to hold on to as Corien wrenched apart her thoughts, searching for a thing he could not find, trying to force from her a power she refused to touch.

Forty-five minutes. An hour. Two hours, they managed, and then three, with no interference from Corien and her guards noticing nothing, until finally, one day, the Prophet said, *Good. Now we move.*

—◇—

The first time, Eliana crept from one side of her room to the other, then bathed on her own for the first time since arriving in Elysium. She opened the doors to her rooms, her heart pounding, and peered out into the broad shadowed corridor that ran left to right. Arched white rafters soared over gleaming marble floors lined with pale carpets.

During all of this, the adatrox remained motionless and quiet. Even

Jessamyn seemed oblivious. Eliana stepped outside her rooms, barefoot, and waved her hand before Jessamyn's face. Nothing.

The Prophet guided her to an unused sitting room not far from hers, draped in fineries and hung with gold-framed paintings of angelic glory.

Inside it, shielded by the Prophet's calm presence, her heart a frantic bird in her chest, Eliana reached for her power with deliberate intent—not letting it erupt due to anger, not allowing her fear to overtake her reason and force out her power without her permission. It was the first time she had done so since arriving in Elysium, and her mind felt clumsy as it stretched and fumbled. She concentrated on the familiar lines of her castings, slender and cool around her hands and wrists. She pushed her thoughts out along the stone floor and into the air.

A simple goal: move the air, command it to knock over the golden candlestick standing proud on its table.

Simple, and yet she could not do it. The air remained still. Her power was used to hiding and felt reluctant to emerge from that deep place into which she had shoved it. A faint hum at the back of her mind, a slow tingle along the lines of her palms—nothing more. She looked over her shoulder, mouth dry with fear, expecting Corien to come slamming through the door, but the room remained only their own.

Good, said the Prophet. *Now try again. Never step out of that little river. Keep your feet cool and grounded, even as your hands begin to blaze. He cannot find you here, little one, not in these waters.*

Eliana obeyed, but it was the same. Clumsy and distant, her power. Her hands itched, and there was no way to scratch them.

Quickly, now. Back to your rooms. The Prophet's voice was urgent, but never frightened. As if they could see a hopeful future Eliana could not.

She obeyed, slipping back down the hallway and into her bed. Her blood punched through her veins even as she focused hard on the calm flow of her river. It was a more challenging exercise than anything she had ever done as the Dread—to balance the Eliana who was a prisoner steeped in pain and despair and the new Eliana, who was beginning to dip her

fingers into the pool of her power once more. Its texture and rhythm—
how she had missed it.

How terrified she was to awaken it again.

A film of sweat painted her skin as she settled back in her bed. *What did my guards see while I was gone?*

Your rooms as they should be, the Prophet replied. *You, sleeping fitfully in your bed, as they would expect. Now, though, I must go. Sleep, Eliana. You will need it.*

Wait. What are we working toward? What is it we're going to do? Tell me.

Not yet, the Prophet replied after a moment. *It's not safe yet. You're not strong enough. But you will be.*

—◆—

Occasionally, Corien would visit the Sunderlands, where mammoth mechanized pieces of weaponry called vaecordia kept the cruciata at bay.

Sometimes the palace would erupt in raucous revels that lasted for days. Corien would drag Eliana to them, ply her with food and drink, dance with her beneath a ceiling glittering with buzzing chandeliers until she collapsed dizzily into his arms. He drugged everything she consumed, she knew, hoping some combination of ingredients would draw out her power.

But they never did.

With each new failure, he would rage, and those were the worst days, when he would strap her to a chair and pummel her mind with his or chase her through the palace with horrific illusions that left her feeling mad and violent, her vision black, her ears buzzing as if clogged with angry bees. What she did in those moments, she never knew. She would wake later in her rooms with her throat raw, blood caked under her fingernails, and vague memories of someone begging her for mercy. She would stumble to her bathing room and scrub herself with scalding water as her guards watched, ever vigilant. And Jessamyn too, sharp-eyed and strangely restless in a way Eliana had never seen from her.

Sometimes luck would bend in her favor, and the revels would take place without her, or Corien would shut himself up in his rooms, reaching out to generals across the world or gorging himself in the mezzanine of his concert hall as the harried orchestra played furiously below.

And these were the hours when the Prophet came and Eliana practiced escape.

—◆—

The corridor just outside her rooms, at first, and the little sitting room. Then the stairs at the corridor's northern end. The music room downstairs, where Corien liked to pound away on a massive piano. A ballroom of rose, midnight blue, and ochre. The dormitories where the palace servants slept. The horrible dark gallery full of Rielle's likenesses.

Days passed, and then weeks, and with each journey outside her rooms, Eliana's muscles began to remember their former strength. She had not yet managed to knock over the candlestick, but she had learned much about the massive palace, its twists and turns, and was beginning to feel steadier in body as well as in mind.

Good, said the Prophet. *When the day comes for you to leave this place, you will know how to do it well and will be able to defend yourself.*

Eliana bit her tongue. Dozens of times, she had asked the Prophet the reason for this work, what day they were waiting for, what schemes the Prophet had designed.

But each time, the Prophet refused to answer. *Not yet. Not until you're stronger and I can be sure every new corner of your mind is well shielded from him.*

How am I to know this isn't some demented game? Eliana asked, bristling. *You lead me through the palace night after night; you push me through these exercises of my mind and my power. And for what?*

The Prophet sent her a gentle plea, followed by that fondness Eliana so craved, its warmth sweeter than any wine.

Please, trust me, little one, the Prophet said. *I have deceived many in my life, but not you. Never you.*

And Eliana had no choice but to believe this strange friend whose face she still did not know and hope she wasn't a fool for daring, yet again, to trust someone who lived behind a mask.

◆◇◆

Then, one night, when the Prophet's familiar greeting came, it pulled Eliana from a dream so vivid it followed her into waking.

Like trying to recall a word only just beyond her reach, a tightness bent in her chest, pulling her onward. Her fingers tingled. If she closed her eyes, she could hear a thin black rumble, as from a nearing storm. If she opened her eyes and unfocused them, ripples of gold danced at the edges of her vision.

I know where we'll go tonight, she said, slipping from her bed.

The Prophet's curiosity curled. *Where?*

I saw it in my dream.

Will you tell me?

Look for yourself.

You know I don't like to do that, the Prophet said gently. *Not if I don't have to.*

I'll show you, then.

Tell me first. Please. I must know where we're going. There was a pause. *I don't want to invade your mind, Eliana. I'm not like him.*

I'll tell you if you tell me what it is we're working toward. What plans you have for me. Where you are, and if I can come to you.

The Prophet fell silent.

Eliana smiled grimly as she crept into the corridor, past Jessamyn's frowning figure. *For weeks, we've been working together. My mind is stronger than it's ever been. We can talk without him noticing. You can hide me for, what, five hours now, as I move about the palace?*

That's true, the Prophet said, thoughts carefully blank.

Eliana turned a corner, hurried unseen past a patrolling pair of guards. *You made me drop that knife for a reason, all those weeks ago. I think I deserve to know it. What is the purpose of this work we've been doing? Is it merely a diversion to pass the time?*

Not a diversion.

Then what?

The silence continued.

Eliana darted like a shadow across the palace's second floor, the strange memory of her dream guiding her through a maze of tiled rooms and curtained hallways until she emerged at last into a soft world of green.

It was a vast courtyard, as large as one of Corien's grandest ballrooms. Walls heaped with flowers, vines spilling down iron trellises, bushes painted bright with berries. Rows of red blooms, oiled wooden tables of seedlings growing roots in glass vials. Enormous shivering ferns, glossy-leaved trees heavy with fruit. Eliana looked up at a ceiling of colored glass. Crimson and gold panes. Vents open to let in the nighttime air.

She cradled the nearest red flower in her hands, caught the familiar sweet scent from her rooms. *So this is where he grows these flowers.*

The Prophet felt tense and a little befuddled. *Your dream showed you this?*

Yes, this exactly. Every last detail. And...over here. It showed me this too.

She crawled beneath the seedling tables and disappeared into the courtyard's thick green gloom. It was absurd, what she was doing, as if she were playing a child's game. But a strange tension bloomed in her chest, tugging her on, and she had to follow it or she would burst. A strange vibration rattled her teeth, and she remembered forging her castings, plunging her hands into Remy's wound. This felt the same—the same vitality, the same urgent thread of power growing taut and golden inside her bones.

I think it's the empirium, she thought. *I think it's trying to show me something.*

A slight ripple of alarm from the Prophet. *Why do you say that?*

Eliana pushed past a tangle of vines. She was deep in the courtyard now, a thick silence all around her. Moss soft under her hands and the air green in her lungs.

Then she saw it, the place from her dream—a tiny dark thicket formed of joined ferns and vines, bordered by the roots of a flowering tree with weeping branches and rough black bark. Hardly large enough for her to curl up in, and yet she pushed her way through the wild growth until she sat hunched in the middle of it, shivering.

"The air feels thin here," she whispered, slowly moving her fingers through it. "Like I could push it aside and find something else behind it."

The Prophet had grown very quiet. *Would you like to try?*

Yes, Eliana replied, trembling. Her castings warmed against her skin. *But I don't think I can.*

Maybe something small, first. Something natural. Not a candlestick, but a tree. Can you coax its roots from the earth?

Eliana tried, her skin soon slick with sweat. The roots remained wedged in the black soil, but the air changed, vitalized with a humming hot charge. Eliana reached out with her power, guiding it to hold on to the feeling. The world buzzed with heat, as did her skin, and she felt herself lifting up off the ground to follow the air's new current.

Then she lost her grip and sank back to the dirt, exhausted and cold. Castings dark, head aching.

You're doing so well, little one, said the Prophet, and Eliana clung to the warmth of those words.

They returned to the garden again and again, and each time Eliana crept on her hands and knees into her quiet, dark thicket, she felt a tiny piece of her old strength return to her. It was slow progress, for Corien's punishments continued, even more vicious than before. He could sense the change in her but couldn't discover its source, and he threw his fury at her with his fists and his mind. After these torments, body and mind battered, Eliana moved slowly, and her thoughts were sometimes too scattered to focus properly.

Some nights, she could not move from her bed at all, and the Prophet simply comforted her, whispering words Eliana's sluggish mind couldn't understand, sending the illusion of soft hands on her back.

Once, Corien spent twenty hours straight in her mind, searching through its every crevice for the answer to what was happening, somehow, right beneath his nose. And Eliana lost all sense of pride and self as those jagged spikes of pain split open her skull. She sobbed on the floor, twisting and jerking in Corien's grip, and mired in that black agony, the only word she could summon was *Simon*.

She screamed it over and over, reaching for the door as if he stood just beyond it. If she screamed loudly enough, he would come for her. If she begged him, he would save her.

And then the door did open, and Simon strode toward her, picked her up from the floor, brushed his lips against her forehead. She knew he was not there. Corien's wicked glee carved down her back like an ax's blade. And yet Simon felt so real, so familiar, that she pressed her face against his chest and clung to him.

He brought her to the little bed at Willow, underneath the slanted ceiling. The glowing brazier in the corner, the rain pattering against the windows. Safe in his arms, warm in their bed, she allowed herself a moment to enjoy the lie.

Then she wrenched herself away, kicked him when he reached for her, scooped hot coals from the brazier and flung them at his face.

Blackness, then, and Corien's voice mocking her as she fell.

For days, she tossed in the grip of cackling dreams, and when she next woke, her rooms were hushed.

She sat up, donned one of her nightgowns, walked unsteadily toward the door.

I'm so sorry, little one, the Prophet said, their voice thick with anguish. *If I could take all of this from you, I would.*

I don't need your apologies, Eliana said sharply. *I need you to hide me.*

And in the garden, wrapped in the Prophet's fierce cloak, Eliana cracked open the earth and pulled roots from it with only her power. She reached for the air, used it to push a path clear through the ferns, deeper into the garden. Delving down into the soil, she coaxed up water until it pooled around her in cool gurgling puddles.

Her castings glowed faintly, washing the thicket in pale gold.

He tries to break you, the Prophet said, voice warm with pride, *and he fails utterly. Well done.*

Simon's echo whispered through her hair. Eliana shook it free, set her jaw.

I'd like to try something new, she thought. Ribbons of pale light streamed unbroken through her veins. Her power mirrored the new strength of her mind. They were connected, her mind and her body, and they in turn were connected to the water at her toes, and the roots she tucked back down into the earth so the tree could drink.

She heard the roots guzzle, ripples of the empirium betraying their primal, unthinking appetite, and she understood the feeling.

Her power was ready and coated in steel. It was hungry. And she ached to feed it.

The Prophet was wary. *What will you do? Tell me.*

It's like I said before, Eliana replied. *The world is so thin here. The air feels fragile.*

Her fingers buzzing and hot, her castings like little stars relearning their light, she thrust her hands forward, then pushed them apart, palms out. A wave of energy detonated, but she stopped it, absorbing it with her own flesh and blood so it would not shake the palace.

The Prophet marveled. *Oh, Eliana. Watching you work is a joy I have not felt in an age.*

Eliana only half listened, her hands still buried in the air. Gold veins of the empirium crackled around her fingers. Each grain of light painting the thicket gold whispered to her, and she listened closely, staring at the impossible thing before her.

A shape floated in the air, dark and thin, like the pupil of a cat's eye. Its insides roiled with stormy color—indigo and violet, a blue so brilliant it was nearly white. At once, Eliana felt pulled toward it, as if it were a mouth greedy to swallow her.

She dug in her toes, braced her hands against the earth. In her mind, the Prophet's surprise hummed like a struck bell.

What is this? Eliana asked.

A seam, the Prophet said carefully. *You have opened many across the world without knowing it in those moments when you called upon your power in fear and anger. This, though—look how even it is, how precise. It was your focused will, Eliana, that opened this door.*

Eliana stared at it. Something pulled at her shoulders, beckoning her forward. She searched the darkness, the angry light shifting inside it, and saw a faint vista of low hills, scattered pine woodlands, a sky purple with twilight.

A door to where? she wondered, her heart pounding, and before the Prophet could answer, Eliana's hands flew to the seam. She gripped the edges and pried them open wider until it was possible for her to slip inside.

The Prophet flew into a panic. *Eliana, wait!*

But the empirium had pulled her to this place, and now golden whispers tugged her forward.

here

HERE

come see

they are everywhere

hurry

Before the Prophet could stop her, Eliana held her breath, shut her eyes, and stepped through the fissure into what lay beyond.

Her feet hit solid ground. She opened her eyes and saw gray clouds moving fast across a violet sky. The hills were shallow and rolling, furred in downy green grass, and there was not another living thing in sight. No animals, no people. There was not even wind. Only a quiet that felt unnatural. An eerie, pale light suffused it all, like a dusk tinged with storms. Black clouds edged every horizon, and below her feet, past the green of the grass, shifted a vast darkness, as if the meadow and hills were only a thin veil cloaking something terrible and lightless.

Then a bird called out, and when Eliana looked up to find it, she saw far above her the shifting faint shape of an enormous winged beast. It fluttered past, sending darkness rippling across the sky, and was gone, but another followed in its wake, and then another, and three more, slithering and serpentine, each of them a behemoth.

Eliana stepped back, staring in horror. What she had thought were gray clouds were in fact the shadows of these creatures, swarming from horizon to horizon.

A sickening heat blossomed at her breastbone and flooded her fingers. She ducked low, searching in vain for something to hide beneath. But the unnatural quiet remained, and when Eliana looked back at the sky, she saw that it looked just the same as before. The monstrous shapes were no nearer to her. It was as if she and this strange green world existed within a bubble beyond which writhed gargantuan beasts—but whether they were far away or very near, she could not guess. At least, it seemed, they could not reach her.

She slowly straightened, forcing her breathing to calm. Cold sweat prickled the back of her neck.

Then, a glottal cry split the air, puncturing the eerie quiet. On the horizon, something long and dark and twisting dropped out of the clouds and began to fly. This was no distant gray shape. This was clear and sharp, long-tailed with broad black wings, and approaching fast.

Eliana spun around and ran for the thin vertical slice of lush green marking her path back to Corien's palace. Long minutes passed before she managed to push through it, for a great force was shoving back against her.

But with a last controlled burst of power, she managed it, tumbling out into the garden courtyard. She whirled to grab the seam's edges. Her fingers tingled as if she had plunged them into water hot enough to burn. The seam sucked at her; that place, whatever it was, wanted her back. But she fought its force, wrenched the sizzling edges back together, and used her power to seal shut the fissure. Only a faint glimmer remained in the air, and then it was gone.

Breathless in the dirt, clammy with sweat, Eliana reached for the Prophet. *What was that place? What did I see?*

The Prophet's voice was breathless with relief and wonder.

You saw the cruciata, they replied. *And you were in the Deep.*

-24-

RIELLE

"The home the Kammerat have built is astounding—a thriving city of dragons and dragon-speakers, constructed in high mountain caves and canyons. Below, a lush green valley provides them with food and warmth. They say the saints helped create this haven after the Angelic Wars ended, and that they have lived undisturbed ever since. Until now. It has been difficult, convincing the Kammerat to fly to the Northern Reach and rescue their kindred. Their isolation is sacred to them, even at the expense of their own captured people. They say they will do nothing more in this war beyond that, and I don't blame them. Leevi, however, still thinks he can persuade them. He'll have to persuade me too, I confess. Why leave this sanctuary for a hopeless war? But Leevi is determined, and so beautiful in his hope for victory that it takes my breath away."

—Journal of Ilmaire Lysleva,
dated February, Year 1000 of the Second Age

Rielle woke in the Northern Reach.

As soon as she opened her eyes, she recognized the bedroom she had shared with Corien. Its black stone walls, the thick white furs draped across their bed, the wide wall of windows framing glaciers and a sky of dimming sunlight. Mountains and sea, industry and fire.

Everything that had happened sat at the edge of her mind, a vivid portrait of her own design, and she shivered to look at it. The bitter taste of ash still coated her tongue. In her ears echoed the crash of a dark sea.

Corien sat at her bedside, watching her quietly. He was in his everyday black—vest of brocade, tunic buttoned at his wrists with obsidian, high square collar, cloak fastened at his shoulders with ebony pins.

She pushed herself upright, her body lighting up with pain, and croaked, "Do not harm that girl more than you already have. Obritsa had no choice but to obey me. If you hurt her again, I'll kill you."

"You assume I've done anything to her at all," he said, unblinking.

She laughed, which made her raw throat burn. "You are an unconvincing innocent."

Only then did Rielle notice the three nurses bustling about her, changing the bandages that wrapped around most of her body. Three humans— two women and a man. Had they chosen to serve the angels in exchange for the lives of their loved ones? Their nervous eyes flitted up to her face and then back to their work. Her skin stung where they had slathered it with salves; she was encased in long white strips of cloth.

And still Corien watched her, pale and still, but Rielle did not flinch from him. She had opened the Gate with her bare hands. She was radiant with pride; she was a force unmatched. And she knew, when he looked at her, that he sensed it too: a change between them. A ripple of new tension, the bend of a current changing its course.

The power she had demonstrated was beyond what either of them had expected.

Rielle shoved the nurses away. The sudden, sharp movement left her burns screaming. "Leave us. I can tend myself."

Then she stumbled to her feet and tore the bandages from her skin one by one. At first, the pain was searing, as if she were tearing off strips of her blistered, blackened flesh. But she set her jaw and pushed through the agony to imagine herself whole and smooth, as she had once been. She sent the thoughts up and down her body. Waves of quick power, sculpting.

By the time she removed the last of her bandages, her skin had healed, and all her pain had vanished.

Unabashed before Corien and the gaping nurses, who had frozen at the door to watch her undo all their work, Rielle went to the enormous mirror that leaned against the wall in the room's far corner. Fascinated, she examined her nakedness.

There was a golden sheen to her skin, and the ends of her hair and fingers sparked like a struck anvil. Her irises were twin circling storms of gold, only thin bands of green remaining. Her lips were pale, bitten, and chapped. Shadows stretched long and deep beneath her eyes, and there was a new hollowness to her face, as if something essential in her had been scooped away. She found she did not miss it, even as her head pounded and her bones ached with exhaustion.

Because there was a clarity to her mind that she had never before experienced, a singularity of purpose. She still knew that she had been born in Celdaria, that she had married a man named Audric and killed a teacher named Tal, but when she turned her thoughts that way, trying to recall the details of their faces, what they had felt for her, what she had felt for them, she could remember very little. Only vague swaths of color and sensation. Every memory that had once tormented her had faded into the shadows of her mind.

In their place seethed golden whispers, fervent and full of appetite, crowding out everything but the now. This frozen fortress, the angel watching her from his bed. Her fingers, still buzzing from the Gate. She would feel that violent ageless charge for the rest of her days, she knew. The cold pain in her teeth, the restless hum of the palms that had gripped the fabric of the Gate and pushed it open wide. These would forever be her companions.

Rielle smiled faintly, touched her face in wonder, then turned to the side and inspected the roundness of her swollen belly. The sight evoked a new fondness in her. She cupped her hands around it, felt the warm pulse of her growing child. This child who had survived the Gate. That she ever could have considered ending her life was inconceivable. No one else in the world would ever know what it felt like to be touched by the Gate's power. That the child belonged in part to Audric was a fact that now left her indifferent.

The child was *hers* more than it was anything else, and bound her to no one, not even to Audric.

When Rielle turned back to Corien, she found him staring at her, rapt. She shot a silent glance at the nurses, and they scurried out of the room.

Rielle walked toward her wardrobe. She felt the gleam of her every step. "How many angels did I free?"

"Five hundred thousand," Corien answered quietly.

She slipped on her black velvet dressing gown with the gold sash, the intricate embroidery of wings, flowers, thorns. "So few? You said there were millions in the Deep."

"There are. The Gate has force to it still, even though you battered it soundly. The weaker of my kindred are finding it difficult to escape its pull."

"Perhaps I can eradicate this force," Rielle mused. "Create a safe passage through which the others can travel."

Corien rose and drew her slowly toward the bed. "You can—of that I'm certain. You can do anything, my star, my fire." He found the hollow of her throat and kissed it. "But first we must do something else."

Faintly annoyed, Rielle considered denying him. Half her mind felt far away, imagining the Gate and how best to alter its fabric to allow the other angels passage. But Corien's hands were warm and were doing delicious things to her skin. She smiled, sliding her fingers down his torso. This too was a pleasure she craved.

They would speak of the Gate later.

"Is this what you mean?" she murmured.

"It's been too long, Rielle, since I've been able to touch you."

She shivered at the rough quality of his voice, how close it was to unraveling. She pulled away from him and bid him kneel before her. He grasped her hips, pushed aside the folds of her dressing gown, and buried his face in her thighs with a moan.

"And then I shall begin our great work," Rielle said, weaving her fingers into the glossy black of his hair.

"And then we shall begin our great work," he agreed. Then he put his mouth on her, and Rielle knew nothing but the supple new strength stretching happily inside her, the luminous glow of her skin, the power beneath it rising to meet Corien's lips.

There was a vast underground honeycomb of chambers and halls beneath Corien's fortress. Weapons lockers, stores of grain and wine, the narrow dark rooms in which the servants slept. Dozens of passages led outward to the laboratories, the barracks that housed the adatrox, the pens where the ice-dragons of Borsvall were caged, dissected, poisoned.

At the heart of this grand labyrinth of stone, a ring had been carved into the floor—a great swirling circle of wings. Acres of pillars fanned out from the circle, each tall and thick as a battering ram.

Rielle stood inside the feathered circle. Corien had told her he had engraved it himself when the fortress was first built. No one had stood within it until now. Until her.

It was an altar meant for resurrection.

At Rielle's feet lay a beautiful young man from a rural province of western Kirvaya. He had been stripped naked and trembled on the cold floor. His skin was pale and smooth, his limbs long and healthy. The torchlight flickering around the circle painted him gold. Chosen for his beauty and strength, plucked from his bed by an eager angelic mind, even laid out on the floor like a slab of meat he was exquisite. His name was Tamarkin.

Corien, standing at Rielle's side with his hands clasped behind his back, held the man fast, waiting.

With her eyes, Rielle traced the lines of Tamarkin's body—every muscle, every sinew, every bone. She saw beneath his skin to his pulsing organs, his veins rich with blood. At his foundation, a sea of gold crashed and ebbed, forming everything that he was. Brightest in his mind and at his heart, illuminating the twin webs of his lungs.

She could have looked at him for hours, watching in fascination the pulses of light and energy that were his frantic thoughts, his rapid heartbeat. Only she could see these things, these deep inner workings of body and blood; not even the angels were witness to them.

"Are you ready, my love?" asked Corien gently.

Dreamily, she said, "Almost." She knelt at Tamarkin's side, ran her fingers along the dips of his pelvis, the ridges of his ribs. His skin twitched at her touch. In Corien's grip, mute and terrified, his eyes were wild. He watched her fingers as if fearing claws.

Around them, the chamber pulsed. Tricks of light teemed in the air, but there was a heft to them, and their intelligence pricked at Rielle's mind, deferent but greedy. The air bent to make room for them.

Angels, waiting in throngs. Their energy was that of a herd of beasts in their pen, muscles trembling, flanks sweating.

One of them hovered over Rielle's head. His name was Sarakael, selected on a whim by Corien as the first to be resurrected. Rielle could sense Sarakael's fervor, how he longed to fall before her in ardent worship.

But she hardly noticed him. Though she could sense every watching angel—how their minds slipped through the air, how their whispers rustled and hissed—her attention was entirely on the man lying before her.

She wondered if she should be nervous, but she was not. The chills traveling along her spine were like fingers tapping her awake.

Corien stepped closer. *Now, Rielle?*

She nodded. *Now.*

At once, Corien killed the man. An easy shattering of his mind, and without the mind, all else would fade. There would be agony, he had told her, for an instant, and then a nothingness, a slip into the long dark of death. Rielle watched the light leave Tamarkin's lovely blue eyes.

His empty body waited for her to begin.

The how of it was easy, but she suspected the doing would not be. She had thought it all out. As Corien slept, she had sat in the fur-draped chair by the windows and stared out over the vast ice, designing her method.

And now, she followed her own instructions. Her breath trembled, her body alive with a surging heat that knocked like fists at a door. She reached out with her power and commanded the angel Sarakael to enter the body, then waited while his faint shadow-self sank through every orifice—the slightly open mouth, the nostrils, the ears. She placed her hands around the skull, for this was the most important anchor. Living mind to dead brain. Bright eyes to dull ones.

The trick, she thought, was to work while the empirium was still bright inside the corpse. Tamarkin's body was warm, and seas of gold still pulsed inside him, but soon they would thin. The more vital the empirium, the stronger the binding would be.

So she began to knit.

She used her hands, because she found the physicality a useful focus and because she wanted to look impressive and unknowable. As she knelt on the ground beside this dead man, rebuilding him into something new and glorious with her deft fingers alone, the angels would look upon her and marvel. The bond would be stronger than if Sarakael had simply possessed the living body. She would stitch them, mind to body, fusing the two together so completely that they would become a single being, stronger than either human or angel. A new kind of life of her own creation.

Rielle moved over every inch of the skull, and beyond her fingers, her power searched and explored. She felt the cool, supple texture of Sarakael's presence, waiting breathlessly. The empirium shone brilliantly in the minds of angels, and Sarakael, young and weak as he was, unable to take true hold of a human body without assistance, was no exception.

Once, it might have hurt her eyes to look at him. Now, she stared right into the blazing inferno.

She worked her power like a seamstress with her needle and stitched the angel to its new body. Incandescent light to fading, dull light. Inch by inch, speck of gold by speck of gold. Millions of stitches, each miniscule and infinite.

Sweat poured down her back and arms. She felt a distant coolness—Corien placing a wet rag against her neck and brow. She had warned him not to interfere with her mind, as it could disrupt her concentration, the flow of power from fingers to angel to body.

But as she worked, she began to long for his familiar touch. Resurrection was an immensity for which she was not truly prepared. With each stitch, she lost a bit of herself and then regained it. Her muscles were torn and rebuilt a thousand times over. Her breath came fast and sharp.

"My love, should you stop?" Corien's voice was tight with concern. "Is it too soon after the Gate?"

"Leave me be," Rielle commanded. She formed the words through a dreamlike fog. "I am both the Maker and the Unmaker. The thing that destroys and the thing that creates."

Her vision blurred and expanded until she could see everything in the vast underground chambers at once, and then everything in the Northern Reach, shrunken to the size of an artist's canvas. Or was it she who had grown, surpassing the constraints of her own body? She saw the mountains encircling them, the vast frozen sea, the White Wastes. She saw the stars in the sky and the worlds that turned beyond them—and that was too much, too confusing. Frightened, full of wonder, she reined in her wandering vision, returned her focus to her furiously knitting hands.

At last, she finished.

Her vision was still consumed by the empirium, and she watched, elated and exhausted, as the body before her, this new creature with his ancient powerful mind and his supple human limbs, rose before her. He tried out his legs, stretched his arms to the high ceiling, and crowed in triumph.

He coruscated, glinting. He experimented with running, jumped and darted. He was faster than Tamarkin had ever been, beautifully limber, breathlessly strong. He gripped a torch bracket affixed to a nearby pillar and swung himself up into the stone rafters. Naked and glorious, he shone faintly, as if he had been dipped in gold.

Rielle watched him from her spot on the floor, holding her body still. She felt Corien standing tensely behind her but could not possibly turn to look at him; she would crumple with exhaustion, and she refused to do that where they could see—this swarm of angels, all chasing after Sarakael. Their jubilant howls were a clamor in her mind.

Sarakael jumped to the ground, then hurried to Rielle and prostrated himself before her. He kissed her fingers, the hem of her gown.

"Thank you, my queen," Sarakael murmured at her feet. "My glorious queen. I do not know how to express my gratitude. To move again, to run and jump. To feel the cold of this stone and the damp of the air, the weight of the mountain above me and the soft glide of my perfect skin. My queen," he choked out, "you cannot know what this means to us all."

"That's enough, Sarakael," Corien ordered, his voice shifting to that of a practiced commander. Rielle could easily imagine him as the angel Kalmaroth, ordering regiments of angels to war. "The rest of you, make yourselves useful. My generals, who are stronger than any of you—strong enough to escape the Gate long ago and to possess bodies of their own accord so they could help me begin to build our new home—these generals have tasks each of you can perform. Until you are summoned for resurrection, you will obey their every command."

Rielle listened to him speak as if from a great distance, her spinning head a whirlpool on the verge of collapse. Distantly, she comprehended that Corien was helping her to her feet, that he was supporting her weight with an arm linked through her own.

When at last they reached their bedroom, Rielle let herself fall.

Corien caught her, kissed her softly. "My beauty, my brave one. You're here with me now. You can rest."

She relaxed her tense muscles, began to shake in his arms. As he led her to bed, she saw her startling reflection in the mirror: lips pale as her skin, all color leeched from them. But her eyes glowed as if embers burned within them. She imagined herself opening her mouth and breathing fire. She imagined biting Corien's neck and injecting him with venom.

A strange thing, to tremble so and need Corien's hands to hold her up, and yet to feel stronger than any of her past selves. It was as if they had all been skins to shed, and she was beginning to uncover the true Rielle beneath them all. A sweet nut of power glowing hard in its shell.

Gaunt and glittering, she grinned at her reflection, watching black-gold shadows roil at her collarbone, in her palms, at her tender pulsing temples.

"When I'm strong enough," she whispered against Corien's chest, "I will give them all wings."

— 25 —
ELIANA

"Many of the saints' writings about the Deep have been lost to time, or to vandalism by radical factions of humans—such as Anima Primoria—who support the angels and decry the creation of the Gate. Those writings that have not been stolen are under close guard by whoever possesses them—usually that country's holy authority—and are not available for study by visiting scholars, a reality that this scholar in particular finds not only offensive but potentially dangerous. Only by understanding what happened in those days can we prevent it from happening again."

—*The Fathomless Deep: A Treatise*
by Tasha Kirdova of the First Guild of Scholars

When the Prophet returned to Eliana, seven days had passed since her journey to the Deep.

You've done well, they said, sending her cautious waves of comfort. *He sees nothing of the Deep in you, and it will not occur to him to suspect it.*

Curled on the floor where Corien had left her, Eliana cracked open her eyes. She swallowed and tasted copper; she had bitten the inside of her mouth bloody. Across the floor, shards of glass were scattered like fallen snow. Corien liked to break things when he was angry. Her windowpanes

stood open to the evening, their edges jagged. Half her guards were duti-
fully sweeping the remnants into pans. The other half, with their blandly
watchful expressions, made sure she didn't lunge for a piece to cut her
throat with.

"Under the rug," Jessamyn ordered, toeing the floor with her boot.
She glanced at Eliana, a troubled expression darkening her face. "Take up
every carpet."

Eliana watched them clean, then climbed into her bed and pretended
to sleep, her face hidden beneath her hair, but in fact she was watching the
doors to her rooms, waiting for Corien to storm back through them. Tears
wet her cheeks, but she hardly felt them. Each sound from her guards
made her flinch. An hour passed, then two. A shift change. Jessamyn left
for the Lyceum, the home of Invictus, where she would sleep.

At last, Eliana felt it was safe.

I want to go back, she thought to the Prophet, the forming of each word
a triumph. *I have an idea. Do you think it can be done?*

Then she sent them her plan, what she envisioned for its end.

The Prophet's pride was unmistakable. *Oh, little one, I like the way you
think. Yes, I believe it is possible, and worth exploring. We will begin tonight.*

◆

In the courtyard, tucked into the thicket where she had first entered the
Deep, Eliana sat in the dirt with her legs crossed, considering the dark seam
hovering in the air before her. It pulled at her like a mouth eager for a taste.
She had to hold on to the tree roots at her knee to keep herself away from
it until she was ready. Everything near the seam—moss and leaves, the
dirt, its pebbles—had turned black and withered. The desiccated remains
shivered, pulled toward the fissure as if resisting being swallowed.

Remember, the Prophet told her, *the moment you can no longer hear me,
you must return to Avitas, just as you did before.*

Eliana would have bristled, had she not been so afraid. *You have said
this already.*

And I will say it again. Your plan is a fascinating one, but it is not without risk.

Risk. Such a small word for what she was about to do. It had taken the seven saints all their power to create the Gate. Later, her mother had opened it with only her bare hands.

And now, here was Eliana Ferracora, her hands damp with sweat and wrapped in gold chains.

Tell me again what it is, she said. *The Deep.*

The Prophet hesitated. *I worry repetition will only add to your fear.*

Please. Talking through this will settle me.

Very well. The Deep is, essentially, an abyss. A void between worlds, as Zahra told you, months ago. No sight or sound. No physicality. Nothing but raw, unfettered empirium. At least, for angels, this has been true. Occasionally one of them might sense a flash of color, a whisper of sound. Visions that pass as if mere thoughts before the empty blackness returns. But it seems your power allows you a different experience. For you, the Deep is a place of continuous, corporeal illusion.

It's also full of countless enormous monsters, let's not forget, Eliana said dryly.

The Prophet sent a flutter of amusement. *Yes. The cruciata that have entered the Deep from their world—which the angels named Hosterah—can indeed survive there. They are strange, ancient beasts that even the angels do not entirely understand. But little else can survive the Deep. The angels could not and lost their bodies.*

Eliana placed her palms in the dirt. The earth beneath her was a familiar anchor. Panic beat a fierce drum in her heart. Images of her body tearing itself to pieces flashed through her mind.

You won't lose your body as the angels did, the Prophet reminded her, though their voice vibrated quietly with tension. *They could not pass through the Deep unharmed, but it seems that you can. Your mother could have too, I think, if she'd had the chance to try.*

As if that were a comfort. Eliana set her jaw, rolled her shoulders. *I will see things I cannot trust, but I have to trust them.*

I think you will see, as you did that first day, faint images of what I believe are worlds beyond our own, as if you are walking through memory. But I think it isn't memory—it is happening now, or has happened, or will happen. Many worlds, all connected by the Deep, in which time has no meaning.

Eliana focused on her steady breathing. *You think.*

It is a theory, the Prophet admitted. *Many scholars throughout history— both human and angel—have posited the very concept I describe. Think about it. You were able to stand in those hills, even though they were mere illusions, echoes through the Deep. So, whatever you see today, be it roads or mountains or forests, trust it. Use it. Believe the illusion. Let your power provide you with reality.*

Or else fall into the endless abyss? Eliana asked wryly. *Be consumed by the Deep?*

I am confident you will manage to avoid that.

And Eliana felt that confidence, sent to her by the Prophet on a steady current.

She wished she shared the feeling.

Instead, a sick fear gnawed at her stomach. She could not shake from her mind the violet sky tinged gray with the shadows of beasts. Though she had survived her first journey to the Deep, there was no certainty she would survive the second. But if she waited any longer, she would be cowed by the sight of this thing she had made.

Eliana held her breath, let go of the tree roots, and stepped swiftly through the fissure, expecting the same vista of soft hills and empty fields to greet her.

Instead, she saw a city crowded with narrow black spires that stretched toward a dark sky scattered with stars.

She froze where she stood, in the middle of a broad thoroughfare choked with people—merchants carting their wares, jugglers tossing glow-ing orbs, children leading animals by knotted ropes. Some of the animals she recognized; others, fleshy and mottled, she did not. If she looked too directly at any one thing, it slipped from her gaze, turned gray and cloudy, then flew out of sight. There was a faintness to it all, a slight discoloration, as if she were looking not at something real but rather at the relics of a dream.

They don't see me, she said, slowly making her way through the crowded street. Dark shapes quivered at the corners of her eyes, giving her the unsettling sense that something vast was closing in upon her. She learned quickly to keep her eyes focused straight ahead, or else the world would start spinning. She could not think about what truly surrounded her: nothingness, endless and dark. The fall of her feet on the illusory road beneath her—that, she lied to herself, was real and true.

You understand, now, how they did it. The Prophet's voice was grave. *The Deep touches all things. The joints between worlds here are thin and pliable, the empirium capable of being molded by those with the power to do so. Like your saints of old, who used their elemental talents to doom an entire race.*

Zahra told me it was a peace treaty, Eliana thought evenly, matching her words to her measured pace forward. *The angels would enter another world, one that was uninhabited, and make it their own. The humans would remain in Avitas, and the Angelic Wars would end.*

Zahra told the truth, the Prophet replied. *It was a terrible deceit.*

The saints did not enter the Deep, though, or else they would have died. Isn't that right?

They worked their magic from Avitas, yes. A pause. *More or less.*

How was this accomplished?

Silence from the Prophet.

Eliana fought a swell of impatience. *How do you know all of this?*

I am a keeper of many stories, was the cryptic reply.

Holding her many questions on her tongue, Eliana watched a boy run past. White braids fell to his waist, and freckles dotted his pale skin. She looked for too long at him; his shape blurred and faded, then flattened, as a shadow would fall across the ground, and was gone. The cobblestones were slick with rain, and Eliana thought she saw drops falling, but when she looked harder to confirm it, pain spiked behind her eyes.

She turned away, her head aching. Not knowing what was real and what was not left her stomach in queasy knots.

None of it is real, the Prophet replied, *and yet all of it is real. I believe what you are seeing is another world, very distant from this one and yet so near that if you put out your hand here in Elysium, you would be touching it and not know it. Many worlds*, the Prophet repeated, their voice soft with fascination, *all connected by the Deep.*

A movement above her, faint at the edge of her vision, urged Eliana to look up, but she refused, afraid of what she would see. She remembered Remy convulsing at her feet, Corien watching coldly from above.

Did it hurt? she thought, knowing the answer. *When you lost your body?*

Another beat of silence. Seldom did they speak of the Prophet's identity. Eliana often feared that delving too deeply into such questions would ruin everything between them.

But Eliana had known the truth from the first time they had spoken: the Prophet was an angel, whether they chose to talk about it or not.

Once again, the movement above flickered. Eliana looked up. Overhead was a night sky with stars more numerous than those she knew in Avitas. Ripples passed through the stars as if they were froth on black water, and in that water swam creatures unseen. Eliana squinted and saw faint dark shapes.

Her blood turned cold. *The cruciata?*

Yes, the Prophet replied.

Do they see me?

It is possible.

Driven by a wild, throat-clenching instinct, Eliana reached an iron gate and hurried past it into a small park, where the trees were heavy with rain. She ducked behind one and clung to its trunk, hidden beneath the sopping leaves.

But then, through her fear, she remembered: None of this was real. She could hide beneath a tree, inside a house, deep in a cave, and none of it would matter, for in reality it would still be only her, Eliana, huddling behind nothing, seen by whatever lurked in the Deep. She couldn't hide—she was alone and vulnerable in an endless abyss, and this tree was not a tree, and the ground she stood on was not ground at all. She existed in nothingness, and nothingness surrounded her.

Abruptly, her fingers passed through the tree, and she stumbled through it and fell. A stubborn part of her brain expected to hit the ground, but instead she kept falling, past the ground that wasn't truly there and into a spinning maelstrom of darkness.

Lights flashed, as if she had passed into a storm. She tried to shut her eyes against them—they were too bright, they were hurting her—but she couldn't. They were everywhere, scorchingly brilliant, as if all the stars she had seen were now erupting in sprays of color. The hot white of lightning and a roiling plum, the punched black-blue of a fresh bruise. She tried to scream, but the air stole her voice. No, not air. *Nothing*. The empirium, the Prophet had said, raw and unfettered.

Distant shrieks and howling roars crashed against each other, building to an awful, discordant cacophony that slammed over and over against her ears, as if she were falling from a high cliff through chaotic mountain winds.

She gasped and choked, struggling to breathe. Heat swept across her skin in painful waves, and with a burst of terror, she wondered if this was the beginning of the end. She would lose her body just as the angels did, her skin peeled away by the Deep.

Eliana, listen to my voice.

She fumbled for the Prophet's faint, distorted words as if they were handholds she could use to climb free of the darkness. *What's happening? I don't understand!*

Listen to me and concentrate on what I'm saying. Remember the city you saw, the road you walked upon? You must recreate the illusion, use it to steady yourself and find your footing once more. Your little river, Eliana—remember it. How it anchors you to your own power. How it protects you from anything that would hurt you.

Eliana struggled to think of the city and its black spires, the boy with the white braids, the juggler's glowing orbs. The images rushed at her, tumbled and frantic, and she grabbed for them, imagining her castings and the power they carried as anchors that could pin the world back into place. And with each image she caught and held came a relief from the roaring noise battering her ears. The brilliant lights dimmed; the spinning blackness slowed and steadied. She began to feel the edges of herself return—the hem of her nightgown kissing her legs, her hair brushing her shoulders, the cool embrace of her castings.

There you are. The Prophet's voice was steady, no longer so distant. *Take a step.*

Eliana obeyed and placed her foot on the wet cobblestones of the spire-city's rain-slicked road. For a moment, she did nothing but stand on her own shaky legs and breathe. She clung to the feeling of her own physicality, hoping it would ground her.

Trust the illusion, she told herself. She held onto the song of her power, thrumming in every vein, and in her mind she drew a picture of the world she had seen. *Rebuild it.*

The boy with the white braids sprinted past her. Dizzy, she turned to watch him as he plunged into the crowded street and crashed into the arms of a man who knelt before a shop front, waiting to embrace him. The man's white hair was bound in many knots. He was, Eliana thought, the boy's father.

Her eyes filled with tears as she watched them. How long it had been since she had been held by someone who loved her.

Come home now, the Prophet ordered. *I should never have allowed this.*

Eliana turned away from the narrow green light in the distance that marked her way home. *I can't. Not yet. I haven't done what I came to do.*

Eliana, you nearly lost yourself to the Deep just then. This is new to me too. If that happens again, or something worse, I may not be able to help you.

Eliana flexed her fingers. The chains of her castings shifted gently around her hands. *But if I go back now, I could die there just as well, so I might as well stay here and finish.*

The Prophet fell silent, their quiet anger a cloud on the horizon of Eliana's mind, but she ignored that and closed her eyes. She concentrated on the slight weight of the gold discs resting in her palms, slowly urging her power to rise until a gentle force tugged at her chest. That same instinct had brought her to the courtyard garden, where the air was thin.

Now, this pull at her chest, at her shoulders and fingers, urged her to move forward. Slowly, she opened her eyes and found the black city painted in incandescent shades of empirium gold. Brightest where she focused her gaze, dimmer at her vision's periphery.

The empirium is luminous here, she thought to the Prophet. *Brighter than anything I have seen in Avitas.*

As it should be. The Deep is the empirium unburdened by physicality. The Prophet's voice softened. *I think this is why you, daughter of Rielle, can walk there without pain. The empirium is the footprint of God. It is the thing that made the worlds. And you carry more of it inside you than any being that has ever lived.*

Except for my mother.

A fluttering pulse, as if the Prophet felt a slight pain. *Yes, little one. Except for your mother.*

As Eliana walked through the winding city streets, following the empirium's call, the buildings grew taller and closer around her. She kept her mind sharp, used it to create a path that was real even if the road underfoot was not. Even if this was an illusion, a mere echo of a world that lived far beyond her reach, she would believe in it. The path led her up a narrow staircase of stone, into a house with its doors thrown open to the night.

Hurry, Eliana, the Prophet said at last. Hours had passed in a blink. *He will come soon. We can try another day, if we must. Do not allow stubbornness or pride to—*

Here, Eliana thought. Inside the house, in the corner of a sitting room that existed in a distant world that was not her own, she had found what she sought.

Oh, the Prophet said, their thoughts soft with amazement, for they could see through Eliana's eyes the place she had found: a thinness in the fabric of the Deep, a pliancy of the empirium itself, just as she had discovered in Avitas. Only here, in the Deep, it manifested as a slight watery sheen in the air. It was made of a thousand colors, as if it were a prism catching sunlight.

Eliana waited another moment, letting her eyes unfocus and turning her thoughts inward, so the empirium could guide her golden sight through the gleam to what lay beyond. She smiled to see it, then called up her power, brought her hands to blazing, and pushed aside the air shimmering before her until a small seam hissed open, spitting white-hot blue light against her fingers.

Past the seam and below her, as if she looked down upon it from a low cloud, stood a city, sprawling and white. Spiraling towers capped with wings reached for a brightening dawn sky. There was the wide chasm circling the city, the bridges spanning it.

And there was Corien's palace, its burnished domes and elaborate parapets resplendent in the creamy light of sunrise.

Eliana sank to the ground and sat back hard on her heels. She braced her hands against her thighs, afraid to breathe too hard, though her head spun from her exertions. The world around her shimmered precariously. She blinked hard and, through a glittering haze, stared at the hole she had made. How weak it seemed, how small and pale. Fingers of light branched out from its perimeter, but so slowly and faintly that Eliana feared the tear might soon repair itself.

That's enough for today, the Prophet said. *Hurry home, little one, I beg you.*

Eliana stood, swaying slightly. *I must make it wider. Wedge it open farther. It's too small now. The cruciata will never get through. Once I leave, it might mend.*

There's no time for that now. We will come back and try again and again until it is done. Or we will craft another plan entirely.

Staring at the faint shapes of Elysium, Eliana felt frantic. *I cannot wait any longer!*

If you try to push your power too hard all at once, you might lose yourself to the Deep, or you could draw the cruciata to you before you're ready—before I'm ready—or you may alert Corien to our work, and he will come for you, and for me, and all will be lost. The Prophet's voice was stern. *You must ruthlessly measure out the use of your power, or you will leave yourself vulnerable when you most need the strength. We must work slowly, and all the while continue our exercises and rebuild your stamina. We decided this when you first presented your plan to me.*

Eliana knew this was right, and yet she turned from the seam with tears of frustration in her eyes. *Is he coming?*

Soon, I think. And you must be entirely yourself before he sees you.

Her heart heavy in her chest, Eliana exited the house and hurried back the way she had come—through the city's center to its outer streets. She saw the narrow door leading back to Avitas, distant greenery framed in angry bruised light.

It is real, she told herself, moving as quickly as she dared toward her exit. *It is real, it is solid.* She made herself slow, forcing herself to feel each footfall against the road. Then she was at the seam and slipping through, its light buzzing against her skin. On the ground beyond, safe in her charred thicket, she turned and drew the seam closed with shaking fingers. Soon, only a faint imprint remained, a trick of the light one could easily dismiss. She watched it fade, the image of that one paltry hole in the Deep lingering in her mind. It sickened her to think of how much work was left to do and what she would endure in the meantime.

There you are, the Prophet said, their voice a soft tremor of relief. *Thank God. Eliana, I think this was too much, too bold. You should not go back again. There are other ways to fight him. The hole you carved may widen by itself in time. The cruciata will sniff it out.*

"But how long will that take?" Eliana whispered. She was too tired to return the mind-speak; she reveled quietly in the ragged sound of her own voice. "I cannot wait for that to happen. I must do it on my own before fighting him takes what is left of me."

The Prophet did not reply to that, but Eliana felt the steady cloak of their thoughts as she fled back through the palace to her rooms. A foul taste flooded her mouth when she caught sight of her doors, flanked by two gray-eyed guards.

It will not be forever, Eliana, came the Prophet's voice, thick with sorrow. *I am working tirelessly to help you in ways you do not even know yet, but the timing must be precise, or else we will lose our opportunity. I will return to you as soon as it is safe. We will go back together.*

Eliana did not answer. Instead, she pushed open the doors to her rooms and shut them behind her in silence.

26

SIMON

"Don't look too close at the woods, my dear,
Don't speak too loud in the night
Stay in the glow of our bed, my dear,
Keep our candle always in sight."

—Traditional Astavari folk song

Corien had filled his city with abducted beauty—faces with remarkable symmetry, minds crackling with talent. Poets and musicians, artists and carpenters. Each building was flawless, designed by angelic minds and crafted by artisans stolen from their beds the world over—promised safety for themselves and their families if only they would live in Elysium and do as His Majesty the Emperor of the Undying commanded.

As Simon made his way through the city to the Lyceum, he found every citizen Corien had collected staring up at the sky—some in wonder, others in fear.

Simon, stalking past them, kept his eyes on the road ahead, refusing to gape like the rest of them, but the light from this thing that had appeared in the air could not be ignored. It washed over everything, illuminating the city with strange colors. White and blue, indigo and plum. It was night, and yet the city hummed with light bright as day.

Only once, at the doors to the Lyceum, did Simon glance up.

Above the city, directly over its heart, gleamed a bright unblinking light, trapped behind clouds. It had appeared some weeks past, and every few days it grew larger and brighter, like the head of a brewing fierce storm. Some described it as a tear in the clouds or a bruise. It was a great eye, insisted others. Simon had heard them whispering during his patrols; the entire city teemed with the mystery of it.

The angels had given the phenomenon a name: *Ostia.*

Across the bridges and the rocky plains beyond, refugees clamoring for entrance to the city had begun carrying out elaborate sacrifices to curry favor with the angelic guards posted at the city's perimeter. The light in the air, they believed, meant that the time was nigh for some great act of either mercy or bloodshed from the Emperor. If they impressed him, their lives would be spared.

If only they knew that the angelic guards watching them did so with nothing but cruel amusement, and that their violent acts would go unrewarded.

Simon threw one last cold look at the sky. He knew exactly what Ostia was, as did the angels and many who lived in the Lyceum. It was a tear in the empirium, clumsy but growing, and beyond it lay the Deep. Soon there would be not just one Gate they would have to guard against, but two. The question was, who had made this one?

The answer seemed obvious to Simon, but Corien had spent weeks tormenting Eliana and had found no evidence tying her to it. Her screams echoed through that wing of the palace day and night with little silence between them.

Simon entered the Lyceum and did not look back.

◆

In the Lyceum, in the receiving hall known as the Rose Room, Simon sat listening to the governing body of Invictus known as the Council of Five, wondering how long it would take them to realize they were being spied upon.

He glanced at the glossy cherrywood doors, beyond which Jessamyn crouched, eavesdropping. Her movements had been too clumsy to go entirely unnoticed; Simon had heard her foot scuff the floor. Like the rest of them, she was no doubt on edge due to the constant eerie light teeming in the sky. There were no true nights anymore; even the darkest hours were painted silver.

Simon looked back at the Five, but they were ignorant to her presence, which faintly disgusted him. They were meant to be assassins of the highest order, and yet they could not hear one of their own students shuffling outside their door.

One of the Five, a pale, sinewy woman named Vezdal, leaned over the council table with a glare.

"So you see, Simon, we cannot delay any longer," she said urgently. "Each moment that creeps by could be our last. You've seen the sky. I refuse to watch angels die and the Empire collapse because we did not act."

"'He has chosen me to guard His works,'" said one of the other Five, Mirzet, a brown-skinned woman lined with age and yet still supposedly a viper with a sword. "'He has chosen me to receive His glory.' So says the Invictus oath. *He* has chosen. Not *they*. Our loyalty must remain to the Emperor."

"And yet the oath also says, 'I am the guardian of His story,'" said another of the Five, his voice smooth and even. His name was Kalan, a tall, bull-shouldered man. "One could argue that His story is the story of the angels—the Empire, the entire race, not only one angel—and that we are not properly guarding it if we let it end, whether or not that means betraying the Emperor."

Mirzet scoffed, pushed her chair roughly back from the table, and stalked away to one of the windows. It was the only one open in the room, admitting a spear of Ostia's eerie blue light.

Kalan turned to Simon and spoke again. "Jessamyn's reports tell us he shuts himself up in the girl's rooms for hours at a time. She hears her screams, and she sees the Emperor emerge afterward, harried and crazed, but still the girl resists him. Is this accurate, Simon?"

Simon watched the man coldly. "It is."

"And Ostia grows every day. Ravikant suspects it will soon open wide enough that the fabric of the empirium there will rupture, and the cruciata will spill right into the streets of our city. Isn't that right?"

"If you are trying to steer me toward betraying my lord and Emperor, you will fail," Simon said, his voice low and even. He rose from his chair. "It was a mistake for me to come here. It was an even larger mistake for you to call this meeting. I will give you one chance to persuade me that you have said these things in error due to fear and a misguided interpretation of the Invictus oath. If you fail to persuade me, I will bring the Emperor here tonight and have you slain on your steps."

Kalan's eyes blazed, his hands flat on the tabletop. "His mind is elsewhere, Simon. You know this. You see it yourself every day. All of us do. This obsession with traveling to the past and reuniting with his lost love… It has ruined him. If he were himself, if his mind were what it once was, he would have broken the Ferracora girl long ago. But he has not, and monsters encroach upon us from sea and sky. We must act. She must seal the Gate, and now Ostia too, or else it is death for all of us."

Simon waited, half his attention on the tense council.

The other half listened for Jessamyn.

"Admiral Ravikant is already at work," Kalan went on, sounding more confident now. He thought his argument was working. "He has assembled his strongest lieutenants. They believe that the combined strength of their minds will be enough to destroy him. But in order to do this, we will need your help."

Suddenly, Vezdal shot up from the table and hurried for the doors. She kicked them, and they flew open wide, knocking Jessamyn to the floor.

The girl jumped to her feet just as Vezdal lunged, a long, slim blade flashing in her hand. Jessamyn dodged it, whirled and kicked. She missed, and Vezdal grabbed her leg, flung her hard to the floor.

"Fool girl!" Vezdal roared. "Traitorous scum!"

Kalan wrenched Vezdal back into the room, brought her whirling around to face him.

"We can use her, Vezdal," Kalan hissed. "She has been assigned to the girl's guard. She has been assigned to watch over her brother. Jessamyn is a valuable pair of eyes in the palace."

Vezdal ripped her arm from his grasp. "Now she is a risk, and we must eliminate her."

But Jessamyn had already fled down the corridor.

Vezdal ran after her, reaching for another knife at her belt. One of the other Five, a formidable archer named Telantes, followed hot on her heels. Simon heard the clatter of blades against the stone floor, the thin whip of arrows.

Kalan turned to Simon, his cheeks bright with anger, but before he could say anything, Simon pulled the revolver from his hip and shot him.

Before Kalan hit the ground, Simon had whirled and shot the others cleanly between their eyes—Mirzet at the window, and Praxia, still seated at the table.

Simon stalked across the room and stood over Kalan, who clutched his gushing belly. Simon raised his gun for a killing shot.

"My apologies, Kalan," he said. "I could not allow you to work against the Emperor. You think Ravikant would be able to do what the Emperor has not? His mind is a bludgeon. He would kill the girl the first time he entered her thoughts, and then we would be defenseless before the oncoming swarm."

Then Simon pulled the trigger. He was out of the room before the gunshot's echo faded.

As he ran out of the Lyceum in pursuit of the others, a single thought screamed through his mind, and even with his feet pounding against stone, his gun hot in his hand, he could not shake it:

I shot him right in the gut.

I shot him right in the gut.

—◇—

A maze of courtyards surrounded the Emperor's palace—one Simon knew well.

He passed under a stone archway from one courtyard into the next, keeping his gaze fixed on Jessamyn. She was not far ahead of him; she'd taken an arrow in the thigh and was slowing fast.

Vezdal leapt out of the shadows and grabbed Jessamyn's arm, spinning her around. Jessamyn dodged Vezdal's knife, then jammed the hilt of her own into Vezdal's nose with a sickening crunch. Vezdal staggered, her nose spurting blood, but she only hesitated a moment before running after Jessamyn's limping form.

A shadow followed fast atop the courtyard walls—Telantes, a quiver of arrows on his back.

Simon cut through another courtyard, then emerged through an arch of ironwork dripping with flowers just as Jessamyn came staggering down a flight of white stairs. She ran into him, and he gripped her hard before she could fall.

"Invictus," she panted, wide-eyed, her face pale from blood loss. "Ravikant."

"I know," Simon said calmly. "I was there, if you'll recall."

Then he moved her aside, took aim, and fired behind her. Two shots— one for Vezdal, the other for Telantes. The archer fell from the wall into a pile of flowers.

Simon helped Jessamyn toward the palace, his arm tight around her back. He glanced down. Her leg was drenched with blood; her eyes were glassy and unfocused.

"Our physicians will see to your wounds," he told her, and then there was a stillness. A veil descended upon his mind. He knew it well. Its flavor, its scent. The astonishing power of its will.

Simon opened his thoughts to Corien, letting him peruse as he liked— the Rose Room, the frustration of Invictus, the treason of Ravikant.

I see. Corien's words floated on a white river.

And then they were at the palace, stumbling into a small parlor near the southeastern entrance. Corien paced, his white shirt open and loose over his dark trousers, his hair a matted mess. He had been with Eliana;

his eyes held a crazed gleam that appeared only after a day locked away in her rooms.

The palace nurses hurried forward, settled Jessamyn on a divan, and began at once to tend her wounds.

Corien stood over her, though Simon knew he was not looking at her. He could feel the distraction rampant in Corien's mind, how entirely his thoughts were wrapped around two women—one dead, and one near it.

"Thank you, Jessamyn, for coming to warn me," Corien said quietly. He pressed his lips to her hand, lingering over it for so long that the nurses—human, clear-eyed, stolen for their skill at healing—exchanged nervous glances.

Simon cleared his throat and stepped forward. "My lord? What are your orders?"

"My orders?" Corien turned to face him. Through the windows, Ostia's light painted him exquisitely. His cheeks glowed as if he had daubed them with rouge made from stars.

"My orders are to open every door to Vaera Bashta," he said quietly, his voice making every word shiver. "Every last one of its prisoners will be free to do as they wish. Every house, every body, every bed is theirs to claim. No more cells. No more wardens. I want my white streets to run red in her honor. Clearly this city is filthy in ways I did not realize. It is time to clean it."

Then he grabbed his coat from the floor and swept out of the room. Simon started after him, but Jessamyn caught his arm as he passed.

"But Remy is still in the Lyceum," she said, short of breath, her eyes hazy with pain, her braid limp with sweat. "Get him, please, and bring him here before the prison is opened. If he dies before Eliana seals Ostia…"

Simon snatched a syringe full of sedative out of the nearest nurse's hand and emptied it into Jessamyn's arm. She went limp on the divan, and he left her with the silent nurses to hurry after Corien through the palace.

27

NAVI

"I know you grieve. I know you look at the life we have lived and what the world has become and feel rage burn in your heart. But think instead of how I love you, and how Nerida loves Tameryn, and how the families we have seen cherish one another as families have always done. Love is the one constant force that no violence or despair can diminish. We must hold onto the light of this truth, Cat, even when the world grows dark. Especially then."

—Undated letter from Saint Ghovan the Fearless
to his sister, Catarina, archived in the Vault of the Ages,
in Orline, the capital of Ventera

Over the past month, Navi and her little army had ferried nearly all of their meager supplies and most of their number from their camp in the Kavalian Bog to Ysabet's hidden cove.

In four days, the ship would be ready to sail. An incredible achievement, and one that had both swamp and cove abuzz with nervous energy.

Navi was not immune. She worked with little rest, hardly allowing her sweat to dry between tasks. Readying bundles of rags, bottled herbs, and canvas tarpaulins; stacking wrapped packets of dried meat, seeds, and rice cakes; boxing sacks of grain and oats. Much of the last month had been spent carefully and quietly visiting a strategically nonsensical pattern of markets on the islands of Hariaca and Laranti, even occasionally venturing back to the port of Algare, where they had first made port after leaving Meridian.

Now, they had a decent supply of their own to add to Ysabet's, and Navi could breathe more easily, knowing her people wouldn't be a burden. If she was to lead Ysabet and her crew on a deadly mission across the ocean to Elysium, at least they would all be comfortably fed in the meantime—if the stores didn't go bad, and if they didn't lose everything in a storm.

Navi shook those worries from her mind and ducked into her tent, searching for a scrap of paper on which to make notes. Her eyes burned from lack of sleep, but whenever she tried it, rest came only in fits. They were all feeling the strain—exhaustion and fear and a wild, giddy sort of exhilaration. At last, they would take to the sea, storm the Emperor's home, and fight for the Sun Queen. They would be legends in whatever world survived. Their names would be whispered at tables, muttered in prayers.

First, of course, they had to figure out how to actually *get* to Eliana. It would not be a simple task to breach the walls of the Emperor's city.

Navi laughed to herself, wiping her brow. She desperately needed sleep. And anyway, they had the entire ocean voyage to engineer a plan.

Merry shouts rang out beyond the tent, followed by the drag of boats up the muddy shores of camp. Ysabet's crew, come for that day's shipment.

Navi froze, paper in hand. She tried to listen past her suddenly racing heart but could hear only her own eagerness, the hot pulse of it in her blood.

A moment later, the tent flap flew open, and Ysabet strode inside, bringing with her the salty smell of the sea. Damp white hair curled at her chin, and her cheeks were red from the wind.

"All is well," she said, hands on her hips, sheathed sword hanging from her belt, white sleeves rolled up to her elbows. She surveyed Navi's neat little tent like it was the deck of her own ship. "We'll be ready to leave in four days' time. An evening sail, which is not my preference, but until we're away from the islands, we'll have to watch hard for imperial ships. Not that the *Queenslight* cannot fight for herself—she can, she's a fierce she-wolf of a boat—but best to avoid battle until we can't any longer."

Navi had been moving uselessly about the tent, straightening papers, tucking Hob's notebook back under his blanket, keeping her face carefully blank. She could not bear to look at Ysabet. For a month now, she had simmered with a longing she had not felt since she first lay with a girl at fourteen. And on the heels of her desire was a terrible fear that Ysabet would laugh in her face if she confessed it. Never mind that she often felt Ysabet's eyes upon her as they worked together, and that sometimes when their hands touched, it was like tinder catching fire.

But then one of Ysabet's words fixed itself in Navi's fretful mind. *Queenslight.* She straightened to stare at Ysabet, whose smug grin lit up her face.

"You named her," Navi said faintly, all the air knocked out of her. "You named her after Eliana."

"It's a good name, isn't it?" Ysabet winked. "Have I earned a kiss at last, then?"

A slow warmth spilled down Navi's limbs. Her eyes filled with tears, and she couldn't stop looking at Ysabet's face, hungry for the quickness of it. Her sharp jaw and cheekbones, her lively brown eyes.

Ysabet's smug expression faltered. "You're crying. Are they good tears or bad?"

Navi shook her head and rushed at her, and they crashed together as if they had been on that course all their lives. She found Ysabet's grinning mouth with her own, wrapped her arms around Ysabet's shoulders.

"Thank God," Ysabet murmured against Navi's lips, her hands at her waist, and then there was no air left to speak. Ysabet kissed like she did everything else: with an easy confidence that turned Navi's knees to liquid. Tender at first, teasing nibbles that left Navi's lips swollen and buzzing. And then, with a quick heated glance, Ysabet slid her hand around to cup the back of Navi's head, and Navi stretched up on her toes to meet her, and this was deeper, this was fevered. Navi's hands clutched at Ysabet's sleeves, and Ysabet's tongue teased Navi's lips until they opened.

With a groan, Ysabet directed her gently toward the small stack of crates in the corner of the tent, and Navi scrambled atop them as if it were the most natural thing in the world. At once, she hooked her legs around Ysabet's thighs, pulled her close. The heat of her, the strong, warm lines of her body. Ysabet seized Navi's hips and tugged them closer. Navi let her head fall back as Ysabet's mouth traveled her throat. She threaded her fingers through Ysabet's hair, delighted by its softness. She wished to bury her face in it.

The sleeve of her tunic had slipped. Ysabet kissed her bare shoulder.

"I didn't name her that only to get in your bed," Ysabet mumbled against her skin.

Navi smiled, her eyes fluttering shut. "I have no bed."

"I do, on my ship." Ysabet lifted her face, her eyes full of stars. "It's big. Captain's quarters and all that."

Then Ysabet's face sobered. She leaned her forehead against Navi's as they found their breath again, and tenderly brushed Navi's silky black hair away from her cheek. Months after her abduction by Fidelia, her hair had finally reached her shoulders.

"I don't only want to lie with you, Navi," Ysabet whispered. "It isn't only about that."

Navi feathered soft kisses across Ysabet's cheeks, her heart aching when Ysabet turned up her face, eyes closed, like a bloom seeking the sun.

"I know," said Navi quietly. "It's the same for me." She shuddered as Ysabet brushed against the hem of her tunic, fingers teasing her naked waist. "Only long ago, when I was quite young, have I been touched like this by someone I wanted. I'd forgotten it could be so nice."

Ysabet paused, then pulled back from her. Her eyes were grave. "So many stories we have yet to tell each other."

Navi touched her face with a soft smile. "We will have much time to tell stories as we speed across the ocean in your beautiful ship."

"Say that again."

Navi's smile grew. "Your beautiful ship."

Ysabet sighed. "I love hearing you say those wonderful words."

A shout pierced the air, followed by another. Navi locked eyes with Ysabet for an instant, and then they hurried from the tent. Outside, their crews grabbed weapons, scrambled to hide supplies. Malik drew his sword, his expression grim. Hob readied his revolver.

Navi squinted into the swamp's gloom, Ysabet just behind her. It was evening; what light passed through the thick net of branches overhead was thin and yellow. Navi glanced at the fissure, but it looked the same as ever—a thin black eye streaked with shifting light, hovering quietly several hundred yards away.

A boat approached, far enough from the fissure that Navi thought the passengers might not even have seen it. Someone stood inside the boat, pushing the vessel forward through the murky water with a long oar.

Navi tensed. Was it only one person, one boat? Or the first of many? Human or angel?

Then the air shifted as if from a breeze. Framed by the still swamp, the disturbance caught Navi's eye at once. Her breath hitched, for she knew that distortion, that faint smudge in the air that flitted and shifted, ever-changing.

Your Highness. Zahra's voice brimmed with relief. *At last.*

Navi surged forward with a sharp cry. "Don't shoot! Lower your weapons!"

Malik looked back at her, frowning, his sword still raised.

Navi pushed past him, laughter bursting from her throat, and waved her arms in greeting. She heard the moment when Hob recognized the oarsman—a short, trim man, pale-skinned, with shaggy copper hair. A choked cry, and then Hob joined Navi at the shore, plunged into the sludge uncaring. He grabbed the boat and dragged it the rest of the way to land.

Patrik's grin was like the sun rising. He tossed his oar to the muddy bank, an unfamiliar scar stretching across his cheek. Navi clasped her hands at her mouth, smiling through her tears. Patrik was much changed since that day months ago when she had met him in the Red Crown hideout called Crown's Hollow. He wore a frayed black eye patch, and he was too thin, his body marked with fresh scars. But he was whole and alive.

Hob cupped Patrik's face in his trembling dark hands, and then, tenderly, as if afraid doing so would end the dream, gathered him close, folding him into his arms. Hob buried his face in Patrik's wild hair, clutched the tattered folds of his shirt. Hob was a man of quiet, but his loud sobs were unfettered, cracking with incredulous laughter.

Patrik pressed his face against Hob's shoulder, his eye closed. He was muttering something barely audible beneath the sound of Hob's relief. His fingers stroked the back of Hob's neck. Navi could barely see him over the great rise of Hob's shoulder, but she managed to catch his eye.

She turned to the others, who were all watching. Malik was beaming, his sword forgotten.

"Go on," she mouthed, gesturing for everyone to move away. "Give them a moment."

Immediately, her little army of strays obeyed, returning to their tasks with Ysabet's crew—except for Ysabet herself, who was glaring sharply up at the trees.

"Something's here," she muttered, hand resting on her sword hilt. "Something angelic."

Navi touched her arm. "Yes, but she's a friend. A wraith named Zahra. She saved me once, and Eliana more times than that."

Then Navi turned to face Zahra—a soft blur in the air, faceless and formless. Unlike Eliana, Navi could not see the echo of Zahra's true form. But inside her mind, Zahra was clear as the cloudless sky.

"Before I tell you how happy I am to see you at last," Zahra said, not in mind-speak but aloud, her deep, smooth voice rich with joy, "and before I tell you where we have been and what we have seen, I must share news with you, Your Highness."

Ysabet let out a low curse. Wide-eyed, she stepped back from where Zahra drifted, though her gaze did not quite land on her.

"I don't understand," Ysabet muttered. "I've never heard an angel speak without a body."

"The mind can accomplish much, if you have the will for it," Zahra said primly. "What you are hearing is an approximation and projection of the voice I once possessed, amplified and unscrambled by your own mind. While not all wraiths can recreate such things, my mind, happily, is strong enough for it."

Ysabet blinked at her, then looked at Navi with an expression so flummoxed that Navi had to stifle a laugh.

"We'll talk more about that later," Navi assured her, gently touching her arm.

"Now. My news." The shape of Zahra in the air, vague as it was, seemed to straighten. "I bring word from the Prophet. Eliana still lives. She fights the Emperor. With the Prophet's guidance, she is learning to use her power covertly. She is working to open a massive fissure between Avitas and the Deep and will soon unleash hordes of cruciata upon Elysium."

A ripple of excitement swept through those who had gathered to listen.

Navi felt wild with happiness. She put her hand to her throat, tears rising fast. "Oh, Zahra. Thank God. Eliana lives. She *lives*, oh, sweet saints. What else did the Prophet say? And who *is* the Prophet? Do you know?"

"I do," Zahra replied, but said no more.

Navi didn't care; her body was bursting with light. "You must tell us everything you know. Where you and Patrik have been, what you have seen. How we can help Eliana. We have a ship, and she's fast. We have dozens of soldiers ready to fight." She spun around, found Ysabet's hands, and squeezed them, grinning. "Eliana is alive. She's *fighting*. I knew she would, and she is. The empirium is guiding her, and..."

When Navi's voice broke and she could no longer speak, Ysabet touched her face, smiling softly. "And now the Queen's light will guide us to her."

―◇―

Navi was not sorry to leave the Kavalian Bog behind, even though it meant living on a ship that was apparently determined to kill her.

Mouth sour from the draught Ysabet had given her, Navi tried at last to move. For the first two days after disembarking, she had not been able to leave her bed and the pail sitting beside it.

But the draught seemed to have settled her stomach, and she left her cabin for the deck. Their winds had been lucky so far, carrying them away from the Vespers at a speed that left Ysabet ecstatic. Navi stood at the door of the main hold, eyes closed. The fresh air washed over her, bringing with it the smells of salt and the thick, oily resin Ysabet's crew used to polish the deck.

Navi opened her eyes, watched her people work. *Their* people. Ysabet's crew of sixty, and her own army of forty-seven. One hundred and seven humans and a single wraith against the ocean, the imperial fleet, and whatever horrors awaited them in Elysium.

She moved past the dark images her worries summoned and walked the deck, learning its steps and curves, admiring the smooth gleam of its railings. The industrious chatter of the crew followed her patrol. She was glad to hear some cheer in their voices now that the Vespers were no longer visible on the horizon. No imperial ships were hunting them; no danger nipped at their heels.

Not yet.

Then Navi glanced at the ship's prow and the elaborate carved figure-head that Ysabet's harried carpenters had been ordered to craft with very little warning: a woman, face uplifted, arms outstretched, reaching for the sky. Her hair fell in waves and curls to her waist, and around her head sat a crown of broad rays.

Beside the figurehead, the air shifted strangely.

Navi paused for a moment. The wraith had told her everything that had happened in the months since they had last seen each other, and Navi was still trying to absorb it all. Zahra, trapped for a time in a blightblade until Eliana had brought Remy back from death and freed Zahra in the process. A reunion with Patrik, and Red Crown spies in the city of Festival. The night of the Admiral's Jubilee, when Festival had fallen to an angelic force intent upon finding Eliana at last and bringing her to the Emperor.

And now, long weeks later, Zahra and Patrik, the only survivors of that awful day, had come at last to rejoin their friends.

Navi only wished they could have been spared everything that had happened in the meantime.

She joined Zahra, standing in silence beside her as she found her bearings at the ship's bobbing bow. She longed to see something more of the wraith than this faint wash of air.

Zahra's voice came wistfully. "I long for that as well, Your Highness."

Sea spray crashed up from the waves below, kissing Navi's face with cold mist. She gripped the railing, her body zipping tight with tension.

"You don't have to stand here with me," said Zahra. "Lie down, if you wish."

"Ysabet gave me a draught to settle me until I find my sea legs," said Navi wearily. "I'd never heard of sea legs before. The term evokes amusing imagery. I'm not sure what I would have. Flippers, perhaps, or fins like a sea maiden." She wrinkled her nose. "Hopefully not tentacles."

Zahra gave a half-hearted laugh, then fell silent once more. So many dark feelings brewed around her that even Navi, inexperienced as she was when it came to deciphering the feelings of angels, could feel the force of them.

She glanced at the wraith, hesitated, then reached out, palm to the sky. "May I, Zahra?"

A pause, and then Zahra said thickly, "Please."

Navi moved her fingers through the air where Zahra's echo drifted. Into her tired mind, she placed the image of what she knew Zahra to look like, as Eliana had described from her visions. She imagined a tall angel with rich brown skin and flowing white hair, brilliant flaring wings, and then imagined drawing that angel into a warm embrace. She would kiss Zahra's cheek, if she could. She would stroke her arms until she slept.

Navi shivered, her skin prickling from Zahra's chill. Touching her felt like drawing her fingers through icy water, velvety and supple.

Zahra's voice rasped with emotion. "Thank you, Navi. That was a dear kindness. And I saw it vividly. You may not be accustomed to speaking to me in that way, but your mind is sharp and clear. With practice, you would excel, I think."

"You have my permission to speak to my mind directly, Zahra," Navi offered. "It must be more tiring for you to speak like this."

"Tiring, yes, but I enjoy being able to project at least some of myself back into the physical world. Besides that, it is more respectful, I think, to preserve that distance. Especially since so many of my kind do not."

"Very well." Navi watched the water, carefully choosing her words. "You can leave, if you want. You can travel faster than we can. You ache to see her, I know."

Zahra's laugh was bitter. "Ache? A small word for what I feel. A girl I love as I would my own daughter was wrenched away from me before my very eyes. I watched them take her on that beach in Festival. I watched the admiral's ship sail away from me and could do nothing. The Emperor kept me from her. I railed against him. I howled for her. It did nothing. I have failed her."

"Oh, Zahra, you haven't—"

"No. Do not comfort me in this."

Navi waited a moment. "I mean what I say. Go to her, if it will help you."

"I cannot. The Prophet forbids it."

This surprised Navi. She frowned up at the place where she imagined Zahra's face would be. "Why?"

"I am to stay with you," Zahra said flatly, "and keep your ship hidden, then help you navigate the Sea of Silarra, which will be choked with imperial ships. It will take great effort to achieve this, but I must do it nevertheless. Eliana does not have friends in Elysium. There is no Red Crown, no one who loves her. She cannot do what must be done alone. You and Ysabet, your crew, your army of strays, Patrik and Hob... She will need all of you, when the time comes. We cannot give her the army she deserves, but we can give her ourselves. And so I will remain here and hide you from searching black eyes."

A moment passed as Navi digested this. "Can you do that? Hide an entire ship?"

"It is what I was born to do. Not to take vengeance upon humans or serve a mad emperor. I was born to serve *her*, to love *her*. This is what I believe. I will bear you to the Sun Queen so you may fight alongside her and help her win this war at last. That is the great culmination of all my long years, the reward for that endless age in the Deep. To serve the world's great hope and guard her friends with all the strength granted by what power I have left."

Navi looked at her hands through a sheen of tears. Humbled, she found her voice slowly. "You are very brave, Zahra. And if you argue with me, I'll get angry."

Zahra laughed. A tender coolness brushed Navi's arm.

In silence, they watched the waves darken as behind them the sun joined the horizon. While the light dimmed, Navi fixed an image in her mind and sent it clumsily in Zahra's direction: Herself, and Zahra as she once was, standing beside her. Navi's head resting against her arm, their fingers bound in friendship, their twin devoted hearts yearning east.

◆◇◆

The night was deep in darkness when Navi at last felt well enough to visit the captain's quarters. The night was quiet. Crew members were at their assigned posts, the waves steady as they crashed and curled.

Navi wished her own heart were as steady. How it fluttered, how it tightened her chest and throat. She touched the latch on Ysabet's door. Wandering the deck after leaving Zahra, she had let her mind ask its questions, imagining every probable doom and possible triumph. She had thought of everything that had happened and everything that would. Zahra had told her of Harkan, how he had died under her care. How Simon had stood cold-eyed at the pier and slain their friends and allies. A pet of the Emperor, declaring devotion even as he plotted betrayal.

Navi could not think too closely of that. She knew of Eliana's feelings for Simon. The death on the beach would have been awful to witness, the realization of her failure a gut punch—but to watch Simon kill their friends, to understand who truly had his loyalty, would have been the most vicious devastation. It was a rare thing, to find someone to trust, someone to receive your love and protect it. Navi knew that truth all too well. And then to have that trust broken, that love proven to be a lie…

Navi would reject violence altogether if she could. But if she met Simon again, she would kill him.

She knocked on Ysabet's door and stepped inside.

Ysabet sat at her desk, its surface strewn with food inventories, weapons registers, maps of the sea and stars.

She turned from her work with a broad smile. "There you are. How do you feel? Would you like more of my wondrous tea?"

Navi pushed on before she could lose her nerve. A rare thing indeed, to find someone she could trust. Someone who would, perhaps, receive her love and protect it.

"What I would like," she said, her voice shaking only a little, "is to do something I fear may come across as presumptuous."

At once, the room changed, the air between them pulling tight. A gilded string, taut and singing.

Ysabet leaned back in her chair, her brown eyes bright with candlelight. "Presume away, princess."

Navi took a moment to breathe, to steady her hands, and then undid the clasp of her cloak. It fell to her feet. "We sail to war, and possibly to our deaths."

"Yes," Ysabet agreed, rapt.

"I told you in my tent that it has been too long since I've been loved kindly." Navi slipped off her boots, undid her trousers, slid them off. Barelegged in her tunic, she watched Ysabet's mouth part, the curve of her lips.

Ysabet's chest rose faster. "Yes."

Navi unbuttoned her tunic's collar, then drew it up over her head. Naked, she asked Ysabet a silent question.

"Yes," Ysabet whispered, and then watched in wonder as Navi settled gently in her lap.

Ysabet's hands came to her at once—one on her hip, the other fingering the ends of her hair. "My God, Navi," she said hoarsely. "You will kill me this night. Look at you."

"Yes, look at me. See me when I tell you this." Navi stroked the silken arches of Ysabet's pale brows. "I also said in my tent that it was not only about lying with you, and you said the same."

She had never seen Ysabet's face so soft, as if all her barbs, all her bravado, had melted away at Navi's touch.

"Yes," she whispered.

Navi lowered her mouth to Ysabet's temple. "Is it possible to love someone you have known for only a few weeks?"

"Yes. Yes." Ysabet fumbled for Navi's face, clumsy in her ardor. She kissed Navi's chin, her jaw, her neck.

"If I am to die soon," said Navi, her eyes falling shut, "I would like to meet it with the memory of you in my mind."

Ysabet's voice floated up to her, thick with emotion. "Yes." She slid her hand up Navi's bare back, tracing the scarred line of her spine. "Yes." She drew Navi down for a kiss, and Navi whimpered against her mouth, for she felt silken and flushed in Ysabet's arms, safe as she had so seldom felt. Even in war, there could be this—love, and hope, and the simplicity of pleasure.

She laughed, joy bubbling to her toes. "Can you say nothing else?" she teased.

Ysabet touched Navi's face, looking up at her as if gazing upon all the world's marvels. "Kiss me," she said, a tiny plea in her voice, an incredulous little bend, as if she could not quite believe what she held.

Navi smiled, ran her fingers once more through Ysabet's soft white hair, and bent to obey.

‹ 28 ›

ELIANA

"I cannot tell my father or my brothers, not yet, for I don't want to raise their hopes prematurely. But I have been visited in secret by one of the Emperor's lieutenants, and he says I am beautiful enough to earn a place in the Emperor's palace as a favored guest! He may summon me today, in fact, and I know just what dress to wear, red like—"

—The last journal entry of Demetra Vassos, human citizen
of Elysium, dated April 3, Year 1018 of the Third Age

In Eliana's shapeless, quiet dream, a single word: *Run.*

Her eyes flew open. Someone was dragging her across her bed, upending her pillows. She tried to wrench free and couldn't. The hand around her ankle was firm and cold.

She saw Corien's face, how giddy it was, the manic edge of his smile. Her bedsheets tangled around her legs. He yanked her hard over the edge of her bed and stalked away, letting her fall.

"Get up. And do something with that tangled hair of yours. You look feral." He was rifling through her enormous wardrobe, shoving past gown after gown. "I have a gift for you, but you must be properly outfitted to receive it."

Eliana scrambled to her feet, looked quickly around her rooms. Her adatrox attendants stood blank-eyed in their white robes. Jessamyn was not there, no doubt sleeping at the Lyceum. Ostia's light painted the windows, casting long shadows across the floor. She had buried her pride deep and felt nothing when she glanced out the window at the enormous dark stain of angry light fixed in the night sky.

A shadow flickered at the corner of her eye. She turned to find the open door to her rooms—and a familiar silhouette.

She had not seen Simon in too many days to count. She was not prepared for it. Her chest flared white-hot, and she flew at him, her anger clean and sharp, her fist raised to strike. She would not unwittingly summon her power, not this night. Her fury burned within an unbreakable cage. He could not get to her, but she would get to *him*.

Simon blocked her with his forearm, and then something grabbed her own, wrenched her away from him, and flung her to the floor.

She fell hard, head knocking against the tile, then looked up at the tilting world to see Corien's ferocious expression. The white knives of his cheekbones, his black eyes reflecting none of Ostia's light. He had not dressed to his usual standards. His thin white shirt hung loose around his pale torso. His hair was rumpled, and his lips wore a burgundy stain.

"Get dressed," he snapped.

A gown awaited her on the bed, glittering like a discarded skin of jewels. She had seen it hanging in her wardrobe but had never touched it. A high-collared bodice in red, dark as a pool of blood and heavy with beadwork. A thick sash of black silk around the waist, fastened with a clasp of golden feathers. Black lace trimmed a narrow, plunging neckline, and the skirt was a layered sea of crimson silk.

It was a gown fit for the Blood Queen.

She hesitated, irrationally afraid of it.

Quick footsteps crossed the room, and then Corien shoved her against the bed, tore at the sleeve of her nightgown. She wrenched herself away from him and then, unthinking, whirled around and slapped him.

He grinned, the thin red line where her casting had cut his cheek fading quickly, then grabbed and turned her, shoving her face down into the gown's glittering fabric.

"I'm waiting," he hissed against her ear, his breath hot and foul. He had been drinking, perhaps feasting in one of his dining halls with whatever lucky citizens had been selected to attend that night's entertainment.

Then he yanked her up and pushed her hard toward the center of the room, the gown clutched in her hands. In Ostia's light, she dressed without shame. She found Simon's silhouette, the faint gleam of his eyes. She locked on to him, held his gaze as she fumbled with the hooks of her bodice. Let them both look at her. Let them see her every scar, her every curve. All shame at her own nakedness had been beaten from her long ago. But her fingers shook as she tied the sash, and she felt worse with the gown's folds around her, this gown that reminded her of the paintings in Corien's gallery. She would have preferred to wear nothing.

"At last." Corien grabbed her arm, pulled her with him as he strode toward the door. He did not give her time to find shoes. "We have an appointment. You've nearly made us late for it."

They swept out of her rooms and into the corridor. The palace buzzed with noise. Servants and revelers bustled past them in plain tunics and neatly pressed coats. Faces drawn, desperate smiles thrown Corien's way.

Simon followed them as they descended one of the palace's grand staircases. An entrance hall gleamed, brightly lit ballrooms circling it like gemstones on a crown. A cold fear was rising inside Eliana, so acute and swift that she felt the absurd urge to laugh.

Corien tugged her down the steps, across the hall, through a set of doors, and outside into the night. His grip on her wrist was punishing, his pace relentless. She stumbled after him, breathless—and then, in the maze of courtyards and gardens encircling the palace, Simon did an extraordinary thing.

He seized Corien's arm, bringing them all to a halt.

"My lord," he said, leaning close, "I believe this to be a grave error. If she is killed—"

Corien backhanded him so hard that he staggered, then caught himself on the thin trunk of a neat square topiary.

"She won't be killed," Corien called out, resuming his furious pace with Eliana in tow. "I don't want to kill you. Do I, darling? No. I simply think you ought to have a good view of this. I think you ought to feel it in your bones. I think that when they come for you, you won't be able to help fighting them. You'll have to, or they'll tear you apart with their teeth. And then what? You'll burst, you wicked child. You'll bleed power down every street."

"When who come for me?" Eliana asked. She tried to look over her shoulder for Simon, but then they were exiting the courtyards, and an escort of angelic guards in imperial armor fell into formation on either side of them, blocking her sight of all but the streets before her.

Crowded with tents and makeshift candlelit altars, every thoroughfare and alleyway, every garden tucked between buildings, was lit as if for a celebration.

There were strings of crackling galvanized lights, torches flaring merrily in their brackets, doors and windows thrown open to let in the cool air. A group of citizens, led by an orator wearing paper wings strapped around his torso, knelt at a fountain. Eliana watched in fascination as they raised their arms to the eerie bright sky in supplication to this thing they did not understand—a second moon, broad and close and menacing. They had heard the name the angels had given it. Whispers at parties, rumors passed from palace to markets, from soldier to servant. *Ostia*. Another Gate, perhaps. A second coming of angels—or of beasts.

Corien passed through the crowds like a ship gliding through the sea, waves crashing apart in its wake. The people of Elysium abandoned their tents, their parties, and hurried after him. They called for the Emperor, begged him for blessings, for invitations to the palace. They even, Eliana was appalled to realize, began to call *her* name. They knew it: *Eliana. Eliana.*

Sun Queen, they called her. *The Furyborn Child!*

The din of their voices crashed against her ears. Her palms were slick within the cages of her castings. She wished desperately that she could reach for the Prophet and ask what Corien had planned, but she didn't dare with him so close.

Then, the air exploded with wailing sound.

Eliana's blood was ice in her veins. The horns of Vaera Bashta. The mournful notes crawled up her arms on thin needle-feet. The Prophet had told her of the prison's cullings and assured her that Remy was still alive.

But every time Eliana heard the horns, she remembered Remy whispering about a room underground and imagined him dead at a prisoner's hand—throat torn open, head bashed against stone. The stomach she had healed reopened by some crude knife fashioned in the dark.

Simon's cruel words glinted in her mind: *I shot him right in the gut.*

Corien stopped in a pentagonal plaza, each side marked by soaring arcades of white stone, exquisitely symmetrical. At each corner stood a broad pillar topped with a statue of an angel in flight or in battle. On the plaza's far side, several angelic guards flanked a set of broad black doors.

Corien released her to throw up his arms. Around them, the gaping crowd hushed. Some reached for him; others fell to their knees.

"Elysium!" he cried. "Your rot will be cut away! Your filth will be scrubbed clean! Every lie you have told, every secret you have kept from me, will be revealed!" He turned, letting them all look at the shining white glory of his face, its mad grin. "For even a kind master must sometimes beat his hounds to remind them who holds the chain."

The crowd shifted, their smiles dimming.

Vaera Bashta's horns sounded once more—the culling's final call.

"Behold!" Corien cried, laughter shaking his voice. "And be cleansed!"

Then the black doors swung open, revealing a dark, toothless mouth, stone steps descending into shadows.

The gathered crowd understood at once. Their screams rose like the cries of hunted animals baying in dumb fear. They shoved past each other, pushed down the slow and trampled them. A great crush of bodies, fleeing fast.

But not fast enough.

Out of the doors poured a stream of darkness—bent and gaunt, scabbed and howling. Not crawlers, not cruciata, but humans who had been kept too long underground. Dozens of them. *Hundreds*. Beyond the plaza sounded the clank and grind of more doors opening, the distant swell of screams.

Horror flooded Eliana in cold waves. She stepped back, but Corien was behind her. He caught her arms and pressed his cheek to hers.

"I told them they could do anything they wanted." His whisper shook with terrible choked mirth. "I slipped inside each of their minds and told them that if they wanted to be free of their cells forever, they would have to impress me. I do so like being entertained."

Eliana thought of Remy and felt her gorge rise. "Why are you doing this?"

He turned her gently. "Because of you, Eliana," he said, as if it were obvious. "You're keeping secrets from me. I know it. That's fine. I keep secrets from you too. But I can't let you go unpunished for it. And I wonder if fighting through streets painted red with blood will awaken you as I cannot. It matters little to me how many in this city are killed today because of you, but I'm sure it matters to you. My tenderhearted princess. *The Furyborn Child*, I've heard them call you. Evocative. I do appreciate a poetic turn of phrase."

He gestured to one of the guards in their escort, who handed him a parcel wrapped in cloth. Corien pressed it into Eliana's hands and kissed her cheek.

"Don't worry," he said. "I won't let anyone kill you. But the rest of them…"

In a blink, he was gone, as were the guards. Alone, unmissable in her red gown bright as blood, she immediately felt dozens of eyes upon her.

The shape of the bundle she held was familiar. Quickly, she unwrapped it.

Arabeth. Nox. Whistler. Tuora and Tempest.

Her knives, clean and sheathed, clipped to a leather weapons belt. How she hated him for gifting them to her. Even in this chaos, on this awful night, she was glad to see them. Her only surviving friends.

Mouth dry, hands shaking, she clipped the belt around her waist and ran. Elbowed her way through the teeming crowd, shoved past the people who recognized her and grabbed at her skirts. One wouldn't let go—a wizened old man in iridescent brocaded finery. He grabbed her sash, pulled her to him.

"Help us!" Drops of blood already painted his face. He groped for her castings. "Destroy them!"

Eliana whipped Arabeth from her sheath and sliced him across his chest. He staggered back, cursing, and released her. She turned and fled, having no sense of where to run but unwilling to reach out for the Prophet. Corien would still be nearby. He was no marque; he could not vanish into thin air. He had simply concealed himself.

She pumped her legs faster, her muscles already trembling. She had grown stronger during her weeks with the Prophet, but her former strength was still a distant memory. How the Dread of Orline would have laughed to see her now.

Exiting the long arcade, gritting her teeth against the burn of her abused bare feet, she pushed her way down one street, then turned down another before emerging into another plaza, this one much larger than the first. Two metal hatches in the stone sat open. She raced past the nearest one just as a pale woman with ropes of matted hair jumped out of it. A hand grabbed her ankle. She fell hard, tore strips of skin from her hands. Turned around and plunged Arabeth into the woman's throat. A strangled cry, and the woman collapsed, clutching the red river of her neck. Eliana rolled out from under her, yanked Arabeth free, and pushed herself to her feet. Her scraped palms stung; she wiped sweat from her eyes.

A thump behind her. Eliana spun around, ducked the wild blow of another prisoner—a man with scarred fair skin, a white knife in his hand. His blade caught her arm, cut a thin stripe to her elbow.

She cried out, ducked his second blow, thrust Arabeth at his neck. But he was fast. He struck Arabeth out of the air with his own knife, then pounced on her, knocking her to the ground. Her vision flickered. He pawed at her gown, dragged his tongue across her face. His breath was rancid, like meat left out to rot.

She let him slobber at her throat as she gathered her strength, then jammed her knee into his groin. He howled with pain, and she grabbed Nox, plunged the fat blade into the man's concave stomach.

He fell atop her, the warm rush of his blood soaking her gown. She pushed him off, Nox in hand, found Arabeth smiling her crooked smile on the white flagstone, and ran.

But there was no escaping Vaera Bashta. Everywhere she looked, ragged prisoners pounced and clawed, their wild cries tearing the air into strips. Two men went tumbling down a staircase, then scrambled after a clattering pistol.

Eliana didn't see who reached it first, but she heard the gunshot as she raced past. A boy darted past her, climbed up a drainpipe. The shape of his body jolted her, and for a moment, though his skin was darker, she thought it was Remy. An icy fist closed around her heart, squeezing hard as she ran. She hoped she would not find Remy. She hoped he was hiding in some gutter or under a staircase in the quiet dark. What would she do if she turned a corner and saw him changed? No longer the brother she had known, but a killer who dealt in blood instead of stories?

The thought battered her as she ran, a terrible whirling fear that rose in her like a current. She felt a sting at her palms and glanced down to see her castings faintly aglow.

She fisted her hands closed around them and ran up a broad flight of white steps, then up a narrow staircase set in the wall of a large apartment building with cruciata gargoyles yawning at each corner. She climbed until she found a high terrace, its walls frosted with scrolling white stonework. The air was quieter there, Elysium's screams a distant cacophony. Under an arbor draped in ivy, she crouched, heart pounding, Arabeth clutched tightly in her right hand. She breathed until she felt it was safe, until the blood pulsing in her ears had slowed. Then, she formed a single clear thought:

Please, help me.

An answer came at once. *I'm here.*

Eliana sank to the ground. *Is it safe to talk?*

He is rather distracted by the evening's events, the Prophet answered drily. *With his mind in its current state, he is easily diverted by his own perversities. But you were right to run far before speaking to me.*

Can I come to you? She felt like a frightened child, begging for comfort after a nightmare. Her head pounded with a primal fear, and she could think of little else. *I don't know where to go.*

A feeling came to Eliana then, such a tenderness that her eyes grew hot.

We must wait a little longer, the Prophet said gently. *When you come to me, he will find me soon after. Everything must be ready by then, all the pieces in place. Your friends are on their way, but you must keep fighting until they arrive.*

Eliana wrapped her arms around her stomach, let out a single choked sob. She felt brittle, ready to fly apart from fear, as if the night's horrors had ripped from her every plate of armor she had forged in the fire of her imprisonment. She could not even bring herself to ask what friends the Prophet meant. Instead, her skittering mind relived those moments with Corien in her bedroom, how he had smashed her face into her beaded gown as if to suffocate her. Simon at the door, his face hidden in shadows as she stared him down.

You need to focus, Eliana. The Prophet's voice grew firm. *The more scattered your thoughts, the easier it is for him to find you, and therefore find me.*

Eliana's exhaustion was a chasm; soon she would tip into it. *If someone else tries to kill me, I might let them.*

He won't let them. Nor will I.

I have the right to choose my own death.

No, you do not, the Prophet said. *Too much depends on you. I know you didn't ask for this burden, but it is yours nonetheless. Listen closely. We won't have a better opportunity than this for you to enter the Deep. Ostia has been growing. The fabric of the empirium there has become thin and fragile. I think you can do it with one more try. I think you can finish your Gate.*

I cannot go back to the palace, Eliana replied, looking out across the city at the distant turrets.

No. Chaos is spreading fast across the city. It's too dangerous to go all that way. If you are injured, it could undo the progress we have made.

Eliana wiped her face and drew a shuddering breath. *Instead, I must find another place where the empirium is thin. Another way into the Deep.*

Yes, and quickly, the Prophet replied. *When he grows bored of this culling, he will end it.*

Eliana recited the facts she knew, each thought bringing a little more steadiness to her mind. *In the palace, the empirium guided me to that place in the garden. A place where I could open a seam to the Deep. It pulled upon me, and I listened.*

Perhaps that's true, said the Prophet thoughtfully. *Or perhaps it was you who guided the empirium. You who told it what you needed and where to take you.*

Eliana shivered in her wet dress, the blood-soaked fabric already growing stiff. She uncurled her tight fingers. In her palms, her castings held a hint of warmth. *I cannot be afraid of them. I must use them to help me.*

Your castings are of you, the Prophet reminded her. *An extension of your body, your mind, and your power, not a separate thing. It is yourself you must not fear.*

As if that were an easy thing. Eliana half formed a useless rude thought, then tossed it away. Under the arbor's leaves, the screams of Elysium rising to meet her ears, she breathed. There was a chill breeze that raised the hair on her arms. The roof was made of white stone, and she felt the age of it, how long it had lived in the earth before it was carved free. There was water in the leaves shivering overhead, and there was sunlight somewhere beyond the horizon, where it was morning instead of night.

Her palms grew hotter. Even with her eyes closed, she could see their twin flares, how they beamed to see her. She welcomed her power, cupped her hands around it, and in its vast brilliance, she found the river she had first made with the Prophet so many weeks ago.

Never step out of that little river. She recalled the Prophet's words, ran over the grooves of their memory in her mind. *Keep your feet cool and grounded, even as your hands begin to blaze. He cannot find you here, little one, not in these waters.*

Feet in cool water. Mind smooth and hard as a stone. Fire in her hands and stars behind her eyelids. Her veins a web of light.

I rise

The empirium's voice boomed inside her, singular and many. A wave threatening to crest, hungry for the shore.

I rise

I RISE

"No," Eliana whispered. "*I rise.*"

Then she stood. She opened her eyes and looked once more into the eerie, silvered night. She watched Ostia's light shift slowly in the sky and listened to the thrum of her power, how it moved through her body and into the air and back again. Her blood pulsed with the great ancient heartbeat of the world. A map of the empirium expanded before her, its brilliant vastness unspooling at her command. Cords of light rippling in an endless sea. Planes upon planes of shifting gold, and within them an infinite number of paths to walk.

A beat, a held breath. Something pulled at her—the tightness of a sky ready to split with lightning. Arabeth in hand, she found the path she needed and followed it back down into the Emperor's city, the screams of the hunted rising to greet her and the gold eyes of her castings open wide in her palms.

← 29 →

RIELLE

"I have decided not to tell anyone of what I saw in Meridian. Knowing that Rielle killed Grand Magister Belounnon will bring no comfort to anyone here. But I cannot stop thinking of the look on her face as she incinerated him: The shadows on her gaunt face. The furious molten gold of her eyes. One moment he was there. The next, there was fire, and he was gone. And before Annick and I fled, I looked back at Rielle and saw her trembling in the rain. She wept, her skin glowing with a faint gold sheen, and gazed across the sea toward the black eastern horizon."

—Journal of Garver Randell,
dated February 17, Year 1000 of the Second Age

Rielle knew after her first resurrection that it was impossible to continue working underground. All that weight above her, the mountain's cold black bulk. She needed to see the sky.

Corien asked for no further explanation. He ordered a dozen of his soldiers and an outfit of one hundred adatrox to construct an altar on the mountain beside his fortress. A stone walkway led from one of the windows on the highest floor of the fortress, near Corien's own rooms, out across the snow to this towering black edifice, dark against the mountain's endless white.

The altar's structure reminded Rielle of the Gate, which delighted her. Three steps led up to a flat plinth of black rock. There was a table of stone for the bodies to lie upon, and stone pillars flanked the spot where she would stand. The plinth itself was freshly engraved with wings, a whole storm of them, feathers so fine that Rielle knelt in her furs to run her fingers over their delicate grooves.

"They made this so quickly," she said, looking up at Corien. "Four days. How?"

It had started to snow. Whorls of it, tiny swift flakes, danced across the altar. A cold wind ruffled the hem of Corien's black cloak. His collar of dark fur was dusted white.

He shrugged at her question, held out his hand. "They had no choice."

She took his hand and rose. The light was dimming. Near the horizon, past the snow-spitting clouds, patches of indigo sky held the last gold of the sun.

"Bring me the next one," she murmured, and kissed him distractedly. Her fingers tingled, hungry and eager. "I want to do it again."

⬥

Corien came to her at dawn. He stood beside her in the gray light as the snow fell soundlessly from the sky.

In silence, he watched her weave wings for the reborn angel on her table. The body lay on its stomach, naked and stark white in the cold.

Once, Corien had shown her where the wings would join the back—not with joints of flesh and bone, as with birds or bats, but with a simple blooming growth of light. He had drawn pictures for her with his mind, shown her the look of the wings in flight. Not just any wings, but his own, long lost. For the first time, he had shown her himself as he once was: Kalmaroth, warmonger and rebel. His name meant "light undying" in Qaharis, and he had understood that to signify he was meant for greatness. Pale skin and dark hair, tall and slender, blazing blue eyes, and wings flaring out from his back—light at the root, shadow-tipped. Apart from the wings and the height of his body, Kalmaroth had looked very much as Corien did now.

Rielle thought of that as she worked. A smile played at her lips. She liked thinking of him years ago, escaping the Deep and finding a human who reflected his own lost beauty.

Like a patient weaver sitting at her loom, Rielle pulled strands of the empirium from the air. Her eyes saw gold, and in it were many things. There was the long, ridged cord of the corpse's spine. There were the stormy dark places within the mass of muscle and sinew where the wings should begin. Her body churned with aches, hot spools of tension burrowing into her shoulders, her wrists, the small of her back. Despite the mountain's bitter cold, beads of sweat raced each other down her brow.

But her mind was clear. Her thoughts soared like knife-winged birds of prey, swift and amber-eyed. She guided the empirium with the needle of her power, and with each swift silver stab, her blood leapt higher, seeking more.

When it was done, the angel lifted herself from the table and stumbled to her feet. One of the palace attendants, teeth chattering even in his furs, hurried forward to offer the angel a robe to cover herself.

But the angel ignored him and instead pushed herself into the air with a jubilant cry. Her wings were incandescent, twin stars of white light affixed to her back. They did not move like songbirds' wings, that undignified flapping. Instead, they angled subtly when necessary to change the course of flight. They narrowed when diving; they expanded when rising.

Soon, the angel's form had vanished. Only the light of her wings remained, gliding fast from peak to peak.

Rielle licked her chapped lips. "Bring me another."

"We'll eat first." Corien retrieved her fur cloak from the ground. "You haven't eaten since yesterday."

"I don't need to eat."

"You do. And you need to wear this." He placed the cloak around her shoulders, over the thin red gown she had worn for days. The fabric, once fine, now reeked of sweat. "You'll grow ill otherwise."

She swatted him away. "I would prefer to continue working. Bring me another."

His pale eyes were very still. "You've been working for seven days, Rielle, with very little rest."

"I am aware. Bring me another."

"You're still human. You need sleep, food, and warmth."

She laughed. "What nerve you have. You whispered in my dreams for months on end, stealing sleep from me until I came to you. And now you say I need to rest."

Turning away from him, Rielle found one of his lieutenants, an ice-eyed female angel with honey-brown skin and black braids. She could not recall her name and did not care to try.

"You," she said. "Bring me another at once."

For hours, the lieutenant had been watching Rielle with shining eyes. She did not even glance at Corien before hurrying back to the fortress, two angels of lower rank at her heels.

Rielle looked up at the sky. Around her altar rippled a shifting ring of shadows as if she were deep underwater, looking up at the light through shivering waves. Hundreds of bodiless angels crowded near to watch her work. How she delighted in the feeling of their awe. Their eager thoughts tapped against her mind like moths hitting a window, clumsy as they chased the light beyond the glass.

"No, Rielle," said Corien tightly, coming up beside her. "We will go inside now."

"We will not. And if you won't choose another angel for me, I'll do it myself."

She let her eyes unfocus, sent her power flooding out to illuminate the mountainside. In the golden realm of her vision, her power hit the angels' minds like a blazing current crashing against rocks. The patterns of its waves were mesmerizing. With each ripple, sensations flew back to her, reporting. Tastes, sounds, textures.

Ah. There was one she liked.

She directed her power to the left. One of the angels peeled free from the rest and came flying to her open arms.

Queen of light and blood. The angel's voice trembled as she drew him down to the dark table of her altar. *Thank you for choosing me. You have my heart, my queen; you have my love and my loyalty.*

Rielle held the angel steady against the stone, the fabric of his mind stretched between her hands like a canvas unrolled. Impatience prickled her skin. She glared at the walkway that led to the fortress. The snow was falling faster, veiling the black walls.

"Your lieutenants are slow," she observed. "I need a body."

Corien's shoulders were rigid with anger. "Release him and come inside with me, now."

"I want to do it again."

"And you will, my love, but not until tomorrow."

She set her jaw, fighting to still her trembling mouth. She knew he was right; she could feel how her hands shook, the sway of her balance. Her stomach and throat felt on the verge of collapse, dry and pinched, desperate for food.

If only he had not stopped her. While she worked, she noticed none of this.

"I have only resurrected three hundred angels," she muttered.

He laughed quietly. "In seven days. A remarkable achievement."

"We need more than that to do all we have dreamt of."

She sent him a simple thought: *I need more.*

"Celdaria isn't going anywhere," he said aloud, ignoring her silent plea. "The *world* isn't going anywhere, and nothing can stop us."

"My mind aches for more of this." She wanted to cry with frustration; she wanted to punch the stone table in two. "And yet my body is too weak for it."

"You are only human," he said gently.

"I am more than human!" she roared at him. Beneath her voice rang a deeper one, a furious distortion. The rumbling of some creature stirring on the ocean floor. Rielle fixed him with a brittle smile. "And isn't that what you've always wanted?"

Corien was very still. Above them, the cloud of circling angels flinched.

Then Corien came close, mouth hovering beside her cheek. "You know I don't wish to make you come inside with me, but I will do it if you leave me no choice."

"Do that and I'll kill you," she growled.

A soft puff of laughter. "You won't."

He had stayed out of her mind since she had opened the Gate and returned to the Reach, but now she felt him sifting carefully through the outer edges of her thoughts. He was not wrong. She would not kill him. It would destroy her to kill him. There would be no one left in the world who could watch her unafraid.

The angel in her hands vibrated with excitement. *Can you craft my wings to cast iridescent light? Before, my wings shone cerulean and violet in starlight, amber and lavender in the sun.*

Corien's icy-eyed lieutenant emerged from the fortress, flanked by her inferiors. In her arms lay the body of a naked man with dark skin. Rielle delighted in the woman's presumptuousness. Normally, Corien insisted upon being the one to take the human's life.

"Rielle, I swear to you, I will do it," said Corien. "I will keep you dumb for days while I spoon food into your mouth."

"Leave me," she hissed, watching eagerly as the body neared the altar. There was a stirring in her breast, molten and bubbling. "I must work."

As the lieutenant stepped onto the plinth, Corien grabbed Rielle's arm, wrenched her against his body.

Brilliant white rage exploded behind her eyes. She shoved him away from her with a sharp cry. The plinth cracked in two. Corien staggered, nearly fell.

And Rielle did not think before she did it. A furious instinct commanded her, and she eagerly obeyed. The scorching power boiling inside her spilled over, blazing down her arms and legs. She twisted the angel between her hands as if he were a mere plaited rope. The cords of his mind stretched, frayed, then snapped. He was clay in her palms, chunks torn off and squashed.

Ignoring his howl of pain, Rielle clapped her palms together and smashed him into oblivion.

The world fell away from under her feet. The landscape before her vanished. In its place, an endless black sea, a sky full of stars.

Frightened by the hugeness of this place, how it sucked at her like a whirlpool, she fought its pull, reached for Corien with her mind and her hands, but could not find him.

She opened her eyes.

She stood in the black sea that had taken her after she had killed the Obex in Patria. Shallow waves edged with gold lapped gently against her shins. The sea floor was soft and ever-changing, a shifting blanket of tiny pebbles. Above, a profusion of stars—vivid azure, amethyst and rose, gilt and ivory and colors she could not name. So many of them painted the black sky that they seemed a solid mass, a sheet of woven jewels with only a few stones missing.

"You've come at last," came a voice from behind her.

She turned. A child in a simple white gown stood not far from her. She was small and round-cheeked, with pale skin and unruly dark hair that fell to her waist. Her lips curved, a sly, familiar smile.

Rielle stepped back, her skin crawling with cold. "Who are you?"

The girl laughed. "You know who I am."

She did. The tones of her own voice chimed in those words. The child was herself as she had been at five years of age, except that her own eyes had been green, and the eyes of this child were a brilliant gold. An aura of light shone around her, as if she eclipsed the sun.

"I don't understand." Rielle glanced back over her shoulder, as if she would find Corien there. But she saw only the sea, endless and glittering. "Have I died?"

"Not yet," the girl answered brightly. "The shell of your body is there, but the heart of you, your true self, is here with me. It's not death, even though it looks like it. It's *next*."

"I would like to see myself," Rielle said, sick with fear.

The girl wrinkled her nose. "If you insist."

Before Rielle's eyes appeared a vision of herself, still and glassy-eyed, back on the mountain. Her skin and lips were deathly pale. Corien sat on the steps of her altar, holding her in his arms, begging her to awaken. He roared for his officers to fetch the healers from their laboratories.

Rielle shivered, watching this unmoving version of herself. She certainly *looked* dead.

"Don't worry." The girl's voice was high and clear. "Didn't you hear me? You're not dead yet. Now, come. I've been waiting so long for you to arrive. Walk with me. I should like to show you what is here."

Rielle hesitated, then took the girl's hand. They walked through the shallow black-gold sea. The hem of the child's white gown floated on the water's surface.

"Do not be afraid," said the girl cheerfully, leading her on. "It is only me here, and I have no wish to hurt you. I think you will like it here very much. I think you will prefer it."

Rielle shivered. She longed to rip her hand free and also to wrap the child in her arms. "Where are we?"

"We are everywhere. Do not let go of my hand, please. That will make it easier for you. Your mind is still quite crude in its humanity."

Then the girl tugged Rielle forward, and the sky began to move. The stars streaked past them in brilliant streams of color, but the water remained calm, as if somehow every step they took covered a span of many miles above and only a few inches below.

Rielle cried out and stumbled, her mind unable to grasp the incongruity, but the girl's grip was strong. Her laughter chimed above the roar of the sky.

"Where are you taking me?" Rielle gasped.

"I want you to see me," the girl replied. "Am I not beautiful?"

"I cannot look." Tears streamed down Rielle's face. Her chest tightened. The force of the stars streaking past, how they rushed like angry rivers. The sound would crush her.

"I understand. Your eyes are simple, but they will not always be. Already it has begun."

Hours passed. At last, Rielle cracked open her eyes just enough to see her feet moving shakily through the black water. The sea's surface did not reflect the light of the stars. The waves held their own light, as if illuminated by fires that burned deep underwater.

She found her voice, hoarse from disuse. "You are the empirium, aren't you?"

"You should open your eyes all the way and look around." The girl's whisper made her jump.

They had stopped moving and were now sitting in the shallow sea. Something tickled the back of Rielle's neck, urging her face toward the sky. She fought it, though she ached to look up. If she saw whatever hung in the sky above her, she would never want to look away. Instead, she watched the warm water lap against her swollen belly.

Playful, the girl drew her hands across the waves, then smiled up at Rielle. "This is where you belong. Look up and tell me you agree. I would like you to agree."

Rielle hesitated. The seabed pebbles were silky between her fingers, each one pulsing with the rapid patter of her heartbeat.

"Look up, won't you?" the girl said once more. "You will not be sorry."

Rielle could no longer resist. She lifted her gaze to the sky.

Among the stars, globes of light and rock spun slowly—some large and near, others small and distant. Stripes of color ribboned some; others were plain or murky with clouds. Rielle ached to reach up and touch them. She sat on her hands.

"What are they?" she whispered.

"They are worlds. Would you like one?"

Rielle ignored the question. "I don't understand. My world does not look like this."

"It would if you lived in the stars and looked down upon it. It is a pretty thing, Avitas. Green and blue and white. A gemstone streaked with clouds."

Rielle's heart pounded all reason out of her. She struggled to form thoughts. "Tell me: Are you the empirium?"

The girl looked disappointed. "Everything is the empirium."

"But there must be a single place or being more powerful than the others. A place where everything began. A being that began it."

"Must there?" The girl tilted her head. "Perhaps you are the being that began it, for you are of the empirium, and the empirium is all things. Perhaps nothing began it and it has always been." Her bright golden eyes did not blink. "Perhaps I am the empirium, one of many that have existed, and the time has come for me to be reborn as another."

Rielle's breathing had grown thin. "You speak nonsense. Are you the empirium or not? Are you the thing that made us?"

"Would you try to kill me if I were? Usurp my place?" The girl's voice had gone cold. "Your angelic lover might wish you would. His questions are pale. His sight is narrow. Without you to help him, he is insignificant."

The girl stood, found Rielle's hand once more. "There is more to see. You are the first in an age who has been strong enough to see me. I would like to share all of myself with you."

Rielle gazed up as they walked, the waves sloshing around her legs. The sky was a tumult of streaking color, planes upon planes of it, as if the river of stars had fractured into facets that each now streamed in a different direction.

"If you are of the empirium," Rielle began, "and so am I, then I'm not seeing only you. I'm seeing myself. In all of this—these stars, these worlds. I am reflected in them."

The girl's voice bubbled with glee. "Now you are beginning to understand. Come! Hurry!"

Rielle followed, a new deft grace in her steps. How beautiful the sky was, how glorious in its strangeness. She plunged her hand into it, drew down one of the spinning worlds. A little violet jewel, angry yellow clouds swirling across half its surface.

"Do with it as you wish," the girl whispered. They sat at the edge of the sea, their feet dangling. Below them, a waterfall plunged silently into blackness. "Do you love it?"

Rielle examined the world, slowly rolling it back and forth between her palms. "I feel nothing for it."

"What if beings live upon it?"

"Do they? How many?"

"Millions."

Alarmed, Rielle released the world back into the sky. She pushed herself to her feet, watched the stars absorb it. "I wish to leave now."

The girl frowned. "But there is so much more to see."

"I'm tired."

"You won't be forever."

Rielle's eyes filled with tears. She could not tear her gaze from the sky. She never wanted to stop looking at it; she wanted to pluck every world from the stars and run her fingers across them until she had memorized their textures. And yet her body ached for stillness, for the warm comfort of Corien's bed. The conflict soured her tongue, as if she had bitten into metal.

The girl stood. Her grip on Rielle's hand was iron, her smile glittering. Rielle recognized that smile; she had worn it herself.

And she realized, with a dizzying wave of clarity, that she was speaking to the empirium, yes, but she was also speaking to the part of herself that wished to see more, to make and unmake and never stop.

"Come with me," the girl pleaded. "You will see. We are rising, you and I. There is so much more for us to do."

They plunged back into the sea, crossing it beneath the churning stars. The girl's pace was swifter now. The stars and their worlds blurred into unreadable sheets of color.

Movement caught Rielle's eye. She glanced left, saw reflections of herself and the bright-eyed girl holding her hand, the black sea at their feet, the chaos overhead. Countless reflections, infinite to the horizon. On her right, the same thing, and before her, and behind her. An infinite prism of herself. She whirled, searching, and when she called out for Corien, her terrified voice echoed against itself. *Corien?* The single plaintive word expanded, ripples of sound colliding until her ears rang.

"I have so many more things to show you," said the girl, frowning. She tugged Rielle faster. "Come. This way. I'm lonely and I'm tired. It's so nice to have a friend. Please?"

The girl's smallness was an illusion. The force of her dragging Rielle through the water was that of ten thousand rolling storms. Rielle tried to stop, dug her heels into the soft seabed, but the sight of her reflections, all of them doing the same thing, disoriented her. She lost her balance and fell, but the girl caught her.

"Look!" The girl swept her arm across the sky. The stars halted in their roaring currents, then coalesced and shrank. Bright pearls of light dotted the emptied sky, each surrounded by a faint glow.

Weak-kneed with fear, Rielle nevertheless marveled at them. Her blood roared in her ears, just as when the rivers of stars had blazed through the sky. Her power reached out from her chest—dozens of seeking fingers, all groping for more. More light to be dazzled by, more worlds to touch, more speed. She longed to cross an ocean even larger than the one at her feet. To jump from pearl to pearl, those opalescent eyes staring down at her from the sky, and follow whatever path they took.

"What are they?" she breathed.

The girl's cheek pressed against her arm. "Someday you will find out," she murmured, dreamy.

Rielle, please! Come back to me!

Her heart jumped at the distant sound of Corien's voice. The pain of her body returned to her, as if carried on the backs of his words: the pangs of her hungry stomach, her parched mouth. She stepped back, turned her gaze away from the sky.

The girl opened her mouth and howled with furious despair, and the world plunged into darkness.

Rielle ran from her through the water, though it broke her heart to leave this part of herself, so pure and unwavering in its desires. She had so many questions, so many worlds to touch. With each step, she wondered if she would find another cliff and fall off the edge of all things.

"You cannot leave me!" the girl wailed. "I will not allow it!"

Something hot and sharp tugged on Rielle's arms, her chest, her trembling knees. She glanced back and saw nothing. A black abyss, and her feet sinking into the seabed, and a terrible silence that threatened to smother her.

She sent out a thought to Corien. The farther she ran from the girl, the more clearly she could think. *Hold on to me. Don't let me go.*

I have you. His voice was firm and steady. He sent her image after image, each less muddy in her mind. The fortress rising dark and square, the mountains in their coats of snow. Corien, cradling her body in his arms. She saw her own inert body flicker, a candle's flame wavering in the wind. Waves of gold passed over her body's skin, and she knew they were scorching hot, for she could feel that searing heat in her own blood, how it pulsed like water boiling, and yet Corien did not shy away. He held her and held her, whispering her name against her hair, and with his mind he called her forward across the sea. The girl's piercing wails spiraled higher, so deafening that Rielle thought her skull would shatter before she escaped.

Then, a wall of cold slammed against her, shoving air back into her lungs.

She burst back into herself, felt the delicate wet fall of snow on her cheeks and the warmth of Corien beside her, and began to laugh. Tears soaked her face; her chest ached with wild sobs.

"Where did you go?" Corien asked quietly, once her laughter gentled.

She pressed her face against his coat. "I went to what is next," she whispered. "I went inside myself and saw what I am and what I will become. I looked at the stars and pulled them down and held them."

Corien was quiet. She could feel his mind examining her every word.

"Would you like to go back?" he asked at last.

Rielle scanned the Reach, curious what had happened in her absence. Her power skimmed across the empirium, then brought images back to her: The avalanche she had caused when the empirium took her, how it had crashed down the mountain and flattened dozens of adatrox. Boulders of ice had smashed into one of the enclosures that held the doomed ice-dragons. Several of them were now free, fleeing for the mountains. At their sides limped their Kammerat companions, those odd, obsessive little Borsvallic recluses who preferred the company of dragons to that of humans.

And, Rielle noticed with a flicker of interest, they were not alone.

There was Obritsa and her guard, Artem. And Ilmaire Lysleva too, and another young man beside him. Another of the Kammerat.

At once, Rielle sensed Corien's rising anger. Now that she was safe, he would kill them.

"Don't hurt them," she commanded. "Who is that man? I do not recognize him."

"His name is Leevi," Corien told her, his voice thin with anger. "One of the Kammerat, a former prisoner here. He escaped months ago, and now he returns with the king of Borsvall, and more Kammerat too, all come to save their kin." Corien's voice curled. "How heroic."

"Let them go," said Rielle, already losing interest in the frantic little group.

Corien's every thought clenched into fists. "They will think they have beaten me."

"And if they do?" Rielle touched his cheek, turned him to face her. "It won't matter in the end. We will kill them. They will live and watch us rise. They will die at their own hands, unable to bear the agony of their failure. Whichever of these things happens, their joy will be short-lived."

She felt Corien settle, watched the lines of tension melt from his shoulders. He pressed his thumb to her chapped bottom lip.

She smiled at him. "You see? They are nothing to us. Let them flee for their mountains like rabbits running scared. I would like to see them realize the futility of escape. I would like to watch that dawn on their faces. Wouldn't you?"

Corien pressed his brow to hers and closed his eyes. His mind rose to meet hers gently, and when he next looked at her, he was calm.

Then a thought occurred to Rielle. "Did I kill him?" she asked, thinking of the angel she had smashed between her hands.

A pause. Corien's fingers stroked her arm. "You did."

"I hardly remember it," she said, and yet the girl inside her, eyes glittering in her endless sea, could remember every speck of the angel, how it had felt to split him open with her power. Mere dust in her hands, easily swept away.

"I'm sorry," she added, because she felt it was the thing to say.

"He meant very little to me. A child from a common family, neither strong nor clever." Corien paused. "And anyway, you don't mean it."

He was right. The death of that angel had sent her to that place beneath the rushing stars, and she already longed to return to it.

But before she could do that, she would need to be stronger still, in both mind and body, so she could understand what she saw and be worthy of it.

More than that, she needed to look once more into the eyes of those who had feared her. She thought of them all, their names plucked easily from her distant memories: Audric, Ludivine, the Archon, Miren Ballastier, Queen Genoveve. Tal, dead at her hands.

She drew each of their faces to mind and felt a cold white rush of anger. They would be cursing her even now. They would still think of her as human, look at her as if she were one of them. They would perhaps still imagine themselves capable of gentling her.

Corien's lips brushed her brow. She could sense how she baffled him, how carefully he moved around in her mind, as if stepping barefoot around broken glass.

"What is it you want, Rielle?"

"I want everyone to see the wonder of our great work and fall to their knees," she said. "I want to walk the black sea and climb the lights to see what lies beyond them."

She looked up, her vision painting Corien in shades of gold. He sucked in a breath, and gleefully she wondered what she looked like to him now that she had held a world in her palms. When they returned to the fortress, she would go to her mirror before she ate a single scrap of food.

"I want to look once more into the eyes of those who fear me and show them what I have become," she said, her voice trembling as she thought of it. "I will show them they were right to fear me and that I will never again hide from the true reach of my power."

Then Rielle looked past Corien to the dull gray sky and comforted herself by imagining it remade—vast and roaring and incandescent with stars.

30

LUDIVINE

"When the world was young, bright with fire and black with storms, the empirium touched the white sands of Patria's northern shore, and drew up from the dust a creature of such beauty that for a moment all the beasts of the world held their breaths. Into this creature, the empirium breathed the gift of long life, and sent her soaring into the clouds on newborn wings of light and shadow that trailed to her ankles, and named her angel."

—*The Girl in the Moon and Other Tales,*
a collection of angelic folklore and mythology

In her boat, her cloak damp with seawater, Ludivine watched the Mazabatian warships out on the waves. Her stolen human eyes watered from the wind.

There were fifteen ships, their curved wooden hulls and empty decks polished to a gleam. A banner of cyan and emerald fluttered proudly from each mast, and the ships plunged across the sea at full sail—but they were unmanned, propelled forward by waterworkers and windsingers packed into the boats surrounding Ludivine's.

Somewhere above them, silent and unseen in the thick night, Atheria kept watch, ready to dive down and extract Audric if necessary.

"You're doing wonderfully, Lu," came Audric's low voice. He touched her shoulder, for which she was grateful. Even through her cloak and gown, the warmth of his sun-soaked skin was a familiar balm, one that left her chest aching.

It had been so long since he had touched her. She had to look at the thought sideways. Head-on, it would shatter her.

Audric resumed his position at their boat's prow. He was not a sailor, and yet he looked at ease standing there, his cloak fluttering behind him.

Ludivine surveyed the soldiers rowing their boats, the elementals working to push the empty warships across the ocean. When they faltered with fatigue, they looked to Audric, this king who was not their own. Queen Fozeyah remained in Quelbani, overseeing the city's defenses in case of swift retaliation from the Celdarian navy, or the arrival of another storm. Queen Bazati and one thousand Mazabatian soldiers were traveling the land route to Celdaria. In two more days, they would reach the capital.

Princess Kamayin sat behind Ludivine, working as hard as the other waterworkers she commanded, and they were grateful for her. Their thoughts, when they drifted to Kamayin, were bright with love.

But it was Audric, too, whom they loved. They found him in the dark, his curls windblown, his brown skin gleaming with moonlight from without and sunlight from within. Engraved in their minds was the moment when he had plunged into the hurricane's eye and destroyed it from within, his sword ablaze in his bloody palms, the sky blooming gold.

Since that day, his skin had held a new glow. Golden threads of light gilded his curls. He had always been beautiful to Ludivine—those warm brown eyes, that full mouth, his firm, square jaw.

Now, he was something out of saintly lore. The Lightbringer, descendant of Saint Katell, reborn in the belly of a storm.

Her hands trembled. The mental shield she had fashioned to cloak their boats did not waver. But the dark thoughts that had been brewing in her mind for months stirred and swelled, threatening to spill over.

To keep them at bay, she thought through their plan again.

The Sea of Silarra was a blunt spear of water between the southern coast of Celdaria and the northern coast of Mazabat. They had been traveling across it for a week. Ludivine could see the dark line of the Celdarian coast on the horizon.

They had sent ahead a message: *The usurper will fall. The sun will rise.* And now fifteen warships sailed fast for Celdaria. Hundreds of Merovec Sauvillier's soldiers had ridden south from the capital to mount a defense. Ludivine sensed them even now—scores of minds waiting at the shore, others gliding out to meet them on warships of their own.

With the capital emptied of so many of its fighters, Merovec would be utterly unprepared for the arrival of Queen Bazati and the first wave of her army. Ludivine pushed her mind east, toward the road the queen's army traveled, and was pleased to find them on course. They had left Mazabat days before Audric's armada and would arrive in the capital in less than two days, long before the soldiers Merovec had sent to the shore could hurry back to the capital and defend it.

All was as it should be. And yet this was no comfort; Ludivine's thoughts remained a tangled knot of dread and shame.

She licked her upper lip, tasting the salt of her sweat, and marveled. Years in this body, and she had still not grown used to its oddities—the icy drip of anxiety, the hot flush of desire, the sharp pinch of hunger. As an angel, centuries ago, she had of course felt such things. But as a human, each sensation was so much more immediate, the hunger more pressing, the desire more insatiable.

She closed her eyes, fighting the pull of memory. Herself sprawled across Audric's bed in Baingarde, Rielle tucked between them. Audric reading by candlelight, Ludivine absently toying with Rielle's hair. Rielle snoring, her cheek pressed against Ludivine's arm.

Tears turned Ludivine's throat tight and hot. She knew such a moment would never come again.

What is it? Audric scanned the Celdarian shore. *You're troubled.*

It is nothing, Ludivine told him, and she was relieved when she felt the lie pass through him unnoticed.

Rielle would have felt it at once.

Your shield is holding. His thoughts were steady, a firm hand guiding her through a dark maze. *I hope you are proud of your work. It's remarkable.*

Ludivine nearly laughed. *What would have been remarkable is if I had been stronger. If I had managed to fight past Corien's hold on Rielle and get her away from him. If I had persuaded her away from his side and back to ours before she opened the Gate.*

As they plunged across the sea, Ludivine remembered that day in Quelbani when the sky had dimmed and the world had grown still. She had reached for Rielle and seen dim echoes of what she had done—the Gate wrenched open, hundreds of thousands of angels freed. Ludivine felt the memory echo in Audric's mind too, darkening his thoughts. She wished she could hold his hand.

But touching him would only make things harder.

Ludivine pressed her palms together and ran her thoughts once more over the shell of her shield. The more diligently she worked, the less room remained inside her for guilt. Guilt would fade and end. Someday, she would not feel it at all.

Then came a whistling, crackling sound. A hot spear of elemental power shot through the air, and one of the Mazabatian warships burst into flame.

On the horizon, dozens of lights flared bright. Tiny fires, raging and ready.

Audric pointed, running his fingers along the shoreline.

"They're here," he muttered. "And they have firebrands."

Ludivine felt how unsettled Audric was to see the ships his own father had commissioned sailing toward him through the night in the hands of the enemy. Their sails were ghosts, their new House Sauvillier banners gray and black in the moonlight.

"Rowers, hard to starboard!" Audric's voice rang out over the water.

The rowers obeyed. The six boats veered right, a tight formation within Ludivine's shield. Kamayin called out to her elementals in a northern Mazabatian dialect.

"From sky to sky!" she cried. "From sea to sea! Steady do I stand! Never do I flee!"

The windsingers took up the call, chanting the Wind Rite as they worked. And then the waterworkers began, repeating Kamayin's second prayer:

"O seas and rivers! O rain and snow!" Their voices formed a steady chain of sound atop the waves. "Drown us the cries of our enemies!"

They kept the empty Mazabatian armada sailing north without pause, even as each vessel caught fire and burned. The warships met the Celdarian fleet with no arrows fired, no catapults launched.

"Turn, you idiots," Audric whispered, for the Celdarian ships were slow to veer away from the ships bearing down on them.

Ludivine, her back to the flames, could nevertheless sense how confounded the captains were. Fifteen prized Mazabatian warships sailing at full speed to their destruction?

She allowed herself a small smile as their six little boats circled wide around the chaos toward the Celdarian shore. Through Audric's eyes, she saw the fiery Mazabatian ships encircle the bewildered Celdarian fleet, and once they were in place, Audric shouted a single command.

At once, the elementals lowered their arms. Heads drooped onto shoulders. Some leaned out over the water and heaved.

But there was still the shore to reach, and after a few moments' rest, Kamayin called out encouragement, and their tired cloaked fleet resumed course for Celdaria.

Ludivine stared ahead at the dark coastline. Her heart was a wild thing, its rhythm like the clop of a horse running scared.

Audric knelt beside her. "Only a little while longer, Lu," he said. His thoughts were tired; she could sense how the mind-speak had wearied him. "Then we can rest, catch our breath. You have done so well."

She set her jaw against the warmth of his voice. How she had craved its return these long weeks. And now, how she fought to push it from her mind.

Yes, they would reach the shore soon. They would rest.

And then, she would run.

The waterworkers quietly sank the boats in a deep cove off the Celdarian coast some hundred miles from Luxitaine, where there was little but tiny farms and fields of sleepy goats. They made a crude camp in a scrubby woodland near an orchard of olive trees. The air was warm, but in Âme de la Terre, high in the mountains, it would be crisp with the spring snows.

Ludivine waited until most of their party was asleep. Only two people remained awake: a pale, burly woman and a brown-skinned reed of a man, neither of them an elemental. Soldiers, cursing quietly to each other about their aching arms, their hands blistered from rowing. But Ludivine could sense the bloom of their pride, how glad they were to have seen Audric safely to shore.

Her throat ached as she sent them to sleep. They would wake in a half hour or so, embarrassed to have dozed off. They would promise each other to never confess it.

The camp was silent, the moon a thin smile. A goat bleated in its dark field.

Ludivine's knees shook as she left the soldiers behind. There was no need to creep; the power that had shielded them across the water shielded her still. They would hear none of her footsteps, not even feel the air her body moved.

And yet she crept as if across a frozen lake. A sort of madness had taken her. Her thoughts screamed; she could not calm their wild spin.

At a bent oak, she paused. Her nape itched with sweat. For a moment, she stared at the dark countryside, the farmhouse on the hill to her right.

She could have gone then and been done with it.

But she could not resist one last look at him.

Audric slept beneath the oak, the Sun Guard in a tight circle around him and Sloane not far off, sleeping with her arms folded and a frown on her face.

Ludivine knelt beside Audric, held his face in her hands. She could hardly bear to look at him, at how soft and dear he was in sleep. The elegant straight line of his nose, the furrow of his serious brow. Even in repose, he looked a king.

She kissed him as he slept—his temples, his cheeks. Pressing her forehead to his, she breathed the air he exhaled, circled her thumbs against the turn of his jaw.

"I love you, my friend," she whispered. "I have never not loved you." She remembered the words he had given Rielle, how tender his face had been as he spoke them. "My light and my life," she whispered, then pressed her mouth to his cheek.

Tears rolled down her face, her chest so tight she feared it would collapse in on itself. Rising, she did not look at him again. When she stumbled away from him, it felt like what she imagined death to be. In his sleep, he was innocent of her cowardice; when he woke, he would be battered with it.

She put her hand to her chest, willing her heart to stop aching. But she knew it would never. She knew this, and still she left him, trusting that he would be able to sneak through Âme de la Terre and into Baingarde without her there to protect him. He had the Sun Guard, she told herself. He had forty elementals and twenty-four skilled soldiers and a princess of Mazabat.

They do not need an angel, she told herself, and because they were asleep, because she had hidden herself so completely, she cried without fear as she fled. Her sobs gripped her chest like a glove of steel. She climbed a little ridge of rock, wiped her face with dirt-smeared hands.

At the top, she sat on a flat boulder cracked down the middle. It wobbled as she wept. She hugged herself and sent to Audric every memory she had of their years together. Every lazy afternoon stretched out on the rug by the open windows in his rooms, every warm night nestled in his bed. His arms around her, her arms around Rielle. His dark head tucked over her fair one, and Rielle's face smashed into her neck, or his, happily nuzzling them as she drifted off to sleep.

When he woke, he would see the memories, and he would hate them. He would hate her for sending them, reminding him of what they had both lost, and he would hate her even more for leaving him. He would not understand it, and she would not leave him with an explanation, for the truth was too craven.

For years, she had dreamt of a future with them. They would age and have children. Rielle's power would grow, and she would use the empirium to solidify the hold Ludivine kept on this body she had grown to think of as her own. Rielle would help her truly join with it at last, become *human* at last, or at least near enough—stripped of her long life, diminished by Rielle's godly craft to something crude and fragile. And Ludivine would finally be able to rest, no longer fighting to remain intact inside a body but instead simply existing. A being no one would fear or revile. She would love and watch over Rielle and Audric and their family for the rest of her days, and grow old, as they would, and die, as they would, and never be required to live without them.

But instead, she had failed them both utterly. She had known it for months. Either one or both of them would die in the fight to come, perhaps at each other's hands, and Ludivine could not bear to see it.

She rose, shaky, and brushed the twigs from her skirt. Then she turned and saw a looming dark shape among the trees. Monstrously tall, horribly still. Even in the shadows, Atheria's black eyes were unmissable. They fixed on Ludivine as if she were prey.

Ludivine froze. Under the godsbeast's gaze, the shield of her mind felt pitiful and childish. She had never felt more keenly like the coward she was.

"My love was not enough to save them," she whispered, clutching her stomach. "If I stay and watch them die, it will kill me."

The chavaile stared. Her tail flicked savagely.

Ludivine turned away, fled fast through the orchard and across the fields beyond, climbed over a crude wooden fence, and then, at the banks of a small stream, looked back.

Atheria had not followed her. Audric would wake to see the chavaile at his side. Maybe he would see in her great dark eyes the truth she had heard.

Ludivine squared her shoulders and faced the northern horizon. There were hills, and mountains beyond. Patchy woodlands, rivers rushing to the sea. She knew not where she would go, what she would do. She knew only the drum of her heart, her footsteps stamping out *Coward*, the hot racing fear that told her to run.

If she ran, she could hide.

And if she hid, when the world ended, she could live content inside the cocoon of her memories and pretend she heard nothing.

31

AUDRIC

"For weeks, the magisters and I have been suggesting to Merovec that he implement the reinforcements and defensive measures you outlined in your last letter, but he refuses. He insists the true danger is inside Âme de la Terre's walls. He continues his interrogations of elementals and refuses to look past our borders toward the true danger. I suspect it's because the idea of what's coming terrifies him. He is incapable of facing it. Many elementals have gone missing. Rumors of bodies stacking up inside Baingarde race through the streets like wildfire. My heart grieves to send you this news, but I can also tell you this: Red Crown is ready. Everything is in place for your return. A series of instructions sent via several different messengers will shortly be en route to you. Patience and courage, my king. Soon, you will be home. For crown and country, we protect the true light."

—Encoded letter from Miren Ballastier
to the exiled king Audric Courverie,
dated February 21, Year 999 of the Second Age

At every turn in the narrow, dark tunnels beneath Mount Cibelline, a part of Audric held its breath, hoping the next stretch of darkness would reveal Ludivine.

She would be breathless with excitement. News had come from the north. She hadn't run away; she had simply gone into hiding to safely make contact with Rielle. And now, Rielle was coming home, speeding south on some other glorious godsbeast who had come down from the clouds to save her—which would of course make Atheria jealous, Ludivine would point out. He would laugh and embrace her, and then she would shield them all—Audric, Sloane, Evyline and the Sun Guard, Kamayin and her soldiers—as they snuck into Baingarde under cover of night. And by the time Rielle arrived home, the castle would once again be his.

But the tunnels remained dark, the only sounds those of his breathing, the footsteps of his friends and allies, and the other part of Audric, the less hopeful part, knew the truth:

Ludivine was not coming back.

They climbed a narrow set of stone stairs set into the deep earth. Evyline insisted on leading the way; she and Sloane and the Sun Guard had taken this route months earlier and knew it well. Audric marveled at the passage of time. Though only a little over four months had passed since his doomed wedding, the long weeks since had felt like an entire age, and that he had been married to Rielle on the same night as Merovec's coup—the same night he had fled his home—felt bizarre, even impossible.

As he climbed, the acid bite of shame flooded his mouth. Sloane and Evyline, the Mazabatian queens, and Princess Kamayin had all told him many times that it was not cowardice that had driven him away, but he still found it difficult to believe them.

This was a moment in which Ludivine would have reached out to him. *It was not cowardice,* she would have told him in that low, steady voice of hers. *It was wisdom. You could not know what allies remained to you. The vision Corien sent had already thrust the night into chaos. You are the heir to the throne. If you had stayed that night and died, then the reign of Saint Katell and her descendants would truly have been lost.*

But Audric's mind remained his own, empty but for his whirling thoughts. With each footstep, even as he climbed through the mountain, he felt himself sinking back into the heavy, dark place from which he had only just begun to emerge in recent weeks. He longed to sleep, to tuck himself into a cold corner of these tunnels his ancestors had built and close his eyes forever.

But then Evyline, at the head of their procession, opened the hidden door carved into the mountain, and they emerged into the overgrown gardens behind Baingarde.

Audric stood aside at the tunnel's mouth, allowing the others passage, and gazed at the familiar green world around him. So far from the castle, the gardens sprawled untamed. A profusion of ferns and tangled moon-flower vines grew thick around the hidden door. A carpet of pine needles softened the ground, and overhead the trees grew tall and close.

The scent was so familiar that Audric felt lightheaded—the thick green spice of the shivering trees, the sweetness of old leaves rotting in the dirt. Past the wild growth near the door, far out in the jade gloom, a sorrow tree stood, its thin branches heavy with bright green buds and tiny pink blossoms. The first blooms of spring.

Audric could not tear his eyes from them. He had kissed Rielle for the first time beneath one of those trees. He knew he shouldn't think of it, and yet he could not help doing so. The warmth of Rielle in his arms, the softness of her mouth. The eager noises she had breathed against his ear, her trembling hands in his hair. The sweet ache of happiness at finally allowing themselves to kiss.

Sloane touched his shoulder. He waited until his eyes were dry, then turned away from the sorrow tree. Kamayin was muttering instructions to her elementals, their castings faintly aglow. Evyline and the Sun Guard stood in a circle, all of them reciting the seven elemental rites.

Audric could hardly bear to look at them, these people who had decided they would fight at his side. They were so soft in the dim garden light, so breakable. If he had never loved Rielle, would they be standing there? Would a usurper sit on his throne? Would his father be dead and his mother a shell of her former self?

It would have been easier, he knew, if he had never loved her.

And yet, given the choice, he would do it again, even knowing what was to come. He would lose her a thousand times over if it meant he would first have the chance to love her.

They crossed the gardens to the catacombs, where another network of tunnels led into Baingarde itself. They connected to the mountain tunnels at several underground junctures; there had been no need to come to the surface. But Audric had wanted to see the gardens, even though he had known it would hurt him.

Near the catacombs, the seeing pools gleamed flat and black, like polished stones set into the ground. Memories of himself, Rielle, and Ludivine, young and uncaring, flitted across the pools like shadows.

Sloane kept near him as they hurried through the trees. Her short black hair shone blue in the pale moonlight. The polished obsidian orb of her scepter buzzed with ready power, and the shadows clung to her lovingly, like children to their parents' legs.

"It's strange, isn't it?" she murmured. "Remembering the last time we were here? It was such a wild night, so long ago, and so rife with terror. I hardly remember what Baingarde looks like."

"I remember it," Audric said at once. "I see it in my dreams. I taste the cinnamon cakes I used to steal from the kitchens for Rielle. I can smell the old leather of my books. I can feel the cold hoof of Saint Katell's stone mare in the Hall of the Saints. I used to sit on it and pray when I was a child, when I couldn't sleep. I could tell you every stair that creaks in the servants' wing. There is a tapestry on the second floor, near my father's old study. It depicts Saint Nerida standing in the middle of a crashing sea, the waves splitting apart on either side of her. There is a golden thread on her trident that's come loose. Right on the shaft, below the middle prong."

They had reached the catacombs. Sloane watched him steadily, saying nothing. The others waited in the shadows, weapons at the ready, scanning the trees for enemies.

"I remember everything," Audric whispered.

A call shattered the night's quiet: three long blasts bellowing from the old watchtower at the city's perimeter. Audric had only ever heard the sound when Miren and her acolytes from the Forge had visited the horns to make repairs and refresh the magic woven into their metal.

The sound of that horn meant that enemies had been sighted.

Another horn answered, this one higher and brassier. Kamayin, grinning, lifted her chin; her soldiers stood taller. It was the Queen's Horn of the Mazabatian army, announcing their arrival. Queen Bazati would be with them, and General Rakallo. One thousand Mazabatian troops. More would come, once they had retaken the city. The real battle was yet to come.

Audric turned to face his own little army. The faintest sliver of light escaped the top of Illumenor's sheath, lighting the faces gathered around him with an eerie glow.

"May the Queen's light guide us," he said without shame, for Rielle may have left them, but the prayers spoken in her name had lost none of their power.

And there was still another queen to be found, if the prophecy was true. *She carries a girl*, Ludivine had told him weeks ago, and whenever he thought of it, his heart ached with love. Was it his child's light they now followed? Or was it simply the light that came of believing there was reason to keep going?

Audric caught Kamayin's eye. She nodded once, her castings humming gold at her wrists. Then he found Evyline, towering above them all. The lines around her mouth looked deeper than Audric had ever seen them, the gray of her hair that much closer to white.

How the last few months had aged them all. How stretched thin with grief they had become.

"May the Queen's light guide us," Evyline answered, and the Sun Guard echoed her prayer.

There was nothing else to say. Audric hurried into the cool darkness of the catacombs, the air heavy with the weight of lives lived and lost, and led his fierce little army into the tunnels that would take him home at last.

Baingarde buzzed with chaos.

Servants gathered weapons and supplies, fled to their rooms, took up posts at the windows to watch the battle unfolding outside. Soldiers of House Sauvillier ran from storeroom to storeroom, then out into the castle yards.

Audric, Kamayin, Evyline, and Sloane each led a team of fighters up through the castle from its cavernous foundations. Audric had drawn diagrams of Baingarde, gone over the maps again and again until everyone from the boats that had crossed the Sea of Silarra knew the number of rooms, the stairwells to avoid, where guards would most likely be posted. Anyone they encountered, they were to incapacitate—no killing, if they could manage it—and to avoid detection, they were to use elemental magic only when necessary. The common soldiers sworn to serve Merovec Sauvillier, Audric had told them, were not to blame for the crimes of their lord.

Audric approached Baingarde's soaring entrance hall, his team of six at his heels. They crouched in the shadows of the second-floor mezzanine. A polished wooden arcade ran the length of each corridor of the mezzanine, and heavy green drapes curtained private sitting rooms. Three enormous staircases joined the mezzanine to the hall below, where the polished marble floor gleamed.

Audric watched the massive front doors open, thick wood reinforced with stone. A stream of Sauvillier soldiers rushed out into the night, their commander barking orders. Even once they had closed the doors behind them, Audric could hear the sounds of battle in the city. He glanced out the windows that spanned the length of the front wall, saw the streets of his city sloping down to the wide, saint-made lake and the broad grassy Flats beyond.

The Flats were alight with magic—angry bursts of fire, soaring streaks of sunlight. The Mazabatian army was a great dark river pouring through the wide pass between Mount Taléa and Mount Sorenne. Scattered shapes spilled across the Flats to meet them.

Audric watched grimly. With so many of Merovec's soldiers still making their way back from the coast, those left in the capital would be overwhelmed by the brutal efficiency of Queen Bazati's one thousand troops. Miren's reports had estimated that only a few hundred Sauvillier soldiers had remained at their posts in the capital, and those would be listless and agitated, undisciplined, as all Merovec's soldiers had become.

They would not stand for long against the Mazabatians. It was a fantastic diversion to direct attention away from the castle and a startling demonstration for the citizens of Âme de la Terre of how inadequately Merovec had prepared the city for angelic invasion.

But Audric still had to move quickly.

From under the hood of his cloak, he watched the shadows, his fighters tense behind him. At the far end of the entrance hall, the great polished doors of the Hall of the Saints stood closed. A dozen guards flanked the doors. Two dozen more were stationed around the entrance hall.

Audric frowned, recalling Miren's encoded instructions. *He will be in the Hall of the Saints*, she had written. *I will get him there and keep him there.*

But with so many soldiers surrounding the doors? Miren had assured him they would be lightly guarded, and the sight of three dozen watchful fighters left Audric feeling uneasy. Had Miren's messages been intercepted? Had their spies betrayed them?

Nerves buzzed under his skin; he itched to move. A light flashed softly across the mezzanine—three times in rapid succession—marking the arrival of Sloane's group. Another set of flashes, then a third—Evyline's and Kamayin's groups. The guards below looked up, drawing their blades.

Audric hissed a command to his fighters, and they rushed down the stairs, the other three groups doing the same across the room. Audric did not draw Illumenor. Merovec's guards may have suspected he was somewhere in this fight, but he would keep them wondering for as long as he could.

As they charged the Sauvillier soldiers, he braced himself for the slam and burn of magic—but none came.

He watched in shock as his people easily dispatched three dozen soldiers. There were no elementals among them, he realized. Miren's letters had told him of Merovec's new fear of magic, how he suspected all elementals to be secret allies of Rielle. But to protect himself with guards who stood no chance against attackers who would of course fight with magic seemed a foolishness too astonishing to believe.

Kamayin and her elementals blasted the soldiers with wind and water—moisture drawn from the air, wind held waiting in their palms. Sloane's scepter slashed blue light, summoning shadow-wolves that sent the soldiers cowering. Evyline and the Sun Guard blazed a path toward the Hall of the Saints. They were a fierce storm, pouring all their fury and grief into the blows of their swords. Evyline let out a ferocious guttural yell and cut down the last of Merovec's guards.

She turned and found Audric across the hall. Bodies littered the floor. Some of the soldiers groaned, clutching their wounds. But most were still.

Breathing heavily, Evyline bowed her head. "I tried my best to spare them, my king, but when someone runs at you with a sword, you do what you must." She paused. "When they saw what Merovec was doing, they could have fled. They could have defied him."

Audric stepped over a body at his feet.

"Not all of them could have," he said quietly. "He could have held their families prisoner. He could have threatened them with torture. I don't blame them, and I grieve each of their deaths."

Then, his people behind him, their castings and swords raised and ready, Audric pushed open the doors and entered the Hall of the Saints.

Inside the massive room, shadows reigned. The only light came from the prayer torches affixed to the base of each enormous stone saint. Queen Genoveve's and King Bastien's empty thrones sat on the dais at the far end of the room. Above them curved a wide loft in which rows of polished wooden chairs awaited the Grand Magisters, the royal councils and advisers, and invited nobility. Beyond the loft, elaborate stained glass depicted the saints in peacetime, the Angelic Wars far behind them. And towering between the loft and the thrones was the statue of Saint Katell on her white mare, her head crowned with a polished halo of gold.

Here, Audric's father had questioned Rielle after the Boon Chase. Here, the Archon had crowned her Sun Queen, and Ludivine had come back from the dead. The weight of the room's past pressed against Audric's skin.

He glanced around quickly as he strode past the watching saints. A dozen Sauvillier archers stood in the loft, their arrows trained on him. Around the room, swords raised and arrows nocked, were more soldiers, each of them tracking his people as they followed him inside.

And standing on the dais was Merovec Sauvillier himself, resplendent in the mail and armor of his house—a sash of russet, silver tassels, a fine tabard of thick wool dyed midnight blue. His blond hair fell in waves to his shoulders, and his eyes were as sweet a blue as Ludivine's. Save for his jaw, which was firm and square where Ludivine's was soft, the resemblance was uncanny.

In his arms, he held Queen Genoveve. Her back was to his front, a thin silver blade at her throat.

"Come closer, and I will cut her throat," Merovec called out, his voice booming in the empty room.

Audric stopped, gesturing for the others behind him to do the same. It should have terrified him to see his mother held so cruelly. Instead, a calm fell over him, leaving his mind sharp and clear.

"You're already a traitor and a criminal, Merovec," Audric said. "You would add murder of your own aunt to that list?"

"My traitor aunt." Merovec wrenched Genoveve's head closer to his own, his hand wrapped in her hair. "She insisted I stay here rather than go out with my soldiers to meet the Mazabatian army. First Bastien is killed, then her son disappears, and her niece. She said she couldn't bear to lose me too." He hissed against her ear, "Do you think I am unaware of where you've been sneaking off to of late, dearest aunt?"

Genoveve did not flinch in Merovec's grip. Her graying auburn hair gleamed copper in the torchlight. Her eyes were twin coins of steel.

"I think you are unaware of many things," she replied evenly.

"Red Crown, they call themselves. House Courverie loyalists." Merovec spat on the floor. "My own people, plotting behind my back as I work to keep them safe, as I undo the evil their own prince allowed into their country."

Audric locked eyes with his mother, took a single step forward. In the shadows atop the loft, the archers shifted but did not loose their arrows.

"And what have you done to keep them safe?" he asked. "I saw no bolstered defenses at the city borders, no additional watchtowers constructed in the mountains. I have heard of no education given to the people about angels or how to strengthen their minds. Nor do I hear talk of Merovec Sauvillier forging alliances with Borsvall or Kirvaya."

"Borsvall and Kirvaya." Merovec's handsome face twisted. "One without a king, and the other without a queen. Both of them fled into the night, leaving their countries in chaos. I want nothing to do with them."

Audric took another step. "I heard what you did to Ilmaire Lysleva. He was a guest in your own home, and you beat him, imprisoned him." Another step, each one measured and careful. "I would say you should be ashamed, but I know you have no capacity for it."

Merovec barked out a laugh. "Ilmaire? He was weak. A sop of a king who wanted us to open our arms to Rielle, let her do as she wishes. *Forcing Rielle to choose between good or bad, light or blood, is folly,* he said. *It will be our undoing.* I see why you like him. He's as big a fool as you are. He didn't want the crown, anyway. I did him a favor."

"And now you hide in my castle and terrorize my people." Audric kept moving forward, another step with every sentence. The archers would not hurt him, not without Merovec's command. "You interrogate them and invade their homes. You question their faith and tear apart families."

"I cannot be sure which of them you and your murderous bride managed to corrupt before she left you." Merovec tilted his head. A sharp grin widened his mouth. "Tell me, do you pleasure yourself while imagining her moaning in the arms of her new lover?"

But Audric was impervious to him, his mind a spotless shield. "Fear has consumed you, Merovec, and you have turned Âme de la Terre into a nest for it. A place of suspicion and distrust. You have done nothing to prepare our people for what's to come."

Merovec looked around the room. His blade cut into Genoveve's throat. A thin trickle of blood dripped down her white neck, but she did not cry out; her face didn't even flicker with pain, and Audric's heart swelled with love for her.

"Where is my sister?" Merovec snapped.

Audric had reached the sun engraved in the polished stone floor, where Rielle had stood during her deposition, only a few paces from the dais. He stood in the sun's heart, Illumenor humming at his side.

"She isn't here," he replied.

"Of course she is." Merovec's smile turned bitter. "I know what she is now. The angelic wretch in my sister's body. Ludivine!" He roared her name, pressed his knife harder against Genoveve's throat. "Ludivine, or whatever your filthy true name is, show your face!"

"She's gone, Merovec. Not two days past, she disappeared into the night. I've no sense of what's happened to her."

"You lie. How else could you sneak into Baingarde unseen?"

"Because it's my home." Audric took another step forward. "I was born here, I was raised here, and it was here that my father taught me how to rule a country, just as his mother taught him and her father taught her. I know secrets about Baingarde that you will never know, and I know my people too."

"You're holding her hostage somewhere. You think you'll be able to trade her life for your mother's."

Genoveve stared at Audric, her expression turned inward. Nothing showed on her face—no pain, no fear. Nothing but a hard light in her eyes that reminded Audric of the woman she had once been before Bastien's death had ravaged her.

"It's not possible to hold Ludivine hostage. To avoid capture, she would enter my mind and dissuade me from binding her." Audric glanced at the stained-glass windows beyond the statue of Saint Katell. He needed to stall a bit longer. "I'm sure you wonder when it happened. Do you remember when Lu caught a terrible fever when she was sixteen? She was gravely ill for weeks."

A flicker of memory on Merovec's face. "You try my patience."

"I know the feeling. Lu died that night. An angel took possession of her body and her name. The transition was seamless. She wanted to be close to Rielle, to observe and protect her. Your sister did not suffer." Then he added calmly, "I thought I would send you to your death knowing that, at least. Or you can release my mother and relinquish the throne you stole from me, and this bloodshed will end. We can talk more of these things. You and your soldiers can join my own and help us ready our country for war."

A low boom exploded outside, shaking the castle—the unmistakable sound of two elemental magics crashing into each other. In its wake, the silence was woolen. A single Sauvillier soldier shifted to Audric's right.

"Is there nothing you have touched that isn't ashes?" Merovec said, his eyes bright. Only now did his voice waver, cracking to show the fear underneath. "You and Rielle both leave death in your wakes. There is nothing we can do to stop what is coming, and you know it. We cannot live while she survives. I will hang your corpse from Baingarde's gate, and beside it the bodies of everyone in Red Crown. My soldiers will have seized them by now. Their faces will rot in the sun, turn swollen and black. And those who pass this monument of ruin will remember what happened to King Audric the weakhearted and everyone who loved him."

Audric looked once more to the stained glass. A faint shadow swooped past it. His hand moved slowly to Illumenor's hilt.

"The Scourge was a dark time in our history, Merovec," he said. "That you would insist on recreating it, this time not hunting marques, but rather anyone you suspect of working against you, is proof enough that you are unworthy of your stolen crown."

"Not another step!" Merovec bellowed. Three quick swipes of his knife left red gashes on Genoveve's arms and cheek. She did cry out then, a muted yelp of pain that made Audric's vision pulse black.

"I'll cut her open and let her bleed out on this throne you think I don't deserve!" Merovec's face was wild. "And you'll have ruined yet another life!"

A piercing explosion swallowed Merovec's voice. The stained glass windows shattered. Colored shards flew across the room, and Atheria followed close behind, her mouth open wide to bare her fearsome sharp teeth. She trumpeted a cry of rage that hit Audric's bones like ice.

Merovec released Genoveve, fumbling for his sword. Genoveve elbowed him in the ribs, then whirled and tried to punch him. He caught her wrist and flung her to the floor bright with glass, kicked her in the side again and again.

The Sauvillier soldiers in the loft shot their arrows. Audric dodged them, ran for the dais. To his left, Sloane pulled shadows from the hall's corners, cast them into sharp-beaked hawks. They dove fast, repelled every new arrow shot. Evyline and the Sun Guard rushed forward, their swords flying. Some of Merovec's soldiers tried to flee, screaming in terror as Atheria snapped at them. Kamayin whirled, her wrists blazing. She reached for the seven prayer basins lining the room and smacked the fleeing soldiers with foaming fists of water.

An archer crouched in the loft sprang to her feet and shot an arrow at Atheria. It struck her right shoulder, near her wing joint. She shrieked and dove for the archer, who shot her again, this time in the thick muscle of her upper left leg, but didn't have time to nock a third arrow before Atheria reached her. She grabbed the archer by her throat and flung her hard to the floor below.

Audric raced up the steps of the dais and unsheathed Illumenor. His power raced through his body, crashed into the sword, then ricocheted back into him, flooding his veins with blazing heat. An endless cycle of power, blade to blood to blade again. Gold danced before his eyes, but instead of obscuring his vision, it enhanced it.

He swung Illumenor. The sword's brilliance erupted, blasting the room free of shadows. Everyone fighting staggered, shielding their eyes.

Merovec left Genoveve bleeding on the glass-strewn floor and spun to meet Audric's sword with his own. Their blades crashed together. Audric bore down on him, Illumenor crackling with trapped sunlight. Merovec cried out, looked away from the impossible brilliance, but held his sword fast.

"You won't win, Merovec," Audric told him. "Surrender, and you will live. Resist, and I will destroy you. I don't want this for you or for me. We are family. We are children of Celdaria."

Merovec thrust the weight of his body up against Audric's sword, unlocking the grip of their blades. He swung wide for Audric's neck, unable to aim in the glare of Illumenor.

Audric spat a curse. There would be enough death in days to come, but Merovec was leaving him no choice.

He focused his mind, sent bolts of power streaking down his arms. Illumenor scorched white-hot, its power extending past the metal until the blade became as solid and thick as a spear.

With the dawn I rise, Audric prayed, raising Illumenor. *With the day I blaze.*

He brought Illumenor down across Merovec's torso, slicing clean through his armor, bone, and muscle. The two halves of his body dropped to the floor, the wounds steaming and clean, bloodless. Audric stared at the carnage in Illumenor's unforgiving light. He would never be able to burn from his mind the image of those glassy blue eyes, frozen in shock.

The room plunged into silence. What soldiers of House Sauvillier still stood let their weapons fall.

Audric knelt at his mother's side, making sure no one else could see his face. He didn't trust it not to show his horror, how he loathed the destructive potential of his power and the fact that he had been forced to use it in such a way.

He inspected Genoveve's wounds. The cuts on her throat were shallow, but she breathed carefully, her face white. Broken ribs, he guessed, and hopefully nothing worse. He held her head, and she turned her face into his palm and let out a single fractured sob.

"I thought I would never see you again," she whispered. "I'm sorry. I'm so sorry. I should have stopped him. I shouldn't have let him…"

She gasped, her voice lost in pain. Audric pressed his brow to hers. On the floor beside them, Illumenor trembled in a bed of glass.

"I don't need your apologies," he said. "What I need is for you to live and help us through these dark days. My brave mother. I love you. I've missed you."

"I hate what I've become since your father died," Genoveve choked out.

Audric shook his head, kissed her cheek. "I don't."

Then he rose. Everyone in the room was watching him—his people, the surrendered soldiers on their knees. All their eyes upon him were a terrible weight, even those of his friends. What were they to do next? They waited for him to tell them. Someone would always be waiting for him to declare war or peace, or dispense judgment, or grant mercy.

He had never imagined having to do all of that alone.

"Evyline," he began, "send two of your guards for Garver Randell, and tell him King Audric requests his presence at the castle. Kamayin, you and your elementals will guard the captured soldiers, hold them here in the hall. Sloane, help me bandage Atheria's wounds, and then we'll need to find a sack or fashion a sling in which to carry this."

He knelt by Merovec's torso, made himself stare at the horror of it.

"I must ride out to the Flats," he said quietly, "and show the brave soldiers of House Sauvillier that the man they fight for is no more."

Then he closed Merovec's eyes and retrieved Illumenor. The heat had burned away any trace of blood. The blade gleamed silver and clean, as if it had never in its life known the taste of death.

32

ELIANA

*"Kalmaroth and I were boys together. Once, I even loved him.
We brought back to our houses injured birds and nursed them
to health before releasing them into the wild. We played in
our mothers' gardens, read books and practiced mathematics
in his father's study. Our houses crawled with happy, fat
cats; Kal never met a stray he didn't want to bring home and
spoil. But whoever that boy was is gone. In his place is a man
who burns with dissatisfaction, with unanswerable questions, with disdain for anyone whose mind cannot match his.
His jealousy of humans and their power is consuming him.
I no longer recognize him. I see in his eyes a cold gleam that
freezes my blood. He must be stopped."*

—Writings of the angel Aryava,
archived in the First Great Library of Quelbani

In a narrow alleyway near Elysium's factory district, where massive
buildings churned out smoke day and night, Eliana found her way back
into the Deep.

Inside the factory walls, mechanized creations designed by angels and
operated by human prisoners clanked and whirred, producing armor and
weapons. The streets were slick with soot and oil, and still every stained
cornice was exquisite.

Eliana knelt near one of the refuse pits, where those humans whose beauty the angels had tired of sorted through scraps and shoveled waste. The hot, acrid air stung her eyes. She tasted metal on her tongue. Behind her, violent cries rose throughout the white city. Vaera Bashta's prisoners were sweeping through the streets on tides of blood, and Ostia—the great eye in the sky, rimmed in blue-white—shone its light upon all.

In this place of rot and ruin, Eliana raised her trembling, tired arms into the air and drew it apart. Her mind held fast to the image of the fissure she had already opened in the sky above Elysium. *There.* She sent the thought through the veins of her power, guiding it. She needed not only a door into the Deep, but a door that would lead her *there*, to the fissure waiting and widening and the air stretching thin within it. Her castings were fire in her palms; in her chest, the empirium turned in searing blades. It had guided her to this alleyway full of smoke, and she clung to it. A rope in a blizzard of ash, taut and tough.

Or perhaps it was you who guided the empirium, the Prophet had told her. *You who told it what you needed and where to take you.*

Eliana shivered, her skin soaked with sweat. Her ruined gown clung to her, its jewels winking cruelly.

Somewhere, Corien brooded, nearing the end of his amusement.

The Prophet's voice was thin with strain. *Hurry, Eliana. The world spins ever faster.*

The moment the seam she had opened was wide enough, Eliana held her breath and stepped through it—and walked into a world at war.

She faltered at the sight before her, then set her jaw and moved through it. This world the Deep was showing her, this echo of a place that existed elsewhere, was different from the one she had seen before. Lavish sculptures of bronze and gold ornamented rooftops and shop fronts. Squat towers blanketed in ivy flanked a wide gray road down which armored soldiers marched in gleaming lines.

They held long spears with wicked points, swords polished to brilliance. The people they marched upon fled in screaming chaos, dragging their children and animals behind them. Some knelt with guns on their shoulders and fired, but when they hit their targets and the soldiers fell, only moments passed before they rose unsteadily to their feet again, their wounds closed, and resumed their inexorable forward march.

Eliana's blood ran cold at the sight of them. Their eyes were not black, and yet...

What's happening here? She tried to block out the echoes of screams tumbling down the road. *What is this place?*

My sight through your mind is dim just now, but if I see correctly, it is a world called Sath, the Prophet said, their voice so distant that it frightened Eliana. *I recognize it. I have seen it myself. When your mother died, the shock resounded through the Deep. Holes opened into many worlds. Some angels lost faith in Kalmaroth long ago and have no desire to return to Avitas. They are making homes elsewhere.*

Eliana's bile rose. *Why would any of them wait in the Deep to return to Avitas, then? When they could go to other worlds and escape the Deep's torment?*

The Prophet's voice came quietly. *Because Corien is a force unmatched, and has ingrained in so many angels a thirst for vengeance that cannot be slaked. Because some angels would endure a thousand more years of torment if it meant they could someday come home.* A pause. *Others despair at the devastating futility of war and want to protect humans from extermination. There are many reasons.*

Eliana felt trapped between a great sorrow and an anger pure as ice. *Is there no end to the ruin my mother has wrought?*

Eliana, you must hurry. Do not allow the Deep to distract you. Remember what you must do.

She obeyed. A dim blue-white glow on the horizon caught her eye. She fixed on it and ran, her feet slamming hard against the road that wasn't there. As the world of distant Sath sped by, darkness flashed and fluttered at the corners of her eyes: the true Deep, cold and endless, choked with beasts and raw power. The sky was teeming with cruciata, close enough now that Eliana's tongue tingled with the hot rank stench of their massive bodies. Wings fluttered against her skin; something sharp and thin cut her upper arm. As she ran, she felt the air surge behind her. If she looked back, she knew she would see horrors swarming fast on her heels.

The beasts had been waiting for her. They were ready.

So was she.

Ignoring the dark brimming sky, she kept her gaze on Ostia, its light growing brighter and nearer as she ran, until at last she reached the fissure she had made—a jagged glowing cut through the Deep, and into Avitas.

Eliana went to its sizzling edge and sank carefully to her knees. Her original small cut had expanded to an area some sixty yards square. Shocks of light and color bloomed across it. Beyond and below rippled the faint shapes of Elysium.

Eliana's pulse beat fast in her throat. She unfocused her eyes and let the empirium wash over her. Waves of gold, surging at her fingers. She could see how thin the fabric of the Deep had become within Ostia's jagged ring. Only a thin membrane of power remained. A brittle pane of glass, ready to be shattered.

She pressed her toes against the hard road beneath her and believed it was real. She said a silent prayer that this would be enough. She gathered her power into her mind, imagined it as spears, sharp and ready.

Then she plunged her hands into Ostia's bright edge and let her power explode across it. White light crackled against her fingers and snaked up her arms, as if she were elbow-deep in frothing water. Her castings blazed so hot that her instinct was to rip them off, but she gritted her teeth and kept pushing her hands outward, the pain shooting up her arms so specific and supple that it approached pleasure. Her vision lost all colors but gold.

Then, at last, the fabric of the Deep stretching thinly across Ostia's mouth gave way.

There was a great hot shudder beneath her hands as of a beast heaving its last breath. A bolt of energy shot up through Eliana's arms, and she fell back onto the road, gasping. Quickly, she braced her palms against the illusion of stone. She had to keep hold of the lie, for the thing happening before her eyes was so unthinkable that her head spun in protest.

Ostia had been opened. Angry light crackled across its mouth. It had at last become what Eliana had hoped for from that first moment when she awoke in her white rooms and thought of carving a door in the sky.

Her mother had opened the Gate.

And she had opened Ostia. A hole in the Deep. A door leading out from the abyss. Through it, Elysium was clear as a spotless reflection.

You've done it, came the Prophet's voice, dim but triumphant.

Then the cruciata dove.

They tore down from the sky, plunging out of the Deep and into Elysium, a monstrous river of fury. Their clamor was so great it was as if all the beasts in Avitas had lifted their heads to the sky and howled as one. They screamed and wailed, clawing at each other, hungry to be the first to fly through and feed. Some were immense and bulbous, hulking beasts with flat snouts and paws like bludgeons. Others were slender and serpentine, and still others were avian, their hides a mottled mix of scales and feathers.

Eliana's blood iced over as she watched the raptors fly. She remembered them from the attack outside Karlaine. One had grabbed Patrik and flung him to the ground, breaking his leg. Eliana had killed another with her dagger. The light of Ostia scorched them as they passed through it, leaving their feathers charred, but they flew on uncaring, their fanged beaks open wide.

The cruciata had come from another world. *Hosterah,* the Prophet had called it. They were mighty enough to survive the Deep.

But Elysium would not survive them.

Her gut clenched with horror as she thought of the innocent lives below that would end in claws and teeth. How many beasts had she already loosed from the Deep, and how many more would fight their way through?

But she did not see another way to fight him, not without this distraction to help her. And if she did not fight him, they were all dead anyway.

Only once did she allow herself to imagine Remy, pursued down a blood-stained street by a monster with gaping jaws. Then, slowly, her hands trembling, she crouched at Ostia's threshold, its ragged hem sizzling around her. The force emanating from it threatened to hurl her back into the Deep. She clung to Ostia's bright rim, watching the churning stream of cruciata. Not all of them were able to escape the Deep's pull. Some were tossed away from Ostia; others clawed at nothing, pinned immobile by a force they could not fight.

But the stronger among them were able to escape. Eliana saw a nearing raptor and liked the look of it. The Prophet said something, a warning, but Eliana ignored them and threw herself onto the raptor's back as it passed her. She hit it hard, flung her arms around its meaty scaled neck, and braced herself for the fall.

A ring of heat burned past them as they dove, peeling scales and feathers from the raptor's hide. But then they were through, the beast shrieking as it steadied its wings. It tried bucking Eliana off in midair. Its tail caught an angelic statue and sent it smashing to pieces on the road below.

Eliana, her eyes blurred with tears from the wind, saw a rooftop nearby. She tried to roll as she landed, but she was out of practice and fell badly. The impact jarred her knees, and she cut her arm on a jagged slate tile. She slid down the roof, grabbed on to the cornice and clung there, legs swinging, until she realized the ground below wasn't far and let go. On the road, she stumbled forward, gritting her teeth against the starbursts of pain that lit up her legs. As the Dread, she could have jumped onto that roof and felt nothing. The thought came and went swiftly, an echo of her former life.

She raced through Elysium with no sense of where to go next, desperate to call for the Prophet. Ostia's light had darkened, washing the city in an angry purple-red, as if every tower had been dashed with blood. The Prophet had told her that her friends would soon arrive and then they could act, they could meet at last. But when? And *who*?

But she asked the Prophet nothing and kept her mind firmly shut. Corien would be looking for her. Using her mind to seek the Prophet would light her up like a beacon.

Instead, she imagined her river, the cool satin currents of it carrying her swiftly into the city's congested heart. She climbed a low wall, raced up a slowly winding staircase to one of the city's higher levels. Cruciata streamed past her, their tails lashing, their wild calls a ravenous chorus. Some— feline, quick and yowling—darted over rooftops and up walls with ease. Shrieking flocks of raptors glided fast overhead. They dove and pounced, feasting upon anything that moved—the prisoners of Vaera Bashta, ripped from their own kills, and the citizens of Elysium in their shredded finery.

None of them touched Eliana, but she didn't think their gratitude would last forever. She needed to find a safe hiding place before their mood changed.

Remembering the rooftop courtyard from earlier that night, she turned sharply left, then right, then up two broad flights of stained stone steps. She could have wept with relief to see the familiar narrow staircase, the apartment building with its yawning cruciata gargoyles.

Over her shoulder, she glimpsed the cruciata still flooding down from the sky. They spread fast across the city in rivers of darkness. Soon they would find the bridges, the tent cities sprawling across the rocky fields beyond.

She turned away from the sight, hands in fists as she ran. She would kill them once they had served their purpose. When the Emperor was defeated and the Empire had fallen, she would destroy any beast that still lived and close both Ostia and the Gate.

She only had to survive until then.

On the rooftop, on the terrace bordered with curling white stone, she found the ivy-draped arbor she had hidden beneath only hours before, and froze. Under the arbor, two small boys huddled in the arms of an old man and a woman plump with child.

The elder boy had his hand clamped over the younger one's mouth. All of them stared at Eliana until she held up her hands, shook her head, and smiled. They relaxed, smiled back. The woman even scooted aside to make room for her.

Then Corien found her.

He appeared suddenly, striding across the terrace. His coat was pristine—long and black, pressed and embroidered, buttoned at his shoulder with a set of gold wings.

One of the little boys cried out. Corien snarled under his breath, flung out his arm. The next moment, everyone hiding beneath the arbor crumpled to the ground, their eyes empty.

Eliana knew it was futile to run but tried it anyway. Corien kicked her legs, sent her crashing to the roof. Her castings, dull and dark, clattered against the stone.

He grabbed her hair, wrenched her hard to her feet. She cried out, scalp stinging and eyes watering, and tried to whirl and punch him. Her exhausted mind remembered too late the knives strapped to her waist.

Corien found them first and ripped her belt from her. Arabeth skidded across the stone and into the shadows. He tossed the other knives over the side of the roof. He said nothing, which terrified her. He loved to hear himself talk, loved how he could make people squirm with his words. But even his mind-speak had vanished. His face was a beautiful white mask of fury.

He dragged her toward the steps, one hand in her hair and the other clutching a handful of her gown. The simple, primal part of her mind that knew only that she was prey pounded on her skull, begging her to scream for help. But any scream would go unnoticed in the demented arena Elysium had become, and if she screamed with her mind, Corien could find the Prophet.

She gasped for breath as he pulled her down the stairs, his iron grip sending hot spikes of pain down her spine. But she would not allow her power to rise and defend her. She could feel its anger; it had not been long since she had used it. It would be so easy, it told her, to let it out.

WE RISE

The empirium roared at her, its blazing fists punching through her veins.

"No," she whispered, begging it to quiet. "No, no, no."

Corien paid no attention to her, his pace relentless. She had never prayed harder in her life. A single, simple word: *No*. No power, no fire, no light. She pushed her entire body into the word. Her castings stayed cold in her palms.

A cloud of black bloomed before her eyes, lifting only when Corien threw her to the ground.

She blinked, the wind knocked out of her. Rielle's flat, brass eyes stared down at her. They were back in the palace, in the gallery of her mother. Eliana lay inert as Corien swung a sword through a spun-glass rendering of Rielle, slashed an oil painting with the blade's tip. He seized the brass statue perched on its pedestal above Eliana and flung it into the shadows. The noise was deafening, all the more so for his silence.

Eliana panted, sweat burning her eyes. She couldn't move much, but she could see he had cleared a space around where she lay, a circle of destruction.

At last, he spoke.

"This is it, Eliana," he said, his voice vibrating with something she couldn't name. Appetite, or fury, or maybe exhaustion. "This is the end of our game."

She strained to look at him. If she saw his face, would she know what he felt? She could sense nothing of him in her mind. He was keeping himself away from her.

Then his wide grin appeared. He was not alone.

Simon stood rigid at his side, Corien's hand tight around his wrist. Simon's lip was swollen and bloody from Corien's backhand hours earlier. For a fleeting moment, Simon's eyes locked with hers. Blue of ice, blue of fire. The look shook her, unraveling what was left of her fraying calm.

"Simon?" she whispered.

"Yes, Simon's here too," said Corien. "I assume you remember what he can do? He's going to do it for me, here, now. I'm going to tear your god-damned power out of your veins once and for all. I'm going to batter open your mind and dig until I can twist everything you are around my fingers."

She stared at Corien, her mouth dry, her heart beating so fast it left her buzzing. There was a twitchiness to him that she had never seen before, his face pulsing at the temple, at the corner of his upper lip.

She dared to look hard at his black eyes and wondered how many minds they held inside them—and how close they were to slipping from his grasp.

"I'll die," she told him. "Then you'll have nothing."

He crouched to stroke her cheek. "What do I care, once Simon has sent me back to her? I'll have your mother. I can be rid of you at last."

Frantic, she tried to rise. "You don't want to see her. You failed her once—you lost her once. You'll do it again."

Corien stood, looking down upon her coldly. A madness lit his eyes. "No, Eliana. I see now the mistakes I made. I won't make them this time."

Then he plunged inside her. An inferno flaying open every fold of her mind, scorching clean every corner she had worked so desperately to hide. Everything he had done in her months at the palace was nothing compared to this. The pain sucked her breath from her, left her writhing soundlessly. She clawed at the slick floor, her gasps choked and hoarse. She tried to say a single word, to focus on a single image. Blue eyes, locked with her own. Instead of *No*, her prayer shifted.

Simon. Her mind screamed it, and every image of him her mind had ever stored away flew at her. She reached for them, tried to grab hold of one and press it close. *Simon!*

"Come, Simon!" Corien howled, jubilant. "How long can you stand to watch her like this? Hours? Days? Weeks? I am ageless. I am infinite. I can burn her until the world falls apart around us!"

"I will watch for however long it takes you to succeed, my lord," came Simon's flat voice.

"Such a loyal pup you are, such a beautiful crag of a man. But even you, ice-cold as you are, will tire of her screams. The human mind can only stand to witness so much pain." He shoved Simon. "Put up your hands! Find me a thread, Simon! Do it!"

Simon obeyed, his arms rising stiffly.

Corien's fingers, wedged deep in Eliana's thoughts, twisted savagely. A scream did burst from her then. She was hidden in her thicket in that lush courtyard garden. In the Blue Room on the admiral's ship. At the glittering masked ball in Festival, in her warm candlelit room at Willow. She was in Orline, black and lithe, leaping from rooftop to rooftop with Harkan at her side. She was in her bedroom, listening to Remy read her a story about the saints.

She was in Ioseph Ferracora's arms, watching the sun rise, looking shyly up at the crumbling statue of the Lightbringer, noble and tireless on his winged horse.

Her scream found a word. "Simon!" Her fingers were rigid; her bones would soon pop from her skin. "Simon, *please!*"

"Simon, please! Simon, please!" Corien burst into wild laughter. "Can you feel the threads, Simon? Can you sense them coming? She won't last long. I can feel her every shield cracking. Poor little Eliana." He leaned close, shouted in her ear. "Poor little Eliana! So brave, so noble, so needlessly fucking stupid! You could have been happy, you idiot girl. You could have had everything you wanted, and instead you wriggle on the ground like a caught worm, soaked in your own piss!"

Eliana sucked down air like a child newly born, but it wasn't enough. Her lungs were burning, her mind a shrieking white storm. Her castings began to warm; her power had tolerated this indignity for long enough. It swelled fast inside her, a boiling sea rushing for the shore.

She couldn't clench her fingers; instead, she slammed her palms against the floor, willing her castings dark. A vision came: herself smashing her head on the tile until it split. Corien's delight slithered inside her. He would allow her that after she had given him what he wanted. She could bash her head open to her heart's content.

Soon, her mind would slip altogether. Her power would burst out and awaken Simon's marque blood, and that would be the end. It would all have been for nothing.

The breath she drew rattled in her chest, an inward wail. *"Simon!"*

Then Corien flew back from Eliana, and his mind tore free of her. Something had come between them; some cold door of stone had shut on the reaching crawl of his fingers. He stumbled into a toppled statue, crashed inelegantly to the floor.

"It's her," he breathed. "She's here." And then laughter shook him, bubbling up until it became a cackle, shrill and beastly. Where Simon was, Eliana didn't know. She reached feebly across the floor, hot red-black pain surging up to drown her.

Corien's wild howl hurt her bleeding ears. "Show your face to me, you snake! Where are you? *What have you done?*"

And then, another voice, quiet and thin, only for Eliana to hear: *Stay with us, little one. Just a little longer. Help is coming. Help is close.*

The Prophet. The last two words Eliana's mind formed before a gentle hand, a familiar tenderness, guided her into blissful oblivion.

⭐ 33 ⭐

LUDIVINE

"When alone in your bed at night, the dark all around you, horrors without and within, you may wonder: Is this all there is? War and death? Fear and despair? But this is the wrong question to ask. Instead, ask yourself: What will I do when he comes for me? At the moment of my death, when I look back upon my life, what will I see? Will I be proud of what I have done? Or ashamed of what I have not? Think carefully. I know shame you cannot imagine. I know guilt that crawls through the blood like disease."

—*The Word of the Prophet*

In her private chamber at the heart of a vast underground labyrinth, Ludivine sat in her favorite chair: deep cushions of lavender velvet, polished cherrywood that gleamed red in the light. Three squat candles flickered on polished stone pedestals—one to her right, one to her left, one before her against the curving stone wall.

One for Rielle. One for Audric.

One for Eliana.

Her rooms were never without them.

An ornate sword rested in her lap, vibrating quietly. On its golden hilt, a tessellation of carved suns. On the dark leather of its tasseled sheath, an elaborate tapestry of tridents and daggers, spears and arrows, hammers and shields. Rays of sunlight and godsbeasts in flight—a chavaile, an ice-dragon, a firebird.

Ludivine shifted, making herself comfortable. Her stone halls were quiet, but they would not be for long. Once, they had been a wing of Vaera Bashta, collapsed and abandoned. Now, after decades of painstaking work, they had been rebuilt and scrubbed clean of everything except for her seven acolytes, their weapons and supplies, her vast collection of books.

The corridor outside her chamber whispered like wind through rushes as her acolytes prepared for the arrival of their guests. She made sure to keep seven with her always. She liked the number, and disguising any more minds than that would require her to divert too much attention from her efforts around the world.

Their excitement was orderly but obvious. They had prepared endlessly for this day, and Ludivine had seen to it that their minds were disciplined, but they were still human, still flimsy and volatile and bursting with contradictions. Their little flittering fears and hopes darted through her mind like tiny gold fish in a dark sea.

She saw herself through their eyes as they passed the door to her chamber. Pale and quiet, a young, sweet-faced woman sitting tall in her chair. Long golden hair twisted into a braided knot at her nape, a woolen gown of lilac and rose buttoned at her throat. The shoulders were square, the bodice a cunningly concealed breastplate. Even she had to watch her abdomen. Wounds there required more time to heal.

Her acolytes wondered, as they glanced at her, what she was seeing. They looked at her black eyes, half-lidded as she worked, and shuddered. Even though they loved her, the sight of her sometimes unsettled them. After all, her eyes were black like his. Her mind was ageless and unknowable like his. Even if she did tell them what she saw as she sat motionless in her chair, they wouldn't be able to understand it—how she could see so much at once, how her mind could be so immense and yet remain hidden right under his nose.

What did she see?

A city once grand and white, obnoxious in its swaggering beauty, now overrun with monsters.

A bruised eye hovering above the city. Crimson and pulsing violet, like a fresh wound, and edged with crackling blue light. Out of it poured a black river of wings and scales, claws and fur. Clever sinuous heads with gnashing teeth. Sharp beaks snapping for prey.

Once, Ludivine would have grown angry to see the destruction Corien had wrought. The hysterical fear of his citizens, how hopelessly trapped they were. The people of Elysium had traded their families and their freedom to escape the savagery of war.

And now look at them.

But Ludivine was past anger now, had been past it for hundreds of years. She no longer knew grief or loneliness. She felt no regret, no shame, no lingering ache of lost love. All feeling had fused inside her, plating her insides with steel.

The only thing left was the end. It had burned in her chest for centuries, an immovable blue flame that grew as she did, brightening as the pieces of her plan fell into the places she had made for them.

She stretched her mind a little further.

There was Navi and the Red Crown captain Ysabet. Hob and Patrik. Navi's brother, Malik, and ninety-two others. Zahra was leading them toward the city through the rocky fields, cloaking them from sight. Ludivine watched Zahra closely. The wraith had used much of her strength to hide the *Queenslight* as it navigated the Sea of Silarra, evading dozens of imperial warships.

She would die soon. Ludivine could see that clearly. Only thin threads of strength kept the wraith's mind in one piece.

Hurry, Zahra, Ludivine commanded. The link between them remained steady, guiding the wraith through the city's pandemonium. Centuries ago, she would not have been able to achieve such a thing—to find Zahra, one wraith in a sea of minds, and guide her halfway across the world.

It was astonishing what a millennium of heartbreak could do. Centuries of working alone in the dark to make her mind what it now was.

She smiled a little. What was Corien so fond of saying? *I am infinite.*

Now, he was no longer the only angel who could make such grandiose claims. Now, she was strong enough to match him.

Maybe strong enough to beat him, for she had been smarter than he had. More careful, more sparing with whom and what she chose to control.

She stretched her mind a little further.

There was Remy, wiry and silent as he followed her path through the city. He had an open mind, clever and pliable, and he accepted her guidance as his own instinct. She saw the scars Elysium had left in his mind—the horrors of Vaera Bashta, the torment of Corien, his parents' deaths, Jessamyn's brutal tutelage—and was pleased. He would be more helpful to Eliana this way.

And in the end, if they succeeded, his scars wouldn't matter.

Remy climbed up one of the palace gutters and slipped inside a smashed window. Someone had thrown a head through the glass. The prisoners of Vaera Bashta were gathering at the palace doors, roaring to be heard, pounding on the walls, begging for entrance. Corien's troops had scattered through the city to fight the cruciata, desperate to avoid the bright blue sprays of blood. Using vaecordia, the same massive mechanized cannons that Corien had sent to the Gate, a regiment of angels fired at Ostia and the cruciata scrambling out of it.

Ludivine, sitting quietly at the outermost edges of Remy's mind, led him into a small chamber on the palace's third floor. The nurses' ward, where Corien's physicians patched up mutilated human bodies until they were suitable for angelic use. Remy had stolen weapons from the Lyceum before the prisoners had invaded it—two little daggers and a sword strapped to his back. Jessamyn had trained him well in their short time together, and the four adatrox hovering listlessly at the doors were useless fighters. Angels no longer guided their movements. They moaned wordless cries of agony, swung their blunt fists, tried to ram Remy against the wall.

He darted between them, slashed their throats, then hurried inside the room.

There was Jessamyn, gritting her teeth as she pulled on her boots and jacket over her bandages. Ludivine felt them lay eyes on each other. Jessamyn: surprised relief. Remy: weary gladness. He hadn't thought he would be lucky enough to find her.

The cruciata have invaded the city, he told Jessamyn.

I can see that. Her wry reply.

He approached her carefully. Ludivine sensed how prepared he was to kill her if she tried to stop him. She was wounded; he might manage it.

I need your help, he said. *I don't know the palace. You do. And you're a better fighter than I am. We need to get Eliana out of here.*

Jessamyn nodded. *I'd thought of that. Who else can stop the beasts? The Emperor certainly can't.* She eyed his belt. *I need a knife.*

He tossed her one, and they ran. Ludivine watched them weave through the palace toward Corien's favorite theater. Music began to play, accompanying their quick, light footsteps. Brass horns set high in the rafters crackled with sound. Lights flashed at each juncture of wire that connected them—galvanized power, sparking as it worked. Lamps flickered in their casings.

The music was choral, sweeping, triumphant. Ludivine recognized it as the symphony Corien had commissioned from a recent acquisition—a young composer from Mazabat, prodigiously talented, who had surrendered to save her wife.

Ludivine dared to brush her mind across the theater, the barest sweep of a touch. She saw Corien lounging in his favored curtained box, flush with wine. He had locked the doors; he was brooding. The city was falling down around him, and he was ignoring it. He had nearly killed Eliana, and realizing that had frightened him. So there he sat, furious and terrified, unwilling to face the reality of his failure.

Or so Ludivine supposed; she would not dare touch his mind. But after thousands of years, she knew him well enough to guess.

Below, the audience—bloodstained and wild-eyed, plucked from the city by Corien's generals to enhance the evening's entertainment—applauded frantically for the orchestra. Ludivine felt the frenzied buzz of their thoughts: maybe, if they cheered loudly enough, the Emperor would let them stay inside, locked away and safe.

And sitting in a chair near Corien was Eliana, unconscious and horribly pale, sweating out nightmares Corien had left wedged in the brittle glass of her mind.

Only when she looked at Eliana did Ludivine feel pain. Her face was the perfect combination of Rielle's and Audric's. His full mouth, her arched brows. Her sharp jaw, his lovely brown eyes.

If Ludivine allowed herself, she would be able to remember their warmth, their arms wrapped around her, the soft fragility of their skin. Her rage, his grief. Her passion, his strength. Soothing Rielle to sleep after yet another night of dream-horrors. Audric howling in Ludivine's arms on the floor of his rooms in Mazabat.

How desperately and fatally she had loved them.

But Ludivine did not allow any of this. Her mind was silver and clean, sharp as death.

Stay with us, little one. She didn't dare touch Eliana. Corien would feel it. Instead, she said it to herself. *Just a little longer.*

She began her slow retreat from the palace. No movement too swift, no movement unplanned. Everyone was running where they should. There were Remy and Jessamyn, sneaking through the palace toward the theater. There were Navi, Ysabet, Zahra. Patrik and Hob, their soldiers. All of them fighting their way through the city.

There was another person Ludivine needed to find, perhaps the most essential piece of all. As always, when reaching for him, she sent her instructions with a silent apology—for everything she had done to him and everything he had lost.

But she would do it again if she had to, and he knew it. She would destroy his mind and remake it a thousand times if she had to.

It's time, she told him.

Understood, he replied with a tiny shiver of joy, for even all the abuse she had dealt him had not destroyed his love for what his blood could do, for all the fearsome secrets it held.

She felt him draw his gun, heard him stalk through the corridors of the palace. Wailing adatrox intercepted him, bewildered and terrified. A human man in a ruined blue suit, bold and delirious with trauma, crawled through a smashed window and leapt onto his back. But his shots were clean, his blades precise and deadly. She knew that better than anyone, had made certain he was more weapon than man long before Corien had gotten the chance to do the same.

It was the only way, Ludivine told him, as she had told him many times before. He did not answer her; she did not expect him to. She left him to his work.

She sat in her chair, watching her three candles burn, but her mind was everywhere. She held her sword and waited.

⤺ 34 ⤹

AUDRIC

"Dearest sister. You'll not believe the story I have to tell you, so I'll wait until we meet in person and you can see for yourself the extraordinary circumstances of my new life. Suffice it to say, there are dragons, and there's a boy, and I love them all. We're on our way home to you—though not directly—along with a marque and her guard, and several others whom we freed from a secret angelic prison in the far north. I must sound mad to you, but for the first time in my life I feel like myself. I'll see you soon, and I know I'll need to do much to earn back your trust, but know this: I'm ready for war at last. I'm ready to fight for our home. And I'll not be leaving you again."

—Encoded letter from Ilmaire Lysleva to his sister, Ingrid, dated March 30, Year 1000 of the Second Age

Audric was sitting in the gardens behind Baingarde when his mother found him.

"I thought I might find you under this tree," she said, without insinuation or scorn and settled beside him in the soft, spring grass. The earth was black and damp, the trees heavy with that morning's rain. Twilight painted the gloom a soft violet, and the pink blooms of the sorrow tree overhead were finally beginning to open.

Audric forced a small smile. "If anyone else caught me moping under the tree where I first kissed the Kingsbane, they might try to take my crown again."

Ludivine, he tried once more, *are you there?*

He had been trying all afternoon, had wasted four hours under this tree as the sun faded from honey to lavender.

Wherever she was, she still refused to answer.

"All the Mazabatian soldiers have been assigned lodgings," Genoveve began. The gray folds of her linen gown pooled atop the wet grass like fallen petals.

"You'll ruin your dress," Audric pointed out.

"I have many dresses," Genoveve said mildly. "The commanders and as many of the infantry as we could accommodate are in the barracks. The rest of them are lodged throughout the city. So many people opened up their homes. Odo has set up rather luxurious makeshift barracks in his rooftop gardens."

"I would imagine the commanders in our barracks are jealous of whoever was lucky enough to get those beds."

"Undoubtedly."

Audric huffed a soft laugh. Talking about procedure should have helped clear his troubled mind, but his thoughts still felt clouded. He shifted them to the piles of notes stacked neatly on his desk.

"I've sent letters to Ingrid Lysleva and the Kirvayan regent," he said. "Queen Fozeyah will come with more troops once they're ready. Ten thousand by the first of May."

Genoveve nodded, her hands white and still in her lap. Her cheeks were sunken, her every bone pronounced, but the braided twist of her auburn hair was immaculate, and her gray eyes were flint.

"In the Archon's absence," she said, "Grand Magister Guillory has assumed leadership of the Church. The other magisters agreed. It was unanimous."

Audric thought of Tal's empty chair in the Magisterial Council chamber, how Miren—straight-backed, square-shouldered—refused to look at it.

"A sunspinner in command of the Church," Audric said, smiling faintly.

"And a sunspinner on Katell's throne."

Genoveve was looking at him now. He kept his eyes fixed on the black seeing pools, sitting quietly in the sea of grass some twenty feet away.

"And the watchtowers?" he asked.

"Construction has begun on the eight that will surround the city."

"And the builders I assigned to the remaining sixteen?"

"They and their supplies are en route to the northern roads. By month's end, we'll have a line of towers from here to the northeastern border, each of them magicked by earthshakers and metalmasters."

Audric nodded. "And I have riders set to depart in the morning for the seats of all the major houses. Gourmeny and Montcastel. The Valdorais holdings in the Far Fallows."

After a pause, Genoveve cleared her throat. "And what will you do with the soldiers from House Sauvillier? Our prisons are overflowing."

"I'll meet with them individually, then reinstate them if I can. We can't spare a single sword."

"And if there are some who don't wish to fight for you?"

"*I* don't wish to fight for me."

Genoveve reached for his hand. "Audric..."

"They can go if they wish. I won't have a mutinous army fighting at my back. But they'll be safer here than they will be elsewhere, and I'll remind them of that. Every elemental from here to Borsvall will be gathering in Âme de la Terre. If they leave, they will have to face the angels on their own. I think the majority of them will stay and fight and keep their dislike to themselves."

"They don't dislike you, Audric," said Genoveve delicately. "They dislike her."

"In fact, they do dislike me, and some of them even hate me, and perhaps wish Merovec had cut *me* in half, because I was foolish enough to love her. And I would rather not talk about Rielle, Mother."

A long moment of silence. "Sloane told me about the weeks following your arrival in Mazabat. She told me about the weight you've been carrying. The change in you."

Something flared in Audric's chest, a hot spark of anger. He was grateful for it. When he was angry, he couldn't think about everything else.

"I'm still the same person I always was," he said tightly. "I can still lead fighters. I can still discipline traitorous soldiers." Illumenor, sliding quick through Merovec's body. The memory liked him, showed itself to him a dozen times a day. "I can still kill."

"I see the sadness in your eyes, Audric."

At last he glared at her. "And I see the sadness in yours. What good can come of this conversation?"

Genoveve watched him steadily. "For years, you urged your father to study the prophecy. You begged him to read the books you brought him, to educate himself on the writings of the great elemental scholars. And he never did. Do you know why?"

It was a turn in the conversation that Audric had not expected. He blinked. "No."

"Because he was frightened." Genoveve gazed at the seeing pools, the catacombs a distant gray ghost beyond them. "Katell's line had been without true sunspinners for generations. And then you were born and started playing with sunlight while still in your cradle, even before the forging of your casting. Your father knew what that meant, and so did I. Whenever he looked at you, he saw the portent of a war he had long ago convinced himself would never come in his lifetime. The world was at peace. The Gate stood strong. And then you were born. The Lightbringer. More powerful than he ever was, and braver too. You were always willing to consider the worst and face it head-on. The fact of your power, the idea of a war—these things never frightened you, nor did Aryava's words of doom."

Audric shook his head. She had lost him with that one. "I'm always frightened."

"And yet the people who fight for you don't know it. In their eyes, you are Katell born again. And now you draw to you the crowns of Mazabat and

Borsvall. Our allies, descendants of the saints, just as you are. Borsvall nearly became our enemy, but you forged a new friendship with them." She paused. "Was it an angel who assassinated poor Princess Runa two years ago?"

"That is my guess," Audric said grimly. "Hoping to spark the fires of war between Celdaria and Borsvall."

"And yet you did not allow that to happen. You dared friendship, and now Borsvall may come to fight alongside us. You build watchtowers and order our metalmasters to forge thousands of new swords. You walk the streets of your city and talk to your people not as if you are a king and they your subjects, but rather as if you are a Celdarian and they are too. They are frightened, but you are not. That is what they see.

"And, Audric," Genoveve added quietly, her fingers gently pressing his, "I worry that if you don't talk about her—at least to me, or Sloane, or Miren, or Princess Kamayin—then everything you're feeling will rise up and crack you open. Our people can't see that. If they're to face their deaths at the ends of angelic swords, they must never look at you and see how deeply you've been hurt. They must look at you and see an icon. Not a man, but a symbol. Not Audric, but the Lightbringer. It isn't fair, but neither is the crown, and only if you wear it do we have any hope of surviving what's to come. Of that I am certain."

She sighed, and silence followed. They watched Atheria playing among the distant pines, trilling happily as she chased bright jays from their nests.

"Maybe if I had been a mother to her," Genoveve said, "if I had welcomed her into our family with graciousness and warmth, we would not be where we are now."

Audric took a moment to breathe. He hadn't been lying—he did not want to talk about Rielle. But his mother was beside him, and she would not always be.

"It's not as simple as that," he told her flatly. "Maybe if the Archon hadn't forced her to endure the trials. Maybe if Lord Dervin hadn't caught us kissing in the gardens. Maybe if I hadn't pushed her away on our wedding night."

He blinked back his tears. "Or maybe none of that mattered, and regardless of what we did, we would have ended up right where we are. Maybe Aryava's prophecy means exactly what it says: there is a queen of light and a queen of darkness. And maybe Rielle was always the latter, and nothing we said to her could have changed that."

Genoveve made a soft sound, considering. "Have you wondered where the other queen is? If Rielle truly is the Blood Queen, then—"

"She is with child." It was the first time Audric had said it aloud. The words ripped something from him; in their absence, a hollow place opened inside him.

"My child," he added quietly. "Our child. Ludivine told me before she left."

Genoveve put her fingers to her mouth. A little choked sound shook her shoulders. A dove made its mournful cry high in the sorrow tree's blooms.

"Ludivine told me the child is a girl," he went on. "So maybe she is our Sun Queen, our unborn salvation."

Genoveve pressed his knuckles to her lips and closed her eyes. A long moment passed before she released him and wiped her face.

"I wish Ludivine were here to help you," she whispered.

"I'm sorry I didn't tell you the truth about her," Audric said, though he didn't feel sorry. He only felt tired. He imagined his bed, how enormous and lonely it was, how small he felt inside it.

"I understand why you didn't. You needed her—both of you did—and if I had known the truth, I would have had her exiled, or at least tried to. I would have tried many different ways to be rid of her and failed, and then I would have been regarded with even more pity and disgust than I already am."

His mother spoke with no hint of self-loathing, no bitterness. Now Audric was the one to watch her carefully—the thin straight line of her nose, the painful sharpness of her jaw, how she held herself with such stillness. Was it because she was afraid of breaking? Or because she had been broken so many times that the idea no longer frightened her?

"Mother," he began. "That's not how it is."

Genoveve smiled at him. "I don't need comfort. I only want you to sit with me. I want you to come to me when the weight of this becomes too heavy for even your shoulders. I cannot take it from you, but God help me, I wish I could."

She cradled his face in her hands, touched his cheeks, pushed the curls back from his eyes.

"My brave boy," she whispered, and then brought his head down to kiss his brow.

They sat in silence, hand in hand, and waited for nightfall. Audric watched Atheria spin slow shadows through the trees.

I fear no darkness, he prayed. *I fear no night.*

I ask the shadows to aid my fight.

— 35 —

ELIANA

"Sometimes it's strange to think of them together and in love, even after all the stories I've read—the Lightbringer and the Blood Queen. One kind, one cruel. One good, one evil. I wonder what their daughter would have been like, if she'd ever been born. I wonder which parent she'd take after."

—Journal of Remy Ferracora,
dated May 24, Year 1014 of the Third Age

The nightmares were shapeless and vast, but Eliana let them sweep her along on their savage current. She held herself carefully within a fraying net. If she fought too hard against her bindings, if she tried to turn against the nightmares and swim through them to shore, the net would break, and she would fall.

Eliana.

She turned away from the voice. It was him again. He had returned to bash her head in, and this time she would let him.

Eliana, please, wake up!

The voice calling her name was not Corien's. It was familiar, soft, urgent. Beyond it soared music carried high on strings, punctuated by the brassy blasts of horns.

Slowly, Eliana opened her eyes—and saw, crouching behind her chair in Corien's private theater box, a lanky boy with dark, mussed hair, his face shining with sweat.

Remy.

She stared at him, breathed in and out slowly. It was an illusion. It was a lie. She held herself still, waiting to awaken.

But the orchestra played on, and Remy was beckoning to her, and her mind was clear. Corien had said nothing—no taunts, no cruel laughter. Eliana stared at Remy, her blood roaring. She recalled the voice that had called her name only moments ago and recognized it.

It had been the Prophet, urging her awake.

Only her long weeks working with the Prophet could have prepared Eliana for such a moment. Though her mind was battered, her every muscle pulsing with pain, she reached for calm and found it. She thought of her cool little river and stepped quietly inside it.

Then she held Remy's eyes for a moment, telling him not to move, telling him to hold every part of himself still, and turned carefully in her seat to look at Corien. She remained slumped, her eyes half-lidded. Her vision tilted even at that slight movement. Pain stabbed her temples.

There he was, standing near the polished railing with his drink in hand. The music on stage was deafening, and still he yelled for more.

"I can't hear you!" Corien cried, then gulped down the rest of his drink and flung his empty glass at the stage.

In the rows of seats below, the citizens of Elysium echoed his disdain, throwing jeers at the musicians sweating on the stage, tossing shoes and half-eaten food, whatever they could find.

But the musicians did not dare stop, the conductor's arms were tireless, and the sweetness of the music continued—triumphant and joyful, perversely incongruous with its audience.

Eliana watched Corien lean against the railing, his shoulders hunched, his hands white-knuckled. He shook his head in fury; he looked ready to burst. Any moment now, he would reach for another glass to throw.

He would reach for *her*.

Eliana could not move, frozen with indecision. What should she do? Feign sleep? Offer herself to Corien once more so Remy could run?

Then the choir in the grand curving loft above the stage stood as one. Four soloists dressed in long glittering coats began to sing in an angelic tongue they had no doubt learned at swordpoint.

To Eliana's left, beyond where Corien stood, two adatrox dragged up the stairs a man Eliana did not recognize. His head lolled; his black-eyed expression was listless and fuzzy. An angel, but who?

Corien threw up his hands, overjoyed. "Ravikant! What a delight that you could join us this evening. And just in time for the finale too. What luck!"

Ravikant. Eliana looked hard at the admiral. She had not seen him since he lived in Ioseph Ferracora's body. He had found a new body, it seemed—a short, skinny man with smooth brown skin and a shaved head. The adatrox released Ravikant, and he fell to his knees. He had dressed for the occasion in an immaculate suit of soft cream.

Corien knelt beside him, placed his hand on Ravikant's sweating cheek. The admiral began to sob.

The orchestra quieted. The music became a playful march, chirpy and sly, accompanied by tiny rhythmic chimes.

"Did you think you would get away with it?" Corien asked softly, cocking his head. "Did you think I wouldn't find out that you meant to ruin me? And here I was, thinking we were friends."

Ravikant gasped, twitching on the floor, and Eliana's body jolted with remembered pain. She breathed in and out through her nose and kept her hands relaxed on the arms of her chair.

Only then did she notice the floor of their lavishly appointed box.

It was strewn with corpses.

Corien stood, and Ravikant's body grew still. Instead, another body nearer to the door began to convulse. A young, pale girl in a silken gown, perhaps selected from the audience below.

Eliana watched her body shudder as Ravikant's screams, his pleas in Lissar, tore free of her throat.

"So easily I can toss you from body to body," Corien mused, standing over the girl. "Could you do this? I don't think you could. I think all of you are rats next to me. I think you ought to feel ashamed of your own stupidity."

"The city...my lord..." Ravikant tried next in the common tongue. "It is overrun..."

Corien snarled with fury. The girl's body stilled, and that of a white-haired, dark-skinned man sitting propped up in a chair began to twist in agony. His voice was deep; his words were Ravikant's. The orchestra below played on, frenetic strings pushing a melody higher and higher.

Eliana tensed in her chair, fighting for calm. Corien was not watching her. He was distracted, drunk on wine and violence. She could run. Remy still waited behind her; she could feel his tension, how he ached to reach for her. If he had somehow gotten inside, there was a way to escape. If he was real, that is—if she could believe anything she saw.

Corien's back was to her, but not entirely. His mind might have another focus, but his stolen eyes would see if she moved.

The orchestra grew quiet once more—only hesitant pulses from the horns, cautious echoes from the reedy winds.

Eliana held her breath.

Then the full orchestra returned, and the full chorus, in a triumphant, pounding passage that shook the theater from floor to ceiling.

Run, Eliana. The Prophet, faint as a distant dream.

Corien leaned closer to Ravikant, tilting his head so his ear was near the angel's sobbing mouth—and putting his face completely out of view. He was howling as Ravikant did, mocking him. His voice split with laughter.

Eliana did not waste a moment. She slipped free of her chair and followed Remy into the box's shadows. The music pounded in her chest; Corien's furious invectives, hurled at the admiral in tongues Eliana did not know, rang in her ears.

Remy grabbed her hand, helped her down a small flight of stairs in the darkness and out through a door left unlocked. Once outside, they ran. The narrow corridor circling the theater was eerily empty. Unease coiled tight in Eliana's chest. Whatever Remy was doing, he was not doing it alone.

"How did you get inside the theater?" she asked quietly as they hurried through the shadows. "He locked every door."

Remy cut her a quick glance. "Not all of them. One was left unlocked."

A chill nipped her neck. "And you trusted that?"

"I didn't have time to think about it. I only knew you were inside."

His voice was so strange—it was his, and yet not. There was a new steel to it. His face betrayed nothing. Her brother, and a stranger too. Eliana wished there were time to hold him still by the shoulders and make him look at her dead-on until she knew him again.

They raced down a flight of stairs. At the bottom, hidden against the far wall, waited Jessamyn. Her leg was bandaged and her color wan, but her blood-spattered face was hard and eager for a fight. Three dead ada-trox lay at her feet.

"That took far too long," she hissed, then gave Eliana one assessing look. If she felt shame at having been a witness in that white room of pain, she showed none of it. "No one saw you leave?"

"If they had, we wouldn't still be standing here," Remy said darkly, moving to the nearest window to peer outside.

Eliana glanced from Jessamyn to Remy. Remy's trimmed hair, his tunic and trousers that were certainly not prison wear. "You know each other?"

"I'm her virashta," Remy said, as if that explained everything.

Beyond the glass, Ostia's crimson light flooded the world, but it was Remy Eliana couldn't tear her eyes from. How comfortable he looked with a dagger in his hand. The grim set of his face, the scars rimming his knuckles.

"Can you close that thing in the sky?" Jessamyn asked, gesturing at the window.

"Yes," Eliana said, not saying the rest—that she would do no such thing until she had won and Corien lay in ruins.

"Somehow we've got to get you to it safely," Jessamyn muttered, glancing out the window. "And the whole city's gone mad."

Remy shot Eliana a glance. She could see on his face that he knew what she had not said, and his mouth twitched with a small smile.

I will guide you to me. The Prophet's voice came quietly. *Tell them you know where to go. They will follow you.*

"I know how to get there," Eliana said firmly. "I know the safest path."

Jessamyn's eyes narrowed. "How?"

Eliana forced a wry grin. "I'm the Sun Queen. I know everything."

He is distracted, but he won't be for long, the Prophet warned. *Exit the palace on the southern side. You will encounter several adatrox on the way out. Prisoners too. The beasts are swarming toward the palace. Some already cling to it, trying to bash their way inside. Go to the plaza where Corien brought you before he opened Vaera Bashta.*

Eliana drew a deep breath, shifted her hands to feel the slide of her castings' chains. *Can I use my power?*

Try not to. He will only remain ignorant of your escape for so long. The farther you get from him, the more easily I will be able to hide you.

Eliana swallowed against a cold knot of fear. She felt the Prophet's presence, a supple layer of water coating her mind, but it was too thin for comfort.

"I need a knife," she said, and Jessamyn pulled a long dagger from her boot. Eliana recognized it as a standard adatrox weapon. She tested its weight, her grip. She nodded once at Jessamyn in thanks.

"Follow me," she said, and ran, Remy and Jessamyn close behind.

The palace was a cavernous tomb, its stone walls muffling the chaos beyond. The low boom of vaecordia cannon fire, the shriek of swarming cruciata. Eliana raced down a broad hallway lined with windows, the shadows sliced open by streams of red light. Adatrox clustered at the far end like animals huddling together against the cold. Abandoned by their angelic masters, their minds left in ruins, they turned at the sound of Eliana's approach, bellowing wordlessly. Eliana rushed at them, gutted one, and by the time she whirled around to find the others, they were already dead. Jessamyn wiped her dagger on her sleeve. Remy wrenched his own knife from the belly of his kill.

Eliana turned away from him, guilt sitting hard in her throat. There was only ever supposed to be one Dread of Orline, and now the city of Elysium had given birth to another.

They raced down two flights of stairs, out into a great hall in the palace's southern wing. Dark shapes slammed against the windows, then skittered up them, climbing the walls.

Adatrox rushed across the hall, straight for them. Eliana flung her knife into one's throat. Jessamyn held another while Remy drove his dagger into its chest. Another stumbled out of the shadows. Jessamyn hissed something at Remy, and Remy ripped his knife from the first adatrox, spun around, and slashed it across the newest one's neck.

They felled another five on their way out of the palace, then six more as they raced through the ring of courtyards surrounding it. A prisoner in rags leapt for Eliana, his eyes gone mad with fear, and with a fierce cry, Jessamyn threw herself in his path and slashed open his stomach. Another prisoner burst through the hedges and swung a huge club at her, metal spikes protruding from the wood. Remy leapt onto his back and slashed open his throat. The courtyards crawled with prisoners shrieking for blood, adatrox stumbling and flailing their swords.

Eliana let Jessamyn and Remy fight for her, but her head spun, and the world was a choppy haze of red and gold. Her power was desperate, chomping for release. Instead, she used her knife and picked up others from the soldiers she slew. She still wore her filthy jeweled gown and wished bitterly for a belt, hidden pockets, holsters, anything useful.

At the border of the city proper, they hid against the courtyards' outermost wall to catch their breath. Jessamyn, her skin soaked with sweat, clutched her right leg. In Eliana's tight fists, her castings buzzed with need. The sky was dark with raptors, the streets teeming. Nearby, two vipers tore at a knot of bodies between them.

Eliana looked back through one of the courtyard gates and saw a sea of cruciata rushing through the maze of hedges toward the palace. Streams of darkness rose swiftly up its walls and towers, slipped inside windows and bashed in doors. Above the palace, fogged in red clouds, shone a smiling crescent moon.

"That ought to hold him for a while," Remy said grimly. "If he touches any cruciata blood—"

"He won't," Eliana said at once. "He's too clever to get beaten that easily."

But a palace crawling with monsters would at least distract him for a few more minutes. She hoped.

Hurry, Eliana, came the Prophet's voice. Stronger now, but tense with effort.

Overhead, at the courtyard's edge, a brass funnel standing tall on a pole wrapped with wires blared a crescendo of brassy horns. Eliana blew out a sharp breath, then launched herself into a relentless sprint. She heard Jessamyn's measured breaths behind her, ragged but constant, and Remy's quick footfalls. Bodies and feasting cruciata clogged the city's larger roads. The stink was hot and rotten, the bite of blood sour on Eliana's tongue.

She turned into an alleyway. People huddled in the shadows, covering their ears, keening over the dead. They cried out as she passed, every head soaked with blood. The alleyway narrowed at the end, and Eliana had to turn sideways to escape it. Emerging from it, she looked down a slope washed red with Ostia's angry light. Low walls and a network of squat white steps separated manicured gardens and wading pools capped with fountains. She raced toward them, jumped over a wall to the path below, landed hard, pushed herself up, ran on. Remy and Jessamyn dropped behind her a few seconds later.

Overhead, a fluttering ribbon of dark color. Eliana looked up. A scarlet-winged raptor had found them, swooping down from the sky with its black beak open wide.

Eliana stared it down, her castings sparking in her fists, her power roaring for release—and at last she let it rise. She reached for the empirium, seized the beast with fingers of gold, and slammed it furiously to the ground. More raptors dove, and she knocked each one out of the sky, her fists flying. Soon, the sky was empty, and Eliana stood panting in a heap of their steaming, ruined bodies.

"Shit," Jessamyn muttered quietly just behind her.

The plaza, now, and hurry, said the Prophet, tense with desperation. *They're coming for you. You just showed them the way.*

She looked around wildly. *Who's coming?*

Angels.

But not him?

He is rather occupied at the moment. The cruciata have flooded the palace, and he cannot control them. Their minds are too strange, too strong. But his soldiers here in the city are eager to impress.

"This way," Eliana said over her shoulder, then raced down the road with Jessamyn and Remy close on her heels. She descended a flight of stairs, then sped across a stone bridge arching over a road that buzzed with cruciata. The creatures burst through doors and windows, flung people screaming into the streets.

Eliana glanced ahead and saw the five angelic statues surrounding their destination. She remembered the pentagonal plaza and the arcades of white pillars that bordered it. The twin black doors, and what had burst out of them at Corien's command.

Jessamyn's blade whizzed past her ear. A skinny raptor with slick black wings dropped from the sky. Eliana dodged it, then raced down a spiraling staircase of white stone and tumbled out into the plaza. She stopped, gulping down air. Remy crashed to a halt beside her, Jessamyn right after him.

"This is madness," Jessamyn hissed. She found an abandoned sword wedged beneath a body shredded beyond recognition, tugged it free. She jerked her head up at the red sky. "Are you going to close the damn thing, or aren't you?"

Eliana looked around the plaza but could see no sign of the Prophet, no escape route, no reinforcements. Instead, she saw angels—ten of them, twenty, *fifty*—streaming down from the upper roads and racing toward the plaza, resplendent in stained golden armor. Cruciata followed, snapping at their heels. One of the angels threw a spear. It spun silver through the air, then pierced a raptor's scaled chest and sent blue blood spraying. The nearest angel fell, then another. It was not enough; soon, they would reach the plaza.

But Eliana didn't dare use her power again with those eyes so near. Corien would feel it, slip into one of their minds, and seize her.

I'm here, she thought, wiping sweat from her eyes. *Now what?*

Something stirred in her mind. A familiar presence that left her cold as ice.

Pain exploded in her skull, searing and brilliant. The world went white, and she crumpled to her knees. The dim cries of battle spun around her, but she saw only this—an armored angel towering over her, his hand outstretched, slowly turning as if working the handle of a door.

It was not an angel she knew, but through the slit of his helmet, in the depths of his black eyes, Eliana saw Corien's smile.

There you are, he thought, slipping into the wrecked grooves of her mind. *My little runaway. I thought I'd lost you.*

Eliana gasped for air, her back arching violently. Her hands scrabbled for purchase on the blood-slicked ground. Every muscle in her body strained against her skin.

Pinned and helpless, she gazed up through a film of tears at the thing that would kill her at last. This angel she had never seen, controlled by another gone mad from centuries of grief.

Then, out from the angel's throat plunged a strange blade—an iridescent copper, shadows shifting across it. *Blightblade*, Eliana thought, shaky and reeling. Fountains of blood spurted from the angel's neck. The blade tore free, and the body twitched, then fell hard. Empty now, nothing more than a corpse.

And over it stood Simon in imperial black, his scarred face streaked with blood and grime. His expression was furious. A dark cloak lined with crimson fell to his knees, and across his torso cut a red sash like a bloody smile.

His bright-blue gaze found Eliana's, locked on for one blazing instant. Something metallic crashed behind her. She turned, still unsteady on the ground, still woozy, but Simon was faster. He darted in front of her, blightblade in one hand, revolver in the other, and shot three angels as they leapt for her. All three copper bullets struck under their chins, where their helmets left them vulnerable.

There is a door in the far wall, the Prophet instructed. *Narrow and plain. White stone. Run to it now. Remy will follow. I must protect him. They are confused, but that will end soon.*

It was as if someone had turned the world inside out. Eliana blinked, searching the plaza, while above her Simon fired shot after shot. Out of bullets, he flung his gun aside and drew another from the belt at his waist. *I must protect him,* the Prophet had said. Because now, Simon was the one drawing their ire. Simon, the Emperor's favorite.

When Eliana found the Prophet's door, a sick heat rushed down her body. A moment ago, the door had not been there—she was sure of it. Thick swaths of blood, both red and blue, slashed across its surface.

Now, Eliana!

Eliana pushed to her feet, searching for Remy. More cruciata were slinking over the walls. They tackled the angels, lashed them with their tails.

In their midst, Jessamyn fought a single angelic soldier. She swung her sword at him; their blades crashed together and locked. The angel swore at her, the ripples of his fury ricocheting through the plaza. Eliana knew that look. He was trying to get at Jessamyn's mind but couldn't.

Her skin prickled. A hidden door. A thwarted angel.

The Prophet was everywhere.

The angel fighting Jessamyn spat a curse in Lissar. Eliana had come to know the word well. Corien shouted it at his servants, often flung it like a knife into Eliana's mind. The Prophet had translated it for her. It meant whore.

Jessamyn bared her teeth at her attacker. Sweaty strands of red hair had come loose from her braid and clung to her neck. "My name," she shouted, her voice cracking, "is *Jessamyn.*"

The angel shoved her to the ground and raised his sword. Eliana looked away before it could fall.

Simon was running toward the Prophet's door, an unconscious Remy slung over his shoulder. He locked eyes with Eliana's. "Go, now!"

Eliana ran for it, but she saw at once that there was no latch. Her power rose like the heat of an explosion. She punched her fists toward the door, castings ablaze inside her clenched fingers.

The door shattered. Shards of stone went flying. Beyond it, narrow stone stairs descended into darkness.

Eliana ran toward them, choking on clouds of white dust. Once Simon passed over the threshold with Remy, she whirled back around and flung her palms at the door. Rock and dust reassembled in seconds, flying back into a solid wall of rock, sealed tight against the city beyond.

In the darkness, Eliana heard only her own ragged breathing, her own pounding head. The tunnel had swallowed all sounds of battle.

She found Remy slung over Simon's shoulder, cradled his cheek in one hand, and held her other before his mouth. A faint puff of hot air, then another. He was breathing. Weak with relief, she stepped back, away from the heat of Simon's body. They stood for a moment, the silence thick and scorching between them. Eliana's castings threw a faint golden light across the scarred lines of Simon's face and the iridescent blightblade still clutched in his hand, dripping blood.

Eliana glanced at it. "Is he in there?" she said tightly.

"No." He would not look at her. "I tried long ago. He's too strong for blightblades. They can't hold him." Simon flicked the blade a little, as if scorning it. "It's the other angel in here, the one whose body he momentarily took possession of to find you. The blade will have weakened him, though. That will buy us time."

Eliana stared at Simon, hardly seeing him. It was too strange, standing in the near-dark beside him. As if the past months hadn't happened and they were back where they had begun.

Come to me, little one. The Prophet sent her a feeling too muddled to decipher. *Simon knows the way. I'll explain everything once you're here.*

Simon shifted Remy on his shoulder and turned away from the steady gold burn of Eliana's hands.

"Follow me," he said, his voice flat, unreadable.

She wanted to seize him, burn his face with her castings until he writhed as she had, until he screamed her name as she had screamed his.

Only the Prophet's gentle voice stayed her hands. *I'm sorry it had to be this way. I took no enjoyment in it.*

Eliana said nothing more to either of them. By the light of her castings, she followed Simon down the stairs. She couldn't look away from the dark blond crown of his head, mussed and bloody from battle. She imagined grabbing it, then smashing his face against the stairs. Her head ached from Corien's last attack, ready to split open, and she almost wished it would, for then she wouldn't have to face what came next. She felt numb, as if she had entered another world, one in which she understood nothing. Her legs moved of their own volition, carrying her deeper into the endless darkness. Her throat ached with each frigid inhalation. The air had grown cold.

At last, the stairs ended. Beyond them spiraled a web of tunnels and chambers. Three people with the bustling efficiency of soldiers hurried by with weapons, packs of supplies, clean folded linens. Their eyes, when they found Eliana's, were clear.

They stopped to watch her, and then four more hurried out of the shadows, breathless, their eyes shining. As she passed them, they sank to their knees and bowed their heads. They kissed their fingers and touched their closed eyes, murmuring prayers in her wake.

Beside the entrance to a chamber flickering with candlelight, Simon stopped. Still he wouldn't look at her. He placed Remy on a bench outside the chamber, so tender and careful, even in his stark uniform emblazoned with wings, that Eliana nearly went for his throat with the knife Jessamyn had given her. Her imagination went crystalline with anger, showing her how the blade would sink into his chest and scrape bone. She thought of

Jessamyn, how at the moment of her death, she had still believed Eliana intended to close Ostia and save the city, and felt the sharp rise of tears.

"You dare pretend kindness," Eliana whispered.

A moment of silence. Then Simon turned to her, his eyes lowered. Her pulse drummed against her throat. Since that night on the shores of Festival, his face had been steel from brow to jaw. Now, every hard line had softened, haggard with weariness.

She wanted desperately to look away but could not. He seemed to shrink from her, as if she were too brilliant to be seen.

"It was the only way, Eliana," he said, the first time he had uttered her name in months. His voice broke beneath the word, and his fingers flexed at his sides, as if he longed to reach for her. "That's what she told me. It was the only way." He drew a ragged breath, then at last lifted his gaze to meet her own.

She stepped back from him. That piercing blue, the full force of it like a strike to her chest. Once, it had held the heat of desire, the flint of anger.

Not once until now had she seen his eyes raw with grief.

A voice spoke from within the chamber. Gentle and familiar, though different than it had felt in her head. There was a clarity to it now, as if a veil had been lifted.

Eliana gratefully turned away from Simon, her knees liquid and her throat sour, and entered the chamber to her right.

In its heart, positioned between three flickering candles, a young woman sat in a polished chair. Pale and golden-haired, she wore a gown of rose and lilac that buttoned at her throat and mimicked the look of an armored breastplate. She held a sheathed sword in her lap, and her eyes were twin drops of ink. Colorless and ancient.

But Eliana was not afraid.

"You are the Prophet?" she whispered.

The woman smiled softly. "You may call me Ludivine. I knew your parents."

She lifted the sword from her lap. The weapon's strength pulsed against Eliana's skin. Her power rose in greeting, making her teeth ache and her castings flare with heat, and she knew, though she had never seen it before, exactly what sword this was. Her blood knew its flavor, knew each engraved line of its hilt.

Ludivine held up the sword, the sheathed blade flat on her palms. Above it, her black eyes shone. A strange sight: Eliana had never before seen an angel look upon anything with love.

"The last surviving casting of the seven saints," said Ludivine. "It has belonged to your family since Saint Katell used it to strike the angels from the sky. It survived the death of your mother. And now, little one, it belongs to you."

— 36 —

RIELLE

"We have done all we can do. The watchtowers stand tall in the mountains. Earthshakers and waterworkers have deepened the lake. The forges burn day and night, churning out weapons by the dozens. Hundreds of civilians have fled the city, making for Luxitaine. Everyone able to stand and fight has stayed behind to bolster the Celdarian and Mazabatian armies. The angels are approaching. Well, let them come. We're as ready as we'll ever be. For crown and country, we protect the true light. And may God, or the empirium, or whatever damn thing is out there urging these dark tides—may something, anything, help us."

—Journal of Odo Laroche, merchant and member of Red
Crown, dated April 24, Year 1000 of the Second Age

Rielle knew she was alive. She knew she was standing. Beyond that, she knew very little of her body.

Her thoughts careened through the stars. Each one brought her back a new piece of information about the mountains on the western continent, the endless black space beyond the clouds, the other worlds residing within it. Her skin was afire, her blood bubbling hot. The empirium insisted on pouring a million pieces of the world into her mind. It was too much and too fast, but Rielle could not stop herself from drinking. Her ears ached, her temples boomed like drums, and still she consumed.

Corien arrived at her side. His presence pulled her thoughts back to her human body, which rankled her. She stared at the horizon until her irritation subsided. She could see things now—close things—that she hadn't been interested in before.

There were the mountains surrounding Âme de la Terre. Twelve mountains, carpeted with pines, and the highest of them—fearsomely huge, snowcapped—towered over the castle at its feet.

There were the armies she and Corien had made over the past weeks and months. Ten thousand gray-eyed adatrox, puppeted by angels. Countless angels remained bodiless, their only weaponry the cunning power of their minds. And five thousand more walked the countryside of Celdaria, exquisitely crafted by her own hands and tethered solidly to the human bodies that housed them. Some flew; others strode. Scintillant and giddy, ravenous for revenge at last, their angelic glory would be obvious to the people watching their approach—the soldiers trembling nervously in their watchtowers, the children looking wide-eyed over their parents' shoulders as they fled the city for the sea.

There was the soft light of dusk, amber and tangerine to the west, violet to the east. There were the farmlands rolling in neat lines toward the capital. Spring seedlings turning quietly in the soil.

And there was the roundness of her belly and the little life growing inside it. Rielle regarded it askance, this tiny assemblage of lit-up fibers kicking hard against her palms. Maybe allowing it to live after all was unwise. *Two queens will rise,* Aryava had said. *One of blood, and one of light.*

She scratched her stomach, her nails catching on the delicate threads of her gown. It was a dramatic garment. Unadorned blood-colored sheer silk from collar to hem. Long slits to her thighs left her legs free to move. The skirt began high on her waist, falling loose around her belly. She wore no shoes; she didn't need them. The night air of spring was cool, but her blood was high summer. She curled her toes into the dirt. The soles of her feet were black from traveling.

She had designed the gown herself the morning before they left the Northern Reach. The first five sketches had ended in a frenzy. Each time she recreated the lines of her protruding stomach, a wildness came over her. That girl on the mountain. Audric's eyes in a frightened face. Skin lighter than Audric's but darker than her own, a light brown like the sweep of pale sand. Dark brown hair in a thick, messy braid, uncertain power trembling at her fingertips, her hands adorned with thin gold chains. *My name is Eliana.*

Rielle had blacked out each scribbled drawing until the girl vanished from her mind and ink stained her fingers. The nib of her pen scored harsh grooves into Corien's polished desk. Once she had managed to complete a design, she watched the tailors work frantically through the night to finish the gown, gratified to see the sweat painting their brows.

Would her own daughter be the queen to rise up against her? Her palms tingled against her belly.

Corien put his cool hand over hers, scattering her thoughts.

"Look at them," he whispered, sweeping his arm through the air to encompass the staggering ocean of their troops. There were the orderly lines of angelic soldiers. The generals wore black velvet cloaks hemmed in gold. There were the beasts Corien and his physicians had engineered under the northern mountains—crawlers, cruciata imitations, deformed and bulging. Their flapping, fleshy wings, armor embedded in their feathered, scaly hides. Controlled by angelic minds, the blank-eyed elemental children sat astride the beasts, their wrists and necks bound with castings.

Rielle examined the beasts' inner workings, blazing gold and complex. There was the muscled might of the Borsvallic ice-dragons; there were the scars left behind by the knives of Corien's mad underground surgeons. The power of the elemental children encircled the crawlers and their forged armor like nets, ready to tug and whip, summon and blast.

"You've done remarkably well," Rielle said serenely. "But I can see where improvements could be made."

Corien lifted her hand to his lips. "In due time, my love. Worlds, remember? We have entire worlds to make our own after this."

"To unmake and remake as we see fit," she whispered. An insatiable appetite stirred in the marrow of her bones.

"Rielle the Kingsbane." Corien turned her face to his. "Rielle the Unmaker."

"I held a world in my hands," she whispered, closing her eyes as his mouth brushed against her jaw. Her thoughts sang as they returned to that endless glittering sea, the girl in the white gown pulling her into the stars. "I want to do it again. Tell me we will. Tell me it won't be long."

"Soon, you will have everything you desire," he said, his breath hot on her mouth, "and so will I. You will pluck worlds from the stars and set them spinning to please you. You will find God and demand something better than what we have been given."

Then he bent to kiss her. The soft warmth of his lips, his tongue opening her mouth. Rielle's blood leapt savagely at his touch. She tightened her arms around his neck, heat pouring down her thighs. Their army parted around them and thundered past. Their generals shouted out a call in Azradil; the infantry responded in kind, a chorus of war cries in the most lilting, most achingly lovely of the angelic tongues.

Rielle sent Corien a blazing image. There was a copse of oaks on a nearby hill. He would lie in the grass beneath her, hold her hips as she moved. She would have him there in the shadows, and when she rose to face Âme de la Terre, it would be with the memory of his passionate cries ringing in her ears.

He choked out her name against her throat, stumbled after her through the marching troops and into the trees, and when they had finished, he lay trembling in the dirt. With shining eyes, he watched her rise.

She hardly noticed him, lightly kicking him away when he reached for her. Already, she was forgetting how it had felt to have his hands upon her. She stood beneath the trees that had sheltered their lovemaking, her skin ablaze with heat. Her vision pulsed with drumbeats of gold. These days, she knew few other colors. Gold gilded her nightmares, swam sparkling on her tongue. Through an amber sheen, she watched the flood of their army rush swiftly toward the city she had once thought to be her home.

Little fires bloomed in the night—a path of flames snaking through the mountains. A thin wail of horns sounded, quickly drowned out by the chanting army.

Rielle smiled, eyes closed, and tilted her face to the sky. As if it would help them to have a warning. As if watchtowers and horns could be anything but an embarrassment.

Corien joined her, silent and dark at her elbow. She could smell him on her skin.

"Are you ready?" he murmured.

She opened her eyes, and he drew in an astonished sharp breath. She could understand that. The empirium was a vast golden mirror before her, and in it she could see her reflection. Her dark hair, wild to her waist; her silken gown hugging her body; her feet bare and black. Each vein painted with a golden pen, two blazing coins of light for eyes.

"I am infinite," she replied, taking up the words he was so fond of saying. She tried not to think about that too closely. That he could consider himself infinite in any way made him seem silly.

She stepped away from him to join her army as it marched relentlessly forward. She could see past them, past the mountains, past the Celdarian and Mazabatian armies assembled and waiting. She could see past all of it to a castle dark and tense, its halls rustling with urgent whispers, and a courtyard near the armories, where a king mounted a winged godsbeast and prepared to ride into battle.

~ 37 ~

ELIANA

"You don't think I long for her coming as desperately as you do? Friends, not a day, not a moment, goes by that I do not imagine the Sun Queen appearing to us at last, battered and bloody and blazing with light, ready to give herself to our enemy so that we may live again. She is with me in dreams and in waking. She roars in my blood like a passion unmatched. And so must she live in yours, so you will be ready to fight alongside her on the day of reckoning we know awaits us all."

—*The Word of the Prophet*

The seven acolytes who served Ludivine moved quietly as cats. They brought a hot stew of beef and vegetables, cups of fresh water, a second chair, a small table.

Eliana had been given a soft tunic and trousers to replace her ruined gown. She sat very still as the acolytes came and went from the circular stone chamber. She watched Ludivine replace the three candles, which had nearly burnt out. In the dim light, shadows flickered across Ludivine's pale face. Her golden hair, bound in a tidy knot, glinted softly. Her gown whispered at her ankles; she made hardly a sound as she moved. She was mighty in her stillness, a quiet river with floods waiting inside it.

Clammy with nerves, Eliana recalled the Prophet's voice and tried to match it to the woman gliding across the room. *Never step out of that little river. Keep your feet cool and grounded, even as your hands begin to blaze.*

Ludivine settled in her chair, quietly ate a few spoonfuls of stew, then placed the bowl on the table between them.

"There was no other way to get you safely across the Great Ocean to me," said Ludivine, as if they had been talking for hours, "and no other way for you to become what you are now. I needed you to break, and then I needed you to rebuild yourself into something stronger than you were before. Into a version of yourself capable of facing your mother at the height of her power. What you were before was not enough. What you are now will be, I hope."

Ludivine's face shifted slightly, as if gathering itself. "I cannot express how sorry I am for what you have endured. But I'm not sorry for what I have done. Regret is poison. It would kill me."

Her black eyes flicked to Eliana's untouched bowl of stew. "I don't want to force you to eat, but I will if I must. You need strength for what lies ahead."

A jolt of anger flashed hot through Eliana. "Is my brother being fed?"

"Of course. My acolytes will also tend to his injuries. All of them are skilled physicians. And no, I will not allow him to hurt any of them, nor will I allow him to hurt Simon, nor will I allow him to escape. He is comfortable. His mind is resting."

"Your mind is forcing his to rest, you mean. Keeping him docile."

Ludivine inclined her head. "Eat."

Eliana imagined picking up her bowl and throwing it at Ludivine's face. Maybe the stew was hot enough to scorch her. She thought through every beat of the image so that Ludivine would see it. But Ludivine said nothing, only watched her mildly. Eliana's fingers trembled around her spoon.

"You have questions." Ludivine folded her hands in her lap. "Ask them."

Her first few bites had awoken in Eliana a ferocious hunger. At first, she said nothing, shoveling food into her mouth. After a few minutes, she wiped her mouth on her sleeve, let her spoon drop into the empty bowl. Then she fixed her eyes on Ludivine's.

"You say it was the only way to bring me here safely," Eliana said. Unspoken words hovered between them, vibrating and tense. Images battered Eliana's mind: Simon standing on the pier's edge and shooting down their friends; Remy on the deck of the admiral's ship, being dragged away from her; their father falling to his death.

She placed her feet flat on the floor, seeking calm. "Why couldn't you have come to me? You're clearly powerful enough to evade Corien's detection. Why hide here and wait for me? Something could have happened. A storm could have sunk the admiral's ship. I could have managed to kill myself."

"A storm was unlikely. The passage you took is well traveled for a reason. And I have demonstrated that I wouldn't have allowed you to kill yourself," said Ludivine. "As I told you, I needed you to break and then be reborn as your truest self. If I had come to you, none of this would have happened. You would still be small and human, frightened of the power in your blood." Ludivine tilted her head. "You are familiar with the legend of the Kirvayan firebird? To rise, first one must burn."

Eliana glared at her. "I am still human."

"Not entirely. Humans cannot do what you can do. Humans cannot do what your mother could do. You are something more than that, and so was she. You know this."

"You could have come to me," Eliana insisted. "You could have done to me everything that Corien did, remade me as you saw fit. There was no need to bring me here. Remy would have been spared what he's gone through. Maybe my father would still be alive."

"Centuries ago, the city of Âme de la Terre occupied this land. Now, it is Elysium. Corien constructed his palace not far from where the castle of Baingarde once stood." Ludivine paused. "It is difficult enough for even the most skilled marque to travel through time. To ensure success, I eliminated the need to travel through space as well."

"Traveling through time." Eliana swallowed, her throat dry. "You want to send me back, to find my mother. Or to kill her?"

A slight flicker of feeling on Ludivine's placid face. "Hopefully, it will not come to that. You will come upon your mother in a moment of peace, when her mind is clear and open and her loyalties are still firmly with Celdaria. You will attempt to reason with her, convince her to turn on Corien and kill him. If she attacks, you will fight her until she surrenders or you reach an impasse. Or you will come back, and we will try again. Another day, another moment. We will try until we cannot anymore. We will try until we run out of time."

"You mean until Corien finds us."

Ludivine inclined her head.

"And then? Once we've run out of time?"

Ludivine paused. "Then you will return to the past a final time, and you will kill her and Corien. You will close the Gate as soon as you can, before any more angels can escape the Deep." The silence was thunderous. "As I said, hopefully, it will not come to that."

Eliana's bile rose. "But if I kill her before I am born, how would any of this work? How could I go back to kill her if I never existed?"

"I have been assured by someone much more intimately familiar with the art of time travel than I am that if the threads are pulled in the correct sequence, if the magic is calibrated precisely, this paradox can be avoided. If you are forced to kill her, if she leaves you no other choice, you will kill her—and thereby yourself, past and present. I sincerely hope it does not come to that. You must not let it come to that."

Eliana felt nothing at the thought of her own death; she had long ago surpassed such small, narrow fears. But at the mention of time travel, a bubble burst inside her. She could no longer contain the question. Her fingernails dug into the table's polished wood, leaving tiny gold crescents behind.

"Simon," she bit out. "Tell me."

Ludivine lifted her glass of water to her lips. "You'll have to be more specific."

"No, I won't. You can sense my questions, and you are no fool. You know what I'm asking." Tears rose fast, but she was too angry to dash them from her eyes.

Ludivine watched her thoughtfully. "Do you remember when Simon sent you back to Old Celdaria? You attempted to reach Rielle. She fought you, and you were too weak to match her."

"Of course I remember. How could I not?"

"Corien was there that day, in Rielle's mind. When you arrived, he skimmed your thoughts."

Eliana tensed. She would never forget the words. *Ah, Eliana. This is not our first time to meet, it seems. How curious.*

Ludivine nodded. "The Emperor had touched your mind before, but only distantly and without much success. He knew you existed but could only find your thoughts intermittently, much to his frustration."

"Because of you?"

"Because of me. But that day, you were far from me, in another time, and *that* Corien was able to find you, if only for a moment. And he said something else, didn't he?"

A chill moved slowly down Eliana's arms as she remembered Corien's words. *What a life you have led. What interesting company you keep.*

"I remember," she said, a mere whisper.

"In that moment, he did not see everything we had worked for, but he saw enough of it," Ludivine continued. "He saw Simon and knew he was a marque. He knew you loved him but was not sure if he loved you. He knew that you meant to end his Empire before it truly began. He knew enough, and when you returned to your present, it was altered."

Ludivine leaned back in her chair, looking suddenly weary. "I, of course, saw all of this too. I saw it in Rielle's mind when she came home that night. But I kept everything I knew from her, and from Audric too. I was a coward then. I was too afraid of what this all might mean, and I didn't act until it was too late. I could not face the scope of my own failure. So I went into hiding. I watched Rielle kill Audric. I watched the angels invade

Âme de la Terre. I watched the world end, frozen in the grip of my own fear. After the invasion, I protected the boy Simon so Corien would not find him. Then I watched Simon summon threads and attempt to travel with you to the kingdom of Borsvall. I told him to hurry. I told him he was strong enough, and he was. But it didn't matter."

Ludivine closed her eyes. Her voice became a whisper. "The force of Rielle's death knocked the threads of space askew and summoned forth threads of time. Volatile and unpredictable. I watched them snatch both you and Simon into darkness, and then I watched as Baingarde collapsed, the mountains around Âme de la Terre crumbled, and everyone living in the city was extinguished. I watched the angels crawl from the ashes. Those who had managed to cling to their stolen human bodies could no longer taste and see and feel as they had only moments before. Their eyes were black, and so were mine. I listened to them howl, Corien loudest of all, for he had lost her."

A long moment passed. Eliana's heartbeat pulsed in her temples. "But Simon said that we would be the only ones to notice any changes. Anything that us being in the past would have altered. I thought..." Words tangled in her throat. "I thought that meant..."

"That he would be protected from any changes to the altered future? He *was*, Eliana. But don't you see? It was the only way. I made sure that the child Simon was there on the night of your birth. Rielle urged him to take you to safety, and I encouraged him, thinking I would join the two of you later. That I would protect you as I had failed to protect your mother. While the world healed from Rielle's death, I would raise you and Simon as my own. Then, when you were old enough and strong enough, I would send you both back to the past to save Rielle before she began losing herself to Corien and to the empirium. Of course, Rielle died before Simon could travel, and the shock wave jarred his work. Both of you were thrown forward in time, and I was left alone in a shattered world."

Eliana's mind worked quickly. "Corien didn't die, either. He survived."

"He was beside your mother at the moment of her death, so his injuries were...severe. It took him centuries to recover fully, and his mind, while still powerful, was never the same. And I knew then that what Rielle had seen on the mountain—you, and threads pulled by a grown Simon—that future was coming true. And I knew that I must act."

A sick heat rose swiftly in Eliana as she began to understand. "In the past, Corien had glimpsed Simon. And though Rielle's death had damaged his mind…"

"I knew that might not be enough to protect Simon, when the time came," Ludivine agreed. "I knew that I must be on the lookout for him myself, and shield my efforts and my very existence from Corien. When Simon at last appeared—hundreds of years later for me, but only seconds for him—I knew the only way to keep him safe from Corien, and therefore protect our one hope of traveling back in time, was to send him right into Corien's hands. Corien would have to believe him to be utterly his own. He would need to serve the enemy to be saved from the enemy."

Ludivine's gaze was steady and bright. "I taught him discipline. I taught him how to withstand pain. As best I could, I ensured that the scars I gave him matched the ones I had seen. Months passed. Then I left him in the wilderness of Vindica and made certain that Corien would find him."

"In the wilderness," Eliana said, numb.

"Simon did exactly as I had instructed," Ludivine said, smiling faintly. "We had practiced until he believed the story he was meant to tell. When Corien found him, Simon was desperate with loneliness. He had lived alone for months, and he was scarred from his accidental journey through time, and here at last was someone from the home he had lost. Rielle had destroyed his city. She had killed his king. It was her betrayal that had brought the angels to his city, her death that had sent him hurtling into a future he did not understand, where he was alone and afraid. He suspected Rielle's daughter had been brought there as well. He would help Corien find her. He would serve without question if it meant he would no longer be alone, and if Corien would help him find his magic again. That was the story Simon told."

Ludivine's smile flickered. "And though he tried for years, Corien could find no evidence of deceit. He was suspicious. He recalled fragments of that old memory, of seeing you on the mountain and seeing Simon through you, but he knew that whatever time travel you had attempted had likely changed your circumstances, perhaps in his favor, and he could not turn away such a gift as Simon. Rielle's death broke the empirium. If her daughter were here, her gifts would not be obvious; they might even be deeply dormant. He would need help to find her, especially since the immense task of growing his Empire had worn thin his already-damaged mind. And what better helper could he find than this boy who had seen everything happen that night he had lost his great love? A boy he could mold. A boy who had held you in his arms. A marque with angelic blood."

Eliana closed her eyes, clenching the arms of her chair.

"From his place at Corien's side," Ludivine continued, "Simon would serve two masters. He would find you, push you to awaken yourself, and then help break you, all while pretending loyalty to your greatest enemy. But he was always mine. He has been from the moment I found him alone in the snow, clutching your little scrap of blanket."

Then, pity softened Ludivine's voice. "I'm sorry, little one. It was the only way. If it helps you, his love was no strategy of mine. I had hoped, of course, that he might grow to love you. Love would make it easier for him to hurt you, and it would therefore hasten your path toward destruction and then rebirth." Eliana opened her eyes, momentarily stunned out of her anger. Ludivine smiled, magnanimous. "And now look at you. A glorious creature."

The moment ended.

Eliana moved like fire. She knocked the table and bowls aside, then struck Ludivine hard across the face.

Ludivine made no sound, showed no sign of pain. The pink mark on her cheek quickly faded.

"You hurt him," Eliana said, her voice tight and soft. "You hurt his mind so severely that he could serve both you and Corien without his true loyalty ever being discovered. You scrambled him, tore him apart, sewed him back together."

Ludivine wiped the blood from her lip. "That's true."

"And I suppose Corien hurt him as well, over and over, to ensure he was not being deceived."

"For every night of peace Simon enjoyed in Corien's palace, he endured ten of torment," Ludivine said simply. "But Corien could never find anything amiss. I ensured it would be so. Until today, he believed Simon to be his entirely."

Eliana's eyes stung with tears. She hardly noticed them. Her chest was hot with fury. "You're a monster. You tortured this boy who had lost his father and his home, and then you sent him off to another monster to be tortured further."

Ludivine was implacable. "I don't need to tell you that sometimes we must make difficult choices and commit acts of violence to benefit the greater good. Look at what you did for your family when you lived in Orline. Look at what you've done for Red Crown, for Remy, for the people of this world. You are no stranger to sacrifice, Eliana, nor to cruelty."

An acolyte appeared suddenly at the door, startling Eliana from her rising grief. They were too quiet for her liking, these acolytes, their gazes too direct. Eliana wondered what torment they had endured at Ludivine's hand. Was it love that kept them loyal, or was it fear?

"They're here, my lady," the acolyte said with a bow.

"See that they are fed and their wounds treated," Ludivine commanded. "We will join you shortly."

The acolyte nodded once and then was gone.

"We will speak more later," said Ludivine, rising from her chair. "Until then, I leave you with this thought. The only way to end this—this war that has for millennia gripped everyone in this world and others—is for you to return to Old Celdaria. Convince Rielle to kill Corien and close the Gate. Fight her if you must. Destroy her if it comes to it."

Eliana stared at her, full of too many warring sadnesses. "You loved her."

"I did."

"And yet you speak of her so coldly?"

"I have had centuries to grieve for her," said Ludivine. She plucked a piece of carrot from her sleeve. Her unfinished stew streaked the floor. "I no longer fear her death as I once did."

The cool mask of her face unnerved Eliana. "I don't understand how we would even do this thing. Simon tried traveling many times in the palace. He could not find his power."

"Because you wouldn't let him."

A deafening silence fell between them.

Ludivine smiled gently. "You understand, then, what you must do. You reawakened his power when your love for him was nearing its peak. Once when you healed Remy. Then again during your time at Willow. The world's magic is dead, Eliana, the empirium wrenched and distant. Only through you does it live again. And with your trust in Simon lost, beneath the iron press of your angry will, his power has become dormant once more, and unreliable, as you have seen. You must truly accept him into your heart once more, allow him to find his power again, if there is to be any hope of doing what we must."

Eliana shook her head. She found her chair and sank slowly onto it, her knees suddenly unsteady. "How can I? After what he's done, after what he's seen and heard..." She closed her eyes, struggling to find her voice. "I could say, 'I forgive you' until my throat bled, but it wouldn't be true, even knowing what you've done to him."

"I didn't say forgive. I said accept."

Hearing Ludivine kneel before her, Eliana opened her eyes and stared at her through a simmering field of hate.

"You could choose not to," said Ludivine kindly, considering her. "You could continue to refuse him his power. We could sit in these rooms waiting for Corien to recover from the blightblade and find us. He'll kill all of us, including Simon, and me, and you, perhaps, because he has very little sanity left now, and then this will all have been for nothing. Everything you've endured. Every moment Simon spent sobbing at my feet as I dissected his mind. I know that's not what you want to happen."

Eliana looked away, her shoulders aching under a terrible new weight. Arguing with Ludivine would be futile. She knew what Eliana thought as surely as she herself did.

"And if we do this," she said quietly, "what will happen to everyone living now? Remy and Navi, everyone I've ever known and loved?"

"They will no longer exist. They will never have existed. At least not as they are now. Remy may still be born someday to Rozen and Ioseph Ferracora, but he will not be the Remy you know, not entirely. Nor will Rozen or Ioseph, nor even the city of Orline. If you succeed in convincing Rielle to kill Corien, then the world will begin again at his death. There will be peace. She will repair the Gate, and the angels will remain sealed in the Deep."

They will never have existed. Eliana, numb with horror, remembered her discussions about this very thing with Simon. While he practiced threading in Willow's gardens, they had spoken of altered futures, lives snuffed out. She had not truly been able to fathom the concept then, and now was no different. It was too colossal, too terrible. Navi, Patrik, Hob. Remy. Her Remy. All of them changed, or maybe not even born. Maybe alive, maybe not. Maybe themselves, maybe not. A whole world of people, blinked out of existence.

Her mouth went dry, her insides a plunging hot swoop of revulsion. She felt somehow dislodged, as if Ludivine's words had shaken loose her deepest foundations. She stared at this golden-haired angel before her but found no comfort in that steely black gaze.

Then Ludivine rose and stepped back from Eliana's chair, her expression shifting. From down the hallway came sounds of a brief struggle. Running footsteps approached, and a woman with warm brown skin and tangled black hair that fell to her shoulders stopped abruptly at the door. Her clothes were filthy, streaked with blood and grime.

Eliana's shock bloomed swiftly, sweeping her mind clean. Her voice was a soft puff of air. "Navi?"

Navi let out a strangled cry, then rushed for Eliana and pulled her into a crushing embrace. Eliana clutched her shoulders, held her fast. Navi pressed her face into Eliana's neck, saying things Eliana could barely hear, for there was a ringing in her ears, as if her joy were a struck bell.

She looked past Navi's shoulder to where Ludivine stood pale and still in the shadows.

"Is this a trick?" Eliana whispered.

No, little one, Ludivine replied. Her black eyes glittered in the candlelight.

Navi pulled away, her cheeks wet with tears. She brushed Eliana's hair behind her ears, looking ready to say a thousand things. How lovely Navi was, even with the blood drying on her arms, the smell of death clinging to her. Bright blue drops spattered her collar. Eliana held Navi's face in her hands, and still she couldn't speak. She shook her head, laughed a little, tried to pull her friend close once more.

But Navi stepped back, her hands warm around Eliana's own. "Zahra is here. I think she's been waiting to see you before she..."

Navi's voice trailed off. She looked back into the hallway. Beyond her was a woman with chin-length white hair and ruddy freckled skin. Eliana blinked, her mind racing to catch up with everything she saw. Patrik was there, and Hob too, and Navi's brother, Malik, and dozens of others Eliana didn't recognize.

And drifting slowly toward the door was a figure faint and gray. Hair streaming like ripples of wind across water, eyes dark and flickering. An echo of the angel she had once been, drawn in thin shadows.

"Zahra," Eliana whispered, reaching for her. At that single word, Zahra cried out softly, faded, and then reappeared only to float slowly to the ground.

Eliana knelt to meet her. Her hands hovered over what she could see of Zahra's shrinking form. She had diminished to the size of a child. The shifting lines of her body were like curls of fading smoke.

"What happened, Zahra?"

"My queen," Zahra mumbled. A thin hand of shadow moved toward Eliana's cheek. "My queen, my queen. There you are."

Navi knelt beside them, her hazel eyes shining. "She was wonderful, Eliana. She hid our ship for the entire journey across the ocean. She guided us through the Sea of Silarra, helped us elude dozens of imperial warships. She shielded us on the road to Elysium, through the city, and down here to you. The Prophet..." Navi glanced at Ludivine, her brow furrowed. "The Prophet guided her to you. All of us survived the journey. One hundred and seven of us, alive and well thanks to her."

"Zahra, you marvel, how did you manage such a thing?" Eliana drew a picture in her mind: the two of them embracing, Zahra in her angelic form, as Eliana had seen in that vision so long ago. Rich brown skin, white hair falling like spider-silk to her hips. Platinum armor bright with sunlight, gossamer wings streaming like rivers of starlit shadow from her back.

But before she could send Zahra the image, Ludivine stopped her with a gentle press in her mind. *She cannot bear it, Eliana. Her mind is losing cohesion from so much strain. Be gentle.*

Eliana stared at the floor, where only the faintest black wisps marked Zahra's unraveling. The vague dark print of her eyes were but a suggestion of shadow on the stone. Eliana shook her head, her throat aching. Her tears washed away all color from the world.

"Zahra, why did you do this?" she whispered.

A fractured voice replied, a mere breath of sound. "For you, my queen."

Then, a slight tremor against Eliana's skin. A soundless give, as if the air had previously held a great weight, a mammoth intelligence, and now held nothing but itself.

→ 38 →

AUDRIC

"Rise with the dawn, my brothers, my sisters, my friends!
Rise with the light! With the sun at our backs, we meet
our enemies without fear or despair or doubt! We know
only the rage blooming bright in our hearts! The love for
those we have lost! The love for the home that has been
taken from us! And love for the day we know will come
tomorrow, and the next, and the next, until the sun rises
and looks down upon a world of peace at last!"

—A speech delivered by Saint Katell of Celdaria
to the elemental troops at the Battle of the Black Stars

Audric rode Atheria to the highest slopes of Mount Cibelline and stood in the quiet, thin air, watching the horizon. From such a height, the puny watchtower flames seemed laughable. Beyond them churned a relentless black sea—the angelic army, scattered with white starbursts of light that hovered and glided and sometimes soared.

Audric knew what those lights meant. He had read every account of the Angelic Wars he could find. He had seen the illustrations in his books and had drawn his own sketches when he was young. Angels in flight, wings of light and shadow carrying them past mountaintops and into the clouds. They could glide through an army and leave dozens of glassy-eyed, empty-minded soldiers in their wake.

Rielle had given them bodies, which was no surprise. But it seemed she had also given some of them wings.

Audric watched the distant angels fly until he could no longer stand on his own. He turned to Atheria and leaned hard against her, his knees unsteady. She watched the horizon, ears flat and teeth bared. She snapped her tail as if longing to whip it at someone.

He breathed hard and fast against her coat. When he returned to Baingarde, he would be not only a king but a commander. He would show no fear. He would neither balk nor cower.

But on Cibelline, sheltered by the ancient whispering pines, he clung to Atheria, seeking anchor in a storm. She covered him with her wing, and he gladly hid beneath it. Long moments passed. On the mountain, the world was quiet. A few bird calls, a whistle of wind. No marching boots, no crackle of elemental energy, no clank of angelic armor.

Evyline and the Sun Guard were waiting for him in the grid of armory courtyards. He would dress soon, and he would need their help to fasten the plates of his armor, secure his cloak of emerald green, violet, and amber.

And then, he would need to face this. Face *her*. He would need to show himself before his army, and the Mazabatian troops, and the elemental regiments sent from the temples, and somehow rally them to face their inevitable doom. How many thousands could they claim? And how many more could Corien?

He wrenched himself from the solid warmth of Atheria's belly and climbed clumsily onto her back. Even kneeling, she towered, and he was too shaky for grace. He huddled there between her wings, then climbed off and tried again, and again, until he had shaken the nerves from his skin and could swing easily onto her broad back.

Long weeks ago, they had ridden out to meet the eye of a storm.

A storm, an army—one was not so different from the other.

He held the lie in his mind as Atheria shot down the slopes, swift and silent over the treetops. These were his last moments of peace. He knew somehow that he would never again be able to breathe without also drawing a sword or watching a soldier sworn to him cut down by an angelic blade.

As Atheria rode the wind, Audric tried once more to reach for Ludivine. Surely she would not leave him to this. She would reappear at the last moment with some great piece of information or brilliant strategy, or with Rielle on her arm. Ludivine, triumphant. Rielle, bright-eyed and giddy with relief to be home at last.

An embarrassing thing to imagine, like a child spinning fantasies.

Audric set his jaw. *Ludivine? Are you there?*

But she didn't answer. In a city of thousands, in a country of millions, he was utterly, irrevocably alone.

✦◇✦

It was night when he faced his soldiers. Ten thousand troops, mounted and on foot. Armored and cloaked, swords at their hips and castings aglow with waiting power. Metal bands and daggers, tridents and spears, shields and hammers, all scattering the city with light.

Throughout Âme de la Terre, those who had not fled the city, too young or old or weak to take up arms, gathered on rooftops and crowded at windows for a chance to see him and Atheria as they passed through the city on their way to the Flats.

The ground shook with the marching footsteps of the enemy, a storm unlike any that had ever darkened the sky. Soon, the angelic armies would breach the mountains. Earthshakers had been working for weeks to bolster the mountains themselves as a defense, blocking passes with avalanches, cutting through solid rock to create canyons, sheer cliffs, mazes of rock. The winged angels would be able to fly over such obstacles, the stolen elemental children would perhaps manage to flatten them, but his earthshakers were stationed at the pass, ready to reinforce the barriers as needed. He hoped this war of stone would slow the angels' progress. Even the broad, sloping pass between Mount Taléa and Mount Sorenne, a huge gap in the encircling mountains, had been fortified. Audric glanced at the pass as Atheria flew. Almost two years ago, Audric had nearly died there during the Boon Chase. It was strange to recall a time when Borsvall was the enemy rather than a desperate ally. Even stranger to remember the chaos of that day—the earth flying apart around him, swift tongues of fire streaking across the Flats toward the city.

Rielle, wild with fear and glorious in her rage, tearing apart the world to save him.

He drew a breath and urged Atheria out onto the Flats, where his armies waited in orderly ranks. Archers, foot soldiers with pikes and spears, elementals holding fire and wind in the palms of their hands. They had erected a towering stone wall around the city proper, twenty feet thick and two hundred feet high. Archers and elementals were stationed atop them, arrows at the ready and fists crackling with power. Once the army had marched onto the Flats, earthshakers had demolished the city bridges spanning the lake that bordered most of the city. Now, the water gleamed unadorned, a deep and broad expanse curving around from one side of Mount Cibelline's foothills to the other. If the angels managed to both traverse the lake and breach the wall, they would meet the second army—another thousand soldiers and elementals, ready to defend the streets of their city.

Audric's traitorous mind fixed on the thought that it was not a matter of whether the angels would breach the wall. It was a matter of *when*. There was no hope of defeating the army marching on them. Not all of the angels had wings, but his surviving scouts had told him about the beasts among the angelic ranks—perverse creations, mutilated and malformed, just as Kamayin's spy had reported. Elemental children rode atop these creatures, gray-eyed and deadly, their castings bound to the beasts' forged armor. *Monsters unholy*, one of the scouts had called them before he burst into hysterical tears on his knees before Audric's desk. Beasts in flaming armor. Children who stamped apart the earth without flinching.

Audric guided Atheria to the top of a tall stone platform Grand Magister Florimond had constructed at the lake's outer shore. He dismounted Atheria and looked out upon the Flats. Twenty thousand soldiers turned to watch him—his own troops, and those from Mazabat. He touched the forged amplifier at his belt, a gift from Miren. His father had used it the day of the Boon Chase. *To celebrate another year of peace in our kingdom.*

He raised Illumenor until the soldiers quieted. Citizens within the walls would be listening, too, watching the Flats with fear in their hearts. Many of them knew this fight was hopeless. Far fewer understood that the true fight would not be on the battlefield between humans and angels.

It would be between him and Rielle, wherever it was that he found her. If he could convince her to use her power against the army she had created, then perhaps the tide would turn.

Otherwise, the city, the country—the *world*—would fall. Of this he was certain. *The world will fall*, Aryava had said centuries before. *Two queens will rise.*

Only once in recent months had Audric allowed himself to look upon those words with hope. Alone in his bed in Mazabat, Ludivine's news sitting in his gut like a stone, he had recited the familiar words. *Two queens will rise.* Rielle, after he had won back her loyalty. And then, in the aftermath of war, their daughter. A princess of peace, and someday a queen.

Atop the tower of stone, Audric lowered his sword. Around him, the air pulled taut with tense silence.

May the Queen's light guide me, he thought, and held in his mind a fuzzy imagining. The shape of his daughter's face, the weight of her soft head in his arms. What would she look like?

"You are afraid," he said, his voice booming through the amplifier. Even with its aid, he had to shout to be heard. The night was thick, close, as if the world knew what lay ahead. "You see the darkness coming for us. You hear its roar. I see it too. I hear it in my bones. And I too am afraid. But more than that, I feel love. I feel love for you, for this city we live in, for this country and the people in it, for every farm and every forest, every river and every mountain."

He began to pace the platform. His cloak whipped at his legs. The air shivered, stirred by the presence of so many gathered elementals.

"We can feel our fear. It is allowed. It is right, and it is human. Our blood will race, our knees will quake. But our hearts..." He shook his head, looked fiercely out at them. Thousands of them, elemental and not, wide-eyed and rapt, their helmets burnished to a shine. Wrists ablaze, swords gleaming silver, fear pulsing at each and every throat.

"Our hearts will not fail us today," he told them. "This is not a day for fear. It is a day for love. Hundreds of years ago, our saints fought these same enemies and won. They lit the sky with fire, they cast mountains into the sea, and they drove the angels into the Deep. Now they are back, and the saints are long dead. But we are not dead, my friends. We *live*! And on this day, it will be *our* swords that bring the enemies to their knees! It will be *our* power that turns them to ashes where they stand!"

He paused, letting the soldiers' shouts and cheers rise and wash over him. The sound made him sick with love. He wanted to gather each of them to his chest and hold them there safely until dawn came. He blinked until his eyes cleared.

"Our prayer for so long has been this: May the Queen's light guide us." He allowed the words to linger in the air. He knew what they would think, who they would think of, and allowed them to think it. "But I say that *we* are the light! *We* are the salvation we have prayed for! *We* stand on this earth that is our home, and it is *we* who will drive from it every creature who would dare try to take it from us!"

He turned toward the northern horizon. A black crescent teemed on the mountain pass. For a moment, he considered sending out his thoughts, as Ludivine had taught him. Maybe she would answer. Maybe she had found Rielle and would guide him to her.

But instead, he raised Illumenor. The sun was gone from the sky, but the echoes of its light remained, and still more burned distant beyond the horizon. He pulled every scrap of it his power could find toward the silver flat of his sword, then sent it streaming to the ground in brilliant rays.

"*We* are the light!" he cried.

They took up the call—his army on the Flats, his people in the city. They echoed him again and again.

Sloane, at the head of her regiment of shadowcasters, her armor black as obsidian, thrust her scepter into the air. The orb at its top glowed blue like the white-hot center of a flame. Its light drew shadows from the earth—wolves and hawks, prowling mountain cats with raised hackles.

Miren's ax flashed in Illumenor's light, and the two hundred metalmaster acolytes she commanded punched their castings into the air.

Princess Kamayin held up her fists as if preparing to engage an attacker, her castings glinting at her wrists.

Queen Bazati drew her long, curved sabre, whipping the air into a cyclone.

The Sun Guard, standing below the wall, turned their horses toward the mountains. Evyline's yells thundered like an anvil's blows.

Magister Duval and his regiment of windsingers, the city guard, the Sauvillier soldiers who had declared their loyalty to the throne. Odo's private army of paid knife fighters and archers, all of them now proudly sporting the livery of House Courverie.

Every soldier gathered raised their voice in a furious chorus.

"We are the light!"

Their shouts roared like waves.

"We are the light!"

Audric climbed swiftly onto Atheria's back. She launched into the air, and the archers on the wall knelt at his departure. They touched their lips, then their eyelids. The prayer of the House of Light.

"We are the light!"

The Sun Guard a gleaming V below him, Audric flew low and fast over the deafening cries of his army. He lifted Illumenor high, cast its light in bright beams through the night. Beneath the steady pound of his heartbeat came a roll of thunder as his army began to charge, following Illumenor's light. The sharp neighs of eager warhorses, their huffing breaths. The clang of armor, the zip and crackle of elemental magic gathering to strike.

Power raced through Audric's every vein, warming the plates of his armor. White light shot from his fingers like sparks from a fire.

"*We are the light!*"

His words broke into screams of fury. Below and behind him, the ocean of his army crested, their war cries splitting open the air. They had reached the wide stretch of the open Flats. A broad field, miles long and miles wide, slightly damp from recent rains. The horses tore up mud with their hooves. Waterworkers pulled rainwater from the ground and spun foaming spirals in the air.

Audric watched the horizon. The angelic front lines had breached the mountains at last and were charging toward them. Beasts plunged across the Flats on grotesquely large forearms, blunt paws, splintered hooves. One—bear-like, enormous, with a mottled hide that looked tough as rocks—whipped its armored tail and shot ribbons of fire. Eerie light flashed—bright and liquid, like moonlit rivers bleached of color. Angelic wings, approaching fast.

But Audric did not falter. In his hand, Illumenor was an inferno. It would dazzle them. He heard the shrieks of the monsters below and saw angels veer quickly away, as if they had been pummeled.

He stared them down. Beyond the mountains, night reigned. But Illumenor turned the battlefield to a scorching, merciless dawn. He heard the awful sounds of two armies crashing together. The ring of swords, the wild cries of felled soldiers.

"*We are the light!*"

And still they shouted his words.

Audric's breaths matched the urgent beat of Atheria's wings as she plunged ahead toward the mountains. Illumenor cut a broad line of white fire through the angelic army. He heard the whistle of arrows, the hissed curses of angels lashing the air, but nothing and no one could approach the blinding brilliance of his casting.

He would not be able to hold such power steady for long.

He turned his thoughts to the battle raging below and searched the chaos for Rielle.

~ 39 ~

ELIANA

"'Tell me,' said Morgaine to her love, 'will you think of me when I am gone? So far from you I must go, such a journey lies before me.' And Morgaine wept furious tears, ashamed for him to see her, but Gilduin held her hands and kissed them, and looked upon her anguished face, and suddenly Morgaine felt at peace, for in Gilduin's eyes was naught but love. 'There is nothing in this world that I could look upon and not then think of you,' he said, 'for in you lies everything I have known, everything I am, everything I will be.'"

—"The Ballad of Gilduin and Morgaine,"
ancient Celdarian epic, author unknown

In the room Ludivine had set aside for her, Eliana lay beside Navi, arms tight around her, cheek pressed against her arm. She listened to Navi breathe and waited for her to reply. With a twinge of nerves, she remembered that she would not be able to wait for long.

Corien would not stay weakened by Simon's blightblade forever. Ludivine had shut herself away in her room to keep watch for him. Every passing moment brought them closer to when he would regain his strength and come hunting. Hours, Ludivine had guessed, and only a few of those.

Eliana burrowed against Navi's side, greedy for her warmth. She thought of how Navi had kissed the sharp-eyed, sharper-mouthed woman, Ysabet, before retreating to Eliana's room. How their fingers had interwoven, a lingering touch, before moving apart. It should have brought her nothing but joy to know her friend had found a lover. But it only made her think of how little time she herself had had with Navi, and Zahra, and everyone she so fiercely loved, and how all of that time had been while they were at war.

At last, Navi blew out a sharp breath. Her left hand stroked Eliana's hair.

"Well," she said, and then said nothing else. Eliana looked up at her, studied her face. The fine cut of her jawline, her thick black lashes. She fiddled with the hem of Navi's sleeve, glad she was saying nothing else. She didn't need to; Eliana could see everything she felt on her face.

She asked quietly, "Are you ashamed of me?"

"Because you pity him?" Navi's voice was gentle. "Of course not. I admit I pity him myself. But I pity you far more, and I am glad that I nor any of my people have seen him today. He is wise to keep himself hidden away. I'm not sure I could have restrained Ysabet, and she's never even met the man."

Eliana smiled a little. Silence fell between them, a long, unhurried pull of peace.

"I'm angry that I have to do this," she whispered into the quiet.

Navi's fingers were tender in her hair. "As am I, my darling."

"I'm angry that I *want* to." Eliana pushed on before Navi could respond, "I shouldn't want to let him in again, to accept him, to allow him his power. For months, I've guarded myself against memories of him. I've wanted to hurt him. I've tried many times. But now, when I think of what's been done to him, I hate him less. When I think of seeing him again, knowing what I now know, I feel this awful relief. He has suffered, and so have I. All those weeks of pain in Corien's palace... He has lived through years of that. He understands." She drew a quaking breath. "And then I hate myself for thinking about this when there is so much else to think about, so much else to—"

She swallowed against the hard ache in her throat. The words danced on her tongue. *If I do this, Navi, if I manage it, we will never have met. Maybe you will never have been born.*

Or maybe Navi *would* be born to her lovely family in Astavar. She would grow up in Vintervok without a dark future on the horizon. No war, no spy work, no suffering in the Orline maidensfold.

"There is too much hate in the world already," Navi replied after a moment. "Why direct more of it at yourself?"

Then Navi shifted until they were both on their sides, facing each other. She pressed her brow to Eliana's.

"We don't have much time," Eliana whispered. It could have been said about any of them, about any part of this, but she knew Navi would understand her meaning. "I don't have to forgive him, she said. I just have to open my heart to him again." She laughed a little, tears on her lashes. "What little of it there is left."

"Then go to him," Navi said quietly. "And be kind to my friend. Her heart is stronger than she thinks, no matter what evil tries to break it."

Eliana kissed Navi's cheek. She closed her eyes and lingered there against Navi's soft skin. Then she rose from the bed and did not look back.

◆

She found him in a small chamber situated far from the others. Her steps carried her there on fluttering wings of nerves, and when she knocked and heard his summons, every muscle in her body tensed. Panic splintered swiftly inside her, a widening crack in thin ice. She considered turning away, leaving him, demanding of Ludivine another solution. How could she accept or even face this man who had hurt her?

This man who had suffered just as she had. This man who, like her, knew very well the true breadth of Corien's cruelty.

She did not turn away.

She entered the room, found Simon sitting at the edge of a tiny bed that looked too small for his tall frame. Was it here that he had spent those months under Ludivine's tutelage? Had she visited him as he slept, sent him nightmares within these very walls?

He looked up, realizing too late who stood before him. He was unable to hide the open mess of his face, his bloodshot eyes and reddened cheeks, the wildness of his hair. He caught her eyes and looked immediately away.

"No," she told him, going to him at once. "If I don't get the relief of not having to look at you, then you have to see me too." She lifted his chin so their gazes locked. His lashes were wet. He tried to look away again; she did not allow it, holding his face still. He had kept himself clean-shaven while in Corien's palace, but these last few wild days had not allowed him the time. His cheeks were growing rough again, and she wanted to rub her fingers against them until she could remember no other sensation. She longed to hurt him in whatever vicious way she could imagine. She longed to run from him and everything that awaited them.

"I know what has been done to you," she told him firmly. It was difficult to speak. She put a metal stamp on every word. "I know what you've endured. You have my pity. You do not have my trust."

He nodded, his mouth held tightly. He had been expecting her to say that. Against her palms, she could feel the muscles of his jaw working.

Too many words crowded her throat, many of them brutal. She could have screamed with frustration. This was moving too fast for both of them. There was too much hurt between them, too many lies and too many days apart.

"But you do have my love," she said furiously, as if it were a curse.

Simon watched her, hardly breathing. He did not blink.

"I wish you had nothing of mine," Eliana said through her teeth. Her cheeks burned with anger, and her heart ached in too many places. "Not my love, not my anger, not my memories. I wish you hadn't seen what he did to me. I wish…"

She could no longer speak. Simon reached up to cover her hands with his own. He barely touched her; she was an eggshell in his palms.

"I wish I could hurt you as you hurt me," she whispered. "I wish I didn't want you still or care for you at all. I wish all I wanted was to help you find your power again." She shook her head. Her voice teetered on the edge of something sharp. "But I want more than that. Even now, even after everything."

When Simon closed his eyes, tears slipped out. He turned his face into her palm, whispered her name against her fingers.

She watched his mouth, fighting ferociously against her own misery. It split her vision into diamonds. "He hurt me," she said softly. "I called for you. I screamed for you to help me."

Simon let out a single sob. Fumbling, he reached for her. His face against her ribs, his hands clutching her shirt. The tender weight of his palms sent a fierce bite of joy up her arms. Her instincts were at war. To leave him aching, to lean into his warmth. Two paths and no answers.

"God, I know," he said, voice muffled. "I heard you. I heard every word, Eliana. I heard it every time he hurt you, and I could do nothing. There were times he made me watch, and you were so delirious with pain you didn't even realize I was there."

His words spilled like shards of glass against her belly. Each one stabbed her, and yet she clutched his shoulders, held him fast, wished she could press him inside her until he no longer existed anywhere else.

She held his shoulders and watched the wall as he wept. His tears were as silent as hers, his body rigid. They were both used to that, she supposed. They were used to hiding the signs of their pain.

And suddenly, she could no longer bear to remain standing. She didn't care that she had wanted to hurt him, that for months she had watched him stalk through the palace and imagined his murder at her hands.

She bowed her head to kiss his crown. "I'll miss you," she told him, not meaning to say it, and then a sob burst out of her, unexpected and savage. She could hardly breathe; tears seized her like fists.

There was more to say, more than could ever be said, but Ludivine was shut away in her eerie candlelit room, fighting for every moment. There was no time to say anything more, no time to mend or heal. Not forgiveness, Ludivine had said. Only acceptance. And Eliana had come to Simon's room determined to do nothing but talk, to work at opening her power to him and helping him search once more for his.

But when he turned his face up to hers, his hands trembling at her sleeves, Eliana lost all sense of the wrath she wished he deserved and knew he did not, and she met his mouth gladly.

He waited until she had settled in his lap before wrapping his arms around her. The sensation nearly split her chest in two. Such a solid cocoon of warmth. She cried out against his lips, opened her mouth to receive his kisses. They spilled inside her like knives warmed by fire. Hot steel glinting red, blades that slipped and sliced. He smelled of salt and smoke, murmured her name until she wore the syllables on her skin.

This would bring no relief, Eliana knew, even as she clung to him. His fingers found her, and she clenched her thighs around his arm. They would finish, and they would ache in body and in heart, everything they had locked away now once again unleashed. His power would return if they were lucky, or maybe unlucky, and then he would send her back to do the impossible thing she must do, and she would never see this version of him again, never see any of them again. If she succeeded, if her unborn self survived, she would grow up in Old Celdaria, ignorant of everything she had once been, or had never been.

She wove her fingers into Simon's hair, pulled hard so he would look up at her. His eyes landed on her face, just as searing hot as she remembered, and his hand moved just as it had the first time until the fire rising inside her spilled over, roaring. Despair came fast on its heels, and she knew she could not stop, not yet, not ever.

Frantic, she moved to lie flat on her back and then pulled him atop her. Guided him into place, hooked her legs around his. He must have sensed her desperation, the wild sorrow building in her chest like a storm spinning with pitiless thunder. He moved sharp and hard, as if he could imbue in her the memory of every night they would never have. An apology for every time he had hurt her. A plea for forgiveness that would never come.

She arched up against him, tightened the grip of her thighs. Tugged at his hair, dug her fingernails into the scarred flesh of his back. When he latched on to her throat, sucking gently on her skin, she whispered for more, begged him, commanded him. Her mind was a cascading shower of light. She knew nothing but him—the map of his scars under her palms, the rough plane of his jaw scraping her cheek, his mouth on every trembling slope of her body. His hoarse voice, hot against her ear, and how beautifully it cracked open under the weight of her name.

After, cooling in the damp sheets, soft and sticky in the nest of his arms, Eliana pressed her face against his chest. Her jaw aching with tension, her legs and arms heavy and tired, she listened to the steady rhythm of his heart.

"I don't love you," she whispered fiercely against his skin.

A moment passed. Then she felt Simon's hand cup the back of her head, cradling her to him. His lips touched her brow.

"I know," he replied, his voice choked with sadness. "I don't love you either."

→ 40 →

SIMON

"In the stars I draw your hair
In the moon I find your eyes
In my blood I hold your name
In my bones I feel your lies."

—Traditional Kirvayan folk song

A t first, when he woke, Simon could do nothing but look at her.

He'd kept his eyes open for as long as he could, relishing the sound of her breathing. But exhaustion had finally pulled him under into a light sleep that left him, as it always did, fighting through a wilderness of dark dreams.

And then he woke with Eliana curled tightly against him, her face knotted with anger even in sleep. He hardly breathed as he watched her. The tangle of dark hair falling over her cheek, her chapped lips, her bruised and tender skin—not from his own hands, though it might as well have been.

He would never forget her face that night. As they danced in the glittering Festival ballroom, she had clung to him. Afraid, but loath to show it. Only the tight, sweaty clamp of her hand around his as they waltzed betrayed her true terror. And then, on the admiral's ship, he had stepped forward in his imperial uniform and had watched without feeling as all the light left her eyes.

Without feeling. Yes, just as Ludivine had taught him, and right from the beginning, he had been an excellent student.

And yet, there had been moments when he had nearly thrown it all to ruin.

He carefully moved away from Eliana to swing his bare legs out of bed. He dragged his hands through his hair, then held his head and stared at the floor.

He could not banish from his mind the image of her writhing as Corien crouched over her, mocking her screams with his own. The gallery of shattered glass around them, and Eliana reaching across the floor for him.

She had screamed for him, wept his name, and he had only stood and stared, a pillar of faultless stone, awaiting his orders. In his mind, Ludivine had said nothing, but he had heard her all the same.

Break, and doom us all.

Simon's heart began to race, his breathing to quicken. He raised his trembling arms into the air and nearly laughed aloud, because even with these memories battering his tired mind, his power sprang to life at once. Threads spun easily from the air and clung to his fingers like burrs drawn to the rub of linen. Energy pricked at him; the air hummed with distant song.

He imagined the smooth stone corridor just outside his room. Low ceiling, iron brackets for torches. He would try that first, only a small jump from room to hallway.

The empirium lies within every living thing, and every living thing is of the empirium, he recited, heat rising fast in his throat.

Its power connects not only flesh to bone, root to earth, stars to sky, but also road to road, city to city.

Moment to moment.

But as Simon tried to focus his mind, it jerked and slipped away from him. The threads at his fingers flickered.

He set his jaw, his body stiff with tension, his hands alight with power gone uncomfortably hot. He was not used to working magic, and he could not quite fix his thoughts on the hallway outside this room. *His* room. Many nights he had lain awake as a boy, cold with dread, wondering if Ludivine would come to him for the next morning's lesson silently, in his mind, or instead come padding quietly down the hallway outside his room. A tray of breakfast in her hands, and her steady black eyes holding inside them some new terror meant to unravel him.

He blinked sweat from his eyes. He didn't even blame Ludivine for everything she had done. He blamed none of them—except for the angel licking his wounds up above and the monstrous queen he had so loved.

Simon nearly laughed to think of her. The Kingsbane, they had called her. How he had once adored her. Even near the end, when nasty rumors flitted up and down the streets of Âme de la Terre and music halls rang with the sound of foul songs written to insult her, even then Simon had believed their Sun Queen would come back to them.

But now his mind wouldn't fix on the Kingsbane's memory. He could barely recall her true name. He tried to force it, and his body twitched with pain.

Ludivine had taught him all too well not to think of her. And Corien… Corien liked no one to think of her but him.

Simon frowned at his rigid hands. They shook in the air as if straining against an unseen door. The threads brightened once, then faded.

He wedged his fingers in his hair and bent over his knees, a scream of frustration lodged in his throat. He squeezed his eyes shut against the tumult of his mind. Too many images, too many voices. Too many cuts, too many scars.

Then something stirred behind him—a small sound, a question—and he held himself still, tense with wanting and hot with fear. When Eliana touched him, her soft hands tender on his arm, he let out a harsh sob. He reached for her hand and brought it to his lips. But he could not look at her. Even should they have a lifetime of years to share between them, he wasn't sure he would ever be able to convince himself that he deserved to look at her.

"I was trying to remember something," Eliana said quietly after a time, "but I'm having trouble. I wonder if you could help me."

Simon closed his eyes. He could have listened to her speak for the rest of whatever life was left to him. Her voice held shadows, but it was still hers. How he had missed it. How he had agonized in his quiet room at the palace, trying to ignore the distant echo of her screams.

"Of course I'll help you," he rasped.

"Well, it's a bit of a funny thing. When we first met, you and I, in my house in Orline. We fought. You wore your mask."

Simon reached for the memory. It was ragged, as were all the rest. Flashes of chaotic color trapped behind churning darkness. Ludivine shut up in her room, Corien shut up in his palace, each of them fighting the other—the ripples of their war battered him even now, protected in the deep heart of Ludivine's home as he was.

"I remember," he said at last. "We fought. You were very good."

"I was," Eliana agreed, "but here's the thing I can't quite recall." She paused. "How many times did I punch you in the face? Three? Five?"

Harsh laughter burst out of him. He was not used to laughing. It sat strangely in his throat, left him dizzy.

"I pulled a gun on you," he remembered. "You called me a cheater."

"You were," she said lightly. "I would have beaten you otherwise."

"Unlikely."

There was a pause. Then Eliana moved closer to him, her leg touching his. "I've tried to remember other things."

He knew what she was doing. He felt the steady heat of her power reaching for him, as if she were indeed the sun come down to warm him. Already he could feel his power rising to meet hers. The air around him began to clear, and his thoughts along with it.

He blew out a long breath and raised his arms once more.

"What other things?" he asked. Light bloomed softly at his fingertips. A good burn.

"What your father's name was. You told me once."

"Garver," he replied. The name dropped awkwardly from his tongue. His father's face was but a faint smear of memory. "Garver Randell."

"He was a healer."

"Yes."

"And a marque, like you."

Simon nodded.

"Tell me, Simon," Eliana said gently.

"Yes," he replied. "A marque, like me." He licked his dry lips. "What else do you want to remember?"

"The names of our friends you shot at Festival," she said without judgment.

Still he struggled to speak. "Darby. Oraia. Ester. Dani, and her son, Evon."

"And many others."

"Yes."

"All in service of me."

"Always, Eliana." His voice caught on thorns. *Always.* A cruel word, a lying word.

He held his breath, waiting for her to speak again. Beyond his hands spun a dazzling circle of light. Threads, waiting to be traveled.

"I'm also trying to remember what it felt like, that first night we were together," she whispered at last.

"It was everything," Simon answered. He heard the brittle sound of his voice as if he no longer belonged to his own body and was listening from somewhere distant, somewhere golden and warm within the light of their rising power. "You were everything that night. You were the entire world, and I was safe inside you. For once, I felt safe."

Eliana slowly wrapped her arms around his torso, then pressed her cheek between his shoulder blades and held him.

"So did I," she whispered.

Simon let himself live there for a moment, then stood and drew on his trousers. He took the feeling of her quiet embrace with him through the threads and emerged in the room's far corner with her name on his lips. The threads' light snapped closed at his heels, throwing off a slight bitter tinge of smoke.

He turned to find Eliana watching him. The sight of her nearly felled him. Bare in the rumpled blankets, echoes of violence marking her skin, she held her head high and looked at him steadily. The air around her glimmered with power. A queen in his bed, lighting the world awake.

It took everything in him to turn away from her, and try again, farther and more easily each time, until he had traveled to the far end of Ludivine's compound and back to his room in the space of a breath.

He sank to the cold floor, shaking with things he could not name. He heard Eliana rise from the bed, tug on his discarded tunic, and come to him. She knelt and touched his face. So careful, the fall of her fingers on his skin, as if afraid he would fly away from her. That she would wake, and it would be another dream sent by the enemy.

Simon glared hard at the floor. What lay ahead terrified him. Only twice in his life had he attempted to travel through time, and both instances had ended in disaster.

"When I was younger," he said thickly, "I didn't need this kind of help to work magic."

"There isn't anything wrong with needing help."

"No, there isn't. I had just forgotten what it felt like to receive it."

He sensed a change, then, a shift in the battle that seethed at the perimeter of his mind. He knew what it meant and raged against it. He drew Eliana to him roughly, and she grabbed him just as hard and held him close. Her breath was hot in his hair, her body too thin under his hands.

"We are more than our anger," she said, her voice low. They were the words she had said in Willow, the gardens soft with rain around them, her hands warm on his scarred chest. The memory drifted sweetly, the last leaf falling before winter.

"We are more than what has been done to us," he said in reply, and felt her smile against his neck.

The door opened. One of Ludivine's nameless acolytes, unabashed, crisply efficient. Eliana whirled to glare at the man over her shoulder.

"Yes?" she snapped, and the sharp sound of her anger made Simon ache with love.

"She says it is time," the acolyte said, looking each of them in the eye. "He has found us."

➤ 41 ➤

ELIANA

"It isn't the concept itself of threading through time that so frightens those who decry the practice. Rather, their fear stems from the potential repercussions, the unpredictability. Time is not a clock that can be calibrated, no matter how skilled the traveler. Time is endless, brutal, and as untameable—and changeable—as the sea."

—*Meditations on Time* by Basara Oboro,
renowned Mazabatian scholar

Eliana hurried into Ludivine's favored chamber, Simon close behind her. They both wore fresh clothes provided by the acolytes. Eliana's coat buttoned at her shoulder and fell to her knees, flexible enough for her to move but thick enough to offer some protection. She wore a hefty weapons belt, laden with daggers, and felt a pang for her own lost knives.

She glanced at Simon only once. Moments ago he had been holding her, his face open and soft. Now, he was armored for battle. A long coat like Eliana's, and beneath it a vest of mail. Revolver at his hip, knives in his boots and in sheaths strapped to his forearms.

Inside the room, Ludivine sat with Remy as she had with Eliana—in two chairs facing each other within a wide triangle of three flickering candles.

Ludivine glanced up, her skin pale as bone. Eliana startled to see how much she had changed in only a few hours' time. Shadows darkened the hollows of her face, and sweat dotted her upper lip.

But her voice was still as cool water. "Is everything working as it should?"

Eliana could have happily struck her again for that. Such coldness in her voice, as if she didn't know exactly what had happened, as if she could not feel the state of their hearts.

"All is as it should be," Simon replied, his gaze bright as lit steel.

Ludivine didn't flinch, but Eliana heard her voice, soft and sad in her mind. *I'm sorry, little one. I was not always as I am now. I wish you could have known me when my heart was still whole.*

Eliana sent her nothing in reply. No pity, no kindness. She had no room for it. Her body was taut and trembling; she pushed hard against herself as if fighting a rising flood. She heard soft footsteps at the room's entrance and glanced behind her to see Navi and Ysabet, Patrik and Hob, Malik, and several others just behind them.

Navi reached for her. Eliana gratefully took her hand, then faced Ludivine once more. She didn't look directly at the back of Remy's dark head, too frightened to think about what he and Ludivine might have been discussing.

"Your acolyte said Corien has found us." She bit off each word, teeth hard and tongue sharp. "Now what would you have us do? Where is he?"

Ludivine stood. Serene, she breathed in and out, then tilted her head slightly, as if listening for a distant sound.

Eliana tensed. A thick moment passed, and then she heard it: a rumbling vibration, a distant high shriek. Faint but unmissable. The air tightened, grew still. It was the moment before a storm broke open.

Behind Eliana, the others shifted nervously.

Ysabet marched forward, hands on hips, eyes narrowed. "She's done something. Can you feel that? The stone is vibrating under our feet." She jerked her head. "What have you done, angel?"

Beside Eliana, Simon shifted. She glanced at him. He would not look at her, but she sensed it was now for a different reason.

Ludivine gestured at the two acolytes flanking the door. At once, they began emptying the room—the chairs, the carpet, the pedestals on which the candles burned. Only the candles themselves remained, and Katell's sheathed sword.

Remy silently came to Eliana's side, found her free hand. The ache that now lived in her throat blossomed ruthlessly. If they did this, none of it would matter. Not Vaera Bashta, not Invictus, not the hard new glint of Remy's eyes. He would be born to Ioseph and Rozen Ferracora and live a happy life in the city of Orline, writing stories and baking cakes. She refused to acknowledge any other possibility.

"This chamber lies at the heart of a labyrinth," said Ludivine, very still as her acolytes bustled around her. "There are dozens of chambers, hundreds of passages. Some lead to rooms. Others lead nowhere. This will buy us some time. The cruciata are intelligent, but their bloodlust dulls their wits."

Navi drew a sharp breath.

Just behind Eliana, Simon stood quietly, hands fisted at his sides.

Tentatively, Eliana reached for Ludivine's mind. At once, Ludivine showed her the truth, her black eyes unblinking and unashamed.

"You've brought the cruciata underground," Eliana whispered. Shrill, rasping cries, still distant, followed her words, as if the beasts had heard their name.

Someone behind her—Hob, she thought—muttered a sharp curse.

"Why?" Navi whispered harshly. "How?"

The chamber thrummed with rising vibrations. Something was approaching them, some ruthless marching weight. The beasts? Or worse?

Eliana's stomach dropped. Clarity swept through her, heat chased by cold.

"Because the angels are coming for us," she said, "and the cruciata will protect us."

"Protect us?" Patrik scoffed, glaring at Ludivine. "They have no love for us, and now two enemies will soon be upon us, thanks to you."

It had been so long since Eliana had seen Patrik that the sight of his furious pale face rested strangely on the surface of her mind, like oil topping water. He was familiar and yet not, flesh and blood and yet a memory. He glared at Ludivine, his ruined eye hidden behind a frayed black patch. And there was Hob, tall and frowning at his side, fresh scars on his dark-brown skin. Navi, her eyes bright with tears, her mouth thin with anger. Ysabet behind her, looking ready to tear out Ludivine's throat with her teeth. Malik at the door, his face so like Navi's—lovely straight nose, warm dark eyes. And crowding in the hallway, everyone Navi had brought with her across the ocean. Dozens of refugees and sailors and hardened fighters, all now trapped underground.

Looking at them, a slow tingle of horror spreading across her skin, Eliana understood why Ludivine had waited to guide her here. She had been waiting for Navi's little army to arrive—a disposable infantry. *Help is coming*, the Prophet had told her. *Help is close.*

Ludivine smiled faintly at everyone gathered. "It's time. Hurry. She needs you."

One by one, their faces changed. A ripple of feeling passed through them like a shimmering wave of heat. Fear hardened into anger. Tears dried and mouths set. Patrik was the first to turn away and draw his sword, pushing past the others to hurry down the hallway. Hob followed shortly after him, then Malik, then Ysabet, with a ferocious growl.

Navi choked out a sob, pulled Eliana hard into her arms. A moment later, she was gone, the last of them to leave the chamber. Eliana stood frozen, the sounds of their war cries muffled by the blood pounding in her ears. Another breath, and her dread lifted. Sound came crashing back to her. She called Navi's name, tried to run after them. Hands pulled her back against a strong chest. Too enraged to scream, she shoved Simon away with a burst of power from her castings. She didn't realize she had tackled Ludivine to the ground and started punching her until Remy and Simon yanked her away.

"Every moment you helped me, every day you worked with me to strengthen my power," she spat, "you knew what you would do. You saw

Navi and the others coming to Elysium and guided them down here. You knew you would send them to fight the cruciata, sacrifice them without a thought if it bought us some time. You knew, and you never said anything to me."

Ludivine sat up, wiping her mouth. As Eliana watched, her lip stopped bleeding. "Of course I didn't."

"Because you feared I would fight you."

"I feared nothing. I knew you would react as you're reacting now."

A sob burst out of Eliana as she imagined Navi's face. "I love them."

"And they love you. Even those who have never met you. They love what they have been told about you. They believe in your ability to save them. And if they must die to allow you that chance, then they must die." A smile touched Ludivine's lips. "Navi draws irresistible pictures of you for anyone who will listen. Of course they love you. One night at Navi's side, listening to her stories about you, and anyone would believe what she says. That you are a queen for the ages."

Eliana wrenched her arms free of Simon and Remy. Her feet were stones on the floor. "You got inside their heads just now, sent them away to fight. You could have done that with anyone, recruited dozens of people from Elysium. Two hundred, five hundred. Why *them*?"

Ludivine let out a thin laugh. It did not move her face. Her mouth was pale, her eyes grotesquely dark in the bleached canvas of her skin.

"I'm not sure you understand how angry he is," she said, her voice smooth as a polished blade. "It requires so much of my strength to keep him out of this room. I have very little left to spare, only enough to encourage people already inclined to die for you to go and do just that. I could not have shepherded people from the city down to us. I could not have gotten inside their minds and made them into puppet soldiers. It would have left me too vulnerable. It would have left Simon too vulnerable, or you. And now, every part of me that still lives is fighting him."

Eliana pressed her fists to her thighs. A hundred people paled in significance against the entirety of humankind. She knew this.

And yet she clung to her anger. "You gave them no choice," she whispered.

"They chose to sail to you," Ludivine said. "They chose to follow Zahra through a city tearing itself to pieces when at any moment she could have died and they would have been discovered. One chink in Zahra's mental armor, and a warship could have found them, blasted them to pieces on the high seas. I merely made a suggestion just now. A slight breeze at the backs of warriors already prepared to die and eager to fight."

Eliana was too numb with sadness to protest when Ludivine took her hands. She wished Zahra were before her instead of this black-eyed angel with a hollow space where her stolen heart should be. She formed the thought viciously, slammed it at Ludivine's face.

It remained unruffled, porcelain smooth.

"Five of my acolytes died twenty minutes ago while drawing the cruciata into my home," Ludivine said quietly. "I have spent long years with all of them. I grieve their death. But I did not flinch at sending them to it, nor did they flinch at going. When Navi, Ysabet, and their crew left the Vespers, they knew they would sail to their doom. They did so gladly. They did so for *you*. It was their choice to fight then, and to fight today. We should now honor that choice by doing what must be done."

Eliana held Ludivine's black gaze, then turned away to face the empty door. Navi had stood there, and Patrik and Hob, only a moment before. Behind her, Simon and Ludivine were speaking. She ignored them, listening instead to the distant sounds of battle. Monstrous shrieks, wet guttural roars.

Swords crashing.

"I hear swords," she said, the words foul on her tongue.

"My acolytes, before they died, managed to tempt one hundred cruciata underground," Ludivine replied. "And Corien has sent five hundred angels ahead of him. They will move slowly, avoiding the cruciata blood our friends have spilled. This will give us some time. But their sheer numbers will eventually overwhelm the beasts. They will be the sea that clears a path for him. Before an hour has passed, he will stand in this room. But by then, you will be long gone."

Eliana turned. Simon stood in the center of the room, his back to her. He pulled threads from the air, a weaver of light.

Ludivine put her hand on Remy's shoulder. "Remy and I have been practicing Old Celdarian. In case something should happen to Simon, Remy will know how to speak with whomever you encounter. The common tongue was different then, and Celdarians will be more likely to trust you if you speak their language. Luckily, Remy's vocabulary was already quite robust. He learned much in his time with Jessamyn." She smiled fondly, tucked some of Remy's dark hair behind his ear. "If only we had longer to spend together, Remy Ferracora. Your mind is a fascinating one. It holds so many dreams, even after months of living in darkness."

Watching them, Eliana felt ill. She snatched Remy away from Ludivine, then walked with him to the far side of the room.

In the shadows, she steeled herself. Pressed her brow to his, held his cheeks. His eyes were her whole world. Bloodshot and blue, rimmed with dark lashes.

"I would say you can't go with me," she said, "but somehow I don't think you'll accept that."

A tiny smile lifted the corners of his mouth. "If I stay here, I'll definitely die. If I go with you, I might live."

She bit her tongue. It was not the moment to talk about time, what might or might not happen, what would or would not be changed.

"There is that," she said weakly.

Remy put his hands over hers, gently pressed her fingers. "You can do this, El."

It felt wrong to hear the pet name in his new cracking voice. This boy before her, this wiry killer with watchful eyes. She pressed a fierce kiss to his forehead. If she didn't look straight at him, she could pretend away the past few months and imagine her room in Orline. The lace curtains, her mother's quilt, Remy's voice lulling her to sleep as he read of saints and angels, godsbeasts and kings.

From the corridor came horrible sounds, the crash and tear of teeth and swords like lightning splitting open the earth. A sharp cry burst free of the chaos. Eliana thought it sounded like Navi. Her neck went cold with sweat.

Ludivine moved past them to the door. The light from Simon's growing threads lit the walls strangely, a wan white-gold that carried with it a sharp, acrid scent like the silver charge of spitting storm clouds.

"When you step through the threads, you will find yourself in the royal gardens behind Baingarde," Ludivine said. Her hair was liquid gold in the growing light. "It was a peaceful evening. Audric, Rielle, and I were resting under a sorrow tree at the end of a long day. Long, but good. The trials were over. We had not yet left for the tour that would introduce her to the kingdom. Her father had recently died, and Audric's too, and there was grief in us, and fear, but when it was only us three, there was also peace."

She glanced back over her shoulder. The threadlight gave her eyes a golden sheen. "Simon?"

"Nearly there," he said, his voice tightly coiled.

Eliana went to him and stood at his side. She felt Remy join her, caught a glimpse of how soft with wonder his face had become as he watched Simon work. The expression made him more familiar.

"Is there anything I can do?" Eliana asked.

Simon tightly shook his head. "No."

"You're doing wonderfully."

His mouth quirked. His temples gleamed with sweat. "How would you know?"

The truth was, she didn't. But it was beautiful, as it had been before, to watch his long, deft fingers draw light from the air. The serious furrow of his brow, the set lines of his jaw.

She placed her hand on his arm. His body relaxed, and the swirling threads of light gathering at his fingertips solidified, brightening.

Despite the fear turning coldly in her chest, Eliana smiled.

"Thank you," Simon whispered, his voice thin beneath the growing hum of his threads, and though he could not remove his hands from the air, she felt him shift toward her. Their legs touched. Remy hooked his arm through hers, pressed his cheek to her shoulder. He muttered a sentence in Old Celdarian over and over. At the corner of Eliana's eye, one of the candles flickered.

Then, an explosion of sound from the hallway, a titanic cascading clatter of metal against stone. Past the door flew a slain cruciata, flung by something out of sight. The raptor's sleek black-green feathers painted bright blue streaks across the floor.

"He's coming, and faster than I thought," Ludivine announced. Her voice betrayed nothing, but Eliana felt the slightest of tremors in her mind.

"You'll send us through and then come right after us," Eliana said firmly to Simon. "Close the thread behind you. Don't look back."

Simon nodded. A slight shudder passed through his body. His threads—dozens of them, maybe hundreds—were gathering into a solid ring of spinning light. And as Eliana watched, darker threads joined the lighter ones, consuming them. They snapped like whips, lashing a spitting blackness through the air. The ring of light flickered, dimmed, then brightened. Dark threads twined with threads of light. Shapes manifested beyond the ring—tall green shadows like enormous soldiers marching in clean lines. Trees?

Eliana's skin prickled. *The royal gardens behind Baingarde.*

She retrieved Katell's sheathed sword and hooked it to her weapons belt, then drew the sword out for inspection. It was more elegant than she had guessed it would be, the golden hilt carved to resemble rays of sunlight, the blade polished to a high shine. Though it looked enormous, it felt light and nimble in her hands. She stood, marveling at how easily it moved through the air. Her castings sang against the hilt, their brilliant light kissing the metal.

Horrifying screams ricocheted through the halls outside. Someone whose voice she did not know begged for mercy.

A dark pressure rippled against her mind and brought with it a faint whisper:

Eliana.

Heart pounding, she returned Katell's sword to its sheath. Pangs seized her, terrible longings for her room at home, for dear brave Zahra, for the warm embrace of Navi's arms. Watching the threads, she held the knot in her throat so it could rise no further. She rolled her shoulders, shifted from foot to foot, shook out her hands and fingers. Her castings threw light across the ceiling.

Beside her, Simon's arms trembled in the air as if holding up an unthinkable weight. She reached for him, then thought better of it. If only she could wrap him in her arms, bury her face once more in the hot space between his shoulders.

Instead, she faced the spinning ring of light, its sparks spitting across the room, and prepared herself to run. Her muscles tensed, Katell's sword an unfamiliar slight weight against her leg. Beside her, Remy held a dagger in his right hand. At his hip gleamed another. His face, turned haggard by his time in Elysium, could have been carved from stone, perched atop one of the temples in Orline as a tribute to the fierce saints of old.

The moment Corien arrived, Eliana felt it like the fall of night across her skin. The air pulsed, suddenly so thick and close that Eliana gasped for breath. A roar of fury punched the walls. Metal hit metal. Did Corien also have a sword? What did it look like, two angels locked in combat of both blade and mind?

She kept her eyes on the threads, felt Remy start to turn, and grabbed him, swung him back around.

"Don't look at him," she muttered. "Look at Simon. Look at the light."

She could feel Corien's fingers scrabbling at the edges of her thoughts, digging for her. Her calm splintered like wood.

Eliana. His whispers tumbled like falling rocks. A rush of furious sound. *Eliana.*

"Go."

Simon's hoarse voice rang out like a shot. Eliana eyed the spinning threads as if they surrounded a chasm, cold and bottomless. A wave of fear swept across her skin, sharp as needles.

She resisted the urge to touch Simon and instead moved as close to him as she dared.

"Now?" she whispered.

Tears stood bright in his eyes. His mouth twisted. "Now. *Go*, Eliana."

From behind them came a sharp cry. Some blazing instinct compelled Eliana to turn. Corien's white shirt, half-torn from him, shone wet with red and blue blood. Veins of black drew a dark map across the winter of his skin. He drew wheezing breaths, and each step was unsteady, but whatever the cruciata blood had done to him, whatever lingering pain the blightblade had left in him, he was fighting it. A lesser angel, so drenched, might have died at once.

But Corien bared his teeth and raised his sword high. Ludivine stumbled. One of her hands flew to her temple. With a scream of fury, Corien swung at her. The blade sliced clean through Ludivine's neck. Blood spurted like red rain. Her head dropped to the floor and rolled. Her body crumpled, and her sword clattered to the ground.

A whine of panic erupted in Eliana's skull. She spun back to the threads and launched herself at them. She grabbed Remy's hand, pulled him with her through the ring of light.

A gunshot cracked the air.

Behind her, Simon cried out.

Eliana turned back to reach for him, but something yanked him away, out of her reach. She saw a flash of his face, bright with pain, and then he was gone. His threads shifted sharply, veered, then righted themselves, as if a cloud had passed over them and then the sun had returned. The darker threads, those hissing tendrils of time, split and reformed. They grabbed Eliana and Remy, flung them forward. Her mind screamed with fear. Something gripped her throat, stole her voice.

Then she set foot on solid ground. The threads snapped closed behind her, singeing her heels.

She took a breath, desperate for a cool, quiet world of green. *The royal gardens behind the castle Baingarde. It was a peaceful evening.*

But then a bolt of fire zipped over her head. Breathless, she ducked, pulling Remy down with her. They hit the ground hard. Mud sucked at their feet and hands. The twin black smells of blood and smoke sent her head reeling. Something barreled past them, some great beast with a mottled furred head and a long serpentine tail. With each of its thundering steps, the earth quaked. Something glinted around its ankles as Eliana watched them streak by. Flat strips of metal embedded in swollen skin, each piece glowing with a familiar light.

Horror swept through her. This creature was not quite a cruciata, at least not like any she had seen, but it was close enough, and it wore *castings*. On its back sat a gray-eyed child with wrists that snapped fire. Eliana's blood turned cold. An elemental child, controlled as the adatrox were.

She pushed herself up. Remy scrambled to his feet beside her. The world was an uproar of sunlight and fire, darkness that moved and howled. Something was burning nearby. They ran, choking on smoke, and found a rocky ridge to hide behind. They wedged themselves into a crevice slick with mud and blood. Beside them lay a man in armor, his glassy eyes open wide and one of his legs torn away.

Eliana hid the light of her castings against her chest and stared over the rock at the chaos beyond.

It was a battlefield, so vast it could have been the entire world. Soldiers in armor swung their swords, flung their spears. A horse with no rider raced by, its reins trailing. Eliana flinched as a shadow-hawk flew shrieking past them. It dove at an armored soldier, talons first, and expanded. A cocoon of darkness wrapped quickly around him, smothered him, and slammed him to the ground.

Night had fallen, and yet bursts and beams of light illuminated the fight in erratic flashes. Eliana saw a pale woman with short black hair swing a black staff topped with a glowing blue orb. The orb drew shadows from the ground, and soon a pack of dark wolves bounded away from her and into the battle, their jaws open wide. A man struck the ground with a glowing shield, cracking the earth open. Five soldiers stumbled clumsily into it, and Eliana saw one of their eyes as they fell—gray and cloudy, expressionless.

Her blood chilled. Adatrox.

"Look." Remy, crouching beside her, pointed to her left, where the silhouette of an enormous mountain loomed in the distance. A thousand tiny lights spilled across its foothills. Fires marked an enormous stone wall. It was a city built on the hills that rose up toward the mountain, and at its apex stood a faint gray castle with towers reaching for the sky.

"Baingarde," Remy whispered. In his voice, she heard the same reverent awe that had kept him reading about the Old World night after night, year after year.

Something exploded nearby. Fire bloomed and grew. A soldier flew—*flew*—away from the inferno, carried swiftly away on spears of white light tipped in shadow.

For a moment, Eliana could only stare. She had spent a dark lifetime in the palace of an angel, but never before had she seen one with wings.

Remy tugged on her arm, drawing her down. They flattened themselves behind the rock. Eliana's castings trembled against her palms. Breathless, face pressed into the dirt, she tasted magic on her tongue. It choked the wind, sparked cold and metallic in her mouth, as if she'd kissed a bolt of lightning. Her vision was sharp as glass. Her blood roared, jubilant. Words floated to her mind on currents of gold.

Rielle was alive. The empirium had not yet been broken. Eliana dug her fingers into the mud, resisting the upward pull of the magic-ripe air. Was it possible to fly without wings?

"This isn't the night Ludivine spoke of," she said.

"No," Remy agreed. In the shifting, bursting light, his eyes were glittering jewels. "This is spring, the last year of the Second Age. It's the Battle of Âme de la Terre. The battle that ended the world."

AUDRIC

"We will ride for you as fast as we can, but Audric—it is many miles between Styrdalleen and Âme de la Terre, and my people have been ravaged by a hard winter of blizzards, constant quakes and avalanches, and continued attacks in our villages. Thousands are dead. The capital is overflowing with civilians who have lost their homes, their children, their parents. And we are running out of food. My brother has written to me that he comes with aid, but he has yet to arrive, and I worry he never will. You are the best hope we have to survive this, Audric. Stand fast against the enemy, and keep an eye on the northeast horizon."

—Encoded letter from Ingrid Lysleva, Lord Commander of the Borsvallic army, to King Audric Courverie of Celdaria, dated April 19, Year 1000 of the Second Age

He could not find her.

Audric had imagined it would happen immediately, that some incredible burst of power would erupt within minutes. The rest of the battlefield would pale in comparison to her. She would stand at the heart of it, arms flung wide, power streaming like lightning from her fingers.

And Audric would dive toward her, throw such blinding sunlight at her that even she would stagger. He would jump from Atheria before the godsbeast hit the ground, raise Illumenor to strike. Maybe he would say Rielle's name. Maybe she would not allow him even this.

But he could not find her.

And they were losing.

He watched the battle below as if it had seized him in his sleep, some horrible feverish nightmare rolling on and on before his disbelieving eyes. Angels fell by the dozens—speared by castings of fire, sliced in two by spinning shields flung hard by their elemental masters—but seconds later, they were whole again. The ruined pieces of their bodies simply crawled toward each other and reassembled. They found their dropped weapons and stormed back into battle.

Some left their bodies to be trampled and forgotten and instead fought unseen. Celdarian soldiers dropped in silence. No wounds, no blood. Only contorted pale faces, mouths frozen in the beginnings of screams. A windsinger lashed her whip through the air, summoning sharp gusts that knocked angel after angel to the ground. A moment later, the light of her casting went out. Her body jerked, her face shifted, and she slipped off her horse and was gone, trampled beneath a sea of hooves and claws.

Audric's hand shook around Illumenor. The sunlight streaming from the blade was dimming, and angels teemed just beyond the reach of his light. They hissed in Lissar, shouted for him to drop his sword, crashed their blades against Illumenor's bright beams until his ears rang with the sound of fists against glass.

He could not drop his light. They would swarm him in seconds.

But he had to do something for the dozens, the *hundreds* of soldiers being cut down around him. He searched frantically for even the smallest triumph. The zipping blue-white of Sloane's casting, the spark and spin of metalmaster hammers hitting their targets.

It wasn't enough.

A dark tide of beasts churned relentlessly toward the city wall, abominations with castings sewn into their skin and mighty roars like rocks falling. Gray-eyed children rode atop them, their wrists blazing with fire, shadows flying from them like arrows. A flock of avian beasts streaked across the lake on naked wings and dove at the wall. They plucked archers from their posts and tossed the bodies between them, tearing at flesh and bone until only scraps remained.

Audric lay flat against Atheria and closed his eyes. At once, she dove fast for the battlefield. Angels followed on either side, their wings flashing. Their war cries were the howls of wolves.

Before hitting the ground, Atheria pulled up sharply, then wheeled around and cut across the battlefield like a sleek ship through dark waters. Illumenor burned a flickering path through the angelic ranks, scattering them. Audric gulped down air. The wind streaming past him was knife-sharp, black with smoke. He looked back over his shoulder, saw the destruction left behind in their blazing wake, and felt a small burst of hope.

Then a huge weight slammed into Atheria and knocked her hard from the air. Audric fell, lost Illumenor, went tumbling. Hands grabbed at him. Someone thrust a spear into the dirt beside his shoulder. He twisted, dodged another, then scrabbled through the mud for his sword. Something shrieked, a terrible snarling scream. His hand landed on metal. A familiar rope of power snapped into his palm.

He grabbed Illumenor and spun back toward his attacker—a towering angel in gold armor. He thrust his spear once more. Audric dodged it, and Illumenor burst into brilliant light. The angel dropped his weapon, shrank back, shielded his eyes. Their blades crashed together. Other angels converged on them, swords raised. He felt their minds groping for his, fingers digging into the edges of his thoughts, but something was shielding him—a familiar, supple barrier that repelled their attacks.

Ludivine. He hoped it was her. A sickening flash of terror swept through him as he imagined someone else keeping him alive, drawing him on through this battle toward some end he could not see.

He spun to meet the angel's swords, Illumenor sparking brighter with every metallic crash. He dodged their blows, stabbed one angel in the groin, carved a streak of white light across another's plated chest. He looked for Ludivine in the chaos, but she was keeping herself hidden. Was she watching the fight unfold from some sheltered mountain cave? Had she truly left them all to die?

A furious scream drew his eye. Atheria was locked in battle with one of the beasts—shoulders high off the ground, back ridged with fur and bone. Atheria reared up, ears flat and wings snapping. Red gashes striped her stomach. She kicked out with her forelegs, clobbered the beast with her hooves.

Something hard and cold knocked the back of Audric's head. He fell, his vision spinning black. He tried to stand but was pushed flat to the ground. A plated boot on his chest pinned him in the mud. He looked up, blinking hard, and saw the shape of an armored angel framed by radiant white wings.

A blade touched his throat. His skin gave beneath it, a needle-sharp prick of pain.

Then the air bloomed with sound. Rich and warm, like voices raised in song.

The pressure on Audric's chest lessened. He surged upward, Illumenor blazing, and sliced the angel's torso in two. The body fell, its two halves smoking, and did not rise again. Whatever angel had lived inside it had fled, and Audric could see why at once.

Across the Flats, great winged shapes were dropping out of the sky. The spinning light of casted magic illuminated them as they hurtled into battle. They swept fast through the fight and knocked scores of angels to the ground.

Audric stared in wonder at their mighty furred bodies, their huge hooked wings that boomed like drums as they flapped.

They were dragons. *Dragons*, which no one had seen for an age. Dozens of them, some skinny and lean, the size of horses, others broad and muscled, large as warships. Figures rode atop them carrying staffs and swords, cloaks flying like dark wings behind them.

A passage from one of Audric's favorite stories flashed through his mind. *At the dawn of the Second Age, with the angels banished to the Deep, the saints began carving new cities out of the war-ravaged ground, and during these first years of peace, the godsbeasts fled the human cities. Where they went, it is not known, but some believe the ice dragons, the bestial champions of Saint Grimvald, retreated to the far north. They allowed only their chosen companions, the Kammerat, or dragon-speakers, to join them in those frozen reaches. Any others who have dared seek them have perished, their bodies returned home in the night, wrapped in the dark hooded plaincloth the Kammerat favor.*

Audric watched in awe as the Kammerat raised polished horns of bone to their lips. They rode the dragons as easily as if they had born atop them. It was they who filled the air with song, the cascading calls of their horns ringing through the night.

The beasts tormenting the archers at the wall dropped their prey and shot back across the lake to meet the new arrivals, their shrieking calls piercing the air. Two winged battalions raced toward each other through a sky of smoke and sparks. For a brief moment, the sight rendered both armies dumb. Angels and humans alike cowered in fear.

Then came a thunderous clamor from the pass between Mount Taléa and Mount Sorenne. Audric squinted through the smoke, and a chill passed over him. His pounding heart flew to his throat.

For there, spilling down the pass, the earth rearranging itself neatly to provide a safe path, was a sea of flashing blades. Huge silver-dappled warhorses with streaming white tails, and rippling banners showing the colors of Saint Grimvald and House Lysleva—fiery orange, deep blue, and lavender soft as sunset, all snapping on a field of charcoal.

The Borsvallic army, three thousand strong, roared down from the mountains. Their fresh castings flashed; their horns blasted high, sharp battle cries.

Cheers erupted across the Flats. Celdarian and Mazabatian thrust their swords into the air.

Relief burned through Audric's body, leaving him lightheaded. He had not let himself hope for their arrival, but now the sight of them thundering into battle lit a fresh fire in his heart.

He heard a clatter behind him, spun around, and cut three angels in two with three swift strikes, his arms blazing with power. They dropped, their ruined bodies hissing like wood afire.

He whistled for Atheria. She came to him at once, her nostrils flaring wide, her coat spotted with blood. He hesitated at the sight of her wounds, but she snapped at him, impatient; her wings trembled to fly. He swung atop her, and then they were in the air, racing to meet Borsvall's army in the foothills. Illumenor lit the way, and he knew that across the Flats and in the city, his people would be watching him. They would see the light of Illumenor streaking toward the mountains, see the warriors of Borsvall riding to their aid, and they would stand taller and dare to think of tomorrow.

Atheria swooped low, brought Audric level with the leader of Borsvall's troops—a rider on a white warhorse, fearless and fast. Two bannermen followed her, flying the colors of her house. It was Ingrid Lysleva, commander of the Borsvallic army and regent in her brother's absence. She had not taken the throne, Audric had heard, even at the urging of her magisters and advisers.

Ingrid glanced up as Atheria began to fly beside her, matching the pace of her horse. She wore a silver helmet crested with horns, and when she met Audric's eyes, it was with a fierce, wild grin.

Beyond her, one of the dragons spun down from the sky to fly alongside them. A smaller dragon, lean but ferocious, with snapping teeth, clever gold eyes, and a crest of patchy white fur. Her rider lay low against her neck. He was a fair-skinned man with dark hair whose face Audric did not recognize. He was dressed in a long loose coat and cloak sewn from dark plaincloth. One of the Kammerat, then, Audric thought. Behind him, clinging to his waist, was another man, similarly garbed, bearded and blond and thinner than Audric remembered.

Their eyes met across the wild space between them. Ilmaire raised a hand in greeting, and Audric's heart lifted to see his friend. He had never believed the rumors that Ilmaire was dead. To see him alive and well, riding a dragon alongside his sister, as all three of them flew into battle, brought new strength to Audric's tired limbs. Illumenor crackled to brilliant life.

Hundreds of angels had turned to face the charging Borsvallic army, their pikes at the ready. The sky rained black arrows. Audric heard horses cry out behind him, heard soldier after soldier fall. But still they charged, Ingrid's shrill war cries piercing the air, and just before they met the angelic ranks, Audric reached out with his power, gathered every speck of casted light sunspinners across the battlefield had managed to summon, and thrust it all in one fell blow toward the enemy.

Light detonated across the Flats, knocking half the angels to their knees. The rest staggered, shooting without aim. The Borsvallic army tore through the enemy lines like fire through a forest. Battle sounds swallowed Audric whole. He glimpsed the flash of swords, the white of snapped bone. The mottled gray of a beastly hide, a dragon's clever furred head. Angelic breastplates marked with that proud crest of wings.

Audric drove Atheria through the fray. He cast light left and right, throwing angels from their mounts, knocking swarming beasts away from their kill. The Borsvallic army churned behind him, following the path he blazed.

Then the air tightened, prickling Audric's skin. A voice drifted toward him as if carried on the wind, only he knew at once that no one else could hear it.

Audric, it whispered.

Sweating, breathless from the use of his power, Audric shivered on Atheria's back, for it was *her* voice calling to him, and it trembled with something he could not name.

Gold burst at the corner of his eye. He whirled, pulling Atheria up from the battlefield, and looked back over the Flats, past the lake and the towering wall, and across the city toward Baingarde.

From the castle rooftops sprouted light so radiant, so sharp in its purity, that even Illumenor seemed to dim. The light shot into the night sky, volcanic, and then assumed a shape—two massive wings in flight, bold and familiar. The same symbol stamped on every angelic chest now hovering in the air above Baingarde, tall as storm clouds. A declaration: *Here I am.*

Audric's mind told him to ignore the bait. But a fierce clean anger shot through him, jolting his bones like cracks of lightning, and his mind's warnings were easy to ignore.

"Go!" he roared, leaning hard toward the city, and Atheria obeyed. Angels raced after him, their wings blazing. He hardly noticed them, knocked them easily from the air with his brilliant sword. Ludivine, wherever she was, was still helping him, or else it was Corien allowing him passage, toying with him for entertainment. Audric cared nothing for the reason. The angels' mental attacks bounced off him, useless as tiny pebbles thrown at a mountain. His power raced hot through his body, irradiating his vision. Illumenor moved without his command. He thought only of Baingarde, the wings incandescent above it. The woman standing within it.

Atheria sped over the lake, dodging winged beasts. Soon they were at the city wall—its parapets burning, the elementals atop it in desperate combat. Beasts clambered up out of the lake and up the stone. The angelic army's elemental children had created bridges to provide easy passage over the lake. Gray-eyed soldiers raced across with huge black ladders, hissing beasts guarding their passage; hundreds of others had reached the great stone wall and began to batter it with a huge fat beam of steel and wood. Each impact exploded like thunder.

Audric looked over his shoulder, tempted to circle back and use Illumenor to blind every angelic soldier on the new bridges, give his own people time to demolish them. But the light over Baingarde pulled at him, and he turned back toward the wall with fury in his heart.

Just as Atheria reached the wall, a swarm of black birds flew at Audric with tiny claws like needles and jabbing beaks. Their cries were hoarse, strange, more canine than avian. Atheria faltered, tried to shake her head and wings free of them, but they clung to her like drops of oil.

Audric scanned the ground beyond the wall. He knew these birds. They weren't trying to attack him; they were trying to turn him away from the city. When he found the blue glow of Sloane's scepter, he hissed her name in fury. Atheria dove fast; the birds made of shadow peeled off of her. By the time they landed, she was clean. At the doors inside the wall, soldiers hurried to make barricades. Elementals on the ground aimed their castings at every climbing beast. The enormous wings hovering over Baingarde washed everything in a hundred shades of gold.

Sloane hurried over, her pale face streaked with blood, eyes snapping as blue as her casting.

"What do you think you're doing?" she shouted.

Audric dismounted. Atheria tossed her head and stomped on the fading remnants of Sloane's birds.

"I'm doing exactly as we agreed," he told her, his voice as angry as her own. "Find Rielle. Win her help if I can. Stop her if I must." He flung his hand at the castle, the wings shining above it. "There she is. So I'm going to her."

"You won't defeat her alone, Audric. At least if you met her on the battlefield, you would have help, a chance to speak to her while the rest of us provided cover." Sloane grasped his arm, her face desperate. Her drenched black hair carved harsh lines across her pale cheeks. "Let us come with you."

He looked past her. There was Miren, hurrying down from the wall, red hair pulled back into a messy knot. Evyline and two of the Sun Guard were at her heels, their cloaks dripping. Kamayin arrived just behind them, riding a wave of water over the wall. She had carried them all across the lake from the battlefield. The tails of her long leather coat whipped around her like tongues. She landed with a splash, crossed her wrists in front of her chest like a shield. Her castings flashed; the water subsided, shrinking into twin orbs of rushing foam in her palms. On her shining brown face beamed a triumphant smile.

Evyline reached Audric first. Panting, she knelt before him. "We saw the wings, my king. We knew you would fly for them. We could not let you face her alone."

"You'll have a better chance with us at your side," Miren added grimly, standing a little apart from them. She tightened her grip on her double-headed ax. A tight cloud of metal spun to life around her—shattered dagger blades and tiny metal stars with deadly sharp tips.

"Or any chance at all," added Kamayin dryly. She pushed through the others, flung an arm around Audric's shoulders. Her face half-buried in his collar, she said quietly, "Don't be an idiot, you idiot."

Audric gently detached himself from her. "Rielle might want to keep me alive, or Corien might, long enough to talk to me."

"Taunt you," Miren corrected. "Gloat and preen."

"Perhaps. But you… Why would they care about any of you? She could burn you to ashes the moment she sees you."

"Maybe that'll give you enough time to stab her," Kamayin said cheerfully. But her eyes were hard, and her jaw was set.

Audric turned away from them, dragged a hand through his sweat-soaked curls. He didn't know what to say to them. He wished they hadn't stopped him. He could have ridden that tide of rage all the way to the castle, faced Rielle without a moment to think about it. No time to remember her, no time to feel fear. Now, that wildness was gone. His body ached with bruises, reminding him of his own fragility.

A few paces to his left, a light began to spin. A ring formed fast, sparking white, and out of it stepped four people. Two Audric didn't recognize—a thin woman, fair of skin and hair, with angry blue eyes, and another woman, tall and plump and copper-skinned with graying black hair in a crown of braids around her head. The sight reminded him of Ludivine, how she had popularized that very hairstyle in the north. His throat tightened painfully.

Two more people emerged from the ring of threads. A man with pale brown skin, dark brown hair and eyes—and a girl with white hair, her skin a similar light brown, her own eyes alight with power.

Audric stepped back in shock. "Obritsa." The man was her bodyguard, the silent, stoic Artem.

The queen of Kirvaya nodded sharply, her face a grim mask of determination. "What do you need us to do?"

Audric glanced at all of them. The pale woman's fingers glowed, as if she too were ready to summon threads. Two marques, then. Clearly, they all had a story to tell, but there was no time to ask for it.

A chorus of battle cries made them all look up. Another regiment of winged angels had reached the city, joining those that had already made it past the elemental chaos of the Flats. They flew over the wall and darted up the winding streets. Elementals chased after them—windsingers gliding atop the currents of their own power, earthshakers burrowing up through the ground. A formation of dragons raced over the wall in pursuit, black-robed Kammerat riding atop them.

Audric turned away from the sight of his people fleeing in terror. These streets had been their home. Now, they burned with the fires of war.

"Help them get out," he said hoarsely. "Take them south, help them hide. As many as you can."

Obritsa did not hesitate. She exchanged a sharp look with the pale woman, the other marque. Immediately, they summoned threads, waited for Artem and the woman with northern braids to hurry through, and followed soon after. The rings of light snapped closed.

Audric went to Atheria. He held her long face in his hands, pressed his brow against her velvet snout.

"You can do more good out there than you can with me," he told her quietly.

For a moment, she was still. Her ageless black eyes watched him gravely. Then she snorted and stepped away from him. Her wings brushed like silk against his cheek. She launched herself into the air and flew fast for the battlefield. She gave a sharp cry, hawk-like and terrible, as she disappeared over the wall.

Audric turned away, blinking hard, and faced the castle. No more words were said. None were needed. Miren and Sloane on his right, and Kamayin, Evyline, and the two Sun Guards on his left—Fara, he was pleased to see, and Maylis, two of Rielle's favorites.

Together, they raced through the city. Audric stifled his power, kept Illumenor dim. For now, he would let the others fight for him. Eyes focused on the streets ahead, he heard the crash of his friends' magic, the whip of their swords.

He was, perhaps, running to meet his doom.

But he would not meet it alone.

~ 43 ~

ELIANA

"Feel the earth beneath your feet
and the wind that moves the trees
See the shadows shift across the fields,
the tide that pulls the seas
Hear the whip of metal forged in prayer
The crack and spit of flame
Watch the sun climb up the sky and burn—
A fire no sword can tame!"

—"The Glory of the Seven," traditional Celdarian war hymn

Bodies marked the path toward the city of Âme de la Terre. Armored bodies abandoned by their angels. Adatrox, disposable infantry, their armor crude and their faces frozen in expressions of horror. Steaming elementals, their magic slower to die than their bodies. Horses and archers, and the beasts that fought for the angels, creatures that looked like perverse imitations of the cruciata Eliana knew.

Many more still lived. They fought on foot on the battlefield wet with mud and blood, crashed together in the air. And hundreds, perhaps more than a thousand, flooded the city in churning waves of hide and steel. The defensive wall had fallen, its thick stone bashed clean through.

Eliana raced to join them, Remy at her side. They used the fallen as shelters, running from corpse to corpse. At each one, they knelt, watching for a break in the fight, then ran on, slipping on the slick, trampled ground. A dragon swooped by, chasing after a pack of beasts that scrambled toward the wall. The dragon's mighty wings turned the air to thunder, knocking Eliana and Remy to the ground.

Remy, his face splattered with mud, stared after the dragon. Eliana let him stare as she ripped helmets from two angelic bodies lying nearby. She shoved hers on, trying not to gag from the vile scents coating the helmet, the ground, herself.

Eliana tugged on Remy's arm, yanked him up, shoved the second helmet at him. They ran. At the wall, they didn't hesitate. Hesitation would draw angelic eyes. They brandished their weapons—the sword Remy had retrieved from a fallen adatrox, and Katell's sword, dimmed to look like any other weapon. Eliana gritted her teeth as they joined the angelic companies streaming through the shattered stone. Beside her, Remy mimicked their battle cries. Eliana didn't dare. She bore down hard on every muscle in her body. The air was ripe with magic, the empirium wide awake and watching. Her bones ached with the effort of stifling her castings, ensuring Katell's sword stayed dark.

She ducked the swinging blade of a young, wide-eyed soldier—not an angel but a human, trying in vain to defend his city. He was clumsy; she pushed past him easily and tripped him with her sword.

They were through the doors, clambering across a plaza that was perhaps, in times of peace, a sprawling marketplace. Now, it was chaos. Beasts scrambled up the walls of buildings; gray-eyed adatrox marched up the plaza's wide stairs and poured into the narrower neighborhood streets. Angels with bright wings punched through high windows and dove inside.

Eliana glanced up toward the mountain that loomed over the city. At its base was Baingarde, now marked by a pair of enormous golden wings half as large as the castle itself. Whenever Eliana looked at them, her blood surged dangerously, and she had to clench her fists tighter to keep her castings from bursting to life.

There was no question of who had made those wings or how desperately Eliana's power wanted her to reach them.

Remy panted as they ran, his helmet painted with fresh blood. When they reached a swarming intersection on the city's second level, he darted behind a large square pillar, pulled off the helmet, and tossed it toward a doorway of arched stone where a gate stood smashed open, its ruined ironwork half-melted and sizzling. The helmet rolled across the path of two girls running hand-in-hand. Even the shadows teemed with people desperate for escape. One of the girls jumped over the helmet and screamed. The other yanked on her arm, let out a harsh sob. They ran on.

"I had to kill a child to get through the wall," Remy said dully, watching them flee. His fists opened and shut. "Some idiot boy with no armor and a knife as big as his face. He wouldn't get out of the way."

Eliana couldn't find the words to comfort him. Her throat closed in anguish; the air was hot and rotten with death. She pressed herself flat against the pillar and looked past it at the carnage beyond.

People of the city, arms laden with wailing children, tore screaming through the streets. They fled toward the castle, for it was the only place left to run. Angelic troops marched relentlessly up from the city's lower neighborhoods. They unleashed arrows; they charged with swords raised high. Dozens of citizens fell, though no weapon had hit them. They dropped like shot birds from the sky, rolled down the stairs, knocked others off their feet.

A company of elementals in robes of charcoal and orange, scarlet and gold, rushed out from a side road, planted themselves between the angels and the fleeing humans. Fire snapped from their gleaming shields. Abandoned weapons flew up from the ground and whipped through the air at the angelic troops, slicing open necks.

Eliana searched for the best route to the castle. But every street and alleyway, every set of stairs and parapet seemed to crawl with more enemies by the second. A dark beastly shape jumped from rooftop to rooftop, then slithered down a wall and barreled into a crowd of people rushing toward a building for shelter.

Eliana's palms began to burn. She clenched her fingers tight and turned, pressed her back flat against the pillar, tried to catch her breath. A screaming crowd rushed by. An elbow jostled her. A man with a shrieking child thrown over his shoulder ran past. From somewhere in the chaos came an explosive crash of glass and wood. Screams rose and were quickly silenced.

"You'll have to fight them," Remy said quietly at her side. "We'll never make it otherwise. There are too many of them."

Eliana squeezed her eyes shut. "I can't. She'll find me. *He'll* find me."

"And they'll come for you, and you'll fight them here instead of there."

"Or they'll kill me where I stand without ever having to leave the castle."

Something tugged at her breast, a familiar urgent pull. Her castings sparked and popped like a growing fire.

A voice of thousands, of millions, neither kind nor cruel, spoke in her mind. A single cold instruction, spoken not with words but with feeling, with a particular flavor of power veering left in her veins.

there

Eliana's eyes flew to the smoldering iron gate. She pushed off the pillar and shoved her way through the running crowd. Remy hissed her name, grabbed for her sleeve. She pulled free, crawled over the wrecked gate, and entered a small courtyard. One of many, she could see, of various sizes and designs. Immaculate stone arcades connected them, and narrow passages capped with vine-draped arbors created a maze of walking paths. Pale statues lined the walls, hidden in private alcoves piled with flowers. Others stood proudly on the elaborate cornices, robed and stern. Eyes turned to the sky, shields in hand.

"These must be temples," Remy whispered, joining her with his sword raised. "There's Saint Marzana. And again, over there. You can tell by the shield she holds."

But Eliana hardly heard him. She was staring at the far end of the courtyard, where a man and boy knelt beside a woman twisting in pain. The man was pale with graying hair, his skin lined but his movements deft as he cut an arrow from the woman's shoulder. She screamed past the cloth stuffed into her mouth, turned her face into the boy's arm. She crushed his hand, her knuckles white with pain, but the boy did not flinch. Ash and dirt streaked his sweaty face, but his eyes were keen, a watchful bright blue.

Eliana, watching him, could hear little but her own pounding heart. The screams and crashes of battle faded. Remy murmured a question, then spotted the boy and drew a sharp breath.

The sound unstitched her. Her eyes filled with tears as she watched the boy pass a jar to the man beside him, then bandages with which to dress the wound. Everything about his face was familiar—the stubborn jut of his jaw, the set of his serious brow. His hair, ashen in the dim light, shaggy and mussed, in need of a trim.

His name was in her throat. She clutched the front of her coat, and then Remy's hand, because if she didn't hold on to him, she would rush across the courtyard, all reason abandoned, for the chance to look even once into Simon's eyes, innocent and not yet full of hurt.

A few moments later, the man patted the woman's shoulder. Simon's father, Eliana assumed, her head spinning wildly. Garver Randell. She watched Simon help the woman to her feet. His father fastened a cloth wrap around her torso, gingerly placed a fussing baby inside it. The woman nodded weakly, then pressed a kiss to Simon's head and limped away through one of the narrow courtyard passages.

Simon's father hurried through another passage at once, and Simon followed close behind, their bag of supplies strapped to his back.

Once, before he disappeared into the shadows, Simon paused and looked back over his shoulder. Such a frown on his face, such a fearsome little glare. There were echoes of the man she loved, the man she had left to die at the hands of his tormentor. Thinking of it, the air left her lungs; she gripped Remy's hand hard and tried to push from her mind the image of Simon, alone at Corien's mercy.

Then the young Simon was gone, hurrying after his father, and the courtyard was empty—except for one shape, long and dark and lithe, like the one she had seen only moments ago slithering down a building.

And now it was here, darting into the passage Simon and his father had taken.

Eliana launched into a fevered run across the cobbled stonework and into the shadows, and when she emerged into another larger courtyard, she saw the beast crouched to jump—scaled and bulbous, yet feline in its grace. Dragon-shaped, but a mutilated, vicious version. Charred castings had fused with its body, but it seemed not to care. It stared at the people gathered nearby. Simon was there, and his father, and several others, huddled around a man lying prone on the ground. They didn't see the beast, nor the three others approaching through the courtyard's garden. Tails lashing the air, long snouts glistening with blood.

Eliana did not think once of her sword or the knives at her hip and in her coat. She snapped her wrists to awaken her castings and threw herself at the beast she had followed. She tackled it, rolled, then slammed her palms against its hide and sent it flying through the courtyard. It hit a wall with a startled yelp, then fell and did not rise again.

The small group of people cried out and scattered.

Eliana turned away from them, Simon's presence a hook in her heart. The three other beasts converged on her, mouths open wide, their broad malformed paws pounding the ground. A child rode one, pressed flat against the back of its beast. Gray-eyed and silent, the child sent spinning discs of light flying at her like arrows.

Eliana dodged them, then flung back at the child raw waves of power, furious and blazing. In mere seconds, her attackers were ashes. Shards of the blown-apart castings skittered across the ground like sparks, then went dark.

Eliana stood, breathing hard. She saw Remy watching from the shadows, ready to come to her aid. He shook his head at her, his mouth thin. Eliana flexed her hands, wrangled her wild thoughts, commanded her castings to dim.

But was it too late? The people in the courtyard had seen her. Had Corien? Had Rielle?

She held still, feeling for a change in the air, but none came. A moment passed, then two.

She dared to glance back. Simon was gone, as was his father, and Eliana bit back a wild cry. An ache seized her, so hard it felt like a punch to the chest.

A man stepped forward, tall and shadowed. He gestured the others away, sent them scurrying off through a narrow passage between buildings of pale stone. Saints stood at every corner, watching with blank white eyes.

Soon, the man stood with only two others—soldiers, hands on their swords and shoulders square with tension. The man approached Eliana slowly. One of the soldiers hissed, "Odo!"

The man waved them back, and as he came out of the shadows, Eliana saw his face. He had brown skin, smooth and taut, oiled black hair in neat waves, a neat black beard. He stopped a few paces away, narrowed his dark eyes, and said, "Who are you?"

Eliana did not answer, unwilling to trust him yet. Was it Simon the empirium had been leading her to, or this man? *Odo*, the soldier had said. A name, perhaps, or an Old Celdarian word she did not know?

She lifted her chin. She needed him to see that she was unafraid.

"I need to enter Baingarde," she said firmly. "Can you help me?"

Remy hurried over and translated, and the man's eyebrow quirked. Eliana could not understand his reply.

"What a strange answer to my question," Remy translated. The man looked at Eliana's hands, at Katell's sword hanging from her belt.

Before Eliana could work out a response, Remy stepped forward. He spoke in Old Celdarian, his voice hard and clear. She did not know every word, but she understood enough.

"She is Eliana," Remy announced, "daughter of the Kingsbane and the Lightbringer, heir to the throne of Saint Katell. It is Katell's sword she carries, and it is Katell's blood in her veins. She hails from a future when the world is ruled by the angels of the Undying Empire. She seeks her mother and means to end this war."

As he spoke, Eliana stared hard at this man. She took Katell's sword from its sheath and allowed it to shine. A slow chill passed through her, and her power lifted high against her skin, whispering along the sword's blade, *Know me.*

Then Remy said a string of familiar words—the same sentence he had recited repeatedly under his breath in Ludivine's chamber just before they had passed through Simon's threads.

The man before them blinked. Behind him, his two companions straightened, glanced at each other in startled confusion.

"What did you say?" Eliana whispered.

"'For crown and country, we protect the true light'," Remy said quietly. "The words of their Red Crown. This is where it began." He raised his voice. "How do we get inside the castle? Do you know? Can you help us?"

A beat of silence. The man stepped forward and spoke. Remy quickly translated. "My name is Odo Laroche, and I am a friend of the king."

The man's gaze moved to Eliana, sharp and seeking. "You look like them. Your eyes. Your mouth."

Then he glanced at her castings. "Your mother, though, needs no castings. You do?"

"Someday, perhaps, I won't need them," said Eliana. "But I will always want them."

Odo seemed pleased by this answer. His voice softened the slightest bit.

"And how am I to know you aren't an angel?" Remy translated.

Eliana took the dagger from her hip and nicked a thin cut across her forearm. She held it out for him to see. Seconds passed. The wound did not close, a line of ruby marking her skin. She spared a thought for the indestructible Eliana of old. How reckless she had been, jumping off roofs without thinking and taking blows as though they were gifts.

"And yet you do not speak Celdarian," said Odo, "and not even the common tongue I know. Yours is a variant of some kind. I recognize only certain words. How very odd."

"Not odd," Eliana replied. "I was taught to speak one thousand years from now. Things have changed."

Odo lifted an eyebrow. "Clearly." He glanced at Remy. "And are you also a child of Saint Katell, you who speak for the princess?"

Eliana waited for Remy's translation, then took his hand before he could answer. "No. He is not. But his name is Remy, and he is my brother."

Remy's hand squeezed hers.

Odo nodded, looking hard at both of them. Then he turned and beckoned for them to follow.

"You're lucky, Your Highness," he said as they hurried across the courtyard. His companions brought up the rear. "There are many hidden entrances to Baingarde through which one might enter unnoticed, and I know all of them. Though please don't tell your father that."

Her father. Eliana's heart fluttered in her throat. She hoped the Lightbringer, wherever he was, fought far from the castle and its eerie wings of light.

They moved swiftly through a series of gardens and courtyards strewn with debris. Elemental magic streaked the night sky with color. Beastly roars rolled across the rooftops, and the ground shook with marching footsteps. Hundreds of people jostled for entrance at the doors of each temple they passed. They sobbed on their knees, prayed over shivering candles, gathered chairs and tables with which to bar the doors.

Odo knew ways around the crowds, secret ways that took them underground. One such passage brought them to an empty mansion, silent as a tomb. Silken curtains fluttered at the open windows, and the light from Rielle's wings poured golden across the tiled floor. Eliana shivered. They were so close to Baingarde that her tongue felt fuzzy with power.

Odo's companions stood guard at the entrance while Odo himself led Eliana and Remy first into the basement, and then into another room below that, dark and damp. Odo went to a table in the corner, found a scrap of paper and a pen.

"I cannot go with you," he muttered, sketching out a map. "There are many still trapped in this city, and what you must do is beyond any help I can give you."

He gave her the map, then glanced at Katell's sword. So close to the castle, the blade hummed with a light Eliana could not contain.

"You say you seek your mother," Odo said. "When you find her, what will you do?"

Eliana looked steadily at him, feigning a calm she did not feel. "I think you know the answer to that question, Odo Laroche."

After Remy translated, a faint, sad smile touched Odo's face, and Eliana wondered how he knew Rielle, what he thought of her, if they had been friends before everything went so horribly wrong.

"Yes," he said quietly, "I know the answer."

Then he unlocked a plain wooden door and a second one beyond it. He knelt at a hatch set in the stone floor. Somewhere above, a detonation. The house's foundations shook, and dust rained down from the ceiling.

Odo stood. Katell's sword lit his stern, sad face. "Hurry, Your Highness. The city has fallen. Soon, its people will too."

Remy climbed down the hatch, and Eliana followed him. There was a metal ladder, then a slight drop to a flat earthen floor. Her castings illuminated a narrow dark passageway. She heard the locks click shut above them, looked once at Remy. He nodded, his face grim in the shadows, and they ran.

⟶ 44 ⟵

AUDRIC

*"There are mornings when I wake and think I'll be able
to reach out and feel her there beside me. I convince myself
that I won't have to fight her. That she will see me and
want to come home. Then I turn to find my empty bed and
remember the truth of what I must do. 'I don't know how
to both love you and be the person who sends you to war,'
I once told her. If only I had known then what would come
for us. If only we had had more time."*

—Journal of Audric Courverie, king of Celdaria,
dated April 30, Year 1000 of the Second Age

Inside the castle, all was still. Soldiers and servants lay strewn across the
floor of the entrance hall, stiff where they had fallen, their faces drained
of color and their mouths frozen in screams.

Audric moved past them in silence, trying not to think of where his mother
might be. When he had left her, she had been overseeing the citywide evacu-
ation, ushering people south through the once-secret mountain tunnels.

But that was hours ago. Any one of the bodies lying dead at their feet
could have been hers. Or perhaps she was somewhere in the city, her
unseeing eyes turned up to the stars.

Audric did not look at any human shape he passed, too frightened of
seeing an auburn fall of hair.

"What is this?" Kamayin whispered. She stood near one of the hall's stone pillars. Rivulets of gold spilled down it, pulsing with light. They were everywhere, in the walls and across the ceiling. Floating down the stairs from the second-floor mezzanine, they drifted like delicate branches suspended in water.

Kamayin, eyes wide, reached for the nearest one. Her castings sparked brighter as she approached it.

Miren hurried over, caught her wrist. "It's Rielle. She's doing this. Don't touch it, not any of them."

She looked back over her shoulder, and Audric saw on her face the same longing he felt. His power ached inside him—he could scarcely breathe around it—and Illumenor hummed in his hand, as if it truly belonged not to him but to the light streaming golden through the palace.

Audric.

He did not answer Rielle's voice and said nothing to the others. He stepped carefully up the grand staircase, avoiding the slender lines of gold that shifted and hissed, blind snakes seeking heat. Sloane followed behind him, then Kamayin, Miren, Evyline, Fara, Maylis. Seven frightened shadows creeping slowly through a castle seething with light.

As they ascended, the drifting veins of light grew brighter. Audric's heart pounded; the fear was thick inside him. Every step forward sent doubt plummeting through his body.

What would they find at the top? In his mind's eye, he saw Rielle as she had been on their wedding night. Before the vision from Corien, before that awful scene in the gardens. She had been radiant in his arms as they spun across the dance floor, her gown a glittering cloud and her happiness as unfettered as he'd ever seen it.

He held that image in his mind as he stood before a set of stained glass doors on the fourth floor of the west wing. Set in the doors shone twin suns in amber and orange glass, crafted in honor of Saint Katell, each rising over a field of green. Framing the doors was a sea of golden veins pushing their way inside. The air vibrated in Audric's ears and in his teeth, a lightning-charged heartbeat. Beyond the doors was a sweeping terrace that spanned the width of the castle's fourth floor. It had been a favorite place of his father's for private gatherings.

Audric paused, hand hovering over the latch. He didn't look back at his friends, but he felt them nearby, their castings snapping with eager power, their swords at the ready.

He drew a breath and opened the doors.

A blast of heat greeted him, hotter than any he'd felt since childhood, when he had forged Illumenor. He pushed through the scorching air, walked out onto the terrace. Tears filled his eyes. Light was everywhere, the heat of it unbearable. He heard Sloane curse behind him and Kamayin's sharp gasp.

Tangles of light streaked across the terrace and spilled over the railing like waterfalls. And at the far side, looking out over the city toward the battlefield, was a luminous figure. Dark hair threaded with gold, crimson gown edged with cords of light. She faced away from them. Her hands clutched the railing, and from her fingers stretched the wings he had seen from the battlefield. They filled the night sky, too tall and close to see in full.

Beside her stood a man in a long black coat and cloak, a secret smile on his pale face.

Anger exploded inside Audric, anger as he had never felt before. It burned his fingers; it boiled in his chest like oil popping over a flame.

Corien's smile widened.

"She told me not to kill you," he said. "I could have, easily. All those heroics, that impressive sword work, the shouting and the chanting. Inspiring, truly. But she wanted you to see her. She wanted to look upon you one last time."

Then Corien stepped aside, bowing graciously, and Audric watched, holding his breath, as Rielle turned to face them.

The moment he saw her eyes, his heart sank.

Her eyes blazed gold. The power she emitted, hot as waves of fire, lifted her hair from her shoulders in dark coils, and the hem of her red gown floated at her ankles. His gaze dropped to her belly, round with their child, and once again, he thought of their daughter. *Two queens will rise*. A princess of peace. Dark-eyed, maybe, like him, but with Rielle's sharp tongue and coy mouth.

He found Rielle's eyes once more. Her beauty was shocking, and he had never been more afraid, not of her, but *for* her. The shadows drawn sharp across her face, the new hollows in her cheeks, the lines around her mouth—what had carved them there? Grief or pain? Her skin rippled, gold waves surging beneath it. It would not have surprised him to see her flesh peel away, revealing whatever great and terrible power lay beneath it. Another undulation of gold, the shift of waves caught in a storm, and every muscle in her face tightened. She swayed a little, reached back to brace herself against the railing.

"Rielle, what's happened?" Audric whispered. He took a step toward her.

The light snaking across the terrace lashed at his ankles. He dodged it, as did Miren and Sloane just behind him, but Fara and Maylis were not fast enough. The light snatched their legs, then flung them over the railing into the night. They did not even have time to scream.

Kamayin cried out in horror. Evyline howled Rielle's name.

Rielle blinked. At her sides, her hands twitched, and when she spoke, her voice multiplied, as if every river of light hugging the castle were replicating her words.

"What's happened," she said, each syllable slightly slurred, "is that I escaped you. I became what you would never allow me to become."

"And what is that?" He dared to take another step toward her. "Tell me what you've seen. What has the empirium shown you?"

She tilted her head, watching him. Her eyes flashed. "*Everything.*"

"Can you be more specific? *Everything* is quite a lot to imagine."

A sneer. "For you."

He continued approaching her, waved the others back.

"Tell him," Corien suggested, leaning carelessly against the railing a few paces from where Rielle stood. "I'd like to watch his mind try and fail to comprehend it."

"I saw worlds," Rielle said, her smile brittle. "I held them in my hands and made them spin. I climbed the stars. I dangled my feet over the edge of all things. I unmade an angel and then made five thousand more. And that is only the beginning."

Audric kept his eyes on her face, ignoring Corien. "What do worlds look like?"

She blinked again. The question had surprised her. A pause, and then a flicker of feeling on her face, something beyond that wild, molten hunger.

"Ours is blue and green," she said quietly, "with white clouds swirling around it like ribbons. And there are others. One that is bright violet, and one that is yellow with storms, and other small worlds that are hardly more than rocks."

"Astonishing." He slowed his approach. A step, two heartbeats, another step. "And the edge of all things? Can you tell me what it looks like?"

"Like a waterfall of a million colors," she said, smiling. Her gaze was elsewhere. "It falls forever and then begins again."

"Enough," Corien snapped. "It's time to end this."

Rielle glanced behind Audric, and some of the gold faded from her eyes. "Where is Ludivine?"

"She's gone," Audric replied. "She left me some weeks ago."

Rielle's brow furrowed. "Why?"

"Cowardice." Corien ticked words off on his fingers. "Selfishness. Shame. Take your pick."

Rielle stared at Audric. Her eyes shone, not with light but with tears. She drew in a shuddering breath.

"Lu," she whispered.

Encouraged, Audric took another step toward her. "Think of what you could show us all," he said, "what you could teach us. Things none of us would be capable of understanding alone. You've surpassed us, that's true, and some people are afraid and will continue to be. Some will hate you. That's true too. But most will love you, even those who sometimes fear you."

He paused, then knelt. Behind him, Sloane muttered a warning. He ignored her.

"I was wrong to turn you away," he said, looking up at the brilliant glow of Rielle's face. "I was frightened. Can you understand why?"

She stared at him. Her mouth was trembling. Corien came toward her, but then the air rippled sharply, shoving him away. Incensed, he glared at her from within brambles of light.

"Rielle, he's trying to distract you," Corien snarled. "I know you can see that. If you force my hand—"

"Touch my mind, and I'll kill you," she said calmly.

Audric kept his voice just as steady. "Rielle, I asked you a question. Please, will you answer it?"

She looked down at him, seas of gold in her eyes. They cast their own light. "You were frightened of me." She spoke slowly, as if deciphering a puzzle. "I understand why."

"But I never stopped loving you, *never*," he told her quickly. The moment was precarious; he had to tell her everything before the air between them snapped. "Not once during these past months have I stopped loving you. Nothing you do can change that, and I know how much you can do, darling. I'm beginning to understand it, just some of it, and the rest I *want* to understand. I want to hear all about the worlds you've seen; I want to sit with you by the fire and hear you speak of how the stars feel in your hands, and if it's cold by that waterfall at the edge of all things, and which of the worlds is your favorite. Ours, so pretty and green-blue, or maybe that fierce storming one, its skies angry and yellow."

Audric watched her eyes shine, felt his own tears rise to match. "But we can't do any of that if we don't first stop this war. Our people are fighting to live when they could do it so easily, if you allow it. Our ancestors couldn't live together, but we can. The saints tricked the angels, but we won't. Help me do this. We can make a new world, you and I. Right here where we were born. Our *home*. We can make it into a place where all of us, even our enemies, can learn to live in peace."

He refused to look at Corien, but he could feel the great rise of his anger.

For a moment, Rielle seemed to consider it. Her face softened.

Carefully, Audric smiled at her. "Come home to me, Rielle. Please. We've missed you."

It was the wrong thing to say.

There was no warning. She lunged for him, tearing light from the air as she moved. He pushed himself to his feet, and when they crashed together, it was with swords. Rielle had made one out of nothing, a searing weapon of pure light and power. She held it in her bare palms, glaring at him over its wide, crackling blade. Audric gripped Illumenor in hands slick with sweat. His muscles burned, and his knees shook.

"They've missed me?" Rielle's voice had fractured once more, hundreds of booming pieces hissing with fury. "Everyone who has feared me? Everyone who told me to pray and pray and pray, to ignore my hunger, to use my power, yes, but only as ordered by church and crown? Kingsbane, they called me. And you never admonished them. In private, you loved me. You put your child in me. You married me. But you let them scream epithets at our gates, curse me and yell for my death. And when the truth was made known, you became just like them, even though you'd swore you never would."

She leaned closer. Her mouth was bright with stars. "*Kingsbane. Monster.* You said it yourself. And now you see you were right in that, at least, and wrong in everything else. You never thought I could become this, never let yourself imagine it. It frightened you. *Not my Rielle,* you told yourself. *She would never. She is good and faithful and pure of heart.* And when glimpses of my true self became clear to you, you shrank from me. You touched me with anger. You looked at me as if you didn't know me. And you never did. You knew a lie."

Audric had gathered his power as she spoke and now used it to push up hard against her. Illumenor flared white. Rielle stumbled, caught herself. Her sword went out like a snuffed candle, but when she spun back around, she had made another one. This one snapped with red fire, and when it crashed against Illumenor, the sparks burned Audric's cheeks and brow. He screamed in pain but held fast to his sword. Shadows moved across Rielle's face. He could see the startling shape of her skull, how it blazed like lit bronze.

The others rushed forward to help, and through an exhausted haze, he watched Rielle fling them away—Miren, Sloane, Kamayin, Evyline, each of them pinned flat to the terrace with hissing tendrils of power.

"Rielle, look at what you're doing!" His knees gave out. He dropped to the stone floor. "These people are your friends!"

"Are they? Is anyone?" Rielle's eyes darted to the others. Her tongue wet her lips. She looked at Sloane. "I killed her brother." Then at Miren. "And her lover." Her eyes found Evyline. "Her friends, just now. They're broken on the ground." And then Kamayin. "And half her people are lying dead on the battlefield. And everyone in this palace is dead, and so is your father, and mine."

Kamayin's wail of furious grief pierced the air. Audric heard Miren struggling against her bindings. Every piece of metal on the terrace quaked with anger.

"And these are my friends?" Rielle whispered. "These are the people who will welcome me home?" Her blazing eyes fixed on Audric. A terrible sadness passed over her face, so swiftly that he realized he had probably imagined it. Some delirious hope, as he lay crushed beneath her, that she would regret this when it was over.

She exhaled, a trembling hot breath. "You don't know what it's like to live like this," she said, and he could not read her voice, could not tell if she meant it as a boast or a plea.

He gasped for breath. Her power would smother him. "Tell me, then! Stop this and tell me, tell everyone. Ask us for help. Let us help you!"

"It's too late, Audric. It was too late years ago, the moment I was born with this in my blood. It was too late when Aryava uttered his last words." Her eyes shone, but her words were cold as stones at the bottom of the sea. "We were fools not to see it."

Where before her face had been soft, now a door closed over it, and Audric knew as he stared up at her that it would never open again.

She shoved hard, slamming him into the floor. Illumenor went skidding across the terrace. Somewhere in the sea of endless light, Corien was laughing.

Rielle no longer held a sword. It was her arm itself that burned, a brilliant red spear of light, and as it plunged for his heart, Audric held her beloved face in his gaze and whispered, "Rielle, I love you."

ELIANA

"I hear Aryava's voice in my dreams—not the voice I knew and loved, but the voice from his last moments, when he sounded unlike himself, his words hoarse and distorted. 'The world will fall,' he proclaimed. 'Two Queens will rise.' And something cold and ancient looked out at me from his fading gaze—something that did not belong to him. In that moment, I was seen for what I had done, what we all had done. What we had to do, and would do again."

—From the journals of Saint Katell,
written in the years after the Angelic Wars,
stolen from the First Great Library of Quelbani

Baingarde was full of light, thick pulsing veins of it that tangled like the roots of a gigantic tree. They drifted after Eliana as she raced up the castle's sweeping grand stairs. They reached for her legs, her castings, the blade of Katell's sword.

It was torment to run past them. They pulled at her like a song, promising her glory and infinite kindness if only she would stop and touch them. As they climbed, only Remy, swift and silent beside her, kept her moving forward. Pangs of longing bloomed in her chest even as her stomach lurched with fear.

At last, they reached a set of stained glass doors through which poured dazzling rivers of sizzling light. One of the doors had been left open.

Eliana stood a few paces away, staring at it. Her heart thudded in her ears. Her hands were slick with sweat. She heard voices raised in argument, the crackle of magic, and someone laughing. A familiar laugh that sent cold spilling down her body.

Remy, beside her, stared at the doors. Beyond them blazed an unthinkable brilliance, and in that glow, he seemed smaller than he ever had, his stolen sword a child's toy.

"Is that him laughing?" Remy glanced at her, his face pale under its coat of ash. "Is it Corien?"

She was too terrified to nod. Weights slammed against stone—four, in quick succession. A woman cried out in wild grief, and then a man, shouting words she could not understand. Something about the man's voice was familiar, though she had never before heard it, and suddenly the empirium was booming inside her, wordless and urgent, pushing her toward the doors.

She could have defied it. She could have run, gone back to Odo's basement and hidden in the dark until the angels came for her.

Instead, she slowly approached the doors and looked out onto a terrace of stone and fire. Cords of light held four people to the castle wall and the terrace floor, their limbs askew like the wings of pinned insects. Eyes wide, voices hoarse from screaming, they watched a pale woman with wild dark hair, her skin painted gold with light, a sword of snapping red flames in her hands. A man fought her—brown skin, dark wet curls plastered to his forehead. His sword shone with the light of the sun, but it was nothing compared to the woman herself. She was glorious, incandescent, and his arms shook as she pressed him flat against the floor.

Eliana stared at the awful bright world beyond the doors, watching them fight as if through the haze of a dream. Names came to her, for of course it was them: Rielle, the Kingsbane, and Audric, the Lightbringer. She heard the grief in Rielle's voice, the fury and fear. Audric's desperation as the sparks of Rielle's sword singed his face and arms. His body dripped with blood, sweat, and soot, and beneath Rielle's gown of flowing crimson was a belly swollen with child.

Eliana touched her own stomach, as if that would somehow diminish the strangeness of watching these people who had made her.

But then Rielle's sword changed, joining with her body until her right arm was a ribbon of red fire. She reared back to strike, aiming for Audric's heart, and Eliana watched him close his eyes, saw his lips move around words she could not hear.

Panic burst open inside her. She raced onto the terrace, and the sea of golden branches crowding the floor parted to make way for her. Rielle's arm flashed, but before it could fall, Eliana threw herself in front of Audric, summoned all her strength, and flung up Katell's sword.

Rielle's arm crashed against Eliana's blade, and the two spears of light locked together. One red and blazing, the other pulsing gold as bright morning. Each blade crackled, throwing off showers of sparks.

Over the spear of her arm, Rielle's eyes widened in shock. The pressure on Eliana's sword lifted slightly, and her relief was so immense that she felt dizzy. She began at once to speak.

"Mother," she said in the common tongue, trusting that Remy was nearby, "I have suffered much to find you. Please listen."

She waited, hardly breathing, and then, over the roar of their weapons and the hot hum of light spilling over the terrace railing, Remy's voice rang out, translating her words.

Rielle's expression darkened. She looked to Remy, then back to Eliana, and spat something vicious, something Remy didn't have time to translate. She shoved hard at Eliana's sword. Power rushed up Rielle's body in streams of light, gilding her red gown, and for a moment, Eliana feared her own knees would buckle.

But then she thought of Remy behind her, braving the end of the world at her side, and Simon, back in the future, and Navi and Patrik and Hob, and Ysabet, and Malik, and everyone else lying dead because they had chosen to fight for her.

She planted her feet firmly on the stone and drew power from it, from the air blazing hot against her skin, from the night sky burning with magic.

Katell's sword became a spear of pure light and power snapping within her palms. White and gold, like the burn of stars. Her castings blazed in her palms, feeding the new sword she had made. Her muscles burned, and her eyes watered from the fire's heat, but she stood tall, holding fast against the might of her mother's power.

Another wave of surprise crossed Rielle's face. She looked in wonder at the sword, and Eliana felt a small surge of triumph.

If there had been any doubt in Rielle's mind about Eliana's true parentage, perhaps there was no longer.

A presence crept near the edge of her mind, simmering like hungry flames.

Eliana found him at once—Corien, but not the one she knew. Pale-eyed and flummoxed, but there was no madness in him, and even his mind, probing hers, felt more settled.

He stepped forward, mouth open to speak.

Rielle jerked her head at him. He went flying back against the railing and slumped to the ground. Not pinned there like the others, but simply thrown. A warning.

Eliana seized the moment. It might be the only one she was given. "You are in pain," she said. "I see it, and I understand it."

Behind her, Remy began to translate. Eliana glanced back at him. He knelt beside Audric, helping him sit. The Lightbringer seemed shaken, his face burned by Rielle's fire. He caught Eliana's eyes, and in his gaze she saw her own, and on his face she saw pieces of hers. His hand was tight around Remy's, and even on this horrible night of violence, Remy's face was lit up with joy, for here he was, helping the Lightbringer lean against him, holding the hand of one of the great kings of old.

"The empirium speaks to you," Eliana said, tearing her eyes from Remy to find Rielle once more. "It speaks to me too. It tells me to rise. It tells me it is mine and that I belong to it. But I belong only to myself. And it is the same for you."

Rielle watched her, light licking up and down her body. She hardly looked human, her beauty mesmerizing and terrible: the sharp turn of her nose and jaw; the defiant curve of her chapped mouth; the shadows like chasms beneath her eyes; her skin flashing translucent. Beneath it roared rivers of power.

Eliana's spine itched with sweat. She jerked her head toward Audric. "You do not want to do this. You love him. You love him so much that after you kill him, after I am born, you see clearly what you have done and take your own life. You destroy this city. You break the empirium. Elementals can no longer work magic, and the angels turn black-eyed in their human bodies, deprived of taste and smell and sight. A thousand years pass. The Undying Empire rises."

Eliana looked at Corien only once. "He calls himself the Emperor. He and his soldiers conquer the world. They kill and pillage. They raze temples and murder kings. Monsters crawl out of the Deep and come for us."

Then Eliana thought of Zahra, and for a moment, she could not speak. When she did, tears choked her voice.

"Some angels defy him," she said, "but not enough."

It was then that Rielle began to lower her weapon. The red fire faded, revealing her pale, unburnt arm. Eliana held her breath, counted to three, and extinguished her own sword. Smoke curled between them. Katell's sword was a simple hilt and blade once more, glowing softly with light.

Eliana knelt, and Rielle followed, staring like an enraptured child listening to a bedtime tale.

"A resistance force called Red Crown fights the Empire, but they lose," Eliana went on, Remy's translation rolling in the lovely, lilting rhythm of Old Celdarian. "He captures me. For months, he tortures me. He tries to force me to use my power. I resist."

The smallest of smiles lifted the corners of Rielle's mouth. Her eyes flashed, and Eliana, startled, thought that little spark might have been pride.

"How did you escape him?" Rielle asked.

Her voice was surprisingly small and singular, nearly swallowed by the hum of power crowding the terrace. How young she was; how young they all were. Remy, his eyes shadowed with horrors. Little Simon, hurrying through the city with his father, mending the hurts of war.

"With the help of a friend," Eliana said at last. She would not mention Ludivine. The very name felt dangerous. "Mother, please listen. Look at what you have done. See all that you are doing."

Rielle's gaze drifted to Audric. Eliana was glad she could not see his face. The hope that might live there, or the despair. She reached for Rielle's hand, expecting the power between them to spark. But she felt only a hand, smooth and small, with bitten nails and a tiny callus on the right thumb.

"It is a great burden," she said, "and a great gift to live with this power we have. It is impossible for others to understand. It is difficult to bear their fear and their adoration."

Rielle laughed, a terribly sad sound. She touched Eliana's cheek. "Little one," she said, "I crave their adoration. I crave their fear."

Eliana shivered. The Prophet's endearment in her mother's voice. "Is that what you crave most of all?"

A beat of silence stretched taut and thick. Then Rielle's expression shifted, a crack in her bright armor.

"No," she whispered.

"What do you want, then? More than anything?"

Rielle's eyes glittered. "Rest."

"And something else," Eliana guessed.

Rielle nodded. A secret, dreamy smile flickered across her face. She looked inhuman, then, as if her flesh would soon fall away and leave behind a creature that knew only appetite.

"This," Rielle said. She looked around at the light she had made, the brilliance of her wings in the night sky. She closed her eyes and breathed deeply. Beneath them, the castle moved with her, the stone contracting and expanding to match her rhythm.

Tears slipped down Rielle's cheeks. Her voice was ragged with feeling. "I want more of this too." And then she shook her head and touched her temple. A weary laugh escaped her. "I don't know how to be what I am, split in two like this. A queen of light, and a queen of darkness. I am Aryava's prophecy, only I am but one queen. One queen with the desires of two. I cannot bear it."

Eliana touched her mother's face, an instinct she didn't think better of until it had already been done. How smooth Rielle's skin was, warm and thin beneath her palm.

"You can," she said firmly. "And you will. We all have light and darkness inside us. That is what it means to be human."

Behind Eliana, Audric drew in a sharp breath. Rielle's eyes flicked to him, then back to Eliana.

"And if I am more than human?" she asked.

"Then you must carry more of the light, and more of the darkness too, and so must I." Eliana tried to smile. "That is our burden."

Rielle's mouth trembled. "I did not ask for this burden. I reject it. I *hate* it." She looked at Eliana, imploring. "No matter where I go or what I do, I will never be free of it."

And she was right, Eliana knew. A horrible hot grief tightened her throat. The power in their blood would always hunger for more. And to be hungry, to want to consume, to desire might and power, to crave becoming more than simply a creature of flesh and bone—these longings would make them enemies of some, hated and feared and misunderstood, reviled and revered in the same breath. And others, those clever enough to see the true reach of their pain, their fear, their wants and hopes, would exploit them without remorse.

Eliana did not look at Corien, but she used the image of him in her mind as a whetstone for her anger.

"You *are* free right now," she said fiercely. "A choice lies before you, and only you can make it."

She did not elaborate further. She did not need to. As Remy translated, Rielle listened carefully, and her face softened. Weary lines marked her mouth and eyes.

"For too long," Eliana said, "we have been tools of those who love us and those who hate us. Those who think they know our minds, our hearts, our strength. The power that feeds us."

She clasped Rielle's hand, then leaned against her, brow to brow. Blood and sweat slicked their palms.

"Rise with me now," Eliana whispered, "and help me show them how strong we truly are."

Rielle's eyes flickered gold, twin godly flames. "May the Queen's light guide us," she said hoarsely, with a tiny wry smile.

Eliana returned it. "*We* are the light. And our fire will wake up the world."

"And then what?" Rielle's gaze turned distant. She gestured vaguely at the battlefield, at the people she had pinned to the floor. She swallowed hard. "After all this, then what?"

"A life here," Eliana said firmly. "A life alone, if you wish, exploring the empirium. A life without someone else's desires whispering in your mind, robbing you of the ability to see clearly. The chance to find peace with yourself, with your power, with the world."

"I have done things," Rielle said, her voice low and thick, "that cannot be forgotten. Wherever I walk, anger will follow. And if I had the choice of whether or not to do them again…" Her eyes gazed at something far away. "I do not know what I would choose."

Eliana could not argue with that. "You're right. You will always be remembered for those things. But you can be remembered for others too, if you choose to be."

Eliana squeezed Rielle's hands and dared to kiss her cheek, skin hot as fire and smooth as polished steel.

Rielle's tired gaze hardened, and she lifted her chin, as if daring exhaustion to try and best her.

Despite the heat of war around them, Eliana gazed upon her mother's ash-stained face and shivered, understanding that she knelt in the presence of every star that had ever burned—and that the same unthinkable power had built her own bones.

She met Rielle's eyes. Their gazes locked. And then, as one, with the world's ageless heartbeat drumming in their blood, Eliana and Rielle rose with blazing palms and turned to meet the fate they had chosen.

→ 46 →

RIELLE

"Suppose something had happened differently that night, when the Lightbringer fought the Blood Queen above a battlefield of elementals and angels. A word or gesture, slightly altered, or a step right instead of left. The fate of the world, held inside a single, fragile moment."

—*The Night That Felled the World: What We Know of the Battle of Âme de la Terre* by Axel of the Silver Shore, radical Astavari scholar, printed in Year 941 of the Third Age

Rielle's eyes flew at once to Corien. He was a still black shape in her crackling forest of light, and before she could think of what to do with him, what to say to him, he was upon her.

Pain exploded behind her eyes. His fingers were black arrows, diving into her deepest thoughts. They struck true, and from them spread horrible ripples of pain. He wouldn't kill her, but he would remind her that he could.

On her hands and knees on the terrace floor, she gulped down air. Her vision was full of stars. She was a brick of soft clay, and Corien was slicing her in two, in four, in eight, a knife unyielding. He could cut forever and never grow dull.

Rielle crumpled to the floor, slammed her hands against her skull. She would fly apart. He would send her spinning.

The light painting the terrace, drifting and golden, flickered, then dimmed. It was only for a moment, a stutter like a skipped heartbeat, but Kamayin, Miren, Sloane, and Evyline tore free of their bindings, scrambling free. The boy, Eliana's companion, ran to join them.

Then every light Rielle had crafted, including the wings glowing overhead, erupted into flames.

"Get out of my head!" she screamed. The fresh fire roared high.

Corien watched her coldly. There was a new anger in his face that she had never seen before. "No. I've tried that. I've allowed it. Never again."

Wild with pain, Rielle pushed herself up and grasped blindly for her power. She shoved her palms into the air. Snapping streaks of gold flew across the terrace, then shot off into the night. Her aim was terrible, her thoughts scattered. She couldn't see, blinded by tears and the pulsing white waves of Corien's fury. All she could feel was the cold fire of his anger.

And still, unblinking, he watched her.

She tried again, flung her power toward him in desperation. Energy pulsed across the terrace, hot and rippling, as if something huge had fallen from the sky. Corien hissed. His head snapped to the right. When he looked back at Rielle, tiny red pricks of blood spotted his face. A moment later, they were gone.

"Rielle, I'm right here!" Audric crawled toward her. His wounds did not vanish, and his face was raw with terror, and yet still he fought to reach her. "I'm right here. Talk to me. Look at me, please!"

The world was liquid. Rielle was underwater, paddling frantically for the surface. She couldn't breathe, she couldn't find the ground.

Tears streaming down her face, she searched for Eliana.

The girl hadn't moved. She stood rigid, her expression hard with anger. Light blazed in her palms, ready to be thrown. Ripe with heat, the air trembled around her. But if she struck Corien, would it hurt Rielle? Would he turn on her next and entrap them both?

The glass doors burst open. Their painted suns shattered. A dozen angelic soldiers spilled onto the broad terrace, followed by three beasts, five, *eight*. One dropped down from the rooftop, skittered forward on the shiny black hooks of its wings. Another, reptilian and clever-eyed, an elemental child on its back, threw lashes of wind from its ash-blackened castings.

"Protect the king!" Evyline roared, drawing her sword. Her arms and neck wore strips of burned flesh. The others hurried to join her—Miren, her army of knives darting like bolts of lightning through the air; Sloane, pulling shadows from every crack and crevice. Silver spirals of churning water flew from Kamayin's glowing wrists, and Evyline charged, wild-eyed, every blow of her sword like the fall of thunder.

But then Eliana whirled around and launched into the fight. Beside her, the others were nothing, clumsy and unremarkable. Even dizzy with pain, Rielle could not tear her eyes from her daughter. She was lovely in battle, her arms and legs quick as a dancer's. Her coat whipped around her legs. She was filthy with blood and dust, and yet the hum of her power painted her resplendent, as if she had been born from the strokes of an artist's gleaming brush. Her hands glowed brightest of all, encased in her castings—two pendants held snug to her palms by slender chains.

More beasts tumbled down from the roof, shrieking stupidly for blood. With a furious sharp cry, Eliana spun to face the nearest one, sent it flying. It crashed through the stone railing and tumbled into the darkness.

Rielle could have watched Eliana for hours. Arcs of light soared through the air, smashed into the angels' armor, sent them clattering to the ground. But of course they rose again and again, and they would for-ever until they claimed victory.

Then Rielle felt the air tighten with malice, the drawn breath before a scream. Her stomach dropped for miles.

The angels had deployed their minds at last, their fiercest weapons. The brute force of their thoughts snapped through the air, seeking targets. They would seize these fighting women one by one and throw them to their deaths, or make them jump off the edge of the terrace themselves, command them to turn on each other until nothing was left but ruin. They would save Eliana for last and dismantle her piece by piece. Rielle drew a breath, dizzy with fear.

But then something dove out of the sky. Nearly shadows, nearly bodies, but neither of these things and both of them at once. It was as when Rielle had opened the Gate—flashes of beauty, supple skin that gleamed as if freshly emerged from the sea, brief flashes of armor and cloaks, gowns and coats riotous with color. Streaming pale hair, long dark curls fluttering with ribbons. They were angels, each of their minds carrying echoes of what they had once been. And with no bodies to contain them, their memories spilled freely.

Watching them descend, Rielle struggled to rise, shout a warning. But these angels, bodiless and roaring, dove to fight alongside Eliana, shielded Sloane and Kamayin. They wove through the attacking angels, wielded echoes of swords they had not held in an age. One of them had eyes black as river stones, white hair like strands of sea foam, shining platinum armor. She dove in front of Eliana, deflecting attacks of mind and claw. Her war cry struck Rielle's bones.

The armored angels, solid in the bodies Rielle had made for them, cursed the new arrivals. Rielle sensed the specific shape of their fury: these traitors would fight not just for humans, but for this girl who had come from the future to destroy the greatest among them—Kalmaroth, reborn, their salvation and their champion.

A piece of Corien sat in each of the angels' minds, ready in case he should need to command them, and the deeper he sank into Rielle's thoughts, the more clearly she could sense their incandescent rage. She choked on it, her throat closing. Foul words shot from their mouths in Lissar, in Qaharis. *Traitors! Filth!*

Mere seconds had passed since the moment Rielle had risen with Eliana at her side. She lifted her head against a great weight—the pressure of Corien, insistent and full of rage, each of his thoughts a vise.

He stood over her, hands clasped behind his back. His voice was quiet, and yet her ears bled from it.

"After everything we've shared," he said, "after everything we've accomplished, you would turn from me?" He glanced beyond her. His face settled into harsh lines of anger. "You would let this girl, this *liar*, come between us?"

Rielle tried to stand, but Corien's mind shoved deeper, pinning her. She heard a scream and twisted on the stone, bleary-eyed, to see Eliana fall to her knees. Her castings shot careening power that blazed a charred path across the terrace. She clutched her head and cried out, and when she tried to rise, something unseen struck her. Her head snapped around, and she fell hard to the ground.

Fury rose inside Rielle on a wave of white light. The pain in her head threatened to split open her skull, but she pushed past it and stood, found Corien, cut the air with her arm, and blasted him clear across the terrace.

She whirled, her heart in her throat. Eliana was up and fighting again, and across the field of fire between them, their eyes locked, and Rielle had never felt such love in her life.

Corien was up in moments. She heard him rise and stared him down as he came limping back for her. Blood trickled down his temple; his hair was wet with it. She felt a pang of remorse, but she would throw him again if she had to.

"You will not touch her," she told him evenly.

"She's a *liar*," he spat. "You would let her come between us? This girl who came out of the night spinning stories designed to hurt me?"

Blackness washed over Rielle, dragging claws of pain in its wake, and when it cleared from her eyes, she found the sky, encircled in flames. She was on the terrace floor, screaming, and each time she twisted to rise, to reach for her power, the floor cracked beneath her. Spirals of light flew from her fingers, and great knots of fire rained down from the sky.

"Rielle, listen to the sound of my voice! Don't be afraid! I'm right here!"

But she could not allow Audric near her. She would kill him, or Corien would. She shoved hard in the direction of his voice and hoped she had sent him far enough away.

Corien crouched before her, watching as she fought for breath. Faintly, she heard Audric, still calling for her. *Stay with me, Rielle! Fight him!*

She held her head, fought to look blearily up at Corien. The sight of him was horrible. His face was monstrous, pale as bone, his eyes a brilliant white that stabbed her eyes like needles. Somehow he had grown wings. Enormous and black, they were made of a thousand birds that spat raucous harsh cries.

Rielle fought to look for Eliana. There she was, being swarmed by dozens of braying beasts. With beaks and talons, they tore her to shreds. Flames shot up Miren's body. In seconds, she was ashes. Eliana's companion, the boy, burst open, and from the place where his head had been poured shining waves of black beetles.

Rielle shut her eyes, but still she saw them die, and still she saw the beetles merge to become a reflection of herself. And she was the fire too, and she was each of the beasts ripping open her daughter's body, and she was every bird teeming on Corien's back.

"That is what you are," Corien said quietly, unblinking. "This is the darkness that lives inside you. See it, Rielle. Remember it. Love it, as I do."

At last, Rielle found her voice. She could not look at him. He would not allow it. He pressed her skull against the floor.

"I remember everything," she rasped, her tears hot against the rough stone. "I remember how you drugged my thoughts, kept me stupid for weeks. I remember long months of you coming to me in dreams. I told you I wanted to sleep, and you kept me awake anyway, whispering to me of resurrection."

"You love our great work," he said. "It brings you pleasure you have never felt before, joy you could never have found with them. You *know* this, Rielle."

She blinked hard against the bursts of pain pounding her skull. She tried to reach for her power, but her thoughts were too scattered. It was like clutching at water with only her hands.

"Let me rise," she choked out.

"No. Not until I know you have come to your senses."

A sob of rage tore loose from her throat. "Release me!"

"You fear yourself a monster," he said, his whisper booming in her ear. "It eats at you. You killed your father. You killed Tal. You have killed and killed, and you will kill again. *The Unmaker.*" His voice slid against her like a mouth in the dark. "And what if it's true? We are all monsters, full of perversities and violence. At least you and I accept this and have the power and intelligence to *do* something with it."

Rielle shook her head, struggling beneath the flat, hard press of his mind. One image rose to the surface, clung fast amid the chaos he was making of her thoughts: Eliana, falling to her knees in agony. Eliana, radiant in battle. Eliana, kissing her cheek.

"I may be a monster," Rielle said, the words thick with pain, "but I am no longer yours."

Corien's shock was as clear and swift as if she had struck him.

"I have loved you," he said hoarsely, "as I have never loved anyone. You know this. You *feel* this every time I look at you."

The stone of the terrace was turning molten beneath Rielle's fingers. She prayed it would suck her through and send her falling. Dirt and pebbles, flung by the wind, stung her cheeks. A storm was rising. *Ten* storms. The mountain shook beneath the castle, and the castle shook beneath their feet.

"Look at me."

She did not. She watched the world ripple gold at her fingertips.

Corien grabbed her chin, forced her to look up at him. "Look at me!" he roared, and then he wrenched her up off the ground and captured her mouth in a bruising kiss.

His thoughts slithered in fast and locked into place inside her. He found the deepest hollows of her mind and settled there. His teeth caught her lip, bit hard. He sent her visions, memories. His bed in the Northern Reach, the furs askew, their bodies bare and flushed. That cave in Kirvaya where she had first kissed him. The warm safety of his arms after she had fled Âme de la Terre, heartbroken and furious. How he had crooned her name, pressed his lips to her hair.

She whimpered, clutching his sleeves. The sound emboldened him. He deepened his kiss, his hands tight around her skull, and she could feel him toying with her desires, stoking them. If she would not respond on her own, he would force her. If she would not see the truth of his words, he would remake her eyes so she never saw anything but what he allowed her.

And it would be easy, Rielle thought, to allow Corien this. In exchange, she would not have to touch anything that hurt her, or face the things she had done, or discover how to live in this world into which she did not quite fit. She could explore her power unfettered and care nothing for what she left in her wake.

She tried to pull back for air, reeling from his kisses, but he tightened his hold on her, yanked her close against him. His anger was a film of tar at the back of her mouth. She could not breathe; her head pulsed with white waves of pain. His grip became punishing, his nails digging into her flesh.

"Mine," he sobbed against her mouth. "You're *mine*, Rielle, and I'm yours. We understand each other. I can't do this without you. And without me, you'll be truly alone. They will never accept you. *He* will never accept you. They will spin new lies every day. They will smile to your face, and then, when the door has closed, they will whisper in fear of you and plot against you, and children will shudder at the mention of your name. You know this. Even him." He shook her hard. "You *know* this."

"Stop," she gasped, her voice trapped in her throat. His mind slurred her thoughts. "Let go of me, please!"

"Never again, Rielle. Look at what you've made me do. I didn't want this." His mouth moved down her neck, his teeth scraping her skin. His presence was a fog in her mind, spreading fast. Soon, it would cover everything. She was helpless against him. When she reached for the empirium, her fingers met mud.

"Mine," Corien murmured. His hand tightened around her throat.

As he moved back to her mouth, the birds shrieking at his back, she caught his little smile of triumph, the flash of his teeth.

She found a faint thread of strength and slammed her hands against his chest.

At once, his coat burst into flame. He lurched back from her, screaming, and tore it off. The white shirt beneath it was a wet field of red. Thin curls of smoke rose from his charred flesh.

His eyes flew to her, white with rage. She looked behind her, searching frantically for Eliana. Corien's visions had vanished. No beetles, no tearing beasts. There she was, still fighting. Her hands blazing, her heels throwing sparks. Made of light, her daughter, and faltering not even once. What a fearless woman she had made.

Rielle laughed, choking on exhausted tears.

Behind her, Corien spat, "You are an abominable creature." He grabbed a chunk of her hair and wrenched her to her feet. He stank of burnt flesh, and still he was beautiful, his cheekbones painted with soot, his lips flushed from heat and desire.

"I know this," he said, "and I know every corner of your savage heart, your capacity for cruelty, your caprice, and yet I love you still. I would have you right here if you would let me. Fear you? I exalt you. Remember what I told you?" He laughed, tightening his grip on her hair. "You could burn me a thousand times, and I would still want you for my own."

Rielle strained to hear the sounds of Eliana fighting. How beautiful they were, like every song she had ever known.

"I have loved you, Corien," she said, breathless with pain, with a new, muddled understanding. Each of Eliana's blazing strikes struck like a bell inside her, fighting to wash her tired mind clean. "I have trusted you. Part of me will always belong to you. But not all of me." She stumbled on the weight of her tongue. "You saw that I was afraid and worked to keep me that way. You saw that I was lonely and reminded me of it every time I thought of leaving you."

He laughed, stroking her cheek. "Listen to you. Queen of my heart. Is the pain making you delirious? Reject them, as you meant to, and I'll take away everything that hurts you. Rielle." Tears in his voice. "*Please*, do this for me."

Rielle's vision pulsed black. Corien's hands were gentle at her throat, and yet she reached for her power and could not find it. That shove, that bloom of fire on his clothes—she could find nothing more. Her mind was full of him, and if there was anything left of herself, she could not see it. Somewhere, Audric was screaming for her, but it was no use. Corien was inside her, and he would never leave, not now.

The world spun, tossing her. She sagged against Corien's bleeding chest, her eyes fluttering shut. What bliss, to let him hold her. He had promised he would take away the pain, that she would never be alone. Perhaps it was all right to believe him. Strange, that she could have thought otherwise.

Corien kissed her hair, her cheeks. "My love," he whispered, a smile in his voice. "There you are. You've come back to me. Very good, Rielle."

Then, abruptly, relief.

Something cold and sharp dropped between them, severing the cords that bound them. Rielle fell to the floor, and Corien staggered back from her.

His furious gaze shot to the terrace doors.

Huddled on the floor, head pounding as if it had been pummeled for hours, Rielle shivered on the hot stone and watched a pale shape storm across the terrace.

She drew in a sharp breath.

It was Ludivine, grim and swift, her golden hair in a tight knot, her brocade gown of lilac and plum glimmering in the light of Rielle's power. She marched toward Corien with the sword of Saint Katell in her hands.

Rielle's throat tightened with sudden fear. She whirled, desperately searching for Eliana, but Eliana was alive and well, spinning around to fling light at Katell's sword. It crashed into the blade and held there, roaring, and though Ludivine was no elemental, Katell's casting now shone as if she were. She raised the sword high, tossing harsh beams of white light.

Corien, hatred vivid on his face, found Illumenor where Audric had dropped it. A double cruelty: fighting with the sword of the man whose death he craved, and using a casting that was not his to use.

Audric cried out in pain. Rielle searched through the flames, saw only licks of him between bursts of light, and then she could search no longer, for Corien rushed at Ludivine with a roar, and they met in furious battle. Jagged dervishes of shadow and light sparked between the casting of Saint Katell and the sword of the Lightbringer, the blades bewildered to be held by angels.

Ludivine's face was strained, drawn tight and pale. She was no warrior, had never trained for it, and yet she flew at Corien, her strikes brutal.

But it was not only with swords that they fought. Rielle realized this slowly as she watched them whirl and collide. Her vision still throbbed, and her wits struggled to reassemble, but this she knew: for the first time since he had come to her so long ago, Corien was nowhere in her mind.

The strange emptiness sent her into a panic. Pushing herself up onto her elbows, she searched for him, and then for Ludivine, sent them a cautious question.

Are you there?

But no answer came. Rielle's thoughts were entirely her own. It frightened her, the wilderness of it. She had forgotten what it felt like, and the loneliness inside her reared up so ferociously that she found it hard to breathe.

A hand gently touched her own, anchoring her. She knew him at once, though it had been months since she had felt the brush of his skin.

But she could not look at Audric. Seeing the burns on his face would unravel her. She reached for him in silence, found his fingers, slippery with blood. He helped her sit, and she leaned hard against his chest. He was steady even then, a solid warmth, even with his pulse beating wildly under her fingers and his breathing ragged. Behind them, their friends bled to protect them. Their daughter—their astonishing, impossible daughter—fought beasts with hands made of fire.

And before them, two angels were locked in furious combat. Stolen swords crashing, the air around their bodies glinting silver with power. Pale shapes formed at their backs. With each blow, each cry of anger, the shapes rose higher, blooming in the air ripe with magic, until they were twice as tall as their counterparts. One shape was Kalmaroth, the angel

Corien had once been. Tall and fuming, wings blazing from his back. Even the memory of him was magnificent. His sword cracked like lightning.

And there was Ludivine, and Rielle's throat seized to look at her. She had never known Ludivine's angelic name, had been gently turned away from the subject whenever she dared ask, and now she wished she had pressed for it, because this memory, this echo of her true self, was exquisite. She looked to be perhaps Rielle's age, or maybe a bit older, like Audric, and there was a luminous, unbearably beautiful quality to her face that brought tears to Rielle's eyes, for she knew she looked upon an ancient creature that even now, after all she had seen and done, she could not truly understand. This Ludivine, pale and flaxen-haired, shining tresses twisting down her back in elaborate coils, was not as tall as Corien, but her bright eyes were ferocious and her enormous wings were as radiant as the sun.

Rielle's burning eyes moved to Ludivine, *her* Ludivine. Strands of golden hair had come loose from their knot. Fear had stripped her face of all color. She looked quickly at Rielle, a sharp light in her eyes.

And as their gazes locked, the world fell away from Rielle, leaving her weightless. A cold wave of dread dropped down her arms. Audric must have sensed the change in her. He murmured an urgent question. Was it Corien? Was he hurting her again?

But Rielle could not bear to answer him, for she understood the truth of what Ludivine had done. With one look, Ludivine had told her everything. They had shared years of knowing glances across dinner tables, years of sleepy soft looks as they woke in each other's arms, or Audric's, or all together. And now, this.

Rielle's blood roared, her heart howling in protest, and a hundred regrets, a thousand words of grief, lodged in her throat like knots of fire. But she would say none of them, *could* say none of them.

For Ludivine had engaged Corien not only with sword but with every bit of strength her mind possessed. How many times had Ludivine confessed that her strength paled in comparison to Corien's? And yet here she was, throwing herself at him with no hope of survival, drawing him into a battle so fierce that he had abandoned Rielle's mind to fight it.

Leaving her free, for however long Ludivine could distract him, to do what must be done. As if Ludivine were holding closed a door that Corien was clawing through from the other side, giving Rielle time to run. The path was clear, and it would crumble if Rielle did not act quickly. Corien would realize what was happening and unknot himself from Ludivine, and the moment would be lost.

Unsteadily, Rielle stood.

"Stay back," she commanded, stepping away from Audric. Guilt was poison in her veins. Her mouth was bitter with it. With each hammering heartbeat, she thought of the black altar on that frozen mountain, the angel she had smashed between her hands like soft clay. One minute there, the next, annihilated.

I cannot, she thought wildly. Through her tears, she watched them fight. Corien and Ludivine, Ludivine and Corien. Never mind how they had hurt her, how she had hurt them. Their lies, their cruelties, how they had tugged her between them. Losing either one of them would destroy her. Losing both was a thing she could not imagine. And yet Ludivine was holding Corien back, giving Rielle a peaceful mind at last. A mind free of whispers.

A choice lies before you. Her daughter's voice, kissing her memory. *Only you can make it.*

And you must. Ludivine managed a few fragile words. Inside them was a fierce, sweeping love. *It's all right. Don't be afraid.* Ludivine glanced at her once more. There was a weight to that look. A finality.

And then, like a swift jab to the throat, Ludivine was suddenly frantic, her voice breaking at last. She had done all she could. Her strength flickered, fading. Corien's rage bloomed like black waves.

Now, Rielle, please!

Rielle knew she would hear those words for the rest of her life— Ludivine's frayed voice, trembling with fear, begging Rielle to kill her.

She would remember everything that happened in those seconds before the end. How she reached for Corien and Ludivine, held them in her palms as if she were the god that had made them. How Corien realized too late what she intended and screamed for her to stop, his voice shattering. She would remember gathering the empirium—every speck of it, every shimmering strand within reach. How eagerly her power responded and how devastatingly fast it flew at them.

The world flared hot and brilliant—the dark mountain, the burning castle atop it. Rielle's mind, her palms, the air whining as if ready to pop. All went white, and then there was nothing. A silent, booming darkness. The fire, gone. The lights streaming through the castle, vanished, as if they had never been made.

Rielle fell hard to her knees.

Breathed once, twice. Three times, and a fourth.

Shaking, she looked up.

Spots of color bloomed before her eyes. She blinked, the world returning to her. The mountains, the city, the stars beyond. The battlefield somewhere below. A quilt of light and fire, baffled dark shapes darting through the air.

Rielle stared, and stared, and as she looked at the charred spots where Ludivine had stood and where Corien had fought her, she felt something rising inside her. Something savage and lonesome, like the forest at night, like a sea seized by storms. There were not even ashes left behind, some ruin of them that she could touch. Her power still simmered in her palms and in the hollow of her throat, in the crooks of her elbows and the bones of her feet. It hummed quietly, satisfied.

Someone behind her cried out in surprise—maybe Miren, maybe Evyline—and Rielle turned to see that every angel and beast on the terrace had disappeared. A faint glow lingered in the air where they had once stood. Ripples in the empirium, echoes of life suddenly and utterly erased.

Rielle knew what this meant, looked dully at her new reality as if reading scripted instructions. Corien had boasted countless times: *I am infinite*. At any given moment, his mind had been connected with thousands of others—adatrox, elemental children astride their monsters. Angelic captains, eager soldiers. Angels in Avitas; angels in the Deep. And then Ludivine, fighting him, had tangled her mind with his, their power locking together like warring blades, and now they were gone, they were *gone*—Rielle had killed them both at once, efficient, like an arrow through two hearts—and so every mind they had been inside at the moment of their deaths had also been destroyed. Not just dead—smashed into nothing, reduced to ashes so small they could not be seen or touched or tasted. Thousands of them, obliterated at the moment Corien was, leaving the angelic armies in ruins.

The thing rising inside Rielle erupted. An animal howl tore free of her throat. She was beyond weeping. This was a feeling for which there were no words. Her grief left her shaking, and her hands were claws on the stone, nails ragged against it. The air was sour with the things she had done.

Arms lifted her. Audric helped her sit against him, gently caught her hands, and held them against his throat. She felt the beat of his heart against her fingers, the soft vulnerable curves of his neck.

"I'm here," he said, his wet cheek touching hers. "I'm here, I've got you, I'm here." Tears shook in his voice, for he had loved Ludivine too. He had been there in the gardens, at the dinner table, in the warm bed at dawn.

Rielle clung to him, keening against his collar, and then a terrible thought occurred to her. She looked frantically past Audric at the terrace beyond. The bodiless angels who had fought for Eliana drifted above in eerie whispered conference. Alive, but uncertain. What would come next? What now?

But Rielle didn't care about them, nor did she care about Miren, stumbling to her feet, or Sloane, turned away with her hand over her mouth, or Evyline, limping toward them.

"My queen?" Evyline managed, unsteadily, to kneel. Hope erased years from her face. "Are you with us? Is it you?"

Rielle did not answer her. She was looking past Evyline at Kamayin, who was sinking slowly to the ground. Eyes wide, she stared at two faint shapes moving toward each other—a boy and a girl, flickering like shadows thrown from candles.

A word lodged in Rielle's throat. *Eliana?*

She reached for her, wondering where she would go, or if she would go nowhere. If the woman named Eliana would cease to be, now that she had done this thing she had traveled so far to do.

Rielle held her trembling breath.

Blew it out.

They were gone.

— 47 —

AUDRIC

"On this day, Audric Courverie, the king of Celdaria, proclaims, in agreement with the Church, an alliance with the nation of wraiths, who are absolved of all responsibility for the actions of their kindred and with whom the people of Celdaria hope to forge a friendship of peace and communion."

—A royal decree issued by Audric Courverie, king of Celdaria, dated May 21, Year 1000 of the Second Age

At dawn, Audric quietly opened his eyes, and before he was fully awake, he turned to find Rielle beside him.

She slept in a thin nightgown of white linen, curled on her side to allow her belly room. Turned away from him, her face was hidden. A fear gripped him, as it always did in these terrifying moments upon waking, that something had come for her in the night, some vengeful angel who had gotten past the wraiths' defenses.

He held his breath until he saw her chest rise and fall. Relief surged through him, and he blinked until his vision cleared. For a moment, he traced the tangled lines of the dark hair spilling across her pillow. Then he moved toward her slowly, wrapped his arms around her. If she turned toward him, he would see the tired lines framing her mouth and carved into her brow.

He found her hands, clenched in hard fists at her chest. She was fever-
ishly hot, but Garver Randell had pronounced her to be perfectly healthy.
Audric wrapped his hands gently around hers as if cupping water he was
desperate not to spill.

In her sleep, she shivered, and then he felt her soften, the tension she
held even while dreaming beginning to fade. Soon, she was pliable in his
embrace, warm and trembling. She brought his fingers to her lips, drew
his arms tighter around her. Tears dropped onto his hands, and he buried
his face in her hair, his throat aching as she cried. Even with the linens
changed and the rugs replaced, their bedroom smelled of the smoke from
Rielle's fire, as did the rest of Baingarde, as did the ravaged city beyond it.

"Would you like breakfast?" he whispered at last. He hardly dared
move. Mornings were such a fragile time. Another day meant more funer-
als, more patrols sent to the Flats to scour the wreckage for bodies not yet
recovered, more whispered prayers and muttered curses. No one dared
hurt Rielle or even come near enough to touch her. When they walked
the ruined streets to visit healers' rooms and pay tribute at the temples,
crowds trailed them, watching. Some wary, some awestruck. Some even
smiled and knelt in thanks as he passed, Rielle silent and pale on his arm.
They reached for her with pious hands. They glared from the shadows and
dreamed of her death.

"Yes," she said, her voice thin. "Breakfast. Garver told me I should eat.
For the child, at least."

Audric recognized the slight edge to her words for what it was. He
kissed her shoulder, bare where the nightgown had fallen. Then he lifted
her hair and kissed her neck. His hand grazed the curve of her hip, and she
sighed a little, relieved, and pressed her hot mouth to his hands. This, she
knew. This, while she did it, silenced everything else.

He moved gently, his arms crossed tightly across her chest, his lips soft
against her ear, and she clung to him, her fingers digging into his biceps.
When she began her rise, her body arching against him and a soft cry falling from her mouth, she brought him soaring with her. Even in her grief,

she hungered, insistent, and in those slow, sparkling moments just after, the air between them was at peace.

Sleepily, she kissed his arm, then twined her fingers with his and brought them to rest against her belly. Their child kicked against his palms. He thought of the girl who had fought for them on the terrace. Her flashing dark eyes, the wild whip of her brilliant hands. He held her name in his mouth. The syllables had become precious to him. *Eliana.*

Morning painted the windows white. Rielle drifted in and out of sleep, and Audric stayed awake, watchful. There was an ache in his chest that he had given up trying to soothe. If he unfolded his arms from around her, she might come unmoored. If he fell asleep, he might wake to find her gone.

A soft knock at the door alerted him to the time. Weariness dropped heavily onto his shoulders.

"My king," announced Evyline, her voice muffled, "the councils are assembling."

If Audric closed his eyes and held his mind very still, he could almost pretend that nothing about the past few long months had happened. That it was two summers ago, and Rielle was beside him, sleeping peacefully. That Corien was far away and Ludivine slept in her rooms downstairs.

But if he kept the councils waiting for too long, they would spend the rest of the day scowling and make an already difficult thing all the more difficult.

Tearing himself away from the soft haven of their bed was a torment. Audric dressed in silence, and as he fastened the buttons of his jacket, he came around to her side of the bed. The location of the mirror was a good excuse. He fussed with his curls, inspected the healing burns on his cheeks and jaw.

Rielle was watching him, her nightgown rumpled, her gaze soft.

"I love you," she said quietly, and he knew this—he saw it in her eyes and felt it in her touch. He bent to kiss her, and she stretched up hungrily for him, her grip desperate in his hair.

"My light and my life," he murmured against her scorching brow. "I love you, I have loved you always, and I will never stop."

It had become a refrain, a song passed between them over the past few days until the words felt like worn grooves. Her eyes fluttered closed at his touch, and as he pulled away at last, he glimpsed a faint golden light shifting across her face. A sly wink, it illuminated her cheekbones, the curve of her lips, and was gone.

A cold stone dropped between Audric's ribs. He smoothed his thumbs across her face as if he could wipe away whatever it was, this luminescence that sometimes rippled to life under her skin. She gazed up at him dreamily, her sleepy green eyes suddenly swirling with golden currents. Beneath them, shadows stretched long and dark.

"Is it happening again?" Rielle whispered.

He nodded, unable to speak. It had been happening for weeks.

She took his hand, kissed his knuckles. He helped her to the bathing room, then saw her back to bed and sent a page downstairs for food. Her feet dangling above the floor, she watched him gather his papers, his dress cloak, his favorite pen. When he kissed her goodbye, she held his healing face tenderly in her hands, and all the way downstairs, the sweetness of her touch lingered. Yet Audric could not shake the rope of dread winding slowly around his heart.

Yes, Rielle loved him. He knew this, and yet he feared that someday, for her, it would not be enough.

—◆—

The days passed too quickly, each one packed with activity that left him aching with exhaustion by nightfall.

He met with the royal councils, saw to the repair of the watchtowers and the wall, helped the surviving city guard as they slowly cleared the ruined streets. Foul odors drew them to bodies buried in the rubble, both human and not. A disemboweled beast with a stomach full of flies. A child stuck through the heart with a rafter rent from the roof of her bedroom.

Over each body, he knelt and prayed. Sometimes those nearby joined him. Sometimes they stood and stared resentfully. So many had died, and yet he had lived.

He made himself look at their pain without flinching. Sometimes he woke from dreams drenched with sweat, his bones aching from some primal fear, and he knew with biting certainty that he should have died that night. And yet there he was, shaking at the edge of his bed with his head in his hands, alive and whole with only a few scars and one nasty bandaged gash on his leg.

Then Rielle would reach for him, softly call his name, and in her arms he would find a kind of solace until the next nightmare claimed him.

◆

Often, Rielle joined him when he met with his advisers. The larger meetings, with dozens of people gathered in the Hall of the Saints, were one thing—Rielle sat quietly on her throne at Audric's side and offered insight when needed. What was the condition of the Gate? What would be required to close it, and when would she be strong enough to try it? Could it be resealed completely, even stronger than it had been before?

How many angels still remained in the Deep?

And what other creatures might someday escape it?

But the more intimate meetings in the small council chambers surrounding the Hall of the Saints—these Rielle avoided until the day came when her expertise was required.

They sat around a large square table of polished oak. Rielle to Audric's right, and to his left, Genoveve, pale and silent, her auburn hair pinned up in neat coils. Beside her was Sloane, shadows under her bleary eyes. Ardeline Guillory of the House of Light sat on Rielle's other side, followed by Rafiel Duval of the Firmament, his thick black braids tied at his nape. The Archon's chair sat empty, gleaming with polish, and then came Brydia Florimond in her earthshaker robes of umber and soft green, her ruddy skin patched with bandages.

Then there was Miren, rigid and stone-faced. Between her and Sloane, Tal's chair sat empty.

"We have received reports from Queen Obritsa," Audric said, drawing out the papers. "She is requesting aid. Supplies, healers, soldiers. Corien's fortress—"

"Yes," Rielle murmured, her gaze distant. "The Northern Reach."

A pause, silence stretching taut across the table. Magister Duval looked at his hands, his mouth thin.

Audric imagined his mind as a flat, clean plain, free of divots or dust. It was the only way he could move past what Rielle had told him about her time there in the icy far north and focus instead on the papers in front of him.

"Yes," he said flatly. "The Northern Reach. When Corien died, so too did many of the angels there, but not all. Any angels who were not connected to him at the exact moment of his death have survived. Hundreds are still held captive below the mountains in elaborate prisons. Obritsa's army is stretched thin between rescue efforts and the escalating revolution in Genzhar."

He held his breath, then glanced at Rielle. She was lovely in her stillness. Back straight in her chair, chin slightly lifted, the delicate bones of her face carving sharp lines from brow to jaw. Her eyes were fixed on the immaculate shining table, but Audric knew it wasn't the table she saw.

"Before we approve anything," he said, "we will need schematics of the site, a sense of the geography of the Northern Reach. Surely, there are places hidden underground that the Kirvayans have missed, and we need anything that might give us an advantage. Is your memory complete enough to create a map, Rielle?"

Rielle laughed softly. "Of course," she whispered, her voice thick with secrets. "I remember everything."

Sloane shifted in her chair. Magister Florimond looked hard at her pen. Genoveve closed her eyes, her mouth thinning.

But Miren pretended nothing. She glared at Rielle, spots of bright color on her cheeks.

Audric swallowed against the turn of his stomach. For the first time, he felt glad for Ludivine's death. He could not have borne looking at her face and seeing the pity that came from knowing exactly what things Rielle remembered.

"Excellent." His voice sounded hollow to his own ears. He shuffled the papers, withdrew Ilmaire's official report and the letter folded within. "And Ilmaire has written as well. The Gate remains unchanged, but scores of dead fish and other water animals have washed up on shore along several stretches of the Northern Sea. He is concerned that the Gate may be emitting something toxic, perhaps unknown substances from the Deep, and that they are affecting our air and water in ways we have not yet examined."

He paused, gathering himself. When he looked at Rielle, he felt numb. "What does the empirium tell you? Does it offer an explanation for this?"

He struggled to keep a bland curiosity in his voice, and yet he wanted to fall to his knees at her feet and scream at her until that distant, inward look she wore shattered. Shake her until she was free of it.

Rielle absently tapped the table's edge. Her brow furrowed, and when she spoke, it was with a kind of irritated dismissal, as if she were concentrating on something very far away and Audric's question was nothing but a nuisance.

"Yes," she said quietly.

He waited for elaboration. None came. In the silence, his cheeks burned. Magister Guillory cleared her throat. What they must think of him, of Rielle, of all of this.

"What does it say, then?" Audric asked her. "Can you... I'm sorry, this may be a silly question. Can you purify the sea somehow? Prevent further devastation?"

Rielle sighed. The sound seemed to diminish her. How small she was, and how impossibly far away. She glanced at him, mustered up a smile. He hated it. She was trying to make him happy, trying to reassure him, and failing utterly.

"Of course I can," she murmured.

And then Miren could bear no more.

She scoffed, leaning forward. The explosive force of her anger set the brass buttons of Audric's coat blazing with heat.

"Is that all you will say?" Miren said, her voice rough with sadness, her eyes bright. "*Yes* and *of course*? You could say something else. You could look at us as if we're all actually here in front of you. Or you could apologize. You could look me in the eye and say you're sorry." Her voice broke, her jaw square as she fought off tears. "Are you even sorry for what you've done to all of us?"

Rielle stared at her, blinking, and she looked so strange in that chair, so ill-fitting, that Audric's throat clenched with fear. Rielle looked at Miren as if trying to understand an unfamiliar type of weed—not one she was interested in pulling, simply one she hadn't noticed until its thorns pricked her ankle.

He wished he could leave them all, march Rielle up to their bedroom and keep her there. Feed her and love her and rub her sore back until her face found its color again and she looked human once more.

"Miren, you will hold your tongue," Genoveve said tightly. "Rielle saved us, I'll remind you. She destroyed Corien and took many of his soldiers out with him."

"Not before thousands had died. Not before our city was in ruins. Homes destroyed and families shattered." Miren lay her palms flat on the table, her mouth twisting. She had not once said Tal's name, and yet Audric heard echo of it in every word.

"Say it, Rielle," Miren choked out. "Tell me you're sorry."

Rielle examined her hands, then looked calmly at Miren. "If I tell you, will you believe me?"

The room held its breath, the silence fat with nerves.

And then Miren sagged against her chair, her expression flattening. "No," she said at last. "I won't."

Rielle smiled a little, the saddest smile Audric had ever seen. "I don't blame you. But I am sorry, truly. I wish it could be undone. I wish Tal—"

Miren surged to her feet, her ax glowing at her hip. Every piece of metal in the room vibrated, ready to fly at her command.

"Don't say his name to me," Miren said harshly. "Not ever. He loved you more than anything, more than me, and that wasn't enough for you. Nothing we can give you is enough."

Then Miren pushed back from the table and stormed out. A moment later, Genoveve squeezed Audric's hand gently and rose to follow her.

"I suggest we retire for lunch," Audric said into the heavy silence, "and meet again in the afternoon. Three o'clock at this same table, please."

As the others quickly left the room, he gathered his papers. Rielle sat unmoving at his side. He could not bring himself to look at her. If he did, he would see the truth on her face, the thing he feared most of all—more than the angels still roaming the world, more than whatever lurked beyond the Gate and might someday emerge from it.

If he looked at her, he would see the truth: Miren was right.

Without meeting Rielle's eyes, Audric offered her his hand. Wordlessly, she took it, her fingers so light against his palm that it frightened him. As they returned upstairs to their rooms, he clung to the sound of her footsteps, relished each of her labored breaths. Her belly, huge and wonderful. She cursed it, quietly, carefully, as if trying out a joke, and his laughter felt fragile on his tongue.

Lunch awaited them—fresh bread and soft cheese, figs drizzled with honey, a salad of tomatoes and cucumbers. They ate in silence, and not once did Rielle let go of his hand. Her thumb rubbed his, over and over, leaving behind soft smears of gold.

◆◇◆

One night, Audric left Rielle sleeping fitfully in their bed and went up to the roof. The summer air was warm, and night birds called from the thick forests carpeting Mount Cibelline.

He walked the long breezeways of the fifth floor, each bordered with a railing of white stone. Leaning against one of them, he looked down at the scaffolding hugging the castle's western face. Two towers had collapsed during the battle. Great holes torn from the walls by careening elemental magic left Baingarde looking haggard and feeble.

He rubbed the bridge of his nose, willing away the tired burn behind his eyes. With sleep came dreams. He wanted none of it.

Movement shifted at the corner of his eye, smooth and gliding. He watched Atheria fly, smiling to see her nip bats from the air. The sight was welcome—and increasingly rare. When Rielle was awake, the godsbeast stayed far from Baingarde.

Yet more grief for Rielle to carry.

The air shifted beside him like the weight of something moving through cold water.

A chill prickled his skin. He was not yet used to the feeling of wraiths, nor did he entirely trust them, though they had given him no reason not to, other than the fact of what they were. Angels without bodies—angels who had refused resurrection.

Dozens now guarded the city, hundreds patrolled the mountains, and the one drifting near him now was his favorite. His shoulders eased a little when he recognized her—the tall gray reed of her body, eyes black and serene, long thin limbs. Dark hair streamed faintly to her waist, but near Rielle, an echo of her true self shone with power for all to see—gleaming white hair, rich brown skin, and shining platinum armor, as she had worn when she'd first entered the Deep.

"Zahra," Audric said warmly. "Is there something you need?"

The wraith inclined her head in greeting. Her voice was resonant, like the toll of heavy bells. "Nothing but company, my lord king. The night is quiet."

"I'm relieved to hear that." He looked at the vast dark sky. Sometimes he still saw the faint echo of wings burning there. Sometimes he felt their heat on his neck, and the memory made his mouth taste sick. He closed his eyes, holding himself steady.

Then Zahra huffed out a breath. Suddenly, the feeling of her was troubled. It was a helpful thing to have loved an angel. He could easily read the moods of wraiths, and now he had an army of them.

"I lied," Zahra said miserably. "In fact, I do need something. I need to give you an answer you've been seeking."

He turned to face her. Shifting and strange as it was, her dim profile held a quiet dignity that he found immensely reassuring. He had been meaning to tell her this.

"An answer to what question?" he asked.

"You're wondering why I fought against my own people, why I have pledged loyalty to you and your family. You've been wondering it since the night I knelt at your feet, and the answer we gave your councils has not satisfied you."

Stunned into silence, for a moment he could only stare at her. A rising anger helped him find his words. "You've been reading my thoughts. This was not part of our agreement."

Zahra turned, eyes wide. "No, my king. I have broken no part of our agreement. The treaty between us was well written, and all of us who put our names to it did so because we believe in the potential of this new friendship."

"Then how—"

"My lord king." Zahra's voice was fond, and he was reminded at once of her agelessness and his smallness in comparison. How she had lived for centuries before his birth and would drift through hundreds more after his death. "You are a man of exceptional strength, of both mind and heart. But your curiosity is swift and often defies your efforts to remain inscrutable. Your questions dart from you like birds. I cannot help but see them on your face, even the ones you decide not to ask."

He raised his eyebrows. A bold thing for her to say, but there was a strange relief in feeling so seen. "Tell me what you have to say, then."

She hesitated. "It is a long story. Perhaps I was wrong to approach you now. It is only that...oh, my lord king, it is such a wild tale. I have been waiting weeks to tell you." She shimmered, brimming and eager, fiddling with the ends of her hair. "We should retire to your study, perhaps, where you can sit comfortably."

"I am comfortable here. The fresh air is a balm. Tell me, Zahra. You said you have answers for me."

"Yes, my king. You wonder why we fought for you that night, why we betrayed our people to ally with their enemy. Part of the answer is simple, and we told your councils as much: We did not agree with Kalmaroth's mission of vengeance. Not every angel who lived in the Deep was a creature of violence and anger. Forgive me, my lord king, but it is unjust to look at the many millions of us and reduce us all to one feeling, one philosophy, one desire."

Abashed, Audric nodded. He opened his mouth to speak, but Zahra held up her hand.

"Please, if you'll allow it, I must tell it all at once. There is much to say, and you have meetings in the morning, my lord king. At some point, you will need sleep."

He gave her a wry smile. "I suspect I may not sleep much after you've told your tale."

"Perhaps not. I called it wild. An inadequate word for this story, but I cannot think of another." She paused, drawing in a breath. A sad, strange habit of wraiths, she had taught him—they did not have lungs, but they did still feel the instinct to breathe. "You'll remember," she said, "the girl Eliana. Your daughter, my king."

The beloved word struck him. He had not expected this. "Of that night I remember many things, but her most of all."

"We fought in the city that night before we came to you. We shielded your people from angels. We cloaked them from the beasts that hunted them."

He did know this and started to thank her, as he had many times before, but she hurried on before he could.

"As we fought, I sensed her," said Zahra. "Eliana. She was different from everyone living in the world, everyone but the boy at her side. The two of them were from another time. I knew it at once. All of us did, and it was this that brought us hurrying to you and that brought the angels storming through the castle to fight you. We all ached to touch her mind, to understand her strangeness, but I ordered the others to shield her and your friends, and while they dove to protect them, it was I alone who read her thoughts. My king..."

She knelt, overcome. Shadows pooled around her, as if she knelt in shallow dark water.

"I saw everything she had seen," she whispered. "I saw the world in which she had lived. I saw the Undying Empire and all it had done. I saw the people she loved and those who had hurt her. I saw *myself* through her eyes. In that time yet to come, in which your daughter had lived and fought, I was her friend. I loved her, and she loved me."

Slowly, Audric sank to sit beside her. The soft night winds kissed his hands. Overhead, Atheria dove for her supper, chirping gaily.

"I felt everything in that moment my mind touched hers," Zahra said thickly. "I saw all that she had endured and what would happen to the world if she failed. I died for her in that future world. I died in her arms, and she wept over the place where I had been. My lord king, this is what I saw. This is why I fought for her, and for you, her father, and why I always will. I died for her, and I would again."

Zahra reached for his hands. Her dark fingers passed through his like smoke. The cold, supple press of her nearness made him shiver. Tenderly, she touched his cheek. Presumptuous, and yet he sensed nothing would ever be typical between them, not for as long as he lived.

"May I tell you the rest?" she asked. "May I tell you the story of your daughter?"

Tears in his eyes, completely undone, Audric nodded, and then he listened through the night as Zahra spoke of a future that would never be.

◆

It was as if she had heard him, his daughter.

The next day, Sloane came bursting into his study, her eyes shining. Her excitement summoned the room's shadows. They rose trembling from their corners and stretched across the bright windows.

He knew it before Sloane drew breath to speak. A light broke open inside him, warming all the tired bones of his body. A single word rose, blooming through his thoughts:

Eliana. Eliana. Eliana.

For of course, that would be her name.

"I've sent for Garver," Sloane said. She was sparkling at the door, her wide smile a welcome sight. The days had been hard, but this joy was easy and desperately needed. "Your mother is with her, and the nurses. The pain hasn't come for her yet, but she insists it will happen very soon. She's asking for you. She's nervous, but I'm not sure I've ever seen her this happy."

She waited for him to stand, but he couldn't. His knees would surely give out if he tried.

Sloane was merciful. "Come upstairs," she said gently, helping him rise from his chair. "It's time."

– 48 –

RIELLE

"To the skies you were born, to the skies you return
Back to the high places, the far moon, the cold burn
But why did the great song call you so soon, child of the stars?
And why oh why did you listen?"

—Traditional angelic lament

It was dawn in the burnished glory of autumn, and Rielle could no longer hold her tongue. Today was the day. She would tell him as soon as he awoke.

Eliana, full and happy, had fallen asleep on her chest. It was five months since she had come into the world, eerily quiet, staring at everything with those huge brown eyes, and Rielle had still not grown used to how beautiful she was. Her smooth skin, a pale brown like the cheek of a fawn; her soft head, impossibly small; the silken dark hair swirling atop it. The warm weight of her, how perfectly she fit in Rielle's arms. The gentle burbling noises she made while waving her tiny wrinkled feet, hands clenched as if ready to punch.

Rielle kissed Eliana's head and laid her carefully in her cradle. As morning sunlight crept across the room, she watched her daughter sleep. Sometimes her mouth moved, suckling nothing. Sometimes her eyelids fluttered—a dream—and Rielle laughed, in awe of this little person sleeping below her, this person she had carried through month after awful, glorious month.

She hadn't known what to expect when Garver had laid the child in her arms. Nearly twenty hours of excruciating labor, pain so unthinkable that it had drawn her deep into its heart, where everything felt gold and hot, and she glided down a molten fall. And then, at the end of it, a child. Audric holding her hand, laughing through his tears, and this creature, this tiny girl, staring up at her. Squashed and tiny and utterly perfect, her eyes wide and dark, as if already thinking of questions to ask.

It would have been easier had Rielle felt nothing in that moment. She could have feigned love easily enough. Without Ludivine to out her, she could have fooled everyone. The wraiths avoided her, except for Zahra, who was infuriatingly reverent. Never mind that she was capable of killing angels. The mother of Eliana was to be protected and loved without question.

But one look at Eliana's face, and Rielle had been done for. Relinquishing her to Audric in exchange for sleep felt unreasonably devastating. She could spend the afternoon kissing Eliana's fingers and forget to eat entirely. She could watch her for hours and never grow tired of staring.

Love left her dizzy, reeling, giddy. She woke in the middle of the night to comfort Eliana, propped her legs up on a settee and laid Eliana on her thighs. Crooned at her, bounced her gently. Audric would wake later and greet Rielle with a kiss on her brow. He had stopped commenting on her fevered state, for which she was grateful. He would shift Eliana to his shoulder and walk slowly through their rooms. If the night was warm enough, he would open the windows, let the breeze in to cool Rielle's overheated skin. She would watch him from their bed, quietly burning, eyes heavy, and as he sang nonsense songs to their daughter by the light of the moon, she would fall asleep to the sound of his voice.

All of this, this love sitting hot as tears in her throat, and yet, when Rielle returned to bed on that autumn morning, she felt the same restless, weary disquiet that she had felt in the hours before Eliana's birth, and in the days before that, in every long week that had passed since destroying Corien and Ludivine on the terrace.

As she settled against the pillows, it happened again, just as it had only an hour earlier. Each time it came for her, less time had passed since the one before. Audric slept peacefully, sprawled on his back as always, mouth half-open, curls mussed. Rielle turned away from him, pressed her mouth against her shoulder.

A pulsing heat bloomed at her every joint, as if something buried deep in her marrow were pushing her apart. Her power illuminated her every vein; she closed her eyes and saw the blinding crystalline tree that was her body and all its paths of blood. The pain was deafening. When it came, she could hear nothing else. She closed her eyes, clenched her teeth, holding her breath until the feeling passed. She held it for so long that her vision began to spot, but she couldn't let go until it was safe. Never before in her life had she been able to hold quite so still.

When she opened her eyes, gasping quietly for air, Audric was watching her. He reached for her, and she found the strength to push herself away from him. A pressure remained in her fingertips, at her temples, tight and hot, tenuous. If he touched her, she would burst.

"What can I do?" He was sitting up now, fully awake. "Should I send for food? Water? Shall we walk in the gardens? The evening is cool. It might bring you some relief."

Rielle looked at him, blinking the spots from her eyes. How long had she been sitting there, finding her air again? It could have been hours. Her body ached as if freshly bruised, but when she looked at her bare arms, she saw only gold. It crashed against her bones, burrowed into her fingernails.

It wanted out.

"Nothing. You can do nothing, Audric. There is no relief for me, and I think you know that." And then she risked gathering his hands in hers, because she could not live another second without telling him what must be done. She kissed his wrists, breathed out slowly against his knuckles. "I have to leave, my darling. I cannot stay here."

He laughed a little, his brow furrowing, as if she'd told a bizarre joke. "What do you mean, leave? To go where?"

She closed her eyes. "You're not stupid. Please don't pretend to be. Every word I speak costs me. I have to leave. I cannot..."

She paused, swallowing hard, as if trying not to be sick. But it wasn't sickness ripping through her. It was hunger, it was *need*, it was every unseen scar etched into her bones raising its voice in anguish, it was the little golden threads in her blood winding up like coils, ready to snap.

I rise

The empirium's voice, wordless and strange, was gentle. There was no kindness there, no regret, but there was something like acknowledgment. This would be difficult, it seemed to tell her. And yet that was no reason to spare her.

we rise

"I know," she whispered, her voice ragged. "Give me a little more time. I need just a little more."

"What is it saying?" Audric took her face in his hands, his eyes bright. "Tell me. Let me speak to it."

"It hears everything you say, Audric, and it doesn't care. It's not a person or a being. It is everything that lives. It's you, and me, and all of us."

"I'll make it care."

"Don't be ridiculous."

"I'll give it anything. I'll give it myself. *Anything.*" His voice wrapped tight around stifled tears. "There has to be something. An exchange to be made."

Rielle touched his cheek. "Listen to yourself. As if the empirium is a thing that bargains. You're not facing down an enemy, Audric. This is not a negotiation. It's trying to help me. I've grown beyond this body. I'm in pain, and it's offering relief. I have only to let go of the rope and drop."

"Please," he whispered over and over. Eyes closed, mouth tight against her palm. "Please, don't, not this."

The longer she looked at him, the less strength she had to stay solid, to sit earthbound on the bed.

"I've told you what the past months did to me," she whispered, dry-eyed, and yet she could barely speak, her chest in knots. "Something has awakened in me, and I cannot put it to rest. I pushed my power beyond its limits, and now it races on, dragging me behind it. You have to let me go."

"No, I don't. I *can't*. That's not the only way, Rielle."

"It is. Look at me. I don't belong here anymore. Maybe I never did. We used to have that conversation all the time. None of this should surprise you."

"Yes, we had that conversation, and every time, I told you that of course you belong here. This is your home, your family. I still think that, even after everything that's happened. Your power is not all of you. It is only part."

She smiled fondly at him. "Even if I had no power at all, you would love me just as you do now."

"I would. I *would*." He looked away, glaring fiercely at the bed. "We'll find healers—we'll scour the world for them. Scholars of the empirium, the finest surgeons in Mazabat."

"Audric—"

"And the wraiths—their angelic minds are spectacular. They'll help us engineer something to help you, something to quell the pain and calm your power—"

"Audric, *look at me*."

Little shakes of his head, disbelieving. He would not accept it, and he would not look at her. He dragged a hand through his hair, made a sound like choking.

"Please don't do this," he said hoarsely. He pressed his forehead against hers. "Don't leave us."

"I can barely hold myself together," she said, stroking his hair. "I fight it every day, this turning inside me. Someday, I will lose my grip, and then what will happen to all of you? Can't you see the danger?" How dear it was, the soft slide of his curls through her fingers. Each caress of her fingers gilded the dark strands gold.

"You're stronger than you know."

"And yet, what kind of life is it to fight constantly against yourself?"

"I'll help you," he whispered, eyes closed tightly.

"You *have* helped me. You welcomed me back into your life. You defend my goodness and honor every time you enter a temple and some-one shouts in your face, denouncing me. You gave me Eliana."

"And you would leave her anyway? You would let her grow up without knowing you?"

A stab to her heart. She ripped herself away from him. "Do you think I haven't thought of all this a hundred times over?"

He lowered his gaze, wiped his face. At last, heat rose behind her eyes. She had told herself she would not cry, but he looked so ashamed, slumped on their bed. Bare-chested, tears dropping onto his hands.

"I know you've thought of it," he whispered. "I've watched all of this turn in your eyes. I've told myself it was just my imagination. Every morning, I wake thinking this will be the day you tell me what you've just said."

"And every day I live is another day of pain I can hardly bear. Another day in which you and Eliana and everyone we have fought so hard to save are in danger. Look at me."

She lifted his chin, saw the bright shine of his eyes. She pressed a hard kiss to his mouth.

"I must go," she told him, each word a struggle. "You know this. You've seen me suffering."

His face was a tapestry of despair. "I have."

"You've seen the changes in me. The lights beneath my skin, how I burn hotter than fever."

"You cry in your sleep some nights," he said, touching her cheek with the backs of his fingers. "Some days, you're far from me, from all of us. I wonder where you've gone."

"And yet you would ask me to stay?"

Helplessly, he shook his head. "I hate myself for it."

She heard it in his voice, the loathing and the guilt. Their bedroom, soft with morning, glinted with her tears. She kissed his beautiful hands, each rough with new scars. She wished she had been there to see Atheria carry him into the hurricane. From the shore, Sloane had told her, he had dazzled. An orb of light, racing unafraid into darkness.

"You are not deserving of hate," she whispered. "Eliana will learn from you how to love herself. Be kind to your own heart, if only for her sake."

"Rielle," he said, the word splintering against her skin, "I don't know how to live in a world without you in it."

"You will learn."

"But the Gate," he said desperately. "Who will close it, if you leave?"

"I wouldn't leave that for you to face alone, Audric, I—"

She shut her eyes, turning slightly away. The pain was rising once more, sharp-toothed and churning. Gold bit at the insides of her eyes, and a great force pulled at her palms, the soles of her feet, the top of her skull, the small of her back. Fists sank into her muscles and twisted, grinding bone against bone. Soon she would fly apart, and what a relief it would be. She thought of the endless black sea, the rushing sky bright with stars, the little girl holding out her hand.

Come with me, the girl had said. *We are rising, you and I. There is so much for us to do.*

"Stay with me." Tenderly, Audric gathered her hands in his. His palms were clammy, his voice trembling with worry. "I'm right here, Rielle. Listen to my voice. Please, God, stay with me. Please, my darling."

Sweat rolled down her back, pooled under her breasts. If she dove into frozen water, she would melt every iceberg. If she stepped off the bed, if her toes touched the floor, she would fall forever.

"I'm here," she whispered faintly, once she could speak, and he held her, hardly breathing, until this latest burst of agony had faded—the bed linens soaked, her skin blazing like polished copper, tears streaming like rivers down her cheeks. She turned into Audric's body, hid her face in the curve of his neck. Slowly, carefully, he stroked her damp hair, as if she were a bird blown from glass or a beast he dared not provoke.

"I love you, Rielle," he whispered, trembling. "I have loved you always, and I will never stop."

I wish you would, she wanted to tell him. *It would be easier for you, to stop loving me.* But there was no need to stab a dying man, and his voice was already calming her, coaxing her into a woozy lull—her name on his lips, his voice torn to shreds. She fell into a shallow red sleep.

◆◇◆

Rielle waited long enough that Audric began to suspect she had changed her mind. Every morning, he woke to find her still beside him, and hope broke open across his face, lit his eyes warm and soft. He began to sleep more soundly, no longer waking every time she shifted.

Then a chill night came. A sharp wind thumped its fingers against the windows. Clouds black against the stars, the moon new and dark.

Rielle awoke from sleep that hardly deserved the word. Waves of scorching light pulsed behind her eyes. Each dull boom chipped away another piece of her skull.

She held her breath, listening. Eliana slept in her cradle, fist at her mouth, little breaths coming steadily. When Rielle climbed out of bed, Audric did not wake. Shadows darkened the soft skin beneath his eyes. He would deny it, but now she was only a source of grief and endless worry for him.

She hurried quietly across the room in her bare feet. At the door, she had to stop for a moment, put her hand over her mouth until the sob building in her throat subsided. How desperately she wanted to kiss him once more, bow her head over Eliana's tiny warm body and press her face to her daughter's round cheeks.

But she could not risk waking them. She stepped into the hallway, closed the door behind her. Never had a sound held such terror and such bone-shattering relief. Knees shaking, she leaned hard against the door, held up a hand to silence Evyline before the woman could speak.

"Send the others away," Rielle muttered, staring at the floor. She found it hard to look at Evyline, who had asked Rielle many times for permission to replace Maylis and Fara. But Rielle would not allow it. She wanted to look at the two empty places in her old guard. She wanted to feel the remorse it brought, let it sit prickly in her gut.

Evyline obeyed her at once. Soon they were alone.

"What is it, my queen?" Evyline placed her broad hand on Rielle's back. "Is it an angel?"

Unthinkable, that Evyline could have forgiven her, and yet when Rielle finally found the courage to look at her, she saw only love in the older woman's tired eyes.

"I'm leaving," Rielle whispered. "I need you to help me reach the mountains. I cannot be in the city when it happens."

Evyline's eyes widened. Rielle watched her swallow her protests, the dimming of her face as she accepted this command.

"Very well, my queen." Evyline offered her arm, and Rielle took it gratefully. "Where shall we go?"

"Mount Taléa. The foothills, near the pass." Rielle squeezed her eyes shut. Power rippled at her fingertips, pushing hard at the beds of her nails. The ends of her hair sparked white.

Evyline's face was tight with worry as they hurried down the hallway. "Will we have time to get there? My queen, forgive me, but your face...it is full of light. Stars beneath your cheekbones."

"I know." At the stairwell, they stopped. Rielle leaned against the wall. Her mind first went to Ludivine, a horrible mistake that left her breathless with sorrow. She pushed past Ludivine's memory, and Corien's just behind it, and instead formed a picture of a different angel in her mind.

Zahra? Please, hurry.

A moment later, the wraith emerged from the nearby wall, her hair streaming behind her in white currents. Evyline flinched in surprise, spat a curse.

Zahra knelt at once. "What can I do, my queen?"

"Two things," Rielle said tightly. "I need you to guard us as we walk through the city. No one can see us. Keep them far away from me."

"Yes, my queen."

"And I need you to ensure that Audric doesn't wake, not until I'm far enough away from Baingarde that even if he ran full tilt, even if he raced for me on Atheria, he could not stop me." She gritted her teeth, blinked the bright spots from her eyes. "You understand why I am doing this."

Zahra's face held a grave sadness. "Of course, my queen."

"And you can do both of these things at once? I trust no one else, Zahra. I need you and you alone."

"I can, and I will." A ripple of power shifted across Zahra's face, as if the current of her mind had changed course. Her voice lowered. "The king will not wake until you reach the Flats, my queen."

"Good." Drawing thin breaths, Rielle looked down the dark tunnel of the stairs. Each step seemed a mountain. Needles of light pushed their way into her muscles. When she moved, pain scraped her insides, as if every bone had grown sharp black bristles.

"I have much to tell you as we walk," she said, and stumbled toward the stairs before Evyline could catch her. "Listen carefully, for what I do tonight will touch everyone who lives."

She had to stop speaking, then, until they had descended the endless stairs and left the castle behind. Evyline took her to a door near the kitchens, and they emerged into the gardens. Rielle glanced only once toward the dark seeing pools, and when she searched the gloom, the empirium showed her a faint memory, etched in gold—herself running fast across the slippery stones, Ludivine following steadily behind, Audric watching nervously from the grass.

She wept then, even as her blood roared for her to walk faster. She was almost there; she was nearing the end. Soon, she would feel no pain, and there would be no reason to cling to what was left of her fraying body. Her jaw ached so brutally that it was difficult to speak. Some nights, she had thought she would awaken to find she had ground her teeth to dust in her sleep.

Only once they were in the city did she retrieve her voice.

"Tonight I will die," she said, "and when I do, I will send the empirium here in Avitas into something like sleep. It will lie dormant for years.

People will be frightened when they wake and find their power has been silenced. I'm sorry for that, but it must be done."

"Why?" Evyline whispered, the word thin with horror.

"To close the Gate," Zahra said quietly. "And to stop more war before it begins."

Evyline stared. "More war? But we have fought a war, and we have won it."

"But revolution blazes in Kirvaya between those with elemental magic and those without, and if left unchecked, it will spread." Zahra's words came swift and soft. "Marques will hear of the Eliana who traveled to us from the future, and they will experiment with corners of magic they ought not to touch. The princess will be in danger. Many angels still live, and their grief for Kalmaroth is vicious. They will come for you again and again. They will find a way to call others from the Deep, unless the Gate is sealed."

Evyline paled. "I see."

Rielle forced her eyes open even as the blinding world urged them closed. Each building they passed burned with a thousand white fires. Her every step sent waves of power rippling across the ground.

"No new angels will be able to possess human bodies," she managed, struggling to form words—teeth against tongue, tongue against throat. "Those without bodies will remain so, and any survivors I resurrected will find the power of their minds diminished. Elemental castings will go dark. Marques…" She hesitated, thinking of little Simon. How sober and quiet he had been, standing at the ready while his father brought Eliana into the world. "Marques will no longer be able to thread. I will leave only three things untouched: the godsbeasts, the wraiths loyal to the crown, and Eliana."

It was painful to say Eliana's name, as if each syllable were a bludgeon to her ribs. Her heart lurched back toward Baingarde, toward the quiet rooms that held the two surviving pieces of her heart.

"The princess will retain all her power?" Evyline asked.

Rielle nodded. "Someday, the empirium will return. Something will happen to awaken it. Another conflict, perhaps a new enemy. I can see glimmers of this, but the empirium has shown me nothing more. The Gate is a doorway to the Deep, and the Deep is a doorway to every world there is. Something will come. And when this happens and the empirium returns, the world will look to Eliana for guidance."

Her tears crested savagely. "I wish I did not have to ask this of her. I wish I were not leaving Audric to face a world grieving the loss of its magic. But I know no other way of protecting them in the coming hard years, and soon I will no longer be here to do it myself."

"And what of the temples, my queen?" Evyline asked thickly. "What will we worship, if magic is gone?"

"Nothing will stop you from praying to sun and shadows. And if the old prayers become ill-fitting, you will write new ones."

Fresh agony sent her crashing to the ground. Cracks raced across the cobbled road, splintering hundreds of precisely cut stones. She trembled, gasping, and when she looked up, she saw not a road, not a city, but a vast shallow sea. At its horizon, a girl in white.

Evyline tried to help her rise but could only manage to bring her to her knees. The earth pulled at Rielle's neck, its tendrils stubborn and hungry. Fighting it was like fighting the hard press of the ocean. If she was to reach the mountains in time, they would need help. Another body to help her stand and walk, someone she could trust.

Zahra's voice came to her, distant and faint. "My queen, we are near the house of Garver Randell."

"Bring him to me," she croaked, and every word tasted of lightning. "Tell him to hurry."

He came at once, stood quietly for a moment, then knelt at her side. Rielle squinted at him through a white wall of pain. His lined face, his bright sharp eyes.

"You do seem to insist upon the theatrical," he observed wryly, and with Evyline's help, both of them straining, he managed to lift Rielle back to her feet. She felt the gentle press of a worn hand against her forehead.

"Wherever you go, child," he said softly, "I hope you find peace there."

Peace. She laughed, baffled at the thought. Would she be allowed such a thing, even in death?

not death

The empirium scolded her, a bewildered correction. Why would she think anything was as simple as a single human death?

Then what? she asked, gasping for air.

It replied with a feeling, the thin bones of a single word: *more*

They reached the great wall standing battered and charred around the city. Zahra hid them from the guards as they hurried through the freshly built gate. Once, Âme de la Terre had not needed such a wall. Once, none of them had thought any of this could happen, no matter the prayers they muttered by their beds.

And then they were across the lake bridge and in the Flats, stumbling across the ruined ground. Furrows from beastly claws, craters still steaming from elemental magic. The temple acolytes hadn't yet made the necessary repairs to the battlefield, focusing instead on retrieving bodies, cleaning the city, offering counsel to the bereaved. And now, whenever the people of Âme de la Terre looked out their windows, they would see the remnants of war. They would think of the Blood Queen and how she stole their magic from them. Some of them would be grateful for it, find comfort in the new quiet of the air. Some would be wild with grief, but without magic to aid their fury, and with the castle guarded by an army of wraiths, Audric and Eliana would be safe, at least for a few years.

Thunder rolled across the Flats, drawn by the stumbling fall of Rielle's feet. As they neared the pass, the air crackled gold. Evyline looked up, her expression caught between awe and fear.

"Zahra, you may allow Audric to wake now," Rielle choked out, her bare feet slapping through the cold mud. "Go to him. Tell him everything I have said, once he is ready to hear it."

Zahra said nothing, but a cold stream of air kissed the back of Rielle's neck, and then the wraith was gone.

"Tell me what you see, Evyline," Rielle breathed.

"I see golden light streaming across the sky," Evyline replied. "Instead of jagged bolts, like lightning, it is petals, vast and pulsing. They meet, they break apart, they meet again."

"And I see Audric," said Rielle, her voice catching on each word. The empirium was a canvas vast and unending, shapes swirling from ground to sky. She read everything written upon it. "He has awoken. He is running through our rooms, looking for me. He's calling my name over and over. Eliana…" She burst into tears. In her life, she had loved fiercely, but never so perfectly as this. "Eliana is awake and crying. Audric is… He's calling for the guards. He's holding Eliana against his chest, shouting my name again. She's screaming in his ear, and he's going out onto the terrace. He sees my light. He knows what I've done."

"Please don't, child," said Garver. "Don't look. It will only hurt you to watch them."

Rielle fell to her knees into a soft rise of mud. Above her towered trees golden with the last flush of autumn, and above them, the pine-dark foothills of Mount Taléa.

"Get back," she cried out, pushing at Garver's chest. She grabbed Evyline's hand, squeezed once, then shoved her away as well. She waited until they had shrunk back into the trees, both of them standing on a ridge piled high with rocks. Below them in the mud, she shook on her hands and knees. Gulping airlessly, swallowing against the storm rising within her. It was time, and yet she knew not where to begin.

breathe

let go

Rielle stared at her hands in the mud. Pale and small, surrounded by shadows.

we rise

The girl crouched before her—her child self, bright-eyed and smiling. Barefoot, white gown fluttering at her ankles, skinny wrists and wild dark hair.

"Come with me now," the girl said, entirely kind, her voice tender. "There is so much more for us to do."

The world glittered with diamonds. Blistering pain knocked at Rielle's temples, but when she reached for the girl's hand, some of the terrified knots in her shoulders unwound, and at the edges of her vision, roses of shimmering gold light blossomed by the millions. Light burst from her in a thousand brilliant streams, and in the last moments before it consumed her, she saw too many things to name. But some things she saw, and knew, and held close.

She saw the shattered city that had been her home, its seven temples alight with candles of mourning, the lake glittering like a smile around its wall.

In the Sunderlands, the Gate's light groaned and spun, spiraling into itself, a cyclone of violet and gold, until there was nothing left of the door that had once been. Only two great gray stones, the air between them entirely ordinary and shivering with sea winds.

In the high, cold mountains of Borsvall, King Ilmaire slept beside his new husband, Leevi of the Kammerat, the dragon-speaker. The capital of Styrdalleen was once more the winged city it had been in the First Age, for dragons large and small perched on every tower, great wings folded, tirelessly watching the night for enemies. At a wall of white stone overlooking the shore stood Ingrid Lysleva, commander of the army and the king's beloved sister. She looked with narrowed eyes across the Northern Sea toward the distant island of the Gate, where strangely lit clouds turned slowly, like no storm she had ever seen.

In the burnished city of Genzhar, in a palace of scarlet and gold, the young queen, Obritsa, looked coldly upon the traitorous magisters who had sold her city's children to Corien in exchange for places of honor in the new angelic world. The executioner lifted his sword, but at the last moment, Obritsa stopped him, sparing the magisters' lives. She knelt before them as they wept on her hands, and then, smiling a hard smile, told them something Rielle could not hear.

In the city of Quelbani, the pearl of its country, its shattered streets painted pale by the moon, the princess Kamayin Asdalla read by the light of candles in her mothers' room. Behind her, they slept in their broad white bed, their faces soft, their hands entwined. Kamayin looked up from her novel, bare feet on the window sill, and absently tapped her toes. She left her book on her lap and turned to the table beside her, added several notes to the paper at her elbow. At the top of the page was a question, circled twice: *How do we move forward from here?*

And on a small terrace outside the finest suite of rooms in Baingarde, the king of Celdaria cradled his daughter against his chest, watching the horizon bloom bright with farewell.

A BEGINNING
AND AN END

"My darling daughter, my little one. You may not understand what I have done for a long time. You may be angry with me, you may hate me, you may grow up and be indifferent to me. But whatever you feel, know that I have loved you desperately, and that's why I had to leave you. You will have a life now, and though the world has changed, it will be safe for a time. You will be frightened, some days. You're allowed to be frightened. But you are stronger than any flame that burns. Watch over your father. Hold him close to your heart. Cherish your friends. Love yourself and the power I have given to you. Watch the skies and feel the sun on your skin. Swim the rivers and play games in the shadows. In every moment, in every blade of grass, in every path untraveled—there I will be, beside you, and there I will always be. My Eliana. My brave girl. There you are, beginning."

—Letter from Rielle Courverie,
late queen of Celdaria, to her daughter,
Eliana Courverie, princess of Celdaria
and heir to the throne of Katell,
dated November 11, Year 1000 of the Second Age

FIVE YEARS LATER

Eliana sat on her favorite stool in her favorite corner of her favorite place in all the world—except for her bedroom, and her father's bedroom, and her grandmother's sitting room with the godsbeasts painted on the ceiling, and the quiet, cool catacombs, where the pretty statue of her mother marked an empty tomb.

Besides all of those places, Garver's shop was her favorite. She liked the way it smelled of plants and tonics, a sour but clean sort of smell that woke up her nose, and she liked the herbs in their neat little glass jars, the tonics and ointments labeled in Garver's precise letters. She liked the tidy worktables and how Garver had sanded them smooth, how the air grew steamy when they were brewing new mixtures to be bottled and put away.

There was the cheerful garden of flowers and herbs outside the windows, and now, in early summer, it was bursting with color. Sometimes Atheria's shadow would pass across the window as she flew about, searching the skies for lunch. There was the bright silver bell hanging at the door, and there was the broom Garver kept in the corner, and the kettle of tea warming over the fire.

But out of everything in the shop, as wonderful as it all was, Eliana liked Simon best of all.

She snuck a look at him while he worked. He had a very solemn face for a thirteen-year-old boy, everyone said. *Rather severe*, Eliana had heard. But she liked his face and its seriousness. His pale brow furrowed when he read lists of ingredients, and his hair was a dark golden color, falling messily over his forehead. He had deft fingers that chopped up roots and herbs so quickly and carefully that a feeling of warmth came over Eliana as she watched him. The feeling told her that she was safe. When she was with him and his sharp little knives, nothing could hurt her.

"Can I try?" she asked, scooting forward on her stool.

He glanced at her. "No."

"Why?"

"Because the knives are sharp. Do you want to cut off your fingers?"

"No."

"Well, then."

"But *someday* I can use the good knives?"

He smiled a little, finished chopping his pile of yarrow leaves, then scooped them into his palm and dropped them into the crushing bowl.

"Maybe," he replied. "For now, you'll use the bad knives."

He raised his eyebrows, looking at the knives next to her. They were kept dull for her use and therefore were not good for cutting, which meant that when she used them, she was slow and stupid-looking, and she hated looking stupid in front of Simon.

"They're not bad knives," Garver said from his own table. "They're knives for learning."

Eliana made a face at the knives, and then Simon laughed under his breath and bumped her with his elbow. This sequence of events cheered her considerably, so much so that she chopped up her own pile of leaves faster than she ever had before, then shot Simon a look of haughty triumph.

And that made him laugh aloud, his big laugh that he hardly ever used. She beamed at him, watching him smile. It was a rare thing to see him so happy. Often, while they waited for roots to boil or while they hung leaves to dry, Eliana caught Simon looking out the windows with a terrible sadness on his face.

It happened most often when the winds were high, carrying the scent of pine down from the mountains. Simon was quiet on those days, strange and serious, and not serious in the way she liked. On those days, he hardly talked at all. There were shadows on his face, and his eyes were sharp and angry, or else flat and full of sorrow. When this happened, he hardly looked at her.

Once, he had even snapped at her. "Is it possible that you could stop talking to me for once in your life, for even a few minutes?" he had shouted, and then his face had crumpled in horror, for she had immediately burst into tears. Garver had sent him upstairs to his room, not even letting him try to apologize, and then had sat quietly with her until Zahra came to bring her home.

Later, tearful and sniffling on her father's lap, Eliana had asked him why Simon had done this. Why he grew so sad some days, so cruel and short.

And her father—her dear, gentle father, who always had the answers to her questions—held her for a long time, cozy on his lap beneath their favorite blanket. She thought maybe he had fallen asleep.

Then he said softly against her hair, "My darling, you may not understand all of this just now, but I'll tell you anyway, because that's what we do, isn't it? We talk to each other. We tell the truth."

"Yes, Papa," she said, staring up at him. She had heard her father sound sad and serious many times, especially when they visited her mother's tomb, but this was different. This voice held secrets.

"Simon, I think, grieves the loss of his power. You remember what I told you about what your mother did when she died?"

Eliana had seen paintings of her and had heard her father describe her many times. When she imagined her mother—her green eyes, power painting her hair and arms with gold—Eliana sometimes had to hold her breath, because it felt as if she could turn around and see her mother standing there. As if Eliana's mind could bring her back from the empirium, wherever it had taken her.

"She helped the empirium go to sleep," she told her father, her voice falling to a whisper, as it always did when she spoke of her mother. She thought carefully through each word, because her father had taught her how important that was. The magic in their world was gone, he said, but some still remained in the words they spoke, and that power must be respected. She held the necklace her father had given her—a disc of gold on a slender chain, engraved with the image of her mother riding Atheria. Holding it always made her feel a little stronger.

"Someday the empirium will wake up again," Eliana said to her father, "but right now it's asleep, and only I..."

She stopped speaking, her cheeks warming as she stared at the floor. When she wasn't praying at the temples with Miren and Sloane, or reading books about the empirium with her father, Eliana often forgot about the power inside her body. Her power was why she could see Zahra and the other wraiths, while everyone else could not. Her power was why her father sent her to Garver's shop for lessons, and why her father and Miren and Sloane and Zahra taught her so many things that sometimes she felt like her head had grown three times larger than it should be. They wanted her to learn everything there was to know about this magic that lived in her blood, and to not be afraid of it, and to know many other things too, like healing and music and mathematics, so that her power was not the only thing she loved.

Sometimes, when Eliana remembered that she wasn't like anyone else in the world, it made her feel lonely, like a bird perched high in a tree, too high for the other birds to reach.

Her father kissed her head. "Only you can still touch the empirium. That's right, Eliana. And it isn't a bad thing. You shouldn't be ashamed of it. Your mother left your power intact for a reason. Maybe she thought something frightening would happen someday. Maybe she loved you so much that she wanted you to keep this piece of her inside you."

Eliana shivered. What frightening thing might happen someday, and what could she do to stop it?

"This is why Simon sometimes feels sad, I think," her father said. "Why sometimes he even seems angry with you. You have power still, and he does not. His gift was taken from him, as was mine, as was everyone's—for good reason, I have to believe it was for a good reason—but they are gone nonetheless. I think seeing you sometimes reminds Simon of what he has lost."

Hearing this, Eliana's eyes filled with tears. "Should I not be his friend anymore? I don't want to make him sad, Papa."

"No, darling, that's not what I meant. In fact, I think it would make him saddest of all if you stopped being his friend. There may simply be days when he is not himself, and you will need to be patient with him. Maybe you'll even feel that you should not talk to him at all at those times, and that's perfectly all right. You can work together in silence, or read one of Garver's books and leave Simon alone at his table. Do you think you can do that?"

But today was not one of those days. It was a day of light and cheer in Garver's shop, and Eliana stared and stared at Simon as he laughed— laughed because of a thing that *she* had done! Her chest hurt a little, watching him. It was a sweet, quiet hurt, and she didn't mind it. The feeling reminded her of being home in her safe, warm bedroom, watching her father's face as he told a story about her mother.

The silver bell rang at the door, and Eliana whirled to see that Zahra had come to bring her home—but she was not alone. Her father had come with her, all the way down from the castle! Even though he had told Eliana he would most likely have to sit in boring meetings for the entire afternoon, there he was with his broad smile and his dark eyes like hers, holding out his arms to catch her.

Eliana nearly tumbled off the stool in her haste to run to him. She shrieked his name in greeting as she jumped at his chest, and he caught her and swung her high and kissed her hair. And there was his voice, so dear and warm, asking her if she would like to eat lunch with him at Odo's today, and maybe sit on Odo's terrace with the ferns and the flowers, and Odo himself would join them, which meant *stories*. Strange, wild stories brought to him by all the people who worked for him, the wraiths who spied for him, the merchants who sold to him.

Eliana felt dizzy. An entire afternoon sitting at her father's feet while Odo spun stories for them!

She kissed his cheek, which was scratchy from his old burns and because he really needed to shave. She wrinkled her nose and told him so, and he laughed, and tall, wonderful Zahra swooped down to touch her forehead—a cold brush of air like the beginning of winter, when the air smelled of snow.

Eliana turned in her father's arms. "Are we finished, Garver? Can I go?"

Garver's mouth twitched. "No, child, I forbid you to go with your father, the king. Instead, you must stay here for the rest of the day and sweep the dust from my floors."

She gaped at him, a feeling of absolute horror crawling up her arms, and then Garver, chuckling, returned to his work.

"Good day to you, my king, and thank you," he said with a little bow and a wave. "As always, your daughter was very helpful today."

Eliana blew out a sharp breath. She looked at her father, indignant. "You mean he was joking?" She looked back at Garver, even more indignant. "You were *joking*?"

They left the shop, Garver's laughter in their ears and Simon at their heels. He was quiet at her father's side and held open the garden gate for them.

"You'll bring her back next week, won't you?" Simon said hopefully as they started walking up the road. "It's less boring to cut leaves and things when she's here." He paused, his face carefully blank. "You know. Because I have to watch her constantly. Make sure she doesn't cut off her fingers. Teach her how to use her *learning* knives."

Eliana stuck out her tongue at him, but she knew he wasn't really angry, because he was already smiling, and her father was laughing his big warm beautiful laugh that she so loved. Atheria was flying in great lazy circles through the bright spring sky. Zahra drifted alongside them, telling Eliana about the wildcats she had seen in the mountains that morning, and above them, far up the road, Baingarde stood in the hills and pines, waiting for their return. Their *home*.

As they walked up the road, Eliana snuggled against her father's shoulder, watching Simon grow smaller and smaller. He always waited at the garden gate until they reached the top of the road. It was only polite, he said, a show of respect for the king. And the princess, Eliana often reminded him, to which he usually responded with a merry-eyed shrug.

As they neared the road's end, Eliana held her breath, listening to her heart pound. What if he didn't wait? What if he returned to the shop before he was supposed to? Her eyes watered as she stared, and she refused to breathe, even though she was starting to feel a little dizzy.

Zahra sent her a fond, slightly exasperated thought: *Little one, if you don't breathe soon, I will force you to.*

And then—*there.* Simon raised his hand at last, as he always did, just as he had promised. Eliana's heart filled with light to see it, and she giggled against her father's ear, so happy that she couldn't answer him when he asked her what was funny. Instead, she smiled and waved back at Simon until they turned the corner and the little shop she so loved, and its garden, and the boy standing patiently at its gate, fell quietly out of sight.

ELEMENTS IN THE EMPIRIUM TRILOGY

———◇———

In Celdaria, Rielle's kingdom, the Church is the official religious body. Citizens worship in seven elemental temples that stand in each Celdarian city. Temples range from simple altars in a single, small room to the elaborate, lavish temples of the capital city, Âme de la Terre. Similar religious institutions exist in nations around the world of Avitas. In Eliana's time, most elemental temples have been destroyed by the Undying Empire, and few people still believe in the Old World stories about magic, the saints, and the Gate.

ELEMENT	ELEMENTAL NAME	SIGIL	TEMPLE	COLORS
sun	sunspinner		The House of Light	gold and white
air	windsinger		The Firmament	sky blue and dark gray
fire	firebrand		The Pyre	scarlet and gold
shadow	shadowcaster		The House of Night	deep blue and black
water	waterworker		The Baths	slate blue and sea foam
metal	metalmaster		The Forge	charcoal and fiery orange
earth	earthshaker		The Holdfast	umber and light green

SAINT	PATRON SAINT OF	CASTING	ASSOCIATED ANIMAL
Saint Katell the Magnificent	Celdaria	sword	white mare
Saint Ghovan the Fearless	Ventera	arrow	imperial eagle
Saint Marzana the Brilliant	Kirvaya	shield	firebird
Saint Tameryn the Cunning	Astavar	dagger	black leopard
Saint Nerida the Radiant	Meridian	trident	kraken
Saint Grimvald the Mighty	Borsvall	hammer	ice dragon
Saint Tokazi the Steadfast	Mazabat	staff	giant stag

ACKNOWLEDGMENTS

---◇---

Sixteen years ago, I dreamed up a character named Rielle and decided I wanted to tell her story. (*Decided*, as if she gave me some choice in the matter.)

And now, the final book of the Empirium Trilogy—the story of Rielle and Eliana—is complete. Words can't describe how lucky I feel to have gotten the chance to share these books with the world. They have been the soul of my creative life. I'm not sure I'll ever love any story as much as I've loved this one, which is a terribly strange and bittersweet feeling.

Over the years, many people have helped me make this trilogy a reality, far more than I can thank here. To all the readers, librarians, educators, and booksellers who have embraced these books and helped them succeed, thank you from the depths of my heart for your support, enthusiasm, and kindness. And to my loved ones, my friends and family—you know how much I adore you, and how grateful I am that you have never stopped believing in me. I'm so glad you're mine.

For this final book, I want to dedicate these acknowledgments particularly to my publishing team. Without them, without their understanding, commitment, and hard work, this story would still live only in my mind. Their devotion, talent, and skill have made these books a reality, and that is an extraordinary gift I will hold close to my heart forever.

Thank you—a million thank-yous—to my fearless, unflappable agent,

Victoria Marini, whose tireless advocacy and compassion have not only helped my books but also helped me as a person. I'm thankful as well for the team at Irene Goodman Literary Agency—especially Lee O'Brien and Maggie Kane—as well as the ever-helpful Penelope Burns at Gelfman Schneider/ICM Partners, and Renee Harleston, for her insight and expertise.

I must express unending gratitude to Annie Berger, editor extraordinaire, who has been such an invaluable creative partner—and who has such unerring confidence in my abilities—that I sometimes sit back and gawk at my own good fortune.

Huge, heartfelt thanks to the indefatigable Sourcebooks team, especially the endlessly patient Beth Oleniczak, as well as Sarah Kasman, Stefani Sloma, Lizzie Lewandoski, Katie Stutz, Mallory Hyde, Valerie Pierce, Margaret Coffee, Sierra Stovall, Ashlyn Keil, Caitlin Lawler, Heather Moore, Michael Leali, Jackie Douglass, Danielle McNaughton, Todd Stocke, Steve Geck, and Dominique Raccah.

I would like to give special thanks to production editor Cassie Gutman, for her sharp eyes and boundless patience; and to Nicole Hower and David Curtis, for the trilogy's glorious covers. Sourcebooks has been such a wonderful home for Rielle and Eliana, and I am so grateful to everyone who works there for making me and my girls feel like part of the family.

I am particularly grateful to Alison Cherry, exceptional copy editor (and extraordinary friend)—thank you for making this book better and for supporting me, always.

Huge thanks as well to the teams at Penguin Random House Audio and Listening Library—Aaron Blank, Heather Job, Brieana Garcia, Rebecca Waugh, Emily Parliman, and Jessica Kaye—for their work on the trilogy's audiobooks. And my warmest appreciation goes to Fiona Hardingham for her masterful narrative performance.

The process of bringing a book to life involves so many more people than simply the author alone. When I step back and look at everyone who has helped me tell this story, I feel truly blessed and humbled by the outpouring of love and belief. Thank you.

ABOUT THE AUTHOR

———◇———

Claire Legrand is the *New York Times* bestselling author of several books for young readers, including the Edgar Award–nominated *Some Kind of Happiness*, *The Cavendish Home for Boys and Girls*, and *Sawkill Girls*, which has been nominated for both a Bram Stoker Award and a Lambda Literary Award. She lives in central New Jersey.

FIREreads

⑤ #getbooklit

Your hub for the hottest young adult books!

Visit us online and sign up for our
newsletter at FIREreads.com

@sourcebooksfire

sourcebooksfire

firereads.tumblr.com